# The Settlers of Catan

# The Settlers of Catan

A historical novel based on the board game
"The Settlers of Catan"

Rebecca Gable

SKETCHES BY KLAUS TEUBER

Translated by Lee Chadeayne,
translation reviewed by Ingrid G. Lansford

*The Settlers of Catan* by Rebecca Gable was first published in 2003 by Bastei Lübbe in Köln, Germany, as *Die Siedler von Catan: Nach Motiven des Spiels "Die Siedler von Catan."*

Translated from the German by Lee Chadeayne.
First published in English in 2011 by AmazonCrossing.

Published by AmazonCrossing
P.O. Box 400818
Las Vegas, NV 89140

ISBN-13: 9781611090819
ISBN-10: 1611090814
Library of Congress Control Number: 2011909466

# Table of Contents

# Foreword

How do you invent games? This is probably the question a game designer is asked most frequently. For many people it seems to be a mystery how someone can succeed in creating a small world of its own, made of cardboard, wood, plastic, and a few rules. A game world to submerge into, get away from it all for a couple of hours and meet one's fellow human beings in a refreshingly different way.

The motivation—and sometimes even the irresistible urge—to start developing a game always rests upon a story. The story must fascinate me and awaken in me the desire to be able to relive it time and again in a game situation.

The starting point for the game "The Settlers of Catan" was the history of discoveries. I was particularly taken with the Vikings, who—way ahead of their time—headed for Iceland, Greenland, and America in their dragon ships and permanently and successfully settled Iceland.

In the ninth century, Iceland was uninhabited except for a few Celtic monks; the island didn't have to be conquered, but everything had to be created from scratch. Trees were felled in once densely wooded Iceland to build houses and ships. Roads were built, sheep multiplied in rich pastures, and before long, grain grew—although not abundantly—on the then much warmer island in the North Atlantic Ocean.

Pioneering days! Probably, the settlement of Iceland was successful only because people helped each other, peacefully traded with each other, and looked for new ways to build a better society. Around 920, the

Vikings thus founded a people's assembly—the althing. It is the oldest parliamentary institution in the world and exists to this very day.

Well, Catan isn't Iceland, although there are many similarities. Catan is also uninhabited in the beginning and is then developed during the game. Lumber is produced, grain is harvested, ore is mined, and clay is extracted and made into bricks. The resources are used to build settlements and roads; cities develop, and a busy trade between the players helps to overcome shortages. Even though there's a winner at the end of the game, it is more about cooperation than about competition. Things are built rather than destroyed, because the Catanians are peace-loving people.

"The Settlers of Catan" was released in 1995. From day one, the game was very successful. Within three years of its release, over one million copies had sold. Since then, over 18 million copies of the Catan game series have been sold worldwide in over forty countries and thirty languages. Catan has been particularly successful in North America in recent years, especially in the United States. I am delighted by the noticeable enthusiasm of many English-speaking fans, who have expressed their fondness for the Catan games in a host of e-mails, social media postings, as well as at various conventions.

In 1998, for the first time I thought of how delightful it would be to experience the story of the settlement of Catan in a novel. It was a halfhearted thought, however, because I lacked the talent to write a good novel and didn't know anyone I could ask, either. I also had the feeling that the time wasn't ripe yet for a novel.

Since I love to read good historical novels, it was inevitable that two years later I came across Rebecca Gable's novel *The Smile of Fortune*. I was so carried away by this novel set in the Middle Ages that it took me only one weekend to devour the book. I felt very close to the characters Gable so masterfully brought to life—characters who weren't only portrayed as good people but who also had their weak sides, which was essential to make them believable as human beings.

I was impressed by her suspenseful, authentic, and historically substantiated narration of the era of the Hundred Years' War in England.

And then—I probably had read three-quarters of the novel—I suddenly knew it: Rebecca Gable would write the story of the settlement of Catan, or else the story would never be written.

For two years I hadn't thought of a Catan novel, but now I was as if possessed by the desire to have Rebecca Gable as its author. Then, when I visited the Frankfurt Book Fair in 2000, I managed to meet the writer. I actually had little hope; after all, Gable was a bestselling author already back then, and she certainly had no need to get on the bandwagon of my game's success.

To my great delight, however, things turned out differently.

Very soon, we were continuously exchanging e-mails, and finally, in the spring of 2001, we arranged a meeting in Cologne. Meanwhile, I had developed a rough draft of the novel's plot as I envisioned it, and Rebecca Gable had also given some thought to it. When we started to tell each other our ideas for the novel, we were very surprised: they mostly coincided.

The die was cast; Rebecca Gable was willing to put the story of the settlement of Catan on paper. Months of harmonious and constructive collaboration followed. Although my only role was that of a critic—and I never found much to criticize—it was very exciting to experience and accompany the development of the novel "live," so to speak.

The German edition of the novel was published in 2003, and thanks to its success, you now hold the English translation.

I would like to thank Ms. Gable from the bottom of my heart for this time and the wonderful novel you, dear reader, are holding in your hands now.

—Klaus Teuber, August 2011

# Part I: Elasund

# Autumn Moon

"Ye gods, that's cold!" Candamir gasped, for the plunge into the pitch black water had taken his breath away. "Why didn't we do this before the harvest? Only fools go swimming this late in the year."

Osmund slowly moved his arms about to stay afloat. "Stop whining. The nine-armed kraken will hear you shouting and come after us."

"Yes. Or the twelve-headed sea serpent. Boo!"

They laughed. Even in their callow youth they had held their swimming contests every harvest moon, and in those days the competition had been less about who would be first across the fjord than who could scare the other the more with their real or imaginary stories of sea monsters.

"Ready?" asked Osmund. His wet, blond hair shone like a will-o'-the-wisp on the dark water.

"Just waiting for you," Candamir replied.

"Then let's go."

The small white crests sparkled in the moonlight as their arms sliced through the waves. They moved fast and almost silently through the water, like two seals, neck and neck at first. A shimmering white cliff towered up on their right, jutting far out into the fjord and serving as a breakwater for the harbor of Elasund beyond it. When they reached the outer point of the peninsula, they were already past the halfway point in their race.

Osmund could sense he had a slight lead, though he didn't look to see. He was no longer sensitive to the ice-cold water around him—the water was his friend, making him fast and weightless. He took deep, regular breaths and felt he could swim forever, not just across the fjord, but out to the distant island realms his people had founded.

Then he felt a tight grip on his arm.

"Osmund!"

He heard the horror in Candamir's voice. Even the best swimmer could cramp up in this icy water. But it didn't seem like Candamir was in any danger of going down. Perhaps it was the cold or the effect of the moonlight, but his friend's face appeared ghostly pale as he stared toward the shore.

Osmund turned his head and looked in the same direction, to the end of the fjord where Elasund lay.

*O save us, Father of the Gods,* he thought, full of dread. *Not again...*

The village was on fire, and in the harbor were four ships that didn't belong there.

"Let's get to the boat!" he shouted breathlessly.

That afternoon, a slave had rowed a small boat to the narrow, crescent-shaped beach on the far side of the fjord so that Osmund and Candamir could return home more easily after their daring competition. Water and sand flew as the two leapt to their feet and ran to the boat, which had been carefully pulled up onto the beach. Their wet clothes clung to them and the night wind was bitter cold, but they scarcely noticed it. Quickly they pulled the boat into the water. Another building had gone up in flames.

"Uncle Sigismund's barn," Candamir murmured as he slid onto the seat and grabbed hold of one oar.

"Please hurry," said Osmund, full of anxiety for his wife and son.

They lowered their oars at the same time, and soon the boat was speeding like an arrow across the calm, dark water. As they approached the village, they could hear shouting and the noise of battle.

"It's the accursed Turons again," Candamir said softly.

Despite their wet clothing, they had begun to sweat. They rowed silently, concentrating on their rhythm, looking repeatedly over their shoulders. As they drew closer to the village, they could see the battle raging in the harbor. Both Candamir and Osmund realized that they had left their weapons behind on the shore before starting the race.

When the water was knee-deep, they jumped out, waded ashore, and with nothing but their bare hands attacked the first two Turons they saw. The raiders were fearless and experienced, but Candamir pulled a dagger from the belt of one warrior and slit his throat before his opponent even noticed him. With a gurgling cry, the dying man slumped to his knees while Candamir tore the sword from his limp right hand. From the corner of his eye, he could see that Osmund had beaten an unhelmeted opponent on the head with a large stone and then helped himself to the man's weapons. Several of the enemy warriors rushed at the two newcomers, now standing back to back. A heavyset brute with a long, braided beard came straight toward Candamir, his short sword raised over his head, ready to strike. Candamir, caught off balance, couldn't get out of the way fast enough, but instinctively hurled the dagger he was still clutching. The blade whistled through the air and bored into the leather breastplate of his attacker.

As the Turon fell, Candamir had a fleeting view of the harbor and saw one of the enemy boats already casting off. In despair, he realized they had arrived too late. He had known it back in the fjord when he saw the first flames, but he didn't let himself think about who or what might be aboard the departing ship. Neither did he allow himself to be distracted by the cries of men and women, many of whose voices he recognized. Instead, his brow furled in anger; he lunged forward, swinging the captured sword in a wide arc.

It was almost impossible to get through the throng of Turons on the grassy shore. In a blind rage, Candamir lashed out at everything that stood in his way.

In the flickering light of the burning barn he could see Harald the blacksmith holding his sword in his left hand and his hammer in his right, trying to defend himself against two Turons. Before Candamir could come to his aid, he caught sight of Osmund again, who killed one of Harald's attackers. The smith fought off the other and in a brief gesture of thanks raised his fist clenching the hammer. "They have locked up two dozen men and boys in the barn!" he shouted over the cacophony. "I think your brother was one of them, Candamir!"

Stunned, Candamir stared at the wooden building burning like tinder after the long, dry summer. "Help us, O mighty Tyr," he pleaded softly, and almost too late, he raised his sword as a tall Turon warrior appeared, wielding a huge battle-axe.

It had not escaped Osmund's notice that the intruders were dragging mostly women and girls to their ships. He *had* to get home. Yet he couldn't ignore the desperate cries of those trapped in the burning barn and the pounding of their fists on the locked door. For just a moment he hesitated, then leapt forward and slew a Turon warrior who was preparing to attack his cousin Jared from behind.

One yard at a time, the two friends, Harald, and their neighbors fought their way through the tightly packed throng to the door that was still shaking from the pounding fists of those locked inside. Then, with a mighty blow of his sword, Harald severed the head of one of the enemy leaders. On seeing this, the rest of the Turons withdrew from the barn, retreating to other parts of the village.

Osmund and Candamir each took hold of one end of the heavy beam blocking the barn door, as Harald and the remaining Elasund warriors hurried back to the meadow by the shore, where it seemed that the resistance was now more determined and organized under the leadership of the brave Eilhard and Osmund's uncle Olaf. Thick clouds of smoke poured out, along with coughing, hunched figures.

"Hacon?" Candamir grabbed a youngster by the arm and stared into his soot-covered face. But it wasn't his brother. He took a deep breath before stepping over the threshold, with Osmund like a shadow at his side.

The burning walls of the barn should have provided some light, but the smoke was like a black fog. Cinders and glowing pieces of straw rained down on them. When suddenly, out of the darkness, a screaming tower of flame staggered toward them, Osmund pushed the burning man out of the building, tore off his own damp tunic, and wrapped it around him.

Candamir groped his way through the smoke-filled darkness. The heat singed his eyebrows, and his lungs ached. On the verge of panic, he stumbled over something on the ground. Stooping over, he recognized the face of young Wiland. He heard a muffled cracking sound behind him, and as he wheeled around, he saw a burning roof beam on the ground, and then a second one drifting slowly down, like an enormous torch falling into a dark well shaft.

Osmund appeared at his side again, grabbing him by the sleeve and pulling him to the door, along with the lifeless body. "Let's get out of here! The roof is collapsing."

"Hacon," he called, part cough, part muffled sob.

Osmund shook his head. His grip on Candamir's arm was like an iron vise, and without saying a word, he brought his friend out into the fresh air. They were hardly ten steps from the barn when the roof collapsed with a loud cracking sound and a shower of sparks.

Candamir put Wiland down in the grass. When he stood up again, he saw what remained of the living torch—a horribly blackened human form, suspiciously motionless. "Who…was that?" he asked.

"Your uncle Sigismund," Osmund answered calmly. "And now come, Candamir. If your brother really was in there, then there is nothing we can do for him. But the battle is not yet over."

A few moments later, a loud piercing horn sounded and the Turons turned their backs on the slaughter on the shore, as if their bloodlust had suddenly been quelled. As they withdrew to their three remaining ships, the villagers charged after them into the knee-deep water, eager to reach the ships and recover what had been stolen. But to no avail. The Turons were back on board, covering their retreat with a volley of deadly arrows that emerged from the darkness with a terrible whirring sound. They could be heard before they were seen, and quite a few Elasund warriors were hit before they could duck. Just in front of Candamir a man was struck and fell in the water. He grabbed him under the arms, dragging him back to shore.

The three pirate ships sped away, their oars glinting in the moonlight as if made of glass.

It had become strangely quiet on the shore. Here and there soft moaning sounds could be heard, but the clamor had subsided.

Candamir turned his back on the fjord. "Has anyone seen my brother?"

Those standing around him shook their heads, not meeting his gaze. Candamir stared toward the smoking ruins of the barn that had been one of the largest in Elasund. As children, he and Osmund had played there, proving their courage by jumping from the hayloft into a pile of straw, which became smaller and flatter after each successful jump, until the valuable straw lay scattered all over the barn. That had enraged his uncle, who punished them when he found out. Nevertheless, they had always snuck back. Candamir wondered if Hacon and his friends had also abused Sigismund's hayloft for their tests of courage—how strange that he didn't know, that he had never asked Hacon about it. He suddenly felt weak in the knees, but before despair could overwhelm him, a bright voice from somewhere overhead called, "I'm here."

Astonished, the men looked up into the crown of the mighty ash tree standing in the village green. The dry autumn foliage rustled, then two gangling legs appeared, and Hacon jumped down. He walked over to his brother with his head bowed. "A huge Turon with a red beard chased me up there," he explained, embarrassed. Just three months shy of his fifteenth birthday, Hacon was actually ashamed that he had fled the fight. He jerked his chin toward the tree trunk. "Eilhard killed him before he could climb after me."

Candamir let out an audible sigh. He put one arm around his brother's bony shoulders, discreetly leaning on him while taking a close look at his face. Hacon had a nasty gash on his forehead but otherwise seemed unharmed.

"Thanks, Eilhard," Candamir said.

The older man nodded. "Smart lad, your brother," he said in a deep, resounding voice. "The less quick-witted boys burned to death in Sigismund's barn. I never saw Turons behave like that."

"What a bunch of cowards," said Hacon flatly, pointing at a corpse lying face-down on the water's edge. "Bert Sigismundsson. A Turon killed him from behind—I saw it." His eyes moved restlessly from the body to the retreating enemy and then back to his brother's face. "Bert was a year younger than me, Candamir," he said bitterly.

"Yes, I know. I'm sorry," Candamir replied. He addressed his brother, but his words were directed at all his neighbors. "I'm sorry that we weren't here."

Harald the blacksmith pointed to the upper part of his right arm. "For someone who wasn't here, they got you pretty good."

The wound was sticky and wet with blood. Candamir had barely felt the wound, but now he remembered the moment in front of the barn when he had seen the blade coming down and thought he would lose his arm. And he would have, too, if Osmund hadn't suddenly been there to strike down the howling Turon. Candamir turned to look for his friend. His eyes fell upon the tall, unmistakable figure with the blond shock of hair, some distance away. Osmund was heading home. An inner voice urged Candamir to follow.

He let go of Hacon. "Is my Saxon still living?" he asked.

Several men nodded.

"Tell him he needs to take care of the injured. He knows what he's doing—listen to him," Candamir said.

As he was turning away, the gray-bearded, burly Siward took hold of his blood-soaked sleeve. "Candamir, we can't just stand here and watch them leave. We have to go after them!"

The younger man slowly shook his head. "That's pointless, Siward."

"But they took my wife!" Siward grabbed hold of his arm tighter. "She is your mother's cousin—you *must* help me! You have a ship!"

His thumb was pressing down on the wound, and Candamir pulled away. He felt sorry for Siward, but he knew it would be completely futile to pursue the pirates now. The Turons had long, fast warships with twenty pairs of oars, and with the night wind as weak as it was, it would be impossible to catch them in a merchant sailboat like Candamir's. And even if the wind changed and they somehow managed to catch them, a single ship would have no chance against four.

Unexpectedly, Osmund's uncle Olaf took his side. "It would take us at least an hour to get the ship ready," he said in his husky bass voice. "Candamir is right; it would be pointless."

Olaf was the most experienced sailor and the wealthiest man in Elasund. His word carried weight. Siward lowered his head and nodded.

Candamir caught up with Osmund at the door to his longhouse. A withered, gray-haired woman stood at the door, arms folded, blocking the way.

"Let me by," Osmund said in a strangely weak voice.

The old woman shook her head. "Gisla is dead, Osmund, and there is nothing you can do about that."

"I want to see her."

"No, you don't. Believe me."

"A curse be on you, Brigitta! She is my wife!"

"She was. She was also my granddaughter, and I tell you, you won't get to see her like this. She never would have wanted that."

Osmund clenched his fists. "Out of my way, you witch…"

Candamir stepped forward and gently took hold of Brigitta's elbow. "Let him pass; he knows what he is doing," he said. "And it is his right."

She looked at Candamir contemptuously, hesitating for a moment before stepping aside. Osmund went past her into his house. It wasn't long before they heard his cry of anguish. Candamir shut his eyes tightly for a moment.

The old woman cackled. "So he knows what he is doing, does he?"

Candamir backed up half a step. Like almost every man in Elasund, he was a bit frightened of old Brigitta. "What…what happened?"

"There were three of them," she said matter-of-factly. "One I was able to kill, but the other two dragged her into the bedroom, locked the door, and…"

"How is Roric?" Candamir hastily interrupted.

"He slept through everything. They did not find him. I hid him in the manure pile—the only place those greedy swine didn't search."

Candamir nodded. It seemed one of the gods had held his protective hand over Osmund's house tonight after all, if only halfheartedly. Osmund would certainly find consolation in his son's survival. Someday.

"Go down to the harbor and help the wounded," he told Brigitta. She was sharp-tongued and perhaps in league with demons and forest spirits, but she was just as skillful a healer as the Saxon.

"Sure," she said mockingly. "I'll leave the heroes of Elasund, who fearlessly swam across the fjord, overlooking four enemy ships rowing into the harbor in the bright moonlight before their very noses."

Candamir did not respond. He knew there was no point in trying to defend himself. Only someone who had swum the fjord at night would know that even in the brightest moonlight you couldn't see more than ten yards. And that between fighting the cold, maintaining your direction, and trying not to panic at the thought of the bottomless darkness below, it was impossible to notice anything else.

"Where is your great-grandson now?" he asked.

She nodded toward to the longhouse. "I put him down next to his dead mother, but by tomorrow I must find a wet nurse for him."

Candamir nodded. "Then I won't keep you..."

With a knowing snort, she turned away, tightening the black shawl around her shoulders.

Candamir took her place as sentry in front of Osmund's door to make sure no one disturbed his friend in his grief.

"Master, Master, wake up!"

Candamir was startled out of his sleep, seizing the hand shaking him by the shoulder. Seeing that it was only the Saxon, he let him go and rubbed his eyes. A dirty bandage covered the wound on his upper arm, and only a small amount of blood had seeped through. "Why this racket?" asked Candamir grumpily.

"Master, one of the Turon warriors is still alive. They...they want to gouge out his eyes, cut off his...you know what, and throw him into the water to feed the fish."

"Well? What else are we to do with him?" Candamir replied, yawning and passing his big hands through his hair. It fell black and straight over his shoulders, and like most of the men, he wore the strands that framed his face braided into plaits.

The Saxon waved his arms wildly. "People must not treat each other that way," he explained.

"Ye gods, are you starting in with that again?"

The Saxon was a funny little fellow. He came from Britain and had a name that was so completely unpronounceable that for simplicity's sake the people of Elasund just called him the Saxon. Two years ago when he arrived, he had looked even more peculiar than today. He had had a round spot shaven on the crown of his head and had carried neither bread nor gold in his pouch, only an iron cross and a strange object with two wooden covers and thin sheets of dried animal skin adorned with odd little runes. The Saxon had called this thing a "book" and said it, like the cross, came from his god, a god he claimed was mightier than all other gods. The people of Elasund had thought it best to kill him and burn the gifts from his god, fearing they might be dangerous, but Osmund was opposed. Since Gisla had not wanted the stranger in her house, Candamir had taken him as his slave, and he had never regretted it. The Saxon was of real help; he knew all sorts of things about afflictions and illnesses, and he was good with the livestock. But still, he was strange.

Candamir sat up, and only then did the Saxon discover the slave girl beside his master, slumbering peacefully. Candamir slid the fur blanket over her exquisite little breasts, aware that the sight of a naked woman made his slave uncomfortable. The Saxon had claimed that there were many men in Britain who had shorn their heads and were living together with their god in houses they built for him—without women. Candamir concluded that these bald-headed men and their god obviously did not care much for women.

"The Turon is an enemy and has killed our neighbors," Candamir explained patiently. "It is our duty to avenge them. If we don't, their spirits and patron gods will haunt us, and rightly so."

Even the Saxon seemed to understand that. Nevertheless, he argued. "If you spare him, maybe he will tell us why the Turons are always attacking us. And when they will come the next time."

Candamir pulled on his trousers before slipping into his ankle-high seal leather shoes. "That is not a bad idea," he said, wrapping his laces crosswise around his ankles and tying them. "But he will tell us anyway. Believe me, he will tell us everything we want to know."

As the pale sun rose, Candamir hastily downed a bowl of fish soup and stepped out of his longhouse. Returning late last night from his vigil in front of Osmund's hall, he had noticed some of the devastation the Turons had wreaked on his property, but only now in the gray morning light did he see how bad it was. Most of his livestock had been stolen. The cowshed and storage shed were reduced to blackened frames. His slaves, at least, had managed to hide because his house was farther from the shore than most of the others, but Candamir now wondered how he would get them—or anyone else—through the winter.

Elasund was made up of a good two dozen farms, each consisting of a longhouse, stables, barns, and other buildings. These homesteads formed a rough circle, close enough together so their inhabitants could join in defending themselves during attacks like the one the night before. The land surrounding the village was used mainly as pasture for raising sheep and cattle. Only a handful of the villagers planted barley, rye, or even wheat—the climate here was simply too rough and the winters too long. Things just didn't grow well. The Elasunders had to buy their grain in the harbors farther south.

Accompanied by his brother and the Saxon, Candamir walked the gentle slope to the village green where the Elasunders gathered whenever there were matters of common importance to discuss. On their way down, they passed plundered storehouses with gates torn half off their hinges, slaughtered cows, and trampled chickens lying in the mud.

"How many were killed?" Candamir asked the Saxon.

"Your uncle Sigismund, his son Bert, and three of his servants," the slave replied dejectedly. "Turgot Turgotsson, his wife, and a servant..."

It was a long, sad litany: almost a dozen free people and as many slaves were now laid out behind their houses. Seventeen women and girls had been carried off. “This means that the village has lost almost one tenth of its free population,” the Saxon concluded.

“What do you mean by that?” Candamir asked gruffly.

“One out of every ten men and women is dead or has been carried off into slavery,” the monk explained.

“Thor’s hammer…that’s terrible,” young Hacon murmured. Candamir agreed.

The morning was cold and gray, and though a sharp sea breeze brought dark clouds, it had not rained. Near the old ash tree a fire had been lit, and the villagers huddled around it, shivering, their breath forming little white clouds in the cold air. Osmund was there at the back of the crowd, silent and pale, holding his sleeping son in his arms and staring out at the sea.

Two strapping young Elasunders were holding the prisoner tightly by the arms, his hands tied behind his back. The prisoner was a slender, almost gaunt man of around twenty years with ginger hair and beard. Feet apart, he stood between his guards, swaying gently. He was wounded; blood trickled down his forehead and into his eyes. He tried to look indifferent to it all, but he kept glancing at the poker lying in the fire, its tip already glowing red hot.

Siward, whose wife was among those abducted, yelled out, “Stare all you want. This poker is going to be the last thing you’ll see in your miserable life.”

“Master…” the Saxon pleaded, but Candamir silenced him with a look.

The monk, whose real name was Byrhtferth and who was the son of an Anglo-Saxon nobleman, did not find it easy to resign himself to a life of slavery. He had left his British homeland in order to convert these unfortunate savages, well aware of the risks. He had not, however, anticipated the loss of his freedom or status. He had long come to realize that God had imposed this existence on him as a trial, and this made it easier for him to bear the bitter lot of servitude. He suspected that God would not deliver him from his fate until he had been able to convert these wild men to the true faith of charity and brotherly love—yet at times like this his task seemed hopeless.

"Let's get down to business with this Turon," old Brigitta said. "I'm cold, and I have wounded people to take care of."

*If you're cold, go home where you belong,* Candamir thought, irritated. Women had no business being at the *Thing*, the assembly held regularly by all free men of the village. But no one dared remind Brigitta of that.

"Just a moment," Olaf said, taking a few steps forward. He wore a knee-length tunic of the finest dark blue wool, gray trousers of the same material, and shoes of the best cowhide, fashioned by cobblers in the land of the Franks. He was tall and broad-shouldered like so many Elasunders. A few silver strands shimmered in his shoulder-length, blond hair and short, well-groomed beard—just enough to make him look wise but not old. "I would first like to ask him a few questions," he said, fixing his sharp, light blue eyes on the prisoner. "Why do you carry off just our women?"

The Turon's shoulders tensed as he looked him directly in the eye and replied, "Because our own women were also carried off—we need women." Turonland lay much farther south than Elasund, so his dialect was nearly incomprehensible to the assembled group.

"Who took your women?" Olaf asked.

"Kuwans," the prisoner said.

A murmur went up in the crowd like a breeze in the forest treetops; the Kuwans were a wild race of warriors from a land beyond the eastern sea.

"And why don't you want any male slaves?" asked Candamir. Noticing the disapproval in Olaf's gaze, he knew it was impertinent of him to take over the questioning. But deference was not one of his strengths, and ever since his father had failed to return from a trading voyage the previous autumn and Candamir had become head of his little household, it was harder than ever for him to show his elders their due respect.

The prisoner kept silent, as if it were beneath his dignity to answer such a question.

That angered Candamir, who turned to the two youths holding the Turon and said, "Take one of his eyes and let's see if that will make him talk."

"They don't take men as captives," the Saxon interrupted, "because they have lost so many of their own people and fear the slaves will rebel."

Candamir shot him a glance over his shoulder. "You're really living dangerously today, aren't you?"

The Saxon gave him a long-suffering smile.

His master turned back to the Turon warrior and asked, "Is it as he says?"

The prisoner nodded reluctantly.

"And you thought you could just come here and do to us what they did to you, is that it?"

"Everyone has to see to his own needs," the prisoner replied, without a touch of remorse.

Candamir snorted and took a step backward. Siward fetched the poker out of the fire with a leather cloth and moved toward the prisoner.

"No!" the Saxon cried out, throwing himself between the prisoner and the vengeful Siward, who hesitated, astonished at the slave's outrageous behavior.

"You must not take revenge!" the Saxon pleaded. "'Mine is the vengeance, saith the Lord.' Only if you show kindness will he grant you mercy and protect you."

Osmund handed little Roric to Brigitta, pushed his way forward, and seized the monk by the arm. "Your weakling of a god who let himself be nailed on a wooden beam by his enemies? I think we can do without his protection." He struck the Saxon on the chin so that the little monk tumbled backward against the Turon warrior.

Osmund turned toward Siward. "Do it, or give me the poker. I am tired of waiting. He is one of those who burned our neighbors, sent your wife into slavery, and killed my wife. He owes us his sight and his life."

"Osmund," said Hacon, speaking up in spite of his shyness. "This man didn't do any of those things." Hacon had great respect for his brother's friend and was even a bit afraid of him. But he loved the Saxon slave and was fascinated by the stories he told, so for his sake, he gathered up his courage and continued. "This Turon didn't touch any of our people. You knocked him down with a stone before he had the chance. I saw it with my own eyes." He pointed to the treetop where he had been hiding the night before. "Of course we can take out our vengeance on him instead of his comrades, but the gods will not punish us if we don't."

Kicking the Saxon aside like a bothersome mongrel, Osmund, his forehead wrinkled in concentration, looked at the prisoner and nodded reluctantly. "Hacon is right—this is the fellow whose sword I took. But I want him to die just the same," he added. "I want to see him shed his blood just as they shed Gisla's."

Harald put his hand on Osmund's shoulder. "But if the gods do not demand his life, we could keep him, Osmund. We lost many good slaves last night, and we need workers."

"I'd rather rebuild my barn with my own hands," Siward said.

"Well then, let's vote on it," Olaf suggested.

Because Gisla had been his nephew's wife, he joined Osmund and Siward in favor of the Turon's death. Candamir sided with Osmund as well, out of respect for his friend as well as for his dead uncle and cousin. Like everyone present, Candamir regarded an attack on a relative as a personal threat; after all, a family was as strong as it was large. However, the majority considered the prisoner's capacity for work more useful than his death.

Osmund was having trouble holding back his anger, but before he could pull out his dagger and take things into his own hands, Olaf nodded to his sons. They led the Turon to their farm, locking him in the sauna for the time being.

"Be my guest tonight, Osmund," Olaf offered. "You need a nurse for your son, Brigitta tells me, and surely you will find one among my maids. Eat and drink with us, and let us comfort you in your grief."

Osmund folded his arms and lowered his head. He would rather have declined, but in contrast to his friend, he knew what was proper. "Thank you, Uncle."

Olaf turned to Candamir. "And you should teach your slave some manners."

Candamir nodded and regarded his Saxon without speaking, his sea-gray eyes glinting angrily. The monk lowered his head in a gesture of humility and, with a furtive grimace, realized that blood would flow in Elasund that day after all, and it would be his own. Whatever was required to bring him closer to God, he concluded.

"It is time for us to decide what to do," Harald said. "Things can't go on like this. In the spring the Turons attacked us and stole our cattle, and now they come back to steal our hay and our women. Where will it all end?"

"We must send a messenger to the king," said Siward's son Wiland. Upon seeing his words met with nothing but surprise and laughter, he added furiously, "He is the Turons' king as well as ours! He can order them to leave us alone and to give back my mother..." His voice broke, and he lowered his head.

Osmund felt sympathy for the boy, who was barely fifteen. He had no memory of his own mother, who had died of lung fever just a few weeks after his birth. His father had taken him to the neighboring farm where a firstborn had also just come into the world of wintery gloom. Only after his foster mother had died eight years later—just after the Yule festival, when Hacon was born—had Osmund experienced the fear and loneliness of that long-ago loss. It was the bitterest memory of his childhood, and he remembered clearly how both he and Candamir were ashamed to share their grief—just as Wiland was ashamed now—both retiring to a silent corner to shed their tears. Perhaps the first time they had ever done anything separately.

In a strange way, the loss back then made the present loss more bearable. No happiness can last forever, his father had warned—that is not man's fate. It is only a loan from the gods. So as devastated as Osmund was by Gisla's death, he was not surprised.

He laid his hands on Wiland's shoulders. "Tell me, who is your patron god?"

"Odin," the boy answered hoarsely.

"And mine as well. That's good. He will give you the consolation of his wisdom. Your mother is gone forever, just like my wife, and even the king cannot change that. Who is he, this king? Who has ever seen him in Elasund? He is as far away as the stars. Place your confidence and hopes in Odin, who watches over your happiness and at least sends us one of his ravens, or a dream, now and then. He is closer to us than the king."

Looking up at Osmund, the boy squinted, his face still smeared with soot and his eyes dilated from the horrors of the preceding night's narrow escape from the burning barn. "But how can that be? Shouldn't the king protect his own people?"

"Indeed," Osmund declared. "A good people should have a good king who safeguards their laws and their land. Unfortunately, it is not that way for us."

"If we put our confidence in the king, we might just as well go down to the fjord and drown ourselves," said Brigitta grimly.

"Then let's board our ships, take off for Turonland, and bring back our women and livestock," Eilhard suggested. His beard was as white as snow, but he could wield a battle-axe with the best of them. "The Turons are weakened by Kuwan attacks—the prisoner said so himself. It shouldn't be hard."

But the suggestion found little support. Two of the seven Elasund ships were still at sea and would not return from their long voyages until late autumn or after. And with the losses of the previous night, there were barely enough free Elasunders to man the remaining ships, to say nothing of deploying a group of warriors. The unanimous opinion was that any attempt to invade Turonland would lead to disaster.

"Perhaps you're right," Siward said impatiently, "but if we do nothing, we will surely have a difficult winter. My cattle have been stolen or slaughtered, and my stores of dried fish and grain have been burned. We will starve, and many will die. Then we will certainly no longer be able to defend ourselves."

Candamir looked across the fjord at his own ship tugging on its mooring in the breeze. "Sometimes I wish we could just go away," he said. "Find a place where the winter is not so dark and where we are not always cold. Where we have more than three moons in the year to fatten the cattle and plant a few stalks of grain."

Wistful murmurs could be heard all around; Osmund had finally put into words what all were thinking. "Yes, my father and even my father's father, and *his* father before him, dreamed of a new homeland. But they waited too long. Those of our people who settled in Ireland no longer welcome newcomers. Britain belongs to the Angles, the Saxons, and the Jutes, and now there is no more land."

Olaf disagreed. He had long been thinking of leaving Elasund, not just since the frequency of the attacks had increased. The land was poor and could no longer feed the ever-growing population. And though he was the richest man in the village, he had five sons to think of and saw no future for them here. Leaving in search of a new homeland seemed to him the only way to secure the continued survival of his family. However, such ideas had to be carefully weighed before being discussed. The Elasunders were still in a state of shock; it was not the right time to make such important decisions.

"There are two things we must do," Olaf said to the gathered villagers instead. "First, we must lay in new supplies for the winter. This means we must fish every day the weather permits. There is no time to dry the fish, but we can smoke them. The cattle we have left must be slaughtered and salted—after all, without hay we won't be able to get them through the winter. And we ought to take a few wagons farther inland, to the south where the Turons have not wreaked havoc. Perhaps we can even buy a few sacks of flour. And finally, we must plan how to defend ourselves from future attacks."

Olaf's house was the only one in Elasund that was surrounded by a high wooden palisade. The gate was damaged and blackened from the previous night's attack, but it had held. And thus wealthy Olaf was the only one not to have suffered any losses, neither of people, cattle, nor other possessions.

Candamir expressed what many were thinking: "Not everyone has as many slaves as you do and is able to spare them to cut and carry wood to build a fence." It sounded sharper than he had intended.

Olaf replied with an indulgent smile, "Well, if you are short of workers, how come you bought a new slave girl last summer instead of a strong lad? Maybe it would be a good idea if you thought with your head once in a while."

His words were met with a spontaneous, if muted, snicker by the crowd—the first display of cheerfulness since the attack. Blushing, Candamir laughed too.

It was almost noon when Candamir, Hacon, and the Saxon returned home. No one spoke—they were all deep in thought. The slaves exchanged worried looks when they noticed the gloomy mood and brooding silence of the three. Their fears were confirmed when Candamir took out his whip.

"Candamir…," Hacon stammered.

"Be quiet," he commanded his brother sharply. "Otherwise it will be your turn next. I wouldn't mind that at all, you know. If you hadn't stuck your nose in like that, the damned Turon would be dead now and Osmund wouldn't be cheated out of his revenge."

*And what good would that have done him?* Hacon was tempted to ask, but he didn't dare.

Candamir seized the Saxon by the arm more roughly than necessary and dragged him outside, across the small grassy yard toward the stable. A cow lay on the path, its throat slit and its head twisted grotesquely backward. On the right, the storehouse was in ruins, but the stable that held the sheep and horses in winter was still standing. It was at the far end of the yard, beyond which pastures and fields rose up to the hills behind. Fir and pine trees were scattered here and there, providing shade to the animals in the summer, forming a dense forest past the river.

"Well then," Candamir said, absentmindedly.

The Saxon regarded his young master, who towered over him by more than a head. He took in Candamir's broad shoulders, his large, powerful fist holding the whip, and his cool, almost expressionless gray eyes. With a sinking heart, the Saxon realized how angry Candamir was.

"Well, if it is your will, my Lord...," the slave sighed.

"No, not really," said Candamir, misunderstanding the object of the Saxon's address. "But this time you have really gone too far, don't you think?"

"If I only believed that you cared what I thought, then I would try to explain why I did it. It was for the salvation of your soul and that of your neighbors."

"Enough of this foolish talk. Take off your tunic and turn around."

Obediently the Saxon removed his threadbare, faded gray garment. He was wearing neither a shirt nor a vest underneath. He carefully folded the tunic, placed it on a nearby woodpile, and leaned over, supporting himself with his hands on the bare wall of the stable. Then he waited there in the cold, clenching his teeth.

When nothing happened, he ventured a glance over his left shoulder. "May I ask what you are waiting..."

Candamir was looking across the fields. A figure, still too small to make out, had appeared over the crest of the hill. It seemed to be swaying slowly, as if carrying a heavy load.

Shading his eyes with one hand, for despite the clouds he was blinded by the bright yellow autumn light, Candamir suddenly exclaimed, "O mighty Tyr!" He dropped the whip and ran off, jumping effortlessly over the fence, and jogged up the hill toward the figure.

"And the Lord performed a miracle and saved his unworthy servant," the Saxon said to himself. "At least for the time being." He picked up the whip, rolled it up, and hid it behind the woodpile.

He saw now that the figure was that of a woman, and quickly dressed. Candamir had reached her, and for a while they stood together, talking or perhaps arguing. Two of Candamir's horses grazing nearby raised their heads and eyed them curiously. Finally, Candamir took the bundle from the woman, and they slowly descended to the yard. The bundle was thrashing about—a child. Candamir was carrying the child on his left hip and had placed his right arm around the woman's shoulders.

Her hair was dark, and the Saxon was certain he had never seen her before, though after three years he thought by now he knew everyone in Elasund and in the hamlets along the river. Curiously he gazed at his master and the newcomer, opening the gate as they approached.

They walked past without so much as looking at him, and he followed them to the house. The woman was not even twenty and would have been very pretty, he thought, had her face not been tear-stained and pale from exhaustion. In addition, she was very pregnant, and she looked so much like Candamir that the slave knew exactly who she was.

Hacon had been sitting by the fire, miserable and lost in thought, but when the door opened his worried face broke out in a joyful smile. "Asta!" He jumped up and ran toward her, but when he saw her face he stopped and said again, uncertainly, "Asta?"

She took his hands in hers and smiled back. "My word, Hacon…I can hardly call you 'little brother' anymore. You're tall enough now to look down on me!"

"I wouldn't dare," he replied, embarrassed.

Candamir put down the squirming bundle. "Hacon, this is our nephew, Fulc."

Just three years old, little Fulc looked suspiciously at his new surroundings, and when Hacon tried to pick him up, Fulc kicked him in the shins. Hacon suppressed a cry as he jumped back.

Heide, the fat old maid who had been the cook here since Candamir was in diapers, observed the scene with a stony face, crossed her mighty arms, and grumbled, "Just like his father, I'd say."

Asta's face darkened as she grabbed hold of her son. He hid his face in her skirt, and an uncomfortable silence came over the room.

It was Candamir who finally spoke up. "For anyone who does not know—this is my sister Asta. She was married and living in Elbingdal, but the Turons also attacked their village yesterday and killed her husband. So now she has come back home."

*I am sure this isn't the whole story,* the Saxon thought to himself. His suspicion was soon confirmed when Candamir turned to the cook and said, "We will forget what happened in the past—that is no longer of any importance. My sister and her son are welcome in this house and will be treated with kindness and respect. Do you understand, Heide?"

"Certainly, Master."

"Good. I'd be sorry to have to order you or anyone else out of this house with the hard winter coming."

Heide's wrinkled cheeks lost their color, and she lowered her eyes and nodded.

For a brief moment, Candamir closed his eyes. He had not the slightest idea how they would ever make it through the winter. His sister's unexpected arrival and the whole matter of the old feud which she brought with her would be a heavy burden. He settled into his high seat—a slightly elevated, wide chair with beautifully carved posts that stood in the middle of the room to the right of the longfire. It was reserved for the head of the family and had accommodated a long line of his ancestors. Candamir remembered the first months after the death of his father, and how he had felt like an impostor sitting there. But not anymore; the high seat gave him a feeling of strength and self-confidence.

"Bring a bench for my sister and my brother. You, Saxon, go and get us beer. Gunda, take charge of the boy. The rest of you, leave us alone," Candamir commanded his servants.

Trestles were hastily brought in and set up along the fireplace, and a tabletop was laid over them. Then a bench was placed alongside and padded with pillows and furs, on which Hacon and Asta took their places. Gunda, the pretty Frisian maid the villagers had teased him about that morning, quickly gained the confidence of little Fulc. She sat with him on a seal-skin blanket by the fire and fed him bread and honey. He soon leaned his head against her knee and closed his eyes. Gunda gave Asta a conspiratorial smile, then lowered her eyes again politely.

The Saxon filled a large pitcher from the beer keg and put it on the table along with three earthenware mugs. Then he looked questioningly at Candamir, jerking his chin toward the door to inquire if he was to leave. Candamir shook his head, so the servant withdrew into a dark corner next to the beer keg where he also slept at night.

It had started to rain, and a sea breeze kicked up, whistling around the house and tugging hard at the boards of its outer walls. But it didn't reach the people inside: the building had both a half-timbered outer wall and a wooden inner wall, and a tightly packed layer of earthen insulation between. The main hall had no windows, though, so the only source of daylight, aside from the door, was the small, round hole in the middle of the roof, through which the rain now came pouring in, falling into the fire. Yet this arrangement made the main room with its longfire cozy and warm throughout the year. Here, inside, you were as sheltered from the elements as a bear in its cave.

The fire crackled cheerfully, and now and then a drop of resin burst, spreading a pleasant pine fragrance through the room.

Candamir took a deep draught of beer, then filled his cup again. "Asta, tell us what happened."

"Do you mean yesterday, or in the last four years?"

He shrugged. "Both."

The attack up the river in Elbingdal had followed the same pattern as the one in Elasund. The Turons had killed everyone in their way, stolen the provisions and the women, and locked up the men, boys, and cattle in the biggest barn before setting it on fire.

"Nils, too," Asta concluded. "He was burned to death like all the others."

Candamir nodded. He could not honestly say he grieved for his brother-in-law, but he was sorry for Asta. It was strange to see her there again, so suddenly.

For as long as anyone could remember, there had been a blood feud between the families, and Nils and Asta had incurred the anger of both their fathers by marrying. Their father never pardoned her, but Nils's family finally forgave the renegade son and accepted him in Elbingdal along with his wife. The marriage had guaranteed a temporary truce between the two families, at least. Candamir had to admit that this was a good thing. It had finally done away with the constant threat that had hung over his childhood.

And they had been good years, Asta concluded defiantly. Nils had made out well and had even planned on ordering a ship with eight pairs of oars from Berse the shipwright. His family had never warmed to Asta, but she had been treated politely, at least.

"But this morning..." Asta paused, quickly reaching for a mug in order to hide her emotion from her brothers. "In their anger and their grief they turned on me like a pack of hungry wolves. I...fled. I had to run. Nils's uncle had a hunting knife in his hand and called Fulc a damned brat from Elasund. I was thinking that if they killed me and Fulc, you would learn about it and things would start all over again. So you see, I had no choice, Candamir."

He nodded, and then after a moment's silence said, "It is good that you came."

Asta sighed. "I can imagine you are wondering how you can feed your people, even without me and my child." Glancing down at her curved belly, she corrected herself. "My children."

"Oh, we'll manage somehow," Candamir replied.

"How serious is it?" she asked.

He didn't try to fool her. "Well, pretty bad. We still have our sheep and horses, because they were out to pasture, but the cattle are all dead except for an old ox. And the storehouse...you saw for yourself."

Candamir heard a faint whisper from the shadows behind the beer keg and turned around, frowning. "What did you say?"

The Saxon raised his head and looked at the three siblings. "I said, 'Behold the ravens.' It is something from my book that just came to me. But you don't believe in any of that."

"Well, you are quite right," said Candamir, annoyed. But he was curious just the same. "What does your strange god know about ravens?"

"My god knows everything about everything," the Saxon replied. "And he says, 'Behold the ravens: They neither sow nor reap, they have neither storehouses nor barns, for God takes care of them.'"

"That's brilliant!" Candamir scoffed. "We don't need a lecture to know that the ravens are better off in a hard winter than we are. They always make it through because they are the birds of the gods."

The slave was about to start in with an explanation of the biblical allegory, but he was cut short by Asta. "That reminds me of our grandmother's story about the winter ravens," she said, looking into the fire with a sad smile.

It was a memory long forgotten that now came rushing back when Asta mentioned it: their father's mother had often taken the two grandchildren under her large fur blanket and told them stories. She had the cracked, harsh voice of an old woman, but she knew how to bring distant worlds to life in the children's imagination.

"Winter ravens?" Hacon asked blankly. He had no memory of this grandmother, as he had been too young when she died.

"Yes, our grandmother often told us about the far-off island," Asta said, passing her hand through his hair. "But if I remember correctly, you only wanted to hear the stories about great battles and warriors. I can see you now standing over there by the fire with your wooden sword, battling bravely with the shadows." She pointed to her son, who had fallen asleep on Gunda's lap. "Soon you can tell Fulc all your favorite tales."

*If Fulc survives until next spring,* Hacon thought uneasily.

As if reading his mind, Asta became serious again and turned to Candamir. "I am sorry that I just showed up here and added to your worries, brother. I know I have no right to ask your help..."

"Nonsense," he interrupted gruffly. In a way he was happy she was back and surprised by how much he had missed her. "But we must plan. Saxon, come here; put some wood on the fire and sit down with us." He knew that the Saxon was smart and resourceful, and good with numbers. Candamir wouldn't have admitted it, but he trusted this man's judgment over that of many of his neighbors and often took his advice without letting him know it.

The Saxon fetched an armful of logs from the wood box by the door and laid them on the fire. Then he sat down next to Hacon and shyly bowed his head before Asta.

She smiled at him and asked, "What is your name?"

"Byrhtferth, Mistress."

"What?"

"Byrhtferth."

"Just call him the Saxon," said Candamir. "That's what everybody calls him here."

"But Candamir," she objected, "everyone needs a name."

Candamir shrugged impatiently. "So far he has gotten along without one." And speaking as if the slave were not even present, he told his sister all about the Saxon and his bizarre god, and how he had come to live with them. "Now and then he is quite useful," he concluded, "but often he's a nuisance. Actually, I was about to give him a good whipping when you arrived."

Asta saw how embarrassed the young monk was. "What do you want me to call you?" she asked. "Pick out a name I can pronounce, and that's what I will call you."

The Saxon blushed to the roots of his flaxen hair, but finally, an idea came to him that seemed as bold as it was ironic. "Then call me Austin, Mistress, if you will be so kind."

"Agreed!" Asta nodded contentedly, clasping her hands together on the table.

Candamir frowned. He was not pleased that his sister, who had just returned home, was already having an influence on the way things were done in his house. He knew his resentment was childish, but he secretly swore to himself that he would never call him Austin.

"Well, can we perhaps get down to the matter at hand?" he said impatiently.

"There is a very simple way to get us all through the winter, Master," the Saxon began.

"Indeed? I am eager to know what that may be."

"Load your pack animals into your ship and head south to one of the big trading ports. Sell your ship there, and with the money you can buy grain, peas, and dried fish to bring back with the pack animals." He spread out his hands. "We will live like kings."

Candamir cast him an incredulous look. "The *Falcon* is the most precious thing I own. If we have a good hunt in the spring, I will take the seal furs and walrus teeth to the land of the Franks and exchange them for the excellent weapons they forge there. For that, I need a ship."

"You won't be going anywhere with your ship if you die of hunger first," the slave replied.

"It's out of the question," Candamir repeated firmly. "Perhaps it would be best if I just sold *you*."

The monk did not reply, as he knew his master was not serious. Instead he just shrugged his slender shoulders and said, "Well, it's still just September...Autumn Moon, I mean. We can fish, as Olaf said, and perhaps we will even catch a whale, which would last us about a month. We won't get much more from the sea, but this is just the right time for hunting in the forest. You can find nuts there as well, and edible mushrooms, and if you look hard enough, all sorts of berries and wild herbs."

The Saxon knew that the idea of eating animals from the forest was suspect to the Elasund villagers. Scarcely anyone here knew how to hunt on the land, and those who did hunted bear, weasel, and fox for their fur, not their meat.

"Well then, starting tomorrow and on every day the weather permits, you will go into the forest with the maids and gather berries, mushrooms, and so forth," Candamir decided. "Hacon and I will go fishing with Osmund."

"Master, if you could give me a bow and arrow to take along..."

Candamir shook his head. "No." An ancient law forbade slaves to bear weapons, and Candamir suspected that his Saxon was offended, so with a mixture of compassion and impatience, he added, "It is not that I distrust you, but if anyone saw you, I would be in trouble."

"You could send me into the forest with him," Hacon said. "I could take the bow."

"You have the strength of a little bird," Candamir scoffed. "You can't even draw the bowstring halfway back."

"That's not true!" the boy protested indignantly. "I can..."

"I said you will go out fishing with us, and that's it. We need you in the boat."

Hacon knew only too well why they needed him. From sunrise to noon he would be sitting with a bloody knife in the stern of the boat cutting open cold, slippery fish, taking out the slimy guts and throwing them into the sea in order to attract more fish. The work was arduous and disgusting, so against his better judgment, he tried again. "You could just as well take along one of the slaves."

Candamir gave him a solid rap on the head. "I could, that's right, but I am taking you along instead."

He didn't approve of how much time his brother spent in the company of the Saxon. He suspected that Hacon was quite taken with his strange stories. The Saxon was a good-natured, docile fellow to be sure, but Candamir doubted that his god was as harmless.

The people of Elasund burned their dead, mourned those who had been carried off, and prepared hastily for the approaching winter. Hardly any of the cattle and pigs slaughtered by the Turons were fit for consumption because they had not been bled, but their hides were removed for processing into leather before the carcasses were burnt. The servants were sent into the forest to cut wood and rebuild the storage sheds that had been destroyed. The women and children set to gathering and harvesting what the forest could provide for their survival, while the men went off to sea every day, all hoping and praying that the snow would come late this year.

Osmund looked glumly at their day's catch as he took down his boat's mast and pulled in the oars. All they had were a few small whitings and a half crate of herring.

"Not enough," he murmured.

"It is never enough," Candamir agreed gloomily as he jumped off into the knee-deep water, pulled the boat ashore, and tied it to its mooring. Motioning to Hacon, he pointed to the little box containing the herring. "Take it to Osmund's house."

"They are yours, Candamir," Osmund said. "I got yesterday's catch of herring."

Candamir snorted. "That was hardly anything. Do what I say, Hacon." He waited until the youth had shouldered the box and left before he said to Osmund, "You may not care whether you survive the winter, but you must also think of the people entrusted to you, and of your son. He needs his father."

Osmund nodded curtly. He knew that Candamir was right, even if he didn't like hearing it.

Silently they spread his nets out to dry in the grass by the shore and removed the remainder of the meager catch from the boat.

"Asta wraps the fish in herbs, smokes them over a fire of oak wood, and pours a ladle of beer on them from time to time. You must try that, Osmund, it tastes wonderful."

Unexpectedly, Osmund felt his mouth watering. "Sounds good," he admitted.

"Then come over tonight."

"I can't. You know I'm going out into the backcountry tomorrow with Olaf and Jared to get provisions, and I still have a great deal to do."

Candamir nodded, suppressing a sigh. He had noticed that Asta and Osmund were avoiding one another. They had been betrothed before Asta had eloped with Nils. That had not upset Osmund especially, as he had eyes only for Gisla at the time. But the fact remained that Osmund had been avoiding Candamir's house since Asta's return.

"I wish you success with your trip," Candamir said. He had entrusted almost all the silver he had to his friend in order to buy flour, oats, peas, and perhaps a little hay and seed for next spring.

Osmund stood bent over the open case of whitings and divided up the catch as best he could. His hands were cracked from the ice-cold seawater.

Candamir looked down at his own hands, which were no better. "Maybe Hacon's right," he said. "It *is* drudgery and hardly worth it. Perhaps we really should try hunting in the forest."

Osmund stood up straight and put his numbed hands in his armpits. He was wearing a heavy sleeveless vest over his coat and a warm hood, but he was stiff with cold just the same. "It's just that none of us has had any experience hunting deer or wild boar. We would come back empty-handed and just waste the few precious days we have left to catch fish."

Shivering, Candamir shrugged his shoulders. "I don't think we will be risking much if we try for one or two days. Our situation is desperate—reason enough for us to try something different."

Osmund was accustomed to Candamir's abstruse ideas and had realized years ago that the best thing was simply not to respond. "Perhaps we'll catch a large codfish in the next few days, and when the weather gets really bad we can slaughter the sheep since we don't have any winter fodder, anyway."

"Sure, Osmund. It's just that this won't be enough," Candamir said impatiently.

Osmund looked straight at him and nodded. "I know. But there is nothing else we can do."

There were five men on the trip—Osmund, Olaf, Olaf's eldest son Jared, and two of Olaf's slaves—and it took five days. It rained the entire time, and on the way back they were overtaken by an icy downpour that brought their progress to a near standstill. Even in good weather, the narrow, rutted roads would have been a challenge. Huddled on the box of the middle wagon holding his long coat around him as tightly as possible to shield himself from the wind, Osmund guided his team of oxen with patience and skill, hoping the storm would soon pass.

Business had been brisk, and the three wagons were heavily loaded. The farmers had had a good summer—warm and moist. They had been spared attacks, livestock disease, and other catastrophes. Their barns overflowed, and they were willing to share with the neighbors on the coast—in return for good silver, of course.

Olaf was happy with the way things had gone, and that morning he told Osmund he intended to keep a small portion of everything they had procured for himself before distributing the rest in Elasund.

"But Father," Jared had said indignantly, "they are our neighbors and they are in need. We are well enough off—why do you want to…"

Olaf silenced him with such a hard slap in the face that Jared nearly fell from the wagon. "Enough? What do you know," Olaf said, and they continued their trip in silence.

The storm had since worsened, and now the wind was driving wet snow into their faces, making progress very difficult for both driver and oxen, and nearly ripping off the skins they had used to cover their load.

"Look up ahead," Olaf shouted above the storm's ruckus, pointing to a wood-shingled roof, just visible through the pine forest. "There is a farm. Let's stop there and wait for the worst to pass."

*Until spring, perhaps?* Osmund thought glumly.

But Jared murmured, "Thanks be to Thor!" He feared the raging storm, and Osmund couldn't blame him. The old pine trees were bent almost to the ground by the force of the gale, and at any moment the travelers could be crushed by a falling tree.

Before reaching the secluded farm, Osmund's wagon became stuck in the mud, and he, Jared, and the two slaves had to summon all their strength to free it again—the oxen could simply not do it themselves. Osmund was grateful when they got to the barn without breaking a wheel or an axle.

Olaf walked over to the house to arrange accommodation for the night. While the slaves unhitched the oxen, Osmund and Jared collapsed on two bales of straw in the barn. Jared pushed his dripping ginger hair off his forehead and wrung out the slender braids that framed his face. Then he gently touched the cut on his lower lip made by his father's ring. "I wonder when he's going to stop that," he said glumly. "I'm almost nineteen!"

Only three years younger than himself, Osmund realized, and yet his cousin seemed still very youthful to him. "Get married," he advised succinctly.

The younger man laughed in astonishment. "And what then?"

"It'll make you grow up in no time. And no father raises his hand against a married son."

Jared leaned back against the wall, stretched out his legs, and looked at Osmund thoughtfully. "Then you don't know my father very well," he replied. "He knows how to control people. And he rules with an iron fist."

"Yes, I know."

"I'd like to marry," Jared said. "Siward's daughter Inga, for example. But Father won't allow it; there's no dowry."

"You should listen to him. These things are more important than they appear to you at the moment."

Jared laughed and shook his head. "And I had to hear that from you, of all people! You didn't have anything but your little piece of land and a drafty, ramshackle house. Your wife had no dowry. How long ago was that? Two years? And today..."

"I am still just as poor today as I was then, Jared." By working hard day and night, and with Candamir's help, he had built a new house for himself and Gisla when little Roric was on the way, but that was about all he had been able to do. In any case, he had nothing to fall back on to stave off the impending famine. Of the provisions on the wagon, he would get only what Olaf had promised him for coming along, as he had no silver to buy anything.

"Well, you have twice as many sheep as two years ago," his cousin pointed out.

"But no ship to take their wool south to sell it," Osmund replied. "Our grandfather was a wealthy man, Jared. But my father quarreled with him, and so your father inherited everything—all the land, the ship, and the money. My father got nothing, and so I am poor and my son will be poor, and all his sons as well. This land is too exhausted for a man to make out on his own. Be smart and don't make the same mistake as my father."

Jared propped his chin in his hand and thought for a moment. "At least your father was free."

"No poor man is free."

"Free from the tyranny of his father, I mean. I will never be, as long as he lives."

"But no man lives forever. And he really isn't all that bad."

"That's what you think. All you see is his bright side. Recently he has taken a real shine to you. You must have something he wants. What could that be?"

Osmund pulled a piece of straw out of the bale, placing it between his teeth. "I thought maybe you could tell me."

Jared raised his hands. "I have no idea. Your land?"

How tempting—his land! A barren field and a few stony meadows. Osmund laughed softly.

Olaf laughed much louder.

Jared was startled, anxiously wondering how long his father had been standing there.

Whatever Olaf had heard, it apparently hadn't dampened his spirits. He took his son and his nephew by the shoulder and said, "Come, the farmer's wife has pork and beans for us and will cook us a leg of mutton." He twisted Jared's ear so it hurt, but casually and inconspicuously without letting Osmund out of his sight. "Don't worry, nephew. You have nothing to fear from me."

"I'm not afraid of you," Osmund replied quietly. He didn't mean it as a challenge; he was just stating a fact. Since Gisla's death, he was indifferent to most things, so nothing really frightened him anymore.

Olaf patted Osmund's bearded cheek. "I'm convinced the sparkle will come back into your eyes when you learn what it is I want from you, lad."

Osmund wasn't overly curious, but since Olaf held his gaze, he finally did him the favor and asked, "What is it?"

Olaf let go of his son's ear. "Leave us alone, Jared."

Relieved, the young man left the barn and headed over to the house, where a pretty woman greeted him with a warm smile and a pot of hot stew. When the worst of his hunger had passed, he spent some time talking with her. The house was warm, and the air was heavy with the fragrance of meat roasting on a spit over the longfire.

By the time Olaf and Osmund entered the house, the leg of mutton was already crispy and brown. Jared raised his head when he heard the door. He was not surprised to see that his father had been right.

Osmund's eyes were sparkling.

# Hunter's Moon

Hacon was predictably the first to wake up. Since early youth he had been plagued by bad dreams, and ever since his brother brought the Frisian slave girl into the house, they were often wet dreams. These disturbed him more than the nightmares of years past, though he knew from speaking with his friend Wiland that he was not alone. But it worried him just the same, particularly since the Saxon had said that such dreams were an expression of unclean thoughts.

Hacon sat up and looked around the dimly lit hall, illuminated by only the weak glow from the longfire. He was sleeping on two benches that were pushed against the wall of the main room and padded with soft covers and furs. That was the privilege of the younger master of the house. The slaves lay on the hard, straw-covered ground wrapped up in blankets.

Candamir and the Frisian slave girl lay on two adjoining benches, their arms wound tightly around each other—but that was an exception. Ordinarily, the master of the house and his companion occupied the small private chamber behind the hall, but he had let Asta have this room for the birth of her daughter the previous afternoon. She had named the baby Hergild, after their mother.

Without making a sound, Hacon tiptoed to the door and opened it. He was dazzled by the unexpected glare, as a small pile of powdery snow slid onto his bare feet. The lad stood motionless in the doorway and took a deep breath of the fresh air, marveling at how pure and silent the world seemed after the first snow.

"What's going on?" Candamir asked drowsily.

Hacon stepped aside so his brother could look out. Candamir sat up and rubbed his eyes with both hands.

Gunda stirred at his side, looked up, and turned up her nose in disbelief. "Snow? A whole month before the Yule festival?" she asked.

"That is not unusual here," Candamir snapped, often feeling the need to defend his homeland against her Frisian arrogance. "How much is it, Hacon?"

The boy stuck his foot into the clean, white snow outside the door and laughed softly as the snow tickled him. "About half a yard," he estimated.

Candamir sank back into the covers. "Good, that won't interfere with today's plans."

It wasn't long before the virgin snow cover was crisscrossed by little paths, the widest being the one leading to the outhouse. Breakfast was skimpy, just a bowl of thin fish broth for each, since they had to carefully ration their supplies. Only the master of the hall and the new mother were given a few bits of the meat and onions used to make the soup.

Heide returned from the bedroom with the empty bowl and nodded in response to Candamir's questioning look. "She is well, Master, and the baby too."

He was relieved, secretly dreading the long hours of screaming, but the birth had been mercifully fast and without much wailing. Asta had forbidden him to send for old Brigitta. She told him she would rather die than be touched by that witch, to which Candamir reminded her that it was the old witch herself who had delivered Asta, as well as Candamir and Hacon. But Asta couldn't be persuaded and gave birth to her daughter with the help of only the two servant women.

Heide picked up little Fulc from the bench and took him to the bedroom door. "Go now, and see how your mother is, little one. Don't be afraid." Turning to Candamir she added, "What your sister needs is a bath."

Candamir tapped Hacon on the shoulder and said, "You heard. Go and heat up the sauna, and take the Saxon along. Make sure you heat enough water—we'll have to wash the wool after the sheep have been shorn." Candamir stood up, beckoning his two other slaves to follow him. "We'll get the animals from the meadow." He slipped on his lambskin waistcoat, and as he walked by he put his hand briefly on Gunda's slender neck, leaned over, and kissed her on the lips before disappearing outside.

Hacon and the Saxon followed a moment later. It had stopped snowing, but the sky had darkened and gradually turned to the unmistakable gray color that presaged more snow. The wind had died down, and it was cold.

The sauna was a little wooden hut on the west side of the yard with an entryway where you could take off your clothes and, if you wished, cool off with cold water after the steaming bath. Behind a heavy wooden door, the bathing room itself featured a hearth in the middle which was used for heating and making steam.

Hacon looked at the wood box—it was empty. "Of course," the boy grumbled. "What would you expect?"

Candamir often scolded his brother for being lazy, but the Saxon thought it was only natural that an adolescent would rather spend his time with his friends than do chores. He had been the same way. Picking up the empty box, he said, "It's all right, I'll go."

When he returned shortly after, groaning under the weight of the heavy box of logs, Hacon felt guilty. He jumped up from the bench and started piling the wood on the hearth. "Thank you, Sax…Austin. That is a strange name, you know."

"Really? I'm quite happy with it." In fact, nearly the whole household had started following Asta's example, calling him by that name—much to Candamir's annoyance.

"What does it mean, 'Austin'?" the boy asked, placing a handful of straw on the wood and reaching for flint and steel.

"It is the Saxon form of a Latin name, Augustinus, that means in your language 'The Illustrious One.'"

Hacon raised his eyebrows and scrutinized his friend meaningfully from head to toe. "How appropriate," he observed.

The Saxon couldn't help laughing. "You are right about that. I chose it because it was the name of Britain's first bishop. It fit *him* perfectly."

"What's a bishop?" Hacon inquired.

"What a nobleman is in the world, a bishop is in the church."

"I see—and what is a nobleman?"

*Poor child,* thought the Saxon, sighing. *What a barbaric, chaotic world you are growing up in.* "A mighty warrior who owns much land and rules over everyone and everything in his land."

"Sort of like Olaf?" Hacon asked.

The Saxon grimaced. "Not exactly. A nobleman serves his king, not himself and his own desires. Ideally, he should be a wise, upright man—at least the bishops are upright."

Austin picked up the big cauldron, carried it outside, and filled it with snow. As he stopped to blow on his freezing fingers, he saw Osmund crossing the yard toward the stable where Candamir had herded a dozen of his sheep. Candamir's anxious face lit up in a broad smile when he saw Osmund coming.

Lugging his burden into the bathhouse, he shut the door and hung the cauldron over the fire. Then he sat down on the stone bench alongside Hacon. Now they could only wait for the water to boil, not the most disagreeable task a slave could be required to do on a freezing day like this. He rubbed his hands together over the crackling fire and said, "Osmund has come."

Hacon was not surprised. "He is helping us to shear the sheep that are to be slaughtered. Nobody can shear the way he can."

"Why are the sheep shorn before they are slaughtered? Wouldn't it be much simpler to do it after?" the Saxon asked.

Now it was Hacon's turn to laugh at the Saxon's ignorance. "Wool is better when it comes from living animals."

Austin could hardly believe that the wool would have enough time to change quality between the killing and shearing, but he had to admit he knew little about it. The Benedictine brothers raised sheep and planted wheat and vegetables for their own use, but because he was so good with his hands he had been instructed in the art of writing and producing books, not in tilling the fields or caring for livestock.

"He seems better," the Saxon said after a lengthy silence. "Osmund, I mean. He no longer seems to be brooding as he was just a few weeks ago. Clearly the Lord has led him out of the Valley of the Shadow of Death."

Although Hacon did not understand this last remark, he nodded. "Yes, that's what Candamir says, too. But Osmund still avoids all women. He doesn't seem to be in a hurry to marry again."

"No," the Saxon said.

"You think that's right?" the boy asked in amazement.

"Indeed. He is grieving over the loss of his wife, as he should."

"But that has to end sometime. Little Roric needs a mother, and a man needs a woman."

"According to my religion, men and women should be married only once and remain single if their spouse dies," the monk said. "The only reason to marry again is if they are in danger of succumbing to the sins of the flesh."

Hacon frowned. "The what?"

"Lust. You know what I mean…" Austin blushed and looked into the fire.

Now Hacon knew what he meant. The Saxon only blushed when the conversation turned to men and women sleeping together. "I have never understood exactly what you mean by 'sin.'"

"Committing a sin means breaking a law or ignoring a divine commandment, doing something evil."

"But what men and women do is not forbidden or evil. Beasts do it as well, and they don't know anything about good or evil."

*This young fellow is almost a philosopher,* the Saxon thought, amused. "In my religion, it is a sin if you do it without God's blessing."

"And God gives his blessing to each man and each woman only once? What happens if they realize that they just don't get along and they separate?"

The Saxon shook his head. "That doesn't happen with true Christians. They enter into a bond for life, and it is sanctified by God. But, as I said, if one of them dies, God looks the other way and permits remarriage in order to avoid something worse."

"Strange, how your god interferes in the life of his people," Hacon said thoughtfully. "And that he has time for that."

"Well, he is all-powerful and therefore can do a hundred things at the same time."

"I think you mean he can interfere in a hundred lives all at the same time," the boy said. "But tell me, what good is it to your god if men and women don't lie with each other?"

"No, it's the other way around. It's a good thing for men. Chastity elevates the soul."

*Then my soul must be floating in the clouds,* Hacon thought gloomily—he still had not lost his innocence, though he would have been all too happy to be rid of it. "So what you mean is that Osmund is a better man than my brother, for example?"

The Saxon nodded. "In this respect, yes."

"Do you think that's why your god is rewarding Osmund with the best herd of sheep?"

"No. God rewards the righteous in the hereafter. You know, I have told you all about that."

Hacon nodded.

"You couldn't say that Osmund is richly blessed with earthly rewards, in spite of his good flock of sheep," Austin continued. "He works day and night trying to make something out of this worthless bit of land, and to no avail. Now, on top of everything else, he has lost his wife whom he loved more than I have ever seen a man love a woman. Between you and me, Hacon, sometimes even I find it hard to understand what measure God uses to assign good or bad fortune to people here on earth."

Hacon thought for a moment before responding. "Why should you feel sympathy for Osmund? He always looks down on you and treats you rudely."

Austin shrugged his shoulders and smiled. "He is bright enough to fear the power of my god. Sometimes he takes it out on me, but I don't mind. After all, he saved my life when I came here."

"And was that such a big favor? Now you live the miserable, shameful existence of a slave. If they had killed you instead, you would be a martyr and sit beside the throne of your god, wouldn't you?"

The Saxon laughed softly, laid his hand on the boy's shoulder, and replied, "Good point, Hacon. But apparently I was not yet ready for that. Look, the water is boiling. Let's fill the cauldron again before your brother catches us idling and makes martyrs of us both."

Nothing could be heard except for the muffled sound of shears cutting through the heavy wool. Osmund worked with regular, confident motions, and it was a joy to watch him. Candamir, however, was not paying much attention to what his friend was doing—his thoughts were far away on the wide, blue sea, on foreign shores.

Osmund finally broke the silence. "Well? What do you think?" he asked impatiently.

"I don't know," his friend said as he stooped down, picked up an armful of wool, and stuffed it into a large wicker basket nearby.

Osmund straightened up, releasing the sheep he had clamped between his legs. The animal bleated and scampered away, casting a disapproving glance at Osmund over its shoulder.

"Well, go ahead and bleat as long as you can," he said softly. "If you only knew what's in store for you this afternoon, you'd cry a lot louder."

Candamir chuckled, but then he became serious again. "Leaving this place...," he murmured uneasily.

Osmund took off his thick fur vest and passed his arm over his forehead. Shearing was hot work, even in this cold. "It's not like you haven't thought about it before."

"No." Candamir caught the waistcoat that Osmund tossed to him and hung it over the fence. "You know that I've been dreaming about it for a long time."

"But dreaming about it and seriously considering it are two different things," Osmund said, before calling out to Hacon. "Where are you, lad? Bring me the next one."

Hacon came out of the barn leading a large gray sheep by a rope that he placed in Osmund's outstretched hand. Then he put an armful of wool in the already overflowing basket and whistled for one of the slaves to carry it over to the hall.

But Candamir shook his head and tapped the boy on his skinny chest. "*You* will carry the wool. It's time you built up your muscles."

Hacon clenched his teeth at the insult, then slung the basket strap over his shoulder and staggered to his feet. He headed for the hall as quickly as he could, but not fast enough to escape Candamir's and Osmund's scornful laughter.

Alone again, Osmund took the patient sheep and started removing the fur it wouldn't soon need, as Candamir's gaze wandered across the meadows that rose up to the dense pine forest. The trees looked sublime under their thick caps of snow, and though Osmund was looking down at his hands, he guessed what was going through Candamir's mind. "We wouldn't be leaving very much behind here. You more than I though."

Candamir snorted. "The land yields less and less every year, and half belongs to Hacon. When he is grown up and demands his portion, there will be hardly enough for either us to live on. Maybe we'll even become enemies like your father and uncle," he said, folding his arms. It made him restless to watch Osmund at work while he stood idly by. "I've been mulling that over for a long time," Candamir admitted after a brief silence. In fact, it was his greatest concern for the future, and Osmund was the only one he could confide in. "No, I tell you, no matter how beautiful this place may be, I wouldn't mind leaving. This land isn't good for anything anymore except to drive a man to despair. I'm just worried about Olaf."

Osmund nodded. "I know."

"I don't trust him."

"I know," Osmund repeated in a sharper tone. He was never quite sure how he felt about Olaf either, but since he was his uncle he felt obliged to defend him when Candamir or anyone else said something disparaging about the rich merchant trader. His prosperity certainly made him an object of envy. But Osmund concluded, "Just because you would set sail with him doesn't mean you have to trust him."

"It doesn't? What do you know about that country? Where is it? What's there? Only your uncle knows the answer to all these questions. If we sailed with him, we would be completely at his mercy."

"Admittedly." Osmund let go of the shorn sheep, stretched, and walked over to Candamir. They stood there leaning on the fence. "But he certainly has no intention of sailing his ship into disaster. He only does things he thinks will be profitable for him, but his advantage could also be ours. The risk is great; there is no doubt about that. Even Olaf doesn't know exactly where this island lies. He just found it by chance when he ran into a bad storm that lasted twelve days and drove him off course. On the way back he hit another storm, and he believes it was only with the help of the gods that he finally made his way back to familiar waters. So nobody knows exactly how to reach this place, and it seems that only if we find the storm again will we find the island. But *if* we can find it, Candamir…" He paused, shaking his head.

"Well, if we find it, what then?" Candamir pressed.

"It's somewhere southwest of the land of the Franks," Osmund continued. "That means that the winters are short and mild, and the ground is fertile. You can harvest your crops twice a year. Can you imagine that? Olaf doesn't know how large it is, but he tried to sail around it and in three days had still not reached the southern tip before bad weather forced him back. Enough land, Candamir, for every family in Elasund and the villages along the river—that is, for every family willing to take the risk."

"Hm," Candamir replied. "But it is unlikely that such a wonderful, fertile land would be uninhabited."

Osmund shook his head. "The people there are peaceful and small in numbers. The only weapons they have are those used for hunting and fishing. It would be child's play to take their land and make them our slaves."

"It sounds like it, anyway. But how can Olaf claim to know all about that?"

"He lived among them for two weeks and studied their ways. They were friendly and simple people and helped him get his boat back in the water again."

Candamir had to admit it sounded tempting.

Finally he said, "You know, I believe I'll just have to think it over for a while."

Osmund nodded and went to get his next victim from the shed. "Olaf says if we want to do it we have to decide soon so we can build up some interest for this venture among the people by the river. Soon the snow will be so deep that we can no longer reach them even on skis. He's right about that of course, but we need to think it over carefully. If we set out and really do get caught in a storm like the one he described, there might well be no turning back."

"And how come he chose you, of all people, to confide in first?" Candamir asked. "You're not on such close terms with him. After your father died, he didn't lift a finger to help you, so why this sudden burst of interest in his family?"

"It doesn't have anything to do with interest in the family," Osmund said. "But all his money won't make this happen if he doesn't have the support of Elasund. And Olaf is a man who's at least honest with himself. He knows very well that many people distrust him. He is counting on me to convince you, and then on both of us together to convince all of those Elasunders who would reject Olaf's plan just because it came from him. That's true most of all of Harald the blacksmith."

Candamir shook his head. "In any case, we'd be sailing off into the unknown, and everyone would have to think about whether they wanted to expose their families to such dangers. And that's what makes me so suspicious. Ye gods, why would Olaf be ready to take such a risk? He's rich! His farm is a fortress, and the Turons can't do him any harm."

"You're wrong," his friend said. "Olaf doesn't want word to get around, but he lost a lot to the Turons, too. A burning arrow set fire to his stable and all his horses were killed."

"O mighty Tyr," Candamir murmured, feeling sorry not for Olaf but for all the wonderful horses.

"He won't starve on account of this," Osmund continued, "but he had plans to ship half of his animals south and sell them in the spring. It's a hard loss for him, and don't forget that Olaf has five sons. Perhaps he does have a good deal of land, but he still doesn't have enough for them all. Jared and Lars are already sworn enemies. Olaf worries about dissension in his family and is concerned about its survival, Candamir, just as you are."

Candamir stroked his beard. What Osmund was saying sounded reasonable, but it didn't ease his doubts about Olaf. "Perhaps," he murmured hesitantly, "but I'd be a fool to support a venture like this when the outcome is so uncertain."

Yet even as he said this, he was seized by the longing he sometimes felt when he wandered to the promontory and looked out over the open sea. It was the restlessness and love of adventure in his blood—what a temptation simply to leave behind all your cares and wants and seek your fortune in far-off places…

By twilight, they had shorn eight sheep and slaughtered, bled, and gutted four—no small task for a short day, they thought. Then they washed up with the warm water waiting for them in the bathhouse and headed over to the hall. Everyone was busy there. Hacon, the Saxon, the two other slaves, and the two maids were all sorting and washing the wool.

Asta was sitting on the bench by the fire, right next to the high seat, and holding her tiny, sleeping daughter in her arms. Fulc sat next to her, mother and son pushing a little, clumsily carved toy ship back and forth between them on the bench. The boy was making soft but remarkably realistic wind sounds.

Candamir was pleased to see that his sister had dressed up: she was wearing a dove-gray, long-sleeved gown, and over it a reddish-brown jumper that the two men recognized at once as belonging to her mother. They remembered the oval bronze buckles fastening the straps above her chest and connected by a short chain of polished, semiprecious stones.

"May the blessings of the gods be with your daughter in all of her journeys, Asta," said Osmund.

"Thank you, Osmund," she said, looking up and smiling, but she could not fool him. He saw that she had been crying.

They hadn't seen one another very often since Asta had come home, and when they had, their meetings were brief, and they only exchanged a few inconsequential words.

Asta was three years younger than he, and when they were children they had been like brother and sister, but they had always taken for granted that one day they would marry. Their fathers had decided it for them, and it seemed a natural thing to do. But everything worked out differently, and they both felt a bit guilty about it now. Four years had passed since Asta went to Elbingdal, and they had grown apart, but now as they looked into each other's eyes and saw the pain they were each suffering, the intimacy of their youth suddenly returned.

"I've been assured a number of times that it will pass," Osmund heard himself saying.

Asta blinked briefly and nodded. "Yes, people tell me that three or four times a day."

Passing his hand through Fulc's hair, Osmund said, "Handsome lad. Favors his father."

"That's what the cook says, anyway, when he misbehaves. I think he looks like Candamir."

"Probably the one he got his bad manners from."

Candamir rolled his eyes, retreating for a pitcher of strong beer. Asta and Osmund laughed softly, and then he sat down beside her. Candamir took a suspiciously long time to return with the beer. Then he and Osmund each downed a giant mug before removing their coats and settling down to work.

Water was heated over the longfire and mixed in wooden washtubs with cold water and soap containing lime, ash, and fish oil. The fleeces were soaked and washed twice as steam rose and spread through the room like a fog. The slaves rolled up their trousers and the maids gathered their skirts, then they all climbed into the tub and stamped the dirt from the wool. They sang and laughed, urging each other to speed up until the water splashed over the side onto the floor. Gunda was the most spirited of them all. The rising steam reddened her cheeks and frizzled her curly blond hair, which fell to her waist. It looked more like she was immersed in a joyful dance than in a tub washing wool, as she freely flaunted her well-shaped calves.

Candamir had taken the washed fleeces outside to rinse them in cold water. When he returned, he saw how his friend was watching Gunda. As he put the dripping washtub down next to the fire, he asked him casually, "Why don't you stay the night?"

Osmund quickly turned his eyes and shook his head regretfully. "Believe me, I would only too gladly, but…"

"But what? Come now, it's time you began to live again—and it would please Gunda, you know," he added without any special emphasis. "Ever since the midsummer festival she has been watching you with longing eyes."

Osmund began to waver. "But I thought you—I mean you and she…"

Candamir smiled, shrugging. He didn't like the thought of sharing Gunda, but in this instance it was for a good cause.

He pulled his friend over to the longfire, settled into the high seat, and gestured for Osmund to sit down opposite him in the place of honor. He ordered the maids to put the wool aside until the next day and start preparing the meal. "Bring us beer. Take the large pitchers and keep them full," he ordered the Saxon. And before his sister could object, he added, "We'll start tightening our belts tomorrow."

Even before the meal was served, Osmund and Candamir had downed so much strong beer that the Saxon was sure he would have collapsed half-dead in the straw if they had ordered him to join in—something he knew from past experience. This time he was spared, as the foster brothers had turned their attention on Hacon instead, urging him to match them tankard for tankard. "Come now, little brother," Candamir teased. "Drink, drink, drink! Are you a man or a mouse?"

Tables were set up on both sides of the longfire, and the maids served a stew of fish and mushrooms. There was even a small slice of bread for everyone. The servants sat on the bench on either side of the high seat, and Osmund, the only guest, sat alone on the other side of the fire.

"So if we did it, Osmund, when would we set out?" Candamir asked between mouthfuls.

Osmund's gaze had momentarily wandered over to Gunda again. "In the spring," he answered, "as soon as possible. Before the accursed Turons come back to finish us off."

"Set out to go where?" Hacon asked, flabbergasted.

"Never you mind," Candamir replied brusquely. "Drink your beer." Turning to Osmund, he continued, "Was it a spring storm that took Olaf there?"

Osmund looked into his cup and nodded.

"When would that have been, and why hasn't he ever told anyone about it? He doesn't make a secret of any of his other adventures and supposed glorious deeds."

"Two years ago. He did not talk about it because he'd intended to trade with the people there, and naturally he wanted the market all to himself. But now that things are looking so bad here, and getting worse, he says he understands why the gods led him to this island."

"Island? Gods? What are you talking about?" Asta asked.

The Saxon, experienced in interpreting mysteries, had no trouble making sense of these odd allusions. "Olaf wants to leave Elasund and find a new home?" he asked in astonishment. "And where does he think this island lies? Off the coast of Scotland, I presume."

Candamir shook his head. "Much farther away, in the western sea."

"Oh wonderful," Austin muttered to himself. "The sea of no return."

He sat to the left of his master, which was a place of honor, but unfortunately it also meant he was always within reach. He was rewarded with a swift kick to the shins. "How come my guest's mug is empty, you loafer? And mine, too. Get moving!"

The slave stood up quickly and reached for the empty mugs.

"And don't forget Hacon's," Osmund said with a smirk.

The boy smiled bravely. "We are going away, Candamir?"

His brother raised his hand dismissively. "No, it's only a crazy idea. Olaf thought it up because he's probably crapping in his pants at the thought of the Turons returning in the spring."

"Then he's not the only one," Hacon mumbled.

*That's for certain,* Candamir had to admit to himself. "I just don't know," he finally said. "In any case, I would have to learn a lot more before I could make such a decision. And it doesn't just depend on us alone. We can only succeed if we set out with a fair number of ships."

"Oh, I see," said the Saxon, putting the mugs down in front of them, spilling a little froth onto the table. "You mean that unfortunately the secret island is already inhabited and you plan to treat the inhabitants the way the Turons have treated you."

"Or the way the Angles and Saxons treated the Britons," Osmund said with a sly smile.

"Well," Hacon offered, "the Turon we captured was right, in a way: everyone has to look out for himself. He who can't defend his land doesn't deserve it, right?" He reached for his mug with feigned eagerness and put it to his lips, then tipped slowly backward until he fell off the bench. The room broke out in laughter.

Candamir, who was still steady on his feet, arose and pulled his brother up. "Don't you dare to throw up all over my hall," he warned.

Hacon shook his head vehemently and then passed out. Catching his brother and throwing him over his shoulder like a rag doll, Candamir took him outside and set him down on the snowy ground, leaning his back against the outside wall of the house. He knew that in his brother's condition the clear, cold air was the best remedy. He was sure Hacon was too drunk to freeze to death, but he decided to bring him back into the house in an hour nonetheless. Candamir checked to see there was nothing wrong with the boy, and then he gently wrapped him in a fur cover.

Returning to the warm hall, Candamir stopped to have a few quiet words with Gunda. She listened carefully and then hesitantly replied, "If it is your wish…"

Gunda was a proud girl, claiming to be the daughter of a chieftain who had been snatched from her family during a night raid by pirates. But they all said that. It was just as likely that her father had too many daughters, was financially strapped, and sold her off to the travelling slave-trader Candamir bought her from last spring. It didn't matter to him, but he didn't want to offend her. "Just this one time," he said with a smile.

"All right then. I'll admit there are things that would be harder for me to do, Master."

Although he'd known that, he wished she hadn't said it. "Well, there you go then," he answered coolly.

"But I am pregnant."

*O mighty Tyr, save me,* he thought in astonishment. In contrast to Osmund, he considered fatherhood anything but appealing. The very thought frightened him to death. But all he said was, "So?"

"I just wanted you to know, so that it's clear he's your son—in case it's a boy, I mean."

"And now I know," he replied noncommittally. "Go now, get him something to drink and sit down with him before my sister goes to bed."

Gunda smiled. "Ah, now I see what you have in mind."

Candamir realized that he *really* didn't like the idea of sharing his Gunda. "Somebody has to see to it that they get together, since the gods don't seem to be much concerned about it."

They had barely finished the slaughtering, salting, and smoking at both Candamir and Osmund's farms when the first serious snowstorm arrived, putting an end to any work outside. Thus, people sat by their longfires and did all the necessary things they had not had time to do in the weeks since the Turon attack.

Tjorv and Nori, the two slaves Candamir had inherited from his father, were hollowing out a big piece of soapstone and smoothing the underside. You could already see that it was going to be a cooking pot. Tjorv was a skilled stonecutter, and if he felt restless enough in the course of the long winter he would probably decorate the outside of the pot with wolves' heads or goblins' faces—anything to annoy the old cook. The women were spinning wool, all except for Asta, who was busily sewing a new lambskin jerkin for Hacon, since he had outgrown the last one. Hacon was carving a skate from a thigh bone—with varying degrees of success. An especially violent burst of wind howled around the house.

He paused in his work and looked up toward the roof, but he was not worried about the shingles. The roof had acquired such a thick covering of ice and snow that the wind could not tear it off. How homey it was in the hall when the storm was raging outside. He stood up to add more wood to the fire, but Candamir stopped him. "Take it easy, Hacon, unless you'd like to go fetch more wood before the storm lets up."

"No, not really," the boy grinned.

"Go on, Heide," Candamir nodded. "So the king of the giants had stolen Thor's hammer and demanded Freyja's hand in marriage in exchange. I can imagine she wasn't too pleased."

"You are right about that, Master," the cook confirmed, nodding grimly and continuing her tale. "Her anger shook the whole Hall of the Gods, and she refused. No one had any idea what to do, as the gods knew they could not withstand an attack by the giants without Thor's hammer. Finally, the wily Loki suggested that the only way out was for Thor to dress up as a bride, go to the hall of the giants, and pose as Freyja. This enraged Thor, as he feared that the gods would think him unmanly and his reputation as the boldest and most valiant warrior would be besmirched. But the smooth-talking Loki pointed out that this was the only way. So they wrapped Thor in bridal linens, dressed him in women's clothing and a towering headdress. When he arrived at the hall of the giants, the king's eyes shone with joy and desire, as he thought he saw Freyja before him. He led her to the bridal feast and was surprised at the huge portions of meat she ate, and above all, how much mead she drank. But Thor explained to him that he had been fasting eight days and eight nights because of his longing for the bridegroom. The giant king was moved and had the promised bridal gift brought in and placed in his bride's lap. Then the disguised Thor leapt up from the bench, tore his bridal veil from his face, swung the hammer that he had now recovered, and slew the giant king and all his kin."

Heide had talked herself into a frenzy, and at the story's conclusion heaved a deep sigh of satisfaction, causing her ample bosom to rise and fall like waves in a storm.

"Magnificent, Heide!" Hacon applauded. "Wonderfully told."

Candamir concurred. He loved this story, savoring the humorous image of the grim Thor dressed up as a woman. He chuckled, then raised his head. "Come here, Saxon."

Austin had been holding the loose, spun wool for Gunda so that she could roll it up into a ball. She claimed he was the best person for the job since he was so good at keeping still. Carefully he laid her string of yarn down on the bench and stood up.

He walked over to Candamir, who was holding his razor-sharp dagger in his hand and pointing to a piece of seal hide that was spread out on the bench. "Put your foot on it," he commanded.

The slave took a step back and asked timidly, "But what have I done, Master?"

Candamir looked at him first in bewilderment and then laughed at his fearful expression. "Nothing. What are you thinking? That I want to chop off your foot? You are going to get a pair of shoes, that's all."

The Saxon heaved a sigh of relief. In his homeland it was customary to sever the heel tendon of those slaves who were too keen on gaining their freedom. Even though this custom seemed to be unknown here, he had worried that under the spell of this grisly story Candamir could have decided to turn him into a limping cripple.

"Shoes, Master?" he asked with a blank look. The past two winters he had not had shoes. In the first year, when he had complained about cold feet, Candamir had explained that slaves were made to go shoeless for the same reason their hair was clipped short—so they would never forget their lowly status.

"Indeed. And a pair of skis as well. If you do as you are told now, that is."

Austin quickly placed his foot on the leather, remaining motionless as Candamir carved the outline of his sole with the point of the knife.

"Now the other foot."

The Saxon obeyed, waiting until this dangerous measurement had been safely concluded before asking, "To what do I owe this honor, Master?"

Candamir began to cut out the leather sole, and Austin watched, admiring how skillfully he worked, the knife never once deviating from the line he had drawn.

"I have a task for you," Candamir began in a hushed voice while keeping a careful eye on his work. "It is not so simple and takes cleverness and skill." He looked up suddenly and smiled at his slave. "So you're just the man for the job."

The Saxon had a feeling this was not going to be anything good. "I always get nervous when you flatter me, Master," he confessed. "What is it?"

Candamir looked around quickly to make sure no one was listening, but Nori had started one of his bawdy stories and the rest were hanging on his every word.

"You saw Osmund's storehouse," he began in a low voice.

"Of course."

"What he has will last him at best until the Yule festival."

"Yes, I know."

"You will go there every night to replenish his supplies a bit. Discreetly, you understand. A dozen herring for his fish barrel, perhaps, or a cup of flour smuggled into his flour sacks now and then. But he must not notice it, under any circumstances, for it would offend him."

The Saxon nodded. "And if he catches me, he'll kill me."

"Probably both of us. You see, I'm putting my life in your hands."

"I'm touched, Master. But won't he see the ski tracks in the snow?"

Candamir waved his hand dismissively. "In the coming weeks it will snow every night; your tracks will be covered up. And even if they aren't, there are so many ski tracks between his farm and mine that one more won't be noticed."

Austin nodded thoughtfully, then took a deep breath and replied, "All right. But have you had a good look at our own storehouse and asked yourself how far *we* will get with what we have? I know that Osmund is your best friend, but it's doubtful we'll make it through the winter, and certainly not if we give anything away."

"I think you are forgetting your place again," said Candamir, cutting him off sharply. Then he pointedly turned his back on him and began to cut out the front and sides of the first shoe.

The Saxon returned to his seat with a feeling of unease. He heard only the end of Nori's story along with the bursts of laughter, but he was certain he had not missed much. He responded to the question implicit in Gunda's raised eyebrow with a feeble smile and picked up the string of yarn again.

"Won't you please tell us a story, Asta?" Hacon asked.

She nodded obligingly and dropped her sewing in her lap for a moment in order to collect her thoughts before beginning her tale. "When the world was still young, before the gods did battle with the giants, Odin was strolling through the lea of the fairies one night. It was springtime and his blood was seething in his veins, as it does with all creatures, when he caught sight of the daughter of the fairy king standing by a brook. Her name was Tanuri, which means Daughter of the Starlight in the tongue of the fairies. So great was Tanuri's beauty that Odin's eyes shone, and he was consumed with longing. For three days and three nights he hid among the flowering trees that stood around the clearing on the bank of the brook, and three times Tanuri appeared at dusk. Finally, on the third evening, he approached her and made advances to her. She turned him down, however, as she was already betrothed. 'Then break your promise, and I will fulfill your every desire,' Odin said. Tanuri asked for three days to think it over, and thus Odin spent three more nights at the bank of the brook. When she returned, she said she would accept his suit if he gave her a land that was perfect.

"And so Odin went to the giants and asked their help. They created for him a perfect land—an island in the sea with neither winter nor drought, neither sorrow nor pain, with mountains rich in gold and minerals, valleys full of fertile, black earth, groves of trees with brooks and the most beautiful flowers, and forests full of wondrous peaceful creatures and sweet fruit. When Odin saw this land, his heart rejoiced, for he saw that it was perfect, and he brought Tanuri there.

"She inspected the land, climbed the mountains, rode through the valleys, the groves and forests, and saw there was nothing in this land that was bad. Finally she said, 'There is no snow.'

"'But the snow brings death to many,' Odin protested.

"'What could be purer and more perfect than snow?' she replied.

"And so Odin summoned a large flock of white ravens to the island, and they settled at Tanuri's feet whenever she wanted, looking like a covering of snow.

"'There is no fire,' Tanuri complained.

"'But fire brings death to many,' Odin said this time as well.

"'What could be purer and more perfect than fire?' Tanuri responded.

"And so Odin thrust his spear into one of the mountains and twisted its point deep into its marrow so that the mountain spewed fire.

"'Now the land is perfect, isn't it?' the god said eagerly. 'I have fulfilled my part of the bargain, now fulfill yours.'

"But Tanuri spoke: 'How foolish you are, Father of the Gods. In this land there is neither sorrow nor pain. How could it be perfect? Perfection lies only in the balance of all things, good as well as evil. No, you have not fulfilled my wish, and I owe you nothing.'

"Then Odin realized that Tanuri, like all women, was full of cunning, yet wiser than he was. He let her go, but he remained on the island for a long time, overcome with sorrow and pain as he had lost the most beautiful of the fairies. And thus the land became perfect when it was too late. In Tanuri's honor, Odin named the island Catan, which in the tongue of the fairies means Land of Starlight. Odin lingered there until his grief had subsided, and then he moved the island far out into the sea so that no mortal might ever reach its shores."

It was very quiet in the hall after Asta had finished. The grinding of the chisel against soft stone and the scraping of Hacon's carving knife had stopped—only the women had continued their silent work.

"That was…wonderful," Gunda said with a deep sigh.

Asta smiled, and with an embarrassed wave of her hand went back to her sewing. "Oh, my grandmother told it much better. Tanuri would sing a song when she came down to the brook at twilight, but I forget how it went. Do you remember it, Candamir?"

"No." He shook his head regretfully.

"That's a shame. You have such a beautiful voice."

Before anyone could urge him to sing, he asked Gunda, "Don't they tell this story in your country?"

She shrugged. "I don't believe so. Some of our tales are different, just as some of the names you give the gods here sound strange to me. And the Saxon's god is becoming ever more powerful in my homeland."

Candamir clicked his tongue disapprovingly. "That's a shame."

"Isn't there also a story in your book about a far-off land?" Hacon asked the Saxon.

The monk glanced briefly at Candamir, and because his master seemed not to object, he replied, "In a manner of speaking. It was a garden, and it was perfect in the same way that Odin understood perfection. God gave this garden to mankind as a gift."

"But?" said Tjorv, urging him on.

And so Austin told the story of the Garden of Eden, the tree and the snake and the banishment from Paradise.

Once the monk had finished, Candamir asked, "And why this strange test?" He sounded annoyed. "How was this tree different from the others?"

"Well, it was forbidden," Austin said.

"Why?"

"Because God ordered it so."

"So first he creates this land and the people, and then he gives the land to them. But he creates man with all his weaknesses and puts him to a test that he cannot pass. What nonsense! Was your god bored? What other reason could he have had to do that?"

"They could have passed the test, in spite of their weakness," Austin objected. "For God gave them a free will."

"Do you mean to say that man holds his fate in his own hands?" Asta asked, with a smile of disbelief.

"Indeed."

"That's impudent," Candamir said angrily as he walked over to his Saxon and, without realizing what he was holding in his hand, started waving his sharp-edged knife in front of Austin's nose. "The Norns decide the fate both of men and of gods, and this is the only way the world can follow its preordained course. How could we presume to know what is right and wrong? Your stories are interesting, Saxon, but their teachings are vain. And dangerous. You are welcome to tell us about the great kings in your book and their battles, but no more nonsense like this. Do you understand?"

Austin moved his head back a bit in order to distance himself from the deadly blade. "Yes, Master," he murmured with feigned humility. But he knew he was lying. He could not stop anymore than he could have willed himself to stop breathing. "There is the story of the mighty warrior Sampson and his fate. I believe you would like it…"

The days got darker and colder, and life in the village came to a near halt, as no one went outside unless urgent matters required it.

The weeks before the Yule festival were not yet marked by real privation, but already by hunger. No one was satisfied with the one or at most two skimpy meals a day they received, especially the men. All were suffering from a constant, gnawing feeling of emptiness in their stomachs.

Austin began his nightly errands. It was the first time in his life he had been on skis. They were made of pine and were fastened to his feet by leather cords pulled through holes in the thin boards. The left ski was two paces long and had a smooth underside, while the right ski was no longer than Austin's arm, and its underside was covered with fur. Candamir had explained to him how to push off with the short ski and glide along on the other one. He was given a long stick to help keep his balance. It took a while, however, until the Saxon could do much more than fall on his face. Despite the cold, Candamir and Hacon stood in the yard watching him and making fun of his clumsy attempts. But as he was young and agile, he quickly mastered this unusual means of locomotion. Austin carried out his mission flawlessly, and he rather enjoyed rising in the middle of the night when the whole house was asleep to venture out into the cold. It reminded him of his years in the monastery when the brothers interrupted their sleep every night for Matins and Laudes. Whenever the weather allowed and there was at least a bit of light from the moon or stars, he went over to Osmund's farm with a sack of provisions and filled his barrels. He was well aware of the danger. If Osmund caught him, he would naturally assume the Saxon was trying to rob him. And God only knew what might happen then.

Haflad the charcoal burner, who was Brigitta's son and Osmund's father-in-law, had caught one of his slaves stealing from him and had beaten him so unmercifully that the man died. Now he lacked a servant, and according to Nori, who had told him this gruesome story, in his anger and despair Haflad now knocked about everyone in the house. And so Austin took refuge in prayer during his nightly excursions. But he also thought it advisable to take some precautions, and so he always brought along a little treat for Osmund's dog. The huge, shaggy animal knew the Saxon by now and did not bark when he came.

So it wasn't Austin who got caught red-handed in a storehouse but Hacon. Heide had sent him to fetch a cup of oatmeal, and smelling smoked fish strung on a cord hanging from the ceiling, he instinctively reached for it. But before he could take a bite, a big fist grabbed him by the neck and yanked him back.

Hacon gave a half-suppressed cry and let go, as if the fish were suddenly red hot.

The fist shook him so hard that his teeth rattled and then yanked him around.

"Candamir..."

His brother let him go, then punched him in the face, something he had never done before. Hacon was thrown against the wall before falling to the ground.

"Today—and how many times before this?" Candamir asked coldly.

The boy propped himself up on an elbow and shook his head. "Never," he mumbled. He had bitten himself on the tongue, and his mouth was full of blood. The whole left side of his face was throbbing with pain, and his head was pounding like a drum from the blow, but it was primarily the shame that brought tears to his eyes. He choked back the blood. "Never, I swear on Thor's hammer! I'm sorry, I don't know what came over me. I'm really sorry..."

"Get up!" Candamir shouted at him. "And stop blubbering."

Hacon got to his feet and wiped his bloody nose on his sleeve. He stood there, arms dangling and head bowed so low that his dark hair covered his face.

"What you were about to do could cost Asta her life," Candamir said more calmly. "Or Fulc. And you know that, don't you?"

The tears flowed faster, and the boy bit hard on his lower lip. "For a moment I just didn't think of it. I...I am so hungry, Candamir. It just came over me."

Candamir sighed and sat down wearily on one of the barrels. "You must learn to control yourself. How often have I told you that?"

"I don't know," Hacon answered in a choked voice. "Often."

"You think you are hungry, do you? You have no idea, little brother. No idea."

Hacon wiped his face on his sleeve again, this time more vigorously, then summoned up his courage and looked at his brother. He was startled at his stern expression. "And what now?" he asked anxiously.

"Now you will learn what hunger really is. You won't get anything to eat until supper tomorrow."

As if in protest, Hacon's stomach growled loudly. The boy pressed a hand against his belly. "Is that all?" he asked, half bitterly, half hopefully.

Candamir nodded, remembering the last winter famine. It wasn't the Turons who had been the cause, but a late frost, a wet summer, a bad fishing season, and a hailstorm that had completely destroyed the meager harvest. Hacon had been too young to remember it, but Candamir was twelve, and his father had caught him at the herring barrel in the storehouse. He still shuddered recalling the terrible beating he had received and the awful fever he had come down with that night. He had almost died. His father had been beside himself with worry, but Candamir hated him. Their falling-out had lasted until the end of the winter, each of them alone in their misery.

"Yes, that is all. And it is punishment enough. You will curse me tomorrow, believe me. But I have to do it so you learn what I am trying to spare us."

Hacon heaved a sigh and looked up at the ceiling. "Maybe you'd better tie me down somewhere. I honestly don't know if I can make it otherwise. Wouldn't it be awful if you found me here again tomorrow?"

Candamir smiled sadly. "Eat snow, if you can't stand it. That helps." Then he roused himself and stood up. "I am in the smithy, in case anyone is looking for me."

Hacon nodded, and to his amazement Candamir left him behind in the storehouse by himself. As soon as the boy noticed this, he unconsciously straightened up, threw a contemptuous glance at the smoked fish, and, after Candamir's steps had faded away, whispered, "Thank you, Brother."

He went outside, firmly closing the wooden door behind him.

"Make me a lock for my storage house, Harald," Candamir asked. "I'll give you a leg of mutton for it."

The blacksmith was silent, waiting for the young man to knock the snow from his shoes and sit down on the wooden bench next to the forge.

As always, the smith's silent composure made Candamir talkative. "I am no better than my Saxon's god," he said. "I have led my brother into a temptation that no man can resist. Not at his age, at least."

Harald nodded thoughtfully, took the chisel he had been working on from the fire, and pounded it with a small blacksmith's hammer. "I'll make your lock," he promised. "Keep your leg of mutton. If you'll help me two days next summer during the hay harvest, that will be payment enough. And now tell me what's troubling you, lad."

Candamir straightened his shoulders, enjoying the heat on his back. His hall was always nice and warm, but the blacksmith's shop was the only place in Elasund where it was hot even in winter. As usual, Harald was working stripped to the waist, and his muscular chest and broad shoulders glistened with a fine film of sweat. Here it always smelled of iron and sweat. The smithy had been his favorite refuge during childhood. Harald had been a good friend of his father, but whenever there had been a falling-out between father and son—a frequent occurrence since they shared the same hot temper—the smith had always taken the boy into his house. Even today Candamir sometimes sought advice here, for in contrast with Olaf or his dead uncle Sigismund or other men of his father's generation, Harald was never condescending.

"Has Osmund spoken with you yet?" Candamir finally asked. "Or Olaf?"

The smith dipped the chisel in water and put it on the workbench to cool off. "I haven't seen Osmund for weeks. He keeps hiding, giving himself over to grief. I think it's time for him to stop, by the way, or he may not live to see spring. And his uncle Olaf and I haven't spoken for a long time—since that day six months ago when his sword broke and he claimed it was my fault."

"I see." Candamir stood up restlessly, walked over to the workbench, and fidgeted absentmindedly with the tools hanging on hooks above it before picking up the new chisel and promptly burning his hand. "Well, as you know, Olaf is not exactly my favorite neighbor, but he made a proposal to Osmund that I just can't stop thinking about."

"Is that so?" Harald was preparing a clay mold lined with a waxed cloth and putting a small iron bar into a stone ladle. Then he put another shovelful of coal on the fire and pointed to the bellows. "Tell me about it."

Candamir worked the bellows slowly and steadily, the way Harald had taught him as a boy. "Olaf thinks we should go away, leave Elasund and try to find a new homeland, just like many of our people did in the past..." Candamir pointed at the odd-shaped, flat mold and said, "What is that going to be?"

"Your key," the older man answered. "Now, you know, I've been thinking about that, and even more so since the Turons attacked us the first time and killed my brother. But where can we go? Some people say Britain, but I don't know...you can't mess with these Anglo-Saxons, even though more and more of them worship this weakling of a god, as I hear."

"No, Olaf is not thinking of Britain, but an island in the western sea that he discovered by chance," he replied, telling the smith all about Olaf's Land.

After Candamir had finished, Harald was silent for a long time, mulling over what he had heard. He seemed to pay no heed to what his hands were doing, but as he poured the white molten iron into the little mold, he did so with skill and caution born of decades of experience.

"It sounds good," he finally said.

"Indeed."

"I have to think about it," Harald concluded thoughtfully.

"Do that."

"Tomorrow I'll come to your house and install the lock. Then we'll talk some more. Now tell me how things are between Osmund and your sister. Will they see the light this time and marry?"

Candamir sighed and sank down on the bench again. "If only I knew. There's no doubt that they get along well. A few days ago they were sitting together all afternoon and talking. But they are like... brother and sister."

"Maybe you should remind them that they are not. Now is a good time of year to arrange marriages—there's not much else to do."

"That's not as simple as you think. When Asta ran off with Nils, Osmund and I were still practically boys. He should have been awfully hurt. In any case, I was, and he had much more reason to feel that way than I did. He was the only one, however, who showed any understanding for her and what she had done. As far as all this is concerned, I don't understand either of them."

The smith raised an eyebrow in amusement. "Really? Weren't you ever in love, Candamir?"

Candamir grimaced in disgust. "I won't have anything to do with such nonsense."

"No? Well, someday I'll remind you of this. By the way, there is some talk your little Frisian is going to have a baby?"

"Talk? Who says so?" Candamir asked, frowning.

"Brigitta, of course."

"And how would she know? I am sure Gunda hasn't confided in her—she is afraid of the old witch."

"Just as you are," the smith replied. "Well, she knows just the way she knows so many other things that nobody told her. Brigitta is closer to the gods than any of us. Under no circumstances should we make a decision affecting our future until we hear what she thinks."

"Then we might as well ask conniving Loki himself."

The smith shook his head. "You are mistaken. Incidentally, she called your Frisian woman's baby a 'child of distant shores.' What do you make of that? Strange, isn't it?"

"Well, Gunda comes from distant shores."

"Hm," the smith grunted.

A few days later, when Harald was shoeing Siward's horse, he mentioned Olaf's island and Candamir's idea. Siward spoke about it with old Eilhard over a mug of beer, who then strapped on his skis and went to visit his two sons who lived in a little village along the river in order to tell them about the sparsely populated, fertile island in the western sea. In this way the proposal gradually spread around Elasund and the surrounding communities.

With the leisurely work pace during the dark winter days, people had plenty of time to think. Some, especially the young people, were so enthused about the idea that they would just as soon have taken their belongings down to the ships and sailed away at once—regardless of the winter storms. Others thought the idea was completely absurd. After all, their ancestors had lived in Elasund, and their children had been born here. What would they do in a foreign land? Their roots were *here*.

But as the men and women sat together at the fire and spoke about their fear of new attacks in the springtime and their worries for their children's future, it began to seem that leaving was the lesser evil.

The news was also joyfully circulating that Osmund had convinced his rich uncle Olaf to invite all free-born people of Elasund to a Yule feast. Nobody else had the resources to put on a meal that would do justice to the important festival. Hacon dreamed of steaming cauldrons and whole oxen roasting on a spit over a big fire, and he was not the only one. But even greater than everyone's joy at the unexpected invitation was the surprise of it. The people of Elasund knew that Olaf was rich partly because he was a miser. There had been hunger and deprivation in winters past, but he had never seemed to care whether his kinsmen and neighbors were able to cope.

"People are thanking me," Osmund told Candamir. "But I have had nothing to do with it."

Candamir shrugged. "Then just tell them that this undeserved gratitude embarrasses you."

"I have. They don't believe me."

Candamir was amused at his friend's despair. "There are worse things than a good reputation."

They were standing in Candamir's sheep barn where it was cold and dark and the air was filled with a pungent odor of sheep dung. Osmund had climbed over the low wooden partition to examine the animals. There were a dozen of them, crowded together and miserable.

Candamir went to look at his horses. He owned four—more than anyone in the village, after Olaf lost his. He had two docile geldings that he used for plowing. They were better suited to his hilly fields than oxen, and besides, he preferred to work with horses. In addition he had a beautiful brown mare and a three-year-old colt that were his pride and joy. The horses were the only luxury he allowed himself. He was generally considered the best horseman in the village, and at the races held during every midsummer festival he was usually the victor. "Let's hope I'll manage to get all of you through the winter," he murmured, patting the mare on the neck. She was pregnant, and he had great hopes for the foal. "We have little hay left."

Osmund had no sympathy for this vain passion. "You ought to take better care of your brother than your horses. He is pale and thin."

"And who isn't?" Candamir replied. "Just look at yourself."

Osmund raised his hand in a dismissive gesture. "I am doing just fine. It's strange, you know, how my provisions are dwindling much slower than I had expected."

"You are more economical than you thought."

"Nonsense." Osmund shook his head, baffled. Then he returned to the subject of Hacon. "The boy is listless. That's not a good sign, Candamir. He's always sitting around with that accursed Saxon. If you want, I'll talk with my uncle. Since he has shown so much generosity lately, maybe he will take in Hacon for the rest of the winter. In his house there is enough to eat and no false god."

Candamir released the mare's hoof, straightened up, and turned around. "Thanks, but I can feed my household by myself."

Osmund raised his hands placatingly. "You can't do that any better than I can, but that's no reason to get angry. Your brother's health should mean more to you than your pride. Asta is worried about him."

"She told you that, did she?" Candamir asked. "When?"

"Yesterday. One of my ewes gave birth, and she came over with Fulc to show him the little lamb." He couldn't help smiling. Osmund loved sheep the way Candamir loved horses.

"A nice Yule roast for you," Candamir teased.

Osmund gave him a reproachful glance. "We'd rather eat straw. Besides, we don't need that, thanks to Olaf's generosity. In any case, Asta mentioned that she was concerned about Hacon. And even though she didn't say it, I know she is worried about her son, too. If you sent Hacon over to Olaf, there would be more food left for little Fulc, Candamir. Olaf can always use an extra pair of hands, even in the winter."

Candamir looked his mare in the teeth and thought it over. When Osmund's back was turned, he gave her a little piece of the oat bread that he had put aside from his breakfast. "No," he said finally.

Osmund gave a resigned shrug, but he asked nonetheless, "Why not?"

"Oh, I don't know...I just don't feel right about Olaf. Jared and his siblings live in mortal fear of their father. Nobody ever talks about it, but we all know that it's no accident your aunt drowned in the fjord the year before last. She killed herself. There's something just not right about that family, and I don't want my brother to become part of it."

Osmund sighed impatiently. "Perhaps Olaf does have a bad temper and is harder on his sons than is absolutely necessary, but your brother is no sissy. You pamper him too much."

"I do not," Candamir said angrily. "You have discovered a strange affection for your uncle Olaf all of a sudden. You want to sail away with him at any cost, and now you're trying to convince yourself he's a good man so that you can do that with a clear conscience."

"But he *is* a good man," Osmund replied, just as angrily, "better at least than many people here think. My father tried to convince me all my life that Olaf is greedy and malicious, but he was just jealous of him, like so many others."

"Why then did Olaf keep your father from getting his land and his inheritance, if it wasn't greed and malice?" Candamir asked.

"Because grandfather set it up that way. And that was father's own fault, and nobody else's. Unlike my father, Olaf is thinking of his sons' future. He wants to bequeath land to them where they can do something more than just eke out a miserable existence. He wants that for all of us. Is that bad?"

"No," Candamir had to admit. "It isn't. And even though I don't trust him farther than I can throw this horse, I will go with him if it comes to that. I am just as tired as you are of lying awake at night and asking myself what we will eat next month."

# Yule Moon

Olaf's hall was three times the size of Candamir's, which itself was not the smallest in Elasund. Valuable wall hangings adorned the large room, making it feel homey and comfortable. For the great celebration, herbs had been strewn over the rushes on the floor, and wreaths and garlands of evergreen and ash hung from the soot-blackened roof beams.

Tables and benches had been set up along the sides and back of the fire. Oil lamps stood on the tables in decorated silver dishes, their light reflecting off the gold leaf vines on the posts of Olaf's magnificent high seat.

In his best ermine-lined tunic, the master of the house gazed down upon the large crowd of guests with an unusually benevolent smile. Despite the losses from Turon attack that autumn, the number of free men and women of Elasund was still too great even for this hall. They sat crowded together at the long tables. Nearly every father and mother had a child on their knees, but the crush of people did nothing to dampen the festive mood. The reality by far surpassed Hacon's dreams—huge cauldrons as large as washtubs hung over the fire, and the aroma of braised fish rising from them would have made even a well-fed man's mouth water. Outside the hall a provisional kitchen had been set up where oxen, pigs, and sheep were being turned on huge spits. There was more than enough wheat and rye bread for everyone. The loaves seemed to Hacon as big as wagon wheels. And along the south wall stood rows of kegs full of beer and mead.

"Well, I must say," Candamir heard old Eilhard murmur from across the table, "even the Yule feast in Valhalla could hardly be more sumptuous than this."

"It's a shame that one man should be so rich," his wife answered in an equally soft voice.

Eilhard shrugged his shoulders. "Since he's letting us all share in his wealth today, you shouldn't complain."

Nevertheless, the jealousy at Olaf's magnificent hall, his fine clothes, and his well-fed children was unmistakable.

The host did not seem to notice. He rose from his luxurious high seat and seized the silver-edged drinking horn that Jared had brought him. The other heads of households in the hall also stood up, and the crowd fell silent.

"So let us now drink to our forebears," Olaf proclaimed in his deep, resonant voice. "May they live on forever in their sons and in our hearts."

He took a long drink of mead and then gave the horn back to Jared, who carried it around to the other men one by one. Before drinking, each let his thoughts wander back briefly to his own ancestors. Candamir used the occasion to ask forgiveness of his father for having taken the disowned Asta back into the house.

The winter solstice was the time of ghostly apparitions. And this tradition of honoring them at the feast was at least partly done in the hopes of pacifying them, so they would not use this dark time of the year to haunt the living. This too was the point of the drink sacrifice.

The Saxon had once mockingly remarked that they had a strange concept of sacrifice, since they always ate the sacrificial animals and guzzled down the drink sacrifices themselves. Neither Candamir nor Hacon ever understood what the Saxon found so amusing, for the only important thing was the thoughts going through your mind when slaughtering the animals or drinking from the horns.

When all the proprieties had been observed, Olaf opened his arms wide in a gesture of welcome. "Now let us feast and be merry, dear neighbors and friends!"

They did not have to be asked twice. The women, to no avail, admonished their children not to eat so fast and their men not to drink so fast, in order that their first decent meal in weeks would agree with them. But the Elasunders ate without stopping. The first ox served up was also a sacrificial animal, and they ate in appropriate silence and reverence, but with unceremonious haste. Olaf's servants had to step lively to keep all the empty mugs filled.

The island that Olaf had discovered in the western ocean and the possibility of finding and seizing it was the dominant topic of conversation at the Yule feast. Many Elasunders, the young men in particular, became starry-eyed when speaking of it. Many women, too, perceived the advantages of such an undertaking. If they could reach this island, it might end their fear of an enemy attack, or their worry that their sons might kill each other someday fighting over exhausted land that yielded less and less each year. The most wondrous things were being told about this island. Trees grew there, Harald's wife Asi told them, that blossomed all year long, bearing sweet fruit that was as large as cabbages. There were no sheep in Olaf's Land, Candamir heard from the other side of the table, but rather huge herds of goats and wild cattle, and a peculiar race of donkeys whose mares gave milk that tasted like mead. Another guest told of schools of bright, shining, two-headed fish that could be caught on the reefs around the island. Candamir and Osmund smiled to themselves at the stories they heard that night. Olaf had not actually reported these strange and wondrous things, the tales had come into the world all on their own, and the two friends took care not to contradict even the wildest exaggerations. They wanted to take off on this bold adventure. So what did it matter if their neighbors imagined the new homeland a little bit more fantastic than it really was. Once they arrived, they would manage with whatever was there. And no one, not even Olaf, could say exactly what that would be.

But the skeptics spoke up too and were not ridiculed for their hesitation. The highly regarded Siward finally shook his head and said gloomily, "What do we really know about this land? Even Olaf can't tell us what we are going to find there. Anyone who knows me also knows I'm not afraid of fighting, but I am devoted to my homeland. In the spring, let's get together with the people from up the river, set sail to Turonland, and take back what belongs to us. Let's spread fear among our enemies so they will respect us and stay away from now on. Then life will be good here. The ashes of my forefathers are buried in the hills behind my home. This is where I belong, and nowhere else."

Many nodded in agreement.

"It's easy for him to say," Asta whispered to her sleeping daughter. "He has good, fertile land, and a lot of it. His children will be taken care of..."

"But his son Wiland would still rather sail for Olaf's Land," said Hacon, who was sitting beside her.

Asta followed his gaze and saw that her brother's friend was glaring at his father, his face red with shame, though he did not dare publicly contradict him.

"Well, in the end every family will have to decide for themselves," Osmund said. "We don't all have to go."

"But there must be a good number of us if we are to conquer this land," Candamir countered.

A lean young fellow with cropped, reddish-blond hair appeared with a large mug and served them some mead. It took Candamir a moment to recognize the slave, and then he said, "Well, well, the Turon! I haven't seen you for a while."

The prisoner stood before him, his head bowed.

Candamir looked him over. "Well, how do you like life as a slave, you scoundrel? Do you think you got what you deserved for making our women suffer the same fate as yours, considering that they have to endure things you'd never have to face? Huh? What do you think? Is that fair, or wouldn't it have been better for us to kill you?"

Because he got no answer, he grabbed the Turon roughly by the arm. "Open your damn mouth."

"He can't answer you, Candamir," Osmund said.

Candamir released the slave. "Why not?" he snapped.

Osmund dipped a piece of bread in the meat dish standing in the middle of the table. "He insulted Olaf three times, so Olaf cut his tongue out."

"Oh." Candamir cast another contemptuous glance at the Turon before dismissing him with a wave of his hand. "Be gone."

Relieved, the slave moved on with his pitcher.

"Your uncle is a cruel man," Asta said softly to Osmund, looking furtively in the direction of their host sitting on his ornate high seat. Olaf was leaning toward the man next to him and listening with a malicious sparkle in his eyes, then, suddenly, he threw his head back and let out a roar of laughter.

Osmund followed Asta's gaze. "Cruel," he repeated pensively. Then, with a slight shrug, he said, "Olaf presides over a large household. A man in his position must sometimes be harsh in order to keep the respect of his people."

"Respect, sure," she conceded. "But fear?"

"For a coward, fear and respect are one and the same. And the Turons *are* cowards."

Asta was not convinced. "Well, I'm happy that we don't have any servants in our house with such hatred in their eyes as this tongue-less slave."

"I still think it's a disgrace we left him alive," Candamir said.

Osmund agreed. "You are right. But I'm sure he's paying for his deeds."

"Which is more than can be said about you," a grumbling voice muttered behind him.

Osmund flinched and turned around. "Haflad," he said with feigned politeness.

"My son-in-law," the coal burner replied drunkenly. "How is my grandson? Or have you fed him to the wolves by now?"

Osmund clenched his fists, but answered calmly enough. "He is healthy and growing, don't you worry."

"How could I do otherwise? When I know he is in *your* care?"

Osmund stared into the fire and said nothing. He always fell silent when treated unjustly, and Candamir, who never hesitated to speak his mind, just couldn't understand it. "You're talking nonsense again as usual, Haflad. Osmund is in no way responsible for Gisla's death, and you know that very well."

"I know that, huh? So where was he when these damned swine got her? Was he standing at the door of his house, sword in hand, to defend his wife and son? No, my mother had to do that. It's only thanks to her that the child is still alive, because his father was a coward and ran away and hid..."

Candamir stood up. "You'll take that back."

Osmund raised his left hand, gesturing for him to calm down. "Just forget it, Candamir," he murmured, without looking up.

Candamir ignored him. He looked the hulking charcoal burner straight in the eye and said, "You know perfectly well where we were when the Turons came. It was a stroke of fate that they attacked us on the night of the full harvest moon. Osmund is not responsible for it. Now take that back." He moved toward Haflad menacingly, who instinctively stepped back. Candamir crossed his arms in front of his broad chest and smiled. "What a fearless warrior you are, Haflad. Where were you, in fact, that night? Who was it that ran off and hid when the Turons came?"

Moving remarkably fast for such a heavily built man, especially one so drunk, Haflad's fist flew toward Candamir's face, but Candamir stepped aside in time. The charcoal burner was nearly knocked off his feet by his own momentum. He staggered into a table, and a few cups clattered to the ground. Asta, Hacon, and those seated nearby jumped up to make room for the brawl. But Candamir shook his head. "Not here," he said to Haflad and turned around. "Let's step outside."

But before he had reached the door, Haflad came rushing at him from the rear. Candamir would have bet his last few miserable herring that he would do just that. He was prepared, and grabbing the huge fist that was closing around his neck, he arched his back, leaned forward, and threw Haflad over his shoulder. The charcoal burner landed hard on his back, motionless and winded.

Candamir looked down at him for a moment, then nodded. "I'll wait outside."

He walked out of the warm, smoke-filled room into the winter twilight. The cold air felt good. He took his stand in the middle of the open space of the courtyard.

It wasn't long before Haflad came out, followed by a crowd of spectators. Candamir's brother and sister were among them, as were Osmund, Harald, and old Brigitta. Except for Osmund, they all seemed more excited than concerned. A village festival without a brawl was like a wedding without a bride.

The combatants stood opposite each other, glaring. Then Haflad raised both fists, but still did not stir. It was not Candamir's style to engage in a long harangue. Impatiently he pointed to the tip of his chin. "Come on now, what are you waiting for?"

Again, Candamir was surprised at how fast the charcoal burner moved. He hit exactly where Candamir had shown him, and Candamir was thrown to the ground. His head was buzzing, but he jumped up again at once, lunging at his opponent and landing a well-placed blow in the pit of his stomach. Holding onto each other, they fell to the ground and rolled around in the snow, groaning and punching each other.

Then Haflad suddenly extricated himself from the clinch, and as Candamir stood up, Osmund cried, "Watch out, Candamir!"

But Candamir had already seen his opponent pull out a large hunting knife whose broad blade gleamed in the fast-fading light.

"Put it away, Haflad," said Harald. "There is no reason to spill blood."

"Do what he says, son," old Brigitta urged, but Haflad shook his head defiantly and raised the knife, moving toward Candamir.

Candamir dodged and pulled his own knife out of its sheath on his belt. Haflad took a mean slash toward Candamir's throat, but missed. The outcome of a knife fight depended on speed and agility, and in this respect, Candamir had the advantage. He fought carefully and cleverly but never attacked, only trying to disarm the charcoal burner. Haflad came charging at him again with his head down, avoiding both Candamir's punch as well as the kick that was directed at the hand holding the knife. Candamir stepped back at the very moment the lethal blade sliced through his tunic, penetrating his flesh just above the navel. His quick reflexes saved his life. The cut was only superficial, but it robbed him of his composure. The only thing that stood out clearly in his mind was, *He means to kill me. He really means to kill me.* With this thought, he cast aside all caution and rushed at Haflad with a shout of rage. Again they rolled around in the snow, each holding a knife and stabbing viciously at the opponent's throat and heart, but none of the stabs hit their mark.

"Osmund, do something," Asta said in a flat voice. Her eyes were huge, and she stared at the red streaks that Candamir's blood left in the snow.

"There is nothing I can do," he answered. He sounded calm, but his face betrayed his fear.

Candamir rolled onto his back, and Haflad was suddenly astride him, his knee pressed down on Candamir's right forearm. He took his knife in both hands and raised it high over Candamir's head. Seeing his chance, Candamir clenched his left fist and struck the charcoal burner on the throat. Haflad's cry of triumph turned into a strange rasping sound, and the knife slipped from his hands, falling harmlessly into the snow.

Bucking like a foal, Candamir managed to throw off his opponent, who landed on his side, writhing and gasping for air. Candamir knelt down alongside him, also gasping for air and pressing his left hand down on his blood-drenched clothing. Haflad's larynx had not been crushed, and he was not fatally injured, Candamir realized, so he grabbed him by the hair and put his knife to his throat.

Then he hesitated. His mind suddenly became completely clear, like an empty vessel. Out of the corner of his eye he could see old Brigitta, her right hand half hidden in the folds of her dark skirt. But Candamir knew the hand was clenched, and only the index and small finger were extended. She would curse him the instant he cut her son's throat, and Brigitta's curses were powerful. In a week he would choke on a fish bone or meet with some other premature fate. He turned his head and looked over at his brother. Hacon was very pale, his face was grim, and his gaze was fixed steadily on Brigitta's half-hidden hand. He saw exactly what was going on and would kill Brigitta if she cursed Candamir—that was his duty. If Haflad died, Brigitta's only living relative would be little Roric, and while he was only one now, the day would come when he would kill Hacon to avenge Brigitta. And what then? Certainly Hacon would have sons who would continue the blood feud, and so one day Candamir's nephew would kill his best friend's son—all because a drunken moron had once made a careless remark at a Yule festival.

Candamir remained silent and motionless for a long time. His instincts, his dignity, all the rules he had ever learned, were driving him to kill the charcoal burner lying there motionless in the snow, his eyes tightly shut and waiting for his end.

"Keep your life, you maggot," Candamir said so softly that only those standing nearby could hear it. "But don't ever forget this day, or what you are." He raised up his opponent's tunic and placed the point of his knife on the charcoal burner's belly on the exact spot over the navel where he had been injured by Haflad's knife. Haflad quivered when he felt the first small cut, but Candamir continued, carving the mirror image of a Fehu rune in the fat, white belly. It stood for cowardice, among other evil things. Then he wiped off the blade on Haflad's pants leg, replaced the knife in its sheath, and rose unsteadily to his feet.

Osmund walked over to him, without even glancing at his father-in-law. "Let me see the wound, Candamir."

Candamir waved him off. "I'm going home. The Saxon can take care of it. Tell your uncle thank you from me."

"As you wish."

"I'm coming with you," Hacon said. He tried to speak firmly, but his voice quivered a bit.

Candamir shook his head. "You'll stay here and eat."

"I can't eat any more, Candamir."

"Then try harder," he said, turning away.

"But..."

Osmund grabbed him roughly by the arm. "Leave him alone and do what he says."

Candamir had to stop twice along the way to vomit. Overeating and drinking after two months of tight rations, combined with the wound in his abdomen, did not seem to agree with him. After the second attack of nausea he was bathed in cold sweat, too weak to go on. He stood leaning against a tree trunk, looking regretfully at all the good meat lying there steaming in the snow, and waited for his knees to stop shaking.

When he finally reached home, he found his servants seated at a table alongside the fire consuming a meager Yule dinner. Everyone looked up when he entered, and they all noticed the patch of blood on his dark gray clothing. Heide clicked her tongue in disapproval, and Gunda gasped, raised her hand to her mouth, and was about to jump up, but Candamir waved her off. He was feeling so dizzy that he leaned against the closed front door long enough to take a few deep breaths, then pushed himself off and staggered to the door leading to the back room. "Saxon," was all he said.

Austin followed him into the bedroom. Candamir stood at the foot of the large bed covered with sheets and furs, his blood dripping steadily onto the straw-covered floor.

"You'd better lie down," the slave said timidly.

Candamir shook his head. "I'd just bleed even more and ruin the good bedclothes."

"Then sit down," Austin suggested, pointing toward the clothes chest along the wall.

Candamir nodded, following his advice while Austin kneeled before him in the straw and carefully separated the upper and lower garments which had been slashed open. What he saw underneath alarmed him. The wound was not very deep, and obviously no internal organs had been injured—otherwise Candamir's face would have been grayer and he would most likely be dead—but the wound was almost a foot long. "That will have to be sewn up, Master. Otherwise it will bleed all winter."

"Then just go ahead."

The Saxon stood up. "Would you like something to drink?"

"No, I'm drunk enough."

Austin left the room and went to the stable, where he took a hair from the mare's long tail. Then he returned to the house and asked Gunda for her finest whale-bone needle.

Candamir had stripped to the waist, and pointing to the clothing which lay in a pile on the floor, said, "Tell Asta to try to get them clean and mend them. They are my best clothes."

"I will." Austin squinted as he tried to guide the thread through the eye of the needle, and after several tries wished he'd asked Gunda to do this job. He finally managed the tricky maneuver, and raising the needle in triumph, he turned to his master, who was sitting on the chest with his legs apart, looking at him apprehensively. Austin knelt before him again, prayed that God might steady his hand, and began the task.

Candamir flinched the first time the needle penetrated his flesh, but it wasn't as bad as he had feared. The needle was sharp and thin and offered little resistance—in contrast with the rough horsehair. Though the Saxon proceeded with great care, the pain was sharp—the hair snagged constantly and could only be pulled through with a tug.

"How many stitches?" Candamir asked.

The Saxon considered the long wound. "A dozen on top, a dozen below," he estimated.

Candamir cursed under his breath. "Then stop dawdling."

"Like so many brave men, you fear the pain of healing far more than that of battle, Master," Austin said.

"In battle you are too busy to be really conscious of it."

"Then try to take your mind off the pain by telling me how it happened."

Amused, Candamir closed his eyes, leaned his head back against the wall, and asked, "Have you ever killed a man, Saxon?"

Austin shook his head emphatically, though his master could not see it. "No, we men of God do not kill, we save," he explained simply, without the condescension he usually showed when speaking of his faith.

"My father took me on a voyage to the land of your ancestors, up the Elbe River," Candamir said. "We stopped in a village and wanted to trade sealskins for wheat. But the Saxons attacked us and wanted to steal the furs. I killed two of them, a bearded old man and a big fat fellow—I can still remember exactly what they looked like. Damn! Don't pull so hard on the thread, you jackass."

"Sorry, Master." Austin kept right on sewing. "What happened then?"

"We defeated them and got the wheat for free. Then we sailed down river to a larger village where there was a whorehouse, and my father bought me a woman. So it all happened in one day—the first man I killed and the first woman I had." At the time Candamir had believed that was the day he had become a man. Now he knew he had been mistaken. It wasn't that easy.

"How old were you?"

"Fifteen."

"As old as Hacon," the Saxon murmured.

"Hm." He had never thought of it, but it was true. Osmund had accused him of pampering his little brother, and only now did Candamir suspect that perhaps the reproach was not completely unjustified. But no doubt by the time they arrived in Olaf's Land, Hacon would have to prove himself as well...

Austin interrupted his train of thought. "And whom did you kill today, Master?"

"No one." Candamir told him everything that had happened at the Yule festival. His voice was flat but unwavering. Now and then, when the horsehair snagged particularly badly, his eyelids twitched, but he held completely still.

"You spared his life?" the Saxon asked incredulously when Candamir had finished his tale.

"That's what I just said, didn't I? Keep going, you good-for-nothing."

Austin shook his head and continued his work. Eventually he asked, "Why?"

Candamir did not answer. He waited patiently until the dreadful job was finally finished and the Saxon had bitten off the end of the thread. Then he stood up, tottered over to the bed, lay down on his side, and closed his eyes.

Austin had already moved to the door when Candamir said, "You are a fool, Saxon, just like your god. But like so many fools you sometimes say things that make sense."

Austin stopped with his hand on the door bolt, totally amazed. "I do?"

"Suppose we really leave and find a new homeland—wouldn't that be the right time for some new laws?"

"Indeed." The slave thought of his own people and their arrival in a new land, a long time ago. "It is the best opportunity to break with outdated laws."

"Then in the new homeland we ought to break with the blood feud tradition."

He spoke in a drowsy, barely audible whisper, and the Saxon wondered whether he had perhaps misunderstood. "Blood feud, Master?"

"Yes."

"But…haven't you told me countless times that it is the gods who demand blood vengeance?"

"Indeed. But it would not be the first time men defied them. Let the gods themselves decide: If I live, I promise to do everything I can to stop blood feuds in the future. If I come down with a fever and die, you will know what the gods think of my vow."

He fell asleep. Austin tiptoed out, fetched the plain crucifix from its hiding place, went into the stable, and knelt down in the straw to pray for Candamir's life.

# Ice Moon

The Saxon was unable to determine whether it was the silent approval of the Aesir or the power of his god that kept his master alive, but regardless, Candamir contracted neither gangrene nor a fever and was on his feet again the day after the Yule festival.

Many other Elasunders, however, became sick, and the double-edged sword of hunger and privation took its toll in the bitter cold weeks after mid-winter. The guests had predictably hidden all the leftovers from the Yule feast under their clothing and taken them home—what use would Olaf have, after all, for the extra loaves of bread, smoked salmon, legs of mutton, and roast chicken? These provisions merely postponed, but did not end, the famine. That would come about only with the spring thaw, the return of schools of fish and throngs of seals, and the sprouting of edible plants—and there were still many weeks to go until then.

Before the end of the Ice Moon, the first month of the new year in the Saxon's calendar, the last of the provisions had run out, and a dozen people succumbed to consumption and fever. Candamir slaughtered one of his geldings. It took him five days to make up his mind—five days in which his family and servants had nothing to eat. Hacon finally went out to the meadow, dug a hole in the snow, and ate the frozen grass. He came down with diarrhea because he hadn't known to cook the grass first. Little Fulc did not stray from the side of his mother, whimpering constantly in vain. Asta had breastfed him as she had his little sister to protect them from the deadly fever, but when famine at last arrived in their house, her milk had dried up. Candamir himself was troubled with fainting fits. His wound and the considerable loss of blood had weakened him, and the lack of food had kept him from regaining his strength, so he occasionally was overcome by dizziness, lost consciousness, and suddenly toppled from his high seat.

On one of these occasions the Saxon picked him up from the floor, saying, "Unless you do something, Master, we will all perish before the snow melts, and you will likely be the first to leave this world."

Candamir nodded, too exhausted to scold the slave for his unseemly words. The next morning he butchered the horse. The gelding was skinny and no longer young, so its flesh was bitter and tough. But it satisfied their hunger. Heide made a strengthening soup from the bones, and Candamir ate it, as he did the meat, grimly and remorsefully, but without hesitation: like his brother, his nephew, and every person in Elasund, he wanted to live.

In spite of the general listlessness, there was a constant coming and going in the longhouses of Elasund. People did not have much to offer each other in terms of food or consolation, aside from their company. The cold winter weather had reached its climax, but the heavy snows were past. The days became a bit brighter, and there was no wind. Finally, the sun even came through the clouds, and the snow-covered hills and pine forests were so beautiful under the bright blue sky that Candamir sometimes stopped on his way from one house to another, put his ski pole in the crusty snow, and admired the landscape while gathering new courage.

Osmund, on the other hand, could not resist the clear night skies and the fascination of the stars. Even though it became so cold you could just about freeze solid by stepping outside the door after the early twilight, the bright, sublime twinkling untouched by earthly sorrows had a strangely consoling effect on him. On one of the last nights of the Ice Moon, as he was standing outside again, he saw dark clouds moving in slowly from the ocean, gradually consuming the majestic sight.

"You had best spend the night here, Candamir," he said to his friend, who had just stepped out of the house. "A storm is brewing."

Candamir nodded. "Nothing unusual for this time of year."

"No."

After a moment, Candamir remarked, "Perhaps it is the last really hard winter we'll have, if it's true that the weather in Olaf's Land is so much milder."

"I'm convinced it is. The island lies south of the land of the Franks, and even their winters are not as cold as ours."

They looked up at the sky once again, giving themselves over to their dreams of distant shores. Then Candamir crossed his arms and stuck his fists in his armpits.

"Let's go inside," Osmund suggested. "It will start snowing soon."

Candamir followed his friend into the warm, cozy hall, settled on the fur-padded bench on the guest's side of the fire, and gratefully accepted a mug of beer. At his own house, they had had nothing but water to drink—melted snow—for weeks, but Osmund actually still had beer. Candamir suspected that Olaf had sent it to his nephew, but didn't ask. He just enjoyed the wonderful, sharp taste on his tongue. "I spoke with Siward again," he said, "but it didn't do any good. He doesn't want to leave Elasund, and as long as he is holding out, the others won't change their minds either."

Osmund sank into his high seat and nodded thoughtfully. Finally he shrugged and said, "Well, then, if necessary we'll just have to sail with the ten families who've decided to leave."

But Candamir was skeptical. That would amount to two ships—Olaf's and his own—or at most three, if Eilhard's sons decided to come along. That would hardly be enough. They would be easy prey for pirates. Moreover, they did not have enough experienced warriors to conquer Olaf's Land. But he did not repeat his misgivings; instead, he turned the cup around in his hands and stared into it. "Osmund..."

"Yes?"

"Suppose we do it...I mean, if we sail to this new homeland..." He stopped and cleared his throat, then started again. "If we do it, that means we'll be founding a new people, won't we? And then it will be important for us to multiply—to grow, I mean."

Osmund sighed, emptying his cup in one huge gulp. When he put it down again, he said, "I'm afraid I know what you are getting at, but…"

Candamir abruptly raised his head. "My sister and you—you were betrothed at one time, weren't you?"

"Candamir, listen…"

Candamir set his cup down on the table, making more noise than necessary. "Why not? What's the matter with you two? Why is it so complicated? Is she not a good woman?"

"That's not it."

"Hasn't she proved that she is fertile and can bear healthy children?"

"She has…"

Candamir spread out his arms. "Well?"

His friend did not answer right away, but finally said, "Asta is very dear to me, Candamir, like a sister. That's what she always was to me, a sister. No more and no less. Gisla…"

"Gisla is dead," Candamir interrupted.

The corner of Osmund's mouth twitched. "Indeed. And Nils, too. I understand why you believe that it would be the most obvious thing for Asta and me to marry, but it's not as simple as that. You don't know how it is, Candamir. Asta cannot replace what I had with Gisla, and I won't settle for anything less. I won't marry until I find the right woman."

"O mighty Tyr, what foolish prattle," Candamir said impatiently. "You need a wife, and Roric needs a mother. That's all there is to it."

Osmund nodded slowly. "When the time comes and not before. I don't want to offend you, and you mustn't think that your sister is somehow not good enough for me. But in this matter she thinks exactly the way I do."

Candamir shook his head in exasperation. "Well, I can't support her forever," he said gruffly. "She has to marry again."

Osmund shrugged. "It won't be hard to force her into it, if you insist. Asta is a gentle person. Like Hacon. She used up all the fighting spirit and rebelliousness that was in her when she ran off with Nils. There is nothing left now, and she will do what you say. But I don't want to be the one to make her unhappy. Find someone else, Candamir."

Candamir rolled his eyes. "Fine, as you wish." He was annoyed and a little taken aback, but that didn't matter much. They had known each other all their lives and had often been annoyed with each other. "Just don't expect me to understand that," he said grumpily.

"No."

"You're a fool. I hope you know that."

"Maybe, but I don't have anything more to say on this matter, and I would be grateful if you would spare me this in the future."

Candamir nodded coolly and decided not to say anything at all for a while, hoping to punish Osmund a little.

Osmund's maids brought in bowls of thin soup and then sat down with them at the table. Furtively, Candamir glanced at Cudrun, the nurse Olaf had given to Osmund for little Roric. She was no longer young, certainly around thirty years of age, and even though her breasts might still have a lot of milk, they looked flabby and limp from having breastfed all her own children. It almost seemed that Osmund had picked out the most unattractive maid he could find. His other slave woman was a quiet, white-haired Frank he had inherited years ago from his father.

"Eat, Candamir," Osmund urged.

Candamir looked down at the bowl he had pushed off to one side. The soup had a dirty gray color, but a few globules of fat were floating in it, and at the bottom of the bowl he could almost make out a little piece of fish. But he declined with a shake of his head. "I'll eat tomorrow morning at home."

"You'll eat *now*," Osmund said. "Just look at you." He cast a concerned look at his friend's pale face that seemed even more hollow-cheeked than it really was because of the short black beard. Candamir looked like someone at death's door.

"You don't look any better yourself," Candamir replied.

"That may be. Now eat. Otherwise I'll have to get your Saxon and hold his feet to the fire until he tells me why my dog always runs toward him wagging his tail."

Startled, Candamir reached for his spoon and started to eat. He had been sure that Osmund hadn't had the slightest suspicion about what had kept his provisions from dwindling away, but apparently he had underestimated his friend's shrewdness.

"Just listen to how the wind is howling," Cudrun murmured anxiously.

Candamir cocked his head to one side and listened. Even though the thick walls of the house were well insulated with earth and muffled the sounds from outside, they could hear the first gusts of wind from the approaching storm. "I hope the ships won't be damaged," he said.

It was to be the worst winter storm in living memory. That night hardly anyone in Elasund was able to get any sleep. People lay under their covers, fearing the wind would tear the roof off their house or destroy the outlying buildings and the few animals they still had. Osmund and Candamir sat by the fire all night listening to the raging wind and the waves crashing on the shore, and finally Osmund said softly, "There are wolves howling in the storm."

Candamir nodded. He heard it too.

Rarely did wolves leave the forests in the winter and venture down to the coast, and it had never happened during Candamir's and Osmund's lifetime. The old women said that the wolves came when they no longer found enough to eat and could sense that people had become weak and would be easy prey.

Candamir pulled up his knees and wrapped his arms around them. For the first time since the Turons had come last fall, he was really afraid he might die.

By daybreak, the raging storm had subsided, but the sky remained dark and full of thick clouds. As soon as the gray twilight had driven away the horrors of the night, Osmund and Candamir fastened on their skis and set out to assess the damage.

The storm had brought with it more than an ell of new snow, and they had to struggle to make their way down to the village green. When they arrived, they were not surprised to find that almost all the men in the village had done the same. Like their neighbors, the two friends stood in the deep snow of the village green looking in dismay at the message the storm had brought.

None of the ships had been sunk, or even looked seriously damaged. But the village's sacred ash tree, under which the men had held their meetings and made their decisions as far back as anyone could remember, lay uprooted in the snow.

"O mighty Tyr," Candamir murmured. It was all he could manage to say.

The ash had been almost forty feet tall and stood close to the shore. Now the bare, slender branches of its crown lay in the gray water, which was still churning restlessly. It looked as if the waves were tearing at the branches and trying to pull their prey into the ocean. The clump of roots appeared only slightly smaller than the crown and rose up obscenely, still half stuck in the soil, no doubt the only reason the tree had not yet been washed away.

"May the gods be with us!" old Eilhard cried. "This is the end of Elasund."

No one contradicted him, but Brigitta was shaking her head. She was the only one who dared to stand right next to the fallen tree. All the others maintained a reverential distance. She had placed both hands on the earth-covered roots and closed her eyes, murmuring to herself. Candamir could not understand what she was saying, but it almost seemed as if she were singing. She was wearing neither skis nor snowshoes, and he wondered how she had managed to get there.

She opened her eyes, stepped back, and proclaimed in a surprisingly resounding voice, "Behold Thor's sign."

The men exchanged looks of astonishment.

"All I see is a bad omen," Eilhard said.

"Because you are an old fool, and old fools get faint-hearted," she replied.

Eilhard's deeply furrowed face turned dark red. "Be careful what you say, old crone..."

She paid him no heed, but turned to Osmund and Candamir. "You were right, and the indecisive ones were wrong. This tree is an arrow pointing the way for us."

Candamir shook his head. "I don't understand what you mean."

Brigitta's lip curled in a smile of contempt. "Well, I said you were right, but that doesn't mean you are any smarter than this old fool here. Thor worked a miracle in order to guide you, and you are too blind to see it, though it is forty feet long. Which direction is the fallen tree pointing in, Candamir Olesson, you who think you are the brightest man in Elasund?"

He had to force himself to look at the tree again, then answered, "To the southwest."

"And where did the storm come from?"

"From the southwest," he repeated, finally realizing the significance.

The other men also understood, and a general murmur of amazement went up. Of course! The tree should have fallen in the opposite direction. It had to be an omen of radical change that the living symbol of their community had fallen and lay at their feet, but they all understood now that it had to be more than just a prophecy of their doom and that the storm god Thor had indeed sent them a sign.

"But...what does it mean?" Siward asked.

"Isn't it obvious?" Candamir replied, joy and excitement suddenly replacing the terror that had paralyzed him only moments before.

Brigitta raised her hand in warning. "Not so fast."

"But didn't you just say yourself that the tree points like an arrow to the southwest, just where..."

"So it appears, and I am inclined to believe that it is so. But we must make sure. It is time for us to determine the will of the gods."

Many of those present bowed their heads as if in sorrow. Most Elasunders—particularly the men—feared oracles and the revelations that they would rather not know, yet nobody protested. The death of the ash tree was the most potent, and possibly the most ominous, sign they could ever imagine. Yet if it was in fact true that they were now standing at a crossroads, and not on the brink of disaster, they needed guidance.

No one hesitated to bow to the will of Brigitta—for, witch or not, she was the undisputed intermediary between the gods and the Elasunders.

Slowly the old woman turned around in a circle *widdershins*—the direction opposite to the course of the sun. She looked into the faces of the men and the few women scattered around.

"You," she told Osmund. "You are *Nordhr*—the north."

He scowled to show his displeasure, but nodded.

The next ones she chose were Siward's daughter Inga for the northeast, Olaf's eldest son Jared for the east, Siward for the southeast, Olaf for the south, and Eilhard's granddaughter Margild for the southwest. Then she nodded to Candamir and said, "Go and get your brother. I want him for *Vestr.*"

"No," Candamir said. Ignoring the disapproving glances of those standing around him, he folded his arms in front of his chest defiantly. "You can forget about that. You never show the slightest concern for your victims, and my brother is half starved and weak. You can take me if you want, but you can't have Hacon."

"Candamir, the west will be the most important position for this oracle, since it stands for distant places, unknown worlds," she explained with unaccustomed patience. "And I want your brother because Thor is his patron god. I need the connection, you understand."

He nodded. "Nevertheless, my answer is no."

Brigitta's unusually tolerant mood vanished, but Jared spoke up before she lost her temper. "Thor is also my patron god."

She looked at him, frowning, and grumbled reluctantly, "That's correct. So be it. Candamir, then you can take the west. Let's go."

"There's one still missing," said thirteen-year-old Inga, the youngest of those chosen, who nevertheless seemed the least fearless.

Brigitta shook her head. "None of you will take the northwest."

"Why?" the girl asked, puzzled. "How can the oracle speak if the world is incomplete?"

"It is not incomplete, but the one who stands for the northwest is not yet with us," Brigitta replied, shrugging her bony shoulders. "Come on now. There is much to do. Each of you must cut one branch from the root and another from the crown of the ash tree. Take care that as much soil as possible sticks to the root."

Silently, they all followed her instructions. Osmund lent Inga his knife to cut the wood and held her around the waist while she leaned out dangerously far over the water to reach the branch she wanted. When she was safely back on the shore, she smiled at him in gratitude and blushed slightly. Osmund realized for the first time what a charming and beautiful girl she was, and he smiled back.

Candamir detested Brigitta's house and never entered it of his own free will. It was only a small hut, solidly built to withstand the winter, but cramped and musty. It had only one room, which the old woman shared with three ravens. For reasons known only to her, they were named Urd, Werdandi, and Skuld after the Norns who determined past, present, and future. Near the left gable wall of the little house, a fire burned in the hearth. Earthen pots and leather sacks were lined up and piled against the remaining walls. Candamir preferred not to know what they might contain. In the darkest corner, beyond the reach of the fire's glow, there appeared to be a place to sleep on the ground. All sorts of things lay around: cooking pots of all sizes, full and empty, and linen pouches containing herbs, roots, and ground-up walrus teeth. On a shelf right over the entry the skull of a dog and a horse stood guard.

Candamir suppressed a shudder as he stepped over the threshold behind his friend. The lintel was so low he had to duck, and as soon as the door closed, he felt trapped. With eight people and three ravens, the little room was hopelessly overcrowded.

Only Inga looked around inquisitively and without inhibitions. Brigitta gave her an approving nod. "Put on a little pot with water." Inga found a medium-sized cast iron pot and then went outside and filled it with snow.

Brigitta walked to a low wooden chest at the foot of her bed and pushed aside one of the ravens perched on the chest's cover. It hopped to the floor, pecked ill-humoredly at one of its fellows, then fluttered away awkwardly before settling on Brigitta's shoulder. She absently stroked its black chest with one finger, then lovingly murmured, "Just stay with me, Skuld."

*How can she tell them apart?* Candamir wondered. To him, all three birds looked exactly alike: big, black, and ugly.

Opening the chest reverently, she took out a tan, carefully folded cloth and handed it to Jared. "Spread it out."

Jared handed one end of the cloth to his cousin Osmund, and together they spread it out carefully on the floor. Eight black lines radiated from the center of the circular cloth, forming a web-like pattern and dividing the cloth into eight equal fields. One of the lines ended in an N-rune, and they turned the cloth around so that this line was pointing directly north.

In the meantime, Candamir and Siward, following Brigitta's instructions, shoveled the embers into a cast-iron brazier and put new wood on the fire. The room became noticeably warmer. Inga had hung the pot on a hook over the hearth, and Brigitte put various other things into the brew as the little pot hissed and bubbled ominously. Candamir did not let the old woman out of his sight, worried she was adding something repulsive to the brew like frog's eyes or chicken blood. But the only things she put in the cauldron were various powders and something that looked like dried mushrooms.

The potion was soon ready, and Brigitta poured the contents of the cauldron into a large cup, commanding the group to go to their places.

Osmund knelt at the edge of the cloth, just where the rune indicated north, and the others followed his example. Siward was the last to join the group and set the bowl of embers down in the middle of the cloth where the lines met. Brigitta knelt down in front of it, facing northward, and with closed eyes raised the cup and murmured prayers to the gods for support and guidance. Then she drank deeply, passing the cup on to Osmund, who followed suit, nearly passing it to Candamir, when the old woman shouted, "Are you crazy, you fool! The other way around! Do you want to bring ruin down on us all?"

Osmund was startled and opened his eyes wide, then excused himself with a gesture and handed the cup to young Inga. Slowly the potion made the rounds. Candamir, who was crouching at the end of the west line, was the last to receive the drink.

"You must empty the cup," Brigitta told him.

"Lucky me," he said crossly, then raised the cup to his lips and drank. The brew was hot, bitter, and had an earthy, though not unpleasant taste. He drained the cup in two large gulps. Then slowly and deliberately, he turned it upside down next to him, outside the sacred circle of the cloth representing the world. It was now very quiet in the room—the fire was crackling and the embers in the brazier were hissing softly. When the raven on Brigitta's shoulder suddenly let out a strident caw, everyone jumped. Inga and Jared giggled. Olaf frowned and glanced menacingly at his son, but Brigitta seemed undisturbed by the young people's frivolity. She closed her eyes and waited. Her eyelids were wrinkled and red, with fine, blue veins running through them, as still as if she were fast asleep. The reddish glow from the fire cast shadows on her motionless figure, lending it a certain nobility.

"Put your branches from the crown of the ash into the brazier and look into the fire."

The branches were wet and burned slowly as acrid, gray smoke filled the warm room.

The potion affected each of them differently. Siward removed his shoes and massaged his feet as if they were numb or cramped. Inga frowned and pressed the fingers of her left hand against her temple. Margild panted heavily and fitfully, and Osmund seemed to feel nothing at all, though his pupils were clearly dilated. Candamir was wondering why everything suddenly looked fuzzy, as if he were under water, when a sudden, sharp pain in the pit of his stomach made him wince. Startled, he pressed his hand to his stomach and the pain returned. "Oh, you treacherous old bitch," he panted. "You have poisoned me."

Brigitta looked at him coldly. "Pull yourself together, boy. It will soon pass."

But it didn't pass—it got worse. He was so doubled up with pain that his forehead almost touched the floor. "Poisoned," he repeated in a flat voice, "because I humiliated your cowardly, worthless son at the Yule festival. I always wondered when...when you would pay me back."

"What foolish talk," she replied brusquely, but not as gruffly as usual, and she laid one of her old, gnarled hands on his sweaty forehead. Immediately the pain seemed to abate, and Candamir relaxed a bit, but only a bit, because he did not trust her. The stabbing pain soon stopped completely and did not return. He slowly straightened up and looked into the fire again, which seemed to his troubled gaze like a reddish, simmering brew. Gradually he became aware of a sound—a monotonous, rattling noise—like a slow heartbeat. Brigitta held a little pouch in her left hand. Candamir had not the slightest idea where this bag had come from so suddenly. It was made of white sealskin and contained pieces of wood and stone inscribed with runes, which she gently jingled. That was the sound, he realized. It seemed to reach his ears in waves, sometimes muffled, sometimes clear, but always with the same rhythm, and Candamir noticed how his own heart started to beat to this rhythm. It had become hellishly hot in the small hut, but even though his eyes were watering and burning from the smoke, he no longer felt the need to flee.

Finally the rhythm stopped. Brigitta opened the pouch and held it out to Osmund. "Here, take a rune in your left hand, but do not look at it," she said.

One by one, they all took a rune. Brigitta was last, and she drew twice, as no one was in the ninth position. Then she carefully put the pouch to one side, cupped her hands, and told those sitting in the circle to give her their runes. When she had all nine runes, she shook them and rattled them around again, but this time faster and more urgently. Then she opened her hands, spread out her fingers, and dropped the runes on the brown cloth on the other side of the brazier, where they scattered like drops of water. Candamir was strangely slow in his reactions, and it seemed to take him forever to find all nine runes.

None of the runes looked like any of the others. The symbols were either carved into long, flat pieces of wood of various sizes, or were cut into small stones, and all were lying with their inscriptions turned up. That was quite unusual, as even Candamir realized.

"It appears that the gods have much to tell us," Brigitta said. For a long while she stared at the nine runes in front of her, checking the angles and distance they were from each other. Just as important as what each rune represented were their positions to each other, as it determined their sequence and relationships.

Finally Brigitta pointed to the rune lying apart from the others and closest to the bowl of fire. It was carved into a smooth, gray pebble and featured a perpendicular line with a small, slanting line through the middle. "Nauthiz," said the old woman in a firm voice. "It is the beginning and stands for what is." She pointed to the others in the order she had determined: "Berkano, Raidho, Hagalaz, Thurisaz, Kenaz, Ingwaz, Jera, and Ehwaz." Then she started over again: "Nauthiz, Berkano, Raidho, Hagalaz, Thurisaz, Kenaz, Ingwaz, Jera, Ehwaz."

She recited the names again, as if they were a magic incantation. Every time she spoke a name, her finger moved on to another rune, and seven pairs of eyes followed. It had become so hot in the room that Candamir felt like he was breathing liquid fire. Sweat ran down his chest and back, yet his face felt cool and his head clearer than ever. He listened spellbound to Brigitta's monotonous incantations while his eyes followed her gnarled finger, and then he heard a second voice that overlapped hers, always repeating what she said, only a trifle faster. The voice was gentle and strangely melodic, the voice of a young woman or perhaps a boy.

"Nauthiz, Berkano, Raidho, Hagalaz, Thurisaz, Kenaz, Ingwaz, Jera, Ehwaz," both voices declared. Then Osmund and Jared murmured at the same time, "I hear the voice of the raven."

"Good," replied both Brigitta and the second voice contentedly while Brigitta continued her litany of runic names.

*Raven?* Candamir wondered in confusion. *How can this clear and beautiful voice be that of a raven?* Suspiciously, he peered at the black, winged bird still crouched on the old woman's shoulder. Its beak was closed, but the two dark, beady eyes looked at him steadfastly and seemed to be mocking his ignorance. The next time around, the unearthly voice in his head became much louder, even overpowering, and soon he felt a hammering in his temples.

"I too hear the voice of the raven," he gasped, and at once the hammering subsided. The bird glared at him and appeared to be saying, *Well, why didn't you come out with it right away?* Then a vague giddiness came over him, like what he felt when he was hopelessly drunk, but today the dizziness did not deaden his senses, it seemed to sharpen all five of them. He smelled the fire and the smoke, felt the heat and the sweat on his skin, saw a multitude of flickering images in the light of the fire, tasted the strange, earthy potion still on his tongue, and above all, he heard.

"Now throw the roots with the soil into the fire," said Brigitta and the raven. "This time Jared will start."

The wet clods of soil hissed, and for a moment the fire in the brazier subsided as an overpowering odor of dampness, decay, and fertile soil spread through the small, stuffy room.

"Nauthiz," Brigitta began, but then she stopped.

"That was my rune." It was still the wondrous voice of the raven that Candamir heard, but the sound seemed to come from Jared's mouth. "It stands for what is—misery and hunger of the body and spirit." Jared batted his eyes like an owl, as if he simply couldn't believe what was coming out of his mouth.

"Berkano," said Brigitta, pointing to the second rune.

"It is the rune of the birch goddess, my patron goddess," said the raven, through Olaf. "It shows what soon will be —renewal, growth, the new beginning of spring, and liberation."

Brigitta's finger moved on. "Raidho."

For a long while no one spoke, but the old woman seemed in no hurry. She sat there as motionless as the bird on her shoulder, with her finger pointing at the third rune.

Finally, Siward spoke out. "I do not hear the voice of the raven because I did not want to hear it. But I know I have drawn this rune. I felt it." Raidho was the only rune stone that was nearly square, and it had sharper corners than all the others. "Raidho is the wagon and stands for a voyage." He bowed his head. "The gods pay little heed to the wishes of an old man. So be it, then."

There was a long silence in the room, but the sweet voice in Candamir's head gradually returned, and he realized now he had heard it whispering for a long time before taking note of it. The voice was whispering the name of the fourth rune—Hagalaz.

The sound came from Margild's mouth: "Hagalaz is my rune, and it tells of the force and destruction of nature, but also of purification through trial."

"The storm," Brigitta explained, and it was her voice alone that was now speaking. "Hagalaz stands for the storm we must meet and overcome in order to find the new homeland." It appeared she wanted to say something more, but then she changed her mind, pointing instead to the next rune. "Thurisaz."

Candamir could hear the strange voice coming out of his own mouth. "I drew it." Despite the heat, a cold shiver ran up and down his spine and goose bumps formed along his upper arms. Thor's rune was the thorn, symbolizing above all virility. He wondered whether this was a prophecy about his own descendents or if it meant their people would prosper and multiply in the new homeland—but the interpretation was something quite different. "This rune stands for the courage of men, their superiority in battle," said the raven.

So Thor wanted them to know they would overcome the native people on Olaf's island, something Candamir had never seriously doubted. But Jared, who sat diagonally across from him, said, "Thor is my patron god, and from my point of view his rune is reversed, so that it tells of evil, danger, and lies. And discord." He was still obviously suffering from the effect of the potion—he did not look at any of them directly, his voice sounded weak and dejected, and he was very pale. But the voice of the raven in Candamir's head confirmed Jared's prophecy. This realization worried Candamir, and he lowered his head and closed his eyes for a moment in order to collect his thoughts. That proved to be a mistake. Once his eyelids had closed, they simply refused to open again. Dazzling brightness alternated with blackness, in time with the beating of his heart, the voices got further and further away, and he saw a confused succession of images. The raven spoke of the rune Kenaz, the torch of knowledge, and Candamir saw his Saxon with arms uplifted at the edge of a grassy cliff, his face turned toward heaven. His face appeared transfigured, yet blood flowed from his hands, feet, and side. And then he saw Ingwaz, the rune of the earth god that symbolized the security of home and family: a beautiful hall on the bank of a river, the wood of its walls so new they were still weeping resins. And Jera, the rich harvest, a field of golden wheat, larger than any wheat field Candamir had ever seen, at the edge of a dark forest with giant trees, and the trees moved, for in place of their trunks they had legs, and they marched in close formation across the field, trampling the golden wheat. The last of the nine runes was Ehwaz, the horse, standing for movement and change. He saw a beautiful, sand-colored foal with a dark mane and tail, galloping wildly across wide, level grassland.

Candamir smiled in his weird dream, for it was a picture of such perfect beauty. But then a voice spoke up in the northwest, not the voice of the raven, but that of a woman, a voice he had never heard before, and it cried out, "It was my rune, and it is reversed. It heralds discord, distrust, and betrayal!" The voice had frightened the frolicking horse, and it stopped, raising its head and swishing its tail nervously back and forth, before it suddenly turned and fled. *No,* Candamir thought in despair, *don't run away.*

He ran after it, jumping effortlessly over hill and dale, but couldn't catch up with it. The woman's voice called after him, a warning it seemed, but he couldn't make out the words. Suddenly it was no longer a meadow, but a ship's deck he was running across. His steps resounded on the planks, and still he was too slow—he could hardly move forward, and he watched with increasing panic as Osmund fell overboard and sank into the foaming waves. At the ship's side, he fell on his knees, seized the dangerously thin rope that secured his friend, and pulled, but what came to the surface was the twelve-headed sea serpent. One of its mouths opened and descended upon him, a gaping hole with two rows of needle-sharp teeth. Frozen with terror, Candamir stared at it, and then the mighty jaw closed on him and he was surrounded by darkness.

Too late, he drew his sword and lunged at the slimy jaws, but he was pulled down, relentlessly, and swallowed by the monster. Deeper and deeper he fell. He heard a sharp cry—it was Inga's voice, he realized, not that of the raven, and then he started to tumble head over heels, spinning as he fell, but still did not hit the bottom.

"Take him outside and lay him in the snow before he drops dead on us," old Brigitta grumbled. Many hands reached out to stop his fall, lifting him up and carrying him back into the world of light.

He came to in a wonderfully cool, clean bed, but what he saw when he opened his eyes was not snow, but a huge flock of white ravens. Smiling, he closed his eyes again and drifted off.

# Part II: The Voyage

# Spring Moon

The rhythmic sounds of hammers and axes resounded over the smooth, silent water of the Elasund fjord. On every ship, busy hands were at work caulking and building. Sails and boltropes were tested and repaired as the ships were readied for the long voyage.

"Tomorrow," Osmund said, almost incredulously.

"Indeed. If we get a bit of wind by then, and if Berse arrives on time," Candamir said.

Osmund sat down beside him at one of the rowing seats in the stern, and with a grateful nod accepted the mug that Candamir offered. "Oh, he will. Who would ever want to miss the great day?"

Who indeed? After the fall of the ash tree and the oracle, the Elasunders decided to start out in search of Olaf's Land. Siward declared himself too old to rebel against the will of the gods, and his well-reasoned change of heart persuaded the other skeptics to join. More than two dozen clans would set sail the next day in nine ships, and not all of them were Elasunders.

A few families, including those of Thorbjörn and Haldir, Eilhard's sons, had joined them from the villages along the river. Berse the shipwright, who had lived with his family near the mouth of the river far from any town, also wanted to leave, especially since no one would be left who might need his services. In all only four families had decided to stay: Torke the fisherman and his family, who had always been a bit strange, keeping mostly to themselves; then two families who had too few young men and too many old men and small children to set out on such an adventure; and the clan of a merchant sailor who had not returned last autumn. They still hoped of his return and did not want to leave without him.

Candamir was far more concerned about the people staying than those heading to sea with him. How could they defend such a small community if the Turons, or other pirates just as bloodthirsty, returned? It saddened him to think what might await them, but he couldn't force them aboard the *Falcon* against their will.

Osmund drank deeply from the pitcher. They still only had water to drink since nothing had yet grown from which to brew beer, though the famine was over. Once spring had arrived, fish and seals returned in great numbers, and the Elasunders had slaughtered all the farm animals they could not take along on their voyage.

Work on the ships had begun as soon as the weather permitted. All of them, except for Olaf's *Sea Dragon*, had been used only for travel along the coast, and thus their holds, between the high half decks fore and aft, were open. They had been able to store many goods there on their trading voyages in the past, but no one could venture out into a storm on the high seas in such an open ship, or it would founder and sink like a stone. Thus they had reinforced the beams and planks and closed the holds. The ships now had a deck that went the entire length of the vessel, allowing sufficient room for the travelers. The hold could be reached through two hatches, of which the forward one was large enough to accommodate the animals.

"We will never have enough room for all the things people want to take along," Candamir said.

Osmund nodded thoughtfully. "Well, everyone has to stick strictly to the agreement. Basically, we don't need much other than food, sheep, and seed. Everything else we can get on Olaf's island."

"Yes, but you don't seriously believe I will leave my horses behind, do you?" Candamir said with a grin, ignoring Osmund's sigh and tilting back his head. He pointed a long, slender finger at the clouds coming in from the west, some of which were shaped like dragon heads. "Just look, we're getting a breeze. Obviously the gods also want us to set sail tomorrow."

Berse the shipwright had outdone himself. Many Elasunders came down to the harbor to see the new ship arrive. It was a clinker-built plank ship with a shallow keel. Its bright red- and yellow-striped sail billowed in the wind, and artistically carved wolf heads adorned the prow and stern. It appeared weightless, almost as if it had wings, as it sailed majestically over the calm, steel-blue water of the fjord.

"How sturdy it looks," young Inga murmured, deeply impressed, "as if it could never sink."

"*Any* ship can sink," Candamir said and immediately regretted his thoughtless, though no doubt accurate observation. What they needed, at least as urgently as good ships, was confidence. "But you are right," he hastened to add, "it's a real wolf of the waves."

"Is that what it's called?" Hacon asked, pointing to the figures on the bow and stern. Candamir nodded.

Inga was shivering in the cool breeze and pulled up her shoulders. "Can't we sail with Berse? I wouldn't be afraid of anything on his ship."

"Maybe you can ask Berse," Candamir suggested, a little gruffly. It had been settled long ago that Siward's family would sail in the *Falcon*, and Candamir was a little piqued that Inga looked down on his beautiful ship. "If you promise him a kiss, he will certainly take you on board."

Inga grimaced in disgust, and Wiland and Hacon broke out in laughter. Berse was an outstanding craftsman and sailor, but he was small, hunchbacked, and gnomish in appearance. He had once claimed that he was descended from dwarves, and ever since Brigitta had referred to him as "Durin's grandson."

As the *Wavewolf* neared the shore, Berse's sons hauled in the sail and cast anchor, and the small crew disembarked. Berse, bowlegged and in the lead, waded ashore.

Olaf stepped toward him, but Berse made for Candamir instead, who had visited him regularly all winter trying to gain his family's support for the great adventure. The ship's hull had already been completed in the fall, and after the thaw set in, the shipwright and his sons had prepared it for the demands of a trip on the high seas. Candamir had frequently called on Berse for his expert advice on converting the Elasund ships and to admire the progress of the *Wavewolf.*

"If all you were doing was waiting for me, then we can leave," the shipwright said calmly. His voice was rough and unmelodious, perfectly matching his appearance.

Candamir shuddered, half in fear and half in happy anticipation. Looking briefly at the sea, he replied nonchalantly, "Tomorrow morning. Brigitta consulted the runes again, and they say tomorrow is a good day."

Berse lowered his voice. "Are you sure she speaks the truth? Perhaps she consulted the runes to determine the best day to bring disaster upon us. Please excuse me, Osmund, I know she belongs to your wife's kin, but that old witch is capable of anything."

Osmund nodded. "But since she is coming along, it is improbable that she wants to destroy the fleet."

The shipwright opened his eyes wide and cast a quick glance at the old, haggard woman in the black cloak. She stood at least thirty paces away, but she answered his gaze with a malicious, amused look, as if she could hear every word the men were whispering to each other. "She is coming along? What's the purpose of such an old, shriveled tree in new soil?" Berse seemed honestly troubled.

Osmund shrugged his shoulders. "Her son wanted to stay, but she convinced him to come along." Brigitta had not told anyone exactly what she had learned from the oracle or how she had interpreted it. She had merely said that anyone declining this venture was risking the wrath of the gods. Naturally the stupid, drunken Haflad didn't dare defy her.

Berse said, "She'll never set foot on my ship, I swear."

"Olaf will take her," Candamir told him impatiently, growing weary of this topic. "In two hours we'll meet with him and the other captains to set the course. Until then we need to attend to loading the ships."

It was a difficult task. The rules had been laid down weeks ago about who could take what quantity of provisions and how many domestic animals, but everyone had just one more barrel of herring or sack of grain, and everyone believed that in his case a little exception could surely be made.

In spite of all the careful planning, massive confusion ensued in the harbor. Everything, apart from the passengers and livestock, had to be put on board that day. Piled up in the meadow were provisions, weapons, tools, and indispensible though useless keepsakes. Struggling under heavy loads, the villagers loaded their possessions on their assigned ship, laughing as they got in each other's way or fell in the water. Everyone knew they were voyaging into the unknown and that numerous dangers awaited them, but their thirst for adventure and the promise of a new home in a fertile land and a future without famines and land shortages made them all a bit tipsy. Not even Siward was immune to that.

Osmund, Candamir, and Olaf had worked untiringly, leaving nothing to chance. Every family knew not only what ship they were on, but exactly what part of the limited storage was allocated to them and where. Since Candamir's and Osmund's households were relatively small, two other clans were assigned to the *Falcon*. Siward's family was the largest, with his young, new bride whom he had wed the previous month in a little village along the river, his two sons, two daughters, a son-in-law, daughter-in-law, and three grandchildren, as well as nearly a dozen slaves. Harald the blacksmith also had asked for a place on Candamir's ship and brought along his wife, his son, and five slaves.

"First we'll head for the Cold Islands northeast of Scotland," Olaf began, as they gathered around his longfire for the last time. "That will take five days. Some clans of our people have settled there, and we can replenish our water supplies, but we mustn't linger there too long. We have to hurry if we wish to sow our fields this year in the new homeland."

The others nodded, even the shipwright, who was not very fond of the vain, rich merchant.

"From there we head northwest around Britain. We can stop one more time in Ireland to trade, though I think it unwise, as you can never predict the mood of the people there. Today they will welcome you as a brother, and tomorrow they'll draw their swords against you. From there, we head straight south for about two days until the western horn of the land of the Franks heaves into view. Then we leave the coast and head southwest."

Just like his father before him, Candamir knew nothing but coastal navigation, and he wasn't ashamed to ask, "How do you set your course without a coastline to follow?"

"By the sun," the shipwright chimed in. "Some even sail by the stars at night."

Olaf nodded. "And even if the sun is not out, there are enough signs to show us the way: the migration of birds, whales, and dolphins, for example, and reefs or small islands. We continue heading southwest for about four days. There we should meet the storm."

"And if not?" Berse asked.

"Then we will wait for it."

"And are you sure it will come?" the shipwright inquired skeptically.

Olaf nodded. "I found it there twice."

"But you only made it to this island once—if at all!"

"I think that's enough, Berse," Candamir said. "Olaf never said he knew the exact way. If anyone knew where it was, this land would have long ago been taken over by some tribe of our people. Its uncertain location is our greatest hope, and at the same time, our greatest peril. We all understand that."

Thorbjörn nodded. "It's a little too late for your misgivings, shipwright."

Berse backed down with a reluctant grunt.

"We ought to sail in the kind of formation geese use," Olaf continued. "That's the best way to avoid a collision or taking wind out of each other's sails. At night we'll tie the ships together so we won't drift as much or risk losing sight of each another."

"And who will lead this swarm of geese?" Berse asked, half belligerently and half in amusement.

Olaf looked him in the eyes. "I will. I am the most experienced sailor among us and the only one who ever ventured away from the coasts."

Candamir could see that Berse was not entirely happy with that. And he himself felt equally reluctant to accept Olaf's demand for leadership.

But, of course, Olaf was right: only if they entrusted themselves to him could they expect to reach their goal. They could thrash out who would take which role in the new homeland when they got there, Candamir thought. *If* they got there…

The hall already looked abandoned—there were no dishes on the shelves, no hangings left on the walls, no sealskins on the benches, and no cauldron over the fire. Everything had been sold, given away, or packed. The high seat had also been dismantled, the posts tied together with leather straps, and taken on board. The master of the hall was not there, anyway, as Candamir spent the last night before the departure on his ship, just like all the other captains.

Together with Asta, the Saxon, and the other servants, Hacon sat on the bare bench by the fire with his shoulders hunched up. The long silence made him uncomfortable.

"I thought Osmund was coming over with his household," the boy finally said. He was startled to hear his voice echoing in the empty room. "Didn't you say they were going to close up the house today and spend the night here, Asta?"

His sister nodded. "Apparently everything is taking a bit longer than planned," she answered casually. But she thought to herself, *Above all, saying goodbye.* Twice in the last few days she had found Osmund standing behind his house by the little mound of earth under which Gisla's ashes lay buried. The earth still had a freshly turned look to it, and he had placed a rune stone on top, a small boulder that he had polished for a week and which bore an inscription:

*This stone was placed by Osmund in memory of his wife Gisla, the mother of his son, who was killed by the Turons when they came in the autumn. She was a good woman.*

Asta reflected, not without envy, how much she wished she could have placed such a stone for Nils.

The Saxon seemed to guess her thoughts. "Sometimes it is better to move on to a new place and start afresh. It can help you forget what is lost forever."

During the course of the winter, Asta had learned the same bitter lesson as Osmund had, that people quickly become impatient with those who grieve. She felt criticized and answered hotly, "That's easy for you to say, especially for a man who has given his life completely to some god and has renounced human intimacy. That's wonderfully simple, isn't it? After all, you cannot lose a god." It sounded sharper than she had intended, and her voice echoed eerily in the empty hall.

But Austin was neither intimidated nor offended. He smiled at her sadly and said, "Oh yes, Asta, you can lose your god as well. For example, when he has torn you away from your parents and your brother whom you love."

She raised her left hand in a weary gesture of apology. "I'm sorry. Don't pay any attention to what I say. I always become unbearable when I'm afraid of something—like this voyage."

The monk nodded and after a thoughtful silence said, "Well, you were not actually so wrong. I have found my god again, and he gives me assurance and confidence of a kind that none of you have known."

No one contradicted him. In view of the great adventure they would all embark on the next day at sunrise, each one had to struggle with his own fears and doubts, and no one was as calm as the Saxon.

He stood up and nodded toward Hacon. "Let us do what the master has told us and bring the animals in from the meadow."

The boy got up willingly.

At the door, Austin stopped briefly and turned to Asta. "By the time we return, it will probably be almost dark. If you wish, I will go with you to Elbingdal. No one will see us there, and you can visit your husband's grave in peace."

She looked up. "You would do that?"

He nodded. "Just make sure your brother doesn't find out about it."

Without waiting for her answer, he followed Hacon out into the clear spring evening. Dusk was falling, and the sky over the pine forest was a deep indigo color. A soft breeze tousled Hacon's dark head of hair as they walked across the yard and out onto the meadow.

A few weeks ago, Candamir had to slaughter the second gelding as well. Among his horses, only the colt and the pregnant mare had survived the winter famine. Hacon and Austin brought them into the stable and then the dozen sheep that were to come along on the trip. They went about their work silently, and Hacon appeared deep in thought, almost withdrawn.

Austin did not press him, as he knew from experience that the boy would tell him what was on his mind when he was ready, and not before. Hacon was sensitive and a perpetual skeptic, in contrast to his brother. But Austin had learned that the boy could be just as quick-tempered and brusque as Candamir when he was urged to listen to his feelings and examine his own heart—in short, when he was "treated like a girl." He was, after all, at an age when all boys were intent on proving their manhood—not just those raised by their older brother. The Saxon had to admit that Candamir fulfilled this task as best he could, but rarely with patience or sensitivity. Since her return to Elasund, Asta had tried to provide her young brother with the kind of warm nest he had always had to do without, but she was too shy to stand up to Candamir when he treated the boy unfairly. And in any case, Hacon was too old for her maternal care. He really did not have it easy, Austin knew.

When they came back to the yard, Hacon stopped at the well, lowered the leather bucket to get a drink, and then offered the bucket to Austin.

"Thank you."

Hacon sat down on the rim of the well, waited until the slave put the bucket down, and then asked, "Do you often long for your old homeland?"

Austin was surprised. "What makes you think of that today, of all times?"

The boy shrugged his slender shoulders. "Because you said something about parents and a brother. You never spoke of them before."

"No." Austin flashed a quick smile and sat down next to him. "It's better this way. It was God's will that I should lose them, or rather, that they should lose me. I have come to realize why I had to leave my family and everything dear and precious to me. I had to become completely empty in order to become God's vessel and bring his word to the world."

"So you believe that your mighty god, who can do a hundred things at the same time, is following a plan in all he does, and that everything that happens to his people has a meaning?"

"That's right. Nothing happens without God's will, and his will always follows his divine plan. Naturally, we often lack the far-sightedness to understand his purpose. But it's always there."

"So our trip to the new homeland is also his will?"

Austin looked into his eyes and raised his shoulders a bit. "At least our departure is. We have to wait to find out the rest, I would say. It may well be that God is sending us on this voyage as some sort of trial, and that we will only find the promised land if we can prove ourselves."

Hacon nodded thoughtfully. Austin knew the boy was struggling, fighting some inner battle, but it took him completely by surprise when Hacon finally asked, "What must I say to him if I wish to ask him to show us the way?"

The slave sat there dumbfounded. "Hacon…you wish to pray to my god?"

The boy waved him off, embarrassed. "No reason to sacrifice an ox. I only thought it might not do any harm to pray to all the gods I know and have a better chance that one of them would hear me."

"And do what you ask," the Saxon added with a smile. "It is very simple—you can speak with him the way you speak with me. If you turn to him, he will understand you no matter what words you use or what language you speak."

The boy nodded and smiled shyly. "Fine, but don't tell anyone, you hear?"

Solemnly, Austin shook his head. He was careful to conceal his excitement, but secretly he rejoiced. It was perhaps only a small step, but after all the years of frustration, a great victory. He had always suspected that this clever lad, who was young enough in years so that his mind could still be molded, represented his greatest hope. Now the first crack in the wall had appeared, and the monk decided to water this crack constantly with the word of God, so that one day the wall would burst and Hacon would become a believer—unless, of course, Candamir should bash his head in first when he noticed what influence the Saxon had on Hacon.

He put his hand on the lad's shoulder. "You have my word. Now, go to bed. Tomorrow is a big day."

Hacon willingly followed him back to the house. At the doorway, the lad stopped briefly again and looked down at the village, the harbor, and the fjord.

"Will you miss it?" the Saxon asked softly.

Hacon pondered his question for a moment and then shook his head. "Elasund isn't a good place to live. Too little land, too many attacks, too much misery, too cold in the winter. But it is the only thing I know. The unknown..." *The unknown frightens me*, he almost said, but it was unthinkable to admit that.

The nine ships put to sea just as the sun rose behind Elasund, driving away the gray of dusk.

Candamir stood at the helm, looking intently at the steel-blue fjord. The *Falcon*'s red and white sail billowed proudly in the morning breeze, so that the men sitting at the sixteen rowing benches—eight in front and eight in the rear—could take it easy.

Osmund, who was standing at his friend's side, was about to turn around, but Candamir put his hand quickly on his arm and said, "Don't. My father always said it's bad luck."

Osmund resisted the temptation of taking one last look at Elasund. He folded his arms and squinted at the *Sea Dragon* gliding over the gentle waves on their port side. His uncle's ship was no larger than the *Falcon*, but more impressive: the dragon heads at the prow and stern were painted in bright colors, and the dark green, square sailcloth was neither patched nor faded. Its boltropes were fashioned from a bright yellow material that shimmered almost like gold. Behind Olaf, parallel to the *Falcon*, was Berse's new *Wavewolf*, and behind them the other six ships.

Before they rounded the breakwater and Elasund finally disappeared from view, the Saxon furtively looked back, in part to prove that he was above the superstitions of these pagans. The village with its spacious longhouses lay peacefully in the morning sun. Only a few people were on the shore to watch them leave, for in the preceding weeks a noticeable rift had opened up between those leaving and those staying behind. Each group thought the other was doomed, and they avoided one another as if they might become infected with the other's inevitable misfortune.

They followed the *Sea Dragon* westward, past the tongue of land, and Elasund disappeared. Before them lay the open sea. The tops of the gentle waves sparkled in the clear morning light, and the sky was wide and blue.

Candamir breathed in the fresh sea air deeply.

"We ride deeper in the water than the *Wolf* and the *Dragon*," Osmund observed. "Do you think we are overloaded?"

Candamir nodded. "I think all the ships are overloaded, and because we have the blacksmith on board with his tools and supplies, it's a little worse for us. But don't worry. When my father came home from his trips, this ship sometimes rode so deep in the water that the falcon head on the prow got its beak wet with every wave."

"I'm not worried," Osmund said. "I only wonder if Olaf will sail away from us."

Candamir shrugged, unconcerned. "If necessary we can row. Take the tiller for a moment, if you will. I want to make sure the cargo is safely tied down." Osmund took over the rudder attached to the ship's rump on the right-hand side, which for this reason was called the steerboard or starboard side, while Candamir walked toward the cargo hatch in the stern. As he went by, he instructed the Saxon, "Tell the women to make breakfast."

Austin looked up. In his hands he held a crude wooden stick and was carving something into it with his table knife—the only type of knife a slave was allowed to carry. "In just a moment, Master."

"Not in a moment, but now. What are you making?"

"A calendar." The Saxon held out the wooden stick. "Do you see? Today is the twenty-first day of the Spring Moon, or March, as we would say in my country. For every day of our trip, I'll carve a notch in this stick. When we arrive, we will know how long we were at sea and be able to calculate the date of our landing. Then later we can keep a calendar like civilized people." *And I can figure out when it is Easter or Pentecost,* he thought to himself.

Candamir nodded and couldn't help being impressed. "Not bad. Then make sure you don't lose your stick when we get caught in the storm." He laughed at his slave's frightened look and continued on his way.

The trapdoor to the rear hatch led down a short stepladder into the hold that took up the entire belly of the ship. Candamir was met by the pungent odor of manure and the pathetic bleating and lowing of the animals. The sheep lay on their sides, their legs bound together, something they clearly did not like, but the only safe way to transport farm animals. The only animals Candamir would tolerate on deck were Osmund's and Siward's dogs that were smart and clever enough not to be washed overboard by the first serious wave.

Every family had taken around a dozen sheep along, as he had, but no cattle, as Olaf had told them about a wondrous race of fat, brown, long-haired cattle on the island that could probably be domesticated. It therefore didn't make sense to take along the big, heavy animals that were far more delicate than they looked and prone to illness.

Candamir checked the ropes on his two horses. They were lying on their sides tied up like the sheep, but struggling much harder to free themselves. It was easy to see how agitated and miserable they were, and he felt bad about it. The mare rolled her eyes and tried to nuzzle his hand, and he patted her slender neck with a reassuring murmur. Then he arose and checked the ropes used to secure the kegs, baskets, and sacks. *What a collection of provisions and objects,* he thought as he glanced around. Siward had even smuggled a crate on board filled with ordinary, wooden drinking cups, and Harald had brought along a seal fur, bald in patches and smelly, whose purpose Candamir could not imagine. Superfluous things, but perhaps everyone was trying in their own fashion to take along a bit of the old homeland, he concluded.

The wind blew constantly that day, finally subsiding at dusk. They lowered the sails and roped the ships together as planned, pulling them so close that only a step separated one from the other. But even on this floating island, none of the captains allowed a cooking fire aboard his ship. That would be too dangerous, Osmund patiently explained to the grumblers. Ships were made of wood, as everyone knew, and wood burned. The women prepared a meal as best they could of cold smoked fish and sheep's milk cheese. Inga tried it bravely and mumbled some indistinct words of protest while she chewed. After she had swallowed, she exclaimed with a laugh, "Oh, that really tasted terrible."

"If it were up to me, it would taste much worse," said Asi, the smith's wife. "Then your Osmund would perhaps change his mind about the cooking fires."

Inga blushed. "He is not *my* Osmund."

Asi filled some bowls with the cold fish supper and cast a glance at her. "But you wish he were, don't you?"

Asta could see how uncomfortable young Inga felt. "Well, I'm convinced we'll all get used to this diet," she said to change the topic. "After all, we have practically no other provisions."

The others nodded and sighed. Since the end of winter, nobody had had any grain left except for a little seed, so they had not even been able to bake the hard, unleavened loaves of bread that kept easily and were usually taken on long voyages.

Some of the men had climbed down into the hold to look after the animals. The horses and some of the sheep were particularly restless, and on Candamir's instructions, Hacon and Austin took the shackles off them for a while to allow them to stand up and get their blood flowing again. When they were done, they came back on deck again and tackled their supper hungrily, though without great enthusiasm. After supper the travelers walked around from ship to ship, exchanging their experiences of this first day with each other. They soon returned to their places, rolling up in a fur blanket, so it became quiet on board. Quite a few wondered at the spectacular sight of the starry firmament, especially those who had never put to sea before. Yet it wasn't long before the boat's gentle swaying had rocked them all to sleep.

With a good wind they arrived at the Cold Islands on the morning of the fifth day. They headed for the main island, because, according to Olaf, that was where the largest village, and best place to trade, was located. But he had also warned them that Cnut, the self-appointed king of the Cold Islands, was a greedy and deceitful fellow who would pull a fast one on anyone fool enough to let him.

"Do the people here speak our language?" Hacon asked, looking out toward the foreign coastline.

Osmund nodded. "Their ancestors came from an area not far from Turonland."

They sailed into a long bay that ended in a rocky shore with a large village situated on it. The houses were smaller and much closer together than in Elasund. You could see workshops and storehouses but no barns. The people on these islands lived from trade and fishing, as Olaf had explained to them, so they hardly had any livestock and did not farm.

They cast anchor close to the beach. "We should not all go ashore," Candamir said. "It can't hurt to have enough men on board to guard our belongings."

Osmund agreed. "I'll go with Olaf and see if a friendly reception awaits us."

"Please, please, take me along," Hacon begged, his eyes shining.

"All right then," Osmund said. "But keep your silence when I speak with the foreigners, do you hear? You never know what..."

He stopped short because a small disturbance had broken out aboard the *Sea Dragon*. Olaf and his two older sons Jared and Lars were standing around the Turon slave who was waving his arms excitedly and uttering inarticulate, angry sounds. Finally Olaf took his whip in hand and began to beat the slave. The poor wretch wrapped his arms protectively around his head and fell to his knees, but Olaf kept beating him mercilessly.

"What's all this about?" Hacon asked.

"I assume that Olaf doesn't want to take his Turon ashore," said Osmund. "The people here are practically his kin, and the slave might get the idea of running away and hiding among them."

The sons finally calmed down their angry father, tied up the bleeding Turon, and stashed him below deck.

"This Olaf is a monster," the Saxon murmured.

Candamir looked at his slave pensively. "But not stupid. Maybe I should lock you in the hold, too. It isn't far from the Cold Islands to Scotland, is it? And south of Scotland is your homeland. Why don't you look straight at me, Saxon? Have you also been harboring thoughts of running away?"

Austin raised his head and looked him in the eye. "Would I not be a fool if I hadn't?"

"Indeed," he said. "So, get down in the hold with the rest of my sheep." He made a pointed gesture toward the hatch.

"No, Candamir, don't do that," his brother pleaded with him. "Make him swear by the blood of his god that he will not run away, and then you won't need to worry about letting him go ashore. Don't lock him down in the hold—it's so horrible there."

And that it was, indeed. Sheep smelled bad enough in large pens or outdoors, but the stench in the hold was appalling. "Very well, then, swear to it, Saxon."

The monk placed his right hand on his heart and raised his left hand. "I swear by the blood of Jesus Christ that I will not run away while we are on the Cold Islands, Master."

"Then go along with Osmund and Hacon. Keep your eyes open. It is impossible to say how we will be received here. And don't think I missed the qualification of your vow."

Osmund, Olaf, and Berse were to go ashore with their attendants, and they conferred at some length about what they would say before going to meet Cnut.

The island leader resided in a huge hall with magnificent wall hangings. His high seat stood at the end of the longfire, contrary to Elasund custom, and was wide enough to share with his wife, though she was presently indisposed, he explained regretfully.

He welcomed them and invited them to take a seat. "Drink with us, brothers from the old homeland."

King Cnut was perhaps fifty years old and wore his beard, but not his hair, in a braid. A narrow, ornately decorated gold coronal adorned his furrowed brow. His clothing, like that of his men, was colorful—green, blue, and even red—and seemed gaudy to the Elasunders, accustomed to dressing in dark and earthen colors. The language of the islanders also sounded strange, as it had been many generations since their forebears left the mainland, but it still had the singsong, melodic sound of the Turons.

The guests took their seats at the table to the left of the longfire, opposite Cnut's men, and Olaf began to speak. "Thanks be to you for your hospitality, noble king. I hope things are going well for you on the Cold Islands."

"Better than they have for years," the island king replied. He recounted in great detail the wars they had waged against the wild Scotsmen. The guests listened politely, congratulating him on his victories.

"And what may bring you here?" Cnut asked finally. "You have come in a fleet of nine ships with women and children aboard, I am told. This is something we have not seen in a long time." He tried to hide his concern, but without much success. Osmund could imagine what he was thinking—Cnut did not want to appear inhospitable, but he had no room for such a large group of settlers on his islands.

"Life is grim in the old homeland," Osmund reported solemnly. He told about the repeated attacks and the winter of famine but did not mention the Turons by name, as that would have offended Cnut. "There was nothing left for us to do but leave," he concluded. "We hope to find a new homeland in Ireland, and if we are unable to do that we will seek to conquer land in the south of Britain." Osmund noticed Hacon's astonished look and was a little disconcerted himself at how easily the lie had slipped off his tongue. But Olaf had warned them not to tell Cnut where they were really headed, and Osmund knew his uncle was right.

Cnut raised his drinking horn and took a deep draught. "That will not be easily achieved," he said, "but I will do everything in my power to ease your voyage."

Osmund bowed his head almost imperceptibly in a token of gratitude and took a sip from his beer. It was the first one he'd had in months. Rarely had anything ever tasted so delightful to him.

"We are not looking for charity," Berse said. "We would like to fill up our water barrels and take additional food on board, but we have silver to pay for it."

The men seated opposite them looked at the strangers with renewed interest. Some exchanged furtive glances, and Osmund had an uneasy feeling that perhaps Berse had made a blunder and these people might flout the rules of hospitality and attack the ships.

But the king said, "We are happy to trade with you and have something here that you may not have heard of before. We call it dried meat. It is ideally suited for long trips because it never spoils. I am sure we could spare a few barrels of it, but it is not silver we need."

Olaf was familiar enough with the Cold Islands to know what Cnut was referring to. Calmly turning his cup between his hands, he said, "We have plenty of wool. No one will have to freeze here next winter, no matter how cold your islands are—if we can come to an agreement."

Cnut relaxed. Osmund could see that Olaf had hit the bull's-eye. These islands were unsuited to raising sheep, and wool was a desired commodity. He gained confidence. Wool was in fact the only thing they had in abundance, because you could not eat it.

Cnut signaled to one of his servants, who left the hall hastily and soon returned with a pewter plate piled high with something that looked like shoe leather.

It did not taste any better, either, Hacon thought as he chewed laboriously on the piece he had been given. But King Cnut was a good salesman. "You will never get sick on it the way you do on raw fish or mutton," he told them. "You don't need to cook it, and it lasts for months, even when it's very hot. It's perhaps not a great delicacy, but it will help you keep up your strength until you reach Ireland or wherever you may end up."

Osmund washed his piece down with a big draught of beer and exchanged glances with Olaf and Berse. They understood one another with just a nod. The stuff tasted awful, but it was exactly what they needed.

"Assuming we bought it, how many barrels could you spare?" asked Olaf, with apparent disinterest.

The king exchanged a few whispered words with his steward before turning again to his guests. "Nine, one for each of your ships. It will be enough to feed you for weeks."

"And what do you ask?" Osmund inquired.

"Eighteen dozen fleece," the king said.

Osmund and Olaf exchanged glances again before Olaf replied, "We cannot part with so many. A dozen fleece per barrel is the most we can offer."

Cnut and his men laughed. "Two dozen fleece," the king insisted. "It is below my dignity to haggle."

The visitors arose and bowed before the high seat, but their gestures were clearly more reserved. "I fear in this case we will have to do without your dried meat, as delicious as it is," Olaf said politely. He nodded to the others, and they started toward the door, but before they could reach it, the guards had stepped up to block their way, standing shoulder to shoulder. They made no threatening gestures, but none of the visitors failed to notice the battle-axes that Cnut's men wore on their belts.

"We need your wool," Cnut said in a conciliatory voice, but even Hacon understood they were being threatened and that the king actually meant, *We will take it if you don't give it to us voluntarily.*

Berse and his son reached furtively for their swords, and Austin, praying silently, moved in front of Hacon to protect him. For a few heartbeats, no one stirred, and it was so quiet in the room that you could hear the crackling of the heavy logs in the fire. Then Olaf turned slowly to the high seat again. His expression was unchanged, and if he was afraid, his looks did not betray it. Osmund, however, felt the sweat breaking out on his chest and back. He admired his uncle's cold-blooded composure.

"If that is the case, make us a better offer," Olaf said firmly, but not impolitely. "Eighteen dozen fleece for nine barrels of dried meat and what else?"

Cnut stroked his braided beard pensively and whispered back and forth with his steward and with some of his men who had left their benches to join him.

"What do you need?" the steward asked. He was a thin little man with a sparse, mouse-brown beard.

The travelers exchanged glances, not knowing what to say. They certainly could use flour, but it was unthinkable to waste two days here baking bread. With their provisions of fish and cheese, and the dried meat, they would have plenty of food, and they had no room for more animals. So what should they ask for?

The Saxon had an idea and whispered something to Osmund. He nodded and looked relieved. "Could you by any chance spare a few barrels of mead?" he asked Cnut.

The king seemed astonished and then roared with laughter. "Well, if you don't have anything better to do than to get drunk while you are travelling..."

Osmund smiled politely and refrained from explaining to Cnut that mead not only was intoxicating but extremely nourishing.

"Well, then, I think we can agree on that," the king announced. "We captured a lot of honey from the Scots, and therefore we have more mead than we can stomach."

The details were quickly agreed on, and as if by magic the threatening atmosphere vanished. The king and his men became cordial again and invited Osmund, Olaf, and all the Elasunders to come ashore for a feast that evening.

Candamir supervised the exchange of their goods and the filling of the water barrels. Like most of the men on board the *Falcon*, he preferred to stay away from the feast. He didn't trust these island people, and what Osmund, Hacon, and the Saxon had told him of their meeting with the strange king confirmed his suspicions.

Just enough of the men returned to the great hall at dusk, among them those who had bargained with the king that morning, so that Cnut had no reason to feel offended. This time, however, Candamir kept his brother on board and had him share the first watch with young Wiland. "And if either of you falls asleep, you'll be in real trouble."

"I'll be dead sure not to fall asleep," Hacon replied. "And I won't feel right again until we set to sea tomorrow and these islands disappear over the horizon."

Candamir smiled and patted him on the shoulder. "Then you feel just the way I do."

He warned everyone on board to be especially vigilant and advised them to keep as quiet as possible and not put their weapons away when they rolled themselves up in their blankets for the night. At an early hour, quiet descended on the *Falcon* and the other ships. Hacon and Wiland performed their patrol duties well, one on each side of the ship, silent and watchful.

When the moon rose, Osmund and the others returned from the festival—roaring drunk. They staggered into the surf and obviously were having trouble getting to the ships. Berse stopped halfway, leaned way back—perhaps to admire the stars—and keeled over with a loud splash.

One of his sons jumped into the water and fished out the old shipwright. Candamir also jumped overboard, swam a few strokes, and then waded toward Osmund. "Come," he said, "let me help you." He carefully avoided any hint of criticism in his voice. There was no sense in admonishing a drunk, as he knew only too well, but he was annoyed. How in the world could they have ever let themselves get so drunk with these foreigners—how could they have been so careless?

"Very kind of you," Osmund babbled. "Believe it or not, in front of the king's hall I saw a three-headed dog."

"Sure," Candamir said, "next to a dragon with green scales, I presume."

"You don't believe me?" Osmund asked angrily.

"Every word."

Osmund pulled back from his friend and then pushed him away with amazing strength. "Who are you, anyway?"

Candamir stared at him, bewildered. He knew all about the strange things and creatures that Osmund thought he saw, especially after drinking mead, but something like this had never happened before. "I'm Candamir, your foster brother. Remember?"

Osmund seemed sickly pale in the moonlight, and his expression was blank. He was breathing fast as if he had been running. "I swear, I've never seen you before in my life!"

Candamir felt his throat tighten. He was hurt, and above all he was scared. But for once he was the one who kept his head. "Just the same, be assured I'm your friend. Get on board and rest a bit. We'll talk in the morning."

"All right, all right," Osmund growled, still full of mistrust.

Candamir had some trouble hoisting him on board. Osmund seemed to have lost all sense of balance. When they finally both stood on deck dripping wet, Osmund suddenly collapsed and fell to the ground unconscious. Candamir dragged him roughly over to his resting place. "May your head throb in the morning," he whispered to him.

Cudrun the nurse, who was sleeping with little Roric in her arms right next to his father, woke up and looked anxiously back and forth from Osmund to Candamir, then carefully covered her master and turned on her other side. Osmund slept like a log.

Candamir also lay down. Gunda was already asleep, and he moved close to her to warm up. She did not wake up. Carefully he put his hand on her curved belly and pressed his nose in her blond locks, but he could not sleep. He tossed and turned restlessly and finally lay on his back, looking up at the stars. He wished they had already left these inhospitable islands far behind. He wished they were already there. Ever since they had made the decision, he had been filled with a keen longing for this abundant land, this new home that would not be his foe, but would reward his hard work with a secure existence. He pictured the house he would build there: a large hall at the top of a gently sloping, grassy hill, with a view over the ocean. These thoughts almost always put him right to sleep—but not tonight. Not a breath of air was stirring, the night was peculiarly silent, and the strong odor of sheep dung seemed to creep through all the cracks in the deck. Candamir breathed as shallowly as possible and tried to imagine the mild, fragrant sea breeze that would waft through the door of his new hall someday…

When Hacon returned from his watch, he didn't need to waken his brother. Candamir got up silently, generously offered the lad his warm sleeping place, and left to take up his watch. The waxing moon shone bright, but Candamir soon realized that two men were not enough to secure the ship. It was not possible to walk up and down freely, as he had to step over and around the sleeping people and their belongings. That took too long. He awakened the Saxon and Siward's son-in-law and ordered them to keep watch over the front of the ship. As he was returning to the stern, he suddenly felt the ground go out from under him. For a moment he staggered, but he was young and agile, and reacted quickly. Even as he fell, he jumped back and managed to keep his balance. Some careless fool had left the cargo hatch open to let out the odor of the manure; an unsuspecting watchman could easily have broken his neck. Candamir bent over to close the trapdoor but hesitated. He took out his long knife and climbed down the short ladder into the hold.

Down below it was almost completely dark, yet he moved confidently and silently because he knew exactly where each part of the cargo was located. He advanced slowly in the darkness, listening intently. The animals were silent, but he could hear them breathing. He had almost reached the middle of the hold, the widest part, when he felt a slight breath of air on his left cheek. In the same instant he arched his back and flailed out with his fist. It hit something soft, and he heard a suppressed groan, somewhat like a gasp, between clenched teeth.

Candamir grabbed hold of an arm and pulled the figure closer to him. "Who are you?" There was no reply. But as he now could make out a human form, he put his dagger to the throat of the mysterious intruder. "You'd better answer," he hissed.

"Do not kill me," a voice replied just as softly. "I will help you, if you will help me."

He lowered his dagger in amazement, then loosened his iron grip a little, pulling the intruder back to the trapdoor to examine in the weak light of the moon who it was he had captured. He had not been mistaken: it was a woman.

"Who are you?" he asked again, bewildered.

"Siglind, Cnut's wife." She looked him in the eye. It was too dark to see the color of hers, but he thought he could make out smooth features, young skin, and a wavy, silvery, shimmering cascade of hair in the moonlight.

"Cnut's wife," Candamir repeated, dazed. He feared that nothing good would come of this.

She nodded. "Are you Osmund? The leader of this ship?" Her tone was strangely peremptory, as if it was beneath her dignity to negotiate with anyone else.

Pretty impertinent for a woman who had hidden among his supply kegs like an escaped slave, he thought. He folded his arms. "My name is Candamir Olesson, and I am the captain of this ship," he declared, and at the same moment was furious at himself for sounding so pompous.

He thought he saw her lips curling in contempt. "All right, then, Captain Candamir. As I said, I'll help you if you will help me."

"I really don't think we need your help, and I advise you to return to your husband's bed, where you belong, before he misses you. And if you do not, I shall have to take you back myself tomorrow. We were trading with him and drinking in his hall and…"

"Tomorrow you will be dead if you don't listen to me," she interrupted.

Completely taken aback, he stared into her face, though he still was unable to see very much. He would have laughed at her were it not for this inexplicable uneasiness that had been tormenting him all evening.

Uneasiness was not the right word, he admitted to himself—rather, it was fear. "I'm listening."

Siglind took a deep breath. "They put henbane in everyone's mead when your men were at Cnut's hall tonight." She stopped, because Candamir uttered a sound of suppressed horror and was on the point of turning back toward the ladder. "Oh, ye gods, Osmund…"

Siglind put her hand lightly on his arm. "Wait. It wasn't enough to kill them, because Cnut feared the anger of the gods if he murdered guests in his hall. But none of your friends will wake up until tomorrow noon, and that applies to everyone who drank the mead you bought from them. Did *you* drink any of it?"

Candamir shook his head. "No one here on board." The temptation had been great, but they had allowed reason to prevail and decided to put the mead aside for the time being. "But I don't know about those on the other ships. And what intentions does your noble husband have now?"

"He was disappointed that not more of you came to the feast, I was told, but he considers you weakened enough so that even a coward like himself can attack you at dawn, slaughter you all, and steal your wool and ships."

"I see," Candamir murmured bitterly. "Thank you for your warning, Siglind, you are an honorable woman. But I must ask you to leave the ship now, as we must sail at once."

She shook her head. "Wait until midnight. They have arrows they can use to set your ships afire if you attempt to flee. You must wait until they have gone to sleep. And the price for my warning, Captain Candamir, is that you take me along."

He had suspected as much. He looked at her uncertainly out of the corner of his eye and had no idea what to do. His first thought was to talk to Osmund, but nothing would awaken his friend from his poisoned slumber.

At a loss, he sat down on a barrel and finally asked, "Won't Cnut wonder where you are?"

"No. I pretended to be ill this morning as soon as I saw your ships coming into the bay. Cnut hopes I am finally pregnant and will stay away from my chamber."

"Why don't you just leave him? I mean, why don't you return to your family instead of entrusting yourself to strangers?"

She snorted softly, or perhaps it was a sigh of resignation. "The laws of the old homeland don't apply here, you know. He won't let me leave. He never asked me if I wanted to be his wife either. He simply took me from my father's house and killed my family."

Candamir was shocked. For a moment he sat there feeling as if all the strength had left his limbs, his head bowed and his hands on his knees. Then he looked at her again. "I am really sorry."

She did not move. "So? Will you take me along?"

He didn't hesitate any longer. Hospitality was clearly not the only time-honored law that was abused here in the Cold Islands, and this woman was entitled to his help, even if, as he feared, she was a haughty bitch.

"I'll take you along," he replied. "But perhaps you should first know where we are going."

"Well?"

"We are in search of an unknown land. One of our people found it by accident, but…you have to go through a storm to reach it. A rather bad storm."

She laughed. It was a merry, melodious laughter, but it abruptly stopped. "You don't mean it seriously, do you?" she asked.

"Oh yes, I do." And he told her about the attacks by the Turons and the famine at home, about Olaf's accidental discovery of the unknown island, its docile inhabitants, and all the wondrous things he had seen there. And he told her how they had all placed so much hope in the storm.

When he had finished, Siglind remained silent for a while. Then she said softly, "At long last I have a chance to flee, but as it turns out, my escape just leads to certain disaster. That's the way it has always been with me and fortune. The gods hate me."

"I can't believe that," Candamir heard himself say. "Perhaps they will reward your courage and your luck will change."

"Perhaps," she conceded. "And no matter what, even your crazy trip is better than life here."

Candamir got up from the barrel and extended his hand to her. "Come now. And cheer up. You don't have to hide down here any longer."

After a moment's hesitation she took his hand. Hers was warm, dry, and rough-skinned. Not a hand afraid of work, Candamir concluded.

He brought Siglind up onto the deck, where she gratefully took a deep breath of the night air—but she crouched down low for fear that someone on land might recognize her.

"How long until midnight?" she asked.

Candamir closed the hatch and then looked up at the moon. "One hour. I'll swim over to the other ships now and see who can be roused, and in an hour we'll row silently out of the bay." At least he hoped they would. Whistling softly through his teeth, he said, "Saxon, come here."

The slave approached, climbing nimbly over the people sleeping motionless on the deck. "Yes, Master? Oh…" He was startled at seeing the stranger.

In the moonlight Candamir could see Siglind a little better. He was not surprised that her hair, falling to her waist in numerous braids, was blond, even though he could not yet make out the exact shade. She was probably no older than seventeen and beautiful enough to delight the gods. Candamir looked away quickly and turned to his slave. "This is Siglind. She will tell you what happened, or is about to happen. Look after her, be polite, and do what she wants, do you hear?"

"Of course, Master," Austin said, dumbfounded.

Candamir nodded. "I had better not hear any complaints about you. Awaken my brother and all the other men that you can. I'll be back as soon as possible."

With these words, he removed his shoes and knee-length tunic, put aside his weapons, and swung first his left leg and then his right over the side of the ship and slipped into the dark water.

Like Osmund, Olaf could not be roused from the poisoned slumber, but Jared awoke immediately when Candamir shook him by the shoulders.

"What's the matter?" the young man asked drowsily.

"Your lookouts are worthless, Jared—I got on board without them noticing me," whispered Candamir. Then he told him of the imminent attack.

Jared was suddenly wide awake. "How do you know that?" he asked anxiously.

Candamir was aware that if he told him about the woman, there would be long discussions about whether or not to trust her. He put all the authority he could summon up into his voice. "I just know, now get up!"

It worked. Jared was only three years younger than he, but he was accustomed to taking orders. It gave him a sense of security. He struggled out of his soft fur cover and jumped up. "I must waken my father."

"Save yourself the trouble. We must hurry. How many of your men were onshore this evening?"

Jared thought for a moment, and answered, "Four, in addition to my father."

"And did any of you drink the mead?"

"No, father ordered us to save it for the trip."

"Good. Wake up your people. The first thing you must do is wrap the anchor chain with cloths and blankets so that it doesn't rattle. The part that is under water as well, do you understand?"

"Yes."

"Then have everyone take their places at the oars. And no one must make a sound, Jared. That's the most important thing. If we wake up Cnut and his men, our voyage will end here. Is that clear?"

"Yes, Candamir, I'll do everything just the way you say."

Candamir gave him a quick tap on the shoulder, slipped back into the water, and swam over to the *Wavewolf.*

At midnight, the ships started to move, slowly, like a ghostly flock of geese. None had more than eight pairs of oars, for they were built to be sailboats, and the oars were used mostly for docking and casting off. The men had to work hard, leaning into the oars to make the large boats move at all. Candamir had put Hacon in the rudder position and taken over one of the oars himself. No one beat the time—the men found their rhythm by copying Candamir's movements exactly. Slowly, very slowly, the oars dipped into the black water, were pulled firmly and steadily, and then raised up again slowly. It was imperative to avoid even the slightest splashing sound. The oarsmen hardly dared to breathe and began to sweat before their ship had moved even a stone's throw away. Many of them were inexperienced, and each feared he would make the fatal error.

They had almost reached the open sea when lights appeared on the shore and shouts could be heard.

"Pull!" Candamir's voice echoed across the bay. "Pull as hard as you can, and make as much noise as you want. All together!" He quickened his rhythm, pressed his bare feet against the sloping back wall of the rowing bench in front of him, and summoned up all his strength. The other oarsmen did the same, and the sluggish ships picked up speed.

The torches on the shore became little points of light flying across the sky toward them.

"O mighty Tyr, do not forsake us," Candamir prayed softly. Everyone called upon their own personal patron god, and Austin prayed to St. Peter for his support. Their prayers were heard. One of the fiery arrows struck the sail of the *Sea Eagle*, which was taking up the rear, but the sturdy sailcloth burned fitfully and could be hauled in and the fire extinguished before any great damage occurred.

"Set the sail!" they heard young Jared calling up ahead from the *Dragon.*

"Much good it will do you," Candamir murmured. "There's not a breath of air stirring in this accursed night."

"But what shall we do?" Hacon asked anxiously. "Don't you think they'll follow us?"

"Oh, indeed," his brother replied dryly. "Certainly when they notice that their queen has disappeared. But they won't have any more wind than we will, Hacon, and I didn't see any ship in the harbor with more pairs of oars than ours. The only question, then, is who has the stronger oarsmen."

And so they rowed for their lives, and Candamir took care that the oarsmen rotated frequently so they could all keep up their strength.

At daybreak a breeze set in from the east that filled their sails, yet they kept rowing nevertheless. The sea behind them was wide open with no sign of any pursuers, but they wanted to get as far as possible from the Cold Islands.

Not until the sun stood high in the sky did Candamir allow himself a rest also. "Saxon, bring me a bucket of seawater and then take my place."

"Yes, Master."

Candamir nodded to Harald, who was seated across from him on the port side, and they pulled in their oars. The captain of the *Falcon* took his hands from the smooth, wooden shaft and looked at them appreciatively. His hands ached, but they were not bleeding. He rolled his shoulders and wiped his brow with his forearm.

When he looked up, he was surprised to see Siglind with the bucket of water. "Here, take something to cool you off." A little embarrassed, he got up from the seat and took the heavy bucket from her. While Austin and one of Siward's slaves went to sit on the empty benches, Candamir stepped a few paces backward and poured the water over his head. It was ice-cold, and his skin began to tingle at once.

After he had thoroughly shaken himself off like a dog, he handed the bucket back to Siglind with a smile. "Thanks, that really feels good."

She returned his smile, and that made his wobbly knees even weaker. Siglind's eyes were blue—how could it have been otherwise? They were blue, large, and encircled by long, golden lashes. Her smile made her eyes sparkle like the sea on a golden autumn afternoon. And her hair, it was quite impossible to tell what color it was. Some strands were bright like ripe sheaves of wheat and others dark like wild honey. Candamir had never before seen such hair. Her dress was the deep-red color of wine from warm southern lands that you could buy in the big seaports, and the brooches that held the straps were of shining gold studded with rubies. Siglind truly looked like a queen.

When he realized he had probably been staring at her for quite a while, he quickly turned away. "Gunda, I'm hungry," he said, more gruffly than was customary for him.

The pregnant slave nodded. She was clearly hurt and about to turn away without speaking when he took her by the elbow and said more affably, "Bring an extra ration to everyone who rowed, and tell the other girls to help you."

"Yes, Master."

"And I should go to see Osmund and the others who drank the poison. Does anyone know a remedy for henbane poisoning?"

He had addressed Austin, but it was Siglind who answered. "Wait for it to pass and thank the gods that you survived."

Osmund was no longer in the deep, unnatural sleep he had been in earlier that morning. When Candamir shook him cautiously by the shoulder, he stirred, groaned softly, and opened his eyes. His pupils were enormous.

"Osmund."

"What's…what's wrong with me?"

"They poisoned you and the others, but we're safe now. In a few hours you'll feel better."

"I find that…hard to believe." He doubled up with a sudden cramp and closed his eyes tightly. Candamir felt his forehead. When he realized that Hacon, Siglind, and the other rowers were watching, he barked, "Hacon, put up a tent, and hurry up about it. And don't tell me you don't know how to."

Hacon handed the helm to Siward and set to work with the wooden tent shears, crossbars, and rolled-up strips of canvas that until now had been in storage. Skillfully and in no time at all he had set up a little tent that was really not much more than a roof. Without returning any of the anxious gazes, Candamir brought his friend under the shelter, where he would have at least a minimum of privacy. He stayed there with him, cooling his feverish brow and now and then offering him a drink of water.

Everyone who had been in Cnut's hall felt ill that day. Some of them suffered from paralysis and vision impairments, others like Osmund from fever and muscle cramps. It was dreadful to watch. The cramps made him writhe and shake, leaving him exhausted and breathless when they subsided. Candamir did not move from his friend's side, but by the time they tied the ships together for the night, Osmund was feeling better, and when the sun rose, it had all passed.

Candamir was so exhausted that he fell into a deep sleep alongside his friend in the little tent, and when he woke up didn't realize where he was at first. Anxiously he propped himself up on one elbow and leaned across to look at his friend. Osmund's eyes were open, and he was awake. With Candamir's help, he sat up enough to drink a few sips. Then he said, "I had a dream of a three-headed dog."

"Hm. You told me about it."

"And a beautiful woman," Osmund continued, "with hair as I have never seen before. Every shade of blond that you can imagine, and a red dress."

Candamir nodded and smiled. "That was no dream. She was the queen of the Cold Islands and is here on board now."

Osmund sank back and put one arm over his eyes. "Then may the gods preserve us."

No one even suggested stopping in Ireland. The reception there couldn't have been more dangerous than that in the Cold Islands, but since they had led Cnut to believe that their goal was the Emerald Island, they were afraid to drop anchor there.

Life on board settled into a routine, and Siglind adapted to her new surroundings without much trouble. She was a foreigner, and thus an attraction, and if she had come to Elasund as such, it would have taken years to be accepted into the community, or perhaps it would never have happened. But Elasund was a thing of the past. This trip, and everyday life on board, was so new and strange that one more foreign element scarcely seemed to make any difference. All the men were very cordial to her, but she usually lowered her gaze and spoke little, doing nothing to incite the jealousy of the other women. She slept with Asta, Inga, and the other unmarried women in the bow. At night, when they stopped and tied the vessels together, she helped prepare the meals. She ate sometimes with Siward's kin and sometimes with Harald's, but mostly with Osmund, Candamir, and their families. She never mentioned her past or her life as Cnut's wife, but one evening, when she was invited aboard the *Sea Dragon*, along with Osmund, Candamir, and the other captains, Olaf treated her like a real queen, taking her by the hand and leading her to a small table that had been especially set up.

The other passengers on the *Sea Dragon* and the adjacent ships were jealous and astonished when they saw what was served at Olaf's table. He had dark, hearty bread no doubt purchased from a baker on the Cold Islands and now a bit stale. None of the Elasunders had eaten bread since the Yule festival. And there was goose grease, and smoked eel in the finest herbs, and...beer. An audible murmur went through the crowd when they saw the beer foaming into the mugs.

Candamir felt dreadful. He ate and drank because he was unable to withstand the temptation, but at the same time was ashamed to be enjoying these delicacies in front of all the envious onlookers. Sitting there mute, he cast dark glances at his host out of the corner of his eye. Olaf seemed not the least bit embarrassed, sitting at the table in his fine, fawn-colored clothes, his eyes shining when he gazed upon the queen of the Cold Islands. He joked and chatted with her lightheartedly and spoke of distant seas and great ports that Candamir had never seen, mentioning at one point just in passing that his wife had died two years ago last autumn.

Siglind accepted his attentions with polite reserve, as something she was accustomed to. But she laughed at Olaf's witty remarks, and when she reached out her hand to say goodbye, she allowed him to press it for a moment against his forehead.

Candamir had half a mind to spit out Olaf's precious beer at his feet. He couldn't understand what was wrong with him or what it was about this evening that was tormenting him. He was young and poor, with little experience in life, while Olaf was a worldly man in his best years who could probably clothe a woman with gold and jewelry from head to toe if he had a mind to. It was only natural that Siglind was so impressed with him that she had scarcely looked at Candamir or Osmund all evening. Candamir knew that was to be expected, yet it oddly bothered him.

He was in such a foul mood when he got back to his own ship that no one dared to speak a word to him.

They continued their course southward, within sight of the Irish coast. Since leaving the Cold Islands, the wind had been changeable, but at noon on the fifth day, it died down completely and they had to start rowing again. Candamir ordered Hacon and the other boys his age to take up the oars along with his slaves.

Hacon found the first two hours quite easy—after all, he was accustomed to hard work, and his hands were hard and calloused already. But then he began to feel a strange pulling in his shoulders and neck, and after another hour he felt as if he were carrying an iron yoke.

His oar was the last one on the starboard side, and he knew that was no coincidence. Candamir was standing just a few steps away from him at the helm, facing the sea. Hacon understood exactly what his brother expected of him. He was to outlast and outperform all the others of his age and set an example for them. And so he rowed on, and when he got dizzy and thought he couldn't continue, he closed his eyes and counted the oar strokes. He counted from one to twelve, and then started over again, as counting and arithmetic were not his strong points. But he didn't faint and fall off the rowing bench, as did Wiland, and then Harald's son Godwin, who was more than a year older than he. Shortly after that, Olaf gave the signal to stop.

Candamir handed the rudder to Osmund and walked over to his brother. "Good job," he said softly.

Hacon smiled. It was not often that he heard words of praise from his brother. Candamir took the palm of Hacon's right hand, examined it carefully, and said with satisfaction, "No blisters."

Indignantly, Hacon pulled his hand away. "I'm not a child anymore, Candamir."

"I know. Nevertheless, you will exchange places tomorrow with the Saxon so that your right arm takes the strain your left took today."

"As you wish."

Seated adjacent to Hacon, but on the port side, was Austin, and Siglind went over to them to hand them a little dish containing a handful of fresh crabs they had fished out of the sea that morning. "Here, for the worst hunger pangs."

Like all the boys on board the *Falcon*, Hacon was so hopelessly in love with Siglind that the blood rushed to his head and his throat became dry. His "thank you" was just an undignified croak.

Siglind seemed not to notice. Hacon's heart missed a beat as she placed her hand briefly on his arm and said, "If we ever reach this island, you will go down in history and people will sing about the brave Hacon whose strong hands brought his people to the promised land."

Hacon was sure she was teasing him.

The Saxon's head snapped up, and he asked, "Did you say 'the Promised Land'?"

She turned away without acknowledging him, but when he looked down, he noticed something unusual. Though there were far fewer crabs in his dish than in Hacon's, it also contained two short, red woolen threads, arranged in the shape of a cross.

Weak gusts of wind arose around noon the following day. The oarsmen stayed at their stations, as they had to be ready for pursuit from the Cold Islands as long as they remained close to shore.

Hacon suffered the worst case of sore muscles he had ever had. After a couple hours his arms and legs loosened up a little and he felt better, but he was grateful for the noticeable assistance provided by the gentle breeze.

Austin sat in his rowing seat, raising and lowering his arms mechanically and staring out at the coast of Wales to his left. He was in agony. The rugged, black cliffs were scarcely a quarter mile away. It seemed as if he needed only to stretch out his hand in order to touch them—no distance at all for a good swimmer. And he could swim like a seal, even though he had always concealed the fact from the Elasunders. He had grown up on the Sussex coast and in his youth spent much of his summers in the water. Perhaps he could even swim faster than Osmund and Candamir, who considered themselves unbeatable. It would be worth a try, in any case—and there, in front of him, lay Wales. It was not Anglo-Saxon land, but it was thinly settled and the Christian faith was already widespread there, too. It probably would not be hard to cross it, and then, in a day or so, he would be with his family. It would take one more day to get to the monastery he had left so long ago, full of enthusiasm and ambitious plans. Home was within reach. He needed only to jump overboard, and he'd have a good chance of making it.

The days of servitude would be over, just like that, and he would be a well-regarded man again, the son of an Anglo-Saxon thane, a respected scholar. One thing was clear to him: this was his last chance to see his father, mother, and siblings again, and the abbot who had taught him to read and write. Tomorrow they would catch sight of the horn of Brittany, and he would sail off with these wild men into the unknown, to find a new world, or what was far likelier, a watery grave. So it was now or never, and he could scarcely comprehend his own hesitation; it made him furious. He wanted to be *free*. But God had ordained that his years of vain endeavor just now seemed to be bearing their first fruits. Young Hacon was almost ready. He had become receptive to the Word; the field was open for sowing. And now, this woman—of all things, a woman!

Once again he looked over at the coast. His longing for freedom and friends tugged at his heart and made it heavy as lead. His hands started to sweat, and his head became light at the thought of the bliss awaiting him if he only took the leap. It would be so easy.

But he knew that was not what God had in mind for him. Oh, God had great plans for him, that was certain. "For where two or three are gathered together in my name, there am I in the midst of them." It almost seemed as if He had spoken those words because He knew that one day an Anglo-Saxon monk would be sitting at a rowing bench, wrestling with the temptations of freedom.

Here, on this very ship, two or three had gathered in His name, and that was no accident. The will of the Lord had never been clearer: *Here is your place,* He said, *carry my word out into the new world of these men and lead them into the bosom of my church.*

Austin understood the message perfectly, but he didn't want to obey.

"Pay attention, Saxon, you are off your stroke," shouted Candamir, who never failed to notice when one of the oarsmen slackened his pace.

Slowly and deliberately, so it appeared, the Saxon drew in his oar, stood up, and walked toward Candamir.

"Would you perhaps tell me what's going on here?" Candamir asked.

Osmund glanced from one to the other, then slipped into the empty rowing seat and grabbed hold of the oar. After two strokes he had gotten into the rhythm.

With his head bowed and arms dangling at his side, Austin stood before his worldly master. "Let me go," he said quietly. He motioned toward his left. "Over there is my country. I'm aching to be home. Let me go."

Candamir turned his gaze away and squinted as he looked out across the water, then pretended to busy himself with a slight correction to the ship's course. He was moved by the desperate plea of this man who had worked for him for three long years loyally and willingly. It was a hard lot to live in servitude far from home, and Candamir knew that he deserved some reward. His conscience told him that it would be only right to let him go.

"Tell me, Saxon, can you swim?"

"Yes, Master."

"Well enough to reach the coast?"

The Saxon raised his head and nodded mutely as tears ran down his face.

"Then why didn't you jump?" Candamir asked. He sounded angry. "Why do you come here and ask me?"

"I...I can't just...without saying farewell. I can't do that."

Bewildered and not knowing what to say, Candamir shook his head and stared out at the horizon, as if some answer could be found there.

"Candamir…," Hacon began, but his brother would have none of it.

"You will be quiet!" he said sharply. Then he turned to the Saxon again, who was standing there like a wretch, and told him, "No, I will not let you go. I cannot. We will need you."

"For what purpose?" the slave asked, his voice choking.

Candamir didn't have the slightest idea. He could remember only small bits and pieces of what he had heard and seen when the runes were read, but it seemed to him that they had said something about the Saxon. "I somehow feel you might know better than I," he replied. Then he repeated more firmly, "No, I will not let you go."

The Saxon lowered his head, and his shoulders were shaking.

Torn between contempt and sympathy, Candamir looked down at him. "You are a fool, Saxon. You have sealed your own fate by asking me instead of just jumping overboard. You know that, don't you?"

Austin nodded, shrugging his shoulders in defeat. It was true, he realized: he was a fool. He had given God one last chance to let this chalice pass from him, as if God would ever do that.

"This is cruel, Master," he said. "A final farewell. I have a brother who is as old as Hacon. He was eleven years old when I last saw him, and now he is almost a man, and I shall never see him again. I don't deserve that," he concluded defiantly, his words directed more toward God than Candamir.

"No, you do not deserve that," Candamir replied. "But as I said, the fault is your own. Now you have no choice but to accept Hacon in place of your brother." It was something Candamir realized the Saxon had done long ago.

Austin nodded.

"Osmund, can you take the rudder?" Candamir asked.

His friend pulled in the oar and joined them without even bothering to look at the Saxon, who stood there mute and crying like an old woman.

Candamir led his unhappy servant back to his place and tied him to the oar. "You leave me no choice," he said. And because his conscience still troubled him, he added, "Only until we leave the coast."

The Saxon emerged from his despondency long enough to ask, "And what do I do if I have to pee?"

Candamir couldn't help but grin. "Then I'll untie you and keep an eye on you."

On the twelfth day of their voyage, they sighted the point of that large peninsula Olaf called the Horn of the Franks, but which actually, as Austin knew, was the small country of the Bretons. There they finally put the coast behind them, and he was glad, not just because Candamir kept his promise and undid his fetters as soon as the land had disappeared over the horizon, but also because it eased the torment in his soul. Now that the fleet had left the known world behind and was out on the open sea, the course of his own life was set, and though he grieved for his loved ones at home as if they had died, he was infused with the thirst of adventure and curiosity as he scanned the broad expanse of ocean. With new, unwarranted confidence, he looked ahead to the future, and he was not the only one to do so.

The wind freshened noticeably, and shortly after noon they pulled in the oars. Arrow-like, the nine ships raced across the waves, sending up sprays of foam from the bows and repeatedly drenching the passengers with an icy downpour.

Late in the afternoon, Olaf gave the signal to stop. The seas had become heavier, and when the ships came to a halt, they pitched and tossed violently on the waves, triggering the first cases of seasickness. Aboard the *Falcon*, it was Gunda and Siward's young daughter-in-law Hylda who suffered the most, as both were pregnant, but brave Harald and almost all the children were afflicted as well.

The captains met on board the *Sea Dragon* to discuss the situation.

"We must pick up speed," Olaf began, addressing the other men, "if only because of our provisions. I suggest that from now on we no longer stop at night but continue sailing whenever we have wind. Divide the oarsmen into three shifts, have the slaves each do two shifts, and..."

"No one can keep up that pace," Berse protested, "and certainly not if we have to ration the food."

Olaf frowned. He didn't like being interrupted. "There is a simple way to encourage the unwilling."

"Not on my ship," Candamir said emphatically. "We need healthy, strong men when we arrive, not overworked wrecks who might die on us."

Most sided with him.

"All right," Olaf said. "But if we miss the storm, don't say I didn't warn you."

At least this concern was unfounded. For three days and nights they sailed on a southwesterly course under a steady, brisk wind. And on the morning of the fourth day, they encountered the storm, exactly as on Olaf's legendary voyage.

You didn't have to be an experienced sailor to see it coming. Heavy black clouds drifted in from the north, engulfing the sun, the sea took on a blue-gray hue and became suspiciously quiet, and the daylight turned into a sickly yellow-gray.

"Let's go now, each of you knows what to do!" cried Osmund. "Women and children below deck, and remember to take the dogs and your things along, because what you forget you will probably never see again."

They had discussed and planned for this moment countless times. Siglind opened the back cargo hatch and Asta the one in front. Then they helped the children down the short ladders, took babies and bundles of bedclothes and passed them down to those below, supported the old and seasick, and finally they themselves disappeared into the hold. Meanwhile, Osmund and Siward had distributed pre-cut ropes to all on deck. Those who were cautious tied themselves on, while those who thought they had to prove their valor slung the coil of rope over their shoulders for the time being, Hacon among them.

"Go back to your position and tie yourself up," Candamir ordered him.

"But Candamir…," the youth protested.

With alarming suddenness the wind started to howl, filling the sail and making it crack like a thunderbolt.

Candamir slapped his brother, but at once had both hands back on the rudder. "You're making a habit of contradicting me, Hacon, and that's not a good idea. Now, do what I tell you." He had to shout for all to hear. "That means all of you! Tie yourselves on! Anyone going overboard is lost."

He had scarcely finished speaking when the rain started coming down in buckets and the wind intensified. The men quickly followed his order, wrapping one end of the rope around their waist and tying the other end either to the rings in the ship's side, or to the firmly anchored rowing benches.

The howling of the wind sounded like the voices of the furies, and the ship's old mast creaked ominously.

"What about the sail, Candamir?" Siward asked.

"We won't haul it in until Olaf lowers his," Candamir said, wiping his dripping, black hair from his face.

"But..."

"The sail will stay where it is, I say! Don't worry, Siward, the storm is taking us in the very direction we want to go. And remember what the oracle told us. The gods have sent us this storm. If they want to take the mast, so be it, but until then, we'll sail on." There was a strange gleam in his eyes that Siward found less than reassuring.

There was little difference between day and night in this hellish weather, but as the total darkness of night gave way to a brownish gloom, Austin concluded that somewhere on this earth, in some happier place, the sun must have risen. With trembling hands, he took the stick and the table knife out of his pack and cut the seventeenth notch. There would have to be more than ten others, he knew, before they could hope to reach the island, but try as he might, he couldn't imagine he would live to see that day. He was miserable and exhausted, and though he had nothing left to vomit, he was constantly retching. Many of the men felt the same. Cold and wet to the bone, they cowered on the deck, clinging to their safety lines. Some prayed, some just stared straight ahead, and only Candamir and Osmund seemed to still be on their feet.

During the night the Saxon had seen first one, then the other at the rudder, whenever a sudden flash of lightning had lit up the darkness. Now, in the ghostly gray of morning, it was Osmund who was at the helm, while Candamir, leaning into the wind, strode to the mast. It seemed to Austin that as the morning broke, the storm had gathered new strength. The ship was being tossed about like a leaf in a raging torrent, and huge waves came crashing onto the deck from all sides. But with each step, Candamir found something to grab onto, one time hooking his foot under a rowing bench and another time seizing a rope.

The sail had made it through the night in astonishingly good shape. The shrouds and stays, which were made of seal leather and were relatively new, would probably hold up a while longer. Candamir was more concerned about the mast itself that was set in a keelson, so that it could be let down. The mastheel and keelson were old, and Candamir knew that the mast had too much play. It probably would not break, but might simply fall over if the heel was exposed much longer to the wrath of the storm. He clung to the shrouds and attempted to look out through the gray light and heavy rain. The waves towered up, as tall as three men, and Candamir had to stare from the crest of a wave intently for a long time to locate one of the other ships in the trough below. But he was relieved to find them—farther apart, but still in sight, and all still under sail.

He gave the mast a pat of encouragement. "Don't let me down."

Then, leaving the safety of the shrouds, he worked his way carefully up to the bow and climbed through the hatch into the hold to have a closer look at the keelson. It was dark down below, much too cramped, and stank of vomit and the fear of man and beast. Only a very faint light came through the open hatch, but after a moment Candamir could recognize some dark outlines, and he slowly continued on his way. Just like the men above decks, the women here were huddled down on the floor, their faces rigid with fear, embracing their children and soaked to the skin, as the heavy waves came not just through the hatches but leaked through the joints of the decking as well.

"Here, Hylda," Candamir said, pointing to the sacks of seed that had slipped from atop the heavy supply barrels. "You must pick up these sacks of grain, or they will soon be in the water." Hylda nodded faintly, and clenching her teeth, staggered to her feet. A few other women did the same.

"See to it that you secure them better," he told them. "I know you feel paralyzed by this storm, but you must pull yourselves together and watch the cargo. When we arrive we'll want to have something to sow, won't we?"

"Do you still seriously believe that?" Inga asked. She had an ugly, bloody scratch on her forehead, and her eyes were wide with fear.

"Of course I believe that," he said, winking at her. "Come now, Inga, it's only a little wind."

She gave him a wan smile. A sudden lateral gust caused the ship to roll so violently that some of the women screamed, and Inga was knocked over. But she got up again at once, ignoring Candamir's outstretched hand and reaching for a sack of grain.

Candamir turned away and struggled to climb over the crowd of people and animals in order to check on the horses. He was more concerned about them than about the patient sheep and his two-legged passengers. The mare lay in ice-cold water, sweating and rolling her eyes and frightened to death. He had no idea what to do if she were to foal now. The colt was even more restless and had once again begun to struggle with his fetters. Candamir stayed with them for a moment, speaking comforting words to them. They pricked their ears when they heard his familiar voice, but remained terrified.

He sensed a shadow over him and raised his head.

"Splendid animals," Siglind said, laying her hand on the mare's nostril. "But I don't know how long they can last."

Candamir nodded. "I couldn't bring myself to leave them behind in Elasund, but now I see it was rash and cruel to take them along on this trip."

Siglind raised her head, surprised by this frank confession. "Isn't it the same for them as it is for you? If they live to reach our destination, they will have a better life than before."

"It's just that they had no choice," he answered with a rueful smile.

*Just like your women, children, and slaves,* she thought, but she just shrugged.

Candamir cast a furtive glance at her. Her blond hair was wet, and she had tied the strands together in a braid so that they were not in her way. Her costly red skirt was also dripping with water, but she seemed strangely untouched by all the horrors and troubles of this storm. Perhaps it was the self-control she learned as a queen, he thought. In any case, her calm was clearly no pretense, as it seemed to spread to the horses, who could never be fooled. The mare rubbed her head against Siglind's arm, and her breathing became more regular.

"Would you stay with them?" Candamir asked. "You seem to have a calming influence on them."

Siglind nodded willingly, and somewhat relieved, Candamir set out again through the hold. He fell twice before finally reaching his sister.

"It's a wonder you haven't broken all your bones yet," she said. She was holding a small child in her arms, and when he looked closer, he realized it was Osmund's son Roric.

"Is everything all right?" he asked.

Asta stared at him with a look of disbelief, but then nodded and pointed to Roric, who was looking at her with wide eyes. They were Osmund's eyes. "His nurse is so sick that she can't take care of him. We must see how we can get him fed. I have scarcely enough milk for Hergild."

"Eventually everyone gets over seasickness," Candamir answered confidently.

Yes, but for some it takes weeks, his sister could have replied, but instead she dipped the cup she was holding in her free hand into a barrel that was securely tied down and held it out to Candamir. "Here, drink quickly, before it all spills."

He took the water and nodded in appreciation, but before he drank he poured half of it back into the barrel. Of all the vital provisions they carried on board, water was the most precious. He closed the lid of the barrel and secured it. "Don't ever leave it open."

"But it's less than half full. Nothing can splash out any longer."

"Don't count on it."

She looked at him closely, trying to figure out if he knew anything about this storm that he was keeping from her. She put her hand protectively around the little boy's head. "The water is rising, and it just keeps coming in. Everyone is wet and will probably get sick."

"There is nothing we can do about that. But you are right, we have to bail. Our ship is overloaded, and water is heavy. I'll send down a few men to help you form a line to pass the buckets along."

She nodded. He was about to turn away when she reached out to hold him back. "Candamir…"

"What?"

"If you can spare a moment, please see how Gunda is doing."

He frowned. "Gunda? What's wrong with her?"

"She fell when the ship tossed to one side, and a loose barrel fell on her. She's bleeding."

"O mighty Tyr," Candamir murmured. "Where is she?"

Asta pointed, and Candamir fought his way through the hold.

Gunda lay on two soaking wet blankets, and even in the half darkness he could see that the ankle-deep water around her lower abdomen had turned red. The smith's wife was crouching at her side, seemingly indifferent to the cold, the water, and the violent pitching and tossing of the ship. She tried without much success to make Gunda drink the contents of a cup she was holding.

Candamir kneeled down on Gunda's other side and took her hand.

The girl turned her head and looked up at him, squinting. "The child, Candamir. I am so afraid of losing it. I wanted so much to give you a son."

He exchanged glances with Asi, who slowly shrugged her shoulders. "We just have to wait and see, though it doesn't look good."

Candamir put his free hand against Gunda's cheek and wiped away a tear with his thumb. The ship rolled again and almost threw him down on top of her, but at the last moment he caught himself against its curved side.

"Leave, before you fall on her and kill her," Asi said in a firm though not unfriendly voice. "Go, Candamir. I'll do what I can."

He straightened up. "We must see that she gets to a drier place," he said hesitantly. But there was no place that was much drier.

Asi shook her head. "The cold water will stop the bleeding. Eventually."

Candamir stroked Gunda's hair briefly once more and said, "Stick it out. You will have a dozen children yet, you'll see."

She closed her eyes and nodded.

He moved on, worried and discouraged, lent a hand wherever he could to help secure the cargo, and told the women and older children to take cups and pitchers to bail water.

Once he got back up on deck, he took Osmund's place at the helm. "Asta is caring for your son, and he is well, but we must get the water out of the hold or the ship will go down."

Osmund nodded and worked his way forward to join the other men. "I need ten of you below to bail water. And eat something if you can. In an hour the next ten will have to relieve us."

Hacon, who wasn't seasick, was glad he was given something to do. He jumped to his feet at the very moment the ship rolled so far to port that even Osmund thought it was the end. With a shrill scream of terror, Hacon tumbled overboard.

Candamir violated his own rule, let go of the helm, and rushed to the side of the ship. Osmund and the Saxon had already grabbed hold of the safety line. It was stretched so tight that all the water was squeezed out of it.

"Careful!" Candamir's voice was hoarse with fear. "Be very careful. It can tear like a woolen thread."

Candamir leaned over the gunwale farther than he should have, seizing the lifeline with both hands, but he saw nothing of his brother. Then he hesitated. *Let it go,* an urgent voice whispered in his head. *Let him drown. When you pull him back up, he will have changed into the twelve-headed sea serpent and will destroy you. You will be crushed and devoured in its black jaws.*

The thought was just as absurd as it was powerful. For an instant, Candamir loosened his grip, and the rope almost slipped from his hands.

With one hand, Osmund gripped Candamir on the upper arm, and with the other he clung to the safety line. "What are you waiting for?" he calmly asked his friend.

Austin prayed to God and all the saints he could think of and kept calling out, "Do hurry, Master! He will drown!"

Candamir shook his head to free himself from the eerie vision. Wedging his left foot firmly under a rowing bench, he pulled, bit by bit, and when the next wave came over them and the ship rolled to the side, Hacon's hair briefly appeared in the water below, and no trace of a sea monster.

"Come and help me grab hold!" Candamir shouted over his shoulder.

Austin crept up to his side on his hands and knees, seized the rope in both hands, and pulled with all his newfound strength born of fear. Osmund was holding Candamir's legs, so that the next wave would not sweep him overboard as well.

They pulled the upper part of Hacon's body out of the water. Then Candamir leaned as far forward as Osmund would allow, stretched out his left arm with a desperate groan, and managed to get hold of Hacon's tunic. "Pull, Saxon!" he shouted, and the slave braced his feet against the ship's side and pulled.

Finally, Candamir got his arm around his brother's chest and was able to haul him back over the side of the boat.

They lay on the deck, panting and dripping wet. Candamir held Hacon in his arms and stroked his hair with his left hand. The rain drummed down on them unabated and with such force that every drop felt like a sharp pebble. Hacon's eyes were closed, and he did not stir.

"Is he alive?" Osmund shouted at the top of his voice—the ruckus caused by the raging sea was unbelievable.

"No idea," Candamir panted. "Take the helm, Osmund."

Candamir closed his eyes. *Don't take him from me*, he implored the gods. *Take what you want, take my ship, but don't take my brother.*

Hacon suddenly doubled over, coughed spasmodically, and flailed around with his arms in panic before opening his eyes.

Candamir held him a bit tighter and said, "Hush, hush. It's fine, everything's fine, Hacon. You are safe now."

Hacon stopped struggling, stared at Candamir for a moment—his eyes open wide with shock—and then buried his face in his brother's chest.

Neither of them moved for a few moments. Finally, Candamir sat up and took Hacon's face in both hands. "Are you all right?"

Hacon nodded slowly. "I…I was certain I would die. It was as if a sea monster had swallowed me."

Candamir shuddered. For the first time, he asked himself whether their trip might be doomed, and if it wouldn't have been wiser to stay in Elasund, content with what the gods had provided for them there.

For eight days and nights they were battered about by the dreadful storm. Afterwards, Candamir had only a sketchy memory of this time. The days and nights were dark. Everyone on board the *Falcon* and the other ships was constantly wet to the bone and completely exhausted. They were cold and thirsty, and their misery weighed the heaviest on Candamir. Everyone on his ship looked to him expectantly and with a trace of reproach. He had no more idea than they of how to still their thirst, overcome their fatigue, and master their fear of death. He suffered as much as they did, and his doubts about the whole undertaking grew from day to day. If it weren't for Osmund, who never expected as much from the gods as he did, he might not have made it through. Osmund's calm and grim determination shamed him, tapping reserves that he had never realized he had. Just the same, Candamir was sometimes tempted to bring an end to it all by cutting his safety line and letting himself be carried away by one of the heavy waves.

But nobody on the *Falcon* was washed overboard, or perished in any other way. When the mast finally fell on the fifth day, it landed on one of Osmund's servants and broke his leg. The victim stole a knife and tried to end his agony by slashing his own throat, but Osmund was faster, and in spite of the raging sea, they were finally able to set the fracture and make a splint for the leg.

Everyone on board became hollow-cheeked and pale, and when the mast fell, most of them believed it was the end, that now they were alone and forsaken on the raging sea. But Olaf saw the mast go over and finally gave the prearranged signal to the fleet to lower their sails. Then, in the middle of the eighth night, the storm simply came to an end.

The silence was deafening. The men on deck just sat there stunned, and it was a long time before anyone dared to raise his head. The night was still so dark that you couldn't see your hand before your eyes, and the rain was still drumming down, but after a while the black cloud cover gradually parted. A waning half moon appeared, and here and there a few faint stars. The men sat up, unbelieving, and many walked over to the ship's side and looked out at the sea. It was still restless and churning—short, choppy, treacherous waves shook the ship—but the wind had fully subsided, and compared with the raging storm of the preceding days and nights, the shaking felt like the gentle rocking of a cradle.

"Does this mean it's over?" Hacon asked, his voice sounding both incredulous and suspicious. He had no faith in the sudden calm.

No one answered. Gradually, one by one, the women and children appeared on deck, hesitant and fearful, as they took deep breaths of the fresh night air. Men and women who had scarcely seen one another for a week embraced in their relief. Osmund sat leaning against the side of the ship holding his son on his knees. Tjorv and Nori brought Gunda up from the hold. Candamir was relieved to see that she had neither lost the child nor become feverish. She had fallen asleep from exhaustion and didn't even wake up when the slaves carefully put her down on her blanket, but she did not seem to be ill. Candamir sat down beside her and regarded her distended belly. All this happened in almost complete silence, and the silence continued as people took their accustomed places, as if they were afraid of breaking the spell by speaking aloud. And so it was not long before the completely exhausted travelers had fallen asleep.

The delicate, pink light of the rising sun awakened them. The salty air was still and the sea calm and deep blue. The people arose from their damp beds and looked out on the sea. Far away, they saw the *Sea Dragon* and the *Wavewolf.* On the starboard side they could make out two other dots that were probably two of the other ships. Except for that, there was only the wide, blue ocean, from one horizon to the other, but no land as far as the eye could see.

"Five are still there," Osmund murmured. "More than I dared to hope."

Candamir shrugged. "Who knows, maybe the others are still around somewhere."

"After everyone has eaten, we must man the oars and try to catch up with the *Dragon*. We have things to talk about."

"Oh, I can't wait," Siward muttered.

Osmund looked at him in annoyance, but Siward persisted. His doubts about this trip had never been greater than at the moment. "We can talk until we are blue in the face, but the fact remains that the storm is over and we have not found Olaf's Land."

A heavy silence followed this sober assessment, then two of the children broke into tears and soon the others joined in.

"Great, Siward," Candamir said. "I hope you are happy now."

Mothers and fathers tried to calm their youngsters, even though they themselves looked as if they were about to weep.

Osmund thought it best to find something for everyone to do, and that was easy. The mastheel and keelson had to be inspected and, if possible, repaired. The tattered sail could not be salvaged, and a new one had to be put up. There were a hundred different things to do.

Candamir went over to Siglind, who was standing on the port side and looking to the south, her arms resting on the railing.

"Did you make it all right?" he asked.

She turned toward him and nodded without smiling. "The horses are still alive, but just barely. They have to be brought up into the sunlight where they can move a bit and dry out."

"I know. We'll do that as soon as we've reached the *Dragon* and the *Wolf* and secured the ships. Thanks for your care."

She shrugged. "It's not actually my doing, but they are really tough. It's a miracle, after the harsh winter you had."

Candamir decided not to reveal to her that he had sometimes gone without food himself so that he could give them a little something to eat, especially the mare. He just shrugged and asked, "And the sheep?"

Siglind shook her head slowly. "Some have died."

"Then we should throw the carcasses overboard as quickly as possible."

As the sun rose higher into the clear, blue sky, it became hot. Osmund pulled his tunic over his head and let the sun warm his skin. It was a positively marvelous feeling to finally be dry again. His skin was an unhealthy gray color, and in some places it was covered by a red rash and had a strange, spongy feeling. When the other men followed his example, he saw that they all looked the same way. Too much salt and too much water, he presumed.

After a skimpy meal of dried meat and a sip of water they all took their places on the rowing benches, but Candamir warned them not to overexert themselves, for no matter how great their thirst, no one could hope for more than half a cup of water in the evening. And again he warned them all against the fatal temptation to drink saltwater.

Deliberately and with great determination, the men started to row. The women and children, too, were subdued—they neither laughed nor sang. They were thankful they had escaped the storm but worried about the endless expanse of the sea. They had not the slightest idea where they were. Perhaps they had gone right past Olaf's island in one of the dark and stormy nights without even noticing. It was possible they were headed straight for the edge of the world, and not even the gods knew what terrors awaited them there.

By noontime the two small dots off the starboard side had become ships, and gradually the others came into view as well. "The gods have not forsaken us," Candamir said softly to Osmund. "All the ships survived the storm, and we have found each other again—no small wonder, I should say."

Osmund nodded and refrained from saying what was on his mind—that it made little difference whether they died of thirst together or individually.

They caught up with the *Wolf* and the *Dragon* and tied the ships together, waiting for the others who arrived one by one over the course of the afternoon. Finally the little fleet looked like a wooden island again, gently bobbing and drifting on the calm sea. Fourteen people had either died of exhaustion or been washed overboard. Almost everyone on board the *Sea Eagle* had come down with a fever, and a half dozen of them had died, all children. Everyone felt helpless, thirsty, and exhausted, but those on the *Sea Eagle* were in despair.

Together with Siward and Harald, Osmund and Candamir boarded the *Sea Dragon* to discuss their plight. Olaf's once magnificent ship now looked just as battered as all the others. The proud dragon head at the stern was missing.

"We lost it during the third night," Jared reported. His eyes were bloodshot, and he spoke with a peculiar drawl.

"Are you sick?" Osmund asked his cousin.

Jared shook his head. "Just tired."

"Where is your father?" Siward barked. It sounded curt and impatient, as if he had asked before and received no reply.

Jared jerked his chin toward the little tent that had been set up in the bow. "He's sleeping—I think for the first time in a week."

"Well, wake him up. We have a few urgent questions for him," Siward said grimly.

Jared gave him a pitiful look. "It's not his fault. He didn't force anyone to sail with him." *Except for me and my brothers,* he could have added, but he kept that to himself.

Siward snorted with contempt, and Berse the shipbuilder disagreed as well. "He misled us with his tall story about the fruitful island! He misled us into taking this trip to nowhere, and now what?" Furiously, he opened his arms wide toward the empty, dreary sea. "We will all die because we listened to him! He…he…"

"That's enough," old Brigitta interrupted him gruffly. "It was the will of the gods."

But the shipwright wouldn't be silenced. Raising his finger, he moved toward her. "That's what you say."

"That's what the oracle says," Osmund said.

Berse paid no attention to him and continued speaking, turning again toward Brigitta. "Perhaps it is true and the gods wanted us to leave on this voyage. But they don't seem to want us to reach this distant land."

"Perhaps not," the old woman conceded, unmoved. "But we don't know that yet. Save all your yammering for the end, you weaklings." And because one of her favorite habits was to pour oil on the fire, she added, "Durin would certainly not be very proud of his grandson today."

The shipwright blinked, his huge chest rising and falling visibly. "Ansgar…my son. He drowned," he said in a flat voice.

No one knew what to say. They all lowered their heads to show their respect for the deceased and for the father's grief. Candamir wondered if Berse, too, had kneeled on the deck at the ship's side in the raging storm. Had he held his son's thin safety line in his hands, paralyzed with fear, and cried out to the gods?

When Berse had gotten control of himself, he continued, "We don't have a drop of water left on the *Wavewolf.* We're on our last legs, and I want Olaf to come clean with me."

"But of what use would that be?" Osmund asked quietly. "Nothing Olaf can say will change anything. Instead, we should try…"

"Who asked you?" said Haflad, interrupting his son-in-law. "Olaf is your uncle and saw to it that you had enough to keep you alive through the winter. You would lick his boots even if he led us all to the edge of the world! And if you ask me…"

Osmund was spared the rest by a calm voice behind them. "Do you have anything to say to me, charcoal burner? Or you, shipwright?"

Everyone wheeled around. It seemed as if Olaf had appeared out of thin air. There were dark shadows under his eyes, and his clothes were more threadbare than before the trip, but he seemed calm and haughty as usual, completely in control of the situation.

"Indeed we do," Haflad replied. "You misled us! We were foolish to believe your promises, and we will all pay for our folly with our lives."

Olaf seemed unmoved. "I promised you nothing except the chance to find a new home. Everything else is in the hands of the gods."

"And now the gods have abandoned you," Berse said.

Everyone within hearing shuddered—it sounded so definite and final.

Olaf frowned, and his blue eyes seemed to grow a shade darker. "Maybe they have abandoned *you*, if indeed the gods were ever with you. One thing I have learned is that the gods help those who help themselves. The storm let up too soon, and now we have to row to get ourselves out of these doldrums and find another storm. This is my suggestion: we will rest two hours, then we will start rowing."

The shipwright threw up his arms in a gesture both of anger and despair. "Didn't you hear what I said? My people cannot row—they are dying of thirst!"

Without taking his eyes off him, Olaf said, "Jared."

His son came forward. "Yes, Father?"

"Divide up our water reserves. The *Wavewolf* and all the other ships that have no water left will get equal shares of it."

"You still have water?" Candamir asked, astonished.

"Of course," said Olaf. "All during the storm we collected rainwater with a tarpaulin and saved it in barrels. Two of them are full to the top." He turned to the shipwright and the charcoal burner and added, "We'll see whether or not the gods have forsaken me, but none of us will die of thirst today or tomorrow, that's for sure."

The sea was as smooth as a bronze mirror, and it reflected the dazzling light of the sun burning in the clear blue sky.

"I didn't know it could ever get this hot," Hacon said, untying the lace around his neck to remove the tunic.

But Candamir, standing at the rudder, gestured to him to stop. "Don't take it off, or your skin will burn."

Hacon made a rebellious face but didn't argue. He went back to the seat at the rowing bench where his brother could keep a close eye on him. He had gotten used to the strain of rowing, but he was tormented by thirst. In spite of Olaf's contribution, they still had to ration the water severely, as no one could say how long it would have to last. Austin had given Hacon a small, round pebble to suck on. Hacon didn't feel it gave him much relief, but perhaps, he thought, the thirst would be even worse without the stone.

Osmund was below deck with his slaves and some other men in order to repair the mastheel at least temporarily. Up above they could hear the muffled but consoling sound of the hammer on wood. In view of the complete lack of wind, Candamir had ordered his servants to bring the remaining sheep and his horses up onto the deck for a few hours so they could move around and see the sun again. At first the animals were a pitiful sight. Some of the sheep needed help getting up the ramp, and they staggered around as if they had forgotten how to walk. But soon the deck began to look almost like a pasture in the summertime, and the Saxon wondered if he had told Hacon the story of Noah and the Ark.

The animals were emaciated and practically dying of thirst, and Inga, along with some of the other young girls and boys, gave each of them a half cup of water.

Siglind sat on the deck in the stern with her arms around her knees, oblivious to the general hustle and bustle. She seemed perfectly content simply to do nothing. She squinted out over the sparkling water. "Are you familiar with the sun down here in the south?" she asked Candamir.

He shrugged. "Once I sailed with my father to the land called Aquitaine, where everything is so brown and dried out in the summer that you would think nothing could grow there ever again. It was always windy, so you didn't notice how fast you burned in the sun. My father's cousin had such a bad burn that his skin peeled off, he became feverish, and died."

Siglind nodded. "Aquitaine," she murmured, lost in thought. "I once bought some silk that came from there."

Candamir's throat, already parched, became a little drier still imagining her in a silk dress. At the last moment he refrained from asking her about the color. Instead, he said, "We bought silk there also, and wine, but mostly we bartered for them with our furs. The people down there are wild about ermine and beaver, which is strange because it's so warm there." On the way home they had sold the silk and wine again in the major ports of call.

"Where else have you been?" she asked curiously.

But he shook his head. "That was the only long trip I ever took. Usually my father left me at home to take care of the farm and do the chores," he said matter-of-factly, trying to look dispassionate.

But Siglind saw through him. "I can imagine you didn't like that."

A lopsided smile came over Candamir's face. Every spring since he had been old enough to sail with his father, there had been a terrible row that often lasted days but always ended the same way. "My father had an unfailing way to convince me of the wisdom of his decisions," he said dryly.

Siglind returned the smile. "Like all fathers."

"Or brothers," Hacon murmured to himself.

Candamir looked at him sharply. "What was that?"

"Oh, nothing. Nothing at all," Hacon assured him with a feigned look of innocence, and Candamir realized that his once docile little brother was gradually turning rebellious.

By early afternoon, the *Falcon*'s mast had been raised again, but it did them little good as there still was not a breath of wind. With their eight banks of oars they kept the ship moving. Candamir had the oarsmen work in two-hour shifts, as it was backbreaking work, particularly with the heat and short rations of water. They moved ahead at a snail's pace it seemed, and when the sun stood deep in the western sky, the sea looked just as empty and desolate as it had that morning. The sky clouded over and it became damp and oppressive, but still there wasn't a breath of wind. Finally, a quiet, gentle rain began to fall. Following Olaf's example, they spread out the largest tarpaulin they had to catch the water and collect it in a barrel. Not much had accumulated, however, before the rain let up and finally stopped altogether.

Every now and then Siward stared out across the water. He had become increasingly grim and tight-lipped. His younger children, Inga and Wiland, wisely steered clear of him, but his new wife, who was scarcely older than Inga, didn't yet know the warning signs well enough and was treated with a few slaps and a sharp reprimand when she turned to him with an anxious question.

Such behavior was just as common here as in his homeland, Austin knew, but it was regarded as a lack of control when a man and wife engaged in violence in public. Well, the Saxon thought to himself with a sigh, there had been practically nothing that wasn't public since they left on this trip. Yet he thought Siward's outburst was an ominous sign.

When the slave expressed his concern about morale to Candamir, the latter replied, "Then that makes two of us. But there is absolutely nothing we can do about it." He looked over at Siward, who was standing with his older son and son-in-law, talking quietly. Candamir felt strangely relieved when the smith went to join the little group. "Harald will talk some sense into them," he said confidently.

"At least he will try," the Saxon said.

Candamir gave a small shrug. "Siward has always been a grouch, and now that he's getting old, he's also becoming a coward. Most of the men, however, have more common sense. Only a fool would believe that a trip like this could go smoothly without setbacks and losses."

The Saxon was silent a moment before asking, "Do you really think that Olaf is as confident as he pretends to be? Do you think he actually knows where we are?"

"No, and no," Candamir answered bluntly.

They stopped again as night was falling, and Siward and his people returned immediately to the *Wavewolf.* Candamir and Osmund called for a few slaves to come and help them take the livestock back into the hold. The mare was the most difficult. When she realized where they were headed, she balked, laid back her ears, and began to sweat. But when Nori whipped her with the end of the tether to get her to move along, Candamir tore the rope out of his hands and whipped his slave instead, hard enough so that he cried out. Candamir paid no further attention to the slave and spoke soothingly to the anxious animal to calm it down until finally it followed him down the ramp. Candamir stayed below deck with the mare and the other animals longer than necessary, ashamed of his outburst.

Osmund, who had been looking after the other cargo in the hold, said, "Come on up, the heat will no doubt be letting up soon."

"I'm no better than Siward or Berse," was Candamir's answer. "I'm looking for a scapegoat for my own fears."

"What of it? We are all doing that. Nori took it out on the nag, and you took it out on him. That's the way of the world."

Candamir grumbled unhappily.

Osmund leaned against the mast and looked at his friend, his head tilted to one side. "Do you know, sometimes I fear you listen too much to your Saxon's idle chatter. You are brooding. That's not like you, and it's bad for your health."

"Well, you're the expert," Candamir said. "Who would know more about brooding than you?"

Osmund smiled, patted him on the shoulder, and then both of them went back on deck.

There they were surprised to see old Brigitta waiting for them. "I went to see your little Frisian," she told Candamir, though he had carefully avoided asking what business she had aboard his ship. "You think your Saxon knows so much about healing, but he doesn't know a thing about pregnancies. All you have to do is to say the word and he blushes. Your Gunda is lucky, you know. You should thank the gods that she didn't lose your child and didn't bleed to death."

He nodded and said, "I'll hold off on my thanks to the gods until Gunda, the child, and everyone aboard my ship has solid ground under their feet again."

Her smile was mirthless. "That can happen faster than you think."

"You mean the bottom of the sea," Candamir said.

Brigitta cackled her appreciation. "Sometimes you *are* a bright lad. But don't lose heart—we have plenty of cowards already."

Candamir could be just as sharp-tongued as Brigitta if he chose. "Your son Haflad, for one."

The old woman was not offended. "Only too true. Come on over to the *Dragon*. You too, Osmund, and bring the smith along. Olaf would like to talk things over with you, but without Siward and Berse."

Olaf asked them to come with him below deck. "It's cramped and dark and it smells awful," he warned them, "but nobody will overhear what we say." He had Jared stand at the forward hatch and the mute Turon at the stern hatch in order to keep anyone from following.

"You trust this damned Turon?" Candamir asked in disbelief.

Olaf gave a slight shrug and smiled. "Well, at least he is the most discreet of my slaves. By far. But if I were ever foolish enough to trust a slave—as you do, Candamir—it would be the Turon, whether you believe that or not. He has become very devoted to me."

*On the Cold Islands that hardly seemed the case,* Candamir thought sarcastically.

When they got to the wide center part of the hold, they stopped, and Olaf said, "I'll tell you frankly where things stand. The part of the ocean we are in now is completely unfamiliar to me. I have no idea where we are."

Harald the smith folded his powerful arms. His expression was serious, but not hostile. And that was peculiar, Candamir thought, for the dispute between Harald and Olaf over the allegedly defective sword had never been settled. What a wise man the smith was to be able to put aside this old animosity in their hour of need.

Osmund leaned back against the ship's side without betraying any emotion.

"There's nothing we can do but continue rowing until we catch a breeze again," Candamir said. "The storm didn't last long enough, as you said, but we are on the right course and will have to get to your island sooner or later."

Olaf shook his head. "The truth is, I don't know if we are on the right course. It's possible, but it's just as possible that the storm drove us too far south, and the island is off to our northeast now. I simply don't know," he repeated.

Olaf spoke in a calm voice and without a trace of despair, but when Candamir realized the implications of this confession he felt fear as sharp as an icicle being driven into his belly. So they had gotten lost on the wide open, endless sea. They couldn't go back because no one knew exactly where "back" was, but if they kept rowing or sailing southwest, they could all die of thirst before they reached land. "So we are lost?" he asked. He was thankful he was able to sound so matter-of-fact.

"Well, there may still be a way to find our island, if we are not too far away from it." He stopped, no longer seeking to hide his doubts. That was very unusual for Olaf, who was always so determined to keep up appearances, Candamir thought uneasily.

"Won't you continue, Uncle?" Osmund asked politely. "What is this possibility?"

"The ravens," Olaf answered.

Brigitta looked suspicious. "Ravens?"

Olaf nodded. "I need not explain to you what smart birds they are, do I? They have a knack of finding land. We must send out your ravens, Brigitta—one to the southwest, in case we are still on the right course, which I believe; one to the northwest, in case we have passed east of the island; and one to the northeast, if we have passed west of it. The ravens that find no land will return. We must follow the one that does not return."

"And what do we do if none of them return?" asked the old woman, her voice sounding unusually shrill.

Olaf spread out his hands. Candamir presumed this meant that Olaf would then be at his wits' end.

Brigitta did not answer right away. She quietly moved one step backward into the shadows so the men wouldn't be able to read the expression on her emaciated, wrinkled face.

"Brigitta," the smith began cautiously, "everyone here knows how attached you are to your ravens..."

"What do you mean, I am *attached* to them?" she interrupted him sharply. "They are wise, they are Odin's birds. They..." She stopped.

"They are sacred to you, I know," Harald continued. "But we need them—unless you think that an oracle can help us now."

She stepped closer again and shook her head without hesitating. "An oracle would not work; we wouldn't even know what questions to ask."

Everyone fell silent, and finally the old woman nodded. "Go, wait above. I will bring them to you before dawn." Brigitta hugged her elbows, stared at the ground, and didn't look up as the men quietly slipped away.

The night was cool, but strangely muggy. With burning eyes Candamir stared up at the milky light of the moon shining through a thin layer of clouds. He was exhausted, yet he knew he would not be able to sleep. Restlessly he threw back the cover that he shared with Gunda, turned on his side, and looked at his Frisian slave. She slept so peacefully, one hand under her cheek and her lips slightly open. He would have liked to awaken her—he had done so often on this trip, mostly late at night when everyone on board was sleeping. Other couples were not so discreet, but Candamir had become uncharacteristically bashful since Siglind boarded, even though she was the reason that he had to wake up Gunda. But Brigitta had told him he would have to leave the little Frisian slave alone if he wanted the child. And so, for the time being, he had to refrain from his usual way of relieving his spirits as well as his body. This annoyed him and filled him with a dull, vague anger toward Gunda, even though he knew perfectly well that it was no fault of hers.

Sullenly he rolled over on his other side and discovered Osmund's tall figure standing in the stern on the port side. He got up quietly and joined him.

"I see I'm not the only one who cannot sleep," he said.

Osmund turned his head slowly. "And we are not alone," he replied softly. He stepped aside and only then did Candamir notice Siglind standing next to Osmund, her arms resting on the railing.

"Oh, I'm sorry," Candamir murmured. He was embarrassed and at the same time felt an unmistakable and disturbing pang.

Siglind pointed toward the east. "The sky is clearing over there. We were looking at the stars," she said. If she noticed how uneasy the two friends had suddenly become, she didn't let it show.

Candamir nodded, exchanged glances with Osmund, and smiled almost reluctantly. "Your specialty. The stars, I mean."

Osmund shook his head modestly. "Siglind knows more names than I do."

"I learned it all from my father," she said. "He was a great seafarer and knew everything about the stars. Nevertheless, he never went to sea without taking two or three ravens. More than once they helped get him out of a tight spot."

"So you know," Candamir said.

Siglind nodded. "That we have lost our way? Yes."

"I told her," Osmund said, and he seemed quite ready, in fact unusually eager, to justify this indiscretion.

But before Candamir could think of a reply, she said, "Well, it was bound to happen, wasn't it? What can you expect when you put your trust in a storm?"

"But nevertheless you came along with us," Candamir said.

She was quiet for a moment and then replied, with a sigh, "Anything seemed better than to stay where I was. But I must admit that tonight I have doubts about the wisdom of my decision."

The two men chuckled. "So your father was a seafarer?" Candamir asked. "Did he meet Cnut as a trader?"

She shook her head. "Cnut has a fleet of warships with twenty banks of oars that he uses to raid the Scots and the Anglo-Saxons."

"Just as well they weren't in port when we arrived there," Candamir said. "They would have easily overtaken us."

"They're on the other side, on the western side of the island," Siglind said.

Naturally, they realized—the side facing Britain.

"The kings of Scotland and Northumbria would give almost anything to be rid of this constant threat," Siglind continued, in a seemingly casual tone.

"You think we should go back?" Osmund asked in astonishment.

She nodded. "You ought to at least think about it. Even if we don't know where we are, we would be bound to arrive in familiar waters sooner or later if we just sailed northeast from where we are."

"Perhaps," Candamir nodded coolly, "but I wonder if you aren't just looking for a few foolhardy adventurers to help you take revenge on your husband."

Osmund scowled in disapproval, but Siglind simply shrugged, then turned again to look out over the sea and said, "Who knows? Perhaps I am."

At daybreak, the three were still standing at the railing watching Brigitta and Olaf release the three ravens. Squawking and cawing angrily, each took off in a different direction, and everyone watched as they became little black dots that soon merged with the pale, leaden light of dawn.

Shortly thereafter, the other passengers aboard the nine ships awoke, but many were so exhausted from thirst that they remained on their blankets, staring up at the rising sun. Osmund and Candamir went from group to group and told them they would stay there for a day to rest.

"Rest?" Siward asked suspiciously. "Why?"

Candamir didn't answer but looked down at Siward's young wife, whose name he seemed unable to remember. She was groaning and rolling around in the sweaty covers. It was clear that she was feverish, and she had vomited. "What's the matter with her?" Candamir asked.

Siward raised both hands. His face expressed both sympathy and desperation. "Saltwater," he said. "She drank saltwater."

Candamir put his hand on Siward's arm, but Siward angrily pulled away. "This is the second wife I'm losing in six months, Candamir. And both times this scoundrel Olaf is responsible!"

"Siward, that's just not true." Candamir beckoned to his sister, who was standing nearby. "Asta, go and get the Saxon. Quickly." As she hurried away, he turned to Siward and continued: "I'm terribly sorry for your misfortune, but it's pointless to try to place blame on anyone—and irresponsible."

"Who kept us from pursuing the Turons back then? *He* did," the older man responded with barely concealed vehemence. "And now *he's* the one again who got us into this hopeless plight."

Candamir knew there was no point in continuing the discussion, and so he was relieved when the Saxon appeared, bowed deferentially before Siward, and knelt down next to his wife. He took her hand and put his other hand on her forehead. "Britta, can you hear me?"

*Britta, of course,* Candamir thought. If the Saxon, who generally ignored women, could remember her name, why couldn't he?

She did not respond and seemed only to get more restless.

Austin looked up at Candamir with a frown. "We can't do much, Master. The only thing that could save her would be water—a lot of water. But even then it isn't certain she could pull through."

Candamir thought for a moment and then said, "Find out how much water we have left and how much each person will get today. Then ask if anyone is willing to give his share to Britta. Bring to me whatever you get, and you can start with my own ration. Then go to the other ships and ask there as well."

The Saxon nodded and hurried away.

Siward bowed his head in shame. "Thank you, Candamir."

The young captain shook his head. "Let's wait and see if it does any good. But if you want to show me your gratitude, Siward, then do your part to avoid bad blood."

Siward, however, was too upset to be reasonable. He stayed with his wife, looking back and forth between her and the open sea to the northeast. He spoke softly of Elasund, the beauty of its forests and meadows, herds of seals and huge schools of fish, and everything they had left behind. Many of those who heard him felt how foolish it had been to leave.

Austin's begging brought them an impressive quantity of water. Candamir couldn't decide whether it was due to the generosity of the

Elasunders or the persuasive words of his slave. Nevertheless, at noon, Britta's condition was unchanged.

Within an hour of each other, during the hottest, most oppressive time of the day, two of the ravens returned. Brigitta was the only one who was happy to see them. Everyone else watched their return with a mixture of anxiety and gloom, and at dusk the third one, Skuld, returned. It was named after the Norn of the Future, and Olaf had sent it to the southwest with high hopes. An angry murmur arose on the ships that had tied up alongside the *Sea Dragon*, and a small group of men and a few women, led by Berse and Siward, went to Olaf to have it out with him.

Candamir felt numb. He stared at the big, ugly bird sitting on Brigitta's bony shoulder with its head turned up and chest puffed out. It was squawking excitedly as if it had something spectacular to announce. But the fact that it had returned was proof of its failure—none of the ravens had sighted land. Candamir's head sank, and his arms and legs felt as heavy as lead. He didn't want to look at anyone, above all not his brother and sister. He felt paralyzed by the realization that he had brought disaster down on them all.

Osmund put a hand on Candamir's arm and shook him. "Come on, Candamir."

He hesitated to look up and couldn't keep from squinting, as the gloomy twilight seemed strangely harsh. "Come where?"

"To the *Dragon*."

"But…"

"Just come along," Osmund interrupted urgently. He picked up Candamir's sword that had been lying for days near where he slept and held it out to him. Slowly, with mechanical movements, Candamir strapped on his belt and followed Osmund over to Olaf's ship.

"Just admit that you are at the end of your rope!" the gnome-like shipwright demanded.

Olaf stood at the helm, even though at the moment the ship did not need to be steered. "As long as I am standing here and breathing, I'm not yet at the end of my rope, Berse," he answered.

"But you don't know where to go now," Haflad replied.

"If you would just give me an hour to think about it, perhaps an idea would come to me."

*How fearless he is,* Candamir thought. He had never particularly cared for Olaf and had never been able to shake off the feeling that underneath the fine clothes and his pride there was something sinister, no matter what Osmund said. But now he couldn't help but admire this man's courage, as the danger he faced from these outraged, desperate men was all too clear.

"There is nothing to think about," Siward replied flatly. "Our only hope is to turn back."

Olaf's lip curled in contempt. "That's a great suggestion. If the wind ever comes back, it will be blowing right in our faces, and we will all die of thirst long before we reach any land."

"Right you are," murmured Berse. "We'll all die of thirst, one way or the other, and I'd like to hear how you will answer to your ancestors for what you have done to your kin, your neighbors, and in fact the entire village."

"I'll think about that when we get to that point," Olaf said with a mocking smile that gave rise to an angry murmur and threatening looks from the crowd. There were perhaps thirty others who had gathered here from the other ships, a group of worried, weakened men who nevertheless looked dangerous.

Siward moved a step closer to Olaf. "My wife is practically dead already, and how long will the rest of us be able to hold out—with no water, and lost at sea? We will all die, and because we have nobody but you to thank for it, you should have the honor of being first." He placed his right hand on the hilt of his sword.

Osmund and Jared both stepped forward at the same time and stood shoulder to shoulder with Olaf before Siward and the shipwright could draw their swords.

"You'll first have to kill us," Osmund said calmly.

Berse raised his weapon and rolled his shoulders. "I'd be sorry indeed, but it won't stop me." Berse's surviving son and the repulsive charcoal burner suddenly appeared on either side of him, sword in hand.

Candamir watched this scene incredulously. These were people he had known all his life, who had formed a community for as long as he could remember. They had argued often enough, but when things got tough they had always stood together. Now they had split into two camps, and his head was spinning with the thought of how many blood feuds would result if they now attacked each other with drawn swords. Not that it really mattered—no one would live long enough to carry out these feuds. And with this thought he stepped up beside Osmund. At almost the same moment the smith joined them. Nevertheless, it was just the five of them against almost three dozen.

"You had best step aside," the shipwright advised Osmund and Candamir, and it sounded like the voice of reason. "This scoundrel is not worthy of your protection."

*You are probably right,* Candamir thought, but he said nothing and simply drew his sword.

Siward drew his dagger and moved another step closer. "I am really sorry," he said, looking first at Harald, then Osmund, and finally Candamir. "But he led us into this hopeless situation—and not just us, but your son, Osmund, your siblings, Candamir. It isn't right for you to side with him."

"Sure it is right," Osmund contradicted him in a calm voice, "because Candamir and I also spoke in favor of the voyage, just like Olaf. What isn't right is what you are doing, because you all came along of your own free will, knowing the risk."

Five more men came forward with drawn swords. Berse smiled grimly, nodded in the direction of the reinforcements, and offered Osmund, Candamir, and Harald one last chance. "Now you must decide. Are you with us or are you against us?"

Candamir took his knife in his left hand. Now holding a weapon in each hand, he felt the same familiar rushing sound in his head that he always heard when faced with a life-and-death situation. He wondered if it was perhaps his own blood that he heard coursing through his veins and that would soon be flowing over the sun-bleached planks of the afterdeck. At least it would be a quick and honorable end. Perhaps one day there would even be a song about it—provided anyone lived long enough to tell the tale. Either way, it was better than dying of thirst.

He gave Berse a disarming smile. "What does it look like, do you think?"

Berse squinted and raised his sword with both hands.

"Oh, by Freya's great bosom!" Brigitta cried out. Her voice was so piercing that everyone wheeled around. She had extended her left arm and was pointing to the northeast. Skuld the raven was perched motionlessly on her shoulder, staring in the same direction. "There, just look!" the old woman shouted. "It isn't over yet."

Everyone turned to look in the direction she was pointing.

"Aha," Olaf chuckled. "There it is again, my storm."

Even the least experienced among them could see at first glance that the tempest racing toward them was unlike anything they had ever seen before, making the eight-day storm look like a gentle breeze.

Candamir put his sword back in its sheath and pushed his way through the phalanx of men who just a moment before had been on the point of killing him. "Go, go, move! Everyone back to his ship! Cut the ropes—we must separate the ships, or we will smash each other to pieces."

Osmund leapt nimbly onto the *Falcon*. "Women and children below deck. Siglind, Asta, set an example for the others and go first."

All on board the *Sea Dragon* scattered in every direction, rushing back to their ships, their bloodthirst forgotten.

Only Olaf did not stir. He stared up into towering clouds, and when Jared took the helm he said softly, "Spare yourself the trouble, son. Just go someplace safe. Now we are truly in the hands of the gods."

Soon the others realized that, too. In a very short time the afternoon turned into night, and this time the lightning and huge waves were so terrifying that even the most steadfast among them cowered down on the deck, lowered their heads, and held on for dear life.

Candamir didn't know how many hours had passed like this when another huge breaker crashed over them. The ship spun around, then leaned so far to port that its side disappeared under the waves. Two of the men lost their grip and were washed overboard, screaming. Their safety lines broke like gossamer. For what seemed like an eternity, the ship lay on its side, as if it couldn't decide whether or not to capsize. Then slowly, and with a shudder, it righted itself again.

"Candamir!" Osmund shouted.

"What?"

"We are going to sink!"

Candamir did not reply. Osmund was probably right, but he couldn't think of anything they could do about it. Once more, the ship made one of those sickening pirouettes, and then it seemed to let out a screech that filled Candamir's ears, and he heard an unmistakable sound of wood splintering.

"That...was a reef," he whispered to himself.

He started crawling toward where he had just heard Osmund's voice, and when he was so close he could touch him he said, "We have sprung a leak. I don't know how much time we have, but we must get everyone off the ship, Osmund. At once."

Osmund complied and fought his way over to the hatch, but he asked, "Why are we even bothering to do it? Why not just wait here to die?"

"Because it is a sure thing if we stay here. But if we swim..."

"Swim, Candamir? Where?"

"That was a reef, and where there is a reef, land generally is not far away. If we are fortunate..."

Osmund prayed that fickle fortune would not forsake them now.

He slipped down into the hold, with Candamir right behind him. Water was streaming in through the leak in the port side. Panic had broken out, and people were screaming in despair, pushing their way toward the hatch, tumbling around as the ship continued to lurch from side to side, and then falling back into the quickly rising water.

Candamir and Osmund grabbed hold of those who had fallen into the water and helped the women and children climb up the little ladder as best they could. "Take a barrel, or a board, or whatever you can find and tie it around you. Then jump," Candamir ordered them. He paid no attention to the anxious questions and complaints. "Come on, hurry up. Anyone who stays down here is going to drown. Yes, Hamo, that's right, empty the barrel and tie yourself to it. Here, take your little sister with you and keep an eye on her."

Roric was screaming at the top of his lungs, and Siglind tied him with a rope to a bundle of wooden stakes, which she then handed to Osmund. "Here, tie the loose end around your wrist. Good luck."

Most of them were out now. Candamir nudged Osmund. "Let's get out. Go and save your son."

"And what about you?"

"I'm coming. Now go. You too, Siglind."

Osmund disappeared through the hatch, and Candamir helped the stragglers up the ladder. Then he headed back toward the middle of the hold when suddenly a hand grabbed his elbow and tried to hold him back. "No, Candamir, come now, it's high time," Siglind said.

He pulled himself free. "My horses..."

"They are dead. All the animals that were tied up have died. The water has been rising for hours. Maybe you'd better think of your brother."

"Maybe you'd better mind your own business," he snapped, grabbing her arm roughly and shoving her up the ladder. But he followed close after her and was about to start out in search of Hacon when a wave struck him in the back with tremendous force and washed him overboard. Turning head over heels, he landed in the raging, dark water, and as an experienced swimmer, he concentrated only on which way was up and which way was down. He stayed under water as long as he could in hopes the current would carry him away from the reef and the shipwreck. Then, with long, even strokes, he began swimming toward the surface.

Osmund had no idea how long he had been struggling with the waves to save his own life and that of his son. It seemed like hours to him, but perhaps he was mistaken, his sense of time marred by exhaustion and fear.

He didn't even know if Roric was still alive. Amidst the raging of the wind and the waves it was impossible to tell if the lad was crying or coughing. Siglind had had the presence of mind to tie him to a little float, but it was difficult to swim while holding onto it. He kept on swimming, nevertheless, though he had no idea where he was going. He instinctively let the currents carry him, and then the unbelievable happened—he felt soft but solid ground under his feet. Sand. He dug his toes into it, as if this could somehow prevent the huge waves from carrying him off again. He had at most two heartbeats to examine the ground under him. He stood on his toes, pushed Roric's float ahead of him with both hands, and put his left foot forward. He could feel that the sandy bottom was a little higher there, and he took another step. The next wave came, and he dove in order not to lose his hold on the precious ground. Underwater, he took two vigorous strokes, and when he put his feet down the next time his shoulders were above water.

*Land*, he thought jubilantly, *I have found land!* He grabbed the float and ran, ran until he had left the surf behind and the water only splashed around his ankles. And finally he felt how the sand had changed under his feet. It was still wet, but more granular, not smoothed by the surf, but pockmarked by the rain. And then he stepped on something that could only be a moist clump of grass.

Gasping for breath, he fell on his knees and reached out to feel his son. "Roric…Roric, are you still alive…?" He lifted the child up, along with his float, and felt the little body with his lips. A tiny hand seized his nose, and the child began to bawl, very much alive.

Osmund laughed for joy, or more accurately, as if he had lost his mind. He couldn't see a thing, but he could feel the rope with which his son was tied to the wooden stakes, and he patiently undid the knots. Then he took Roric carefully in his arms and clutched him to his chest. "Hush, hush. Surely you are cold, but you don't have to be afraid anymore, my son. We are safe. We are…" He didn't have the slightest idea where they were. Perhaps it was a desolate island where no man or beast could survive, but he felt the soft sand under his feet, the rough grass growing on it that tickled his toes, and somewhere nearby he smelled trees. "I believe we have arrived," he said.

The storm raged all through the night with unabated fury, and one of the many blinding strokes of lightning hit a nearby tree. Osmund pulled off his tunic and wrapped Roric in it even though it was wet, as this offered more protection than Roric's bare skin. Then he carefully put his sleeping son down in the sand, and in the light from the burning tree looked around the immediate area. There was not much to see—a wall of trees, the white, sandy beach, and behind it the remorseless, raging waves. He turned his back on the sea.

Next to the burning tree he saw some wood lying on the ground. He piled it together a short distance from Roric, then picked up a burning branch that had fallen from the tree. He easily got a fire started, stood next to it, and vigorously swung the burning branch. He hoped fervently that he and Roric were not the only survivors of the *Falcon*, and if others had been washed up there, he wanted to attract their attention.

His efforts soon bore fruit.

The reef that had sunk the *Falcon* was only a quarter mile from the coast, and the current had favored them. Whether they swam against it or let themselves be carried along by it, they all eventually landed there. Only three had drowned, with the land practically within reach, but the others sooner or later saw the fire and headed toward it.

It was almost an eerie sight: the ghostly forms emerging from the storm-whipped darkness. Asta was the first to arrive, along with Hacon and the Saxon, who were each holding one of her children, and then, to his boundless delight, came Osmund's loyal dog. A bit later, Inga appeared with her father. Siglind and Candamir had already met in the surf and arrived together.

Shortly before daybreak the storm weakened, and then it finally died down at sunrise. The *Wavewolf* and the *Sea Eagle* lay stranded at strange angles on the beach, as if drunk, and when the rain stopped and the storm let up, the people gradually came ashore.

Silent and incredulous, the castaways stood around the dying fire and looked around to see where fate had taken them. They found themselves in a long, crescent-shaped cove surrounded on both sides by steep but beautifully shaped rock formations that seemed to be riddled with caves. The beach was around a hundred paces wide, and beyond it there was a forest in which a veritable army of birds were crying. The salty sea air mixed with the full, earthy fragrance of the forest. A flock of seagulls had gathered on the beach a stone's throw away and eyed the newcomers with suspicion.

Inga sank to her knees, exhausted, ran her hands over the damp sand, and murmured, "How beautiful it is here..."

*She is right,* Candamir realized. He looked around again and came to the conclusion that this was no doubt the most beautiful place he had ever seen in his life.

Hacon had no use for the charming contrast of the beach and the cliffs, or the deep blue sea and the green of the trees. "Yes, really pretty," he said impatiently. "But all that interests me at the moment is whether there is a spring over there in the forest." He wanted to head off in that direction, but Candamir seized his arm.

"Stop. Nobody will go anywhere alone, and certainly not unarmed into this forest." With his right hand, he reached to his left side, but the sword was gone. He cursed under his breath and looked down. At least he still had his knife. He pulled it out of its sheath on his belt, and Osmund, Harald, and some of the other men followed his example.

"We will go and look for water and come back as fast as possible," Osmund promised. "Siward, is your wife still alive?"

The older man nodded, pointing to a motionless bundle in the sand. "At least she is still breathing."

"Go back on board and bring back all the containers you can find," the shipbuilder told his people. Then he followed Candamir and Osmund into the shadow of the forest.

They didn't need to look for long. After just a few steps they heard the murmuring of water and followed the sound to a small, clear brook.

The sun shone through the bright spring foliage of the trees lining the little stream that sparkled in the sun.

When he saw the water, Candamir felt such an unbearable thirst that he couldn't believe he had ever been able to endure it. Then, like all the other men, he fell to his knees, scooped up water in both hands, and drank it in long, greedy gulps, even though he knew how unwise that was. At once he felt a sharp headache behind his forehead, and his stomach cramped in warning, but he held down the water. Then he and Osmund both sat up and exchanged smiles of pure joy.

"No beer or mead ever tasted better," Candamir said with a contented sigh.

Osmund rose to his feet and belatedly looked around. "Anyone could have slipped up behind us and cut our throats," he said with some embarrassment.

Candamir nodded, but replied, "There's no sign of people anywhere, no paths, no clearings, nothing."

"We've gone perhaps a hundred paces into the forest," Harald said. "It would be a strange coincidence if we came upon signs of habitation so soon. Olaf says there are not many people here, and the island is large."

"We don't even know if this is Olaf's Land," the shipwright added.

Candamir shrugged indifferently. "Well, it's land, there's water and probably plenty of fish to keep us from starving. That's enough for me, at least for now."

"Let's go back," Harald urged. "Everyone is thirsty, and Siward's young wife is more dead than alive."

Candamir plunged his hands one last time into the wonderfully sweet, clear water and moistened his face. Then he followed the others back to the beach.

In the meantime, barrels, leather buckets, and mead skins had been brought from the ships. Accompanied by an armed escort, the slaves and young men went off to fetch water. After they had all had something to drink, the mood improved noticeably. Soon laughter could be heard from various quarters, and the children played catch and chased after the seagulls. The slaves went back to the ships to get the sheep that were half dying of thirst and drove them down to the river, while the Elasunders sat down in the sand, dried their clothes in the warm sun, and delighted in the feeling of having solid ground under their feet again.

Candamir looked out across the sea. After a while, he discovered the rock where the *Falcon* had foundered. All that he could see was a black mass that rose slightly above the water while gentle waves sparkled in the sunlight as they broke over it. The ship was nowhere to be seen.

Candamir felt more exhausted than ever before in his life, but he knew he could not delay looking for the wreck. "Perhaps the *Falcon* is only a few yards below the surface and we can salvage at least some of our things—tools, wool, and so forth. I'll swim out and have a look before the current carries it away."

"I'll come with you, Master," the Saxon offered, putting down his sealskin bag containing his Bible, his cross, and the calendar that he had saved through both storms. The bag was amazingly tight, and the monk was confident that the word of God had arrived in this new world more or less undamaged.

Candamir nodded gratefully. "Come, then. Let's see how well you really can swim."

The water was cold, and goose bumps formed on their bare arms as they waded out into the ocean. The sandy bottom fell off sharply, and soon the water reached up to their chests. A wave was approaching, so they dived before it rolled over them and swam briskly out to the reef. But when they dived next to it, the fears they had had on seeing the dark blue color of the sea were soon confirmed: the water was unfathomably deep. Candamir felt his way down alongside the reef until his ears began to hurt, and still he did not reach bottom and saw nothing but pitch blackness.

When he finally got back to the surface, his lungs were crying out for air. He clung to the rock next to his slave, panting, and shook his head. "Nothing."

Austin gave a sad nod of his head. He had also dived as deep as he had dared and was able. He had seen a host of small and large fish and shuddered at the thought of what nameless creatures might be lurking down there in the depths. "Let us not waste our time here, Master. The *Falcon* is gone, and there is nothing we can do about it. We, on the other hand, have made it to this unknown land relatively unscathed, and I would not like to be eaten by a sea monster on the very first day."

While Candamir and Austin were out at the reef, Osmund, Harald, and Hacon had climbed the cliffs that formed the bay's western boundary. The rocks were high and steep but contained fissures and footholds so that it was not especially difficult to get to the top.

The lookouts brought good news. "Beyond the cliffs is another bay, somewhat larger than the one here," the smith said. "The *Sea Dragon* and three other ships of ours are moored there and appear undamaged."

"Is anyone still on board?" asked Candamir as he joined them.

Harald nodded. "We couldn't make them out very well, but they saw us waving and took up their oars. Now they are on their way here."

"And what else did you see?" Candamir continued.

"To the south, the forested land rises so that we couldn't see farther than three or four miles," Harald said. "We saw something glittering among the trees that might be a wide river, but the foliage is so thick we couldn't make out what was underneath. In any case, there are hardly any pine trees, and the forest is completely different from ours at home..."

"Everything is covered in green," Hacon interrupted excitedly, "no clearing as far as you see, no villages or boats or ships on the beaches, and..." He stopped short when he saw Candamir scowling at him.

"Please excuse my brother's rudeness, Harald," Candamir said.

The smith nodded indulgently. "He's right, you'd almost think we were all alone here, but of course it's much too early to know. We must listen to what Olaf has to say, but whether it is the island he discovered or not, it is a green land with plenty of water." He was too old and wise to be as enthusiastic as Hacon, but his face looked hopeful.

Candamir turned to his friend with a smile and embraced him briefly. "Well, wherever we may have landed, the gods have given you their blessing, Osmund," he said. "You were the first of us to set foot on this new land."

Osmund seemed a bit embarrassed, but he nodded contentedly. *It is true,* he thought in amazement. *I was the first.* And that was not all. In the morning light he had realized that the bundle of wood that had made up Roric's float was in fact his father's high seat. That surely was a good omen. His line would live on in this new homeland. He kept this to himself, however, and merely asked, "What about the *Falcon*?"

Candamir lowered his gaze and shook his head.

It was just what Osmund had expected. "I'm very sorry about your ship, Candamir. It's a heavy loss."

And that it was. The ship, the livestock, his sword, and not least his ancestors' high seat—much that would be painfully missed by him and the other people who had been on board the *Falcon*. But Candamir realized that it was only the loss of his two horses that he really mourned. He had loved these animals and was convinced they had reciprocated his affection. He had made sacrifices to get them through the winter and had had great plans for them. But he could do without everything else more easily than he had thought possible. He would miss the seed, certainly, and the tools, but they were in a new land. Their old life was a thing of the past, and much of what had gone down with the *Falcon* now seemed to him like superfluous ballast. The loss was a release, he realized, the chance for a really new beginning. And he had not forgotten what he had told the gods when Hacon went overboard in the storm. He put his arm around the shoulders of his pale, skinny brother and said to Osmund, "I got what I asked for."

It took a while before the *Sea Dragon* and the three other ships came rowing into the bay. The tide had started running out, and the current was strong again. Everyone who watched from the beach could see how hard the rowers had to work, and they all thought the same thing—if they had arrived as the tide was going out, they would never have been able to land and everyone aboard the *Falcon* would have drowned. While they were waiting for Olaf's ship, they lit a fire again, and from what remained of their provisions, the women cooked their first warm meal since the Cold Islands. It consisted of dried meat and a few wild herbs that Asta and Siglind had found at the edge of the forest, but their improvised stew seemed to them splendid enough to set before a king.

The sunlight had taken on the coppery shades of late afternoon when the *Sea Dragon* finally dropped anchor in the bay. The Elasunders were relieved to see that one of the three ships that followed belonged to the two brothers from Elbingdal, who brought with them the universally beloved, white-bearded Eilhard. There was however not the slightest trace of the last two ships. The lookouts who had climbed the cliffs on the eastern side of the bay also saw no sign of them. Candamir directed Hacon, Wiland, and a few other boys to light a fire at the top of the rocky cliff as a beacon for the lost ships.

The sun was hovering low on the western horizon like a huge golden coin, turning the cloud-covered sky above a fiery red, when Olaf and his people arrived on shore.

Osmund walked toward them and handed his uncle a cup of water. "I hope that everyone on board the *Dragon* is well, Uncle?"

Olaf placed his left hand on Osmund's shoulder for a moment before grasping the cup in both hands and emptying it in one draught. Then he nodded. "Everyone is alive." He looked around carefully, his gaze passing over the cliffs formed by the wind from the sea, the forest, and the white beach. His sharp blue eyes were sparkling.

"Well?" Candamir finally said, breaking the tense silence. "Is this the place? Do you recognize it?"

But Olaf slowly shook his head. "It is possibly the same island, but I have never been here before. Last time I landed much farther to the east." He nodded toward the setting sun.

Brigitta came ashore with the help of her son, a raven on each shoulder and the third one on her left forearm. When young Inga brought her a cup of water as well, the old woman shooed the birds away with an almost tender gesture, in order to drink unhindered. Her three black feathered companions fluttered up, squawking discordantly, and flew around awkwardly in a little circle before settling down on the sand, ruffling up their feathers.

Suddenly the forest came to life. A fluttering of countless wings commenced, and a flock of birds rose up, so huge that it seemed to the people on the beach that the sky was turning dark. For a few heartbeats they were enveloped in a wave of movement and flapping wings. Some of the children cried out, threw themselves on the ground, and put their arms over their heads. Then the birds alighted, as if following some external command, almost forming a solid mass, one right next to the other. The sand looked almost dirty yellow next to the snow-white plumage of these birds.

The Elasunders stared at them, transfixed. *Ravens,* Candamir thought, *they are white ravens.* The entire beach was full of white ravens, he saw it with his own eyes—they had gathered around their jet-black cousins in a perfect circle and were eyeing them silently, apparently as terrified as the people were. Candamir just couldn't believe what he was seeing—it seemed simply impossible. His head began to spin at this unbelievable sight.

"Tanuri's birds," Asta murmured from somewhere behind him, and her voice sounded strangely deep and distant.

"Winter ravens!" old Eilhard cried out almost at the same moment. "Winter ravens…oh, Father of the Gods…"

Here and there the cry went up: winter ravens! And as if someone had thrown a stone into a body of still water, the whisper moved in ripples outward through the crowd.

The more timid among them—men as well as women—threw themselves to the ground and covered their eyes. All those who had arrived in this bay had survived weeks and months of hunger, sickness, and peril on the mighty ocean. They were physically and mentally exhausted, and they were not ready for such a powerful omen. Many wept in terror.

"Fear not," old Brigitta said calmly. Her voice was almost unrecognizable. It sounded softer, but more powerful, and above all younger than usual. Inga had sunk to her knees in front of her, weeping, and Brigitta put her hand on the girl's bowed head.

"Brigitta, what does this all mean?" Harald asked. Even he seemed worried and confused.

"It means we did not land in Olaf's Land, but in Odin's."

The murmurs died down as abruptly as the soft sobbing.

"That...that is impossible!" Olaf said finally.

She cast him a withering glance. "You are offending the gods, Olaf."

"But...but the land you are speaking of is enchanted! No mortal man can set foot on it."

"Nevertheless, we are here." There was a light in her eyes that no one had ever seen before. It gave her wrinkled features a radiance—an agelessness—almost akin to beauty. Slowly she stretched her left arm out toward the flock of white ravens. Her hand was not even trembling. One of the great birds fluttered up—just as clumsily as his black brothers—and settled down on her wrist, holding out his breast toward her caressing, hooked finger.

Brigitta spread out her arms and for a moment threw her head back. She seemed to extend her arms and face toward the sky, but when the second white bird landed on her right wrist, she turned back to the people on the beach.

"Fear not," she repeated. "This island may well have been enchanted at one time, but for reasons we can never hope to understand, Odin has led us here."

"Led us *where*?" Candamir asked. He was staring straight at her, and it almost seemed to him as if he were seeing her for the first time. She was still an old crone with silver-gray hair and a face that was furrowed like weathered granite. But suddenly he perceived what many an Elasunder had been saying for a long time: Brigitta was closer to the gods than any one of them.

"To Tanuri's island," she replied. "We are in Catan."

# Part III: Catan

# Planting Moon, Year One

*On the fifteenth of April, after twenty-five days of danger and privation, we landed on the northwest coast of what appears to be a fruitful land, which the heathen call Catan. Never before have I seen them so overcome with awe as in the moment the witch proclaimed to them that they had landed on the island created by the father of their gods. Many cast themselves to the ground to thank him on bended knee, an unaccustomed sight among these proud, stubborn people. Some even kissed the sandy soil. Truly, it must have been like this when the children of Israel entered the Promised Land.*

*Even though darkness was almost upon us, a dozen men went forth fearlessly into the forest, and a little later the one named Osmund returned with a young bull tied to a rope. The bull was trusting and docile, as it had never seen humankind, and before it could learn distrust they slaughtered it, roasted it, and sacrificed it to their gods, which among these people means that they ate it themselves.*

*We took up torches and explored the caves in the rocks around the bay, frightening away a huge swarm of bats, but in other respects we found the caves unoccupied and suitable for shelter. We have stayed and rested in this bay for two days and nights. Gradually the people are getting over the horrors of the trip as well as the awe this place inspires, though they do nothing without first asking the advice of the old witch. On the morning of the second day, the* Sea Arrow *arrived in the bay, one of the two ships that were believed lost. It was heavily damaged, but all except a half dozen of those on board survived. In this unexpected salvation the people see another sign of the benevolence of their gods. But there is still not a trace of the second lost ship. They have accepted its loss with their typical stoicism. The passing of dear friends grieves them, but does not otherwise detract from their joy. They are as if intoxicated with this bounteous land...*

"Austin, what are you doing?"

Guiltily the Saxon let go of the pen, an ugly splotch of ink dripping onto the yellow parchment. "Ah, it is you, Mistress. I am writing a chronicle," he replied, breathing a sigh of relief.

"You are doing what?" Siglind asked, uncomprehending.

He pointed to the Bible in his lap, and she knelt down beside him, brushing her hair back and bending curiously over the book. A few of the last parchment sheets were empty. Austin had intended to write down everything he experienced while living among these people, but he had never gotten around to it, primarily out of fear that Candamir might catch him and burn his Bible as punishment. But the departure for the new homeland had finally moved the Saxon to begin, and as early as the winter before, he had secretly made himself some ink from sloeberries.

"Is this the holy book of your god?" Siglind inquired curiously.

"Yes."

"And you are allowed simply to paint some runes in it?"

"No, actually not." He smiled, explaining what he was doing and why.

She nodded, but the chronicle he had begun with such enthusiasm clearly interested her far less than the Bible itself. "Everything in this book comes from your god?" she wanted to know.

"Indeed, it does."

"But only his priests can read these runes, I expect?"

"Well, everyone can learn how, it is no mystery, but as a rule only priests do; that is true."

"Read me something," she asked.

"You would not understand it, Mistress. It is in Latin."

"Is this the language of your god?"

He thought for a moment. "God knows all languages, because he made them, but Latin is the language of His priests."

"I see." Hesitantly, she raised her right hand. "May I…may I just touch your book?"

"Surely." He obligingly held his Bible out to her, and she carefully placed her hand upon it and held it there for a long time. The large book was heavy, so he carefully put it down between them on the dry rock. They were seated before the entrance to the cave that Candamir and his household were occupying for the time being. It was almost dark now, but a fire was always burning here to keep away the bats and other creatures. It was a nice place to sit. From up here you could look out over the forest, the beach, and the sea, savor the gentle evening breezes, and enjoy all the beauty of this land.

"And these runes tell the story of the carpenter who was the son of your god?" Siglind wanted to know.

Austin nodded. "You already seem to know much about it, Mistress. Where did you learn it?"

"Oh…" Her reflective smile vanished, and she lowered her hand. "Cnut likes to raid British monasteries, because there is so much gold there. He always brought the younger, stronger monks back home as slaves. Sometimes he gave me one, and they told me about it. But most of them died of consumption, or some other thing. They were not very hardy."

Austin turned away and grimaced painfully. "And the stories they told you—did you like them?" he inquired.

"Yes. They gave me hope."

"Hope for what?"

Siglind thought for a moment. "Perhaps for something that might fill the void inside of me. Hope for a better life, I suppose, either in this world or in the next. Isn't that what this carpenter god promises to his people? He is not cruel and selfish like our gods."

Austin drew up his knees, clasped his hands around them, and glanced at the open Bible for a moment. For years he had waited in vain to find someone among these wild people who was looking for spiritual fulfillment. Now that God had heard his plea, the monk was suddenly unsure of what to do. He decided to follow his instinct for truth rather than the advice of his abbot. "The God of the Christians is cruel, too, Siglind. Often merciless. But you are right—he is different from the gods your people worship. His power is infinitely greater. And he has made a covenant with mankind, in order to save them. The people who are in this covenant with God are gathered together in a community called the Church. This Church is God's power on earth, the safe home of his Faithful."

"And can anyone join this community?"

"Yes, indeed."

"Tell me more about it."

"Gladly, Mistress..."

"Just a moment ago, you called me by my name—Siglind."

"I did? How impertinent of me. I hope you can forgive me."

She smiled shyly, and the radiance of her deep blue eyes could not fail to move even an ascetic like Austin. "I would rather you continue calling me Siglind," she said.

"No, that is not appropriate," he replied regretfully.

"But you will keep your word, won't you? To tell me about your god?"

"Everything you want to know. But tell me one thing: why are you here and not down there on the beach with your people worshipping the father of your gods? We have been here now for two days, and they have hardly done anything but make sacrifices to him and praise him. They don't ordinarily display such religious fervor, not even at the Yule festival. Don't you believe, like all the others, that Odin has chosen you to find and settle his enchanted island?"

"But I do," she said without hesitation. "Only he can have led us to Catan, for only he knows where it is. But no matter what Odin does, it always serves his own purposes, and no matter how kind he may be toward us at this moment, he may turn away from us the next." She fell silent as if she had to gather her thoughts before continuing. "Perhaps life will be easier here than in the old homeland—mine as well as yours—because the land is better. But if it is really to be a *better* life, we need something...new.

For mankind's greatest misery and misfortune, it seems to me, always come not from bad harvests or cattle plagues, but from mankind itself."

Austin looked at her in amazement. "May I ask, Mistress, how old you are?"

"Oh, I think the next midsummer festival will be my seventeenth."

"Then you are wise for your age."

She shrugged. "I have experienced much for my age."

"We have no time to lose," Olaf said. "In around two weeks, it will be Thor's Night. Seed may well grow faster here than in Elasund, but if we don't start planting soon, we will not harvest anything this year."

All of those gathered around the fire on the beach nodded in agreement.

"But before we can plant, we must clear the land," Siward reminded them. "How can we manage that in such a short time? We have no other choice than to live on what we get from the forest and the sea, for the time being, and plant in the fall."

"Oh, wonderful," Candamir murmured. "And what will we do this winter? Starve, I imagine. Then we will feel quite at home..."

There was scattered laughter, but Siward replied hotly, "Do you have a better idea? According to legend, there is no snow in Catan, so what do we have to fear?"

The fire cast wavering, dark shadows across his face, which made it appear more deeply furrowed that it actually was. After they had realized where they had landed, even Siward had to concede that their trip was in accord with the will of the gods. And in what seemed like a reward for his change of heart, his delicate, young wife Britta had finally overcome her fever. Both the Saxon and Brigitta were confident she would survive. Nevertheless, Siward was sullen as always. Squatting there with his big, bushy beard and hanging shoulders, he looked more like a dwarf than Berse, Candamir thought.

"According to legend, there are no dangerous creatures in Catan either, and yet I almost ran into a bear in the forest this morning," Candamir said. He had walked to one of the many streams that ran through the forest and had taken a good bath. As he was sitting there in the grass along the shore, naked and unarmed, drying himself in the warm morning sun, this huge, hairy beast appeared on the opposite shore, larger than any bear he had ever seen. His heart had almost stopped with fear. Fortunately, all it did was cast him a curious glance before sticking its snout in the water. After it had had its fill, it disappeared again in the woods. But Candamir was warned.

"He is right," Brigitta said. "The legend is old, it may have changed as it was passed down to us, or the land itself may have changed. Whatever the case, we know too little about Catan."

Twice she had sung for them the entire song about the enchanted island. It was much longer than Asta's version, and longer too than the one their grandmother had known. But the song, which recounted the story of Odin and Tanuri in great detail, had much less to say about the location and nature of the island.

Olaf pensively twisted the precious ring on his little finger, and then he raised his head and nodded toward Siward. "It is true that we must clear the land for planting, but not necessarily before we seed it for the first time."

Osmund lay propped on his elbows in the warm sand, admiring the stars again. Now he sat up. "What do you mean by that, Uncle?"

"I was once on an island in the southern seas where a new settlement had been established, and the people there—if I remember correctly, they were Longobards—cleared the underbrush after their arrival and put the seed in the ground between the trees."

An astonished silence followed. Then Siward said, "But you can neither plow nor harrow between the trees." He still couldn't bring himself to look Olaf in the eye. Even though he acted as if nothing had happened, no one had forgotten that Siward was one of the men who had wanted to kill the wealthy merchant just three days before.

"The forest floor was so loose that they didn't need to plow, and it is the same here," Olaf replied. "Naturally, you can't sow in neat rows, as we are accustomed, and the grain also does not grow as well because it is shaded by the trees, but it can be done. It's better than nothing."

"Indeed," Candamir agreed. He was all in favor of sowing as soon as possible—above all, barley. He could do without bread, but it was high time they started making beer again.

Olaf opened his hands briefly. "Then the only question is where we should do it."

A long, heated debate followed. Siward, Eilhard, and many others of the older generation wanted to stay here in this bay that Odin had led them to. For as long as they could remember, they had lived within sight of the sea and did not want to break with tradition. But Brigitta was against it. In the oracle she had seen a place on the bank of a river with a narrow island nearby in the middle of its swift-flowing waters. That was where they should settle, she argued. The younger people sided with her—they were eager to explore the island and see if there might be someplace inland more suited for a settlement.

When Candamir finally began climbing back to his cave, he was euphoric. Long after all the others had gone to bed, he had sat on the beach with Osmund planning for the future. The next morning they would head off to the south, to explore the interior. In the meantime, Berse would voyage around the island with the *Wavewolf*, the ship that had suffered the least damage. Only after their return would they make a final decision about the location of their new village. That had been agreed on in the meeting, and Candamir could scarcely wait until morning. But his face darkened when he recognized the two shadowy forms sitting by the fire at the entrance to the cave.

"Didn't I tell you to go and gather wood, you good-for-nothing?" he said, giving Austin a rather rough kick in the ribs.

Candamir's voice made Siglind jump a bit. As she moved, her wine-red skirt, accidentally or not, covered the open book on the ground.

Austin pointed toward the entrance to the cave. "It's over there, Master, inside where it is dry."

"Hm," Candamir grumbled disapprovingly. "And did you get my shoes?"

"Not yet," the slave confessed. "I am sorry. I forgot."

"Then I'll advise you to do it now."

Austin got up hesitantly. "But most of them are in bed already."

Candamir shrugged impatiently. "The beatings you get when you have to wake people up are no concern of mine. As usual, you richly deserve them. Tomorrow morning I shall leave with Osmund to explore the island, and for that I need shoes." Like almost everyone on board the *Falcon*, he had lost his boots in his struggle with the sea. "And get a pair for yourself also, because you are coming along."

The Saxon could clearly see that Candamir was furious at him, and even though he couldn't figure out the reason, he silently went in search of a generous donor.

Candamir leaned against the rocky side of the cave entrance. "It has gotten late," he said softly, "and too dark to climb about here safely. It would be best for you to stay here." The night sky had clouded over, and the half moon had been reduced to a milky spot above the clouds.

"Thanks," Siglind replied coolly, "but I can see in the dark just as well as you can, and I'll have no trouble finding my bed without breaking my neck." She had insisted on having a little cave all to herself that was located on the slope a good distance above.

Candamir couldn't imagine why she was annoyed at him, but women were often hard to understand. He smiled contritely. "As you wish. But at least allow me to wait here until you have arrived up there safely."

"If you don't mind, I'd like to stay here by the fire for a little while." She couldn't get up without the risk that he would discover the Bible.

He gestured invitingly and crossed his feet. He clearly intended to keep her company. Siglind suppressed a sigh. "So you are going to seek a suitable place for a new village?"

"Yes. And to see what this land is like—what beasts there are in the forest and such."

"You should take along a few women," she said. "The location for a new village has to be selected carefully. Women see the world in a different way than men do and think about things that might not even occur to men."

That was also what Brigitta had said. "Inga and Asi will go with us," he said quickly. "They know all about roots and herbs—not as much as Brigitta, but she is too old, thanks be to the gods."

Siglind ignored the disrespectful remark and declared, "I will come along as well." Candamir lowered his eyes and nodded. He would have preferred for her to stay. There was something about this queen of the Cold Islands that got under his skin. The way he looked at it, there were three kinds of women. There were the young, unmarried girls like Inga, some of whom were shy around men, others were bolder and a bit cheeky, but if you didn't intend to marry them, you were well advised to keep your distance. Then there were the married ones and the widows, and depending on their age and status, you either treated them with respect or flirted a little, and the question of how far you could go depended entirely on how they reacted. And finally there were the slaves. Things were simplest with them. You could take them whenever you wanted, and they couldn't make any demands in return. With a slave girl there could never be the closeness and friendship that you sometimes saw in married couples like his parents. But if you were lucky, as he was with Gunda, and treated them right, they added a lot of sweetness to your life.

Siglind belonged to none of these groups. She was something like a widow, but unlike the others she seemed in no hurry to find a new husband and had no father-in-law or uncle urging her to do so. That annoyed Candamir. It was at variance with his conception of decency and order. And she wore her strangeness and her pride like a coat of armor. Maybe it was only that, the challenge of breaking through her armor that tormented him so badly. In any case, she troubled him, and it was clear that Osmund was troubled by her as well. It was this last point that really worried him.

He glanced at her furtively, her blond hair enveloped in the faint reddish glow of the fire. She looked pensive, perhaps even a bit melancholy. How beautiful she was. Whenever he realized this, he felt a peculiar twinge in his heart. The feeling frightened him because it made him strangely weak, but at the same time he craved it.

Suddenly she raised her head and looked directly at him, as if she could feel him observing her. "And what do you think about our landing on this island, of all places?" she asked.

"I think it is enormously good fortune," he said. "No matter what we may find in the interior of this land, you can already tell that the weather is milder here than in the old homeland. The ground is more fertile, and there is plenty of water. This land is not man's enemy, and we need not painfully wrest every blade of grass from it."

"It looks that way," she agreed. "But don't you think that Odin will exact a price for it? Don't you ask yourself *why* he has led us here?"

He smiled down at her. "Perhaps because you joined us. He probably saw in you the image of Tanuri."

She quickly lowered her eyes.

His smile broadened and then stretched, suppressing a yawn. "Well, we leave tomorrow at sunrise, and it will surely be a long day. Since you have apparently decided to roost on my Saxon's foolish book like a hen on an egg, I'll turn in now. Good night."

She sat up straight and furrowed her brow in displeasure. With a cold glance she wished him good night, rose gracefully from the rocky ground, and headed up the steep path to her cave. Candamir hid for a few moments in the long shadow of the cave entrance, and when he was certain she was far enough away, he stepped out again and watched her. She climbed quickly and agilely in spite of the darkness. Candamir waited until the sounds of her footsteps on the rock had died away, and then he felt the first gentle drops of rain on his face. For a moment he considered leaving the Saxon's book where it lay. If it got a thorough soaking, all the foolish and dangerous stories in it would vanish. But he couldn't bring himself to do it, for he sensed that these strange runes provided his servant with all his strength and forbearance. And so he picked it up carefully by the edges of its wooden binding and carried it into the cave.

The fire at the entrance cast a flickering light into the nearly circular room. The maids had not been idle the last two days. With ferns and branches they had brought from the forest, they had made a soft bed for each person and had even woven a screen that provided their master with privacy. Many had generously donated blankets and furs to the castaways from the *Falcon*, so that no one had to fear the cool nights. It was almost homey. Candamir could vaguely make out motionless shapes along the vaulted sides—Hacon, Asta, Fulc, tiny Hergild, and the slaves in the back of the cave, where the ceiling was low and the air a bit stuffy. Only the Saxon's bed was empty.

Silently he stepped behind the screen, slipped his clothes off in the darkness, and lay down. There was a soft rustling sound as Gunda moved aside.

"You are not sleeping?" he whispered.

"It's kicking so much tonight. I think it will come out soon."

"Good," he murmured. "It can't come soon enough for me."

Gunda smiled in the darkness. She knew that Candamir was impatient for the child's birth, so that her womb would once more belong to him, as he expressed it. She was flattered that he wanted her so much.

"I hope it will be a son," he said suddenly. "We are a small people in a new land and need to grow quickly. I hope it is a son, Gunda."

"And so do I." In fact, she implored the gods every day that the child would be a boy. She knew well that this would make a difference, vital enough to affect her whole future.

Eight people set out at daybreak the next morning. This was a good number, appropriate for the occasion, Brigitta said as she bid them farewell at the edge of the forest in the heavy morning fog. Olaf had ordered Jared to go along with the lookouts, and Harald the blacksmith came too, for he wanted to look for signs of iron ore deposits. He fervently hoped the island held these, as many vital tools and weapons, including his hammer and anvil, had gone down with the *Falcon*. Nobody seemed to realize yet what that meant, and he had not confided his concerns to anyone. But if they found no iron ore, the next generation of Catan settlers would have no axes for clearing the forest and no plowshares to till the fields. For iron rusted when it was unused and wore out when it was.

Candamir stood next to Osmund, the Saxon, Hacon, and Asta, wiggling his toes to test the fit of the donated shoes. "Great," he said, thumping Austin on the shoulder so hard that the slender monk almost fell down. "You really are good for some things."

"It warms my heart, Master, that you value my services," the monk replied caustically. He had had the foresight to get shoes for Siglind as well, and his mission had taken half the night. As Candamir had foreseen, it also had brought him some harsh words and one or two kicks. The Saxon had known for a long time that generosity was one of the finest qualities of these people, and many of those who still had things from the old homeland were ready to share with those who had been on board the *Falcon*. But just as common as their generosity was their violent temper, easily ignited when awakened from deep sleep.

"Candamir, can't I please, please come along?" Hacon begged him for at least the tenth time.

His brother shook his head. "You will stay here and help your sister. Thorbjörn has agreed to take you out fishing so that you will have enough to eat while the Saxon and I are gone. That is your task now, Hacon, and I want you to stop complaining and do your duty well. Is that clear?"

Hacon lowered his eyes. "Yes."

"Good. And do what Asta tells you. In my absence she is the head of the family. I had best not hear any complaints about you."

"Now let him be," Asta said indulgently. "I am sure he will be a great help." She handed her brother his bundle—a few pieces of dried meat in a leather pouch, rolled up in a blanket. That was all he wanted to take along, except for his knife. "Come here, brother," Asta said, standing on her toes and kissing him on the cheek. "Take care of yourself. And Osmund and Austin, that goes for you as well." For her brother's friend as well as the slave, she had prepared the same small travel bundle, which they gratefully accepted.

"It's high time," the smith admonished them. "Let's go."

For each of them Brigitta had a white raven feather on a string made of seal leather. One after the other, they bowed their heads before her, and she hung the strange jewelry around their necks. "In order that

Odin's strength and wisdom may go with you," she explained, shooing them off into the forest with a brusque, unceremonious wave.

The dark forest floor was covered with the same spongy grass that they had already seen, and at least for the time being the underbrush was not especially dense, so they made good progress. Osmund and Jared went ahead, followed by Inga and Siglind, the smith and his wife, and finally Candamir and his Saxon bringing up the rear.

When Austin quickened his pace in order to move farther to the front, Candamir seized him by the arm. "And where do you think you're going?" he whispered.

Austin raised his eyebrows in surprise. "To catch up with Inga, Master. We agreed to look around together to see if we could find any fumitories."

"What?"

"Fumitories. A medicinal plant that could help her father's gall problem. It is rather rare, but if we are lucky it may already be in bloom here."

Candamir's grip turned into something like an iron vise. "Do you take me for a fool?" he asked, a warning glint in his sea-gray eyes.

"Master?" Austin replied, hopelessly confused.

"Do you think I am blind? It isn't Inga you are drawn to, but *her*." Almost furtively, Candamir pointed his thumb at Siglind, who was climbing over a fallen tree trunk. Both Osmund and Jared had reached out to help, but she studiously ignored their hands. "I have absolutely nothing against your taking a wife," Candamir continued softly, "but restrict your search to those of your own state. Don't let me catch you with her again, do you understand?"

It finally dawned on Austin what his master meant. "Master, I have tried dozens of times to explain to you that I am forbidden to have relations with women. My vow..."

"I saw it, you almost crept under her skirt," Candamir interrupted. "And if I catch you doing it again, you will get to know a side of me that you would rather not learn about."

The Saxon realized the seriousness of this threat. Astonished and somewhat frightened he cast a sidelong glance at his master and replied with feigned casualness, "You completely misunderstood the situation."

"It was absolutely clear!"

"No, Master. I…"

"That will do," Candamir hissed. "You heard what I said."

"Yes, Master."

Candamir gave a quick nod. "Then don't forget it."

For a moment, the Saxon considered explaining to Candamir just why Siglind had come to see him. But then he realized that he couldn't risk that; Candamir might get even angrier and forbid any contact between the two of them.

Candamir paid no further attention to his Saxon and caught up with Osmund and Jared. All that Austin could do now was to wait until Siglind had joined the smith and his wife before he could catch up with Inga and keep his promise.

The land continued to rise all morning long, but otherwise seemed to change little. They were in an ancient woodland of mixed deciduous and coniferous trees. One variety of oak, unknown to them, predominated, but they also saw familiar firs and, to their great joy, even ash trees. Although it was still early in the year, the reawakening of nature was already far along, and they discovered many unknown flowers in the long grass. Austin was familiar with some from his homeland, but he could only shrug his shoulders when it came to most. The sky remained a constant blue. As the sun rose higher, it made the new foliage on the trees glisten and cast a wonderful dappled pattern of light and shadow on the ground. It began to get warm in the forest, and the scouts maintained an almost reverent silence in the face of its beauty. All around them they could hear rustling and humming. The forest was full of life.

The last time Austin had gone hunting had been as a boy, before he had entered the monastery. He could not remember everything his father had taught him, but he soon discovered the tracks of red deer, wild boar, and small game, and the hoof prints of a disconcertingly large animal, certainly larger than the bull Osmund had brought back from the forest on their first evening in Catan. A bison? Or perhaps an aurochs? The Saxon didn't know, and he kept his fears to himself. In any case, the men kept their weapons handy and peered attentively into the shadowy forest, the image of the bear that had crossed Candamir's path the day before at the front of their minds. Luckily, they didn't encounter anything more dangerous than squirrels—some black, some red—and a large number of birds.

Shortly before noon they came to a brook flowing in approximately the direction they were headed and decided to follow it, as they could make much better time in the ankle-deep water. The women walked close to the shore, stopping now and then to examine a plant or bush. Inga and the smith's wife were discovering, much to their delight, many roots and herbs that either tickled the palate or were useful in curing fever, pain in the joints, and the like. Siglind, on the other hand, knew all about plants whose leaves or berries provided dyes for the colorful clothing that people on the Cold Islands were so fond of, and she promised that before winter every one of the settlers would have a garment just as red as her own.

"Thanks, but no thanks," Candamir demurred.

Inga and Siglind laughed at his horrified expression. "And why not?" Inga asked. "We have a new homeland, why not some new fashions? If we wanted to keep doing things just as before, we could have stayed in Elasund."

"I left Elasund looking for a better future, not red clothes," Osmund said. "Certainly it would be an improvement if you women all dressed in such gorgeous colors, but I think we ought to stick to our customs, Inga, just so we don't forget who we are," he added with a smile.

*Well, perhaps not all the customs,* Candamir thought, but that was something he wanted to discuss with Osmund at leisure when they were alone.

Up to that point, the smith had been content to let the younger men lead the group and carry the conversation, but now he said, "We need to keep on moving. We probably haven't gone more than five miles yet."

It was just an hour before dusk when they left the creek bed, climbed to the top of a steep hill, and, for the first time since they left the shore, entered a large clearing, dominated by a solitary oak taller than all the other trees around it.

"Let us rest here for the night," Candamir suggested. Everyone agreed that it was a suitable place to make camp, as no one was especially eager to spend the night in the shadow of the forest.

While the women and the Saxon busied themselves making a smooth pit for the fire, and Jared and Harald collected some dead wood, Osmund and Candamir walked over to the solitary tree and looked up into its branches.

"You or me?" Candamir asked.

"You can do the honors." Osmund bent down a little, clasping his hands together.

Candamir placed one foot in Osmund's hands, leaned against the thick bark of the tree, and hoisted himself high enough to grab hold of a branch. After that, it was simple. He easily pulled himself up and disappeared into the dense foliage as quickly and nimbly as a cat.

It was a huge old tree with thick branches that went almost to the top. When they finally became too small for him to climb, he moved sideways and stuck his head out through the leaves. He was at least sixty feet up and well above the other treetops.

The sky was still clear and the visibility unimpeded. There was a slight haze over the blue sea to the north, which already seemed far away. The forest was huge. They had apparently reached the highest point of land. From here, the ground fell off in all directions, so that distances were not easy to estimate, but Candamir guessed that the forest's edge was about twenty miles to the east. Beyond that flat grassland extended out to the foot of a distant chain of mountains. A bit farther south, a river seemed to flow from these mountains, moving through the grassland in a broad bed and finally disappearing in the forest.

Candamir's pulse quickened. *That is our river. If we settle on its banks, we will surely never lack water.* His eyes gleaming, he looked out over the broad, blue-green strip of land, and then, to his great joy, he caught sight of a herd of animals in the flood plain. From their supple, unmistakable movements he immediately recognized what they were: horses.

He turned his eyes farther to the southwest, and in this direction the forest extended deep into the interior of the island too. And where it stopped, all life seemed to end as well. Candamir squinted. He had sharp eyes, but the strange, dark brown plain he could barely see was too far away to actually identify. And then he saw something that so terrified him that he lost his footing on the tree and started to slip.

The first half of his descent was much faster than he had intended, but he caught himself on a branch before he could seriously hurt himself, climbing the rest of the way down with rare caution.

"Well?" Inga asked breathlessly. "What did you see?"

"Did you fall? There was such a strange rustling sound," Siglind added critically.

"Are there mountains anywhere around here?" the smith wanted to know.

"Any signs of habitation?" Jared chimed in.

Candamir raised his hand. "I didn't fall, and what I saw was good, at least for the most part."

He walked over to the fire and sat down on his blanket. Although they were in a clearing, it was still noticeably darker down below than it had been above the trees. Dusk was falling, and as they had already learned, darkness descended much faster here than in Elasund.

"Let's eat while we still have light," said the Saxon, who knew from experience that Candamir was more forthcoming when fed.

The others gathered around the small fire as well, and Inga distributed the meager portions of dried meat.

"Yes, there are mountains, Harald," Candamir finally began his report, pointing to the east. "A whole chain of them, it appears, though they are rather far away." He also told them about the other things he had seen. "I wasn't able to make out any signs of human habitation, but this island is very large. Except for the coast to the northwest I was not able to see the ocean. South of the forest there is what looks like a strange, barren wasteland, at least from a distance. There are no trees, nothing green." He knew there was no point in keeping from them what he had seen in that wasteland, even though it would frighten them as well. "Only the mountain that we know about from the song."

"A fiery mountain?" Jared blurted out. "Are you sure?"

Candamir frowned in annoyance. "No, I just made that up."

For a moment there was an uncomfortable silence.

"Well, it really is no surprise," the smith said. "So far everything else we have seen has been just as in the song. Almost, anyway. The white ravens, the fertile earth, all the beautiful birds and plants. And so we should also expect to find the mountain here that Odin tore open with his spear, shouldn't we? And did you see lots of fire?" he asked Candamir. "Did it shoot fiery balls into the air, or was there a burning river flowing from the mountain?"

The younger man shook his head. "I don't think so. As I said, it was very, very far away in the midst of this wasteland. All I could see was a faint, reddish glow."

He tried to sound reassuring, but the fiery mountain made them all feel uneasy. They knew from the tales of seafarers that such mountains caused earthquakes and sent up poisonous vapors from the bowels of the earth. All too easily such a mountain could be turned into the tool of an angry god. They were troublingly inconsistent with the permanence of land and sea. The Saxon had even read that these mountains, called *vulcani* by learned men, were a bridge between two worlds, an ever-yawning gateway into hell. Since his companions were convinced, however, that this fiery mountain was Odin's creation, he decided it would be best to keep this knowledge to himself.

Candamir threw a branch onto the fire. "Well, it doesn't matter. We have no reason to go that far, or even to go southwest at all. Maybe one of you would like to climb up again in the morning and look around, but I think our prospects are in the south, on the banks of the wide river."

Osmund shook his head. "If you say so, that's good enough for me." He said it without particular emphasis, but it was a remarkable expression of trust. Candamir cast a furtive glance of thanks toward his friend.

Jared considered climbing the oak to form his own impression of the land and the fiery mountain, because he knew that his father would probably expect nothing less. Before he had made up his mind, however, Siglind spoke up. "In any case, we should go and explore those mountains," she said. She seemed to think nothing of intruding into men's business, something that was normally only tolerated from crones like Brigitta. Jared threw the young foreigner an astonished, disapproving look, which she either did not notice or haughtily ignored. She nodded at the blacksmith. "I suppose you haven't talked about it because you don't wish to upset anyone unnecessarily just yet, but isn't it true that our settlement won't get very far if we don't find any iron?"

Harald stared at her. "How did you know that?"

Siglind made a vague gesture. She had often listened to Cnut's discussions with his steward and learned many things, including how vulnerable the Cold Islands were for their lack of iron ore. Iron was a key to prosperity and power. "I saw the cargo aboard the *Falcon*," she said. "Isn't it true that all your materials and tools went down with the ship?"

Harald briefly shrugged his broad shoulders and nodded. "You are right," he said, finally confessing his worries to the group.

Candamir and Osmund looked at each other in alarm. In Elasund, the smith had taken a trip into the mountains once a year to buy his supply of iron ore from the farmers who tilled a few rocky fields, but who lived chiefly from mining. Iron was something they had always taken for granted, because there was no shortage of it.

A dejected silence fell over the group as darkness descended.

"But Harald," Inga finally asked softly, "what...what will become of us if we don't find any iron ore in Catan?" Her voice betrayed her fear, and Jared moved a bit closer to her, wrapping his blanket around her shoulders. She scarcely appeared to notice.

The smith smiled at her from across the flickering fire. "I don't believe that will happen, lass. Remember the song. The giants, as well as Odin, who together conceived and created this land, surely love nothing more than fine weapons. And it says that they have richly blessed the mountains with gold and ore. The only question is *where* they have buried it."

Candamir could tell from Inga's face that she was comforted, as was he. Wrapping himself in his blanket in the dying light of the fire, he soon fell asleep, dreaming of the wild horses he had seen on the grassland at the foot of the mountains.

The next morning, at Candamir's suggestion, they headed as straight south as possible toward the bank of the river. In the course of the day the land gradually changed. The forest became older and the ground damper the farther they got from the sea. They came upon ponds and small, quiet lakes, and began to worry that the land could all turn to swamp. In addition, thick underbrush comprised of elder, blackberry, and other plants unknown to them made progress difficult, as swarms of mosquitoes buzzed around their heads. It was a difficult day, but no one complained.

Their meager provisions were running out, but for the time being they had no fear of going hungry, as Candamir, Osmund, and young Jared were skilled in spear-fishing, and the brooks in the forest were teeming with trout. In a short time they had caught enough so that everyone could eat to their heart's content. It was a welcome change from the dried meat they had all come to detest.

On the afternoon of the third day, they arrived at the river that Candamir had seen from atop the tree. They followed its course upstream until coming to a place where the river turned gently and the forest thinned out, leaving only small, dwindling clusters of young pines and birches.

With the forest behind them and the river on their right, they finally stopped to take in the undulating country before them. Far to the east, they could barely make out what looked like a veil of bluish mist on the horizon.

"Are those the mountains?" Inga asked.

"I think so," the smith said. "How far away is it, Osmund? What do you think?"

"Three days, perhaps four." He looked out at the river that was divided about a half mile downstream by a forested island shaped like a ship. Then he looked across the broad plain and gentle hills that extended from the edge of the forest to the foot of the mountains. He had imagined "grassland" to somehow be different. The ground apparently consisted of pale limestone protruding everywhere through a thin layer of soil with irregular clumps of dark, long-bladed grass on it. Osmund bent down and felt one of them.

Candamir too was disappointed. "It looked better from a distance," he sighed. "Our seed will certainly not grow here."

Osmund shook his head. "The soil in the forest, however, is excellent. We'll have no choice but to clear the land for our fields. Don't look so glum, Candamir—we already expected we would have to do that."

"If we settle here, we'll at least have grazing land for the livestock," Jared pointed out. "We could start clearing the land and then use the wood to build our houses on the river."

"Not too close to the river," Siglind warned. "If there is snow in the mountains during the winter, the river will overflow its banks in the spring and flood our storehouses if we are too close."

Candamir looked at her furtively out of the corner of his eye. She stood very straight, shading her eyes with her slender left hand. Her fingers were long and her skin almost white. A few strands had slipped out of her blond braid and were blown into her face by the gentle breeze. Impatiently, she brushed them away with her other hand. "The grass looks greener on the other side," she said.

"It always does," Osmund replied dryly, "but there's no reason we can't look around on the other bank. I think I'll swim over and have a look."

He slipped off his borrowed boots, and Candamir followed his example. "I'm coming along."

Together they walked down the gently sloping shore and looked out over the river that was around a furlong wide here.

"My father always used to say that one should cross unfamiliar rivers with a raft," Candamir said. His father had had a large collection of sayings that he loved to quote from, especially when he wanted to admonish his careless son.

Osmund nodded. "Your father was a wise man. One can easily drown in unfamiliar rivers."

"Hm."

They looked at each other, laughed, and ran into the water.

Meanwhile, the others explored the bank of the river and the edge of the forest. There were many birds nesting among the reeds, and Inga and Siglind gathered a few eggs.

"I have nothing against trout," Siglind said, "they are always better than dried meat. But can there be anything more delicious than an egg?" She took one, carefully pierced the thin shell with the end of her little finger, and then sucked it out with great relish. "Ah, delicious. You must try one, Inga." She held out a small, green-speckled egg of some water bird. But Inga was not even looking; she was peering out over the river, as if she were looking for something on the other bank. Then she breathed a sigh of relief. "I see them," she said, pointing, "both of them."

Siglind also looked across and saw two figures—one with a dark head of hair and the other flaxen blond—apparently bending over something they had discovered in the grass. "So? Which of them do you want?" she asked Inga curiously.

The girl blushed a little, but answered candidly. "Osmund." She was still looking across at him, her pretty blue eyes shining. Then she sighed and turned away. "But I'm afraid nothing will come of it."

"Why do you think that?"

"His wife has been dead for half a year. Time enough, if he wanted me, to ask my father. But he doesn't even look at me."

"Something you can't say about Jared," the older woman replied dryly.

Inga nodded and finally took the egg that Siglind was holding out to her. She rubbed her finger over the thin, rough shell. "Yes, that's just the way it is. Jared wants me, I want Osmund, and Osmund wants you. The gods must be laughing themselves silly."

Siglind was not fooled by Inga's apparent composure. She had been thirteen herself not long ago and had dreamed of a blue-eyed hero with strong arms and a gentle heart. And even if her dream had not come true, and indeed had turned into a nightmare, she knew exactly how vulnerable a girl was at that age. She took Inga's free hand and squeezed it briefly. "You have nothing to fear from me. I am not interested in your Osmund."

Inga smiled with relief and said, "Then it's Candamir?"

But the queen of the Cold Islands shook her head. "I no longer want a man."

Inga was taken aback and remained silent for a moment, then asked, "But why not?"

Siglind grimaced. Perhaps she was trying to appear amused, but it looked to Inga as if the expression was one of bitterness. And because Inga got no reply, she added, "Don't you think that all unmarried women among us should be obliged to find a husband and have children as fast as possible? There are so few of us in such a vast and unknown land. Our tribe must grow."

"Yes, that is probably the case, but I am not one of your tribe, Inga." Apart from that, Cnut had tried for so long to make her pregnant and it had never happened. She was convinced that she would not be able to contribute to the growth of this people.

"If you don't consider us good enough for you, why did you come with us?" Inga asked. She sounded neither offended nor overbearing, just surprised.

Siglind shook her head. "How could I think that? Be assured I would have been prouder as the wife of a good fisherman than that of a bad king. So it's nothing like that." She didn't know how to explain her motives to Inga without making the poor girl fearful of marriage. "I…I was married for four years and found that was not the way I wanted to live. And I am not the only one who feels that way. Aren't there some widows now and then among your people who don't wish to remarry?"

"Rarely. But you are right, it does happen."

"There you are, see?"

"But what do you want instead?"

"I don't know," Siglind confessed. "I think there must be something else. That can't be all there is, can it?"

"Orache?" Jared asked the Saxon. "What in the world is orache?"

They had retreated under the trees because it looked like rain. Near the edge of the forest they had built a fire in a sheltered hollow, and Austin and the women were examining what grew there.

"Orache is something like cabbage," the Saxon replied. But that wasn't quite correct. He paused for a moment to consider how to explain it. "When the harvest of peas and beans is poor, people sometimes eat cooked nettles, don't they?"

Jared made a face, but nodded.

"Orache is something like that, only it tastes better. The plant grows six feet high and keeps growing until the frost."

"You can harvest the same plant more than once?" Inga asked, uncertain whether she had correctly understood him.

Austin nodded. "If you wish, but it is not really all that tasty."

Asi stepped closer and looked with interest at the plant the young people were discussing, "That makes no difference. At least it would mean we'd have something to satisfy our hunger until the first harvest."

"Well, yes, if it's really orache." Austin was crouched on the ground, feeling the leaves. Then he stood up.

"I thought you said you knew this plant from your homeland. You foreign slaves are all the same," the blacksmith's wife said. "First you pretend to be so smart, and then you really don't know anything."

Asi was really a good soul, Austin knew, but she was afraid of this new land and all the uncertainties involved. He smiled contritely and explained, "There are a number of species of this plant, you know, and I am not quite certain whether this is one of them. And there is a plant with similar triangular leaves that is rather poisonous."

"Well, there is a simple way to find out which it is. All we have to do is to eat some of it," Jared said, looking at Austin and gesturing toward the plant. "It is always practical to have a slave with you. You never know what he will be good for."

He had not meant it seriously, and everyone laughed, but Austin did not join in. He suddenly leaped toward Jared, tore the spear out of his loose grip, and shoved him so hard that he fell to the ground. It all happened so fast that no one could stop the Saxon before he raised the weapon over his right shoulder and flung it with astonishing force. Siglind gasped in fright, and Inga let out a half-suppressed cry. However, it wasn't Jared who lay in the grass fatally struck down, but a large, black wild sow. Though the spear was lodged in its broad chest, it was able to roll on its side. Everyone stepped back in fear as the animal tried to stand up again, but then the small, dark eyes became glassy and rigid, and it lay still.

Austin heaved a long sigh and stretched out his hand to help Jared to his feet. "I'm sorry, but your back was turned to the beast, and it came out of the underbrush so fast and so suddenly that I didn't have time to warn you."

Jared ignored Austin's hand and leaped to his feet. His face had turned red, and he glanced briefly at Inga and Siglind, who were transfixed by the sight of the dead monster.

"By all the gods, how *huge* it is," Inga murmured, shuddering. "And how ugly."

Siglind agreed. "Where did it come from so suddenly?"

Austin pointed toward the trees. "No doubt it has young ones nearby and felt threatened by us. Then they can be really dangerous, because…" He was cut short as a heavy hand fell on his shoulder and spun him around. Before he could say or do anything, Jared punched him in the stomach. The monk fell to his knees and doubled up, gasping and coughing.

"Who do you think you are, taking my weapon from me, you scoundrel?" Jared growled at him, kicking him in the side.

"Jared," Harald admonished him. "Leave him alone. He probably saved your life, you silly boy."

These words did nothing to placate Jared. He didn't know how to deal with slaves in any way other than what his father had taught him.

He kicked him again with unrestrained fury, and the Saxon landed face-first on one of the boulders that were strewn across the ground.

"Answer me!" Jared stepped forward again as if he still weren't finished with the Saxon, but someone seized him by the elbow and pulled him back. "He can't, not while he's still trying to get his breath back, now can he?" said Candamir, who had appeared out of nowhere dripping wet.

Jared pulled free, furious. "Your slave is insolent and disrespectful, Candamir! Father is right—he has no manners!"

Candamir looked at him scornfully. "Yes, I'm convinced that any one of your slaves would have looked on respectfully as the wild sow trampled you to death."

Jared pointed an accusing finger at the motionless form lying on the ground. "He laid a hand on me. I demand he lose the hand."

"You have gone mad," Candamir said, turning away in disgust.

Jared stared at Candamir's back, then at the slave on the ground, and his hand slipped down to the hilt of his knife.

"Jared!" Osmund said sharply. He had stepped up alongside Candamir, equally wet. "I think you are the one who is lacking in proper respect."

His young cousin snorted furiously, but lowered his hand. "You can be sure that my father will hear about this, Candamir," he said angrily.

"Right. And he'll be so proud of the bravery you have shown here today," Candamir replied as he bent over the Saxon and turned him on his back. "Oh, dammit." The slave had cut his nose when he fell, and the blood was streaming out. "Will it be all right?"

Austin shook the well-meaning hand from his shoulder, more out of noble pride than pious forbearance, rose unsteadily to his feet, and staggered toward the river.

"Don't fall in the water!" Candamir called after him, for darkness was falling and the riverbank was dangerous in places.

There was no answer.

Candamir sighed softly, then looked down on the dead sow and said with a shrug, "At least we'll have plenty to eat today and tomorrow." He pulled off his wet tunic and hung it carefully over a branch. It was threadbare and full of holes, but it was the only one he had. "Well, let's go, give a hand. We have to at least gut it before nightfall."

He caught Siglind staring, horrified and yet fascinated, at the long scar above his navel. He passed the palm of his hand over it and said, grinning, "I have a few more. Would you like to see them?"

Surprised at being caught, she smiled in embarrassment before walking over resolutely to the dead sow.

Inga followed her. "The poor piglets," she murmured.

The men laughed at her.

"If we are lucky, they will come looking for their mother," Osmund said. "Then we can catch them and take them back with us. Imagine how happy everyone will be with such a tender roast."

She looked at him disapprovingly. "How heartless you are."

He shook his head. "They won't survive, in any case. They are dependent on their mother."

Asi was busy rummaging about in her pack that was larger than anyone else's and contained the most unbelievable treasures. "It's pretty much the same thing with humans, Osmund, my boy," she said. Then, with a triumphant smile, she held up what she had been looking for—a strong seal-leather rope. They used it to tie the wild sow's hind legs, swung the rope over a sturdy branch, and hoisted the animal up. Harald, Candamir, and Osmund all had to pull together—the sow was much larger and heavier than any pig they had ever killed before.

"Oh, come on, Jared," Osmund said, exasperated. "Stop sulking and give us a hand here."

His young cousin obeyed. Since more animals had been slaughtered at his father's farm than anywhere else, he took on the job of slitting open the animal's throat and belly to bleed it. It took some skill to do this without getting drenched with blood, and Jared mastered the job with elegance and ease, earning murmurs of praise from the three women. This improved his mood, but he remained quieter than usual all evening.

They burned the innards, except for the liver and kidneys. And Candamir set the heart aside on a bed of fresh oak leaves for the Saxon, if he wanted it. They finished long after dark and decided to put off the rest of the work until the next day. Harald hacked away on the carcass with his hunting knife until he had cut out two legs of pork, which they roasted over the fire.

"You were right, Siglind," Osmund said. "The grass is in fact greener on the other side, because it is thicker and richer. That's probably because the topsoil is better there."

"Still, it is not really very good," Candamir added, "and I am not certain if the topsoil over the stone is deep enough for us to be able to plow. Also, we don't have any draft animals. We might try to sow something there, but I think the harvest would be at least as good if we did as the Longobards do and tried to raise grain under the trees."

"But if we do that and the attempt fails, we will lose our precious seed," Asi said.

Candamir nodded. "I know. Olaf and Siward must take a look at the land. They have more experience in farming than the rest of us."

They continued discussing the matter while the leg of pork roasted to a crispy brown. Asi cut the meat from the bone, gave everyone a piece, and put one aside for the Saxon, who still had not returned. They ate in silence, concentrating on the strong, gamey taste of the pork.

Finally, Harald licked his fingers with great satisfaction and said, "The grass on this side is good enough for grazing the livestock, and certainly is so on the other side. We have the river to provide us with food and water and the forest for lumber and for our fields, and if there is iron ore in these mountains, it really isn't that far away. I believe we have found the site for our new village," he concluded.

Only Candamir raised an objection. "Berse and many of the others won't like being a nearly three-day hike from the sea. And they are right, too. Until now we have always lived on what we got from the sea. We can fish in the river, of course, but what about the cod and the herring? What about the seals? How will we do without all of that?"

For the first time in hours, Jared spoke up. "Father said we cannot expect to find any seals here, as they prefer the cold waters of the northern seas. On the other hand, we will have more grain here and raise more livestock. We'll just have to change our ways."

"That's right," the smith said. "Apart from that, we don't really know if the sea is that far away. Maybe there is a shorter way to the coast than going back to the bay where we landed. And..."

"You have only to follow the river," Osmund said, amused that no one had thought of this obvious solution. "It is generally accepted that rivers flow to the sea. And it is very deep. So if there are no waterfalls or rapids between here and the coast, we can row up the river with our catches from the ocean right to the village. We only have to build a dock strong enough to resist the current."

"Thorbjörn and Haldir should know how to do that," Inga said. In the old homeland, Eilhard's sons had lived in a hamlet along the river and built docks there for the large ships.

Everyone nodded.

"So tomorrow we will divide up," Harald said. "I'll go into the mountains. One or two of you should come with me. The others can return to the coast, report what we have found, and lead our people here."

"But Harald, what shall we do if you find no iron ore?" Osmund asked.

"Then another group will have to go out to scout the entire island, even if it takes years. But we can settle here, one way or the other. It is a good place."

"That won't keep my father and Haflad and the other grumblers from reminding us about all the things that are *not* perfect here," Inga said with a sigh.

Harald looked at her across the fire and smiled. "There's no harm in expecting that."

A quiet, gentle rain had started falling some time ago and was now dripping through the forest cover, hissing as it fell into the fire. There was still just a slight breeze, but it was beginning to get cold.

Inga wrapped herself in her blanket. "Oh, this will be a restful night," she murmured in disgust.

"He has been gone for ages," Siglind whispered to Candamir.

"Who? Oh, my Saxon. Well, he'll come back. He can't run away from me here, can he?" He rolled out his blanket and looked around unsuccessfully for a dry spot on the ground.

"If you're not going to look for him, I will," she said.

Candamir raised his eyebrows. "And hope that all the bears and other wild beasts will cast themselves down before Your Royal Highness?"

"He is alone out there, and unarmed," she hissed.

"And it was his choice," he said. "It's cloudy and pitch black. How can I find him?"

She snorted with contempt and stood up.

"O mighty Tyr, give me patience," Candamir grumbled, likewise jumping to his feet and gesturing to her to remain there. "All right, all right. I'll go."

He was not twenty paces from the fire when he could scarcely see his hand in front of his face. The rain was only a light drizzle, but there was no moon or stars to see by. At a loss, Candamir headed off in the direction of the river, stumbling over roots, getting caught in branches, and cursing Siglind. He might never have found the Saxon if he had not already returned from the river an hour earlier and was now sitting under a beech tree, where the ground was almost dry, within sight of the fire.

"Another step and you will stumble over my feet, Master," he warned Candamir softly.

Candamir was startled and looked down. When he caught sight of the Saxon, he crouched down in front of him. "What do you think you are doing, staying away so long?" he scolded him softly. "Do you want to kill yourself?"

"No. The thought is appealing now and then, but my faith forbids it." It was so dark that they could hardly see each other, though Candamir was able to discern the emotion that lay behind the flippant remark.

He put his hand on the Saxon's shoulder. "Are you all right?"

"Of course."

"Is your nose broken?"

"And what if it is?" he said, sounding uncharacteristically brusque.

"Come along then, get some sleep."

Austin seemed not to have heard him. "I once saw a wild boar kill a man," he said softly. "It was horrible."

"I bet it was. Now stop brooding over it. Jared is a fool. He should be grateful for what you did."

The Saxon stirred uncomfortably. "I did not do it to protect him or the others, but out of pride."

"What?"

"I saw the sow rushing toward us and I knew I could kill it—so I did, because I wanted to, out of pride. And that is a mortal sin, you know, especially for a monk."

"Oh, ye gods, don't you think it's a little too late at night for this incoherent drivel? No matter what was going through your mind, you did everyone a service." He nodded in the direction of the camp. "A juicy leg of pork is waiting for you there—and the heart."

Austin was not interested. "You eat it. You are still much too thin."

"Look who's talking."

"But for me, fasting has a meaning. Let me stay here, Master, if you will. I must speak with my God."

Candamir's patience was exhausted. "Enough! You're making an unnecessary fuss over something meaningless."

The monk smiled ruefully into the darkness. "You would not say that if Olaf was going to demand *your* hand. You know very well that this is not yet over."

"I don't care what Olaf demands. We are going to need all the hands we can get in the coming months, and therefore yours are safe from Olaf's vengeance. I'll see to that. Now, let's go. You can continue your silly conversation with your strange god, but do it near the fire, where you are safe. Come on, Austin."

The Saxon raised his head, astonished, but it was simply impossible to see Candamir's face and make out whether or not his name had slipped out inadvertently.

Harald took his wife along, as she was tireless and courageous in mountain areas, and asked Candamir to lend him the Saxon in their search for the ore so vital to their survival.

"Certainly," the younger man said, "but I don't know if he will be of much use, as I don't believe he knows anything about iron and ore deposits."

"That doesn't matter. He has sharp eyes, and that is worth a lot by itself. He can also work with Asi to determine what kind of plants grow in the mountains, and that can be very useful to us." He smiled, and little wrinkles appeared around his eyes. "Moreover, it is sometimes wise not to be where there are bad feelings, don't you think?"

Candamir got the point, replying to his conspiratorial smile with a nod. "Thanks, Harald."

"You're welcome, lad. And who knows. When the gentle Saxon with the fiery eyes and exceptional hunting skill has been gone for a few days, perhaps even the queen of the Cold Islands will notice that we have a few good-looking fellows among us, huh?"

Startled, Candamir looked over his shoulder, but he and Harald were alone on the shore and no one had heard what they said. He lowered his eyes and said, "So you also think she has her eyes on the Saxon? What on earth does she see in him?"

Harald shook his head. "I think you are drawing the wrong conclusion. I would say rather that she has an eye on his god."

"*What?*"

"Hm. In any case, that wouldn't surprise me. She only plays the part of the proud queen. Underneath she is someone quite different—someone restless and troubled. She seems to be looking for something, Candamir, and if you want to be the one she finds, you'll have to become what she is looking for."

Candamir shook his head. "I don't understand what you are saying."

"Then think about it."

Candamir folded his arms and sighed. "I don't know—she is a damned difficult woman, isn't she? I'm not at all sure I want her, to be honest."

"Well then, I imagine you'll have to think about that, too," Harald replied earnestly, but his eyes were twinkling merrily.

And so the five younger explorers set out on their way back to the coast. Their progress was rapid and without further incident, returning the way they had come. Here and there they even found the narrow passage they had made through the underbrush, and Osmund imagined that it would soon turn into a recognizable path if the other settlers took this route to the river, eventually becoming a road if they used it repeatedly to transport their possessions.

Osmund kept a critical eye on his cousin, but Jared seemed to have gotten over his childish grudge. He joked almost exuberantly with the two women and found crayfish and bird eggs for them—even though they still had so much of the pork left. He was cordial toward everyone except Candamir, to whom he spoke as little as possible.

Candamir didn't notice; he was occupied with all sorts of problems and questions that had more to do with clearing the land and building houses than with the things Harald had told him before he left. Though, for most of the way he and Osmund walked behind the young women and Jared, where he could watch Siglind and feast his eyes on the play of sunlight on her hair, and her natural grace. As they forged the shallow brook, he noticed a small birthmark on her calf, and he couldn't help but wonder what else he would discover if she ever allowed him to remove her red dress and dove-gray undergarments. The power of these fantasies troubled him though, and he sometimes wished he had taken her back to her husband or thrown her overboard on the high seas when he had a chance. Instead, he distracted himself with practical questions about how they would survive in the near future, conferring for hours with Osmund, who was just as grateful to have this to occupy his mind.

At dusk on the second day they caught sight of a few deer by the brook, and several times they encountered small herds of cattle that lived in these forests. They were beautiful animals with long, brown coats and large, trusting eyes. On the morning of the third day, the explorers met another herd of such animals, and Candamir tried putting a rope around the neck of one of the cows and leading it a few steps away from the herd. The cow complied willingly, and her calf followed along. On seeing that, he and Osmund decided to drive the whole herd back to the coast with them. "We lost all our sheep," Osmund said, "and it's never too early to acquire a new herd."

There were four cows, three of which had already calved, and two bulls. The larger of these was the only beast that seemed reluctant to let the strange two-legged animals tell them where to go. Candamir tied the rope around his neck and led this bull himself. Patting the animal on its sturdy shoulders, Candamir whispered with a chuckle, "You don't know it yet, my good fellow, but you will soon be a docile ox and help us to pull tree roots out of the ground."

"Look there, Hacon!" Wiland grabbed his friend by the arm and pointed to the edge of the clearing. "There's your brother and the others, and they are bringing cattle back with them!"

The boys had been climbing around on the rocks looking for flint. Now they hastily put what they had found into a pouch they had been careful to bring along and quickly started climbing back down. As they passed the cave where Candamir had set up his household, they heard a heartrending scream.

Hacon raised his shoulders and hurried on. "I can't stand listening to it anymore," he told Wiland. "She's been going on like that since last night. I hope it will soon be over."

"It will," Siward's son said. "Either it'll finally come out or she will die. Either way, it can't be much longer."

As soon as the newcomers arrived at the beach, they were surrounded by a crowd.

"…went with Asi and the Saxon into the mountains to look for iron ore," they heard Osmund saying. "Everyone is well. And we have found a place we think is right for us." With obvious pride, the explorers took turns telling about the great river, the grassland, the mountains and forests, and the little adventures they had had. Hacon and Wiland listened, full of envy.

"Is Berse back yet?" Candamir finally asked.

The bystanders shook their heads.

"We ought not to wait for him," Olaf said. "It will be enough if two or three of us stay behind. I suggest we start out for this river tomorrow morning. Every day counts. And now tell us, Osmund, where you found these wonderful cattle?"

It wasn't Osmund who answered, but Jared. "The forest is full of them, Father." Hacon could not see him for all the others standing between them, but he heard the elation in Jared's voice. "This land really is just as the legend says—it has everything you need to live, and plenty of it."

"Indeed?" Siward asked derisively. "Did you by chance see any sheep? Mine drowned, you know. Or chickens, or goats, or pigs?"

"The Saxon found some tracks of grouse, at least," Osmund replied. "If we look for them, we will no doubt find them."

"And we also saw a wild pig," Jared noted almost casually. "It attacked us, and..."

"I think there will be time enough for the details later," Candamir interrupted. "If we really intend to leave tomorrow, we must get to work. Those who came in the *Falcon* have an easy job, as we don't have anything to pack up. But the rest of you surely do."

Laughing, the people headed back to their caves or to the makeshift pens they had built for their sheep, and started preparing for this new and hopefully final departure.

When the crowd had dispersed, Candamir caught sight of his brother. "Hacon!" he cried, patting him on the shoulder, his eyes gleaming. "Did you hear? We are leaving tomorrow for our new home."

"That's great, Brother. I can hardly wait."

"Why then the sad face? Has something happened?"

Hacon shook his head. "Everything is all right, except...Gunda's child is coming."

Candamir's smile widened. "Is it?" But when he saw that Hacon couldn't look him in the eye, he abruptly turned serious. "Anything wrong with her?"

"I don't know. She's been screaming since last night."

Candamir clicked his tongue disapprovingly. "That's no way for the daughter of a Frisian chieftain to behave, is it? Did you call for Brigitta?"

Hacon nodded. "She was there all night."

"And what does she say?"

"Nothing. You know how she is—she threw the slaves out of the cave, and me too."

Candamir nodded and placed the loose end of the bull's rope in his brother's hand. "Here, tie him up somewhere. Half of the cows also belong to us. See that they don't run off into the forest."

He turned and started climbing up to his cave. Leaning against the warm, sunny rock face next to the entrance, he was relieved to hear that Gunda's voice was still quite strong. He knew he didn't really have anything to worry about unless she stopped screaming before the child came. Nevertheless, he felt sorry for her. Her wailing sounded dreadful, and he pitied her. But he did not suffer pangs of conscience like he had occasionally observed in other men. After all, hadn't the gods ordained that childbirth should be accompanied by pain?

He waited with uncharacteristic patience, and after about an hour the murmurings inside the cave became louder and more excited. "You must press down, girl, or it will never end," he heard Brigitta say, and then, "Oh, what do you mean you can't go on? Of course you can. You must. Come on now, press, press!"

After that, it did not take long. The screaming got louder again and then abated, followed by a tense, almost complete silence. Candamir held his breath, closed his eyes, and prayed silently. And then the furious bawling of an infant could be heard. Candamir opened his eyes again, leaned his head back against the rocky wall, and looked up at the cloudless sky. "Is it a boy?" he asked, stepping into the dark cave.

He had to blink several times before he could make out anything. Asta, Brigitta, and a few young women formed a circle around a bed of ferns in the middle of the room. At the sound of his voice, his sister quickly leaned forward and spread out a blanket. Then she turned to him and said with a smile, "Yes, Candamir, it's a boy."

Candamir stepped closer and looked over her shoulder. Neither Gunda nor the infant were a pleasant sight. The blanket covered only the lower half of her body, and on her naked belly a tiny, messy creature was stirring. Gunda's hair was sweaty and her face marked by exhaustion, but her eyes shone. Concealing his revulsion, Candamir forced himself to smile and nodded to her. "Well done," he said. Then he turned to Brigitta and asked, "Is he healthy?"

The old crone put her hand on his arm for a moment and said, "He is healthy and blessed by the gods, Candamir—the first child to be born in Catan. It is just as I have foreseen. Odin will be his patron god."

Candamir nodded mutely, the lump in his throat preventing a response.

"Wait outside," Brigitta ordered matter-of-factly. "We will bring him to you shortly. Off with you now, you have no business being here."

When Asta finally stepped out into the sunshine and handed Candamir his son, the infant had been cleaned, but he was red as a lobster, and his face was wrinkled like a winter apple.

"It will be all right," Asta assured him. "Believe me, in a few days he will be almost as handsome as you are. Just look, he has your black hair, do you see?"

Candamir nodded, fascinated, and hesitantly took his son. He was as light as a blade of grass. His eyes were open and of a radiant blue, but he seemed to be staring into space. Candamir held the child up toward the sun, spotted his friend down below on the beach, and bellowed, "Osmund! Look! It is a son! He is Catan's first son!"

That evening they lit a bonfire on the beach to celebrate both the birth of Candamir's son and their departure from the bay. The settlers who had remained behind at the bay had not let the six days pass idly. They had boiled seawater to obtain salt and had gone out fishing, discovering that the abundance and variety of life in the waters around Catan was just as great as in the forest. At low tide they had made their way around the rocks, exploring the neighboring bays, where the sandy coast changed to a rocky shore and finally to steep cliffs. In one of these expeditions, Hacon and Wiland had caught sight of small, long-haired goats high up on the cliffs. They could no doubt catch these animals and keep them for milk, meat, and wool, as Hacon proudly told his brother.

"And that we will, Brother," Candamir promised with a laugh. "I swear, before long we will have so much livestock that we won't know how to manage it all."

He laughed, in fact, all evening, bursting with happiness and high spirits. The women had brewed a drink from fermented sheep's milk that didn't actually taste very good, but was marvelously intoxicating. People kept coming up to him with a cup, congratulating him on his son, and Candamir drank everything they gave him. All his neighbors and friends seemed to share in his joy, regarded the birth of his son as a good omen, and were looking forward to the next day and to the place where they would establish their new village. Candamir thought the people looked more alive than ever. Even the eyes of the old folks were sparkling with expectation, and Catan's sun had taken the sickly pallor from their faces.

"What a good, strong people we will be," he said to Osmund and Asta, who had sat down with him in the sand.

Carrying his son on his shoulders, carefully holding the child's hands with his thumb and forefinger, Osmund regarded his friend with a smile. "And what will you name the boy, Candamir? Ole, I assume, after your father?"

It was customary to name boys after their late grandfathers in order to keep alive the memory of the deceased. But Candamir unexpectedly shook his head and looked at his sister. "I thought perhaps Nils, if that's all right with you?"

"You would do that?" Asta asked incredulously.

"Why not? He was young and would have been entitled to sail with us and discover this wonderful land. Fate determined otherwise, but at least his memory should live on here. Moreover, he was my brother-in-law."

"He was," Asta said. "Nevertheless, you never once in your life spoke a word with him, and the only time you met him, you broke his nose."

Candamir shrugged with a shamefaced grin. "I was only sixteen and blinded by Father's hatred and diatribes against Nils's clan. But it is never too late to admit one's errors—at least that's what my Saxon says."

Asta was moved by Candamir's kind gesture and briefly squeezed his hand. "Thank you, Brother. And since you are in such a magnanimous mood, why don't you pay a short visit to Gunda? After all, she played an important part in your great joy, and even though she almost died, you have practically ignored her since your return."

He nodded impatiently. "I will go to her. Later."

"If she had such a difficult birth, she will hardly be able to walk ten miles or more tomorrow," Osmund said. "We'll have to carry her."

Candamir shrugged, unconcerned. "Tjorv and Nori can take care of that. As I already said, we fortunately have nothing we need to take along."

Osmund disagreed. "I have a one-year-old son, a high seat, two cows, a young bull, and a servant with a broken leg, and only one healthy slave to help me."

Olaf came forward with Siglind, one hand on her elbow, a cup in the other. "You can borrow as many of my servants as you wish," he offered.

Osmund shook his head. "Thank you, Uncle, but I can make out all right," he answered politely, though a bit stiff. Candamir suspected that Olaf's hand on Siglind's arm displeased his friend as much as it did him.

"As you wish, lad. You mustn't think I want to patronize or embarrass you, but you are my nephew and have a right to my assistance. Don't forget that."

"I am truly grateful to you," Osmund said.

His uncle turned to Candamir and changed the topic. "I too want to congratulate you warmly and wish your son the blessing of the gods."

"Very kind of you," Candamir replied, making little effort to conceal his suspicions.

"Perhaps you think this is not the right moment, but I must speak with you about your Saxon slave," Olaf continued.

*I knew it,* Candamir thought grimly. "What of him?"

"You know very well. He humiliated my son and tore the weapon from his hand."

"Really? If you think Jared was guiltless in the matter, why is he walking around with a black eye tonight?"

Olaf waved this off. "Because he behaved like a fool and came running to me instead of settling the score himself. But that's not the issue here, Candamir. There are rules each of us must obey—that goes for you, and even more for your servant. He threatened a free man with a weapon. He can fall on his knees and thank his god that all I demand as punishment is his hand."

Candamir stood up slowly. "My slave did not threaten anyone with a weapon, and he will keep his hand."

"Suppose you are wrong about that..."

Candamir shrugged his shoulders. Now that he was standing up, he could feel how drunk he was; regardless, he knew how to conceal the signs. He didn't sway, and his voice was not slurred. "Jared was furious because he looked foolish in front of the women, that's all. His accusations are completely groundless. My Saxon did nothing wrong."

"Well, since there are five witnesses apart from yourself, it shouldn't be hard to get to the bottom of this and prove Jared's accusation, should it?"

"Forgive me for interfering," Siglind murmured with feigned humility, "but I am afraid I cannot testify for Jared, Olaf, as I was not looking and didn't see what happened. Inga, Asi, and I were kneeling on the ground examining a plant."

Olaf let go of her arm and looked at her for a moment. Then he nodded slightly. "I see." He turned expectantly to Osmund, who said apologetically, "I wasn't there, Uncle. When I got back from the river, it was all over."

"So the only one left is the smith," Candamir said, "but after that little disagreement about your broken sword...well." He clicked his tongue as if he regretted this unfortunate combination of circumstances.

Siglind turned away because she couldn't keep a straight face and took Roric from Osmund's shoulders. "Come, little one. You can't keep your eyes open. Shall we go and look for Cudrun?" She took her leave with a gracious nod and disappeared in the darkness.

Osmund and Candamir exchanged a furtive grin.

Olaf was still scowling. For a moment he stared after Siglind, but then he looked Candamir in the eye and shook his finger at him. "You and I know that Jared is telling the truth. He may sometimes act like a fool, but he is no liar."

"I didn't say he was," Candamir said.

"Then we agree. You have seven days' time to bring me the Saxon's hand."

Candamir rolled his eyes. "O mighty Tyr. Were you out in the sun too long, Olaf? I need my Saxon, and I need him healthy."

Olaf came another step closer. "It's shameful, the power this foreigner has gained over you," Olaf said. "For his sake you flout the ancient laws of your people?"

"I said from the start that a new homeland offers a good opportunity to introduce a few new laws. While ours may be old, not all of them are reasonable or just. Whatever the Saxon did, he probably saved the lives of the others, not the least of whom was your firstborn son. And I won't allow him to be punished for that."

Olaf snorted contemptuously. "All right then, since you apparently are not able to understand what I'm saying to you, I will express myself more clearly. *Your* slave insulted *my* son. And I advise you not to pick a fight with me. You owe me something, and if you don't give me what I demand you will have to give me something else, sooner or later. Nobody gets away with not paying me what they owe. Do you understand me now?"

Bewildered, Candamir thought, *So I owe you now? It was just a week ago that I stood by your side, sword in hand, ready to defend you from the others. And though in the end it was probably the storm that saved your miserable life, it would have no doubt come too late had it not been for Osmund, Harald, and myself.* But of course, it was unthinkable to say that out loud. If Olaf really meant to be so dishonorable as to withhold the gratitude he owed him, then there was not the slightest thing Candamir could do about it, and so he simply answered, "I understand you wish to threaten me, Olaf."

"And you would be well advised not to ignore the threat."

Candamir brushed him off. "Right. I'll be so scared I won't be able to sleep a wink." Then he nodded to his friend and said, "I'm going to look in on my son and his mother. Good night, Osmund."

"May you dream of your son's great deeds, and may all your dreams be fulfilled." This was not an unusual blessing on a new father, but the warmth with which Osmund pronounced it left no doubt where he stood in the dispute.

Olaf gave him a strange, almost amused look before turning away and leaving his nephew alone by the fire with Asta.

"Oh, Osmund," she murmured anxiously, "no good can come from this."

"No," he agreed reluctantly, staring for a while into the flames. Then he looked at her again and shook his head. "I have high regard for my uncle, Asta."

"Yes, I know."

"I believe in most cases his intentions are better than your brother will admit. But in this matter, Olaf is wrong. For this reason, Candamir must stand up to him, no matter how it all ends."

More out of sorts than concerned, Candamir climbed back to the cave that was to shelter his family for the last time. He found Gunda and the newborn child in his bed behind the screen. At a safe distance, a small tallow lamp stood on the rocky floor, casting a light on the two sleeping forms. The women had washed Gunda and combed her hair. Except for the dark shadows under her eyes, nothing suggested the difficult struggle she had been through. She had pulled the cover down to her navel. Her son was lying on her belly, his head between her heavy, milk-filled breasts.

Candamir sat down beside them, leaning back against the rock wall. It was a poignant picture, a living symbol of fertility, a promise of a future of blessings. Filled with sudden apprehension, he placed his hand on Gunda's forehead, but she was not feverish. There was no reason to be concerned, Asta had told him. Gunda was robust and at sixteen just the right age. His sister probably was right. The Frisian looked peaceful and radiant. He looked longingly at her swollen nipples, wondering what it would be like to suck on them and taste her milk.

But before he could act on this unseemly thought, Gunda woke up. Her big, blue eyes looked up at Candamir. With her left hand she reached for her son, laying her palm protectively on his little head with a smile.

"Will you acknowledge him as your child?"

"Of course. In fact, I have already, and I've come to tell you how grateful I am to you, Gunda."

With her free right hand she reached out for him. Her fingers closed around his with surprising strength. "I've been thinking, Master."

"Have you?"

"I know you never really believed that my father is a nobleman, but it's true. If we had met in my country, I would have been a girl from a good family with a sizable dowry."

Candamir guessed where this was leading. "Gunda…"

"No, please hear me out," she insisted in a whisper. "Everything turned out differently, and I have become your slave. But now we are in a new land where the old rules no longer have the same importance as before. You said so yourself, didn't you? You…you could take me as your wife—it would not be a disgrace. I am from a family as good as your own. You need a wife, not just a bed companion. You will have an important role in establishing this new community. You may even become a more important man than your father ever was. For that, you need a wife who supports you and can help you maintain that position. I could be that wife—I was brought up to fill that role, Candamir."

He tore his hand away when she said his name.

The corner of her mouth quivered, but she held his gaze.

He shook his head. "No, Gunda."

"Why not?"

The honest answer would have been, *Because you slept with Osmund.* At least that was half the answer, but it was the other half that slipped out: "Because I want someone else."

Once he had put it in words, he knew it was the truth. How simple it suddenly seemed, though it had plagued him since they had left the Cold Islands: he wanted Siglind, even if she was stubborn and had a tongue sharper than his hunting knife, and was not a virgin and could not even bear children—he wanted her.

Gunda was not stupid. She knew who he meant. "The only question is whether you can get her," she said cautiously.

He nodded. It was just as likely that Siglind would choose Olaf, Osmund, or even the Saxon.

"And even if you do," she continued, "how do you think Osmund would feel if you snapped her up from under his nose? Hasn't he just lost a wife who meant the world to him? Do you want to be responsible for it happening again? Isn't he closer to you than your own brother?"

Candamir stood up. "Let's be clear, Gunda. You are the mother of my son, and as I already said, I am grateful to you. The more children you give me, the higher I will value you, but it will not change your state. I don't wish to offend you..." He realized that was a lie as soon as he said it. He wanted to punish her for so readily perceiving his greatest concern and putting it into words. Nevertheless, he repeated, "I don't wish to offend you, but it would be better for you not to have any false hopes. I will not take you as my wife no matter what happens. And if I want your advice or your opinion, I will ask you for it. Do you understand?"

"Yes, Master, of course," she replied in a choked voice.

Furious, he reached for the nearest blanket and lay down next to his sleeping brother on the hard ground. He felt wretched.

Despite their many losses during the voyage, more than two hundred and fifty people started out the next morning for the interior of the island. They drove their sheep before them, heavily loaded down with their belongings and provisions for the three-day trek, but the mood was almost exuberant. Even the light rain that set in early that morning did not dampen their spirits. It was a warm and gentle rain, and the settlers were accustomed to much worse.

Olaf had ordered Jared to stay behind in the bay with his brothers, Lars and Gunnar, and two servants to wait for Berse's return.

The young man was not happy about that, but said politely, "Of course, Father. Just as you wish."

"Wait ten days, and if they are not back by then, follow us. As soon as we arrive, we will build a raft to explore the river, and if we determine it is navigable, we'll come and fetch our ships."

Jared had nodded. "I hope so, Father. It would be sad to have to leave the *Sea Dragon* behind."

All the ship owners felt that way. No one knew for certain if they would ever need their ships again, but for as far back as they could remember the ships had been a symbol both of prosperity and their venturesome spirit.

Before leaving, Olaf had put his hands on his sons' shoulders, one after the other. "I have no objection to your whiling away the time in the forest rounding up a few cattle, but do take care. I want you back unharmed."

Blushing at this unaccustomed display of fatherly affection, Jared, Gunnar, and Lars had promised to be careful.

Tjorv and Nori carried Osmund's injured slave on a litter made of branches and blankets. Hacon and Osmund's uninjured servant carried Gunda and little Nils on a second litter. The other maids and Asta had tied the children to their backs with sheets. Candamir and Osmund each had a heavy pack on their shoulders containing blankets, dishes, and other household goods donated by generous neighbors, and they drove their livestock ahead of them. Siglind, who accompanied them, had the lightest burden of all: the Saxon's sealskin pouch.

Inga was walking with the group in front. "Why didn't you throw all that rubbish into the sea?" she teased Siglind. "You should have filled the pouch with salt instead. The gods only know where we are going to get salt in the future, as we'll no longer be close to the ocean."

Siglind dismissed the thought with an indulgent smile. "As Olaf already said, we just need to go down the river."

The scouts were out front leading the procession, with the rest following eagerly behind and bombarding them with questions. What lived in the forest? The river? In the grassland, and the mountains beyond? As if the scouts had been exploring this land for six years and not just six days. Often they had no answer, and Osmund had to repeat again and again, "We just don't know yet, we'll have to wait and see, but surely Odin must have provided for that."

Candamir enjoyed the leadership role that had fallen to him so unexpectedly. He had realized during their ocean voyage that being responsible for so many people did not feel like a burden. On the ship it had been natural that he gave the orders, as the *Falcon* belonged to him and he was the only experienced sailor on board. Here the situation was completely different. Catan was a great mystery to them all, and yet men of his father's generation still turned to him for advice, and he felt flattered. In addition, it annoyed Olaf, as was easy to see from his scowl, and that added considerably to Candamir's pleasure.

It was not easy to find a camping place for such a large group of men and animals, but Osmund and Candamir kept up a fast pace and by nightfall reached the clearing with the single oak tree. A flock of white ravens rose from the crown of the tree and amid much squawking flew off to the protection of the forest.

Hacon gently put down the litter he was carrying and rolled his shoulders. His brother had spelled him several times in the course of the day, but during the last hour, the boy had suspected his arms might simply fall off. He settled down on the soft earth in the shadow of the mighty tree.

"Thank you, Hacon," Gunda said. She lowered her eyes, as if embarrassed to cause him so much trouble. "Tomorrow I can definitely walk a bit."

He cockily waved her off. "That's not necessary. You hardly weigh more than a feather." He had noticed all day that something seemed to be bothering her. Maybe she was still exhausted from her labor. In any case, he tried to cheer her up, gently passing his finger over the forehead of his tiny nephew and saying, "I think our Nils is already heavier than you. He's a splendid fellow."

His remark produced the intended effect. Gunda smiled, though only for a moment. "Nils?" she asked pensively.

"Candamir told Asta last night that this would be his name. Don't tell me that he didn't mention it to you."

"Oh, but we've hardly had a chance to talk."

"Nils—after Asta's husband," he explained, a bit embarrassed by his brother's atypical—and belated—attempt at reconciliation.

*Of course,* she thought bitterly. *Any name would do, except that of his father.*

Asta came over, offering them each a cup of milk. "Here, it's still warm."

Hacon drank so eagerly that little streams of milk dribbled down from each corner of his mouth. When he finally put the cup down, gasping, Asta shook her head. "You drink like a little boy, even if you have become strong as a man."

He handed the cup back, grinning broadly, held up his arm to make a fist, and admired his muscles attentively. It was true; he was surprised to see that the many hours on the rowing bench had not been in vain.

At just this moment Candamir happened to come by. "Let me feel it, too," he said. "I always wanted to know what such a puny muscle feels like."

Hacon quickly lowered his arm, but Candamir was faster. His huge hand could still easily encircle his brother's upper arm. "Hm," he said, in a sarcastic tone. But when he saw Asta's pleading look, he let Hacon go, passed his hand roughly through his brother's hair, and added, "Twice as much as when we left. That's not saying much, little brother, but you are coming along. Last fall you never could have done what you managed so easily today."

Hacon stared down at the grass, his face beaming.

Wiland sauntered over. "Come on, Hacon, let's climb this tree."

The idea excited Hacon, who had apparently quite forgotten his tired arms. Asta was about to object, but Candamir stopped her with a shake of his head. He went over to the huge tree trunk with the boys and helped them reach the lowest bough.

When he went back to join his sister, he scolded her. "You're holding him back with all your silly fussing."

As usual, she took the reprimand without complaint and gave him a cup of the warm milk that was so marvelously sweet and rich that it soothed his gnawing hunger. "I know you mean well, but you are not doing him any favor," he added softly.

Asta said no more, but gave some milk to her son, who was tugging impatiently at her skirt. Siglind, on the other hand, didn't think much of this restraint that Candamir thought so desirable in a woman. She came over to them with an armful of firewood, dropped it casually on the ground, and said, "No matter how badly you treat your brother, he will never become a rough fellow like you."

"No? And why do you believe that?"

"He's got too much sense for that."

"Well, thanks a lot," he replied caustically. "My father used to say that reasoning power grew along with that of one's limbs. He was a very intelligent man, who even composed songs at times, but still almost always won the stone-throwing contest at the midsummer games."

"Songs?" she asked, interested. "What kind of songs?"

"Oh..." Candamir was suddenly embarrassed. He bent over the wood and stacked it up in order to keep his hands busy and so he would no longer have to look into those unsettling blue eyes. "Songs about his ancestors' great deeds, and the gods...all sorts of things."

"They were very beautiful," Asta interjected.

"Sing one for us," Siglind asked.

"Maybe after we eat," he replied evasively.

Candamir was spared though, as he had hoped, because there was only one topic of conversation during the meal and thereafter—the fiery mountain. Not just Hacon and Wiland, but some of the men also had climbed the tall tree to get a larger view of the surroundings, and they all had seen the same frightening sight: the red glow in the distance.

"One thing is certain," said Brigitta, who was sitting between Osmund and her stupid son Haflad. "Such a mountain always means danger."

Ever since the people had arrived in Catan, they listened to Brigitta more attentively than before, and with more respect. In the old homeland, none of them had felt a need for an intermediary between themselves and the gods, but here they had moved closer to the world of gods and ancient songs than they had ever dreamt possible, uncomfortably close for some of them, and suddenly they appreciated Brigitta.

Nevertheless, Inga asked timidly, “But wasn’t Tanuri right, Brigitta? Fire is one of the four elements. How could a place be perfect without fire?”

The old woman smiled at her. It was no secret she had a soft spot for Siward’s youngest child and wanted very much to pass her knowledge along to Inga. But up to now the girl’s father had always prevented that from happening, as he had a great fear of witchcraft.

“Well, in a certain way Tanuri was right,” the old woman replied. “Unfortunately, her view of the world was not as pure as yours, nor her heart as innocent. Tanuri was a spoiled, selfish child.”

Many of her listeners gasped. “But Odin said that she was wiser than he himself,” Candamir protested.

Brigitta cackled. “Even the father of the gods can sometimes be a lovesick fool, and then his judgment is as clouded as that of ordinary men. Tanuri was clever and underhanded, but not wise. She wanted to play with Odin. That is, she wanted to play with fire, like all foolish children. The fiery mountain on this island is much more Tanuri’s doing than Odin’s. The mountain represents her more than him—it is what she is, and not what he is.”

“And so the mountain is the only evil thing in this land?” Siward asked.

“No,” she replied firmly. “Nothing is evil in this land. The only evil is that which lives in our own hearts, and that we have brought along with us. The land itself is flawless, but the mountain is dangerous, just like a spoiled, selfish child.”

“Unpredictable,” Inga murmured.

“Hm, possibly.” She nodded her silvery head reluctantly. “But you must remember that this is Odin’s land. His will governs all things here, even those with Tanuri’s traits. Therefore it is crucial for us not to lose his good will. He chose us and led us here.” She raised a finger and tapped Osmund lightly on the chest. “You above all, as you were the first to set foot on this island. We all owe Odin something for this, and you in particular."

"Tell me what it is, and I will give it to him if I can."

"Oh, you can, it's not difficult. You must honor him. All of you. And not halfheartedly as you used to at the midsummer festival or the Yule festival or when you had some special request. *Really* honor him, I mean, pay homage to him. To start out, you must not tolerate any god who wants to destroy Odin's power," she concluded, her eyes falling on the queen of the Cold Islands.

Siglind raised her chin, ready for a fight. Asta placed her hand inconspicuously on Siglind's arm, but she shook it off just as discreetly. "Why are you staring at me like that?" she asked Brigitta.

"Isn't it true that you are carrying the Saxon's book and his god's accursed cross in your bag?"

"And suppose I were? How does what I carry in my bag concern you?"

"Didn't you hear what I just said? It is to Odin that we owe our respect and allegiance, not this foolish Christian god."

"I am not contradicting you," Siglind lied, "but what harm can runes on parchment sheets do to a mighty god like Odin?"

"None," Brigitta said. "But they can harm you and young Hacon, and who knows who else. They are dangerous runes, I know."

"That's just ridiculous."

"Oh, is it? Then throw them into the fire."

"No." The full measure of her royal pride, which she so skillfully employed, lay in this refusal, and both Candamir and Osmund admired her courage.

In fact, Siglind was terrified; she could feel the cold sweat on her chest and back. As far back as she could remember, she had always gone on the attack when she found herself cornered. In the four years she had been Cnut's wife, this tendency had brought her many a bruise and a few broken bones. Part of her present fear was based on this memory, but she also feared the power of this spiteful old woman. She was afraid because she was alone and powerless among these strangers, but most of all she was afraid of losing the Bible.

But no one could have suspected her true feelings, not even Brigitta, who saw through most pretenses. She leaned forward. "So you are trying to make us believe that these runes have no power over you, but you still refuse to burn them?"

Siglind prayed to Jesus Christ, as Austin had advised her. She was not really surprised that it worked, but by the speed with which Heaven sent her the flash of inspiration. "It is not the runes of the carpenter god that I wish to preserve, but the Saxon has begun writing a chronicle of our trip and our settlement of Catan in this book."

"A *what*?" Candamir asked with a blank look.

"A…report, so that nothing is forgotten. How Odin led us here, for example. Or all the great deeds that all of you will perform here in the future. Isn't it a good thing to write down all these events for our descendants?"

Brigitta shook her head impatiently. "We will create songs to celebrate our deeds."

"But songs are transitory," Siglind said. "At first they change a bit, then they become garbled, and finally hardly anything of the truth is left. Just take the Song of Catan. Who but you even knew it anymore? And exactly how did it go originally? If it had been written down, we would not have forgotten so much about the story of the island."

"Well, she has a point," Candamir murmured. "There's something to be said for such a…what is it called?"

"Chronicle," Siglind repeated.

Candamir looked at Brigitta and nodded. "For such a chronicle." Not that he cared so much about it, but he suspected that this book was very dear to Siglind. His Saxon, he knew, would no doubt throw himself into the maw of the fiery mountain if he lost it. Candamir had no objection to Brigitta's demand for more reverence for the gods—he knew that he had never really taken it seriously enough—but he couldn't imagine that Odin would take issue with a few animal skins scribbled with runes.

"We need not decide that today, in any case," Osmund said calmly. "I agree with Candamir that such a report can be useful for future generations and more reliable than songs that are only entrusted to people's memory. But we can do something more," he said, looking directly at Brigitta. "We can build a hall for our gods in our new village, a place where we can sacrifice to them on religious holidays and do anything else that you think we should."

It was an unusual, nearly unheard-of suggestion. There were in fact such places of worship in a town in the southern part of the old homeland and in Ireland, Olaf told them, though they were very rare.

Brigitta's eyes began to glow in the darkness. *No doubt she can already see herself as a high priestess in such a temple,* Siglind thought uncharitably.

The old woman nodded at Osmund. "So be it," she declared.

They discussed excitedly what such a hall ought to be like, whether it should be a building like those that people lived in, or a sacred grove of trees, and whether or not a hallowed spring was essential. The Saxon's Bible and the dangerous runes it contained were forgotten, at least for the time being. Osmund caught Siglind's eye and winked at her. She lowered her head and smiled.

Candamir crept away from the fire to gaze toward the southwest, where the fiery mountain stood.

Late in the afternoon of the third day they arrived at their destination. The weather remained dry except for a few gentle rain showers, and at noon the clouds moved away. The sky was blue over the edge of the forest, the river, and the broad grassland. The sight that presented itself to the settlers was of such rare beauty that for the moment not even Siward or Haflad could find any fault with it. The scouts were also seeing the land for the first time under a blue sky and sunshine, and they were more delighted than ever. The grassland stretched out over gentle hills that looked like waves on a calm sea, all the way to the foot of the mountains. In the distance, but still close enough to be clearly visible, a herd of wild horses was peacefully grazing. Calmly and serenely the river flowed toward the sea, and in the reeds along the shore birds were singing.

Brigitta had placed her hands on her hips and had taken her time to look around. "Yes," she finally said, "this is the place."

Work began the next morning. Olaf, Siward, and some other experienced farmers agreed that the grassland on the south shore of the river was good enough to plant rye, which was undemanding and sowed near the surface. It wasn't even necessary to turn over the soil. It would be quite sufficient to make the little furrows for the seed with sharp sticks. But for barley, wheat, and legumes the situation was different—the land would have to be cleared before it could be planted. Thus they couldn't expect to have beer until the year after. However, there were so many wild bees in the forest that they could hope for a good crop of honey, and mead was a sweet, delectable consolation for a lack of beer.

The men used the first trees they felled to build a raft. Then they stretched a long rope across the river. Everyone contributed whatever walrus leather they had, as this was the sturdiest material for that purpose. The raft was attached to this rope, and in no time they had a provisional ferry to take the women safely to the other side in order to cultivate the rye fields. With a second raft, Eilhard's sons set off down river to find a route to the bay where they had landed. The other men cut down trees and dragged the trunks to the riverbank for lumber.

"Timber!" Osmund and Candamir shouted, and Nori and Tjorv jumped to safety. It was a fir tree more than sixty feet high. It fell slowly and elegantly, its needles whistling and crackling as if the wind were passing through them. It landed with a tremendous impact, and the men set about cutting the branches and twigs from the trunk. Then they grabbed hold and everyone pulled together, including Hacon, Harald's son Godwin, Osmund's slave, and some other woodcutters working nearby, and carried the heavy trunk over the already numerous stumps down to the collection point. This was still only a few steps away, but as they progressed they would naturally get farther and farther from it. And they didn't yet know how to move the heavy oak and beech trunks or how to pull the roots out of the earth.

Candamir sat down on one of the fallen trunks and wiped his forehead with his arm. "What we need are draft animals," he said again.

"There are so many things we need," Osmund replied, sitting down next to him. "Not everything is easy to get hold of, but we'll have draft animals in a few days, so stop complaining."

Osmund was right—he worried too much, instead of enjoying the mild spring days here in the forest. The arrival of humans, the noise of their voices and axes, and not least the felling of the trees had at first so frightened the birds that they had fallen completely silent. But they had become accustomed to the echoing, rhythmic chopping and had started to chirp again. The day before, the forest workers had sighted a flock of white ravens.

The fragrant mixture of spring flowers, resin, and freshly cut wood was intoxicating. Even years later, the odor of new wood would remind Candamir of the excitement and energy of these first few weeks in Catan. Chopping down trees was backbreaking work, but he, like so many of the other men, loved to push his limits and prove his strength. An unacknowledged contest was in progress, with each of the men secretly counting how many logs his team had brought to the future village by nightfall, and how many were brought by the others.

"Hacon, Godwin, get us something to drink," Candamir ordered. "Tjorv, Nori, roll the logs to the shore, but not in the water, do you hear? Otherwise they'll float down the river. Later, we'll throw a rope around them, put them in the water, and drag them to the building site. When you have them all down by the river, you can take a break."

Candamir pressed his left hand against his tired back surreptitiously. He waited until the slaves and the boys had left before saying softly to Osmund, "Up to now I haven't actually realized what the sinking of the *Falcon* means for me. I am…destitute."

"But it won't stay that way for long here," Osmund replied optimistically.

More and more, Candamir was assailed by doubts. It wasn't just the sheep and horses they had lost—they had absolutely nothing. The axes they were working with were given to them reluctantly by Haflad, and only at the persistent urging of his mother. Brigitta's support was as valuable as it was unexpected. Candamir and Osmund had earned a reward, she had told her disgruntled son and all those standing around—a reward for having brought them alive and well to Catan on board the *Falcon* and then having found this place. They were beloved by Odin, and the whole community was deeply indebted to them.

And so they had gotten the axes. But Candamir's tunic was so full of holes and rips that there was scarcely any point to putting it on—it provided neither warmth nor protection. His trousers were hardly any better, and Asta didn't even have a needle and thread to mend them with. In addition, since all his sheep had drowned, he wouldn't have any wool in the near future to make new clothes.

"Well, at least we'll soon have plenty of cattle," said Osmund, interrupting his thoughts. "Olaf found five more bulls yesterday."

Olaf was not personally involved in clearing the land but had assigned the work to his four strongest slaves. He himself spent his days in the forest rounding up cattle. He already had a considerable herd, and all the bulls he found he had castrated, just as Osmund and Candamir had done with theirs. Not only were the oxen suited for hard work, but the placid cows could also be harnessed for it, and it rarely affected their milk supply. It just took a few days to get them accustomed to the yoke. Siglind had taken on this task, as she had a way with animals, and not just with horses. In two days, she had promised, the woodsmen could count on having the first team.

But the greatest catastrophe was the loss of the seed onboard the *Falcon*, and neither Candamir nor Osmund knew how to make up for that.

"Clearing the land is now our most urgent task," Olaf had declared the first evening. "Naturally, each of us wants to own and cultivate his own land, but I warn you against each starting to cut wood in a different place. Let's do it all together, and in this way we will make quicker progress. By the fall, we will divide the land we have cleared into equal parcels. We can continue to clear the land all winter long if the weather allows. This new land we'll divide up again in the spring. And so on.

We should keep doing that until every household has sufficient acreage, and after that each one can decide for himself whether or not to clear additional land from the forest."

Everyone knew that it was a sensible proposal, though most of them found it strange not to work on land they could regard as their own, as normally a free man would never think of cultivating land that didn't belong to him. Nevertheless, they all recognized the rationale for proceeding together. When seeding time came in the fall, however, each would go back to his old way of doing things, even though at first on a small scale. And then Osmund and Candamir would stand there empty-handed. The same was true of the summer rye that had to be sown within the next few days.

"Maybe Brigitta will announce that it is Odin's will for everyone to give us a handful of rye seed," Candamir said sarcastically. "I can't think of any other solution."

"Who knows? If you look hard enough, you may even find grain growing wild in this country," Osmund said optimistically.

"Sure." Candamir sighed. "And if we look a little harder, we'll no doubt find trees with ready-baked loaves of bread on them…"

Osmund laughed, but at the same time nudged him in the ribs. "Don't mock what the gods have provided for us."

"You're right. But there's no sense in hoping for a miracle. We need the seed *now*, and you know as well as I do that there's only one man among us who has enough to give us what we need."

Osmund nodded but didn't respond. Instead, he pointed toward the river. "Here comes Hacon with some water for us."

"And about time, too," Candamir said. "You could die of thirst waiting for my brother." And when the boy got closer, he asked, "What took you so long? Did you have to fetch the water from the other side of the river, or what?"

Hacon shook his head with a smile and handed him the pitcher of water. "Berse came back, and guess what? He sailed up the river with the *Wavewolf*. Right behind him came Jared, Lars, Gunnar, and their slaves in the *Dragon*. Fortunately, the wind is blowing from the west."

"Great," Osmund said happily. "The river is navigable; I knew it."

"It took us twelve days," the hunchbacked shipwright told the group assembled around the campfire that evening. "As you know, we sailed down the west coast. At first we saw only high cliffs, until we got to the mouth of this river that has two branches surrounding a swampy, wooded area. Beyond the river the coast is still rocky, but flatter. The land is forested and rises gently as you go inland. But on the morning of the second day, the land changed. All day we saw nothing but a black, stony wasteland. At dusk we cast anchor, and as it got dark we could see a fiery glow in the distance over the wasteland. It must be..."

"The fiery mountain. Yes, we saw it," Olaf said, nodding.

Berse was evidently relieved that this unfavorable news was not a surprise to them and continued his account. Apparently, beyond the wasteland the terrain was flat, richly forested, traversed by many waterways, and possibly swampy. They had stopped for the night near the mouth of a river, where an army of frogs had been croaking so loudly they had been able to hear them out at sea. When they reached the south coast on the fifth day, they saw the foothills of a very high chain of mountains. The lower slopes were forested, but higher up there were no more trees, but either grass or low-growing bushes. Above this region, only bare, gray rock was visible, where many eagles nested. But even on the summits there was no snow.

It seemed the legend was correct—this land had no snow cover in the winter. Beyond the mountains the coast became gentler, and they had seen many bays with long, sandy beaches. In one of them they cast anchor and went ashore for a few hours to explore the countryside. There, too, in the southeast of Catan, they found the soil fertile and mostly forested. More evergreens grew there than here in the northwest, and most of them were of a type unfamiliar to them, with gray bark, wide crowns, and long needles. Their resin had a heavy, aromatic fragrance, and perhaps this was what attracted the countless butterflies. At least Berse had never before seen them in such numbers, many of them large and more colorful than the rainbow. They had seen flowers there, too, such as poppies or thistles that didn't bloom in the old homeland until July. Possibly it was even milder down there than here, but not too dry like the land Olaf and other merchant sailors had told them they had seen on the far side of the Alps or the southern part of the Franks' country.

"The river we came to flowed from the mountains and was full of clear, cold water. We saw unfamiliar birds and animals, even a snake. My son Sigurd tried to catch it, figuring that since this land had nothing evil in it, the snake would be harmless. It bit him and got away. For two days, Sigurd was feverish. He groaned and vomited, but that was all. I told him that Odin and the giants had created this land to please a woman, not a careless fool like him."

Everyone laughed.

"The east coast was almost identical except for a plateau in the middle that we likewise explored by foot. We found marvelous grass there and saw more cattle than you can ever imagine—larger, darker, and shaggier than those you caught here in the forest. But I wouldn't want to tangle with the bulls. In the northeast the coast became more rugged and rockier, and finally we sighted the foothills of the mountains again." He pointed in the direction of the mountains that Harald, Asi, and the Saxon had gone to explore. "It must have been those. Who knows, perhaps there is one single mountain range extending across the whole country from the northeast to the southwest."

"That would explain why there could be a different climate on the east side than here," Olaf said.

Berse gave a slight nod. "We saw mountain goats or something similar, and wild horses. The coastal waters are full of fish and dolphins. There are no seals, as you assumed, Olaf. And nowhere did we see any signs of other human beings. If there are any, they must live far inland and avoid the sea and the coasts. But that would be strange—even though this land is large, it is still an island, and I've never heard of islanders that did not make their living fishing. If you want to know what I think, I believe we are alone here."

Everyone was quiet for a while, pondering all that Berse had told them.

"Here," the shipwright added, sticking his hand in the pouch on his belt and then holding it out for them to examine in the firelight. In his hand was a pearl the size of a pea, shimmering faintly in the light from the flames. "There is a reef in the southeast just off the coast. Sigurd dived there and brought this up with him."

Admiring oohs and aahs could be heard all around.

"And did you discover any place better suited than this one here to establish a village?" Siward finally asked.

"Didn't you hear what I said?" said Brigitta, cutting him short. "*Here* is the place. I saw it in the oracle."

Berse replied just the same, if only to take advantage of the opportunity to question the authority of the crone. "No. You wouldn't have to clear the land, of course, on the high plateau in the east, but it isn't accessible from the sea. Here, with this river, we can continue as seafarers in the future, which wouldn't be possible there. And who knows whether the land there might not turn out to be too dry in the summer. This land here…" He broke off and made a sweeping gesture to include the river, mountains, grassland, and forest.

"…is perfect, just as the song promised," Osmund said softly, finishing his sentence for him.

"So it is," the shipwright agreed.

Naturally, he and his crew had had to leave much unexplored in their circumnavigation of the island. Quite a few expeditions would still have to go out before they could say they knew their new homeland. But that was not urgent at the moment, they thought. A few wanted to set sail for the southeast to dive for pearls, explore the plateau, and perhaps catch the large cattle, but there would be time for all of that. Berse confirmed what Brigitta had told them from the start—in this land they had nothing to fear but the wrath of the gods.

"I know it's late, Uncle, but can I talk with you for just a moment?" Osmund asked Olaf quietly.

His uncle appeared neither reluctant nor surprised, even though Osmund had avoided him the last few days. "Certainly, come along to my modest home. If we are lucky, the new mead will be ready."

"Mead?" Osmund asked, astonished, as they walked along together by the shore. "At this time of year?"

"We still had honey left from last year," Olaf explained.

The settlers were living in temporary cabins. They had driven a few pointed posts into the ground, and the women had woven walls of twigs and evergreen branches or reeds between them. Those who still had tenting material used it as roofing to keep out the frequent rain showers. Those like Candamir and Osmund, who were not among the fortunate ones, covered their huts with leaves and branches, and occasionally got a little wet at night. That really didn't matter much, as the weather was mild.

Space was tight even in Olaf's comparatively roomy hut, Osmund noted as he entered behind his uncle. Nevertheless, the master of the house had a small room to himself, separated from the rest of the cabin by furs and blankets. Inside there was a stool and a trunk that could be used as a table, as well as a wide bed for Olaf and whichever of his young slaves he happened to choose as a companion for the night. One of them, a dainty, dark-haired girl from Ireland, entered and brought the mead to Olaf and his guest. Osmund watched her as she left, and her beauty made his eyes sparkle.

"The gods must truly love you, Uncle," he remarked with a smile.

Olaf raised a finger in warning. "No man should count on that too much." With the large cup in his hand, he sat down on the stool and gestured to Osmund to take a seat on the trunk. "Well? What can I do for you, my boy?"

Osmund could feel his heart pounding right up into his throat, and his hands were clammy. Embarrassed, he raised the cup to his lips and took a long, deep draught in order to gain time. The mead was delicious. For a few moments, the young man concentrated only on this pleasure that he had missed for so long. Then he pulled himself together. "I'd like to ask you for a loan, Uncle," he said. "A little rye and…two or three sheep, if that's possible. I'll pay it all back to you as soon as I can."

Olaf didn't answer at once. Apparently lost in thought, he stroked his graying beard with his left thumb. "I can imagine it is not easy to ask me for this—especially for you."

"I think nothing in my life has ever been that difficult," Osmund admitted. "But I don't know what else to do. When you have a son to think about, pride is something you can afford only up to a certain point."

His uncle nodded. "I don't wish to make this situation even more painful for you than it is already, Osmund, but the answer is no."

Osmund was stunned. Then he cleared his throat, put down the cup, and stood up. "In that case, there is nothing I can do but wish you a good night, Uncle."

"Stay seated," Olaf snapped at him. "We are not done yet."

Osmund folded his arms but remained standing. "Well?"

His uncle looked at him as if he were trying to read his thoughts or get to the bottom of something. "I'd like to help you," he said, and it sounded sincere. "But whatever I lent you, you would share with Candamir, wouldn't you? He is your foster brother, and I know how close you are to each other. Be honest."

Osmund lowered his arms and nodded. "Yes, you are right," he confessed.

"You see, that's the reason I can't do it. I have a feud with your friend, and I would rather pour my seed in the river than let him have bread made from it. I am sorry for you, Osmund, but you must decide. You have not exactly shown me the loyalty in this affair that a nephew owes to his uncle…"

"Does that mean I should have lied for you?" Osmund interrupted him heatedly. "I wasn't there, and I didn't see what happened."

"No, I would never ask you to tell a lie, but that wouldn't have been necessary, would it? We all know what happened, just as we all know that Candamir is in the wrong in this, no matter what the circumstances may have been. He is violating the law, and you took his side instead of trying to reason with him. Isn't that so?"

Osmund nodded reluctantly. "He is so fond of this slave," he tried to explain.

"That in itself is disturbing, for this Saxon has a bad influence on him," his uncle said.

Secretly, Osmund had to admit he was right. "But the facts seemed to support the Saxon. If he had not acted, Jared would probably be dead now."

"Better dead than humiliated."

"Perhaps. But Candamir would say, 'Better humiliated than dead.'"

"There you have it; it's just what I meant. This accursed, unbelieving Saxon alone is to blame if Candamir betrays the principles we have followed and which have defined us for as long as anyone can remember."

Osmund shook his head. "I don't think so, Uncle. Candamir was born with the tendency to rebel against rules such as they are, and to question everything considered immutable. His father stopped at nothing to try to wean him from that, but in vain. It's the way he is."

Olaf shrugged impatiently. "That may be. I have often thought that if it weren't for you, Candamir would have long ago done something foolish that would have cost him his life or at least would have led to his banishment. And I must confess, I would have shed no tears. It is to your credit that you have been so loyal to your friend, but you should take care not to let yourself get dragged into his foolish acts."

"Well," replied Osmund, smiling weakly, "I've done that all my life, Uncle. As far back as I can remember, I've always tried to keep my friend from dragging me into some hopeless jam. I'm not always successful, but it has become a fond habit of mine. And Candamir is right about one thing—so many hands are needed here that it would be stupid to cut anyone's off. Perhaps in a few years, but not now."

Olaf shook his head. "In hard times above all one must be careful not to water down the laws, or they will degenerate." But a moment later his stern look disappeared and he smiled good-naturedly at his nephew. "I can see that your position is basically reasonable and honorable, and that does not surprise me. But you must decide, Osmund, you must take a stand. If you want my seed and my sheep, you must swear to me that you will not give any of it to Candamir."

Now Osmund understood why Olaf took this unyielding position, but it did nothing to change his decision. "I can't do that."

The woolen blanket that served as a door to the back room was suddenly pushed aside, and Candamir walked in. "Lend him the grain and the animals, Olaf," he said brusquely. "You have my word that I won't accept a single grain nor a piece of his wool."

Osmund started to protest, but Olaf interrupted him. "You stood outside listening, did you? Why doesn't that surprise me?"

Osmund jumped to his feet because he was afraid Candamir might throw himself at Olaf, but his friend surprised him.

"No, I don't think you could put it that way," Candamir replied politely. "I was looking for Osmund, and Eilhard said he had seen the two of you together, so I came here. But your walls are only made of branches, and I couldn't help hearing your last words. And that's probably a good thing, because why should Osmund suffer just because there is a feud between the two of us? Give him the seed."

"No," Olaf told him. "He wouldn't have the heart to see you and your family in need."

"In this land no one has to suffer need," Candamir said.

"Be that as it may, you dine often enough at his table." It sounded offensive, as if Candamir were a sponger and not as if they simply visited each other regularly, as was customary between friends.

But Candamir didn't rise to this bait either. Hothead that he was, he wasn't so foolish as not to see that Olaf could be dangerous to him and his family. He knew caution was called for. "I'll get the seed somehow," he said confidently. "Osmund won't be tempted to ignore your wishes."

"And how will you manage to do that?" Olaf inquired. He sounded amused. "Since the death of your uncle Sigismund, you no longer have any close kin left. And your father's friend, good old Harald, lost everything, just like yourself. So tell me how do you intend to get your seed, and if you can convince me, Osmund will not leave empty-handed."

"Stop it," Osmund said. "That's disgraceful."

The two adversaries fell silent so that one might have thought the dispute was settled. In truth, Candamir was casting about for an answer and Olaf was lying in wait like a spider.

Finally Candamir nodded at him. "My brother and I will work for you."

"No, Candamir," Osmund protested. He knew that nothing good could come of that.

Candamir continued as if he hadn't heard him. "Every third day, from the start of Honey Moon until we sow the winter seed. Tell me what you need done, and we will do it—for rye, winter wheat, and barley." Seed was simply more important than sheep, he thought. Those would have to wait another year. In the meantime, someone would give him and his people a few cast-off clothes before their own rags fell off. "And because I will not be there every third day for clearing land, I'll give up one third of my plot."

"I think that would be very unjust," Osmund said, before his uncle could agree. "When the Saxon returns and helps with clearing, there will be three men from your household working every day in the forest, and on two out of three days there will be five, if we count Hacon. I, however, have only one slave fit for work at the moment, and I am still to get more land than you?"

"That's true," Olaf conceded.

"I insist on it," Candamir said. "I can't withhold my labor from the community without paying a price. So what do you say?"

Olaf pretended he needed a moment to think it over. He wanted to see Candamir sweat. But the young man showed uncharacteristic self-control, and neither his expression nor his manner betrayed his true feelings.

Finally, Olaf nodded. "All right. You can start by building me a house, and a decent one, if I may ask. I know you can do that—after all, I saw Osmund's hall in Elasund—so don't be tempted to trick me. My vote on the division of the land this fall at the *Thing* will depend entirely on how happy I am with your work. Now get out."

Candamir turned on his heel and left the little house. Osmund looked at his uncle, speechless, shaking his head, and with forced politeness wished him a pleasant evening, following his friend out into the night.

"Don't say a word," Candamir said between clenched teeth as they walked together through the darkness. "Do you understand? Don't say a word!"

Osmund complied, but just for a moment. “Why did you come looking for me?” he demanded.

“What? Oh, Cudrun came over earlier and said that one of your cows is calving—the reddish one with the little blaze. I went to take a look. It could be a difficult birth, so I thought it would be best to come and get you.”

Osmund nodded, but didn’t rush off to his cow. Instead, he stopped in front of Candamir’s hut and said, “You mustn’t do that, Candamir. You know very well that no good will come of it.”

“Maybe not,” his friend said in a quiet voice, “but you know damned well there is no other solution.”

“There *has* to be one.” Osmund sounded almost desperate.

Candamir laughed, though he felt more like crying. “Don’t worry, I swear to you by all my ancestors that I will not take up arms against your uncle and set off a blood feud between your family and mine. In fact, since the Yule festival I have been of the opinion that the law of blood vengeance is a curse that we need to cast off here in the new homeland. No, Osmund, I will earn the seed with the work of my hands, and that’s all. It will be terrible. Olaf will not let any occasion pass to humiliate me, but I will bite my tongue and put up with it, and someday it will be over. Satisfied?”

“No,” Osmund replied truthfully. “But at the moment I can’t think of anything better.”

Gunda had quickly recovered from her difficult childbirth, just as Asta had predicted. She was still a bit pale and had avoided Candamir’s bed so far, but she was working with the other women in the rye fields on the far shore with little Nils tied to her back in a cloth. The infant thrived. Thanks to the abundance of fish in the river, the good cow’s milk, and the bounty from the forest and river, his mother had plenty to eat and therefore plenty of milk. Nils’s skin had become smooth and had lost its reddish complexion, and the little boy bawled with a strong voice, mostly at night. Hacon, the slaves, and even Candamir cursed under their breath when the child woke them in the middle of the night, but often Gunda found her master looking so lovingly at his son that she became jealous.

The morning after Berse's return, Candamir and Hacon were standing in the grass along the shore, their boots wet with dew. The sun was just rising as Gunda came over from the little fire in front of their hut and brought each of them a bowl of fish soup.

Hacon waited until the slave had left again before asking his brother, "What do you mean we'll be working for him? Why? No one has as many servants as he does."

"I know. But since we have nothing to offer now but the work of our hands, it is the only way to pay for his seed."

Hacon drank his soup and was silent for a moment, his brow furrowed. "I don't like that at all," he said.

"Is that so? Well, you don't have to. I don't like it either, Hacon, but I will do it just the same, and so will you."

Hacon raised his chin belligerently. "Why do you decide things like that all by yourself? You could at least have asked how I felt about it."

Candamir snorted in amusement. "Must I ask my ox for his opinion before I harness him to the plow?"

"So that's how you think of me."

"That's enough now, Hacon. You are my younger brother and have to do what I tell you."

"Haven't I always?" the boy replied. "But you treat me like a child, even though I'm fifteen years old and almost grown up!"

"If you are grown up, then stop whining and accept like a man what you can't change."

Hacon held his tongue. All it would have gotten him was a clip around the ears, and he could do without that.

As if to reward his brother's self-control, Candamir added, "Maybe it *would* be better to do without Olaf's seed, even if it meant that we would lag behind our neighbors by at least a year for the foreseeable future. But if I don't take up Olaf's offer, he won't give Osmund anything either, and I can't square that with my conscience, do you understand?"

"Yes, I understand," Hacon readily conceded. "Osmund has been the poorest among us for such a long time, and through no fault of his own. That has to stop." He sighed and shrugged uneasily. "I only wish there were something else we could give Olaf. The less I have to do with him the happier I am. He gives me the creeps."

"What nonsense," Candamir said impatiently, as if he hadn't admitted exactly the same thing to Osmund just before the Yule festival. "As I said, we don't have any choice, and stop making such a face. After all, it's only a damned house that he wants."

*If only I could believe that,* Hacon thought, shouldering his ax and walking beside his brother along the shore and into the forest.

Siglind kept her word; they got the first two teams of oxen, which sped up the land clearing. The men dug out the roots of the fallen trees until there was enough room to get a chain around them. Depending on how large or difficult the job was, they hooked up two or all four of the draft animals, while five strong men used long bars as levers. In this way they got out most of the roots. Berse's return was also a big help for the woodsmen, as no one was as skilful with an ax as the shipwright and his sons. With the help of the ox teams, the tree trunks could also be quickly transported to the bank of the river and the men could cut more trees in one day than they previously had in two. By the week before Thor's Night, they had made significant inroads into the dense forest.

Berse also convinced them to sort the trunks before taking them to the collection point in the future village. Depending on the size and type of wood, they were better suited for half-timbered construction or roof beams, or wallboards, while others were put aside for building boats and ships. Candamir learned how to make a square beam out of a round tree trunk using his ax, and Berse also showed him how to split a straight tree trunk into boards. While Candamir had some experience with this from his work on Osmund's hall, Berse was much faster and more precise.

"I just can't believe it," Candamir said, holding two boards side by side. "There's not a hair's breadth of difference."

Berse chuckled to himself. “A shipwright needs to be precise, you know. With every stroke of the ax or hammer, you have to remember that you are holding the lives of many men in your hands.”

Candamir nodded, realizing he had a newfound admiration for this funny gnome-like fellow. He dropped the boards and returned to his team of woodcutters, surprised to find them admiring a young ash tree instead of busily cutting beeches and evergreens.

Osmund pointed to the slender sapling, not much taller than himself and straight as an arrow. “What do you think?”

Candamir slowly walked around the ash, examining it carefully from all sides. For a tree that had to grow in the shade of so many older ones, it had a beautiful, wide crown.

He nodded. “It’s perfect.”

They sent Hacon, Godwin, and the slaves back to work and set about patiently removing the little tree from the soil. They were careful not to harm the roots more than necessary, and Osmund wrapped his tunic around them so that no soil would trickle out.

“I don’t know, Osmund,” Candamir said with a sigh, “do you think you can ever wear that again?”

His friend shook his head with a fleeting grin. “Brigitta has already set up her loom, didn’t you see that? And she announced that she will make a tunic from the first cloth she weaves in Catan, with all the magic she knows woven into it, for the man who brings her the new village ash tree.”

“Hm. But she is old and her fingers are all crooked. That may take a while, and by then, you’ll freeze.”

“So what? Come now, take the trunk, but close to the top so that it won’t break.”

The young tree was unwieldy, but light, and they were able to carry it easily down to the grassy riverbank to the place where the settlers were already holding their evening meetings. They had never talked about it, but they all knew that this would be the new village green. And in order to meet, to have a real *Thing*, they needed a sacred tree.

“For the time being, we’ll have to make do with a sacred sapling,” Candamir remarked as they carefully set the tree down.

"That doesn't matter," Osmund replied, "but before we start, we get Brigitta. Who knows all the things we have to observe when we plant it. Maybe she has to recite some incantation, or perhaps she must use runes to locate the exact spot. It would surely be a dreadful omen if the new sacred tree withered and died."

They sent a few children who were playing nearby to go and fetch her. The old woman appeared quickly and was very pleased with their choice. She confessed that she didn't know any rules for planting a sacred ash tree, since nothing like that had ever happened in Elasund during her lifetime. And her grandmother, from whom she had learned everything she knew about the world and the gods, had never said anything about it. So they just chose a location close enough to the bank that the good river spirits could exert their influence on future meetings, but not so close that the attendees at the *Thing* would fall in the water. Brigitta told Candamir to dig a hole and fill a bucket with water from the river, over which she pronounced a blessing before pouring it into the hole. They placed the tree, carefully filling in the hollow spaces around the roots with Catan's rich, dark earth, stamped down the soil, and propped up the sapling with a stake just as thick as its trunk.

"That will be a fine tree someday," Candamir said confidently.

Brigitta nodded. "I will not live to see what it will look like fully grown, but that doesn't matter. Such is the way of the world." Then she regarded the young men. "Both of you deserve a new tunic, and I would say each of you badly needs one. You'll have to be patient a few days, but then the cloth will be finished. Inga and Asta will help me with the sewing."

Candamir and Osmund thanked her awkwardly, unaccustomed to such kindness from Brigitta.

"Look!" Osmund said suddenly. "Here come Harald and the Saxon."

"And they are bringing a horse with them!" Candamir cried out in delight. "But where is Asi?"

Harald and Austin had come over the ridge of the grassy hill closest to them, but the slope on this side extended down gently for more than a half mile to the riverbank. Candamir saw that the Saxon was leading a handsome brown mare at the end of a rope. She was only half broken in and occasionally tossed her head as if trying to free herself. A dark foal was wobbling along beside her on legs that looked much too long. Her ears quivered nervously, but she carried the burden that the men had placed on her back without bucking.

Once the small group had passed the untidy jumble of huts and tents and had come out onto the meadow, Candamir found his worst suspicions confirmed. Asi was nowhere to be seen, and Harald's face was ashen with grief.

"I'll go and get Godwin," Osmund said, turning away.

Candamir stepped forward, took Harald by the arms, and asked, "What happened?"

"She fell," the smith replied. His voice was husky and raw, as if these were his first words that day. "She…fell."

Candamir looked questioningly at his Saxon. Austin also seemed deeply distressed and turned around, casting a long look back toward the east, toward the mountains. "From a distance the mountaintops look almost smooth and solid, but in truth they are craggy and full of crevices and steep slopes. We had to ascend very far before we found the ore."

"Asi…my sharp-eyed Asi discovered it," Harald continued with a proud little smile. "And Austin said, 'No, let me climb up there, it is too dangerous,' but she never listens to what you tell her. She was perhaps sixty feet up when she lost her grip. She…struck the ground almost at my feet, but it all happened very fast. There was nothing we could do. She was still alive. Her shoulder hurt, and was no doubt shattered, and she couldn't move her legs, but she lived for a couple more hours. Then, before nightfall, she died."

Osmund returned from the forest with the smith's son, who was only a year older than Hacon. When Godwin saw his father's face and noticed his mother wasn't there, he stopped as if rooted to the spot, raised his hand slowly, and covered his eyes. Harald put his arm around his son's trembling shoulders and led him down to the riverbank.

Candamir watched the two sadly before turning again to his slave. "What dreadful news, Austin."

"Yes, Master."

"And after it happened, did you climb up there nevertheless and get the ore?" Candamir pointed toward the bulky wooden baskets on either side of the mare.

The slave nodded. "It was the least we could do for Asi, wasn't it?"

It was evening before Candamir learned more details. The small household was gathered around the fire in front of the hut eating crispy, fried trout. They were delicious and juicy, but the mood was bleak. None of them had known Asi well before the trip, but Harald's family had sailed with them aboard the *Falcon*, and their experiences during the voyage had made them close. They all felt as if they had lost a relative, but Gunda was despondent, and tears streamed down her lovely face.

"There is much iron in these mountains," Austin finally said, in a low voice, after Hacon had asked him to tell them what they had seen. "Harald thinks that the vein Asi discovered will take care of all our needs for the coming years, if we exploit it systematically. On the way back we found another deposit, however in a spot just as inaccessible, and if we wish to avoid further losses, we will have to think of a way to make our mining safer."

"And Asi…did she suffer a lot?" Gunda asked.

"No, I don't think so. She said she could scarcely feel her body. Then she became unconscious, and at some point her heart simply stopped beating. Not much is growing up there, but we found some bushes and stunted pines. We put them in a pile and burned her corpse as is your custom, and over the ashes we erected a burial mound of heavy stones. Harald took off his white raven feather and left it there as a burial gift, for she had been the best of all the scouts, he said." Austin stopped and thought for a moment. "No, she did not suffer much, but the smith suffered all the more."

"Indeed, it is dreadful for Harald," Candamir said. "They must have been married more than twenty years. Few couples are that fortunate."

So many women died in childbirth. Men went to sea and never returned, or became victims of a blood feud. It was therefore an exception when a couple was still together in their middle years.

The Saxon nodded sadly. The smith had told him they had lost three children over the years. And he imagined that so much grief must bring a man and wife closer together. "We tied up our tunics to make sacks," he continued, "and carried the ore back down to the plain. Then we came upon the herd of wild horses, and I thought it would gladden your heart if I brought you one, Master, and also lighten our burden. As you know, I am inexperienced with horses, but I was a bit lucky and able to catch the foal. After that, the mare came almost willingly. It took me two days to accustom her to the makeshift carrier I had put together, but it was not wasted time. The smith was able to rest, wander through the grassland, and come to grips with his loss, and I had the chance to discover my love for horses. The mare has a mind of her own, but is a good-natured creature, and I am certain you will enjoy her. On the evening of the second day, Harald returned and said we should name the mountain where it happened after Asi, so that the sacrifice she had made for the settlers of Catan would not be forgotten. And on the next morning we started out again."

"It's good that you are back," Hacon said with a shy smile.

The Saxon bowed his head. "Thank you."

"Certainly the mistress of the Cold Islands will also be happy to see you again," Gunda said, a bit maliciously. "She dragged your heavy book here, all the way from the sea. I'm surprised she has not honored us with her company yet."

"That'll do," Candamir snapped.

Austin suspected the reason Candamir was so touchy on this point was that Siglind had crossed the river with Osmund that evening at dusk, and as far as he knew, the raft had not yet returned. "Well, I must confess, I am happy myself to be back again."

Asta nodded. "Harald must have been a gloomy travelling companion after that happened. He was never a great talker, anyway. The days must have seemed long to you."

The Saxon smiled and shrugged his shoulders. After Asi's death he had in fact spoken more with Harald than in all the preceding days—about death, the meaning of life, and about gods. Harald had not been seeking a new religion, but had suddenly wanted to know what the monk thought about all these things. "On the contrary. The smith is a good man and even in his sorrow was the best travelling companion you could ask for. But this place here…well, you have probably gotten so accustomed to it that you no longer notice, but the memory of its beauty filled me with longing. Even before the accident, the mountains were inhospitable and rough. What's more, they were teeming with snakes. In the foothills you had to beware of the bears, and in the grassland the wolves roam about." He shuddered involuntarily. "I know that Odin likes wolves, but I would be just as happy if he had not brought them here."

The others did not contradict him, and the women especially shared his view. It was every mother's worst nightmare to lose a child to the wolves.

"Well, in a land where there is so much game, surely one does not need to fear Odin's dogs," Candamir said.

"You are right, they were very timid," Austin admitted. "One evening they approached our fire—just out of curiosity, Harald tried to convince me—and we drove them away by throwing a single stone at them."

"Well, you see? Even a scaredy-cat like you should be able to cope with that," Candamir said with a grin.

Austin smiled patiently and said nothing. Even though his ancestors had prayed to the same gods as these heathens, the wolf for his people was a harbinger of approaching doom, discord, and death. Just like the raven.

The festival of Thor's Night, on the eve of the Honey Moon, marked the end of the dark half of the year in their old homeland and the beginning of the bright half. On this day, the settlers put aside their work in the fields and forest to prepare for the feast. Wildflowers were picked to weave wreaths for the young girls and decorations for the houses. Everyone took part, even though their houses were only crooked twig huts that didn't look very impressive, with or without floral decorations. The largest wreath was reserved for Thor's tree—a mighty, twelve-foot high pole that the men had driven into the ground on the meadow.

And for the banquet, the men used traps to catch many small animals and birds in the forest, and even a wild boar and two sows had been caught in the pitfalls. Several oxen had been slaughtered and roasted in honor of the gods, and everyone who had honey left had brewed mead from it.

Once all the preparations had been completed, the people gathered on the shore. The women lined up all the delicious things they had cooked on long, rough-hewn tables, the tempting aroma of roasted meat hovering in the air. First, however, the men had to earn their banquet.

Next to the new village ash, Brigitta stood, a flat pebble with a Sowilo rune in her hand. At her feet were two clay dishes, one containing ox blood and the other a white, chalky slush.

About forty free men took their places in an orderly row in front of her. All had taken off their tunics and shoes, and each was holding a six-foot-long cudgel.

Siward was first. Brigitta took the rune in both hands, shook it a few times, and then dropped it in his outstretched right hand. The rune sign fell face up.

"Summer," she announced.

Siward dipped a small brush made of reeds into the bowl of oxblood and painted a Sowilo rune on his chest.

Berse was next. The stone fell onto the palm of his hand with the rune face down.

"Durin's grandson will fight for winter," Brigitta announced in a solemn voice, but there was a sparkle in her old eyes.

Berse drew an S-rune on his stocky upper body with the chalky, snow-colored slush.

One after the other, they stepped forward, until the men were divided into approximately two equal groups, each with the rune symbol of the corresponding color on his chest. Then they broke into two lines separated by about twenty paces—the winter men with their backs to the north, the summer warriors to the south—and endeavored to frighten their opponents with menacing scowls while pounding the ground rhythmically with their cudgels.

"I simply can't believe they are doing that," murmured the Saxon uneasily.

"And I'd give everything to be one of them," Hacon replied, in an equally hushed voice. But Candamir had refused to let him take part. Maybe next year, he had suggested, but that's what he had said the year before, too.

Brigitta was now holding a red flower and a white flower in her hands and had raised her arms. "Show a little common sense, for a change," she admonished them, "and don't beat each other over the head. We can't afford to lose any of you. Nevertheless, if anyone should die, there will be no blood vengeance, as this battle will be decided by the gods." Then she dropped the two flowers. "May Thor grant you victory!"

It was not the first time that Siglind had been struck by the absurdity of this wish, for naturally only one of the two parties could be victorious. Just the same, she cheered with all the other women, children, and slaves as the men charged at each other. The cheers of the spectators were soon drowned out by the bloodcurdling battle cries of more than forty men.

As in all the previous years since he was allowed to take part in this important ritual, Candamir had wound up on the winter side. It seemed that the rune lottery assigned many of the men to the same side each time. He found that their battle was much harder, because naturally each warrior, as well as the spectators, hoped deep down for the defeat of deadly winter by summer that brought fertility and life to the fields. Nevertheless, the knowledge of being on the wrong side just made their team that much more determined. He didn't look any of his opponents in the face—knowing Osmund was on the other side again, as were Harald and Wiland—instead, he stared only at the red runes and struck away with all his might.

Almost immediately, the two sides were locked in battle. They used not just the wooden clubs, but fists, elbows, feet, and knees. Out of the corner of his eye, Candamir saw the cudgel coming and ducked, but not fast enough. Jared hit him right across the shoulders. The blow winded him, but he didn't go down. Even as he straightened up, he punched the young man in the pit of his stomach, and when Jared doubled over, gave him such a blow to the back of the neck with his cudgel that he fell to the ground unconscious.

"Better luck next time, lad," Candamir growled with clenched teeth, then turned away from the motionless figure to face the next opponent. The field had thinned out noticeably, and everywhere the warriors stumbled over other men lying in the grass in various stages of exhaustion.

An odor of sweat and blood enveloped them like an invisible cloud, and the meadow was so trampled that it looked as if it had been plowed up in places. Five men were still standing on the winter side, along with seven or eight of their opponents.

Bleeding, gasping for breath, and already a little battle-weary, Osmund and Candamir faced one another. This, too, happened almost every year. Osmund had lost his cudgel earlier, shattering it on an opponent's back. He'd then thrown away the splintered end so as not to injure anyone seriously. Candamir threw his down as well before they went at each other with their fists. Eventually they were the only ones still fighting.

A tense, breathless silence had descended on the meadow, interrupted only by the panting of the two warriors and their muffled blows. The fighting slowed down—the opponents had to wait longer and longer each time for the other to get up again. They each had a deep gash across one eyebrow, so that blood was running into their eyes. And Osmund's eye was almost completely swollen shut. One of Candamir's teeth was so loose that he feared it might fall out. Both bodies were bathed in sweat and blood. They stood facing each other, swaying slightly, their arms dangling down seemingly harmless, until the one whose turn it was next found the strength to raise his fist and land one more heavy blow on the chin, neck, or chest of the other. Then they just stood there, blinking and motionless like two oxen in the hot sun, looking hopelessly confused.

Candamir felt as if he was shrouded in a cloud of impenetrable fog, but he could still think clearly. He knew exactly where they were, what they were doing, and why, and he also was aware that they would have stopped long ago if Siglind had not been among the spectators. It was clear they both wanted her, but only one could have her, and so they fought for her in the only way they could. But Candamir also realized that Siglind would not make her decision based on who hobbled off this battlefield as the victor.

He saw Osmund marshalling his last reserves, able to read these eyes just like the Saxon could read his book. *If she is smart,* he thought in that moment, *she will pick you because you are the better man. But I don't know how I would be able to bear it.*

Just a heartbeat before Osmund clenched his fist, Candamir raised his arms, palms spread outward, and dropped into the soft grass.

"Summer has vanquished winter!" Brigitta cried out. Her satisfaction was unmistakable.

There were prolonged cheers, and the women and girls ran onto the battlefield like Valkyries to rouse the fallen heroes. One by one the exhausted warriors rose and, groaning audibly, allowed themselves to be guided down to the river. There they bathed to cool their various wounds and stop the bleeding, most of it minor. This time there had been no serious injuries. Berse's son Sigurd had dislocated his shoulder, howling at the top of his voice when the Saxon reset it. Haflad had broken an arm, which didn't especially upset anyone, and several men had broken a rib or two.

Osmund had collapsed in the grass next to Candamir, and they both lay there, propped on their elbows, their heads thrown back, gasping for breath. At the same time, they turned their heads, fiercely looked one another in the eye, and then broke out laughing.

"Man, what a sight you are," Candamir said, gloating. "I bet it will take a week before you can see out of your left eye again."

"That remains to be seen," Osmund replied calmly.

Inga and Gunda arrived, offering them cups of cool mead and helping them to their feet.

"You were wonderful," Inga said, smiling at Osmund as he gave the empty cup back to her.

He thanked her, passed his hand self-consciously over his bloody brow, and then slipped into the water.

"You weren't bad yourself, Master," Gunda murmured.

Candamir winked at her, supported himself inconspicuously on her arm on the way down to the shore, and turned around furtively looking for Siglind. She was helping a group of little girls put their floral wreaths on. She was already wearing one made up mostly of forget-me-nots. Asta knelt down in the grass in front of Harald and used a damp cloth to bandage what appeared to be a sprained ankle. The smith was gazing out at the distant mountains.

It was a mild evening with a deep blue sky and a touch of summer in the air. The half moon outshone most of the stars. The men feasted and drank with abandon, lit huge fires, and made a racket on flutes made of wood or cattle horn that accompanied the songs they sang of their gods and ancestors. As midnight approached, Brigitta chose Lars to place the crown on Thor's tree. Beaming with pride, and with astonishing skill, Olaf's young son climbed the smooth pole, a rope between his teeth. When he arrived at the top, he waved to the other boys, and they tied the loose end of the rope to the beautiful, big wreath of flowers. Lars pulled it up, hung the wreath over the top of the pole, and slid down to the ground again to the cheers of the onlookers.

"In the Cold Islands, people sacrifice a virgin to Thor on this night," said Siglind, who was standing by the fire next to the Saxon and looking up at the wreathed pole.

"*What?*" Austin cried out aghast.

She couldn't help but smile at his obvious horror. "It is said that on this night the gods mingle with men. But as far as I know, Thor never appeared personally in the Cold Islands, and so it was naturally always Cnut's privilege to stand in for the god and gratify the more or less willing virgin—before the eyes of his cheering subjects, whose fertility he thereby assured. Or at least that is what we were told," Siglind explained, her skepticism seeping through just as clearly as her sarcasm.

Austin shuddered. “I am used to seeing all sorts of things among these barbarians, but at least that didn’t happen in Elasund,” he replied, regaining some composure. Perhaps it had been like that at one time, he thought to himself. He had always suspected that this ritual around the Thor tree had something offensive about it, and now he supposed that it might be a remnant of this abominable heathen custom.

“Of course it didn’t,” Siglind said. “These people have neither chief nor priest, so there would no doubt be a dispute about who would stand in for the god.”

The Saxon nodded thoughtfully. “What happened to the virgin?” he asked.

“Oh,” said Siglind, dismissing the thought with a shrug, “he kept her a while, but as soon as he found that she did not become pregnant either, he sent her back to her family, or her owners, since many were slave girls. Poor Cnut didn’t have much luck with women. As far as I know, none ever presented him with a child.”

“Perhaps that’s just as well for the people of the Cold Islands,” the monk said. “That way, a better man might become king after his death.”

“That’s true.”

They were silent for a while and gazed toward the Thor tree, now the center of lively dances. Around the fire things had become noticeably quieter as couples gradually left the circle of light, seeking some privacy in the reeds at the water’s edge or under the trees.

Candamir was drunk, but it had not escaped his notice that his Saxon slave was again deep in conversation with Siglind, despite the fact that he had expressly forbidden it. But the next morning would be time enough to call the slave to account. At the moment he had other things on his mind. It was not just the mead that intoxicated him, but the Thor’s Night itself, and his blood was seething.

He went over to his Frisian maid who was standing with a group of women, chatting and giggling, grabbed her boldly by the waist from behind, buried his nose in her hair, and whispered, “Find a way to get rid of the child—I’ve waited long enough.”

Her body went rigid in his arms, but she untied the cloth holding her sleeping son to her breast, handed the infant over to Asta, and asked, "Would you take care of Nils for a moment, Mistress?"

"Of course."

Impatiently, Candamir pulled her away from the group standing in the light of the fire. "A moment will hardly be enough," he said.

He didn't waste much effort finding a secluded spot, unable to curb his impatience a moment longer. Behind a hazelnut shrub growing close enough to the shore for them to hear the river's babbling, he pulled her into the grass, pushed up her skirt with one hand, fumbled with his trousers with the other, and then penetrated her with a groan that sounded more relieved than passionate.

Gunda had to suppress a smile. Candamir seemed to her like a boy who finally gets a drink of water to quench his thirst after an overly long day of play. But she couldn't be aroused by his lust. She lay under him silent and indifferent, her hands at her sides in the grass. He seemed to be completely absorbed in himself and not to take any notice of her atypical reserve. His panting was louder than usual and quickened in time with his selfish thrusts. As soon as he had climaxed, he rolled aside and lay there on his back, breathing heavily.

"Is that it?" she inquired. "Can I go now, Master?"

Candamir sat up. "What's that supposed to mean?" he asked angrily. "What's the matter with you?"

"I don't know," she lied. She sat up as well and pulled up her shoulders, shivering.

No doubt he had long forgotten their fateful conversation on the evening after Nils's birth. She had given him a son—his firstborn—but he was not willing to give anything back to her in return. So great was her disappointment that she had lost all desire.

"You don't know," he repeated with an impatient sigh, glancing at her but refusing to recognize how forlorn she was. She had no right to be unhappy, he thought. When she came to him, a frightened child with blond curls, skinny knees, and a narrow face that seemed to consist of nothing but these watery blue eyes, he had treated her well. And when he had finally taken her, he did so carefully and considerately. But he didn't intend to show this kind of forbearance again. By now Gunda had become a grown woman, and moreover, she was his property. "Well, whatever it is, I want it to stop."

"I am sorry if I have not pleased you, Master," she replied with a hint of sarcasm in her voice.

Her rejection hurt his feelings. He could not understand it, and it felt utterly undeserved. With a short nod he said, "As well you should be. Don't think I couldn't bring myself to sell you. You're worth about as much as a sack of winter wheat, which would be more useful to me than a Frisian shrew in my bed."

Gunda raised her hand to her mouth and stared at Candamir in horror. "But...but I am the mother of your son," she reminded him.

He shrugged. "I wouldn't have any trouble finding a nurse for him," he said. Then he got up, undressed, and waded into the dark river.

Gunda stared after him. *You'll pay for that,* she thought. *I don't know how, but I'll see to it that you pay for that.* Then she pulled her threadbare tunic over her head and followed him into the water to placate him.

Osmund walked silently over to join Siglind and the Saxon. He glared at Austin, and with an almost imperceptible jerk of his chin let him know he was unwelcome. The Saxon was glad to have the chance to see if, against all likelihood, there might be a piece of roasted boar's meat still left on the table.

Osmund held out his cup to Siglind, and she took it with a grateful nod. Spellbound, he observed the tiny movements of the muscles in her slender neck as she drank.

"Ah, delicious," she said, handing the cup back to him.

"You had better finish it. I think I've had enough."

She laughed in surprise. "I never met a man before who reached this conclusion on his own."

He smiled in embarrassment, took her by the arm, and led her to a spot on the other side of the fire, just outside the circle of light. There, undisturbed, they sat in the grass. Siglind kept her head down, her hands nervously clasped in her lap, while secretly observing Osmund out of the corner of her eye. His left eye was only slightly swollen. The cool river water and the soothing clove oil that Brigitta had distributed so generously after the battle had worked wonders. Many of their people were well-built and blessed with good features, but Osmund, Siglind thought, was probably the most handsome man she had ever seen. Moreover, he was intelligent, fearless, and had every desirable manly virtue, except wealth—but that was just a matter of time in this land. And yet she would rather have been any other place, even at the foot of the fiery mountain, than here alone with him.

"Siglind," he began softly.

She raised her head. "Yes?"

He hesitated. This was difficult, so different than with Gisla, whom he never had to ask, because everything had been so crystal clear. "When we were on the south shore last night, I told you how I imagine things will work out for me in the coming years and my hopes for the future—the plans I have. Today I'm afraid it might have sounded as if I were boasting."

"No, not at all," she answered truthfully. "Your plans are good and reasonable, and I'm sure you'll achieve everything you have put your mind to. Your son will be proud of you and compose songs about your deeds." Siglind noticed how tense and breathless her words sounded and wished she could jump up and run away, but she stayed put, barely moving a muscle.

Suddenly Osmund laid his large, warm hand over hers and said, "I swear by Odin's eye that you have no reason to be afraid of me."

She shook her head helplessly. "Yes, I know."

"If you know that, then why are you trembling like a cornered deer?"

"But I'm not..."

"Siglind..."

"Stop. Please, Osmund. Don't say anything more."

"I must, because otherwise I'd be wondering for the rest of my life how you would have answered. So—will you be my wife?"

His particular little smile that extended to just one corner of his mouth and made women, and not just Inga, feel weak in the knees, seemed to resonate in his voice, and Siglind had never been more strongly attracted to him than at this moment. She felt a physical desire for this man, a craving she thought had vanished long ago, but she didn't let it show. She had been accustomed to concealing her feelings for so long that it was not very difficult now, a defense that had become second nature.

"No."

"Oh." He didn't pull his hand away. On the contrary, for a fleeting moment he held her more tightly, but then, gradually, he loosened his grip and finally let go completely. "Then I have no doubt been mistaken. Forgive me if I have troubled you," he said, a bit stiffly.

"But you didn't," she replied impatiently. After a brief pause, she continued. "Your proposal honors me. I know there is no better man here I could marry."

"But heart and reason often go their separate ways, and it is Candamir you want," he finished for her, in such a soft voice that she couldn't tell if he was angry, resigned, or perhaps even amused.

Osmund had by no means been certain that she wanted him, but he realized he had not been prepared for this rejection. "You are probably right," he said with feigned indifference. "He may well be the better choice. The gods love Candamir, fortune is always with him, and he deserves it. There is no dark corner in his heart."

"There is a dark corner in every heart," she said. "And you are mistaken. I have no intention of marrying him, because I have no intention of ever marrying again, do you understand?"

"No," he admitted, greatly relieved. "What do you want instead?"

She didn't answer at once. One evening, a week earlier, she had been secretly baptized by Austin, and the monk had told her of the holy women in his homeland who renounced men and the world and devoted themselves entirely to his god. "Brides of Christ" he had called them. They shared in the mystery of this god and knew how to read His book. *Brides of Christ.* Siglind did not yet understand exactly what that meant, but it had a wonderful sound. She suspected that this was the path she might follow, but she could not entrust her secret to Osmund, who hated

Austin's god and had become a passionate worshipper of Odin since they had arrived in Catan.

"I am not yet certain," she said. She kneeled before Osmund and took his hand. "You know what it's like when darkness descends, so that you can no longer find your way, don't you?"

"Yes."

"When life is agony?"

He lowered his eyes in shame, but nodded.

"The darkness is gone," Siglind continued, "but I cannot yet see the way."

"I've experienced that as well. I thought my way and yours were one and the same, but possibly I'm mistaken." He clenched his teeth so as not to beg her to reconsider her decision. Her rejection was a loss that he felt like a physical pain. It made him feel ill. He turned his head and stared into the fire.

She placed her hand lightly on top of his. "Don't be angry at me, Osmund. The last thing in the world I want to do is to offend you. I went into exile of my own free will, but I underestimated what loneliness would be like. It is terrible. But from the very start, you were my friend."

"I still am," he said, though he had not yet decided whether he really could continue to be.

Siglind nodded sadly. She felt dreadful. Why was she not cleverer? Why hadn't she been able to avoid this conversation that was so painful for both of them?

"I wish I were a completely different person," she said. "Someday you will be glad I turned down your honorable proposal, Osmund. I bring nothing but unhappiness to everyone. I have my whole family on my conscience, as Cnut killed them all in order to get me, only to discover that his queen could not bear him a son. You…you really deserve a better wife."

He couldn't help smiling. "What a kind attempt to console me, but quite easy to see through, I fear."

"No, I am quite serious in what I say. That you don't believe me doesn't in any way alter the facts. And…"

Osmund pressed his lips to hers. He hardly knew what had come over him, but he simply couldn't help himself. She reciprocated his kiss and tried to convince herself it was just to ease the pain caused by her rejection. But a soft, traitorous voice in her head whispered that she should be permitted at least one harmless kiss this night. And when Osmund put his arm around her and drew her closer to him, she was tempted to let herself be carried away.

But she knew if she did that Osmund would no longer take no for an answer, and for an hour of bliss, she risked losing everything she really wanted—another life, another god, another way.

She pulled away from him gently, shaking her head.

# *Honey Moon, Year One*

*On the south bank of the river, the rye fields of every clan are separated by furrows and cultivated. It is the very picture of order, created by man and pleasing to God. Summer promises to be warm and dry, but not overly dry, so that everyone ventures the hope of a rich harvest. The clearing of the land also proceeds at a brisk pace, thanks to the strength and untiring industry of these people. It is uplifting to see how they inadvertently follow the divine commandment and take dominion over the earth.*

*The women have finished their work on the south bank of the river. They are spinning and weaving the new wool and roaming the forest in search of more livestock. They are fearless and strong like the goddesses of their sagas.*

Austin paused for a moment and wondered whether he should add the attribute "beautiful," for naturally he wanted the settlers to be pleased with what he wrote about them in his chronicle, fervently hoping one day they might ask him to read his work aloud. But he decided it was inappropriate for a man of God to praise the beauty of women.

*Grouse are apparently not present here in great number and are difficult to find, so we take them into our little huts at night to protect them from foxes and let them hatch all their eggs. The piglets of the wild sows we have hunted are kept in pens and raised with cow's milk in the hope they can be domesticated and bred with the few hogs we brought along. By now, every family has a respectable herd of cattle, and a group of young men has gone off into the foothills to look for goats. Thus, thanks to God's infinite kindness, we gradually are becoming prosperous. The only thing we lack are sheep.*

*Olaf, the unofficial chief of these people, has already started construction of a house for himself…*

The Saxon put his pen aside again. He felt an unpleasant twinge in the pit of his stomach every time he thought of this house being built. Just like Osmund, he had the worst sort of premonitions about what might happen when someone as hot-headed as Candamir was forced to work for the domineering Olaf.

Several people had already grumbled when Olaf chose a piece of the cleared land for the site of his new house. They had toiled here from dawn to dusk to clear land for their farms, Siward declared, and not so that those who considered themselves better than the rest could build a big house there. Olaf countered that he wasn't taking the land from anyone, but was only laying claim to a part of what Candamir had already voluntarily relinquished.

"You could hardly call it voluntary," Candamir grumbled to himself.

Osmund added, "The last word has not yet been spoken about this, Uncle."

Olaf brushed the matter aside with a sweep of his hand. "In any case, I want my house here and nowhere else—close enough to the river to build my own landing for my ships someday. And eventually all of you will also build your houses where you want to, so don't pretend I am claiming rights that each of you don't have as well. The only difference is that I am doing it now."

Candamir and Hacon had started building the house in the week after Thor's Night and spent each third day on it, as agreed. Olaf had assigned Jared, the silent Turon, and two other strong slaves to help them. Having spoken with Olaf in great detail about his wishes, Candamir knew exactly what he had to do. Olaf wanted a hall that differed completely from the ones they had inhabited in the old homeland. It wouldn't have double walls filled with dirt, since Olaf was confident it would never get so cold in Catan that such protection was necessary, even in winter. What he had in mind instead was a half-timbered building like those he had seen in other countries with a milder climate. The walls were to be framed with wooden boards on the outside, and on the inside insulated and filled in with branches and loam—for what Olaf absolutely wanted to have was windows. He had taken a stick and scratched little drawings in the ground so Candamir would understand exactly what he had in mind.

"He wants *two* windows in each long wall?" Hacon asked incredulously. "But then the house is open to all kinds of weather."

"Well, he thinks that during rainy or chilly weather, he can close them with shutters. To be honest, it makes no difference to me if he gets drenched or freezes in his new house."

"And have you ever built windows? Do you know how to do that?"

Candamir shrugged impatiently. "Like doors, I assume, don't you? You put a lintel over it, and that's all there is to it. But what I don't know is how to thatch a roof with reeds." Because of the large quantities of reeds growing near the shore, Olaf had told them to use them as roofing.

"Austin probably knows how to do that," the boy answered. "In his homeland that's the way it's usually done, he told us."

"All right, then, we'll ask him. Now, let's get to work."

Olaf had personally measured his new home's footprint—twenty paces of length and fifteen paces of width—and under his direction Candamir had hammered in stakes at the corners and strung the guidelines. Along these lines they had dug the trench for the foundation. He had sent the slaves into the hills to break limestone and carve the blocks that would hold the vertical beams for the half-timbered construction.

The slaves hauled timber from the collection point, while Jared, Candamir, and Hacon made beams from the tree trunks. Still inexperienced with wood, Jared was more a hindrance than a help. He cursed loudly and frequently and took as much time making one beam as Candamir did making three, and even then the result was crooked and uneven.

Candamir concluded that Jared's contribution would have to be limited to making wooden pins and chocks, but he refrained from commenting on it. He knew that the lad was still angry at him about the foolish matter with the wild sow, and he didn't want to antagonize him further. However, when Jared's ax slipped for the second time, just missing his foot, Candamir suggested he take a break. "It's dangerous when your arms get too tired doing this work."

Jared glared enviously at Hacon, who, although younger, was far more skillful. But contrary to expectation, he didn't get angry, only murmured darkly, "If my father catches me slacking off, I'm a dead man."

Candamir winked at him. "Your father is taking your sheep out to the grassland—he is far away."

"But tomorrow he will count the finished beams and wonder why there are so few."

The Turon put down the trunk he had brought, walked over to them, and pointed to Jared's ax. Then he put his hands together like a pleading child.

Jared snorted contemptuously. "Yes, I'm sure you'd like that, wouldn't it? But you can just forget about it."

Candamir frowned. "Why don't you let him try?"

"Because he's dangerous. Ever since the Turon came at him with a scythe, father forbade him from handling any sharp tools. That was on the day you lost your vicious tongue, isn't that right, Turon? Off with you, get us more wood. I'd better not have to tell my father that you were lolling around, or he'll give you a good whipping."

The slave turned his shaved head away and hurried back to the collection point, but it didn't escape Candamir's notice that he was clenching his fists furiously.

By noon it was hot at the construction site, and Candamir allowed Jared and Hacon to go for a dip in the river. He kept working, for heat didn't bother him any more than cold. The next time the slave returned from the collection site, Candamir stood up straight and looked at him closely for the first time in weeks. The young slave was rather lean. He was probably still rebellious, Candamir thought, and if beatings did no good, perhaps Olaf let him starve. But he looked muscular, wiry, and fit.

"Do you know how to swing an ax?" Candamir asked.

An unexpected smile gave the haggard face a sudden handsome appearance, and the slave nodded eagerly. With his hands he formed a longish vessel, and after a moment Candamir understood. "You are a shipwright?" he asked, astonished.

The Turon nodded.

Candamir took his dagger out of its sheath, held it in his right hand, and handed the ax to the slave with his left. "Then let me see what you can do. But be careful. If you turn around toward me with the ax in your hand, you're dead."

The young man lowered his eyes submissively and turned toward the wooden beam that Candamir had been working on. Then he took the ax in both hands and set to work with skillful blows, obviously unconcerned for the safety of his bare feet. His movements were efficient and of enviable ease. In no time at all, the beam was finished, and the surface he had been working on was noticeably smoother than Candamir's. Finally he buried the ax in the bark of the next tree trunk, straightened up, and stepped aside.

Candamir inspected the work closely, but as hard as he tried he was unable to find any flaw. "Hm," he said, "I think I'll have another talk with Jared."

Changing Jared's mind was no easy matter, for the lad had a mortal fear that his father would learn he let the slave handle an ax. Moreover, Jared detested the Turon with a passion that Candamir could not quite understand, and he treated him with unnecessary cruelty, kicking and abusing him at every turn and for no apparent reason.

Nevertheless, by summoning up all his nearly exhausted patience, Candamir finally succeeded in convincing Olaf's son of all the advantages that would come from permitting the skilled Turon to cut the beams. For his part, the slave was overjoyed to be allowed to exercise his trade again, and he served Candamir from then on with dogged devotion. Thus they were able to begin the roof truss by the end of the month.

"Here, Master, I think you will enjoy this," Heide said, handing Candamir a bowlful of delicious stew made from wild turnips and beef. "It seems you are getting thinner and thinner, no matter how much I feed you," she lamented.

Gratefully, Candamir took a deep breath of the tempting aroma and pressed his free left hand on his stomach under the new, earth-brown garment that Brigitta had made for him. "Nonsense," he said. "On the contrary, if I worked less I'd just get fat, with all the food you stuff into me."

"Indeed, I think we've never eaten as well as in Catan," Osmund agreed, who was a guest at Candamir's fire along with Roric. "Berse and Siward already have an overstuffed look."

His son, who was sitting on his left knee, reached greedily for the spoon in the bowl Osmund had received, but he pulled the bowl away. "One moment, Roric." He held up the bowl a little higher and murmured, "Thanks to you, Odin, for the bounty of Catan and your wise guidance that brought us here."

Everyone sitting around the fire followed his example, except the Saxon. Many of them had made it a habit to thank the god to whom they were indebted at every meal.

"You should learn to humble yourself before our gods or go to bed hungry," Osmund scolded Austin, who lowered his eyes politely. "I prefer to thank *my* god for the food he gives us."

Osmund looked at Candamir in disbelief. Ordinarily he never interfered in Candamir's domestic affairs, but he couldn't help himself this time. "You are all too lenient, it seems to me."

Candamir shrugged. "Perhaps, but what shall I do? You can force a man to do almost anything. You can probably even force him to say anything you want to hear. But no matter what you do, you can't force anyone to believe or not believe something. If you want to keep a man from believing something, you must kill him—which we almost did with the Saxon, if you hadn't stopped us, isn't that so?"

"Perhaps I made a mistake," Osmund grumbled, casting a dark glance at Austin, who seemed to be examining the contents of his bowl with great interest. Finally, Osmund put his arm around Roric's shoulders, took the bowl in his left hand, and used his spoon with the right hand to feed his son. With an involuntary smile he observed the little boy, who ate with great relish, almost greedily. That occupied him for a while, but after Osmund had taken a spoonful himself, he looked at Candamir again and said, "I just hope you will not provoke Odin with your excessive leniency."

Candamir did not answer at first, but continued eating just as hungrily as Roric. He knew that Osmund was right—he took all these things too lightly, and not much had changed in his relationship with the gods since they had arrived in Catan. While Osmund and many of their neighbors had become very devout in their service to the gods—always speaking about the temple they wanted to erect in Odin's honor—Candamir confined himself, as before, to sacrifices on high feast days, and to praying to Tyr, his patron god, to stand by him in difficult situations.

"Odin could hardly punish us any more than he has already," Hacon remarked grimly. "What could be worse than having to build a house for Olaf, of all people?"

In Candamir's opinion, his brother had a point, but Osmund dropped his spoon in the dish in order to give Hacon a good slap. "Watch your tongue. You're offending the gods and my uncle in the same breath, you oaf." As usual, he didn't sound angry, just deliberate. But the slap hit home.

Hacon put his hand to his cheek and looked reproachfully at his brother, but Candamir had no intention of standing up for him. If he had made such a disrespectful remark, Osmund probably would have accepted it with a conspiratorial grin, but Hacon was, after all, not in Candamir's position. It was high time he learned where his place was and what he could—and could not—get away with. Ever since they had left Elasund Hacon had been constantly pushing the limits, and Candamir had some sympathy for that, up to a point. After all, so much had changed. He had become more critical of their traditions as well, questioning much that had once been considered inviolable. Perhaps Hacon was just doing the same. But those who cross the line do so at their own peril, and apparently his brother hadn't learned that yet.

"Where is Asta, anyway?" Osmund asked, breaking the awkward silence.

"With Thorbjörn's wife," Candamir replied. "The baby is coming, but a month too early, Brigitta thinks. She believes it may turn out to be twins; that's why she asked Asta to help her."

Osmund nodded and ate another spoonful before feeding Roric again. "If they turn out to be two girls, we'd better have a word with Thorbjörn as soon as possible," he said.

"You mean one for Roric and one for Nils?" Candamir asked, amused. "You are *very* foresighted, Osmund."

Osmund shrugged impassively. "The first girls born in Catan will be just as blessed by the gods as Nils. Odin would certainly want us to seal their union at an early stage."

"Wait at least until they're born," Heide scolded. "It's bad luck to betroth girls ahead of time."

After the meal, the two friends took the ferry to the other shore to examine the rye and have a few undisturbed words. They walked silently along the edge of the fields, delighting in the first tender green shoots peeking out of the earth in neat rows in the short-mowed grass. Finally, they stopped at a willow tree that stood close to the shore.

"Siward and Eilhard are already talking about building a house, too," said Osmund, gazing out at the river.

"That doesn't surprise me," Candamir replied. "The clearing of the land has moved along faster than any of us could have dreamed. And even though the winters may be mild here, they no doubt bring a lot of rain, and who wants to be living in a hut of twigs then?"

"I suggested to the men that we all devote every third day to building houses. If we do, you won't have to relinquish any of the land this fall that you are entitled to, and we'll all have houses before winter sets in."

"Everyone but me," Candamir grumbled.

"Oh, come on. Olaf's house will soon be finished if you keep working the way you have been. You have such a knack for it, and you'll have had so much experience by then that you'll finish your own house in the time it takes others to build the frame."

Candamir shrugged. "Who knows, maybe you're right. Does that mean that you'll start building as well?"

Osmund nodded, then suddenly turned and looked straight at him. "I'm getting married, Candamir. On Midsummer Day."

For a moment, Candamir was afraid his heart would simply stop. He crossed his arms as if he were cold, stared at the ground, and said softly, "So…you asked her." He took a deep breath and then exhaled audibly. "I always knew you were braver than I am. Now I suppose I'll have to pay the price for it."

"Yes, I asked Siglind," Osmund replied, still looking directly at him. He paused for a few heartbeats in order to torment his friend a bit longer. "But she didn't want me. She says, by the way, that she doesn't want you, either."

Candamir was wrenched so fast from gloom to joy and back again that he felt dizzy. "Oh, by all the gods, she *cannot* mean to marry Olaf…"

Osmund shook his head. "It appears she does not want to marry anyone." He told him what little he had been able to elicit from her.

Candamir sniffed. "What foolish twaddle…"

"Well, maybe you'll tell her that sometime."

*And maybe I just will,* Candamir thought defiantly, before asking curiously, "Well, who is the lucky bride?"

"Inga."

Candamir was not especially surprised. "I was afraid a few times during the trip that she would crawl under your blanket at night and compromise your virtue. I'm sure your fiancée is overjoyed."

Osmund couldn't help but smile. "Yes, I do think so."

"In contrast with her husband-to-be."

But Osmund shook his head. "Oh no, this is the right choice."

"The *right* choice?" Candamir repeated incredulously. Then he raised an accusing finger. "You spurned my sister because she couldn't replace your Gisla, you said, and now suddenly you are going to marry Inga because it is the *right* choice?"

"That was in another life, Candamir. Everything has changed, and Brigitta says she saw in the oracle that Inga and I would wed."

"She claims to see whatever it is that serves her purpose," Candamir replied.

For a moment Osmund looked so disapproving that Candamir feared he was going to receive a slap too. But Osmund merely shook his head and said, "That's not true. She has far too much respect for the oracle to misuse it for her intrigues. You can be sure that she saw it. And it's foolish to revolt against what the Norns have ordained for your life." It sounded as if he were reciting this simple maxim primarily for himself. "I am sure that Inga will be a good wife to me and a good mother to Roric. I have no reason to bemoan my fate."

Inga's girlish, shy devotion had touched him and provided sweet consolation after Siglind's rejection. And Brigitta had seen more—things that he couldn't mention even to Candamir, because the old woman had sworn them to secrecy. But the oracle had revealed that after Brigitta's death, Osmund and Inga would assume great power, that they would be the defenders of the old, true faith—Inga the priestess in the temple and guardian of the sacred spring, and Osmund…a shiver ran down his spine each time he thought of what Brigitta had prophesied for him. And if this prophesy should in fact be fulfilled, Siglind might bitterly regret her decision. Although Osmund knew such a thought was petty and childish, it gladdened his heart nonetheless.

"But she probably isn't bringing much into the marriage, is she?" Candamir asked tactlessly.

Osmund's thoughts had been far away, but now he came back to earth. "What?"

"Inga. We were talking about your fiancée," Candamir said with studied patience. "Siward lost everything, just as we did. The dowry will likely be meager."

"Siward has his resources. In any case, I'll get a few sheep."

Candamir sighed. "Maybe I'm a fool not to court one of Berse's ugly daughters. Marriage is truly a lucrative thing, and certainly not such drudgery as building houses."

Osmund laughed softly. "So what do you think? Are you going to finish building my uncle's house without any blood being shed?"

"We've already started on the roof truss. I can't imagine that anything will go wrong now."

Things had been moving along rather smoothly. Olaf was always happy when he inspected the site, for try as he might, he couldn't find anything to criticize. Of course, he never offered a word of praise, but that didn't bother Candamir. He knew that his work was good, and as Osmund had predicted, in building Olaf's house all sorts of good ideas for his own hall came to him. It was also shearing time, which meant that for the most part Olaf left them alone. Since he had more sheep than all the others, he also had more demands on his time during this season. And displeased with Candamir's acquisition of two horses when he had none, Olaf set out on a rather long trip into the grasslands to catch a few horses for himself.

He soon returned with a stallion and two mares, their foals, and a fair number of black and blue bruises, and for the time being, his venturesome spirit seemed to be satisfied. He took to inspecting his future house more than once a day, which meant that Candamir could no longer use the Turon as a carpenter, which slowed their progress and depressed his spirits.

"Where is your brother?" Olaf asked on one hot, sunny morning at the beginning of Fallow Moon.

Candamir was standing on top of a ladder, putting up a rafter. He lowered his hammer, looked down, and replied, "With Jared and the Turon on the south shore, cutting reeds. We need huge numbers of them for such a large roof, and if we don't start now, we will delay the completion unnecessarily." He was annoyed with himself for justifying his decision.

Olaf nodded. "I see you are quite capable of concentrating and planning something reasonably, once you decide that's what you want to do."

"Oh, thanks very much," Candamir grumbled.

"I imagine you can't wait to finally be done with this onerous task so that you can start building your own house, isn't that so? But remember our deal: you owe me your labor, and that of your brother, until we start sowing."

Candamir didn't answer. Against his better judgment he had hoped that Olaf would show a little decency and give him the remaining weeks off as thanks for the roomy, well-built house. His hope had obviously been misplaced. He raised his hammer to knock in a bolt, wishing it was Olaf's skull. He missed and smashed the carefully formed rafter. Furiously, he closed his eyes tightly and threw his head back.

Olaf pretended not to notice any of this, but walked into the house through the opening where the door was to be. It already looked like a longhouse. The timber frame was complete and covered with evenly made boards. Four window openings in the two long walls allowed the bright sunlight to shine in. The bedroom was sectioned off with a board wall and illuminated by a window in the gable wall. Much to the amazement of his neighbors, Olaf had decided against having a longfire, as that created more heat than needed in this climate and an unnecessarily large amount of smoke. Instead, a round pit had been dug for the hearth just in front of the back room, and where the longfire had formerly been, forming the central axis of each hall, Olaf planned to place a long table, as in a royal hall. As soon as the roof was finished, he wanted to set up his imposing high seat.

He looked up at Candamir through the half-finished roof timbering. "I want a coat of arms above the door to my house."

"A what?" Candamir shouted back, not understanding.

"A graphic symbol of my clan that Jared can carry on after my death—a ship with a raven's head. Can you engrave that on the lintel?"

*Is there anything else I can do for you?* Candamir thought sullenly. "No, but I bet my Saxon could."

"Then tell him to do it."

Candamir nodded and climbed down the ladder. "Aren't you lucky that he kept his hand," he remarked casually.

Olaf walked away without answering.

It wasn't Austin, but Siglind who had explained to Candamir how to roof a house with reeds. Where she had grown up, there was an extensive moor with plenty of reeds, and so it was customary to make the roofs watertight with them. She had once assisted her father and her brothers and knew more or less how to do it.

"No, Hacon, you must cut it much farther down. We need the thicker, lower part of the reed, do you understand? Look." She took Candamir's knife from his hand, seized the bunch of reeds in her left hand, and placed the blade all the way at the bottom. She was standing in shallow water close to the shore, for that was where the best reeds grew. Her feet were bare and her faded red skirt was wet up to her thighs, so that it kept clinging to her legs. That didn't concern her—in fact, in this heat she liked the cool, wet cloth against her skin. But Hacon and the young Turon had trouble devoting the necessary attention to their work. Siglind's legs stood out as clearly as if she had no skirt on at all, and the sight was a distraction to them.

Jared, on the other hand, didn't seem to notice. Bent over, and with his face turned away from the others, he did his work silently and with dogged determination. Ever since the news had gotten around that Inga would marry Osmund on Midsummer Day, he had been in a dark mood.

Hacon forced himself to turn his gaze and his thoughts toward Siglind's hands and took back the big knife with a faint nod. "Got it. I only wish it weren't so awfully hot. I get dizzy when I stoop over."

Siglind frowned. "I hardly think your complaint would evoke much sympathy from your brother. You're standing with your feet in the cool water cutting reeds. He, on the other hand, is building a roof truss in the burning sun. He needs roofing material, and we don't want to let him down, do we?"

Hacon sighed and shook his head. "No, of course not." Reluctantly, he set to work again. "It's really nice of you to help us, Siglind. Why do you do that?"

"Because I owe your brother a favor. He took me on board his ship, fed me, and brought me here. And he is always inviting me over to eat at your house."

"Yes, that's really noble of him," Hacon whispered to the reeds.

Siglind did not reply. But Gunda, who was sitting with Nils on a blanket on the shore in the shade of a hawthorn bush tying reeds together, exchanged a knowing grin with Hacon.

Siglind noticed, but she ignored it, as well as Hacon's disrespectful remark. She was not in a position to reprimand Candamir's brother or slave. She had no standing here and no idea what her future would be among these people. She didn't even know where she would live when everyone had built a house. She was completely alone, as she had said to Osmund, and though it was of her own volition, this circumstance frightened her. It was only in Austin's presence that she felt secure, for he radiated a deep, inner peace and spoke to her of a security that had nothing to do with a roof over one's head. And though Candamir was noticeably gruff toward his slave if they sat next to each other at a meal or spoke too long and too softly together, he tolerated it nonetheless, and for that Siglind was grateful as well.

She checked on her three reed cutters once more, then sat down in the grass along the shore and began, just like Gunda, to gather the wet stalks together into tight bunches and tie them with strong wool yarn to form shingles.

For a while, they worked silently, and the pile of cut reeds got larger and larger. But when the Turon slipped in the mud along the shore and fell backwards into the water, Hacon felt he had earned a little cooling off, too. He thrust Candamir's precious knife carelessly into the mud, dropped into the water, and dove under. He swam a ways below the surface and pulled the legs out from under the Turon, who had just stood up again. He went down with an inarticulate sound of protest.

Hacon and the Turon frolicked a while in the cool water. In the weeks since the beginning of construction, they had become good friends. Siglind walked to the bank and retrieved Candamir's knife, so it wouldn't be washed away, and watched in amusement as the young men splashed each other with water, pushed each other over, went down, and then came back up again, gasping. She jumped at the sound of a sharp voice. "So that's what you call work, is it?"

They were so far away from the ferry that they hadn't seen Olaf coming. Suddenly he was standing there on the bank, hands on his hips, regarding the two young men in the river with a frown.

Their boisterous play stopped, and they emerged from the water.

Olaf grabbed the unfortunate slave by the arm and punched him in the face. "So that's how faithfully you serve me as soon as my back is turned," he said, knocking the Turon to the ground with a second punch and kicking him in the stomach. The slave doubled up, rolled onto his side, away from the cruel kicks, struggled for breath, and retched.

Olaf looked down at him for a moment before turning around to his son. "Why aren't you keeping order here?"

Jared straightened up. "They were just cooling off for a moment, Father, that's all."

"Oh, I can well believe that," he said, kicking his slave in the side once more. "Stand up, you wimp," he commanded. "Get to work, and don't think I am finished with you."

Hacon had been watching, his eyes wide, but now he spoke up. "Please, Olaf. Leave him be. It…it was my fault."

"Oh, is that so?" Olaf stepped toward him, and Hacon instinctively retreated. He felt ashamed that he wasn't better able to conceal his fear, but the violent temper of this huge man with the silver beard had intimidated many a grown-up. "So you're the one who's having a good time here at my expense? Is that what honor means to you? Is that how you fulfill your brother's promise?"

His big hand closed around Hacon's upper arm like an iron clamp, and the boy clenched his teeth, but Siglind said calmly, "If I were you, I'd think twice about what I was doing, Olaf."

He let go of Hacon and wheeled around toward her. "You have a passion for meddling in affairs that don't concern you."

She didn't reply, lowering her eyes in feigned humility, but she had achieved what she wanted. Olaf's fury disappeared as suddenly as it had come, and Hacon got off unscathed, though not scot-free.

"So it was your fault, was it?" Olaf asked sternly.

Hacon bit his tongue so he wouldn't say what he was thinking—*No one here has done anything they need to apologize for.* He nodded meekly.

"And do you think it's right to break your brother's word like this?"

Hacon shook his head. "I didn't, I swear."

"Well, I saw it myself. But I'll give you the chance to redeem yourself. You can guard my sheep tonight to compensate for the time you stole from me."

The Turon hid his face in the grass. It had been *his* chore to tend the sheep that night, but it seemed that his master had other plans for him...

Hacon nodded with relief. "Sure, Olaf. Just tell me where to find them and when to be there."

"It's an hour's walk due east of here in a hollow in the grasslands, where the land is better for grazing. That's where they are. You start out an hour before sunset and take over from Gunnar."

Hacon felt decidedly uneasy, all alone out there under the starry sky. He had never tended sheep at night, for in the old homeland their little herd had been kept in fields that were fenced in, and in the summer there were no wolves in Elasund, so the sheep could be left to themselves.

It was child's play, completely safe, Gunnar had assured him. He just had to make certain not to let the fire go out. If the animals got restless, that was a sign that a wolf was probably nearby, but that almost never happened. If so, all he had to do was to pick up a burning branch and drive the flock closer together, then walk around them in a circle until the wolf left to look for easier prey.

With the new lambs, Olaf's flock numbered more than two and a half dozen. Candamir had never had that many, but that didn't worry Hacon. Sheep were docile and lazy, and by nature preferred to remain together. He was not concerned he might lose one. It was just the loneliness and the darkness that troubled him. All the stories he had ever heard about trolls and moor ghosts suddenly came to mind. He moved closer to the fire and poked it with a stick. Softly, he sang the song of Odin and Tanuri to himself, in order to drive away the silence. But he had not been aware of how great his fear was until he felt a hand on his shoulder. He cried out in terror and wheeled around.

"Hacon." A soft, gentle laugh. "It's only me."

"Gunda..."

"Yes."

His astonishment left him speechless for a moment. He waited until his heart stopped racing before he asked, "What...what in all the world are you doing here?"

"I followed you."

"Why?" he asked, puzzled.

She sat next to him, and now he could see her. She picked up the sleeping infant she was carrying in a cloth on her chest and bedded him down in the soft grass. Then she looked at Hacon, her big eyes earnest and radiant, and seized his hand. "I've been waiting a long time for the chance to be alone with you."

The boy took his hand away uneasily. "I'm afraid that's not a very good idea. What would Candamir say? Won't he be wondering where you are?" he asked anxiously.

She shook her head. Candamir had lately been so tired at night that he fell asleep right after supper if she didn't lie down with him. At sunset that evening she had told him she wanted to go down to the river and bathe. He had not objected, his eyes already closing with exhaustion. "He won't notice anything, don't worry." She took his right hand again, leaned forward, and gently placed her lips on his. Hacon shut his eyes.

His conscience plagued him. He was fully aware that with this kiss alone he was betraying his brother. And he suspected that Gunda had no intention of leaving it at that. Candamir didn't deserve that, he knew. His brother hadn't even been angry when Hacon confessed what had happened on the riverbank and the trouble he had gotten into.

Candamir had merely advised him, with a weary sigh, to use the night hours to meditate about virtues such as loyalty and devotion to duty. And Hacon had had the firm intention of doing just that, but instead, here he was about to commit a truly disgraceful breach of faith.

He turned his head away. "Gunda, no..."

"And why not? No one has to know, Hacon. I'll return before it gets light. There is enough moonlight to find my way back."

"But that's not the point..."

"Isn't it true," she interrupted, "that he is always telling you not to do things, while taking everything he wants for himself? Would you say that's fair?"

"No." Though Hacon had to admit she had found a sore spot.

"So there you are. Come now, Hacon, stop brooding." Her voice was a gentle whisper, and he felt a pleasant shudder. "He doesn't really want me anymore. You know very well who he's pining away for. But you want me, don't you?"

"Yes," he said.

Gunda slipped her threadbare tunic down below her shoulder, took Hacon's hand, and placed it on her breast.

Hacon blinked in concentration. So *that's* how they felt—different from anything he had ever touched, a completely new sensation. He learned a lot of new things that night. Gunda put everything she had into seducing him, thankful for his gentle shyness, his arousal, and his joy. She had followed him in order to take her revenge on Candamir, but she got much more than that. For as clumsy as Hacon was, he gave her everything back that she offered him, and she was comforted at how unrestrained this young man was in his desire for her.

When Olaf found them the next morning, they were still sleeping, exhausted, naked, and in a close embrace. The sheep had scattered widely, and he discovered traces of blood in the grass.

Olaf brought them back, bound and in disgrace. He rode on a nervous mare that was only half broken in, pulling the two malefactors along behind him on a long rope. Little Nils kept crying at the top of his voice, as he was hungry, and whenever there was enough slack in the rope, Gunda tried to calm him down and console him by stroking his hair with her bound hands. But to no avail. Neither she nor Hacon was wearing shoes, Olaf had set a fast pace, and both had bloody feet when they arrived.

The women and girls who saw the sad threesome on its way to the village green needed no explanation. Brigitta sent Inga into the forest to get the men. Soon they arrived in the village, hurrying along in groups of two or three with their axes still in hand, as if a fire had broken out.

They gathered at the new ash tree, forming two circles around Olaf and his two prisoners. The men made up the inner circle, and the women and slaves stood on the outside.

Slowly like a sleepwalker, Candamir moved a few steps closer and stopped in front of Olaf. The skin over his cheekbones and around his eyes looked strangely thin and drawn. He looked at neither his brother nor his slave.

"Six sheep, Candamir," Olaf said, loudly enough so that everyone could hear. He spoke calmly, seeming much more in control of himself than the day before at the river. But his eyes were strangely dull. "The wolves took a fifth of my herd while your brother lost his innocence."

Candamir turned to Hacon. It took the boy a while to summon the courage to raise his head and look his brother in the eye. What he saw was not what he had expected. He had been prepared for fury and disgust, but not this undisguised horror—worse than the night the Turons had raided Elasund.

"Candamir," he began hesitantly, but his brother raised his left hand in order to silence him, and at almost the same instant back-handed Gunda with his right, who cried out in fright and staggered backward. He seized her arm before she could fall, but let her go almost at once and took the infant out of the sling without touching her again. Nils bawled louder than ever, and his was the only voice to be heard in the silent meadow. Candamir turned away and brought his son to Asta. "Take him away." Then he returned to Olaf. "Six sheep?" he asked.

The tall seafarer nodded. "A ram, two ewes, and three lambs. And I'm eager to know, Candamir—how do you intend to pay me for this? What does your brother have, or what do you have, to pay me for my loss that you are responsible for?"

Without looking at her, Candamir pointed to Gunda with his thumb. "Her."

Olaf raised his eyebrows scornfully. "No, thank you. She's not worth that much. I have plenty of young women, and *my* slaves are loyal to me. I don't need an unfaithful Frisian slut, and I have just as little interest in one of your stupid slaves, not even your Saxon. It's too late for that."

Candamir felt his gut shrink to a painful little knot. "You know that I don't have anything else to pay you with," he forced himself to say.

Olaf smiled. In fact, he was beaming with satisfaction, something that Hacon couldn't understand. "All right then. You know what the law prescribes in that case, don't you?"

Candamir looked around, seeking support. The gazes of the other men were full of pity, and nowhere did he see malice, but neither a spark of opposition.

He lowered his head. "Yes, I know the law, Olaf. So do it, and then let us change the law, for it is worthless and wrong."

Olaf raised his finger in warning. "The law is time-honored, proven, and just. Free, well-to-do men pay with silver or cattle. Slaves and paupers like you pay with blood. I think a dozen lashes for each lost animal is reasonable."

Candamir flinched, but he raised no objection. It *was* reasonable. There were no sheep in this land, and therefore the few they had brought along with them were especially valuable. He looked at his brother.

*His face is gray,* thought Hacon. But Candamir's features remained impassive and his voice was cold as he said, "May mighty Thor, who is your patron god, lend your cowardly, traitorous heart a share of his courage. You will need it. *Brother.*"

Olaf led Hacon past the deserted building site of his house to a lone beech that was still standing at the edge of the clearing. The crowd followed him, though no one spoke as they all solemnly assembled around the mighty tree.

Hacon's hands were still tied. Olaf tossed the rope over one of the lower boughs of the tree and pulled on it until the boy's arms were stretched out over his head. Then he wrapped the loose end around the trunk several times and secured it with a tight knot. When he had finished, he walked over to Hacon, grabbed the neck of his tunic from behind with both hands, and gave it a hard tug. The worn material ripped easily, baring Hacon's shoulders and back.

Hacon had closed his eyes and pressed his mouth on his arm. His knees were shaking. He couldn't remember ever being so afraid and so alone, and he realized with pathetic certainty that before long he would pee in his trousers. He felt an almost uncontrollable urge to beg for mercy, even though he knew it would do no good. The only thing that stopped him was the fear of his brother's scorn.

If he had dared to open his eyes and look over his shoulder, he would have seen Olaf murmuring a few words to his eldest son and sending him off to get the whip. When Austin saw what Jared came running back with, he felt sick. In his homeland, whipping was a common form of punishment as well—though only for slaves—but he had never before seen such a barbaric instrument of torture. This whip had three knotted straps, each weighted with little lead balls at the end. Slowly the monk fell on his knees, folded his hands, and started to pray.

Olaf walked behind Hacon, shook out the whip carefully, almost lovingly, until the straps had untangled and the lead weights jingled softly. Then he sent it whistling through the air, striking Hacon on his bare shoulders.

Hacon's screams echoed over the empty brown fields. Three closely spaced welts appeared, and almost at once small trickles of blood started to run down his back. The second blow struck at almost exactly the same spot, and this time Hacon's scream sounded like the cry of a hunted, wounded animal. He threw his head back, instinctively though futilely pulling at the ropes.

The faces of many of the settlers were contorted in pain, and they turned away, not just the women, but a number of men as well, though they believed in the old law and thought Hacon was only getting what he deserved.

After the first dozen blows, Hacon's knees gave out, so that the entire weight of his body was suspended by his arms and his lacerated wrists. His cries became hoarse.

Candamir, who until then had stood firm as a rock in the first row and had been watching the gruesome spectacle without moving a muscle, suddenly stirred. "That's enough," he said quietly, moving a step in Olaf's direction. But Osmund and Harald seized him by the arms and pulled him back.

"You mustn't interfere, lad," the smith warned in an urgent tone. "It is his right. You would just make everything worse."

Candamir tensed his arm muscles and tried to tug free of their grip, but they wouldn't let him go. Their huge hands just gripped his arms more firmly.

In the meanwhile, Olaf went about his work, calmly and with great precision. It was evident that he had some experience in this art. One inch at a time he laid bare the flesh on Hacon's back. When the boy had paid for the second sheep, he uttered barely more than a feeble whimper. His body flinched from the merciless blows, but he no longer offered any resistance. He was almost unconscious.

Candamir looked at Harald. "Let me go."

Hesitantly, the smith released his arm.

Candamir turned toward the other side. "Osmund…"

His friend made no move to let him go. "Only if you swear that you will be reasonable."

"*Reasonable?* Don't you see what's going on here? He's killing him. So let me go."

Osmund looked over toward the beech tree, undecided. His uncle showed no signs of exhaustion or mercy. He had started to sweat a little, but his arm swung the whip with undiminished force. Osmund, too, believed that the law was inviolable and that a public punishment should be severe enough to act as a deterrent for everyone present. Yet cruelty was not in his nature. And he pitied Hacon and was worried about him.

Slowly he withdrew his hand. "But you can't do anything," he murmured anxiously.

"I can't?" His fingers trembling, Candamir loosened his belt buckle, let the belt fall to the ground, then grabbed his new tunic by the back of the neck and pulled it over his head. He placed it in the hands of his astonished friend before walking toward the trunk of the beech tree. There he waited until Olaf started to swing the whip again, and caught the straps with his left hand.

Olaf turned around, furious. "What do you think you're doing?"

Candamir let go of the whip. His hand was wet with Hacon's blood and his throat so dry that he was unable to answer. He shook his head and stepped behind his brother, covering him completely with his own considerably wider back. He reached his left arm around Hacon's chest and pulled the boy to his feet so that he would not choke. Hacon groaned weakly as Candamir's chest pressed against his back. With his free right hand, Candamir supported himself on the trunk of the tree. He glanced over his shoulder, and when he saw Olaf's rapt face he regained his voice. "What do I think I'm doing? I'll take half the blows for him. That isn't against the law, is it? So what are you waiting for?"

Olaf overcame his astonishment and laughed. It was a rough, rumbling sound of satisfaction that seemed to come from deep in his belly. "Didn't I tell you that no man's debt to me remains unpaid?" he asked.

*I owe you nothing at all,* Candamir thought, but he saved his breath.

When the lashes struck his back for the first time with that repulsive, whistling slap, he bitterly regretted his decision. It was dreadful—much worse than he had imagined. The sting took his breath away, and he wondered how Hacon had managed to get sufficient breath for his screams. Before the pain subsided, the whip struck his back again, and the weighted straps penetrated so deeply into his flesh that he thought they would expose his backbone. That was enough. That was all he could take for his unfaithful, devious, treacherous brother. Yet Candamir stayed where he was. He flinched with each of the well-placed lashes, and sweat ran down his body in streams, but he stood there as if he were rooted in the soil, just like the beech tree. He counted the blows, clenching his teeth so hard that he could hear them grinding. His eyes were closed tight, his neck muscles stood out in thick strands, and he was vaguely aware that he was holding on to his brother much too hard, as if he were clinging to him rather than supporting him. The fingers of his right hand dug into the raw bark of the tree trunk, warm in the sunlight, and that gave him some consolation.

When finally the punishment for all six sheep had been carried out, Olaf lowered the whip, panting.

Candamir waited, motionless. Then Osmund came over, his knife in hand, and cut Hacon's ropes while giving his uncle a look of unconcealed loathing. The boy sank to the ground like a sack of grain, taking his brother down with him. Candamir did not let go of him and found himself half lying and half sitting in the grass, his left leg twisted painfully. But at the moment he could do nothing about that. His long hair hung in his face and covered Hacon's head as well.

A group of people gathered around them—Candamir could see their feet, and he heard a woman crying. It was Asta, he knew.

"Go away," he said. "Leave us alone."

Osmund nodded to the others, and Harald put an arm around Asta's shoulders to lead her away. Austin withdrew, but only a few steps. Suspiciously, he eyed Olaf, who was still standing in the shadow of the beech, regarding the fruits of his handiwork with a faint smile.

"Please, Uncle, if you would...," Osmund said brusquely.

Olaf awoke from his ruminations, nodded grudgingly, and left.

Osmund knelt down beside his friend and took Hacon carefully by the arms. "You must let me take him, Candamir."

Without hesitation, Candamir let go of his brother, who sobbed hoarsely when Osmund put an arm around him.

Candamir winced at the sound. "Be careful!"

Osmund nodded. "Come here, Saxon. Take Hacon to your hut and do for him what you can."

Austin bent over the boy and put his hand on his forehead. Hacon had started to tremble, and his face had gone almost white. "Hacon, open your eyes," Austin said firmly.

The boy's eyelids fluttered open.

"Ah, that's better." Austin smiled at him. No one would have suspected how shaken the Saxon was. "I'll carry you now. It isn't far, and when we get there, I'll give you something to ease the pain. Do you understand me?"

"Yes," Hacon murmured, but he looked disoriented and his pupils were dilated.

Austin and Osmund communicated silently with a nod. Then the monk took Hacon's hands, pulled him to his feet, and bent over, so that the boy could rest on his shoulder as he collapsed. Before the Saxon could straighten up again, Hacon had passed out. "Thank you, God," Austin whispered, relieved.

Candamir had used the brief moment when no one was looking at him to get up on his knees. He stayed that way for an instant, one hand on the tree trunk again, and with his eyes closed asked, "Did I scream?"

"No. You didn't utter a sound."

Candamir opened his eyes to see if Osmund was lying to him. But Osmund looked him straight in the face, even smiled a little and added, "My uncle didn't like that at all."

"No, I noticed," Candamir said and started to raise his hand to wipe his wet brow, but quickly lowered it again. It hurt so much that it hardly seemed worth the trouble.

"Come, I'll take you down to the river. A little cool water will surely do some good."

Candamir shuddered at the thought of anything touching his back, even a single drop of water. Apart from that, the river seemed to him as far away as Elasund. Nevertheless, he took his friend's hand and let himself be helped to his feet. The beech was a wonderful tree, and it had helped him to bear this ordeal, but he considered chopping it down nonetheless.

When he got up, he staggered and nearly blacked out. Osmund seized him by the arm and said urgently, "Don't fall, do you hear? That would surely be awful."

"You're right. Osmund..." He felt so sick that he could not continue talking. His throat closed with a dry click, but he willed himself not to vomit. He could not bear having to bend over.

"What is it?" Osmund took a hesitant step, leading Candamir toward the river. "Come, just put one foot in front of the other. You'll be all right, you'll see. Think about something else. What did you want to say?"

"It...it wasn't just."

"No," Osmund agreed, without reservation. "It certainly wasn't."

"He wanted to kill him."

"I'm not sure he wanted to, but that's probably what would have happened."

"Hacon might still die."

"Perhaps."

"And...and you weren't the only one who saw it was wrong. Harald saw it, and many others, even Haflad, who hates me. They all thought the same thing."

"Yes, I know."

"We must change the law, Osmund. The penalty—or the judgment—must be decided by the *Thing*, and not by an individual."

Anxiously, Osmund regarded his friend's sickly, sweaty face. Candamir's voice had become weak, and he was gasping.

"Perhaps you are right," Osmund said, more to calm him down, and not because he really believed it. "Let's talk about it when you are feeling better."

They arrived at the shore. Candamir squinted out at the glittering surface of the river and then at one of the floats they had built for fishing. "Take me down the river a little."

Osmund stared at him. "Don't you think it's a pretty bad time to take a trip? You must go to Brigitta, or to your Saxon if you prefer, and have your wounds tended to."

"They'll take care of themselves. I must be alone for a while." He wanted to think things through, far from Hacon, and Gunda, and all the sympathetic and curious eyes, and give himself over to his misery.

"Candamir, if you only knew how bad it looks," his friend said, pleadingly.

"Osmund."

"All right, as you wish. But I am coming to bring you back this evening."

*First you'll have to find me,* Candamir thought.

Gunda hadn't seen what happened by the beech tree, as Asta had sent her back to the hut with the children and ordered her to wait there. But she had heard Hacon screaming, and when Austin returned with the boy over his shoulder, she broke out in tears.

"I killed him! It's my fault," she cried, burying her face in her hands.

The Saxon was infinitely grateful when Siglind suddenly appeared in the doorway, since a badly injured boy *and* a hysterical woman was more than even he could cope with.

Siglind sized up the situation in one glance. She took Gunda's hands in hers and said in a stern voice, "You must pull yourself together. He's not dead. Come, let's leave, as we don't want to disturb Austin and Hacon. Where are the rest of the slaves?"

Gunda shrugged. "I don't know. They probably just slipped away—as they always do when things get too hot." She sobbed and couldn't take her eyes off Hacon's bloody back, but she did try to calm down.

Austin had put the unconscious boy face down on the bed and turned his head to the side so he could breathe freely.

"I need help," he said.

Siglind reflected for a moment. Gunda would be of no use at present, that much was clear, and it was probably wiser for her not to be here when Candamir returned. "Take Asta's children to their mother. She is at Harald's house." She saw the longing glance that Gunda cast at her son, but she shook her head firmly. "No, leave him here. He's sleeping and doesn't need you at the moment. I will take care of him, don't worry. But go now."

Gunda knew this was good advice, and she certainly didn't feel ready to face Candamir. So she picked up little Hergild in her arm, took Fulc by the hand, and left, with tears still flowing down her face.

Siglind waited until her shuffling steps had faded away before asking Austin, "Will Candamir kill her?"

The Saxon was busy dabbing at the blood with a grubby rag. Without looking up, he shrugged and said, "I suppose so."

She stepped closer. "You said you need help?"

"I need chamomile, so that the wounds don't become inflamed, and marigold and horsetail so they will heal."

"I know horsetail, it grows in the damp meadows by the river, but I have never heard of the other two."

"Anthemis and calendula?" he ventured.

"Yes, both of those grow in the forest. I've seen them, not far from here."

The monk smiled, relieved. "Those are the ones I mean."

Siglind turned around. "I'll hurry," she promised.

Hacon came to with a start and a choked cry, and he started to tremble again. He was bitterly cold, but Austin did not dare to cover him up. Instead, he took his hand, spoke soothingly to him, and told him that the beautiful queen of the Cold Islands had personally gone out to gather healing herbs for him. That conjured up a ghost of a smile on his rigid features.

"Where is Candamir?" Hacon asked.

"I don't know, but no doubt he will return soon." Austin reached for a second cloth, dipped it in a bowl of water, and dabbed the boy's sweaty forehead.

"I'm so thirsty," Hacon complained.

Austin wished he had wine or mead, or at least a sip of beer—anything to give Hacon some strength—but he had only water. Carefully he put the cup to Hacon's lips, and the boy drank greedily. A moment later, his eyes closed again.

Siglind kept her word. Not two hours had passed when she returned, even though she had to go a good distance to reach the forest now that so much land had been cleared, and collecting herbs was in itself a time-consuming task.

"Wonderful," the monk murmured when she put down at his feet the bulging bag she had quickly fashioned from a piece of cloth. "Would you stay with him for a bit while I prepare the salve?" he asked.

"What must I do?"

Austin sighed and shrugged his shoulders. "There is not much we can do at the moment. Try to speak some encouraging words to him when he wakes up. That's probably the most important thing. He thinks his brother will never forgive him."

*He might be quite right about that,* she thought.

"And pray for him," Austin added. "That never hurts."

She nodded, took the blood-soaked cloth from his hand, and sent him on his way with a wave of her hand.

To make ointment, vegetable oil, wine, and beeswax were required, but today Austin was prepared to do without such niceties. Crushing the stems and blossoms took more time than he felt he could spare, and he had no intention of going from hut to hut asking for oil and wax. And he certainly had no intention of asking the old witch for her supply of clove oil and spoiling his ointment with her heathen magic. Instead, he cooked the crushed plants with a little water that he had consecrated earlier, stirred in a spoonful of melted pork fat, and then allowed the rather strong smelling ointment to cool down. Nonetheless, Hacon groaned so pitiably when the Saxon applied it that Siglind struggled to hold back her tears. She gazed down at the injured boy, then at his tiny nephew, wondering what would become of them all.

"Where's Candamir?" Hacon asked again. But they didn't know.

Candamir stayed in the forest for three days and two nights.

He found a small, grassy hollow near the river, lay down in it, and listened to the water, the birds, and the wind, waiting for his back to stop feeling like someone had poured liquid fire over it. He moved as little as possible and soon fell into a deep sleep. He was awakened by Osmund's voice as the golden light of the setting sun flooded the forest. "Say something if you want me to find you."

Candamir kept silent.

"Then I'll just come back tomorrow morning!"

*Thank you, my friend. Only brother I still have...*

That first night he railed against his fate, cursing the Norns and the gods who had led him to this wonderful land that promised whatever a man might desire, only to bring disaster down upon him. He had been betrayed by his own brother and humiliated in front of everyone by his enemy. They had sent him a woman he wanted to spend his life with, but she didn't want him. And they had sent him a son, but the child's mother was a worthless slut. It was almost laughable...

But instead of laughing, he began to cry. And once he started, he found it difficult to stop. He bawled like a little boy until he was finally too exhausted and no more tears would come. He closed his burning eyes and fell into a garish, confused nightmare involving his father, a winter famine, and the storehouse.

He was finally awoken from his restless sleep by something touching him. A little fox was gently nudging him with its damp nose, regarding him curiously, as if sensing that this strange creature was alone and unhappy. The little red fellow sat down in the grass scarcely a yard away. It seemed trusting, and was so amusing that it finally coaxed at least a weak smile from Candamir.

"I hope you are not the cunning Loki trying to lead me into doing something really stupid," Candamir murmured. "I'd probably be inclined to listen."

Osmund kept his word. Every morning and evening he came to the spot where he had left Candamir and called for him, and on the evening of the third day Candamir left his hiding place and went over to him.

"Thanks be to Odin," Osmund said, relieved. "I thought you were dead."

"No, hungry."

Osmund smiled briefly and, as discreetly as possible, cast a glance at Candamir's back. He wasn't surprised to see it was still a dreadful sight—whatever skin was left was colored black and blue, but he was astonished at how well the welts had healed.

"Rest and river water," said Candamir, who had noticed his friend's look.

Osmund nodded. "Do you want to come back, or shall I get something for you to eat and bring it here?"

Candamir was tempted to accept the generous offer, but then shook his head and sighed. "I think if I don't go back today, then I never will."

"Everyone will be happy to see you," Osmund said, matter-of-factly. "Many have come to me and asked about you. They are worried. And all have said they have never seen a man do for another what you did for Hacon. I don't know why you are ashamed, but you have no reason to be. Everyone has nothing but admiration for you."

"Oh, I bet," Candamir replied bitterly. "Especially your uncle..."

"You shouldn't be concerned about what he thinks. By the way, he has very few friends at the moment."

"He never had friends. He doesn't need them." Slowly Candamir walked down to the river with Osmund, and after a short silence added, "I did *not* do it for Hacon."

*Oh, but you did,* Osmund thought. *I saw it.* But all he said was, "He is very sick, Candamir. Your Saxon says it is time you came home."

Candamir did not reply, but silently they headed back toward the village.

Austin, Siglind, and Asta had taken turns watching over Hacon. A fever had seized him the first night, and since then his condition had worsened each day. The fever made him restless, and the wounds would not heal over in spite of the ointment. He was worn down by the pain as much as by his guilt. In his delirium he constantly called out for Candamir, and when he was conscious he asked about him. They couldn't tell him anything, as they had no idea where he was. Osmund had refused to share his secret, worried they'd go in search of him. The only thing he had said was that Candamir would return when he was ready.

For many hours Siglind had prayed at the boy's bedside with Austin, and she was surprised at the peace and strength that gave her. And when Austin baptized the sick boy, all her fear left her, and she realized that now it didn't matter whether he lived or died—he was in the secure bosom of the church, and his soul was immortal.

Evening was coming on when Candamir arrived back at his hut. He stood unnoticed for a moment at the entrance and just watched. Siglind lay on his bed sleeping. She wasn't covered, for the evening was warm, and there even was a small fire in the hut—which Candamir had strictly forbidden. For a moment he became engrossed in observing her slender ankles. Nori, Tjorv, and Heide had likewise gone to bed. Asta and her children were not there. Austin sat quietly on the ground next to Hacon, his knees drawn up, and Gunda crouched right next to the door, nursing her son. She was the first to notice the shadow at the entryway, drew in her breath sharply, and placed her free hand over her mouth. "Master..."

He entered and walked past her without acknowledging her.

Austin raised his head, astonished to see Candamir wearing his new, beautifully embroidered tunic that Osmund had been keeping for him. And in fact, Candamir almost looked the same as always. Only the unusual stiffness of his movements and his slightly narrowed eyes betrayed the truth.

"I am happy to see you are well, Master."

Candamir nodded absentmindedly and looked down at Hacon. "How is he doing?"

Austin sighed and looked at the sick boy, who was breathing heavily. "I'm not really sure," he said, brushing a damp strand of hair from Hacon's forehead. "It's as if his whole body was under siege. His pulse is racing and irregular, the fever isn't going down, and the wounds won't heal. He can't keep down any food. He...he's just slipping away before my very eyes."

*Is he dying?* Candamir wanted to ask, but didn't, as one never knew what a feverish person could hear. He sat down on the ground instead, next to the sickbed, as far away as possible from the hot fire. "Bring me something to eat," he ordered. "I'm hungry."

Austin rose and looked around the small room, at a loss. Gunda had put little Nils down on a blanket. She knew where Heide had put the leftovers of the evening's fish soup and brought Candamir a wooden bowl which gave off a pleasant smell of onions. "Here, it's still warm."

Candamir pretended not to have heard. "Saxon, bring me something to eat, I said!"

Austin took the bowl from Gunda and gave it to him. Candamir nodded briefly, took a sip of the soup, fished out a piece of white meat with his fingers, and ate. Between two bites he growled over his shoulder at Gunda. "Get out."

"But it's dark," she said timidly. "Where shall I go?"

"You can go throw yourself in the river, for all I care." He still refused to look at her.

She stared down at him, her lips slightly parted. Then she hurried out.

Wrapped in a cloak of grim silence, Candamir ate, without paying any heed to what he was tasting. Austin let him be, finally taking the empty bowl from him and casting a handful of dry twigs on the fire.

"Didn't I say not to build a fire in here?"

The Saxon nodded. "I need warm water to tend to him, Master, and for a long time I didn't dare to leave him alone, even for the moment it takes to fetch water outside, especially at night. At night it is the worst."

"It's always that way," Candamir said. If a person was sick or wounded, his resistance seemed to fade with the dying sun at the end of the day. It was as if pain and fever formed an alliance with the darkness, growing stronger. He assumed that was the reason most of those not ordained to die in battle, died at night.

Hacon groaned restlessly. His rattling breath sounded like one long sob.

Candamir looked at him, and an angry furrow formed at the bridge of his nose. "How can he be such a weakling? Osmund was right, I have coddled my brother."

"No, Master, you did not," Austin said softly. "But he is still a boy and for that reason alone cannot be as…indestructible as you. Despite the famine last winter he grew a full head this past year. That takes all the strength he has."

Candamir raised his left hand in protest. "I did everything wrong, simply everything, and now I am paying for it."

"Why do you believe that?" the monk asked, surprised. Since these people had no concept of sin, they could never see a connection between their deeds and their fate. It simply didn't fit with their view of the world.

Candamir hadn't intended to pour his heart out to his Saxon slave, of all people, but he was so weighed down with grief that he couldn't resist. "Everything is slipping away from me. I have failed to teach my brother decency, and now he has brought shame upon both of us. I toil like an ox, but in spite of the wealth of this land, I'm poorer than I ever was in the barren old homeland. Olaf will refuse to give me the seed he owes me, and I wonder how I can live with myself for having built him a house for just a few measly grains of rye..."

"Do not despair, Master," the monk said. "Let peace come into your heart, and then you will find a way, believe me. Above all, forgive your brother."

Candamir looked down at the wounded boy. It grieved him to see him suffer so, and he remembered how Hacon's tormented screams had nearly torn out his heart. He had cared for his little brother since he was eight years old, had taught him how to pee standing up, to shoot a bow and arrow, to use snowshoes and skis, and a thousand other things. It was impossible to stop caring for him overnight. The habit was too deeply ingrained for that. But he could not forgive him.

"Why should I do that?" he demanded.

"Because it is the only way that can lead you, both of you, out of the Valley of Shadow. It will make a wiser, a better man out of you."

"It will make a weakling and fool of me," Candamir said angrily, but in a low voice, in order not to waken anyone. "And what about *her*? Do you suggest I forgive her as well?" he asked.

Austin shrugged, not knowing quite what to say. Theoretically, of course, the answer was yes. Christ had forgiven the adulteress. *Let him who is without sin cast the first stone.* But the monk could not advocate God's boundless, divine mercy. No sin seemed more despicable to him than that of an unchaste woman. "The situation is a bit different I believe, Master," Austin replied. "Hacon deeply regrets his deed. In Gunda's case, I am by no means certain that is so."

"No," Candamir growled. "She doesn't regret what she did. But she will..."

"Are you going to kill her?" the Saxon asked uneasily.

Candamir shrugged, feigning indifference. He had not yet decided. What held him back was not sympathy, or even affection—not even consideration for his innocent, defenseless son. But Gunda was a healthy young woman who could still bear many children, and nothing was needed here more urgently than numerous offspring. It seemed a senseless waste to kill her—and too light a punishment.

"I don't know. Perhaps I will sell her, if anyone wants her. I've got to try somehow to get hold of seed, you know. But she is the least of my worries at the moment. What I do wonder, though, is how I can let Olaf live if Hacon dies?"

Austin sat up straight. "You swore an oath, Master. You swore to break with the law of blood vengeance."

"I know. But if I keep my oath, I will offend the gods and my ancestors, and everyone here will call me a coward."

"No one here would dare to call you a coward after what you have done. Besides, if you break your oath, you also offend your ancestors and the gods."

Candamir nodded with a mirthless smile. "I'd be accursed either way."

Austin knew this wasn't the best time, but he couldn't resist. "Now you see how cruel and foolish your gods are. If that's all they have to offer you, perhaps it's time to turn away from them, to my god."

"You're really clever, Saxon," Candamir said, one corner of his mouth twitching. "But first your god would have to prove to me that he truly is more merciful and mightier than my own, as you're so fond of saying. Tell him to work a miracle and save my brother."

"If he did it, would you renounce the old gods?"

Candamir thought for a moment. "I don't think I could. But I would no longer fight him, or forbid you—or Hacon—from worshipping him."

Austin shook his head with a sigh. "That is a rather poor offer, Master, and I have learned from experience that my god does not like to bargain. But I will see what can be done."

Before Candamir could berate him for this evasive answer, his brother came to. He suddenly awoke from his feverish sleep, rolled to the side, and buried his head in his arms. "Candamir," he moaned in a choking voice.

"I am here, Hacon."

The boy slowly took his arm away from his face and looked at Candamir, blinking. "Is it true? You came back?" Hesitantly, he held out his hand toward his brother.

His fingers closed around Hacon's hand before he could stop himself.

"Oh, Candamir. I…I…"

"Shush."

"Candamir, I'm so scared."

How often had he heard that? *Candamir, I'm scared. I dreamed a monster was sitting on top of me. The wind is howling so loud, Candamir. I'm scared.* And just as each time before, he had the urge to say, *You must learn to control your fear. It's time you became a man, Hacon.* But just as in the past, he moved closer and carefully rested his brother's head on his thigh.

Siglind was not quite sure whether she was awake or dreaming, but she heard a wonderfully clear, bright voice softly singing a song about the twelve halls of the gods:

*The fifth seat is Froheim*
*With golden, sparkling Valhalla*
*Where Odin chooses daily*
*Warriors slain in battle*

Slowly, without moving, she opened her eyes and could scarcely believe what she saw. Candamir had returned, and it was his voice she heard—though it sounded completely transformed. He had taken Hacon's head in his lap, and the boy lay still. But she could see him breathing, and knew he wasn't dead.

Candamir had put one of his hands on the boy's shock of dark hair and looked down at him solemnly while he sang.

*Known to all who visit Odin*
*To admire the hall*
*Shields are the shingles, spear shafts, the rafters*
*Chain mail covers the bench*

It was a gloomy song, since like so many others it told of heroic death and of treason, but Siglind paid scant attention to the words. She was enthralled by the sound of this voice, and the sight of the two brothers. She had never seen Candamir at such an unguarded moment. While he was clearly exhausted and wounded and despairing, there was something else that captivated her, something profound. She could find no easy words to describe what he felt for his brother and what he revealed at this moment when he believed himself to be unobserved. In any case, it was something she never would have expected from Candamir. And something she wanted for herself.

This thought frightened her so much that she shut her eyes tightly like a little girl who thinks she can escape the threatening shadow if only she closes her eyes tightly enough. She lay there motionless, hardly daring to breathe.

*You are drunk, you drank too greedily*
*Muddled is your mind*
*Much did you miss when you went without*
*My leadership and your loyalty.*

Thus spoke Odin to the renegade Geirroed, yet Siglind's newly found god could have accused her of the very same thing. And she had no intention of incurring his anger by deviating from her chosen path. But at the sound of Candamir's voice, her heart was suddenly in her mouth, she felt how the little hairs on her arms and legs stood up, and she was overcome by a strange and uncanny longing.

She was experiencing these odd feelings for the first time in her life, but she well understood what they meant. *No,* she thought, *that's out of the question, completely out of the question.* She no longer wanted any man. No matter what she thought she had just seen in Candamir's eyes, she had also seen that he could be just as brutal and unmerciful as anyone else. All men, her mother had taught her, were alike. They had nothing in mind but battle and mead and planting their seed in as many wombs as possible. Moreover, they weren't satisfied until they had made life miserable for themselves and for everyone around them.

Siglind's experiences bore out this assessment, and she had had enough of it. It was for this reason that she had chosen the Saxon's god as her betrothed, and if she turned her back on him now, she would be no better than Gunda.

Candamir's words suddenly roused her from her thoughts. "Saxon, come here, I think he's dying."

Siglind sat up with a start.

Austin had been kneeling on the ground in front of the hut, haggling with his god and listening to the first birdsong of the new day. But now he came rushing in and put his hand on Hacon's chest.

Then he shook his head, and when he looked up, Siglind saw to her amazement that he was smiling. "No, Master, I don't think so. He's sleeping. For the first time in three days he's sleeping soundly. I think his fever has even subsided a bit. Here, feel for yourself. His heart is beating more calmly than it was just last evening."

Candamir quickly placed the palm of his hand on Hacon's chest, as if he feared that this sign of hope might vanish if he didn't experience it fast enough. But he saw that Austin was right—even though Hacon was no longer moving and was breathing too quietly for them to notice, his heart was beating evenly and strongly.

It would be two more days before they could be sure. Several times the fever and shivering fits returned, and they were still unable to keep Hacon quiet for very long, so the healing progressed slowly. The boy resisted, and sometimes even screamed when Austin applied the ointment, something Candamir could understand after he himself had had the doubtful pleasure for the first time. The stinking salve burned like fire. But it helped—first him and then, finally, his brother. The painful whiplashes healed without becoming badly inflamed.

When a whole day had gone by without the fever returning, and Hacon had eaten his first bowl of soup, Siglind said goodbye. Candamir accompanied her out. It was late, dusk was falling, and crickets were chirping in the grass.

"What a splendid evening," she exclaimed.

Candamir watched her with a secret rapture that he was now so accustomed to. Siglind had thrown her head back, stretched out her arms, and was taking a deep breath of the sweet summer air. With her bare feet, her tanned skin, the faded dress, and the day's last light playing through her hair, she looked like she had spent her entire life on this summer meadow, as if she were a part of this land. Tanuri, he thought, perhaps for the thousandth time. The beautiful daughter of the fairies must have looked like this when Odin first caught sight of her by the brook at dusk.

"Siglind..."

She opened her eyes, and when she looked at him all he could do was smile. It was a moment of perfect happiness, and though it lasted only for a few heartbeats, that didn't lessen its delight.

"Yes?" she asked. "What were you going to say?"

"Oh...I forget."

"Hm," she said, folding her hands behind her and teetering on the tips of her toes. "Let me think. I assume you wanted to thank me, and all that sort of thing."

"I really should, shouldn't I?"

She brushed her hair behind her ear and shook her head. "No, it's not really necessary. I couldn't actually do anything because I don't know enough about such things. Maybe I should ask Austin to teach me about herbs. I think he's the one who saved Hacon."

"Or his god," Candamir murmured.

Siglind laughed softly. "Yes, I heard about your deal."

Candamir shrugged slightly and also brushed away the small braid dangling from his left temple, as if imitating her gesture. "Not an excessive price for a life, it seems to me, even if it's the life of a weakling and good-for-nothing."

Her face turned serious. She reached out with her left hand as if she wanted to seize his hand, but then drew it back. "You must not think so poorly of your brother," she said, shaking her head. "You are only tormenting yourself and doing him an injustice. He is neither a good-for-nothing, nor is he weak, just young. He made a bad mistake and paid dearly for it. Isn't that enough?"

No, he thought, full of resentment, but he didn't intend to discuss this with her any further. She had already seen and heard more about his family affairs in the past few days than he liked. "Maybe," he answered with seeming indifference. "I've got to think about that."

"Do that. And don't take too long."

"Now what does that mean?"

"It means you've got to stop running away and hiding. You've had nothing but a few gruff words for anyone who came to ask how you were, with the exception of Osmund and the smith. You can't hide forever. You must change the law, you've said. You were right. Make sure you do it before everyone forgets what happened. Believe me, not everyone will remember it as long as you and Hacon."

"You always remind me, if I've ever forgotten it, that you were once a queen," he said, thus avoiding a reply.

"Oh, no one in the Cold Island has less influence on the laws than the queen, believe me. Cnut alone rules over the country, and nothing rules over Cnut but his whims."

"Then the people on the Cold Islands have moved far away from the traditions of their ancestors."

Siglind nodded. "In a new homeland, traditions and ancestors quickly lose their significance."

"Yes, that's true."

"That doesn't have to be all bad," she said, anticipating his objection. "As long as it doesn't lead to people losing their values and subjecting themselves to a tyrant just because it's easier." Suddenly she spoke heatedly. "It happens faster than you think. And it can happen here, too, Candamir."

He thought he knew to whom she was referring, but replied with a shake of his head, "I am the last one who could prevent that, as matters stand. I've lost all the respect that I may ever have had, and with it my influence, thanks to my brother, whom you seem to care so much about."

"You are wrong, both with regard to the situation in general and your brother," she said impatiently.

"I really don't think you are in a position to judge that," he said, his voice suddenly harsh.

Siglind expelled her breath audibly. "No, of course not," she murmured, dejected, and turned away. "Good night, Candamir."

"Good night." He watched her until she had vanished in the tall grass in the shadows of the dying day.

The weeks before midsummer were dark ones for Candamir and all those who had the misfortune to live under his roof. While the other settlers enjoyed the splendid summer weather and looked forward with anticipation to the great holiday and to the wedding, darkest winter prevailed in the little hut near the meadow at the edge of the water.

After Hacon had recovered, Candamir went to work in the forest every morning with his brother and his slaves, pretending to be carefree, even laughing if someone grimaced at the sight of his back when he took off his tunic in the noonday heat. But as soon as he got home, his mood changed. He was so abrupt with his slaves that they avoided him as best they could. He treated Hacon with scorn and frosty condescension, insulting the boy at every opportunity. Hacon took to running off whenever he could, eating supper at Wiland's and slinking back to the hut once everyone had gone to sleep.

It was even worse for Gunda. Candamir refused to take any food from her hand and never spoke with her. He had resolved never to touch her again. But when he got drunk on the fermented sheep's milk potion, he occasionally sought her out. Gunda was submissive and pretended to be aroused, no matter how rough he was with her, for she feared above all else that his hatred of her could turn against their helpless son.

And after these nights when he awoke the next morning with a pounding head and a foul taste in his mouth, he felt a wretched mixture of despair and self-loathing.

"Here, Master," said Heide, handing Candamir a dish of orache and goat's cheese. She knew he liked it. "I also have a nice piece of calf's liver for you," she added.

"Then bring it to me."

He shoveled the tasty stew into his mouth with a wooden spoon and was done by the time she brought him the liver—a small piece of dark, juicy meat on a wooden plate.

"Is that all?" he growled.

Heide nodded, deciding not to admit that she had given a piece of liver not just to Hacon but to Gunda as well. The girl was getting thinner and thinner and no longer had enough milk, which was no doubt the reason little Nils screamed so much.

"There's still plenty of stew left," the cook said, trying to placate him.

"Good, bring me some. And see to it that the bawling stops."

She took the empty bowl from him and carried it back to the fire. "Little children will cry, Master, it's normal. You did so yourself, and even louder than your son here. I would know, because I was there. You can't do anything about it."

"I can't? Bring me a stone the size of a fist and I'll show you what you can do about it."

Heide turned pale and gave him a look of reproach, shaking her head. Gunda uttered a little cry of anguish and jumped up from her place at the fire in order to take Nils someplace where his father couldn't hear him.

"You stay," Candamir snarled in her direction, without looking around.

"Master…," Austin started to say hesitantly.

"You be quiet," Candamir told him. "I don't want to hear anything from you."

"I'm sure you don't," the Saxon replied. "Because you would know it was the truth, wouldn't you? And what self-pitying weakling can stand hearing the truth?"

Tjorv, Nori, and Heide stared at him in disbelief. He knew what a risk he was taking, but he had been watching this misery for weeks in silence, and enough was enough.

"What did you call me?" Candamir asked, rising from his seat.

Austin stood and moved away from the fire. "You understood me perfectly well," he replied, with apparent equanimity.

Almost thankful, Candamir rushed at him. His endless brooding had long ago brought him to the conclusion that the Saxon and his accursed god were responsible for all his misery, and now at least one of them would pay for it. He seized his slave with his left hand, and made a fist with his right, but before he could land a punch, two huge arms encircled him from behind, yanking him back.

Candamir didn't need to look over his shoulder to know who was visiting him at this inopportune time. He knew only one man whose tunic was in danger of splitting at the forearms when he flexed his muscles. "Harald..."

"Right you are," the smith answered in his pleasant, deep voice. "Do I have to shake you a little first, or can I let you go?"

"Please be so kind."

Harald released him from the bear hug but did not let him go completely. Placing a hand on his shoulder, he turned him around and asked, "Have you eaten? Then let's go down to the river. I have a few things I'd like to discuss with you."

It wasn't hard to guess what Harald had to say to him, and he didn't want to hear it from him any more than from his Saxon. But he couldn't silence the smith as easily as his slave. Aside from the fact that Harald was one of the most highly regarded men in their community and was his friend, he certainly couldn't have dealt with the consequences as easily.

"Yes, of course, Harald."

With a nod of satisfaction the smith turned away, not without first winking at Austin surreptitiously, and led Candamir down to the river.

The two men took the little ferry across to the other side, as many seeking privacy did. Here on the south shore it was quiet and peaceful, and the fields of rye were an inspiring sight. The grain was thriving—the stalks were already tall enough to sway in the breeze. In five more weeks, six at the most, Candamir estimated, they could begin the harvest. Despite his recent meal, the thought of warm, fresh-baked rye bread made him ravenously hungry.

They strolled southward along the edge of the field. A profusion of flowers was blooming here in the grass, and the bumblebees were still hard at work.

"We will have a rich harvest of honey," the smith noted contentedly. "You know, I have a weakness for mead."

"Who doesn't?" Candamir replied absentmindedly. *Sweet forgetfulness…*

"Listen, lad," Harald began suddenly. "I'd like very much to marry your sister, and she wants to marry me as well. I hope you will give your approval?"

Candamir was astonished less by the question itself than by his uncertain tone of voice. He stopped and looked at the smith. "Harald… *naturally* I'll give my approval."

Harald smiled and nodded briefly. "She spent a lot of time with us during the past few weeks, you know."

That hadn't escaped Candamir's notice, nor had the fact that his sister often did not come home at night, though he'd assumed it was because of the discord at home. He knew very well that Asta was afraid of him when he was angry, so he hadn't been surprised when she sought refuge with the man who was like a father to her. Or at least that was how he thought Asta viewed Harald, though obviously things were a little different.

The smith raised his right hand helplessly. "At first I was almost paralyzed. After Asi's death, I mean. It was as if a part of me had been cut off, a part I couldn't function without. Your sister came and helped us out, even with practical, everyday things. And so I didn't notice at first what was happening. I did not have any intention of ever marrying again."

Candamir smiled. "I'm glad. You are both too young to stay alone for the rest of your lives. What great good fortune that you found each other."

"Yes, the gods have sent us great happiness. And that brings us to you and your fortune."

Candamir's face darkened. "Oh, let's not talk about that now."

"But we must. Come, sit down for a moment. The grass has such a wonderful fragrance. Come, lad."

They sat down in the grass at the edge of the field. Candamir tugged out a blade of grass, put it between his teeth, and gazed west, where the sun had disappeared behind the trees, leaving only a small band of crimson clouds.

A long, comfortable silence followed. The smith was by nature a man of few words, and Candamir had grown accustomed to this harmonious silence.

Today, however, Harald was more generous with his words. "You have made yourself a dangerous enemy with Olaf, Candamir. You knew that, and did it just the same. And it was the proper thing to do, because you were in the right in your dispute. But I'm sure you knew that this enmity would cost you, sometime or other."

"But not like this," Candamir protested, taking the blade of grass out of his mouth. "I figured he would always be against me in the *Thing*, that he would cheat me if I had any business with him, as he has, and that he might even kill me someday in battle. But I didn't anticipate this humiliation. This complete loss of my honor. I never realized how precious a thing it was for me, and I'm glad my father did not live to see it. He would have been so ashamed."

Harald shook his head slowly. "You are mistaken. Your father would have been proud of you. I was proud of you in his place. You…"

"Harald, please," Candamir broke in, his voice flat. "Don't tell any white lies out of pity for me. I think that would be more than I could take."

The smith turned and looked him straight in the eye. "I'm telling you the truth, and you will shut up now and listen to what I have to say. Eilhard himself, who is already immortalized in song for his great deeds in battle, said he couldn't have done what you did for your brother. It is brave and honorable to sacrifice yourself for your comrades in the heat of battle, but to deliver yourself into the hands of your enemy so coolly and consciously takes a kind of courage that very few possess. And I saw how Olaf did everything he could to force you to your knees, to make you crawl away and let Hacon go. Everyone could see that, and with every blow that you willingly accepted, Olaf became smaller and you became greater. Never before have your neighbors had such high esteem for you as now."

Candamir didn't believe a word of it, but he didn't want to offend Harald so kept his doubts to himself. They sat there in silence, and finally Candamir said, "I wish I could go away for a while. Perhaps out onto the grassland, to search for the best horses, to catch them and break them in there, undisturbed. Or go even farther away and explore the wasteland and the fiery mountain, or build a boat and sail around Catan. I miss the sea, you know. But I can't do it. My brother, my son, my servants…they are like a millstone around my neck. Sometimes I feel as if I can't even breathe anymore."

The smith nodded. "Responsibility can be a great burden, and it was thrust upon you much too soon, when your father didn't return home. But the fact that you can't run away from it doesn't mean that you can't change anything."

"What do you mean by that?"

"Candamir, I'd like to ask you to build a smithy for me, and a hall, as soon as possible. I want to provide a suitable home for your sister and her children, and I'll give you wheat seed for it, as much as you need."

That would indeed mean one less worry, but Candamir asked, "Where in all the world did you get wheat seed?"

Harald smiled enigmatically. "A smith always gets what he needs, because everyone depends upon him."

Candamir sighed and raised his hands. "There is nothing I'd rather do than build you a new home," he replied. "But if I don't clear the land, the best wheat seed won't do me any good. You'll tell me, and correctly so, that land without seed won't put bread on my table, either, but…"

"Listen to me," the smith interrupted. "I've spoken with many men—about clearing the land and sowing, about the need of houses before winter arrives, and about you. Berse says you are an outstanding carpenter, better than any of his sons."

"That's nonsense. Any man can split a tree trunk and put together a few beams for a house."

Harald chuckled. "Well, I always think, too, that anyone should be able to make his own knives and plowshares, since it's so simple. But it's only simple for those who know how to do it. You have more experience than you realize. After all, didn't you replace all your farm buildings with your own hands after your father's death? Didn't you build a hall for Osmund? And a new house for Olaf in a very short time? You have a valuable talent, Candamir, even if you take it for granted. Berse agrees, and he should know, shouldn't he?"

Candamir was speechless.

"We've thought it over," Harald continued. "You and Berse could build our houses. Of course you will get as many slaves as you need to help. In return, the other men will clear your land along with theirs, and each will give you some seed and plow and sow your fields. Don't look at me so suspiciously. It has nothing to do with charity. You will be reimbursed for your work, just as I am. In this way, every family might have a house before the start of winter."

Candamir had to admit it was a good plan. It would mean an end to his poverty, and he got along well with the grumpy, dwarfish shipwright; they would work together well. His face brightened a bit. Clearing the forests and tilling the fields were vital but arduous tasks, whereas building houses gave him a peculiar satisfaction. It was only for this reason that he had been able to keep his side of the bargain with Olaf so easily.

"That doesn't sound bad, Harald."

The smith smiled contentedly. "And that isn't the only thing I've been working out for you. Now we come to your brother."

"Shame. I was just beginning to feel better."

"I don't intend to admonish you for showing too little mercy. That would simply be asking too much. And you have done enough for him. The boy is at a difficult age. Believe me, I know what I'm talking about, as my Godwin is only slightly older. Hacon made a big mistake—no more and no less. Someday you will get over the hurt he has caused you, and you may even feel affection for one another again. But until then, the two of you shouldn't live under one roof. Let me take him as an apprentice, Candamir, and in return relieve me of my unbearable son."

Candamir looked at him in surprise.

"Godwin is still grieving over the death of his mother," the smith explained, "and he thinks it's far too early for me to remarry. He makes no secret of it, especially in front of Asta. He is nasty to her and driving me crazy. There is no peace in my house, and your sister is unhappy. Things just can't go on like this."

Candamir was astonished and a little relieved to realize his was not the only household with discord.

Harald smiled, reading his mind. "Every family has its troubles, didn't you know that?"

"Yes, I guess I did."

"Well then? What do you say?"

"I accept. I'll gladly take Godwin into my house as my apprentice and send Hacon to you. I'm just afraid you will soon regret it. He's a lazy good-for-nothing."

"And so is Godwin."

Candamir shook his head. "He wasn't when he was in my team of woodsmen."

"That's the point. Godwin shows his best side when he is with you, and I'm convinced that Hacon will do the same at my house. Godwin has no grudge against you, and Hacon has none against me."

Suddenly Candamir recalled that when he himself had been a youngster, he had often tried to get out of work on his father's farm, but had always been glad to help out in the smithy. Because he admired Harald, while for the most part, he hated his father…

Candamir extended his right hand and they shook, sealing their deal.

"And now we come to Gunda."

Candamir jerked his hand back and looked away in shame.

"You can't kill her, can you?" Harald asked.

Candamir had folded his arms around his knees, propping his chin on them. "No," he said, looking out at the rye swaying in the wind. "Enough blood has been spilled in this accursed affair. And I can't forget what a sweet, innocent thing she was when she came to me. I made her into what she has become. It is not all her fault."

The smith was amazed; this kind of self-awareness was very unusual for a man so young, and especially so for a hothead like Candamir. That could only be the work of the wise young Saxon. In his darkest hours in the mountains, when Asi had died, he had come to know and respect Austin. And he thought it very much in Candamir's favor that he was able to open himself to this influence, ideas that were often in conflict with everything that had been passed from father to son for as long as anyone could remember.

"But I can't forgive her," Candamir continued. "It's strange. Once… just once I gave her to Osmund for a night. It was shortly after Gisla's death. It seemed nothing of great importance. It was different. Perhaps because it wasn't my brother."

"More likely it was because you gave your permission. It makes a difference whether you give something out of generosity or whether it's stolen from you."

"Yes, you are right."

"I agree you should spare her life," the smith told him. "Many people have a different opinion about that, but whatever else she might be, she is the mother of your son, the first son of Catan. Brigitta, too, thinks that for this reason she should live. But you should not keep her."

"I know."

"Ivar told me he would be glad to take her."

"Ivar? The captain of the *Sea Arrow*?"

Harald nodded. "And in exchange, he will give you a sow, a real domestic sow that he brought along from Elasund, with all her piglets."

"But Ivar is fat and has rotten teeth and boils all over his face," Candamir protested.

Harald had trouble keeping a straight face. He had only wanted to see how Candamir really felt about the Frisian slave girl. "Then sell her to me," he suggested. "Asta is very fond of her. Your son could grow up in my house until he is old enough to do without his mother and then return to his father's house. I don't have any female slaves now. As you know, our Tjorvig was swept overboard in the second storm and drowned. But Asta could certainly use a little help in the house and with her children. In payment, I'll make you the best ax you ever held in your hands."

It sounded reasonable. Candamir knew he had to part with Gunda, but what would he do without a warm body in his bed every so often? And that wasn't the only problem with Harald's reasonable solution.

"I would like that ax," he replied with a genuine sigh of regret, "but I can't agree. If Hacon and she both live under your roof, it won't take long before she throws herself at him again, and I don't want that to happen. Hacon mustn't be rewarded for his breach of faith." A feeling of fierce jealousy came over him at the very thought of it, and just the idea that his brother and his slave would live together in peace in the smith's house was repugnant to him.

Harald nodded and shrugged in resignation. "And how do things stand with you and the beautiful queen?"

Candamir shook his head. "Badly. She doesn't want me."

"Did she actually say that?"

"Not to me, but to Osmund."

"He asked her on your behalf? Now really, lad, I sometimes wonder if you don't take things a bit far with your friendship."

Candamir laughed in embarrassment. "No, no, he asked her if she would marry *him*, and when she turned him down, she explained that she didn't want any man. You were quite right, Harald. Siglind has no interest in mortal men, but only in the god of my Saxon. You should see how her eyes light up when Austin tells her about the deeds of his god."

"I'm surprised that you permit it."

"I have to." And Candamir told Harald about the agreement he had made with the Saxon's god.

“I understand. Well, perhaps the queen of the Cold Islands has been so bitterly disappointed by mortal men that she thinks it safer to turn to the divine. But possibly her mind can be changed.”

Candamir shrugged. “But surely not by me.”

“Now I wouldn’t be so sure. Maybe you just have to try a little harder with her. And Gunda is in your way. Think about it, Candamir. Nothing good can come of it if you keep the girl.”

The young man turned away and looked out over the river.

“By Thor’s hammer, what a beautiful bride,” Berse whispered to Candamir. “Your friend is truly to be envied.”

Candamir agreed. Inga was no stunning beauty, but a pretty young girl with soft, rosy skin, and today her eyes were shining. In addition, she wore a new pinafore dress the same deep red color that Siglind’s once had. The queen of the Cold Islands had dyed the cloth herself, and together with Inga’s young stepmother Britta, had sewn the bridal dress. In her braided blond hair Inga wore a wreath of wild pink roses of the type that grew everywhere here on little bushes.

“Yes, she’s stunning,” he whispered.

Brigitta stood in front of the couple, then turned to the bride’s father. “Is the matter of the dowry settled?” the old woman inquired.

Siward nodded. “Due to the loss of the *Falcon*, I don’t have much at the moment, but Osmund has agreed to let me pay the dowry of a half dozen sheep as soon as I can.”

A half dozen sheep were worth far more in Catan than in Elasund, and the crowd murmured approvingly. It was the custom that the amount of the dowry be specified before witnesses, because the bride retained it as a personal asset—along with her morning gift—and in case of separation could demand it be returned.

“Good. Then give the hand of your daughter to her bridegroom,” Brigitta instructed.

Siward seemed a bit melancholy, but he smiled, took his youngest child by the hands, and kissed her on the forehead. “May Berchta bless you, and may you be granted the happiness of many sons, Inga,” he murmured a bit awkwardly. Then he took the hands of the bride and groom and put them together. Inga's dainty right hand disappeared inside Osmund's huge, calloused paw. The sight aroused restrained merriment, and even Osmund and Inga exchanged surreptitious smiles.

A garland of lilies and birch branches had been prepared, and Brigitta took it out of a shallow clay dish. Two little, round wood disks were hanging on its ends, inscribed with a Perthro rune and an Ingwaz rune, which stood for female and male fertility. The old woman wound the garland around the wrists of the bride and groom and tied it in a loose knot. Then she spread out her arms. "Father of the Gods, bless this bond between thy true vassal and thy maidservant."

Inga turned toward Osmund. Her eyes were shining like stars. No one could doubt that on this day her long-cherished dream was being fulfilled. But she spoke solemnly and earnestly. "I will belong to thee alone from this day forward, and together with thee will serve Odin, so that he will bless us with his wisdom, and fortune may never forsake us."

Such a marriage vow was unusual and strange, and the settlers exchanged looks of surprise. Many wondered who had thought up this pious oath, or what its purpose might be. But it left no one unmoved.

"I will belong to thee alone from this day forward, and together with thee will serve Odin, so that he will bless us with his wisdom, and fortune may never forsake us," Osmund repeated with a resounding voice while looking steadfastly into the eyes of his bride. When he had finished, a little smile appeared in the corner of his mouth.

Inga was giddy with happiness, and Osmund put his free arm around her shoulders, hugged her unselfconsciously, and pressed his lips on hers.

This broke the reverent silence. The crowd applauded and laughed, and then gathered around to congratulate the happy couple.

Candamir was the first to embrace his friend. "May you be granted all the happiness in the world."

"Thank you, Candamir."

He turned to the bride and kissed her hand demurely. "Make him happy or you will get in trouble with me," he threatened with a wink.

She laughed. “I’m not worried about that at all.”

Candamir let her go, stepping back to make room for the other well-wishers, and found himself next to Asta and Harald again.

“Well?” the smith said, looking at his wife, his head inclined slightly to one side. “Aren’t you sorry you decided not to have such a moving ceremony? It’s not too late, you know. We could still ask Brigitta to marry us.”

Asta shook her head. “Why? I have no dowry that I could demand back and no father to present me to you solemnly.”

“Only a brother,” Candamir interjected.

She pressed his hand briefly. “I hope you are not angry with me for having cheated you out of this honor.” Asta didn’t care much for Brigitta and thought they could ask for divine blessing for their bond themselves, so she had simply moved into the smith’s hut with her children. No one found that shocking. No one but the Saxon.

Candamir shook his head. “If you are happy, I am too.” And he certainly had no desire at present to be the center of attention. Had the Midsummer Day not been picked as Osmund’s wedding day, Candamir would have made his escape to the grassland and avoided all the festivities. But he couldn’t miss his foster brother’s wedding, so he tried to conceal his gloominess deep inside him where not even Osmund would be able to see it. At the banquet after the marriage ceremony, he ate and drank with his usual abandon, proposing toasts that were as good-natured as they were bawdy. Inga blushed each time.

After the wedding banquet, the Midsummer celebrations began—boxing matches, stone-throwing, tug-of-war, and archery contests, interspersed with music, dancing, and more food. Hacon did remarkably well in wrestling against those in his age group, beating his friend Wiland but losing to Olaf’s son Lars, who pressed his face down into the mud on the meadow longer than necessary, until Hacon started thrashing about in panic and the spectators had to separate the opponents. When Hacon finally stood up, his hair was ruffled and his face smeared with dirt. Then to add insult to injury, Olaf won the stone-throwing contest.

Candamir slipped away without taking part in any of the contests that had filled him with so much enthusiasm in the past. He went down to the little paddock next to his cabin, where both his cattle and his horses were kept, put the bridle on the mare, and swung himself up onto her bare back. In recent weeks he had devoted much time to her, and she had become gentle as a lamb and very attached to him. But he knew it troubled her to be separated from her foal, so he allowed the shaggy little colt to run along beside his mother. In a wide arc, they circled the village meadow and the wretched huts at a walking pace, then turned north into the forest.

Still mostly unexplored country for him, the forest was full of broad-leaved trees and was younger than the forest they had been clearing until now. Candamir assumed that perhaps ten or fifteen years ago there had been a great fire here. In the thick underbrush, all sorts of small game rustled about, and in the little river where he finally stopped, a beaver was busy building a dam.

Candamir dismounted, let the mare graze, and sat down on the shore to watch this incomparable master builder.

"Are you hoping to learn from him?" a gently mocking voice whispered behind him.

Candamir was slightly startled but didn't turn around. "I won't ever to be half as good as he is, even if I had a hundred years of experience building houses," he replied.

His words were met with a peal of silvery laughter. Then, out of the corner of his eye, he caught sight of two small bare feet and a red, faded skirt hem.

"What a coincidence that we should meet here, noble queen," he said, a bit derisively.

"It's no coincidence," she replied. "I followed you. And don't call me 'noble queen.' I'm not a queen anymore."

He turned his head and looked up at her, squinting. For the festival she had done her blond hair in many small braids again, just as when he had seen her for the very first time on board the *Falcon*.

When she saw his expression, she lowered her eyes. "I'm sorry, I didn't mean to bother you."

"You're not bothering me at all," he lied. "And since you're here, you might as well sit down."

She sat down about a yard away to watch the beaver's comical, yet masterful work.

"You're missing the party," she said abruptly.

"That's not prohibited."

"No, but it's not like you."

He looked at her, frowning. "How do you know that?"

"I've known you for a while. Almost three months," she added, a bit surprised, just realizing the fact herself.

*How can you know me? I don't even know myself,* he thought. He drew up his knees, clasping his long fingers around them, and looked out at the river again, whose surface sparkled in the bright sunlight. "I hope you didn't follow me to this wonderful, peaceful place only to nag at me. Because if I wanted to hear well-intentioned advice, I would have remained with my Saxon, my sister, and her new husband who are always so generous in sharing their unsolicited wisdom with me."

Siglind smiled. "No, I came to ask you for a favor."

"Really?" He settled back, propped up on his elbows, and looked at her. "Now I'm curious."

"I've heard there will be a *Thing* tomorrow," she began.

Candamir nodded. "There's a *Thing* every year on the day after Midsummer. I thought that was the case everywhere."

"That may be. I assume this is just another custom that has been forgotten in the Cold Islands, because the king decides everything himself there, and an assembly is thus completely superfluous."

"I see."

"I've also heard that lots will be drawn tomorrow to determine the order in which the houses will be built."

"That's correct. Harald will be the first to get a new house so he can set up a smithy and provide us with the tools we need for building, harvesting, and tilling the new fields. All the others will be determined by lot."

"That sounds very reasonable," she said. "And who will build these houses?"

"Berse and I will, with around two dozen slaves. Sigurd will help his father, and I'll have Harald's son Godwin as a sort of apprentice. That should be plenty."

"And who will do the roofing?" she asked.

Candamir shrugged. "We'll have to learn how. Maybe you can tell me what you know about it."

"I'd rather do it myself."

"What?"

She frowned indignantly. "The roofing. That's what we were talking about, wasn't it?"

"*You?*" He laughed in surprise. "What a silly idea."

"Oh, it is? Well, it happens that I'm the only one with any experience in making roofs from reeds. So why shouldn't I?"

"You're a woman, and once you were a queen. It would be inappropriate," he explained patiently.

"What I was at one time is of no importance and doesn't put bread on my table. I am a woman, that's right, but I'm also single, and so I need a house like every one of you, Candamir. I too need grain and other provisions. How can I get that if not through work? And why not with work that I can do better than any of you?"

He realized that her suggestion was not completely absurd, but he shook his head just the same. "No one would want to work in the fields anymore if you did the roofing on our houses, Siglind. We would starve."

"What? I don't know what you're talking about."

"I'm talking about horny fellows showing up in droves at the construction site to peek up your skirt when you're standing on a ladder."

Siglind lowered her eyes and blushed, and he couldn't tell whether it was from embarrassment or anger.

"There's a much simpler way to get a roof over your head before winter sets in. You wouldn't have to risk breaking your neck climbing around on roof trusses and being pestered every night in your modest little cabin by some love-stricken fool."

"Stop right there," she warned him softly.

But her threatening tone just egged him on and made it impossible for him to stop. "You'd just have to marry me."

She jerked her head up, and the angry glint in her eyes was enough to terrify anyone. "A conceited, arrogant, coarse idiot like you? I could just as well have stayed with Cnut and saved myself a lot of grief!"

Candamir swallowed. "A simple no would have sufficed," he mumbled sheepishly.

He hadn't really thought she would consent, but it was the first time in his life he had made a marriage proposal to a woman, and such a brush-off was devastating.

He bowed his head, and she looked down at his dark shock of hair with a sudden pang of guilt. "Oh, I'm sorry, Candamir, I didn't really mean to say that."

He raised his hand dismissively. "Oh, I'll get over it, don't worry," he said with a grin, though inwardly he wasn't quite so sure. "You're right, I'm all those things."

She sighed. *At times you can be so different,* she thought—*unfortunately not very often.* "You offended me with your coarse remark, so I wanted to pay you back, but I didn't really mean what I said," she replied instead.

He looked at her and shook his head. "First you strike and then you try to pour balm on the wound. That's typical of you women. You can never decide what you really want."

"Oh, but we can, Candamir. You just think we can't because you men never pay attention when we come out with it clearly."

"I didn't mean to offend you, but simply to tell you the truth. I *did* mean what I said. Perhaps I put it clumsily, but I really would like to marry you." She was about to interrupt, but he held up his hand. "No, don't say it. I know your answer, and I'm not crazy about hearing it again. I just wanted to make myself clear."

"And have the last word in this matter," she said with a smile.

"Exactly." He stood up, seemingly calm, but in truth almost in a state of panic. He could bear neither her presence nor her gaze for even a moment longer. With trembling fingers, he took the mare's reins, which he had tossed over a low-lying bough, and gently stroked her soft nostrils with his left hand. Just as gently and lovingly, she took his fingers between her lips and nibbled at them a bit.

"Come to the *Thing* tomorrow and make the suggestion yourself," he said to Siglind as he mounted his horse. "I'll support you."

She looked at him in astonishment as he left. He was sitting straight up on his horse and guided it easily with his knees while holding the reins loosely in one hand. He softly clicked his tongue, and both the mare as well as her foal pricked up their ears. Then the little group disappeared between the trees, Candamir's dark hair and tunic and the horses' deep brown coats merging with the shadows in the forest.

As twilight descended, most of the settlers were too drunk to shout the usual dirty jokes at the bridal couple as they prepared to leave.

Brigitta discreetly led Osmund and Inga along the shore to her hut. There Asta, Britta, and a few slaves were waiting. They took Inga into their care, led her to a shallow spot along the river, bathed her, and finally dressed her in a tunic that Brigitta had woven and tailored expressly for this purpose. It was made of plain, undyed wool but embroidered with strange green and brown symbols and runes.

Nervously, Osmund watched as the women disappeared in the tall reeds along the shore. He wished that Brigitta hadn't ordered him to stay sober, and above all, he wished she would leave them alone so he could have his bride to himself.

"Oh, spare me this woeful look," the old woman scolded him. "Come along and help me, and you will have the chance all the sooner to do what's been on your mind all day."

"I certainly hope so. I have waited long enough," he replied, not in the least embarrassed. Then he joined her at the fire. "What shall I do?"

"Here." She handed him a mortar that was one-third filled with dried leaves and roots. "Grind that to a powder."

"What is it?" he asked skeptically.

"You need not worry about that. It is not *you* who will drink it, but Inga."

"Who is *my* wife. So, what is it?"

"It will give her visions and make her fertile."

"Do you really think that on our wedding night we'll need one of your potions?" he asked incredulously.

"No. But this is about something more important than your wedding night, Osmund. Now do what I say, and believe me, you won't regret it."

He obeyed, and as she stirred the contents of the mortar into a cup of mead, the potion foamed and hissed. He couldn't suppress a shudder and felt ashamed at how relieved he was to not be the one who had to drink it. Brigitta carried the potion outside, mumbling enchantments over the cup, and Osmund followed, though he could not understand a word she was saying.

The women were waiting for them at the shore, and Inga smiled shyly at her husband. Then she took the cup from Brigitta's hands and emptied it, without asking any questions.

"Good," Brigitta whispered, satisfied. "Now take us over to the island in the river, Osmund."

Osmund thanked Asta and the other women, then took his bride by the hand, noticing the strange tunic she was wearing, and led her to the rowboat at the shore. Brigitta crouched down in the stern, Inga kneeled in the bow, and Osmund took the oars.

Darkness had fallen some time ago, but the moon was nearly full and gave a bluish sheen to the night and the water. The island in the river was long, shaped almost like a ship, and forested with old deciduous trees. Osmund had never set foot on it before—it had always given him a strange feeling of unease, as if it were a forbidden place. But he knew that the women often went there, and both Brigitta and Inga seemed to know their way about.

After he had pulled the boat up onto the gently sloping riverbank, they quickly stepped between two tall beech trees and into the forest. In the moonlight, Osmund could just make out a beaten path. He walked behind the women, and after several steps heard Inga's heavy breathing. She was almost panting. He walked a little faster to catch up with her and put his hands on her shoulders from behind. "Is everything all right?" he asked softly.

"Don't speak with her," Brigitta said quietly. "She is now Odin's vessel, his messenger. She cannot hear you."

*Odin's vessel? On my wedding night?* he wanted to ask angrily, but he restrained himself. He could sense the forces at work on this island, even though he couldn't possibly say what they were. They filled him with humility, perhaps even a little awe, and made him more willing than usual to entrust himself to Brigitta's guidance.

Suddenly, Inga veered off the path and into the dense undergrowth, squeezing between two hazelnut bushes. Osmund looked at Brigitta inquiringly, and she gestured for him to follow his bride. This time the old woman followed them. As they went deeper into the forest, the bushes gave way to knee-high ferns and the trees were older. They stood farther apart, so that in places the moonlight penetrated the canopy of leaves. It was very quiet. Osmund could hear none of the usual night sounds, and not a breath of air was stirring. He had an eerie feeling, and drew up his shoulders as he walked on, grim-faced.

Finally, Inga led them to a clearing. He could see no reason why there were no trees there for a distance of around thirty paces, but it didn't surprise him especially, either. Nothing surprised him here, not even the solitary white raven that swept down from the top of a mighty oak tree, settling motionless at Brigitta's feet.

Inga stood in the middle of the clearing, her head tossed back, arms spread outward and slightly upward, and slowly turned around. Her breathing was easier now. Her narrow face shone in the moonlight, serene and yet resolute. Her shadow pointed directly toward Osmund, who stood at the edge of the clearing, spellbound and motionless, watching his bride.

Inga lowered her arms, looked at Osmund wide-eyed, and moved three steps closer to him. He was about to reach out to her when she suddenly fell to her knees.

"Go to her, Osmund," Brigitta murmured. "But don't make any sudden movements—you mustn't startle her."

Slowly he walked over to Inga and knelt down next to her in the tall grass.

"Give her your knife," Brigitta ordered him softly.

He looked at her over his shoulder and frowned. "But won't she…"

"Do it!" She spoke in a whisper, but the urgent tone was unmistakable.

Hesitantly, Osmund undid his huge knife from his belt and handed it to Inga handle-first. She took it as if she had been waiting for it, though he was convinced she was not even aware of his presence. He felt betrayed that she was so far from him on this of all nights. Nonetheless, he carefully watched her every move, worried she might cut herself on the sharp blade.

Inga held the worn whalebone knife in both hands and thrust it into the loose earth as if it were a shovel. She broke up the topsoil and continued digging. She dug up just a small quantity of soil each time, but she worked steadily and without stopping, and after a short time she had made a hole as large as a warrior's helmet. Then she paused and sunk back on her heels, examining her work with a slight frown.

After a few moments, the hole began to fill with water.

Osmund uttered a muffled cry of surprise and jumped back. A shiver ran down his spine, and he had goose bumps on his arms and legs.

Inga laughed, tossed the knife aside, and plunged both hands into the water. "I have found it," she said, not loudly, but nevertheless jubilantly. "Brigitta, I have found Odin's spring!"

"Well done, my child," said the old woman, her voice exultant. She didn't move, but looked over the shoulders of the bride and groom into the well which had already completely filled the little basin. The water, murky from the earth that had been churned up, ran over the brim and across the ground toward Brigitta. Its path was not easy to follow, as it seeped away in the grass, but nonetheless the white raven suddenly decided it had seen enough and flew silently away, just before Brigitta felt the water on her bare feet.

"This is the place, Osmund," she proclaimed unnecessarily. "Here the temple shall be built."

He nodded but didn't utter a word, his eyes fixed steadily on his bride.

Inga took the hem of her strange bridal gown and pulled it over her head. She was wearing nothing underneath. Her light skin shimmered in the moonlight, and when she put her hands back into the spring and moistened her body and arms with the water, they started to sparkle like silver.

Osmund's throat became tight. Never before had he seen anything that aroused him so much.

"Brigitta," he said hoarsely. "When you are finished here, then… don't let us keep you."

With a soft laugh, she passed her hand through his wheat-blond hair, turned away, and said as she left, "Go ahead, my boy, sire your heir, the future king of Catan."

*What about Roric?* he thought anxiously, though he was not in a frame of mind to hold onto this or any other thought. He simply nodded and pulled his bride close. Her skin was smooth and had a subtle fragrance. As Brigitta discreetly withdrew to the boat, Inga extricated herself from Osmund's embrace, lay down in the grass, and held her arms out to him.

Osmund looked tired when he arrived at the *Thing* the next morning. Just after sunrise, Brigitta had returned to the island in the boat. She had astonishing strength in her fingers, though they were bent with age, and could row without perceptible effort. She brought them something to eat and then sent Osmund back to the village, promising to stay with his bride. Inga smiled in her sleep as he kissed her gently on her temple before departing.

Osmund preferred not to know what Brigitta had given her to drink, and he regretted a bit that his young wife had been so intoxicated that she had only a vague idea as to who he was, and would presumably have only fragmentary memories today. But the potion unquestionably had its merits, Osmund admitted, grinning. There had been none of the fear, embarrassment, and clumsiness that had marked his wedding night with Gisla. On the contrary, his bride had been self-confident, bold, and… insatiable. And so it was that this morning he could scarcely stand up.

He was not the only one. Most of the settlers had been far too exuberant in celebrating the Midsummer Night, but nonetheless, Osmund was the butt of most of the jokes. He endured it all with his customary patience so that the men soon tired of ribbing him and Olaf called the assembly to order.

The drawing of lots for the order in which the new houses would be built was generally regarded as the most important thing, and was thus dealt with first. For a long time, they had been trying to settle on a suitable procedure. Olaf's house was practically finished, and Harald was exempt from the drawing, but when the cottages for Brigitta and Siglind were taken into account, there were still two dozen and two places to award. Austin had explained to Candamir that in the strange runes he used there were symbols representing numbers. He suggested they inscribe the number runes from one to twenty-six on little pieces of wood or stone and have each head of family draw one of these lots. But there had been protests against a procedure that only the Saxon could monitor, as there were many who didn't trust him. The shipwright had finally found the solution: he had gone into the forest and come back with a dry branch long and thin enough for his purposes, and broke it carefully into twenty-six pieces.

"The pieces can be put back together again, and because each break is different, there is a definite sequence," he explained to the assembly, pointing to the greasy leather purse he was holding in his right hand. "All the pieces are in here, and each of you will draw one. The first piece is inscribed with a Thor's hammer, and whoever draws it gets the first house after the smithy is finished. Then we can determine who has the piece that fits with the first, and so on."

Naturally, it was Brigitta's idiot son Haflad who hadn't understood the procedure. Some of the men groaned audibly when he asked for clarification, but Berse patiently repeated what was crystal clear to all the others.

Austin, who was sitting in the grass with Asta and Siglind at the rear of the assembly, whispered sullenly, "That will take *hours*." But he was mistaken. Within a half hour the sequence was fixed. Berse and

Candamir carefully memorized it, but advised them all to keep their piece of wood until they got their house. Osmund was standing in the small shadow of the new village ash tree, staring in disbelief at the piece of wood in his hand with a crude Thor's hammer inscribed in ox blood on the raw bark.

Brigitta walked up to his side and looked at him in amusement. "Why do you have that silly look on your face? You should be glad." She tapped him on the chest with her crooked finger. "Just wait, before a month is past, your wife will be expecting."

Old Eilhard was standing nearby, and he chimed in, "If he keeps going like that, she certainly will," and everyone laughed again.

Osmund smiled, shrugging his shoulders. "You're right, and I'm indeed happy about the lot I've drawn," he told Brigitta. "I'm just so unaccustomed to it—I'm *never* lucky."

"Apparently your luck has changed," she replied simply and turned away.

Siglind had also drawn a lot, and she was still standing in the inner circle with the men. She took the occasion to make her proposal now, before she lost her nerve. With her head high and apparently firmly convinced of how essential she was, she described to the assembly the advantages of letting her take on the task of roofing the houses with reeds. She spied one or another of the men casting dreamy glances at her skirt and realized with increasing panic that Candamir's concern was probably warranted. But she bravely made her case despite the realization.

The murmur of disapproval seemed to be louder from the women than from the men. But before anyone could express their misgivings or objections, Candamir rose to speak, as he had promised, and supported her suggestion. He concluded with the compelling argument that the most solidly constructed house was of no use if the rain came through an improperly installed roof.

Unexpectedly, the mood changed. It wasn't just Harald and Osmund who spoke in favor, but Siward, Eilhard, as well as his sons Thorbjörn and Haldir, and a number of other influential men.

The fact that Olaf had voted against it sweetened Candamir's victory, though he was surprised by this unexpected show of support. *Never before have your neighbors had such high esteem for you as now.* Harald's assertion still seemed just as unbelievable to him today as it had a few days earlier when he first made the claim. Yet Candamir had to admit that the men listened to him more attentively today than before.

Regardless of the reason, Candamir decided then and there to seize this opportune moment. "We agreed that each household should provide a slave for help in building the houses."

Everyone nodded.

"The way I look at it, one worker is as good as another—as long as he is diligent—so you may send me the one you can best do without. However, I want the Turon." Suddenly, his gray eyes were directed at Olaf.

The latter straightened up to his impressive size and scowled. "The Turon? You can forget that. I need him myself."

"I insist on it," Candamir replied. "He was a shipwright in his homeland and is a skilled carpenter. Without him, you wouldn't be living in your new house yet."

"Shipwright?" For a moment, Olaf's anger gave way to surprise. "How do you know that? It's hardly possible that he told you himself."

"With a little effort, people can communicate without words, and..."

"Do you mean to say you put an ax in his hand, even though I forbade it?" Then Olaf turned to his eldest son. "And you allowed it?"

Jared turned noticeably paler, but looked directly at his father and nodded. "It would have been a waste not to use his skills. And not once did he threaten anyone with an ax."

Candamir couldn't refrain from adding, "Maybe that's because you weren't around, Olaf. But in any case, he did good work on your house, and I need him for the other houses as well."

Olaf's face was grim. He really was a fearsome sight, his blue eyes flashing through their tiny slits. "I can easily imagine why you want to pick a public fight with me, Candamir, but no matter how often you ask, you won't get my slave."

"*Your* slave? Is he really that?" Candamir asked. "By what right do you claim him for yourself? After the attack last autumn, the *Thing* decided his life should be spared and he should help to make amends for the harm his people caused us. Why then would he have been given to you, of all men, the only one to suffer no harm?"

Olaf found himself unexpectedly outmaneuvered and didn't answer at once. Finally, he replied with an impatient shrug, "It just worked out that way, and now he belongs to me by common law."

"It was no accident," Candamir said. "The rest of us were grieving for our dead or for those who had been taken away. We had serious losses of cattle and provisions and were just too confused to see what you were doing. But once again, you just took for yourself what you wanted, without any right to it—arbitrarily, as you like so much to do, don't you?"

It had become very still, and nothing could be heard but the chirping of the crickets in the grass along the shore and the burbling of the river.

Finally, Thorbjörn, Eilhard's eldest son, spoke up. "Candamir is right. The Turon belongs to the community and not to you, Olaf. It was illegal for you to keep him, and no precedent can be established from that, in my opinion."

Many of them nodded.

Olaf looked around slowly, his contemptuous gaze passing from one face to the next. He was not one to indulge in self-deception—he knew very well that few of his neighbors cared much for him personally. They often followed him—as they had to Catan—because he had much experience, and his intelligence and judgment were superior to that of most of the others. But the envy engendered by his wealth had always threatened to turn to hostility. In Elasund he had been powerful enough to protect himself, but here, where each man would be wealthier—and thus more equal—than ever before after the first good harvest, his power was suddenly slipping away.

"Very well then," he finally said, feigning indifference. "Take him, but don't come to me with complaints when he lapses into one of his dark moods and splits open someone's skull. Remember, I warned you."

Siward, Haflad, and some of the others nodded in satisfaction, and Eilhard passed around a pitcher of mead. For them, the matter was settled.

But Candamir remained standing, his arms folded. "I am not yet finished."

He could feel his heart pounding, his hands were moist, and all of a sudden he was terribly nervous. But he realized that Siglind had been right: if he really wanted to accomplish anything, if he wanted to make sure they had better laws in this new, better homeland, then he had to act soon. So why not now, since the general atmosphere seemed so much in his favor?

"With the same type of arrogant self-assertiveness you employed to acquire the slave, Olaf, you also refused to pay the smith for the sword he made you last summer, and last month you nearly killed my brother."

"That's preposterous," Olaf grumbled.

"It's the truth," Harald stated calmly. "Hacon certainly would have died if Candamir hadn't taken half the blows for him. I saw the boy the next day and had little hope for him. Not even *your* sheep are worth a human life, Olaf. And as far as the sword is concerned, it broke—through your fault, and not mine—before you had paid for it, and afterward you refused."

"If you really thought I had treated you unjustly, why didn't you challenge me to battle?" Olaf asked.

"You didn't have a sword," the smith replied mischievously, to scattered laughter. But Harald turned serious again. "The matter was not worth the spilling of blood, any more than your sheep were."

Candamir picked up the thread. "It's not right that a man only has the choice of subjecting himself to the arbitrary actions of another man, or killing him and risking a blood feud." He raised his hand in an imploring gesture. "No famine, no war has cost as many lives and brought so much misery upon our people as the senseless feuds that we wage against one another, and with which the father burdens his son."

"But it is the law of the gods," Brigitta interrupted. "How dare you question it?"

Candamir turned to face her. "The law of the gods, you say? And yet you were relieved when I spared Haflad at the Yule festival."

"I was relieved," she admitted, unmoved, "but just as disturbed. It wasn't right."

"Mother!" Haflad cried out, obviously hurt by this lack of unconditional motherly love. "I was roaring drunk and was just talking nonsense..."

"Oh, is that so?" Candamir interrupted, half flabbergasted and half amused at this belated confession.

The charcoal burner turned to his mother and continued. "And should I have lost my life just for *that*?"

She shrugged her bony shoulders briefly. "Yes, since you allowed it to come to a duel. This is the law."

"But don't you see what madness that is?" Candamir asked, pointing to his sister. "There was a blood feud between Nils's clan and ours, and I don't even know why. This feud forced my father and me to consider Asta dead when she married Nils. And if the Turons hadn't killed him, I probably would have done so myself someday. Then the feud would have spread to Fulc and Hacon, even though they have the same blood in their veins."

"You should be ashamed," Brigitta scolded him, "for knowing so little about your family. Your great-grandfather stole a ship from Nils's great-grandfather. Then he sailed away, and neither he nor the ship was ever seen again in Elasund. Nils's clan took revenge and slew your great-grandfather's brother. Rightly so! It was a serious, malicious crime!"

"Granted," Candamir agreed. "But what did Nils and I have to do with this ancient story?"

"Blood vengeance is the law of the gods," the old woman persisted.

"Fine. Far be it from me to suggest doing away with it," Candamir said. That was a lie. But he knew that he would never get anywhere with such an extreme proposal, so he decided to pursue his goal one step at a time. "All I want is to prevent blood feuds about matters that the gods would only laugh at."

"And how would you do that?" Siward asked, skeptically.

"Very simply. The *Thing* has a time-honored tradition just as old as the law of blood vengeance, doesn't it? From as far back as anyone can remember, free men gather to make decisions. Why is that so?"

*He is clever,* Austin thought to himself, listening attentively at the edge of the assembly with many of the women. *He probably doesn't even know there is such a thing as rhetoric, but he instinctively makes good use of it.* The Saxon was very proud of his young master.

"Because then the decision will be the will of the majority, and the largest possible number of men will be satisfied," Siward replied to Candamir's question. "And because many heads together are wiser than one."

"*Because many heads together are wiser than one,*" Candamir repeated slowly, permitting one or two heartbeats to pass before continuing. "That's why I say let us from now on pass judgment in the *Thing*. Let us decide with our collective wisdom—and above all, with a majority of cool heads—what is to happen when one man has stolen from another, or owes him money for work performed, or allows his sheep to fall prey to wolves due to his gross negligence. Let us decide that the judgment of the *Thing* is binding on us all. And only in cases where one of us does not submit to this judgment, and only then, may the opponent or the injured party take blood vengeance."

For a moment, there was complete silence, and then everyone started to speak at the same time, so loudly and excitedly that it sounded almost like a riot. It was a new idea, and many of the men were shocked by its strangeness. But many also started thinking. And it crossed Austin's mind that if they had still been in Elasund, none of these men would have even heard Candamir out. But they were in a strange, new world and had crossed over old boundaries, and that gave him hope for his mission as well.

A long and very heated debate followed. Olaf, Brigitta, and old Eilhard flatly rejected Candamir's suggestion. Harald, Thorbjörn, and Haflad, of all people, supported him. Many practical questions were discussed, like whether women and slaves could also sue or be charged in this court, whether it might be necessary to hold the meetings more regularly and on a fixed schedule, and many other such matters.

It was late in the day when they finally proceeded to vote. Candamir's radical proposal won by a narrow majority.

# Hay Moon, Year One

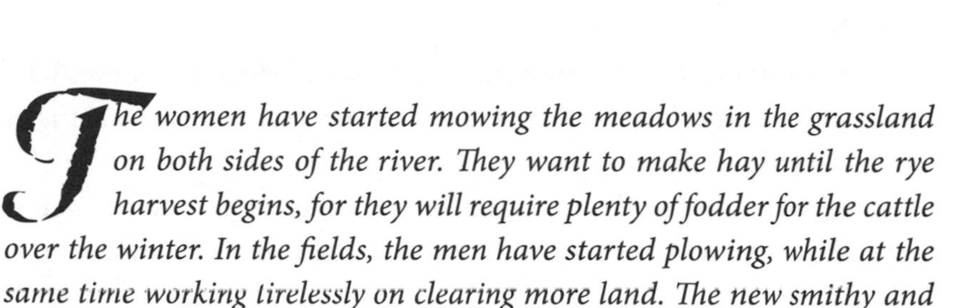

*The women have started mowing the meadows in the grassland on both sides of the river. They want to make hay until the rye harvest begins, for they will require plenty of fodder for the cattle over the winter. In the fields, the men have started plowing, while at the same time working tirelessly on clearing more land. The new smithy and Osmund's house are already finished, and construction is far advanced on the house for Siward and his young wife.*

Austin paused, regarding the small group of new buildings. It held the promise of a beautiful village. The smithy, the mill, which would be built last, and the houses of all who expected to own a ship and set to sea were to stand right on the shore, where once the edge of the forest had been. Another string of houses was going to be built further inland for settlers who were concerned about floods and high water. The houses would be situated farther apart than in Elasund because here there was little fear of enemy attacks. Since some of the finest trees had been left standing, many people would have a shady spot near their houses to escape from the sun that shone here much more often than they were accustomed to. The women had already started planting herb and vegetable gardens. He admired the settlers' untiring diligence that was surely pleasing to God. Austin dipped his white raven feather again into the little wooden bowl holding the ink.

*At dusk, the men go into the forest to harvest honey. The mead that the women make from it is more delicious than anything I have ever tasted. The rye is ripening and turning yellow in the fields, the bushes in the forest are sagging under the weight of wild berries, and small game can be found everywhere. The young men have caught many goats in the foothills, and their coats are so thick and long that they will surely make up for the sheep we have lost. Truly, no misery lasts forever. Praised be the Lord.*

"Put the rafters closer together, Candamir!" Siglind called to him from down below.

He was standing in the roof truss, and she was shading her eyes with one hand and squinting into the dazzling summer sun. "The shingles won't hold like that!"

He looked down at her over his left shoulder. "Quit your nagging, woman. If you had your way, we would seal the roofs with timbers and slats alone."

She shrugged. "When Siward and Britta find the rain coming down on their heads, I'll tell them it was because you were too lazy to build the roof properly."

Candamir sighed and nodded to Godwin and the Turon, who were standing next to him on their ladders. "You heard what the noble queen commanded, men," he said, loud enough for her to hear.

He heard an angry hiss from down below and thought he could make out something like "damned bastard!" He laughed, put his hammer back in his belt, and quickly climbed down the ladder. His face and bare torso were tanned and glistened with a fine film of sweat. "You would be well advised to go back to making your shingles," he told her. "You can start tomorrow morning."

Siglind gave him the large mug of mead she had in her hand. "My shingles have been done for a long time," she shot back, pointing to the bundles of reeds that were carefully tied together and stacked up at the edge of the building site. She'd had enough experience by now to know that the quantity was sufficient.

They sat down together in the shade on a pile of sweet-smelling lumber and amicably passed the mug back and forth. Candamir observed Siglind out of the corner of his eye. Her skin was also tanned, though not as dark as his—she had to guard against getting too much sun—but enough to highlight her beautiful blond hair and blue eyes. Her bare feet, usually so scrupulously clean, showed traces of mud here and there from the riverbank. Asta and Inga had given Siglind a pair of boots and sewn a new dress for her as thanks for the roof she made, but she didn't wear any shoes while working and only her tattered old jumper. The material had faded to an uneven pink, and to everyone's surprise she had fashioned the garment into a pair of trousers. Candamir secretly smiled, remembering the disappointed faces of the men and the shocked expressions of the women when Siglind first appeared at the building site dressed this way. Brigitta and some of the other women had called the attire improper, but in fact it wasn't. Unfortunately, these strange trousers were just as wide and unrevealing as the skirt had been, and Candamir was not the only one to think that. It resembled the ample garments of the Moors, Olaf had said with a salacious smile, where it was customary for the women to wear men's clothing, and vice versa.

Siglind had ignored the criticism and gibes with great equanimity. In her unusual working clothes she could move around freely and safely on a ladder, and that was the only thing that concerned her.

From inside the house, the muffled sound of hammers on wood could be heard. Berse, Sigurd, and several slaves were busy finishing the facing between the timbers and installing the interior wall between the main hall and the bedroom.

"Tomorrow the roof truss will be finished," Candamir promised, "and if you'll show me how to do it, I'll help you with the roofing, along with a few of my people. It's too much for you to do alone."

She didn't disagree. With so many workers, Berse's valuable experience, and Candamir's inventiveness, house construction progressed faster than they had ever thought possible. She could no longer keep up with the cutting, binding, and installation of the shingles.

"Oh, that's not very difficult," she said, then put the mug in his hand, stood up, and went to get one of the reed bundles. "You start down at the eaves," she explained as she sat down again beside him.

"Well, what a surprise," he said dryly. "I'm not as dull-witted as you think, you know."

"If you interrupt me instead of listening, you'll never learn anything," she scolded.

He handed the mug back to her and raised both hands. "Forgive me just this once..."

"The bunches of reeds are attached to the slats. Very close together. The next row has to overlap the one below by two-thirds, or else it won't be watertight. And when you get to the ridge, you start from the inside again at the eaves and tie a rope behind each row of reeds in order to draw the reeds up. That's what ultimately makes them watertight and gives them that shaggy appearance, do you see?"

He nodded, fascinated.

"In any case, I hope they'll be watertight," Siglind added with a nervous little laugh. "The proper time to cut reeds is actually in the winter. Then the stalks are 'ripe.' But of course, we can't wait for that."

"No, but I'm sure that's not necessary. The really important thing is that the reeds dry out and harden before the autumn rains come, isn't that so?"

She nodded.

"Since we have such a dry summer, that ought to be all right," he concluded confidently, "and if you need help cutting, let me know. I'll send you Gunda."

"Better now than later," she answered quickly.

He cast a suspicious sidelong glance at her and then said softly, "Let me guess—you think I'm mistreating her and she could use a little change of pace."

Candamir had forbidden Gunda from leaving the hut without his express permission, and that meant she had to spend most of her days in the dusky half-light with little Nils while all the others pursued some useful activity out of doors.

But Siglind shook her head. "No, Candamir. That's not for me to judge, and I don't think you are treating her particularly badly. On the contrary, I was amazed that you spared her life. And I do understand how you feel. Every other man will look at her as an easy target, and you can no longer trust her."

He stared at the dark brown earth at his feet. "You are right," he said, embarrassed, but it was no longer difficult for him to discuss it with Siglind. They had been building houses together for a month and were strangely at ease together. For both of them, this work was something new, a marvelous adventure, and from the very first day they had shared many laughs. He was still longing for her, almost instinctively sought her company, and felt the hurt of her rejection keenly. Nonetheless, they had become friends.

"But I know she is in safe hands with you," he added, "and I can't lock her up forever, if only because of the boy. He needs light and sun and plenty of fresh air." As always, his features softened when he spoke of little Nils, who was now three months old, thriving, and always smiled in his father's arms.

"Then it's agreed. I really could use another pair of hands," Siglind said almost brusquely, holding the cup of mead out to him. He took it, and for a moment their hands touched. Siglind's were very slender with long fingers, but as rough and calloused as his own. He held her hand a moment longer than necessary and surreptitiously felt the tips of her fingers until she finally withdrew her hand and put it between her knees.

"Come eat with us tonight," he said, as usual.

Siglind would have gladly accepted. She knew that Candamir felt a bit lonely. He missed Asta and even Hacon, although he was still angry at his brother. Osmund no longer came as often to the homey little fire in front of Candamir's hut in the evenings. Inga was jealous and wanted her husband all to herself, and for the time being, he tolerated her possessiveness with an indulgent smile. Osmund was evidently very devoted to his young bride, and everyone whispered and joked about how much time they spent in their new house behind closed doors.

But after a brief hesitation, Siglind shook her head. "No, not today."

Candamir looked away and nodded, not really surprised but nonetheless disappointed. He didn't ask her for the reason, but he knew she avoided situations in which she was at risk of being alone with him, even if just for a few moments.

It saddened her to see him so dejected, and she felt an urge to take his hand and explain it to him, but she knew she mustn't do that.

"Fine, then," said Candamir, rising to his feet, "I'm going back to work. Thanks for the mead."

As agile and quick as a cat, he started up the ladder, but when he was halfway, one of the narrow rafters started to slip and fell, hitting him on the shoulder. He hadn't seen it coming and lost his grip, landing hard on the ground.

"Candamir!" Siglind cried. She came running to him, and Godwin and the young Turon quickly climbed down from the roof.

But Candamir had already sat up, rubbed his left ankle with one hand, and waved them aside reassuringly with the other. "I'm fine, I think."

He got to his feet a bit clumsily, making a face when he shifted his weight to the sprained foot. Then he shook his head disapprovingly at his apprentice and the mute slave. "You two are always dropping something from the roof. It's a wonder you haven't killed anyone yet. You should learn to be a little more careful," he scolded them.

"I'm sorry, Candamir," Godwin mumbled, embarrassed, though this time he was not at fault.

The Turon stood one pace to the right. He was looking down at the ground, but his clenched jaw was visible. He didn't move, but he was trembling and sweat ran down his chest, and not because of the heat. "Pull yourself together," Candamir grumbled in annoyance. "I don't intend to rip your heart out."

The Turon flashed him a fearful glance and swallowed hard. Candamir brushed him off with a wave of his hand and turned away, picking up the rafter that had fallen from the roof.

For a long time, Candamir had been reluctant to admit to himself that he actually was quite fond of the shipwright, who was, after all, a Turon and had brought much grief to his people. But that had been a long time ago, and working alongside him day after day, he couldn't help but like him, for he was not only an excellent carpenter, but an equally agreeable person. Candamir wished he still had his tongue, for he would have liked to know how such a young man could become such an experienced craftsman, how people lived in Turonland, and other such things. It wasn't forgotten how bravely the prisoner had faced the possibility of mutilation and death on the morning after the attack, either. Little was left of that courage now. And it wasn't hard to guess why—his back, arms, and chest were covered with scars from Olaf's terrible whip. Candamir knew how exhausting the effects of pain and physical humiliation could be, and he couldn't help wondering if it wouldn't have broken his spirit as well.

"I don't know what to do, Austin," Siglind said to her confidant and teacher.

It was late in the afternoon, and she had found him in the little paddock near Candamir's cabin and was helping him milk the cows and goats. Candamir already owned a half dozen of each, and it was a lot of work. The Saxon was thankful for the help, especially since the animals were unusually restless that day, determined to kick either the milking pail or the Saxon.

"You must pray," he said. "It's quite natural that you should have doubts about whether you are doing the right thing. That happens to us all."

"Pray?" she asked, a bit disheartened. It was not exactly the answer she had hoped for.

The monk nodded. "Didn't you tell me yourself how much consolation you found in prayer when we feared for Hacon's life?"

"Yes," she admitted, "but that was different. Only God could save Hacon, and just being able to ask him gave me the feeling of not being so helpless. Now this is something quite different. It has nothing to do with God."

"You shouldn't say that," he said sternly. "You decided to devote your life to Him, so everything you do from now on involves Him. You are about to betray Him, Siglind."

"That's not true!"

"It *is* true," the monk replied, his voice regaining some gentleness. "And all of us who have chosen to follow God are faced with this temptation now and then. God sends it to us to test us. Or Satan, to win us over for himself. But either way, you must pray, fast, open yourself to God. Then the temptation will pass, believe me."

She listened to him, her brow furrowed with worry. "I'm not sure I want that," she said.

Austin sighed to himself. "No," he said sympathetically, "how could you? You are still very young, and moreover, you are a woman. But remember what I told you about the origin of sin, and women. Only if you resist the temptation can you really belong to God."

Siglind silently continued her milking. In silent rebellion, he suspected.

"Have you never had the desire to take a wife, Austin?" she finally asked, looking at him intently.

"That has nothing to do with it," he replied.

"I'd still like to know."

"No."

"No? Did you never meet anyone who seemed different to you from all the others? Someone you wanted all to yourself? A woman you wanted to have children with?"

The monk blushed at the very idea and shook his head emphatically. The only women he had ever been around were his mother, his two sisters, and the maidservants on his father's farm. At the age of twelve he had entered the monastery, where he was safe from all impulses and temptations of the flesh. And when more than ten years later he had crossed the sea and landed in Elasund, where he met women once again, he had realized with relief that they no longer tempted him. There were other things that the Almighty used to test him from time to time, or that God's adversary placed in his path. Pride, Austin knew, was his great weakness.

"Naturally, I sometimes regret I have no family," he said, for since leaving the community of his brethren in the monastery, he sometimes felt terribly alone. "But it is a small price to pay for the privilege of leading a life in harmony with God."

"Yes," she said. "I'm sure it is worth almost any price. But if God wanted me, Austin, why did He allow this to happen? I mean...you probably can't imagine, if it's never happened to you, but when I wake up in the morning, it's the first thing I think of, and then...my heart is filled with joy. It pounds and leaps wildly right up into my throat. I never suspected that anyone could feel something like it. It's so...strong."

"It is the temptation of the flesh," he warned her.

"Do you mean, it's only that I want to sleep with him?" she asked, surprised. "No, no, it isn't that, at least not *just* that."

She stood up, poured the contents of her milking pail into the larger one standing in the shade of the linden tree, and moved on to the next cow.

"You won't get very far if you deceive yourself," the monk said gently.

But Siglind shook her head. "I know that, but it's just as I say. It's a feeling I'm familiar with, what you call carnal lust, I assume. Sometimes I had that with Cnut, too. If he had stayed away from me for a long time and then returned in a cheerful mood, not in anger, which sometimes happened. Cnut had his good days, you know." She was pondering it all, and so lost in her reveries that she didn't notice how embarrassed the Saxon was at her candor. "No," she continued firmly. "With Candamir it's something different."

The Saxon shrugged. "Well, it doesn't matter. You must put him out of your mind. You are a married woman, and God loathes adulterers. The only way is the one you were determined to choose just a few weeks ago. You must renounce the world and become the bride of Christ."

"I still don't understand exactly what that means."

"It's a long, difficult path," Austin admitted. "You must learn to read and study the word of God. And when you have taken it all to heart, you must make your vow."

"And what would happen if I broke this vow?" she asked earnestly.

"Then God would show his merciless side. You would be condemned to eternal damnation and all the horrors and torments of hell."

"But…why is He so jealous?" she asked. Her voice no longer sounded rebellious. "What I feel for Candamir really has nothing to do with God. One doesn't rule out the other. Why does he demand all of me?"

"It is not for us to question His commandments, and I told you from the start that He demands a price for the salvation of your soul."

Siglind lowered her head. "I never thought I would find what I want in this world, so it seemed easy for me to renounce it. But now I am no longer so sure I can."

Austin had sympathy for the weaknesses and shortcomings of men. He had a kind heart and did not find it easy to defend God's implacable nature, but he knew that Siglind's salvation was in danger and he could only help her by persuading her to continue on the path she had begun. After a moment of hesitation, he rose from his stool and put his hand on her head to bless her. "You can, believe me," he murmured. "You are stronger than you think. If you pray, God will give you the strength that you may not yet have."

Candamir arrived at the paddock at just that moment. The Saxon saw his master and withdrew his hand from Siglind's head quickly, confirming Candamir's incorrect suspicion. Siglind looked up, surprised, but by no means contrite, when she saw Candamir. "Well? Are we done for today?" she asked, furtively passing the back of her hand over her eyes.

Candamir did not fail to notice the telltale glistening in her eyes. What would have caused her to cry? He suspected that she had thrown herself at the Saxon and he had rejected her.

It was all Candamir could do to control his raging jealousy and not wring the monk's skinny neck then and there. Barely nodding, he said, "As I told you, the roof truss is ready. Now it's your turn." He pointed to the bucket in the shadow. "Full? Then I'll take it along."

Austin stepped aside to make room for him, putting his hand on the flank of the pretty, reddish-brown cow he had just milked. "Yes, I'm almost done. There's just one more…" He broke off because the cow suddenly started to bellow, turned, and thrashed around, stepping on Austin's foot before running off.

Candamir had been bending over the pail, but before he could get hold of the leather handle, the heavy vessel tipped over as if pushed by the hand of an invisible goblin. At the same moment, Candamir heard the cow bellow and felt the ground swaying under his feet. He wheeled around, reaching Siglind in two steps, and threw her to the ground, covering her as the cows and goats ran madly about. Candamir wrapped his arms around his head for protection. When he hazarded a glance to one side, he was astonished to see that his peaceful young ox had rammed his horns into the flimsy wall of the little hut and then trampled the cabin down, just an instant after Gunda had come running out with Nils.

A muffled rumble seemed to come from the bowels of the earth, drowning out Gunda's screams, as well as the sound of the few household goods in their modest home crashing to the ground. The ox seemed to panic at the sight of the destruction he had caused, and stepping back, he pawed the ground, kicked Candamir hard in the side, and galloped off in the direction of the river.

All of that in perhaps twenty heartbeats, and then the earth fell silent and still.

Siglind began to struggle, digging him in the ribs on the side the ox hadn't kicked. "Would you please let me go? What are you doing? Did you think the sky would fall on my head?" she asked, annoyed.

He quickly hauled himself to his feet and let her go. "Excuse me, noble queen," he replied, no less irritated. "I only wanted to protect you from being trampled by the cattle."

"You have succeeded in that. But you have broken my ribs with your huge bulk *and* ripped my tunic as well." She pointed accusingly at what remained of her threadbare jumper.

Candamir clicked his tongue. "Too bad. It was such a fine garment..."

They sat there in the grass for a moment, glaring at each other. Then Candamir rose and walked over to his slave girl, who was now lying on the ground as if thunderstruck, pressing the child to her bosom. Nils had started to bawl.

Candamir took Gunda by the arm and yanked her to her feet. "Come now, pull yourself together. It's over, and nothing happened either to you or to him." His voice sounded almost conciliatory, not as brusque as usual.

Astonished, Gunda raised her head. "You are right, Master," she murmured. "Thanks, I'm fine now." She placed Nils carefully on her shoulder and kissed him on his head, where dense, black fuzzy curls had formed.

Candamir let her go and looked around for his Saxon. Austin, too, had fallen down when the earth began to shake and the cattle went berserk. He was slowly getting to his feet, making the sign of the cross.

"My brave Austin has gone all pale in the face," Candamir said.

The monk nodded. "I can believe that, Master. My knees have turned to jelly."

*Just like my own,* Candamir thought, though he had no intention of admitting it. "Now when they stop shaking, I want you to go off and look for the cattle."

"Of course, Master. Have you ever experienced such an earthquake?"

Candamir thought for a moment. "The summer before my mother died, there was a trembling of the earth in Elasund. I don't know if it was as strong as today. I thought then it was powerful, and I imagined that it lasted an eternity. But my father laughed and said it lasted no longer than a thirsty man needs to empty a mug of beer."

Siglind had also stood up and was flicking blades of grass from her damaged tunic. "I just hope the new houses don't look like your cabin…"

"Do you mean to offend me?" Candamir asked gruffly.

"No, but…"

"Candamir! Are you all right? O mighty Thor, the cabin…" Hacon had come running up and suddenly stopped short.

His brother shrugged and sighed. "The ox did that, but there was no one inside and everyone is fine. How is everyone at your house?"

The boy nodded. "We're all right, too." He looked down at the grass, embarrassed. In the weeks since he had been living as an apprentice with Harald and Asta, he had rarely seen his brother, avoiding him as much as possible. If they did meet from time to time, he never knew what to say. He suspected that Candamir knew exactly how uneasy he was and was enjoying every moment of it.

His older brother regarded him with a cool gaze before turning away. "I'm going to see if anyone needs our help."

"I'll come along," Siglind said.

"Me too," Hacon offered, but far less confidently.

Candamir shrugged. "Are you still here? Go and bring back the livestock," he growled, giving the Saxon a sharp poke as he walked by.

The earthquake had caused a great stir among the settlers. Many had received minor scrapes and bruises from stampeding cows and goats, but none of them had been seriously injured. In addition to Candamir's hut, four others had been trampled down or had simply collapsed. But he was happy to learn that none of the new houses had suffered any damage. Nevertheless, the smithy looked like a battlefield—tools had tumbled from the walls, and sacks filled with iron and charcoal had broken open, their contents strewn across the hard-packed ground. Hacon and Siglind stayed to help, as Candamir headed to Osmund's new home.

His hall was roomy, and the golden light of late afternoon came streaming through the window in the west wall. On the right, next to the window, stood Inga's loom, and the colorful hangings on the walls were testimonies to her tireless work. Just like Olaf and Harald, Osmund had decided against having a longfire, and in the middle of the hall stood the table that Candamir had crafted for his friend upon moving into the new house. But the room was dominated by the impressive high seat that had not only survived the sinking of the *Falcon*, but had also saved the life of little Roric.

Father and son smiled when their guest appeared at the door.

"Come in, Candamir," Osmund said. "I hope you too escaped with no more than a scare." He was busy gathering pieces of a broken clay plate.

Candamir stepped over the threshold and nodded at Inga. She returned his silent greeting without smiling.

"No one is injured, only my cabin is gone," Candamir replied to his friend, "but that is no great loss." Without waiting for an invitation, he sat down on the bench on the guest's side of the table. Roric came tottering to him, and he picked him up, laughing, and set him on his knee. "Good grief, Roric," he said, "what a big boy you are already."

Osmund casually put the broken pieces next to the fireplace and sat down across from him. "Bring your household over here until your own hall is done."

Just two months ago Candamir would have thought of this as the obvious solution, but the scowl on Inga's face warned him that things had changed.

"Thanks, Osmund," he replied with a weak smile. "But Harald already has invited us, and since he is now my brother-in-law, he would probably be offended if we didn't go to live with him."

"Indeed," Osmund nodded, "it's funny how I keep forgetting that." He turned to Inga and asked in passing, "And where is the mead, wife?" It sounded casual, but Candamir sensed clearly that there was discord in the air.

"Thanks, Osmund, but that's really not…"

"You stay seated!" his friend protested. "I insist on it."

Candamir settled back on the bench, and Inga brought them each a large cup of fresh mead. She avoided Candamir's gaze, and despite Roric's loud protests, took the small boy from his arms and carried him into the bedroom. "Shush, little warrior, it's time for sweet dreams," they heard her murmuring just before the door closed.

Osmund's slaves and Cudrun, the nursemaid, were nowhere to be seen. They were alone, Candamir realized to his satisfaction, a little surprised at how relieved that made him feel.

"I'm afraid your wife isn't overly fond of me," he remarked.

Osmund gestured dismissively. "She's pregnant. Gisla was also in a bad mood the first few weeks. The best thing is just not to pay any attention to her, and it will pass."

"That happened pretty fast, Osmund," Candamir congratulated him with a suggestive smirk.

As always, Osmund found the grin contagious. And he was, in fact, proud that his wife was pregnant after barely six weeks. He leaned back in his comfortable high seat, and they talked on and on, just as in former times. They spoke of the rye harvest and plowing and the construction progress.

"And will you lodge a complaint against my uncle at the next *Thing* because he hasn't given you the seed he owes you?" Osmund asked at one point.

Candamir shrugged and turned the cup around in his hands, thinking. "I don't know yet. Don't you think I really should? But I could also choose to forget it—for the sake of keeping peace. My wages for building the houses have provided me with all the seed I can use."

"I never knew you to be so peace-loving. And didn't you put through your new laws to stop, above all, the arbitrary use of power by men like Olaf?"

Candamir looked up. "Indeed. But you voted against it. Why? Out of loyalty to your uncle?"

Osmund raised his eyebrows in surprise. "My loyalty toward my uncle has weakened a little of late, you know," he said. "To a deplorable extent, according to Olaf."

"Then why did you vote against me?" Candamir asked.

Osmund remained silent for a moment as he passed his finger over the patterns and runes cut into the beams of his high seat. "Because I have great reverence for traditions. Perhaps too much so, that may be. But to *you*, they mean too little."

Candamir was not irritated. "Well, who knows?" He took a long drink, adding, "I just think it's foolish to cling to traditions that have the sole virtue of being ancient."

"The law of blood vengeance is not as bad as you think. Because a blood feud always affects innocent people, many a man shrinks from doing an injustice because he knows that what he intends to do could also cost the lives of his sons and grandchildren."

"Yes, Osmund, that sounds so reasonable," Candamir replied heatedly, "except that it never worked that way. Remember Haflad at the last Yule festival—he was much too drunk to weigh the consequences, and that's the way it is all too often."

"But it's dangerous to allow the *Thing* to administer justice," Osmund replied. "Every man in the *Thing* is biased. Let's assume that the same thing happened again today, and this time you killed Haflad. What would happen? Everyone who had a vote in the *Thing* would decide according to whether he felt closer to you or to him—whether by family, or by friendship, or whatever. That's the wrong way, Candamir."

"And what's the right way?"

If he thought he had silenced his friend with this question, he was mistaken. Osmund hesitated, not because he didn't have an answer, but because he wanted to choose his words carefully. "We need a judge. We must elect someone from our midst who is the smartest and the wisest, to settle disputes over violations of the law. Only in this way will there ever be order and justice in a community."

Candamir looked at him in disbelief. "*Free* men, you mean, should subject themselves to the judgment of an individual person, like slaves to their masters?"

Osmund nodded. "A person who is superior, and noble in spirit, and whose judgment no one will dare to question."

Candamir suddenly remembered: "*A good people should have a good king who safeguards their law*," he murmured.

Osmund looked at him in surprise.

"That's what you said to Wiland," Candamir reminded him, "on the morning after the Turons attacked. I never forgot it."

His friend nodded thoughtfully. "Yes, that is what I believe. Good people deserve security, and only a good king can guarantee that."

"Like Cnut on the Cold Islands?" Candamir asked scornfully.

Osmund shook his head. "I mean a really *good* king, elected by the people and confirmed by the gods."

The thought was not unappealing, Candamir had to admit. It would simplify many things to entrust leadership of the community to a single person, the one among them best suited for the task. And yet, the idea filled him with a sense of unease. "But to whom would you entrust such a position? I mean, you can't see into the hearts of even Harald or Eilhard, who are certainly among the wisest of men, can you? Wouldn't we just give free reign to arbitrary use of power if we elevated one among us? How could you know beforehand who would be able to resist the temptations of power?"

"By asking for advice from the gods, as I said."

Candamir placed his hands down on the table and took a deep breath. "The gods too often follow their own devices."

For the first time, Osmund's expression turned severe, almost hostile. "I hear the words of your Saxon. You are slandering the gods, Candamir. That is dangerous."

Candamir grumbled. "My Saxon..."

"Osmund is quite right," they heard Brigitta say suddenly from the doorway. "It's no wonder that Odin in his anger makes the earth tremble, considering how we thank him for his gift."

Candamir looked angrily over his shoulder toward the door. "And how long have you been standing there eavesdropping, huh?"

She ignored him, entering the room uninvited and sitting down on the bench some distance from him. "We have been here more than three months. We are building our houses and soon will be bringing in our first harvest, but where is the temple we were going to build to Odin? It was your idea, Osmund, but you haven't said a word about it."

Osmund looked down at the ground in shame. "You are right," he confessed. "The clearing of the land and the houses seemed more important to me. But the earthquake was a warning, there's no doubt about that."

*A warning, for certain, but from which god?* Candamir wondered. Osmund's accusation—that he was being misled by his Saxon slave—was wrong. Nevertheless, Austin's god had proven his power in the clearest possible way when he cured Hacon. It was the first time a god had ever done a personal favor for him. For this reason alone, Candamir felt indebted to him, and he had to confess he feared him as well. In any case, he was inclined to believe one thing the Saxon said—that his god was mightier than all gods he had known until then.

"We'll build the temple when every family has a roof over their heads, Brigitta," he promised to placate the old woman. "Even before the mill, as far as I'm concerned. But we can't do it at the moment; you must see that."

"It doesn't matter what I see or don't see," she replied sharply. "It's a matter of appeasing Odin. And he has let us know that his patience is exhausted. You must put all the other work aside and start building on the island tomorrow."

"You must be crazy," Candamir growled.

"No, *you* are the crazy one," she said, interrupting him, "and you are a danger to us all if you don't come to your senses. The smith and your sister, by the way, interpret the signs exactly as I do. Harald suggested we announce a *Thing* for tomorrow morning to decide when to start building the temple. Since you so strongly supported the authority of the assembly, you certainly won't oppose its decisions, will you, my lad?"

# Harvest Moon, Year One

*The rye has been harvested, the straw bundled, and on the new fields the sowing has begun, as well as the planting of the parsnips we found everywhere growing wild. The days are getting shorter, but not cooler, and gradually the people are beginning to believe that perhaps there will never be a real winter here. There is no trace of the fear that used to spread as summer came to a close.*

*Each day, the Almighty teaches us something new about this blessed land, and we learn to better adapt to conditions in our new home. We have less wool than before but an abundance of cowhide and, because of all the wood we have cut, bark from trees that provides us with tanning acid. Therefore, more and more we are wearing clothes made of soft leather, which is much sturdier than cloth made of wool. To the great astonishment of all his neighbors, Haflad the charcoal burner found a way to clear the new fields with fire instead of axes. He avoids the danger of uncontrolled forest fire by cutting wide swaths beforehand, and next year we will have as much farmland as we can cultivate. The layout of gardens and the building of houses and outbuildings has also been adapted to the new climate. Carpenters are held in high regard, and this applies especially to my master, who for several weeks has been devoting himself solely to building the temple on the island in the river.*

Unfortunately, the accursed witch, with help from her clever disciple, had succeeded in finding the perfect place of worship for their heathen cult. On the very night of her wedding, Inga had excavated the spring on the little island. Austin didn't want to know any of the details of this ritual, but the settlers were already talking about the magic power of this water. Osmund's slave had immersed his injured foot in it, and the bleeding stopped at once. Old Eilhard swore that his gout hardly had bothered him since washing his painful joints in the spring water, and the poor Turon who was working on building the temple with Candamir drank from the spring every day in the hope of growing a new tongue—so far, without success.

On the day after the earthquake, the *Thing* had decided the temple was to be given priority, and despite Olaf's emphatic objections, entrusted Candamir with the planning and execution. And even though the young master builder had been against giving precedence to this project, he devoted all his strength to it and was consumed with a burning ambition. The hall on the island in the river promised to be larger than any the settlers had ever seen. For an entire week, all the male slaves had been in the grassland cutting blocks of limestone for the foundation, and whoever was too slow or brought stones that were too small met with Candamir's wrath.

The framework for the walls was now largely complete. Candamir chose only the finest, most perfectly formed tree trunks for the hall of the gods, and once the building was finished, the beams were to be carved and decorated with runes and pictures. But that would have to wait until they had the time to devote to such ornamentation.

Building the individual homes still seemed more urgent to Candamir, and it disturbed him that this work was proceeding at a snail's pace now that Berse and his men had to do it alone. But Candamir also had ambitious plans for the temple's roof—it was to have the form of an inverted dragon ship, so that the settlers' descendents would never forget they were a seafaring people and how they had gotten here. To strengthen the effect, he intended to cover this roof with wood shingles rather than with reeds. Siglind had agreed to it, greatly relieved after she had seen the plan for the hall and calculated the huge amount of reeds needed.

The temple construction filled the settlers with curiosity and excitement, and after their day's work, both men and women frequently rowed over to the island to check on the progress. They admired Candamir's work and brought him and his workers little presents and things to eat. But not everyone shared this enthusiasm for the hall of the gods.

"He won't do anything without advice from the shifty Saxon, Harald," Olaf said angrily, "and what he's building for us is a temple to his accursed carpenter god!"

"Nonsense," the smith replied, with a full mouth. He washed his food down with mead before continuing. "The heart of our hall of the gods is not an altar for the crucified carpenter, but the sacred spring, just as Brigitta wanted."

Olaf waved a finger at him in warning. "I tell you, I have seen the temples of the Christians, and they look exactly like what Candamir is trying to pass off as a shrine to our gods."

"He's not passing off anything," Hacon mumbled. "He's doing exactly what the *Thing*..."

"Hold your tongue!" Candamir snapped at him. "Don't you have any manners? Olaf is talking with Harald, and nobody asked your opinion."

Hacon sighed, and his shoulders dropped. He stared into his bowl of stew and stirred it listlessly with his spoon. Whenever he was in the same room with Olaf, he got choked up and his hands began to sweat. His fear of this man always threatened to paralyze him, but nevertheless he had not been able to listen to Olaf's accusations against his brother and Austin without speaking up.

Candamir's entire household, as well as that of the smith, was sitting together at the long table in Harald's hall. Candamir and Austin were quietly eating their supper while Olaf was gesticulating wildly in front of Harald's high seat, admonishing them as if they weren't present.

"If I'm wrong, then tell me this: Why is the temple aligned on an east-west axis and not on a north-south axis?"

Harald gave up hope of being able to eat anytime soon and pushed his bowl away with strained patience. "I don't know, Olaf. I don't understand such things. Why don't you ask Candamir?"

Olaf snorted. "I might as well save my breath!"

"The clearing was too narrow to align the hall facing north, and the spring lies on the east side," Candamir explained, staring at the many specks of fat in his stew. "Brigitta did not allow us to cut even a single tree on the island, but she did agree we should build the hall in an east-west direction, for that is the direction the sun travels."

"You don't say! But I'll bet anything your Saxon suggested that," Olaf persisted.

Candamir did not answer, because Olaf was right in his assumption.

The Saxon looked at the master of the house. "May I speak?"

Harald gestured to him to continue.

Austin had to summon up all his courage to look Olaf in the face, for just like Hacon he feared this huge, violent man. But no one could have guessed that. The Saxon's expression was serious, but not tense. "My master asked me for advice because in my homeland I've seen such large halls that are used for prayer, and he has not. But you are mistaken if you think I wanted to mislead him and have him erect a temple to my god and not yours. My god would not want it, for He hates insincerity."

Harald nodded. "So tell me, Olaf, does that satisfy you?"

Olaf laughed softly. "Are you really so foolish as to believe this wily Saxon, or are you just pretending in order to dupe me, Harald? They always say you are an intelligent man."

"I'm a hungry man, in any case, and would like now to continue eating, with your permission. Your accusations are unfounded, but if you want to, you can bring them before the *Thing*. There will be one in a week."

Olaf nodded briefly and turned to leave. "I only hope that Odin will not send us another warning before that."

They all fell silent until he had left the hall, slamming the door behind him. Then Asta said pointedly, "How he fears the gods, all of a sudden! I always thought…" She stopped as her husband put his hand on her arm and then raised a finger to his lips.

"Yes," Hacon whispered quietly. "I'll bet you anything he's standing outside and listening."

Harald and Asta began an innocuous conversation about how to store apples that grew everywhere in the forest, while Candamir watched his younger brother out of the corner of his eye. Hacon had grown again, and Asta had sewn him some new clothing of the finest, light-brown cowhide. He wore his hair just like Candamir. It was longer than before and had two small plaits framing his face neatly braided and tied at the ends with thin leather laces. It wouldn't be much longer before Hacon would have to shave for the first time, Candamir noted in amazement.

Hacon's powers of observation were no less developed than his brother's, and he didn't fail to notice how thoroughly he was being sized up. "Are you almost done?" he asked with an uneasy smile.

Candamir shrugged, picked up a piece of rye bread, and broke it in half. "I'm amazed to see that gradually you are turning into a man, so it seems."

"I only had to escape your clutches to do that," Hacon shot back.

Perhaps he felt safe because he was sitting out of his brother's reach, but Candamir got up, reached across the table, and gave him a good boxing on both ears. "So that's your thanks, is it?"

"Candamir!" Asta cried out, startled. She was no longer accustomed to such scenes, as it was comparatively peaceful in the smith's house. No one here was hot-tempered, least of all she herself, and this household had become her safe haven.

Hacon tugged his tunic out of Candamir's fist and jumped to his feet. "Yes, that's my thanks: candor. But that's something you could never tolerate, Brother! Ever since I grew too old to unconditionally admire you, you never missed an opportunity to humiliate me. Only since I have been living in this house have I slowly begun to think I could amount to something after all. Oh, not as perfectly and nobly as you, but at least it looks like I could learn to make good tools, because, unlike you, Harald trusts me to do things right!"

Candamir gave a slight nod. He was deeply hurt, and his face had turned to stone.

"Hacon, I'm sorry to disappoint you, but there you go again talking without thinking beforehand," the smith said. "That's something that needs your urgent attention, preferably right away, outside in the fresh air, because I'd like to have a little peace in my house. And I'm convinced that after you've thought it over and come back, you'll have an apology for your brother."

"He may as well save his breath," Candamir said.

Hacon left the hall with his head down. Gunda thought nobody was watching and tried to follow him, but Candamir growled, "Don't you dare."

Startled, she returned to her blanket near the fire where she had been playing with Nils and Asta's children. Fulc had always been partial to Gunda and was gentle as a lamb when she was around. It was Asta's fervent wish that Candamir would change his mind and let her have the slave girl, but the chances of that had probably never been slimmer than today.

"I'm sorry, Harald," Candamir said, sighing and shrugging his shoulders helplessly. He probably would have had more to say if he had been alone with the smith, but he couldn't admit to being wrong in front of Asta, the Saxon, and the other household servants.

Harald smiled briefly and nodded. He could hardly criticize Candamir, for if Godwin hadn't gone to live with Berse and his sons after Candamir's cabin had been destroyed, they would have been at one another's throats at every turn, too.

When the meal was over, Asta asked the maids to clear the table, and she found something for each of the slaves to do, except for Austin, so that finally only the four of them remained seated at the table.

"You should be forearmed when Olaf repeats his accusations at the assembly next week, Candamir," Harald warned.

"Yes," the younger man replied. "At every *Thing* I must be armed against any accusation from Olaf. And who do I have to thank for that?"

"Me," Austin replied. "Let's not forget how it all started. It isn't Hacon's fault. On the contrary, he's the only innocent victim in this entire feud."

"*Innocent?*" Candamir repeated indignantly. "Didn't he betray me and leave Olaf's sheep to the wolves in order to screw my slave?"

Asta and Austin flinched at his choice of words, which had been his intention.

But the Saxon replied, undeterred, "It never would have come to that if you had not needed to do slave labor for Olaf, and that in turn was only because I..."

"No, you're wrong, Austin," Harald interrupted, which was unusual for him in the first place. "Olaf bears a grudge against Candamir, and against Osmund as well, for quite different reasons," Harald continued. "And you'll have to comprehend that, Candamir, and your foster brother too, or else you could both fall straight into his trap."

"What do you mean?" Candamir asked curiously.

"It's a question of power. In Elasund, Olaf was the most powerful man, for he was rich and everyone else was poor. That alone meant he was listened to respectfully when he spoke, and practically everyone had to do what he wanted, because everyone was indebted to him in some way or hoped to get something from him. Moreover, he is fearless, strong, well-travelled, and has a great deal of experience. Well, all of us now are well-travelled, more or less rich in experiences, and many men are fearless and strong. Olaf isn't getting any younger, you know. In the not-too-distant future, his strength will start to decline, his eyes will grow weak—all those things that plague men who do not fall in battle in the flower of their youth. You and Osmund, on the other hand, are young. For that reason alone, you are a threat to him."

"Olaf will certainly have his hands full if he wants to fight against every man who is younger than himself—his own son, to start with," Candamir replied.

"But he can control Jared. And Jared is not in the same position as Osmund and yourself."

Austin nodded. He knew exactly what Harald was getting at. "Osmund has been chosen," he explained to his master. "Odin elected him to be the first to set foot on this land. Above all, Brigitta attaches great significance to that, and Brigitta in turn has far more influence here than in the old homeland. It was *she* who arranged Osmund's marriage to Inga, who is to be her successor. Osmund is...the new darling of your gods. That makes him powerful. Everyone seeks his company. *You*, Master, are the only one to have openly defied Olaf, and in a way that deeply affected everyone here and made clear to them that Olaf's star is on the wane."

"It's just as Austin says," the smith agreed, stroking his beard. "Moreover, you are the one shaping the uncertain future here with your words and deeds. You are building people's houses, their temple, and have shown them they no longer need to submit to power-hungry tyrants like Olaf, but instead have a unique opportunity to make their own rules. Osmund personifies Odin's power over Catan. You represent the creative power of our community. Olaf represents the past, and he knows it. And he will kill both of you, if he can, to take over your roles."

Candamir was staring at the smith in disbelief. Then, with a casual grin, he shrugged. "Well, before he can kill me, he must defeat me in battle. He will hardly come to kill me in my sleep, will he? I don't see what I have to fear."

Harald and Austin exchanged anxious glances. They both thought of Candamir's greatest weakness—the stubborn young woman who lived all alone in a cabin.

"In any case, you should be on your guard," Harald advised earnestly.

Austin agreed. He turned to Candamir. "If you will permit, Master, I'll follow Hacon. It is getting dark, and I'm worried that Olaf might still be prowling around somewhere out there."

Candamir dismissed him with an impatient nod.

Austin found Hacon in the smithy, just a stone's throw from Harald's hall. The boy was busy removing the cold ashes from the forge and filling it with charcoal for the next day. He shoveled the ashes into a leather bucket. Asta made soap from them, and what she didn't need they used as fertilizer for the vegetable garden. He smiled when he caught sight of the monk at the door, but quickly said with a frown, "Did you come to give me a lecture? Save your breath."

"How would you know whether it's worth hearing or not, until you have listened?" Austin inquired.

"Because I know already that you are right. But it won't do any good; I can't ask him for forgiveness, not for tonight and not for what happened with Gunda."

Austin stepped closer and sat down on the bench provided to accommodate talkative idlers—just as it had been in Elasund—who liked to congregate, complaining about the weather, the fishing, or the harvest while they waited for their plowshares. "Why not?" the monk asked.

"Because I'm not sorry," Hacon answered tersely.

"Well, you are right, that does make things difficult. Neither God nor your brother will pardon you for your sins if you don't repent."

"I know," Hacon admitted, busily working. He finally stopped, lowered his hands, and turned to face Austin. And only then did the Saxon realize the grief the boy's heart held. "I…I love Gunda, Austin. I know I'm still too young, but I'd like to marry her someday and make her a respectable woman, as she deserves to be."

*Nothing will ever make a respectable woman out of this harlot,* Austin nearly said.

"But Candamir won't allow that. He doesn't want her anymore and treats her like dirt. He has eyes only for Siglind, but he would rather break her neck than let me have her."

"And how do you know you love Gunda? I mean, are you sure it's really a matter of the heart and not the…" Austin gestured vaguely to a point below Hacon's waist and blushed.

"Yes, I'm sure. Sometimes we get together at night. Oh, don't make that face, I don't mean in that way. We talk. We…" He shrugged briefly. "Well, we have a lot in common and are of about the same age. You can probably say we have gotten to know one another. And maybe your opinion of her will improve if you know she has decided, just as I have, to follow your god. I told her the little that I know about him, and she has dozens of things she would like to ask you, but doesn't dare. She's almost as afraid of you as she is of my brother. And she is pregnant again. And when Candamir finds out, then…"

"She doesn't know who the father is?" Austin asked, slightly nauseated.

Hacon spread his arms. "How could she? Of course not. Therefore Candamir will sell her child, or kill it when it comes, and probably kill her too. But *I* wouldn't mind. I would raise my nephew just as willingly as my own son. The most important thing, after all, is for our community to multiply."

"Indeed. Nevertheless, we are God's children and not rabbits, Hacon, and therefore isn't it desirable to know who the father is? Besides, you are only fifteen years old and can't marry. And you—excuse my frankness—are too good for a woman like Gunda."

"Why do you say that?" the boy snapped. "How do you have any right to judge her?"

"Because she is unchaste and has violated God's commandment."

"But she didn't know anything about His commandments."

"What she did is forbidden by your rules just as much as by mine."

"But didn't you say we are all sinful and therefore can rejoice in God's boundless mercy?"

Austin laughed softly. "Again you are coming at me with my own weapons, Hacon."

Hacon smiled weakly, walked over to him, and sat down. "Help us, Austin," he begged. "Candamir will listen to you. Help us, and I swear to you that we will raise our children in your faith."

The monk was weary of the uneasy compromises that his arduous missionary work forced upon him. He raised his hand in disapproval. "You have chosen to follow God, and you say Gunda wants to do that as well. And so, of course, your children would be baptized, and it ought to be beneath you to tempt me with something like that."

"You're right," the boy said remorsefully. "But we won't ever have these children if you deny us your help."

"Ah!" the Saxon said dryly. "The same sort of bribery in a little different form. You are a clever talker, Hacon, just like your brother."

"Well then, what will you do?" The boy held his breath.

Austin placed his hands on his knees and stared for a moment into the cold forge. Finally, he nodded slowly. "Very well, then. I'll do what little I can. But you must swear to me that you will remain chaste until I can marry you before God with your brother's permission."

"Oh, Austin, that could take *years*!"

"Those are my conditions," the monk replied firmly. "Otherwise I would be complicit in your offense."

Hacon thought it over for a moment, then sighed and nodded. "You're right, I cannot ask that of you." He placed his right hand on his heart and raised his left hand. "I swear it to you by the blood of Jesus Christ."

"Don't forget."

"I won't."

"And to prove your good intentions and contrition, you must go to your brother and make peace with him. He has always done his best for you, Hacon, and no one can demand anything more. I would never say he did everything right, but he tried."

"Yes, I know. But no matter what I say, he will never forgive me."

"Perhaps you underestimate him. Your brother, too, has learned much since we left on this voyage, and he is no longer the same. None of us are. But you must take the first step. It is God's will."

"How can you be so sure?" the boy asked skeptically.

Austin smiled. "'Love thine enemies, do good to those who hate you,' He said. 'Bless those who curse you, pray for those who mistreat you.'"

"But anyone who does that will be called a coward by everyone," Hacon protested.

The monk shrugged calmly. "Christ will not call him a coward. For he also says that when we do as he commands us, '*Then your reward will be great, and you will be called Sons of the Most High, for He, too, is kind to the ungrateful and the selfish.*'"

"Amen," Hacon murmured, lowering his head. "But he had better not count on my ever loving Olaf..."

The bees of Catan turned the countless blossoms in the woods into a wonderful, golden honey, but they defended it with everything they had.

Osmund was a skilled gatherer of honey, an art requiring both patience and skill, especially when you didn't know where the beehives were located. You had to follow the little fellows this way and that through the underbrush, and usually up a tree to get to their hive. Years ago, the Saxon had told them that in his homeland, bees were kept in hives that were set up close to the house or right next to the trees, bushes, or flowers that produced your favorite honey. Osmund thought, as he did every year at around this time, that the Anglo-Saxons couldn't be as dumb as was generally believed, in spite of their crazy religion—this type of beekeeping seemed prudent and convenient.

At the foot of the ash tree where the bees lived, he made a little fire of dry branches and leaves. Then he cut a fresh branch and held it patiently over the flames until it started to burn and give off smoke. With this smoking torch, he climbed the tree and waved the branch back and forth under the hive to drive most of the bees away or stun those that stayed behind. They flew up angrily in a furiously buzzing, black cloud when the smoke reached their hive, but unlike the bees in Elasund who would just flee, the Catan bees dove straight down on the culprit.

Osmund was prepared. He jumped back down onto the forest floor, fled behind his little fire, and stood in the smoke as if it were a magic cloak, rendering him invisible. This tactic did discourage many of the bees, but by no means all of them. He had been careful to put on a long-sleeved shirt with a leather jerkin over it, but his hands, which he held over his face, were badly stung.

"Come on, Jared, what are you waiting for?" his cousin heard him call. Jared could hardly see Osmund in all the smoke, and his voice was muffled by his hands in front of his face.

Cursing softly, Jared climbed the ash tree, breaking open the beehive with his knife, and removed the honeycomb. Jared didn't escape unscathed, either. He felt four almost simultaneous stings on his hands and his arms, but he didn't let it deter him. Being especially careful not to make any sudden movements, he tossed the dripping honeycomb into the bucket he had tied on his waist.

"Done!"

He scrambled quickly down the tree, and the two of them took off as fast as they could. When they finally got to one of the small brooks that passed through the forest, they stopped and gratefully plunged their hands into the water.

At first, their fingers stung even more in the cool water, and Jared drew in his breath sharply. “Why does it have to be like this?” he grumbled, clenching his teeth. “If this land is perfect, why do we always have to pay this price to get honey?”

Osmund looked at him and smiled. “That’s simple, Jared. Just think about it, and you’ll figure it out yourself.”

Jared tried moving his fingers, then immediately stopped again. “Oh, yes, I know what you’re getting at. If the honey were easier to get, our mead would not taste so sweet to us.”

“That’s right.”

“I just doubt whether that’s true. Damn, these little things stung me seven times. How many do you have?”

Osmund shrugged. “I have no idea.” In fact, it was more than two dozen, and he felt a little dizzy, from the pain or the bee venom—he didn’t know which.

His cousin looked him over critically. “You’re sweating,” he said.

“That’s no surprise, it’s hot.”

“And you’re pale as a ghost.”

Osmund clicked his tongue impatiently. “Nonsense, I have as much of a tan as you do. Stop gawking at me. I…” He suddenly fell silent, squinted, and blinked his eyes.

“What?” the younger one asked.

Without warning, Osmund fell forward into the water, motionless.

“Osmund!” Jared leapt up. “What’s the matter with you?”

There was no answer. Worried, he waded into the little brook and fished his cousin out. Osmund was unconscious.

*If he dies, I’ll get Inga,* Jared thought, but he quickly realized how much his cousin meant to him. “Oh, Osmund, what am I to do?” he cried.

Candamir was on his way through the forest, checking traps. He had caught two rabbits and a marten so far, killing the animals with a quick, merciful slash of his knife before fastening his catch to his belt. Martens had a bitter taste, and in Catan nobody needed to eat anything like that, but he wanted the hide.

He set out toward home, satisfied with the results of his hunting trip. A sleepy, late-summer silence lay over the forest. His eyes closed, Candamir took a deep breath of the warm air, redolent with the fragrance of ferns and innumerable berries ripening everywhere on the ground and on bushes. And as hard as he tried, he could not yet detect the slightest hint of autumn in the air. Slowly he spread out his arms, threw his head back, and laughed.

"Only a fool laughs at nothing," a familiar voice behind his shoulder remarked dryly.

He quickly lowered his arms, but took his time turning around. "That may be, but I am laughing with happiness about the lingering summer."

Siglind stepped out of the shadows of the trees to join him. "A good reason," she admitted.

"Isn't it a bit early in the day to be away from work?" he asked.

"I could say the same about you," Siglind replied.

"Actually, I am looking for the Turon. I sent him out more than two hours ago to get new wood for the island, and he hasn't returned, so I decided to go look for him and check my traps while I'm at it."

"It looks like it was worth your while," she said, pointing a slender finger at the animals hanging on his belt. "I have done well myself. I just finished Thorbjörn's roof, and I've come out to look for lady's mantle."

"Lady's mantle?" Candamir repeated, puzzled.

She nodded. "It's an herb for an ailment that troubles me regularly, but isn't anything you need to worry about."

"What sort of ailment is it?" he asked, belatedly realizing what she meant. He briefly raised his hand. "Oh, I know. My mother suffered from it every month, but she didn't know anything about lady's mantle."

"Probably because Austin hadn't come to live with you yet," she said.

Candamir looked at her in amusement and disbelief. "Are you saying that *Austin* knows about remedies for women's ailments? And he can tell you about them without choking up?"

Siglind couldn't help smiling, but nodded. "If it's about medicinal herbs, he's quite able to overcome his embarrassment."

"I'll bet he is," Candamir grumbled. "I'll bet with you he can overcome any embarrassment." He meant it to sound playful, but he wasn't quite able to conceal his bitterness.

Siglind gave him a sidelong glance. "Now just what does that mean?"

He raised both his hands in a gesture of resignation. He didn't want to have this conversation, at least not today. "Nothing at all."

"But you…"

Candamir put his hand on her arm and pointed straight ahead. Between the trees, by the bank of a small stream, he caught sight of something moving. And now he recognized Jared, who was waving excitedly.

"Come here! Hurry!" Olaf's son cried out in alarm.

Candamir and Siglind quickened their pace, and when they arrived, discovered Osmund lying motionless at Jared's feet in the grass along the shore.

Candamir knelt down next to him. "What happened?" he asked Jared.

The young man shrugged helplessly. "I don't know, he just toppled over."

"I'll go and get Austin," Siglind said, about to turn away.

"That's not necessary," Candamir replied, pointing to the bucket with the peculiarly shaped honeycombs that Jared had carelessly cast down on the shore. "Osmund has been gathering honey," he added, as if that explained everything.

"So?" she asked.

"He knows very well that he really shouldn't be doing that, but I don't know anyone as crazy about honey and mead as Osmund. If he gets more than two or three bee stings, he faints. I can't tell you how often I've carried him home from the forest. He was once unconscious for nearly two hours. His father feared he was going to die and after that forbade him to go bee-hunting."

"But that didn't stop Osmund," Jared said.

Candamir nodded. "When did it happen?"

"Just before you got here."

Candamir checked his foster brother's arms and neck—the places where bees ordinarily sting. He was shocked by the number of swollen sting marks, but didn't let it show. "Well, I don't intend to wait here for two hours until Osmund wakes up," he said, giving his friend a firm pinch on his pale cheeks and patting them hard.

Siglind poked him in the shoulder. "Oh, leave him alone, you blockhead," she scolded and knelt down beside him. "Take off your tunic, put it in the water, and then bring it back to me."

Candamir watched jealously as she took Osmund's head gently in her lap, but he did as he was told.

Relieved to have help, Jared watched closely as Siglind dabbed the swollen places on Osmund's face, neck, chest, and arms with cool water, though it didn't seem to help.

"Is he breathing at all?" Jared asked anxiously.

Candamir stood at Siglind's side, his arms crossed in front of his bare chest, and in response to Jared's question, he bent over, pulled out a blade of grass, and held it under Osmund's nose. The blade quivered visibly. Then he placed his hand on the left side of his friend's chest. "Strong and steady," he reported.

"Good," Siglind said, brushing Osmund's blond hair from his forehead. "I think he will come to shortly. It seems to me he's breathing more deeply now."

Soon Jared and Candamir could see his chest rising and falling, and after a moment Osmund stirred and shuddered.

"Shush," Siglind said, carefully dabbing his sweat-covered forehead. "You'll feel better soon, you'll see."

Osmund smiled blissfully. "Siglind…" But then suddenly his eyes widened and he sat up straight, as if singed by her touch.

"Easy, fellow," Candamir said, crouching down next to his friend.

"Candamir…" Osmund sounded confused. "What's going on? Where are we?"

"In the woods. You were gathering honey and passed out once again."

"Oh, yes, now I remember." He smiled wanly. "Where is Jared?"

"Here, Cousin." Jared walked over to him. "You really scared me."

Leaning on Candamir's arm and struggling to his feet, Osmund said gruffly, "It's all over now, so stop looking at me as if I had just come back from the dead." As always, he was greatly embarrassed to have swooned like a maiden.

Candamir was by no means certain it was all over. Sometimes Osmund's mysterious bee-sleep was followed by a dreadful period of nausea. He hoped very much his friend would be spared that this time. No man wanted to vomit at the feet of a beautiful woman, at least not a sober man. "Jared, would you go on ahead with Siglind? I'll stay with Osmund until..."

"That's out of the question," Siglind interrupted emphatically. "I'm going to stay here until I'm convinced he's better."

Osmund rolled his eyes. "But I *am* all right."

"So much the better," she replied, not budging.

The four of them sat together in the grass, just as in those early days on Catan when they went out scouting together. They discussed the progress made building the temple, about whether the winter seed would grow if there was no frost, and about Osmund and Candamir's plans to set out on a long journey to explore the interior of the island in the late fall, after the fields had been tilled and the houses finished.

"But I have come to think we won't really find any other people in this land," Candamir said. "We have been here almost half a year, and if Odin had led any people to the island apart from us, we would have long ago seen traces of them."

Osmund nodded. "I think so too. But I want to see the wasteland and the fiery mountain up close." His cheeks were still pale despite his suntanned skin, but his breathing wasn't as labored as it had been just a quarter hour before.

"Just be careful," Siglind couldn't refrain from saying, though in truth she longed to accompany the two friends.

"Depending on our progress, I'd like to cross the mountains and see what the land is like on the other side of the island," Candamir said, paying no heed to her warning.

"Why?" Jared asked in surprise. "Could it be any better than it is here?"

"Probably not." Candamir shrugged. "I just want to see it. And when we reach the coast, I'll go diving for pearls and bring them to you, Siglind."

She quickly lowered her eyes, but nevertheless the men could see the slight blush that came over her face. "I'll save my thanks for the day that really happens," she said, with an involuntary smile.

"Yes, I guess that's wise," Candamir admitted, and they both laughed.

Osmund felt the old, familiar pang of jealousy. "Don't you think we should get going?" he asked. "We've wasted enough time."

With no apparent effort he jumped to his feet, and the group headed east back to the village. Their pace was slower than usual; Osmund was still troubled with dizziness and as exhausted as if he had fought a long, bitter battle. But he didn't vomit, and he knew that the whole episode would be over by morning. He had gotten off easy this time, he thought, already scheming on how to improve his method for next time.

They took a shortcut through the almost impenetrable underbrush, far from all the paths made by the settlers crisscrossing the forest, but they were familiar enough with the area to know they would soon come to a clearing and another brook that would lead them straight to the river. Jared, who was carrying the bucket, broke off a large piece from one of the honeycombs and handed it to Siglind.

"Oh, many thanks, Jared!" she replied in delight, cutting through the thin layer of wax covering the individual sections and gleefully licking out the honey as eagerly as a child. Osmund and Candamir watched her with carefully concealed pleasure.

Candamir held out his hand. "Give me a piece too, Jared, there's a good boy."

Osmund protested. "I didn't get myself stung just so you would have something to nibble on."

"Oh, just one tiny piece, come on, don't make a fuss like…"

His sentence remained hanging in thin air, because Siglind had suddenly stopped short and wasn't moving. There was such an expression of horror on her face that Candamir thought a bee stuck to the honeycomb must have stung her. Before he could act, Jared let out a half-suppressed cry that seemed to express both disgust and despair.

Confused, Candamir noticed that Siglind and Jared were staring in the same direction, and he followed their gaze. What he saw filled him with such terror that his guts seemed to turn to jelly. The shock and horror of it was worse than any physical pain he had ever felt.

Barely twenty steps in front of them, the Turon was kneeling, bent over, his trousers pulled down around his ankles. His shorn head was tossed back, and his face was twisted into a gray mask of misery. He had braced his hands against a tree trunk to absorb the cruel thrusts of the man who knelt behind him, digging his fingers into the Turon's bony shoulders, raping him. While the four accidental witnesses stood there frozen, he finished, stood up, and straightened out his clothing. The young slave fell on his side and tugged futilely with trembling hands on his trousers.

A wave of nausea swept over Osmund, and he knew he'd be sick after all. Turning away quickly, he disappeared into the hazelnut bushes.

Jared placed his bucket on the ground, turning away slowly, with one hand over his eyes, and stammered, "O mighty Thor" over and over, imploring his patron god to undo what he had just seen with his own eyes.

Siglind stepped hesitantly toward the Turon and his tormenter, finally awakening Candamir from his stupor. He gripped her arm so tightly she was afraid he'd snap her bone like a twig. Candamir caught her eye and shook his head slightly and put a finger to his lips. Emerging from the dense underbrush, he walked resolutely toward the grisly scene, though in truth his knees were soft as butter.

With his head bowed, he knelt down next to the young Turon to help him to cover his nakedness. When the slave saw him, he let out a hoarse sob and hid his head in his arms.

Candamir stood up and turned around slowly. "That's the end of you, Olaf," he said, with a deep sense of triumph and satisfaction.

Now Olaf was the one standing there motionless like a statue, but Candamir was sure it was not fear that had paralyzed him. The powerful trader was looking for a way to talk himself out of his predicament.

Olaf went on the attack. "Why? Because you caught me fooling around with my slave? Do you really think anyone would believe one word you said if you accused me of such a disgraceful thing? I am a respected man, and don't you forget it," he responded, quietly amused, as if he were enjoying a huge joke at Candamir's expense.

Candamir neglected to reveal the fact that there were indeed more witnesses to this disgusting scene, and instead replied, "And now we know what your reputation is based on, don't we? Lies and deception. In truth you are just a…a…"

"Yes? How do you propose to bring charges against me if you are too ashamed even to say the word?"

"I'll bring myself to do it," Candamir promised grimly.

"I'm eager to see that."

"Oh, by all the gods, Olaf, how can you live with yourself?"

The older man gestured dismissively. "It's not as shameful as it looks to you with your limited view of the world, you know. There are places where every man of standing keeps a young boy. If you'd like to try out for this role, you can always come to me."

It was like a punch to the stomach. Candamir felt sick with anger and instinctively pulled his knife from the sheath on his belt as if to defend himself.

At the same moment, Olaf drew his sword.

"Osmund," Jared whispered hoarsely, "whatever you're doing, you must come back here at once."

After a few moments, Osmund emerged from the bushes and, along with the two others, watched the unequal battle in the little clearing. Candamir and Olaf did not have enough room for a duel, which was especially dangerous for Candamir, as Olaf had the weapon with the longer reach.

"How he can fight!" Siglind murmured admiringly. "I had no idea."

Osmund had to agree, though he was far less surprised than she was. Ever since he and Candamir had been old enough to walk, they had practiced handling swords, battle-axes, and knives, and he was all too familiar with his friend's catlike grace and strength. Olaf's sword blade whistled through the air, but Candamir easily dodged it, even getting close enough to wound his opponent on the arm.

"Nevertheless, he will get killed if we don't do anything," Osmund said softly. "You can't beat a swordsman like Olaf with only a knife in hand. Stay here—I'm going."

Reluctantly he emerged from the bushes and walked toward the opponents. Jared and Siglind didn't obey his instructions, but followed him. Fear showed in Olaf's eyes for the first time when he caught sight of Osmund. Yet, without the slightest hesitation, he raised his sword against his unarmed nephew. Osmund would never have thought his uncle capable of something like that, and he was still groggy, so he dodged Olaf's sword far too slowly.

Jared seized his father's arm, preventing the blow that surely would have been fatal, and Siglind took advantage of Olaf's momentary confusion to tear the weapon from his limp hand. Candamir lowered his knife, and silence fell over the little meadow.

Finally, Olaf raised his head. He was so pale that his skin seemed transparent, as he looked at his son in disbelief. "How will you live with yourself, Jared, with your father on your conscience? I don't think you'll be able to do that—you are too much of a coward."

"He's not a coward," Candamir and Osmund said simultaneously.

The young man swallowed visibly, but returned his father's gaze. "I don't know, Father. At any rate, I can't go on living like *this*." His face was strangely expressionless, but the horror in his eyes revealed that Jared was far less surprised by these events than they were. Candamir suddenly imagined what really might be happening behind the closed doors of Olaf's hall, remembering with a suppressed shudder how close he'd come to sending his young, handsome brother there during last winter's famine. "You wanted to kill Candamir, and you even wanted to kill my cousin, just so you could go on like you always have," Jared continued. Then he shook his head. "But I've had about all I can take. If this is to be a better homeland than the old one, why can't it be so for me as well, and for my brothers and sisters and all those who depend on your mercy?"

And so, this time, it was Olaf who was brought back to the village bound and in disgrace. Candamir had untied his rabbits and the marten from his belt and used the rope to bind Olaf's hands behind his back. Candamir and Osmund led him back to the village. They had disarmed him, but were careful not to lay a hand on him, walking a half step behind, one on either side.

Jared had stayed behind in the forest, and Siglind attended to the young Turon. At first he had refused to look at her or anyone else, and did not respond to anything they said. But after the men had left she persuaded him to go with her to the sacred spring on the Temple Island.

It was late afternoon now, and the men had returned from the fields and were working around the house, the women were at their hearths, and the maids were milking the cows. Thus, it wasn't long before word got around that Osmund and Candamir had brought Olaf back to the village in fetters. Soon most of the settlers were gathered around the ash tree to hear what had happened.

"What's the meaning of all this?" Brigitta demanded once everyone had quieted down.

Osmund and Candamir exchanged glances, and then Osmund said, "You ought to send the children away."

"But…"

"Just do it, Brigitta."

She narrowed her eyes, then nodded, and gestured as though she were chasing away a flock of geese. "You heard him. Away with you, go off to your homes."

Candamir walked up to Harald and whispered in his ear. A look of disbelief and shock crossed Harald's face before he folded his massive arms and turned to the assembly. "Candamir says that Olaf committed indecent assault on the Turon."

There was a horrified silence, then a murmur went through the crowd. Brigitta sat down heavily in the grass and turned her back to the assembly. She knew this was a matter that the men had to work out among themselves.

Old Eilhard was incredulous. “Are you sure?”

“There are three witnesses besides myself—Osmund, Siglind, and... Jared.”

The whispering grew louder.

The case was so revolting, so atrocious, that no one felt competent to continue the discussion. Hardly anyone had ever before heard of such a crime. Only Brigitta and Eilhard, the oldest among the settlers, could remember that long ago something like that had once occurred, and so, hesitantly, Eilhard finally spoke up.

He turned to Olaf. “What do you have to say to this accusation?”

Olaf stood up to his full height and with apparent fearlessness returned the old warrior’s gaze. “Nothing.”

“You don’t deny it?” Eilhard said almost pleadingly.

“No.”

The crowd grew silent.

“Then you must die, Olaf,” Eilhard declared in measured tones.

Austin lowered his head and crossed himself. He didn’t care who saw it. *Jesus Christ,* he prayed fervently, *soften their hearts and let them do it quickly.* But he had little hope his prayer would be heard. He knew his unwilling flock—they would do something dreadful. He saw it in their grim faces and the cruel gleam in their eyes.

The Saxon knew that among these people fornication between men was considered the most repulsive of all offenses. And while he agreed it was reprehensible, as he considered all unnatural carnal acts, there was still a difference. For them, who otherwise weren’t very fussy about matters of morality, Olaf’s crime was unspeakable.

“Then give me back my sword and let me do it myself,” Olaf demanded. His voice sounded as strong as ever, without even a hint of a tremble. “Don’t forget, without me, none of you would ever have reached Catan. You at least owe me a dignified death.”

Siward rose from the grass, stepped up to him, and spit in his face. Olaf flinched and jumped back.

“We don’t owe you a damned thing!” the older man said angrily. His hatred of Olaf, which had been smoldering over the last few months, now flared up again. "*You* just led us around by our noses. We only have Odin to thank that we are here. You are a disgrace and unworthy of living in this land! Eilhard is right, you must die. In the old days, men like you were drowned in the swamp."

Olaf sneered at him. "You can look around Catan for a long time before you will find a swamp, brave Siward."

Candamir couldn't help but admire Olaf's courage. He had to be afraid—he was too smart not to know he was facing a horrible death—but he didn't show it in the least.

Suddenly a sharp cry rang out. Everyone was startled, and Osmund frowned at his young wife. Inga had jumped up and was hunched over. She looked at her husband wide-eyed and raised her hands. "Forgive me; it was a snake in the grass. I was startled...please forgive me."

No pregnant woman wanted to encounter a snake; it was a bad omen for the child's future.

Siward raised his head. "A snake? Where?"

"There," she said, pointing with a trembling finger. "It's crawling toward the bank of the river, Father."

Berse headed fearlessly in the direction she was pointing, bent his crooked torso, and quickly seized the light brown and black snake just below the head. It writhed this way and that to get away, but to no avail. The shipwright presented the creature, no longer than his forearm, to Eilhard, Siward, and Harald, who were standing in a rough semicircle around Olaf. "And what do you say to this?"

The three men looked at one another and nodded.

Eilhard turned to Brigitta, who was still sitting in the grass with her back to them. "Is it a sign?"

She did not answer immediately, but finally nodded. "Yes," she said crossly. "It is a sign, there's no doubt about it."

Eilhard stepped up to the prisoner. "You will die by snakebite, Olaf. May the gods give you strength and courage."

Olaf showed not the slightest emotion on hearing his sentence.

"Right now?" he asked.

The old man shook his head. "Tomorrow morning. You will have time to take leave of your sons and put your affairs in order."

For the first time, Olaf seemed to be struggling to keep his composure. "Thank you, Eilhard," those standing closest heard him murmur.

"Death by snakebite? What does that mean?" Austin asked Candamir and Harald as they left the green. The smith marched silently back to his house, his head bowed, and Candamir continued on to the smithy, making a point of slamming the door in his slave's face.

But Austin was not so easily put off when his curiosity was aroused. He asked Hacon, who was sitting with Wiland along the shore near the smithy throwing pebbles in the water.

"They insert the snake into a reed," Hacon explained. "Then they stuff it down his throat. The snake slides down into his stomach and bites him from inside."

"Oh my God," Austin gasped.

Hacon nodded. "I've never seen it, but it must be horrible." He spoke hesitantly, but he knew his Saxon friend well enough to offer a warning. "You had best not do anything to save Olaf from his cruel fate, Austin. If you free him and are caught, you will be the one to swallow the snake."

The monk shuddered involuntarily. "No, thank you. For anyone else I might, but not for Olaf, though not even he deserves that. No man deserves to die like that—it is barbaric."

Hacon had no idea what "barbaric" meant, but he was inclined to agree with Austin just the same.

"Who is guarding him?" the Saxon asked.

"Thorbjörn and Haldir," Wiland replied. "My father thought it should be men who held no grudge against Olaf themselves, in order to make sure that everything takes place in a dignified and decent manner."

Austin nodded uneasily. "Dignified" and "decent" hardly seemed appropriate for this sort of execution, but he knew what Wiland meant.

His keen mind couldn't help but rush ahead to the future. "A lot will change here when Olaf is gone," he said thoughtfully.

"A lot will be better," Wiland replied.

Austin nodded. "Nevertheless, it is not good if the progress of our community is based on such a dreadful and bloody act. It is not a good sign for our future."

"Perhaps not," Hacon agreed, "but some god sent us the snake as a sign, and no other god stopped it from happening."

The Saxon sighed and nodded. "Yes. It sometimes seems to me that He is looking the other way at the decisive moment."

The longer Jared thought about the future, the more he dreaded it. He had remained in the little clearing where the fate of his family had taken such an ominous turn, half hoping that one of the gods would appear before him to at least explain *why* it had happened. He had skinned Candamir's marten and rabbits and gutted them in the meantime, planning to drop them off later at the owner's house—not so much to do Candamir a favor as to keep his hands occupied.

So now he was free. The day he had been yearning for so long had finally come. His father was either already dead or would die in the next few hours. One way or the other, there would be an end to this horror. And Jared himself would now be the head of his family. It would be up to him to make the important decisions, establish new rules, and help his brothers and sisters to forget their father's reign of terror. But how? They would hate him, Lars especially, who envied Jared's role as the eldest son, and who had always willingly suffered his father's abuse, prepared to pay any price for his attention. It was hardly different with his sisters. For his father had ruled shrewdly and was adept at arousing love as well as fear. This had especially been the case with their mother, until finally she could stand it no longer, and on a stormy winter's day had plunged into the icy fjord. Jared had cursed her for abandoning them to their cruel father then, but today he was inclined to forgive her, for he longed to take his life just as she had.

"Jared."

Startled, he raised his head. It had become dark, and he couldn't readily make out who was standing at the edge of the woods. But as he moved closer, he recognized him by the way he walked. It was not Thor who had come to him but Osmund.

"He wants to see you. And you must go and speak with your family."

Jared swallowed dryly. "He is still alive?"

"Until tomorrow morning."

"How..."

"I don't think you really want to know. And you and your brothers and sisters should be far from the village until it's over."

"Oh, Osmund, what shall I say to them? How can I ever explain this to them? They...they will accuse me of murdering my father."

Osmund feared that his cousin might be right. Even though Jared could not have done anything to prevent Candamir from bringing an accusation against his father, the stigma would always remain with him that he had not at least died trying. Olaf's foul deed would be forgotten, because it filled everyone with such shame that no one would ever mention it unless they had to. But Jared would go down in song as the son who had betrayed his father.

"Life is often bitter, Jared, as I'm sure you learned long ago."

"I did."

"The most important thing for you to consider now are your brothers and sisters. You must try to make things as easy for them as possible. And you must bear whatever they say to you. I'm convinced you can do that, for your brothers and sisters are dear to you, and probably no one knows as well as you do how torn they feel and how great their confusion must be. You will be patient and considerate with them, I know."

"Then you know more than I do. I don't want to speak with him, no matter what." The very thought made him sick with fear, even though reason told him that his father was no longer a threat.

"Do it just the same, Jared. Do it for yourself, or else his shadow will follow you all your life, and you will end up the way your mother did. You should not grant him that triumph."

It was quiet for a few moments, and then Jared slipped his knife back into its sheath and stood up. "Here." He held the stick out to Osmund. The rabbits he had gutted were dangling from one end, the pelts from the other. "Give this to Candamir. It would be a shame to waste good meat."

"Thanks. I'll walk back a ways with you."

"To be with me or just to make sure that I don't run off?" Jared asked with a grim smile.

"Because we're going the same away, Cousin," Osmund answered. The words seemed oddly weighty, but it was too dark for Jared to see the expression on Osmund's face.

They hardly spoke in the hour it took them to walk back to the village. The closer they got, the more intense the nervous twinge in Jared's stomach became, but Osmund's presence helped fortify him.

In the meadow, a single torch had been planted in the ground along the riverbank not far from the ash tree. Jared squinted in that direction, and at the edge of the circle of light, he recognized the shadowy figure of his father. They had placed a thick branch over his shoulders like a yoke and tied his outstretched arms firmly to it. His ankles were also fettered. Thorbjörn and Haldir sat nearby in the grass, their backs turned to the prisoner as an expression of disdain. They may as well go to bed, Jared thought. Given the way they had tied him up, there was no danger of escape.

Osmund placed his hand on his cousin's shoulder for a moment before turning away.

With slow, reluctant steps Jared walked toward the torch, past the guards who nodded to him earnestly. Only then did he notice Lars lying a few feet away in the grass, choked with tears. His body was strangely contorted, as if he were suffering from cramps.

"Lars," Jared admonished him in a low voice. "Pull yourself together."

Abruptly, his younger brother sat up. "Don't you talk to me!" he hissed. "I will never speak a word to you again, I swear by…"

"No, Lars, you mustn't do that," his father interrupted. He spoke softly, gently, it almost seemed, though the guards were not close enough to hear his words. "I'll not permit you to quarrel. Your brother did what he had to. I want there to be peace between you, and for you to make sure our family thrives and grows strong. That's my last wish." Pressing against the yoke over his neck, he slowly raised his head and looked at Jared. "Or rather, my next to last. My very last wish is directed to you, Jared."

Despite the mild night, an icy shiver ran down Jared's spine. "What do you want?" he asked coldly.

In the many years he had traveled the ocean as a merchant, Olaf had learned to be a clever, cold-blooded player. Yet never before had he played for such high stakes as he did now. And it seemed to him that his head had never been clearer. With an enormous act of will, he gave his voice a loving, kindly tone. "Do you know what death by snakebite is?"

Suddenly Jared's knees gave way. He collapsed and half fell in the grass in front of Olaf. "Yes, Father, I know."

Olaf smiled at him. "Then take your knife, Son, and do me one last service."

Shortly after nightfall, Candamir went to Siglind's little cabin that stood only a few steps away from the smithy. He felt dreadful—ashamed, besmirched, and guilty—without really understanding why. If Siglind felt equally upset, he thought she should not be alone this evening. But her hut was deserted, and the fireplace in front of the door was cold. Candamir was bitterly disappointed and had to admit he had not come to offer consolation so much as to find it. But then he began to worry. *Where could she be on such a gloomy, stifling night as this?*

He thought she might have sought out his Saxon, but he found Austin sitting with Hacon and Wiland near the smithy, telling them a story. The boys were listening attentively, with shining eyes. No doubt relating some wondrous deed or another by his god. Still, if he was successful in getting the boys to think about something else, then what did it matter? He continued further downriver to Osmund's new hall, but the master of the house was not home, and Inga did not know where he might be.

"I thought he was with you," she said. It sounded like a reproach.

Candamir shook his head. "I suppose he's looking for Jared."

She sighed deeply. "You are probably right. Oh, Candamir, isn't that just a dreadful business..."

He lowered his head, nodding. "Do you by any chance know where Siglind is?"

"Did you look to see if the boat is back? Maybe she is still over there on the island."

A true hodgepodge of boats were docked at the river—rowboats made from hollowed-out tree trunks, rafts, and what was left of the ships that had brought them there. Haldir and Thorbjörn had driven large pilings into the bank, constructing a wooden walkway along the river where they could all be moored securely. But even in the dim light of the waning moon, Candamir saw at first glance that his little boat was gone. It was easy to maneuver, and he had told Siglind she could borrow it whenever she needed it. Inga probably was right.

Candamir stood on the bank for a while, undecided, listening to the majestic murmuring of the river. He didn't want to encounter the Turon just now—even the thought of it made his hands sweat. He wouldn't know what to say to him, or even if he could look him in the eye. But his concern outweighed his embarrassment, so he untied Osmund's boat, jumped in nimbly, and rowed downriver to the island.

In the shadow of the trees it was darker than on the river, but Candamir could have found the way to the sacred spring blindfolded by now. Stepping out into the clearing around the temple, he saw Siglind kneeling on the ground, her head bowed and hands folded, just as Austin was accustomed to doing.

A new burden descended on Candamir's heart. Hesitantly, he walked toward Siglind and saw the young Turon lying at her feet. Siglind's little dagger was protruding from the left side of his chest, and his right hand was still gripping the handle. His eyes were closed.

For a few moments, Candamir looked down at the dead man and the praying woman and realized that he was anything but surprised. Finally, Siglind lowered her hands, but she did not look up. "Austin says that the one true God forbids taking one's own life, but how could I have denied him my dagger? It was all he wanted."

"You..." He had to clear his throat. "You did the right thing, and perhaps this is not the appropriate place to call Austin's the 'one true' god," he reminded her gently.

She shrugged her shoulders and nodded. Candamir crouched down before her and placed his hand lightly on her shoulder. Siglind was startled and raised her head, but she did not shake him off. Tears ran down her face, which suddenly seemed so thin and very young.

"Do you think you could gather a little wood?" he asked.

"Of course. But the Turons don't burn their dead, Candamir. Just like the people on the Cold Islands, they put them in a grave in the ground and build a mound of earth over it."

"Then let's do it that way. But leave me alone with him for a moment."

"That's not necessary. I'll help you, and…"

He took her hands in his. "You're very upset, Siglind. Drink from the spring and rest there for a moment. You helped the Turon escape his unbearable life. You really have done enough for him—I'll do the rest."

"But you despised him."

Candamir shook his head. "No longer, and I haven't for a long time." Then a thought came to him. "Do you by any chance still have the wax from the honeycomb that Jared gave you this afternoon?" It seemed a lifetime ago.

Siglind opened the pouch on her belt and took out a few crumbs of wax. "Here."

He nodded and waited until she had left, then knelt down and pulled the knife out of the dead man's chest. He laid it aside in order to clean it and return it to Siglind later. Then he pulled up the corpse's chin with a strip of cloth that Siglind had already prepared, so the mouth could not open, and stuffed the ears and nostrils with wax as custom prescribed, so that the spirit could not escape from the body and haunt the living.

Finally, while the corpse was still warm, he carried it to a place not far from the clearing where the Turon had sometimes taken a brief nap at noontime. Siglind followed him with two shovels from the building site, and together they buried the Turon. When their work was finished, they both stepped back a pace and observed the small grave mound.

"I don't even know what his name was," Candamir murmured.

"No. Probably no one knows that."

Candamir thrust his shovel into the ground. "What a damn waste," he said, struggling to control his anger. "Olaf deserves what he gets."

"And what is that?" Siglind asked hesitantly.

"A snake for breakfast."

"Oh, Jesus Christ..."

"Spare your sympathy. The Turon was only a slave, but he was a decent fellow, and he's not the first one that Olaf drove to his death. O mighty Tyr, who knows how often it happened before we caught him..." He couldn't continue speaking. The thought was so dreadful that it took his breath away.

"Often," Siglind said. "And when the Turon threatened to reveal everything to the smith, Olaf cut his tongue out."

Instinctively, Candamir wrapped his arms around his body. Then he looked at her. "How do you know that?"

She pointed down at the grave. "We talked for a long time this afternoon—if you can call it talking. I asked questions that he could answer by nodding or shaking his head, and he scratched pictures in the ground with a stick. At first...at first I thought it would be a relief for him to finally get it all off his chest."

"I'm sure it was."

"But not enough to want to go on living," she replied in a choked voice.

"Siglind...it's not your fault. You mustn't think that. Don't do that to yourself."

"Oh, Candamir...if only I could have thought of something else to say."

"No," he cut her short. "No. It's one thing to have to live with something like that happening to you, but it's quite a different thing when the whole world knows." He shook his head emphatically. "I would have done the same, no matter what anyone said to me—believe me, any man would."

Siglind was astonished at this confession. Taking one's own life was viewed as cowardly, no matter the circumstances.

He looked down at the grave again. "I'll miss him; that much is certain. And not only as a carpenter," he added. "And now I'd like to go and take a bath."

"But it's dark," she said absentmindedly.

"I don't care. Wait here for me. I'll come and get you when I'm finished—it won't take long."

She nodded with a tired smile, and he turned away.

The water in the river had a bluish sheen to it as it always did in the moonlight, and the setting moon spread a wondrous light over the crests of the little ripples. When Siglind arrived at the riverbank, she saw the outlines of the two boats, but nothing else. Anxiously, she stepped closer to the river, and just as she discovered Candamir's clothes at the side of the boat, she caught sight of him emerging from the water—first his crop of black hair, then his shoulders, and finally his back. Siglind quietly drew in her breath and bit her lip.

Seemingly lost in thought, Candamir threw his head back, raised his hands, and twisted his long hair behind his head and wrung it out. Then suddenly he said, "I'm going to count to ten, and when I turn around if you're still standing there, I won't answer for the consequences."

"No, please don't turn around," she said, alarmed. "Let me just look at you for a moment longer, but don't turn around."

His hands fell to his sides, but otherwise he didn't move. "Why do you want to look at me if you don't want me?"

She didn't answer.

"One…two…three…"

"Don't you dare!" she cried.

"Four…five…six…"

She didn't protest anymore. He assumed that she had fled. But he kept his word and continued counting: "Seven…eight…nine, and…" He paused, slowly turning around.

Siglind was standing there in the water just a step behind him, naked. The vision of the moonlight reflected on the little drops that ran down her white breasts made his heart race. He looked at her without stirring, completely spellbound.

His lips were slightly parted, and even in the faint light she could see how red they were. His left hand lay on the water, hesitantly reaching out toward her. If Austin was right, she knew she was about to forfeit salvation. But since she had fled the Cold Islands, she had never been as lonely and unhappy as on this night. "Pray if you seek consolation, and the Lord will send it to you," the Saxon had told her innumerable times. And she had tried again and again but always without success—on this night as well, until Candamir had arrived in the clearing. It was probably an unforgivable sacrilege even to think that God had sent him as an answer to her prayer. Nonetheless, it seemed that way to her.

The grief and fear were so clear in her eyes that even Candamir could not fail to notice. Reaching out to her with his left hand, he said softly, "Come here. Just come. I swear that you have nothing to fear from me."

She couldn't help but smile at his promise, and how he misunderstood her fear. She shook her head a little, and the space between them closed. In truth, she had made her decision long ago. She needed the consolation and proximity of flesh and blood. No matter how enticing and promising the Holy Spirit had seemed to her, it was not enough. Christ was not the bridegroom she wanted. She wanted Candamir. If God could not forgive her for that, the consequences would be dreadful, so much was certain, but she cherished the hope that Austin was wrong. He simply knew nothing about the magic between men and women, which, after all, must also come from God, who had created all things.

As soon as she was within reach, Candamir took her by the wrist and pulled her to him as if he feared she might change her mind and slip through his fingers like the water in the river. She freed her hand, wrapped her arms around his neck, and pressed him to her. When she felt his reaction she laughed softly. "My poor Candamir," she whispered. "I hope you can forgive me that I kept you waiting so long."

He placed his hands on her wonderful, round breasts, exploring their firmness and how her skin felt with the water running down it. With a gentle sigh, he pressed his lips upon hers and kissed her. At the same time, he placed his hands around her waist and pulled her farther out into the water. She found his feverish impatience contagious. Wrapping her legs around his hips, she made love to him in the warm, shallow water. And Candamir was vaguely aware that he—of all people—was granted what Odin had sought in vain from the moment he had first laid eyes on Tanuri by the brook.

She slept for perhaps an hour, and he lay next to her on his side in the grass, his head propped on his hand. He used the time to feast his eyes on her naked body. He had given up hope that this would happen. Finally, she awoke because he could no longer keep his hands off her.

"Just what are you doing?" she asked, still half asleep.

"I'm looking for the birthmark. It must be here somewhere on your calf. I saw it when we were wading through the stream on the way back to the shore. But it's too dark, I can't find it."

She smiled. "But it is there. Wait until tomorrow morning."

It felt as if a cold hand was clutching his heart. He turned on his back and put one hand under his neck. Tomorrow morning was not far off.

Regretting her thoughtless remark, she laid her hand on his shoulder and passed it over his chest, allowing the small, dark locks of his hair to slip through her fingers.

Candamir closed his eyes and for a moment gave himself up to this wonderful feeling, pulling her closer. "What changed your mind?" He knew it was a dangerous question, but his curiosity drove him to ask.

"You," she replied.

"Indeed? How did I do that?"

"I'm not going to tell you."

"Perhaps it's just as well. And will you come and live with me in my hall, noble queen, if I should ever find the time to build it?"

"We'll talk about that some other time," she told him.

"Oh," he said, crestfallen. "I assume that means no."

"You're mistaken, but I have conditions."

"Do you?" he replied, permitting himself a grin. "Tell me about them."

"No," she said sternly. "Later."

"Fine. As you will." He could live with "conditions," he was sure. He put one hand on her warm hip and closed his eyes to give himself up completely to the feeling. He longed to turn her on her back, to lie on top of her, and to find out how her skin felt when it was dry. But he knew that now was not the right moment. "It's not long until sunrise," he said softly and sat up reluctantly.

Siglind put a hand on his arm. Her eyes were wide and restless. "Don't go."

He raised his left hand. "I must. As much as I dread it, I must."

"Haven't you done enough?" she asked. "You convicted the perpetrator and buried the victim. Isn't that sufficient? Why do you want to do that to yourself?"

"I don't. But for Osmund this business is even worse than it is for me. Olaf is his uncle, and he always felt indebted to him. I can't abandon him now, do you understand?"

She sighed. "I'll try."

He nodded without speaking. It was no wonder she didn't understand, for he had told her only half the truth. If he had stayed away from Olaf's execution, someone would soon notice that Siglind had disappeared as well, and Osmund would immediately draw the right conclusion. Candamir suspected that it would be a long time before Osmund forgave him when he learned about Siglind and himself. There was really no good time to reveal it, but today would probably be the worst. Candamir pulled Siglind toward him somewhat more impetuously than he had intended, kissing her farewell. "But you should stay here," he said.

She nodded and placed her hand on his cheek. "I'll wait here for you, Candamir."

Theoretically, death by snakebite seemed simple, but things didn't go that way. Though it was small, the snake was unbelievably fast and nimble and had not the least interest in being forced into a hard, dry reed. Siward, Berse, and Haflad worked in vain until, an hour before daybreak, they had to admit their defeat and go to Brigitta to ask for her help.

The old woman was sitting in front of her hut at a little fire, poking at it ill-temperedly with a crooked stick. Her three black ravens sat nearby, sleeping, and as so often before, a white Catan raven had joined them.

The men explained their problem to Brigitta, but when they had finished speaking, the old woman shook her head. "No. I won't help you."

Siward took one step toward her and said angrily, "You said yourself that the snake was a sign! None of us feels good about this, do you see?"

She nodded, unmoved. "It was a sign, but do I have to be happy about what the gods have decided? Olaf is an evil man and always was, but I brought him into the world, as I did almost every one of you, or at least your sons and daughters, and I won't lift a finger to help you with this. Is that clear?"

The men nodded sheepishly.

"Good! Then nothing is keeping you from getting out of my sight, is it?"

They took off as fast as they could.

Siward's young wife Britta finally found the solution. She well knew that she owed her life to Olaf, for he had given her water when she had almost died of thirst, poisoned by the seawater. But she was still fighting for her husband's affection and was willing to do anything to gain it.

When the little snake had bitten Berse and Haflad and the men were about to lose their patience, she had the idea of sewing the snake's mouth shut. And it was just a short step from that idea to the solution of the problem. They sewed in a joint effort, keeping one end of the sturdy horsehair long and threading it through the reed. When it came out the other end, they needed only to pull the snake through. It was child's play.

As the gray light of dawn gave way to the first tender pink rays of sunlight, the settlers gathered in front of Siward's hut—all the free men, a few boys, but only a half dozen women, most of whom had preferred to stay home with the younger children and the slaves.

Osmund and Candamir exchanged glances and nodded, but said nothing. Hardly anyone spoke, and all that could be heard were hoarse and fragmentary whispers.

Old Eilhard turned to Siward. “Is everything ready?”

Siward nodded and held up the reed pipe. Britta had sealed the top and bottom of it with clay so that the snake, whose mouth she had untied again, couldn’t escape. Siward said, “Ready.”

“Then let’s go,” Eilhard said.

In a tight group they set out toward the meadow by the shore. It was enveloped in such a thick fog that they didn’t notice until they had almost reached the ash tree that the guards had vanished.

“Where are they?” Eilhard asked, confused. “Thorbjörn? Haldir?” His voice sounded thin, the same anxiety filling him as it did the others.

A bit closer to the shore they could just make out the fettered prisoner half veiled in the dense fog. He appeared bent over, his forehead rested on his knees, and his hands hung down limply, still bound to the thick branch.

Berse the shipwright stepped toward him, while the others spread out over the meadow.

“Here they are!” cried Harald. “Eilhard, here are your sons.”

And at almost the same time they heard Berse uttering an indistinct sound of surprise. He had seized the prisoner by the hair and pulled his head back. “It’s Jared! Oh, by all the gods…”

A great tumult broke out on the meadow. Everyone was running back and forth like ants. Eilhard, Siward, and most of the others rushed to the place where the smith was kneeling in the damp grass. Eilhard’s sons lay there peacefully, side by side, their hands folded on their chests. Their father held his breath and placed his hand on the chest of his firstborn, then raised his head, blinking. “He’s alive…oh, Thorbjörn…”

“Haldir too,” said Haflad, much more calmly. “If you ask me, they’re just dead drunk.”

“But fortunately no one asked you,” Siward shot back. “Go and get your mother, you stupid ass!”

Haflad gave him an offended look, then turned away and hurried to Brigitta’s cabin.

In the meantime, Osmund and Candamir had bent over Jared and freed him from his undeserved fetters. He had a black eye and a split lip—no doubt the marks of his father’s fists, Osmund thought.

He placed an arm around Jared's shoulders to support him. "What happened?"

Jared moved his cramped limbs and passed his tongue over his teeth. "He…I…" He shook off Osmund's arm, sat up, and looked his cousin in the eye. "He's gone. And it's my fault. Go and get the others, Osmund. I would understand if they made me swallow the snake in his place. But if that is what's going to happen, I don't want to wait."

Osmund nodded and looked at Candamir. "Would you go and get them?"

It took a while before Candamir could convince the other men to come to the shore. They stood around Thorbjörn and Haldir, looking down with anxious faces at the sleeping men, not knowing what to do. Not until Brigitta had arrived and announced that the brave watchmen would no doubt survive did they follow him and take their places in a circle around Jared.

The young man raised his head wearily and was not surprised to be looking into hostile, suspicious faces. "He sent for me," he began his confession. "And he ordered me to either cut him loose or at least kill him and spare him death by snakebite. 'Do one or the other, Jared, but do it,' he said. I thought it was my duty to obey him this one last time…"

"But he had been sentenced by the *Thing*!" Siward interrupted angrily.

Jared nodded. "But be honest, Siward. It horrified you too, and he was not *your* father."

Siward clearly found it difficult to come up with a suitable reply.

"Go on, Cousin," Osmund encouraged him.

Jared took a deep breath. "I pulled out my knife without knowing what I was going to do, and before I could make up my mind, my brother attacked me from the side. He…he had a stone in his hand and knocked me down with it." That upset him more than anything else: Lars had willingly taken the chance that he might kill Jared, his own brother.

"Obviously, they had planned everything. When I came to, they were tying me up in place of Father. And they told me that Father's Irish slave woman had earlier gone to Haldir and Thorbjörn with a cup. She told them she had wanted to bring my father mead, but he refused it, and she asked if they perhaps might want it. They drank it without the least suspicion."

Candamir suddenly understood. "Henbane."

Jared nodded. "It grows here just as it does on the Cold Islands, doesn't it? Yes, she put henbane in it, and soon the guards were knocked out."

"Why…why in all the world did the Irish slave girl help your father?" Candamir asked, dumbfounded. "I can't believe that he was always considerate and kind to her."

"No, he wasn't. Nevertheless, she did it because she is…dependent on him. Just like Lars." Jared was silent for a moment before looking at his cousin and helplessly shrugging his shoulders. "They all left with him, Osmund. Everyone. Lars, Gunnar, Leif, Einar, and Sigrun—and Thorhild too. All my brothers and sisters except Ota. She is only eleven years old, but she…knows him. She saw through him long ago, before I did…"

"They left with him?" Siward interrupted. "But where did they go?"

Jared smiled weakly. "You can't seriously believe they told me that, can you?"

"In other words, Olaf has fled," the smith said calmly. "With your brothers, two of your sisters, and eleven slaves." He glanced toward the dock, and many of the men followed his gaze. But the *Sea Dragon* still lay there at anchor with its mast down, just like yesterday. Olaf had not left Catan.

"He took along more than eleven slaves," Jared said. He wiped the back of his hand over his split lip. It was clear that he was nervous.

"Just what does that mean?" Siward asked, breaking the sudden silence.

Jared looked at Haflad. "When you were at Siward's house struggling with the snake, Lars was in your cabin. If you think your two slaves are at your charcoal kiln in the forest, then you're mistaken, Haflad. They left with him." And they weren't the only ones. Lars had also gone around to a few other cabins where the slaves had suffered under their masters. He gave the discontented slaves the prospect of becoming free men and women if they joined up with Olaf. A half dozen yielded to temptation.

"We must pursue them!" Siward said.

"No good can come of it if we let them go," the shipbuilder agreed.

"How do you intend to pursue them?" Harald asked doubtfully. "This land is huge."

"Such a large group has *got* to leave traces behind..."

"They can't have gotten very far yet..."

Osmund took the reed with the snake and flung it with all his might into the river. Then he took his cousin by the arm and helped him up. No one stopped him.

Jared had by no means been sure that somebody wouldn't come up with the idea of making him pay for his father's crime. Osmund, too, seemed to fear that the angry mood might turn against Jared. "Go home," he told him in a soft voice. "Stay there, I'll come to you later on, and we'll think about what to do."

With a weary nod, Jared turned away.

Harald watched him leave. "He is not to be envied," he said quietly to Candamir.

"No. I don't think he ever was to be envied," his young brother-in-law replied. "But even if all he has left now are his two hands to till his fields, he is at least free."

Harald nodded thoughtfully. "But surely you don't believe this is the last we'll hear and see of Olaf, do you? And whatever we hear and see of him in the future, it won't be good. I only hope that no one ever seriously rebukes Jared for what happened here tonight."

"Harald...Olaf is his father. Every one of us would have done the same thing in his place," Candamir replied.

The smith nodded and said with a sad smile, "But hardly anyone would ever admit that."

Siward put together a group of battle-hardened warriors to pursue Olaf and the slaves who had fled with him. He took along his son-in-law as well as Berse and his sons. Haldir and Thorbjörn also joined them, angered at

Olaf's cowardly attempt at poisoning them. They crossed the river and soon came across a clear trail in the forest on the south shore. But after five days, they returned exhausted, ashamed, and empty-handed.

"We followed them as far as the wasteland," Siward reported. "But there we lost their trail. There is simply no way to track them there—no trees, no bushes we could check for broken twigs, no grass, no loose soil where footprints might be left, nothing at all. A wasteland, indeed."

"What does it look like?" Candamir asked curiously. "Did you see the fiery mountain up close?"

Haldir replied. "Yes, we saw it. It's perhaps ten miles from the northern edge of the wasteland. But it was quiet. We couldn't see any fire, just a bit of smoke over the summit." He leaned wearily on the staff he had cut in the forest, shook his head, and finally turned to Candamir again. "I've never seen anything as barren and lifeless as this land around the fiery mountain. It's hilly and deeply fissured, and almost impossible to cross. The earth consists of brown, strangely porous stone, and nothing grows there except a few half-withered thorn bushes. Nothing can live there. We didn't even see flies. Olaf and his people will die of hunger and thirst."

Candamir nodded silently, but he had his doubts.

"Somehow I just can't imagine that my uncle is destined to die of hunger. He's just too clever for that. Jared said that he's taken almost all the grain as well as the cattle and sheep," Osmund said, putting words to Candamir's thoughts.

"You *can't* drive cattle through the wasteland, Osmund, it's simply impossible!" Thorbjörn interrupted him. "The animals would break their legs or injure their hooves in the numerous fissures. Even for a man with solid shoes it's difficult."

"Well, since you lost track of them in the wasteland and found no animal carcasses, Olaf must have found a way, as impossible as it may seem," Harald replied.

The hunters nodded reluctantly.

"He was at the fiery mountain a few weeks ago," Jared spoke up. He held his head down and spoke haltingly, which was unusual for him. "My father, I mean."

"He never said a word about that," Brigitta said skeptically.

Jared looked up briefly and nodded. "There are many things he didn't tell you, much that you don't know…"

The old woman sighed softly. "I know more than you think, lad. But you're right, he was very secretive, and it sounds just like him to go and explore this land without telling his neighbors anything about what he saw."

Jared looked down at his boots again and said, "In any case, he knew what the wasteland is like. Nevertheless, he took the cattle along, so he must have found a way to drive them through it."

"But we didn't find a single spring there," Sigurd said. "As abundant as water is in Catan, there is nothing but dust and drought there."

"In Olaf's place, I would have had every man, woman, and animal carrying as much water as they could, and I would have tied a double layer of cow's leather around the beasts' hooves," Osmund said pensively. "I would have made them shoes, so to speak. Then maybe it would be possible."

Everyone looked at him in surprise, and Brigitta remarked dryly, "It's obvious you are closely related. You're just as crafty as he is."

Osmund winced. "Oh, thank you very much…"

"Go on, Osmund," Candamir urged him curiously.

His friend gave a slight shrug. "Olaf only needed to get his men and animals across the wasteland once. He could be confident of shaking off any pursuer there. On the other side the land is just as rich and fertile as here. We know that from Berse. But it's impossible to guess where Olaf would turn on the other side of the wasteland."

"Well, to the west lies the sea, to the east, the mountain range. He can only head south," Berse said.

Osmund nodded. "But the south is a vast area."

"That's correct."

"And who knows, perhaps he will even stay in the wasteland. If it's hilly and fissured, as you say, there must be caves there."

"But why in all the world would Olaf want to stay there?" Siward asked impatiently.

Osmund looked at him with a weak, mirthless smile. "In order to stay close to us. Close to all those who brought about his downfall."

Hacon felt an icy shiver along his spine. "What can they live on, if it is a wasteland?"

Osmund did not answer, but he had a bad feeling.

Candamir knew exactly what his foster brother was thinking. He frowned as he looked over at the growing settlement, each house surrounded by a large vegetable garden and paddocks. They lay much too far apart, he realized to his dismay. The settlers had never discussed it, never made an explicit decision, but they had assumed in laying out their new village that attacks from raiders were things of the past. "We simply assumed that in this blessed land we would never have to deal with enemies," he murmured.

"But I warned you," Brigitta said, and he thought he heard a touch of malicious satisfaction in her voice. "I warned you that you would find in Catan all the evil that you brought along. How could you assume that you had left behind your love of strife and battle?"

Her words made Candamir uneasy, but he dismissed them with a gesture of contempt. "I can't remember you advising us to build the houses closer together. Now, in any case, it's too late. And I'm not going to lose any sleep on account of Olaf and his handful of slaves."

They decided it made no sense to send out a second search party; it would have been like looking for a whalebone needle in a haystack, and no one could spare the time from work. Winter wheat and winter rye had to be sown, honey harvested, apples and berries picked and stored away or made into preserves, and the construction of solid homes seemed now more urgent than ever.

The meeting broke up, and Candamir went down to the shore to continue his work on the island in the river. He leapt into the boat, and Jared cast off the lines.

"Thanks!" Candamir reached his hand out to catch the rope, but Jared didn't throw it to him.

Instead he asked, "Can I come along?"

Candamir shrugged. "If you don't have anything better to do with yourself…I would think you'd have your hands full now that you have so few slaves left. Or none at all, isn't that right?"

Jared wasn't put off by Candamir's good-natured teasing. Nimbly, he jumped into the little boat, grabbed the two oars, and without saying a word rowed them over to the island.

"By Thor's hammer," he exclaimed when they arrived at the temple clearing. "The hall is finished!"

"Almost," Candamir said, looking up at the long building with a proud smile. The walls and the roof truss were finished. There were a dozen ladders, with just as many carpenters on them—Godwin, and the skillful, versatile Austin, who had taken the Turon's place, and a number of other slaves. They were covering the vaulted roof with wooden shingles.

"The roof looks like a ship," Jared observed in amazement.

Candamir nodded with satisfaction, relaying his plans. "In one or two more weeks, we can dedicate the temple," he said. "But we won't have it ready in time for the fall equinox as Brigitta had hoped, I'm afraid. We'll have to settle on another day. Come on in, I'll show you the basin for the spring." He seized Jared enthusiastically by the sleeve and pulled him inside the temple. On the east end Osmund had dug out and widened the hole the sacred spring came from and lined it with large, white stones from the river. Now the crystal clear water bubbled out from between the stones, filled the round basin, and ran through a narrow trench, also lined with stones, to the east wall. Beyond that, a small, natural watercourse had formed that flowed into the forest.

"That is...marvelous," Jared said, deeply impressed.

Candamir pointed toward the middle of the hall. "There Brigitta wants to have a large, sacrificial stone, in order to slaughter animals that will then be roasted over the two fireplaces on the left and right."

Jared nodded and looked around carefully. "A truly impressive place to pay homage to the gods."

Candamir cast him a sidelong glance. "Did you come here just to butter me up? Is there something you want from me?" he asked suspiciously.

"What?" Jared seemed completely lost in his thoughts. He shook his head, but blushed noticeably. "No, no."

"Well then? Come on, spit it out."

The younger man finally crossed his arms in front of his chest and looked directly at Candamir. His light blue eyes were just as bright and penetrating as his father's. "Candamir, what I have to say to you is not easy for me. Will you give me your word that you will not interrupt me?"

Candamir nodded reluctantly. "If it doesn't take forever…"

"I want to ask your forgiveness. I have wanted to do that for a long time. For that business about the wild sow back then…"

"Oh, come on, that was *ages* ago…"

"Now, you promised!" Jared protested.

Candamir raised his hands in resignation.

Jared exhaled audibly. "Almost as soon as it happened I regretted it, and I felt ashamed, as I so often did when I tried to be like my father. But I told him about it nevertheless, for I knew he expected that of me. You know, only now that he is gone am I really aware of how much he dominated me. I…I told him because I feared if I didn't, he might hear about it from someone else. Such awful things have come of it, only because I was too much of a coward to listen to the voice of my conscience. I'm really sorry about that."

It was quiet for a moment, and then Candamir asked, "Are you finished?"

Jared nodded, but continued looking him straight in the eye.

Candamir put his hand on Jared's shoulder for a moment. "You know, you remind me of Osmund. It would be just like him to remember such a trivial thing after so many months and take upon himself the responsibility for the consequences. But if two men out on a whale hunt get caught in a storm and drown, the whale is not responsible, Jared. What happened between your father and me had nothing to do with the Saxon or with you." That had become clear to him when Harald showed him the real reasons for Olaf's grudge against him.

"So there is no feud between us?" Jared asked hopefully.

Candamir shook his head and smiled. Jared could not have guessed it, but he had chosen the best possible moment for this conversation. For six days now Candamir had been in a constant state of elation since Siglind's unexpected change of heart. "No, there never was a feud between us, and if you don't run off fast enough you'll have to listen to some advice from me."

Jared grinned and suddenly looked as carefree as a young man of his age ought to be. "And what is that?"

"Don't look back. Get yourself a wife who will bring you a few slaves as a dowry, and tend your fields. This is your chance. Now you can do what *you* want. It's completely up to you."

Jared lowered his head in embarrassment, but his eyes were shining. "You are right," he said softly. "Oh, by all the gods, how right you are, Candamir." It still grieved his heart that he could no longer have Inga. But he was smart enough to realize that in his present situation he could hardly have taken such a poor girl as his wife. Eilhard's granddaughter Margild, on the other hand, though she had no silver or cattle, could at least offer two slaves as a dowry. Since the death of her parents, she had been raised by old Eilhard, who, though he had not become wealthy from his many long-forgotten raids, had brought home many slaves.

"If you need more advice or help, you can come to me anytime," Candamir continued, "but if you're clever, you'll ask Osmund, for his advice is usually better than mine. And he won't deny you his help. You'll find that he will more than make up for the brothers you've lost."

At the thought of Lars, Gunnar, and his other siblings, a shadow passed over Jared's face, but when he turned to leave, he was smiling again. "Thanks, Candamir," he murmured, hurrying back down to the river.

Candamir was up on his ladder, whistling and helping with the work on the large roof. Progress was slower than he had hoped, but as the day wore on, his mood brightened. She had promised to come over before nightfall to ensure that all her advice concerning the attachment of the shingles had been carefully followed.

As always, Siglind kept her word. The burnished yellow sun had scarcely touched the treetops in the west when she appeared in the clearing, barefoot and in work clothes, the way he liked her best.

"I said the shingles had to overlap by two thirds, and that looks more like a quarter," she chided them as soon as she arrived at the foot of his ladder.

"Godwin, Austin, you and the others can quit for today. I've got my hands full just listening to the carping criticism of the queen."

With wide grins, the apprentice and slaves climbed back down the ladders, greeted Siglind politely, and stowed their tools before disappearing into the forest.

Candamir waited for barely ten heartbeats before pulling Siglind to him and kissing her hungrily. She wrapped her arms around his hips, but turned her head away and scolded, "Wait at least until they've cast off. If Austin sees us..."

"Since when do I have to worry about what my slave thinks of whom I am going to marry?" he asked crossly.

She propped her calloused hands against his chest and freed herself from his embrace. "We're not there yet. And besides, while he may be your slave, you know what he is in my eyes."

Candamir grumbled, but took her hand and pressed it to his cheek. "I'm tired of all this secretiveness."

"Yes, I know," she answered noncommittally. "Come, let's have a look at the roof."

Reluctantly he followed her into the interior of the hall, walking slowly alongside her as she inspected the slats and shingles, awaiting her verdict.

Close by the spring, Siglind finally stopped. "It's good," she said.

Candamir nodded and sat down on the ground, where the grass and ferns were thinning now because too many feet trampled them every day and the light was gradually being cut off. He scooped up a handful of water and drank. Of all the crystal spring water in Catan this was certainly the best—cool, sweet, and just a bit earthy. With his wet hand he seized Siglind's arm and pulled her down next to him. Then he scooped up the water with both hands and held it out to her. She bent over and drank a few sips. When he put his hands down, she was looking up at him. Her smile still caused him to shiver a little. He still couldn't quite believe that he was the lucky object of this smile.

"Well, let's talk about your conditions, noble queen," he said matter-of-factly. "What must I do for you to lower yourself and come and live with me in my hall?"

"If you don't stop calling me that, I'm going to leave and never talk to you again!" she fired back.

He grinned. "It's funny that it upsets you so much, so it's not easy to resist the temptation."

"You had better show some restraint in this regard," she warned him darkly. Then she turned her gaze away and pushed her long blond hair behind one ear. "You always say it in such an arrogant tone. It reminds me of how things used to be, the disdainful way I was treated by Cnut's men—when they said 'noble queen' it sounded just like that."

He clicked his tongue a little impatiently, but then raised his hand as if to soothe her. She hadn't told him much about her life as a queen on the Cold Islands, and he wasn't sure he could bear to learn more. To imagine what her life at Cnut's court must have been like, one only had to recall the circumstances under which she had become his queen.

Candamir took her hand. "I promise I'll mend my ways."

She laughed involuntarily. "I can't wait to see that."

"So tell me, don't keep me in suspense anymore. What are your conditions?"

"I want Austin's blessing for our marriage, the blessing of his god."

"That shouldn't be difficult."

"It *is* difficult." And she explained why.

Candamir's expression darkened. "Leave that to me."

"Candamir, I don't want you to put pressure on him—that wouldn't help at all. In a matter like this, he will only do what his conscience dictates. Let me speak with him first."

He couldn't fathom why he should need the permission of his slave to take a wife, but he concealed his displeasure. "All right then. Go on. What else is there?"

She swallowed, raised her head, and looked him in the eye. "I want you to be faithful to me."

"I'm not sure I understand."

"You must swear to me that you'll keep your hands off other women."

"*What?* But why on earth should I?"

"It's God's commandment."

Candamir let go of her hand and shoved back his hair. "O mighty Tyr…I have a feeling there will always be three of us in my bed—you, me, and Austin's god."

"Is it really asking too much?" She sounded uncharacteristically timid. "Won't you ask the same of me?"

*That is a completely different thing,* Candamir thought indignantly. But from the start he had known that this woman was different, and strange, and so it did not surprise him that she set peculiar conditions. He couldn't see any sense in her demand and found it pretty impertinent, but since he had never wanted anything as much in his life as Siglind, he made his decision without long hesitation.

"Agreed."

She looked him straight in the eye. "You will send Gunda away."

There was only one place he could send Gunda. "That means that Hacon will get her," he protested weakly.

Siglind nodded. "Think it over—whether you can accept that without ever holding it against me. Think it over carefully. But you must choose—it's Gunda or me."

"I choose you."

"Then swear to it."

Candamir placed his hand on his heart and swore.

Around midnight, Austin, Siglind, Hacon, and Gunda met in the smithy to celebrate mass. They had been doing that regularly for some time, always on the day of the week which the Saxon referred to as the Sabbath. It was not without risk. If Candamir ever surprised Hacon and his slave girl stealing out of the house together at night, he would naturally have drawn the wrong conclusion, and then who knows how much blood would have been spilled before the true reason for their rendezvous was revealed. And that was not the only risk. Austin knew that if the witch ever found out that he had gathered together a small group of followers to worship his god, then the days of reluctant tolerance would be over, once and for all, and Brigitta would not rest until someone had killed him. Presumably, this honor would fall to Osmund, who had been Brigitta's loyal follower since their arrival in Catan. No, it was smarter to keep the service secret, just as the early Christians had needed to do in pagan Rome.

On the anvil he spread a little cloth that Siglind had lovingly embroidered with red thread, placed his simple cross and a piece of bread on top, and next to it a cup of water, for of course he had no wine. But that made no difference. He was confident that the Lord was ready to make concessions, just as Austin had himself. In any case, it was a consecrated chapel in which they gathered. Austin had used the power of his priestly office to make sure of that. What would Harald have said, if he knew he was swinging his hammer on sacred ground…

Austin waited until his three disciples were kneeling in front of him before raising his hand in blessing: "*In nomine patris, et filii, et spiritus sancti.*"

With heads bowed in reverence, they made the sign of the cross.

He followed the Latin liturgy he had learned, changing it a little here and there, as he knew it would be unwise to make his three faithful believers feel excluded from the holy mystery of the mass. Now and then, he told little stories of the deeds of the patriarchs or the miracles that Jesus had performed, of which they could never get enough. And occasionally he sang one of the hymns that had been a central part of his daily routine in the monastery.

When he had finally consecrated the bread and water and handed it to Siglind, she shook her head.

He looked at her questioningly, even a bit annoyed, but she only shook her head again.

Austin turned to Hacon. "*Corpus Jesu Christi custodiat animam tuam ad vitam eternam.*"

"Amen," Hacon replied, in a voice flat with awe, and took a piece of the bread.

"What was the meaning of that?" the monk asked Siglind once Hacon and the young Frisian slave had slipped out of the smithy after the benediction.

"I was not worthy," she declared firmly, but without remorse.

The Saxon carefully folded the altar cloth and placed it lovingly along with the crucifix and the simple chalice in the pouch that also contained the Bible. Only then did he turn around to her again. "Why do you think that?"

"You said one must only come to Communion with a pure heart, free of sin. And I am not."

Austin sighed. He needed no explanation. He was inexperienced in these things between men and women, but he was neither blind nor a fool. "I have explained to you what confession is, haven't I?"

Siglind nodded.

"If you would like, I can hear your confession here and now. You must attempt to conquer the weakness of your flesh and promise not to do it again. Then God will pardon you."

"It is not as simple as that, Austin," she replied sadly. "Candamir asked me if I would be his wife."

"And how did you answer?"

"Truthfully. But I told him it was possible only with God's blessing and your consent."

Suddenly Austin became weak in the knees. He sank down onto the anvil that had just served as his altar and held his fist to his forehead. "That is…wonderful, Siglind. You have succeeded in making a martyr out of me. Candamir will stop at absolutely nothing to obtain my consent, and I can't give it to you."

"No, he won't do that, I have his word," she said hastily.

*That won't help,* he thought. For a moment, there was silence. Finally, Austin took her hands in his. "I understand that you believe your happiness in life depends on it. But as much as I would like to help you, I *cannot* approve it, because God does not approve of it. It is not my decision. You are the wife of another man, and if you lie with Candamir, you are an adulteress."

Siglind kept looking him straight in the eye. She seemed to him neither as desperate nor as ashamed as he would have expected. "I know," she replied. "You have told me all that many times."

Austin raised his chin. "And I will keep on repeating it until you obey God's commandment, for that is my duty." Suddenly he let go of her hand, raised his index finger, and with a dangerous gleam in his eyes, warned, "I'm cautioning you against your stubbornness, Siglind. It comes from Satan and is your greatest weakness. You think you absolutely must have whatever you want, but you shall not break God's will, he will break yours!"

He loomed over her threateningly, like a king on the throne or a mighty ruler on a high seat, and suddenly she was afraid. "Will you answer one question for me, Austin?"

"Certainly."

"What is it that makes a man and a woman a lawfully married couple?"

"The blessing of the church," the monk answered.

"But Cnut and I never had that."

Austin could not completely suppress a smile of appreciation for her cleverness, but he shook his head. "Since the true faith has not yet come to your homeland, your heathen marriage ritual is binding, I fear."

"Then answer just one more question for me. If a man forces himself on an unmarried woman, are they then married in God's eyes?"

"No. This is fornication. Both are guilty."

"The woman too, who after all didn't have a choice?"

He shrugged slightly and nodded.

"What can she do? Can she confess to find forgiveness for this sin?"

"Yes."

"And after that, can she marry another man and find God's mercy?"

"Siglind…"

"Yes or no?"

"Yes. Ideally, she should marry the man she already lay with, but if need be it can also be someone else," the monk grumbled reluctantly.

Siglind smiled triumphantly.

"But that doesn't change the fact that you are nevertheless Cnut's wife," he insisted.

She shook her head. "There was no ritual, only the will of the king, and no one was asked or gave permission, and no kind of agreement was ever made. What would you call that, Austin?"

He realized at that moment that he had been outwitted, but he had to admit she was right. There was only one possible answer. "Sin."

"Then I would like to confess now," she said, her eyes sparkling exultantly.

He took no special pains to conceal his vexation, fetched the crucifix out of its pouch, held it out for her to kiss, and grumbled, "So kneel down and confess your sins, with the required penance and humility, but be so kind as to spare me the details…"

# Wind Moon, Year One

*The temple on the island was dedicated on the last day of September. For the heathens, this day has no specific significance, but it seemed to me like a sign of hope that this place of worship was dedicated on the Name Day of St. Jerome, who through his translation of Holy Scripture is the forefather of all missionaries. It was he, methinks, who made it possible to spread the word of the Lord throughout the world, and as unworthy as I may be, I am nevertheless continuing his work. And even though I gave assurance to that evil man, Olaf, that I did not want the temple dedicated to my God, I still prayed there on that day to my Lord and His saint.*

*It seems to me that even this heathen temple must be pleasing in the sight of the Almighty, as it was built in humility and in honor of the Divinity. My worldly master truly outdid himself in his art. Verily, he has created a wonderful House of God. Nevertheless, there were no great festivities at its dedication—some oxen were slaughtered, roasted, and eaten, and after that the freemen held a meeting in the temple. However, at the end of the meeting, when the men were about to urinate together in accordance with their custom, the witch chased them outside and told them that this place must never be defiled through bloodshed in anger or human refuse. As always, they willingly did what the old woman ordered.*

*Everyone agrees that this is an excellent building and has shown great respect toward my master, his friend Osmund—who is considered to be Odin's Chosen One—and his wife Inga, who dug out the holy spring. They have decided henceforth always to hold their Thing in the temple in order to be closer to the counsel of their gods.*

Candamir was indeed proud of his work, and he wondered whether Odin wished to reward him for his efforts and had for this reason brought about Siglind's change of mind.

In the meantime, Berse and his people had started building Candamir's house. They carefully followed his wishes, and he could already see how magnificent it would be. Nevertheless, Candamir felt better now that he could put his hand to the task as well. And Berse seemed quite happy that the resourceful young carpenter had finished this huge project and was able to resume building of houses for mortals again, for Candamir's imagination was almost as inexhaustible as his stamina.

"And it's time we finished our work," the dwarfish shipwright announced, "because it's getting colder."

Candamir nodded. There couldn't be any doubt about it—autumn had finally come to Catan. The leaves had changed color, the days become noticeably shorter, and in the morning fog lay over the river and dew was on the meadows. A splendid fragrance was in the forest air. The night after the temple dedication there had been a storm—not a frightening one, but bad enough for all those still living in huts. Worried, Candamir had gone to Siglind's house to make sure her thatched roof had not been ripped off. She welcomed him eagerly, pulling him down onto her narrow bed, but at the same time she seemed uneasy. She clung to him like a drowning person, yet she braced her hands against his chest as if trying to push him away. He knew that secretiveness was repugnant to her, and she saw no reason to hide her feelings now that she had permission from her god, but there was one more thing he still had to do before they could reveal their secret, and Candamir dreaded it so much that until now he had preferred to just put it off.

Instead of joining the others for supper at the smith's house, he asked Asta to excuse him. He pulled on the densely fulled woolen cloak she had sewn for him and set out for Osmund's house at the western edge of the new village. He was surprised to find Osmund and Jared busy working on four sturdy wooden posts with their planes and chisels.

"Osmund..."

His friend spun around, startled, and rolled his eyes. "You are really coming at a bad time, you know."

Candamir smiled uncertainly. "Sorry. I'll go and come back tomorrow, but let me in on what you're doing there."

Osmund and Jared exchanged glances that were half amused and half dismayed, and then the elder of the cousins sighed, "No, no, you don't need to go. Come here and look at this. It was supposed to be a surprise for you, but we're almost done anyway."

Curiously, Candamir stepped closer, and when he saw the posts up close lying there on the two roughly assembled trestles, he knew at once what it was. Suddenly his throat became dry. "A high seat..."

Osmund looked critically at their work. "What do you think? You can see that we don't have a great deal of experience, can't you?"

Candamir shook his head. "It's wonderful." The posts were richly decorated with runes and scrimshaw and painted in dark green, red, and ochre tones. Osmund's high seat was old and venerable just like Candamir's own had been. The carvings on the arms and backrests had been highly polished in the course of generations. This new high seat, however, was made of wood so young that it still had the odor of resin. The wood was light in color and freshly painted—pristine, like this land, and without a past. Candamir found it appropriate.

"I don't know what to say," he confessed in embarrassment. He could scarcely turn his eyes away from his unfinished present.

Inga called to him from the hearth. "Share our meal with us, Candamir. Yesterday Osmund slaughtered a sow, and we have fresh knuckle of pork."

Candamir didn't need to be asked twice, the fragrance was so seductive. "I'd be glad to, thank you."

Jared's sister Ota also sat down with them for supper, as did Cudrun the nurse, Osmund's two slaves, and little Roric. It was a merry, lively group. Inga's pregnancy was quite obvious now, especially since she sat there proudly sticking out her belly while casting furtive, tender glances at her husband from time to time. Candamir couldn't help but chuckle.

They debated the merits and possible dangers of chasing the white ravens away from the freshly sown fields, an issue that none of the villagers could agree on. And they talked about the arduous work of gathering acorns and chestnuts to serve as pig fodder during the winter, and of course the beechnuts from which they made lamp oil, and about the great sensation of the previous week.

Austin had gone to the mountains with Harald and Hacon to fetch new ore, and on the south slope of one of the foothills he had discovered a vine with a few little grapes on it. The monastery where Austin had once lived had grown grapes. He really didn't know much about it, he admitted, but perhaps enough to cultivate the plant. It would take years, in any case, before anyone might taste the first wine from Catan, he warned them. Nevertheless, the settlers' eyes shone at the mere thought of it.

Shortly after the meal, Jared and Ota bade them farewell, and Inga also announced that she and Roric would soon be retiring.

"What do you think?" Candamir asked his friend. "Shall we go for a short walk? It isn't really cold."

Osmund readily agreed. It was the time of the new moon, and since they didn't live far from the sea here, the starry skies were usually clear, a sight he never tired of.

Side by side they strolled in the darkness, each holding a cup of mead in his hand. It was too dark to see where the grass ended and the river began, but they could hear its constant murmuring, and by now they knew this shoreline blind.

"So you didn't just come to spoil the surprise that Jared and I had for you," Osmund said after a lengthy silence.

Candamir frowned. "That sounds as if I needed a reason to come and pay you a visit nowadays."

"No. But you do it much less frequently than you used to."

"Your wife can't stand me, Osmund. Haven't you noticed?"

"What nonsense. She is a little shy." And perhaps a little jealous, for she suspected that her husband cared more for his foster brother than for her. "But why should you worry what she thinks?"

"You're right, it doesn't worry me. And you're right again, because I have come to tell you something."

"And what might that be?"

Just a moment ago, Candamir had imagined that the darkness would make things easier for him, but now he wished he could see his friend's face. "It's about Siglind. She…that is, we are going to get married." *Don't be offended,* he wanted to add. *She really meant what she told you on Thor's Night. She didn't want any man again, neither you nor me. But she couldn't anticipate that she would have a change of heart because something she had never expected happened to her.* He couldn't say that, however. He knew the best he could do was to guide this conversation in such a way that Osmund could save face. If possible, Candamir wanted to avoid things changing between them. And so he confined himself to this simple statement, and he said it in a calm voice, as if he were announcing his plans to sow oats the following week. Then he swallowed and waited anxiously for Osmund's reaction.

He had to wait a long time. Finally, he could sense his friend was putting his cup to his lips and emptying it in a single gulp, before repeating softly, "Married…"

"Yes."

Suddenly Osmund took him by the arm, led him back into the house without even bothering to look at the stars, and gestured for Candamir to have a seat at the table. The servants had gone to bed in the alcoves on the far side of the hall. They were alone. Osmund took a sliver of wood, held it to the fire, and lit an oil lamp. He put the lamp down on the table and took his place across from his friend on his high seat.

"Candamir, I beg you, please think it over."

Candamir was flabbergasted. He had expected coolness and reserve, or perhaps jealousy and anger, but not this open, anxious look. "Why?" he asked.

"Because she is not good for you. She will bring you nothing but misfortune."

Candamir was cut to the quick and forgot all his good intentions. "Not so long ago you yourself were courting her!"

Osmund nodded and gave a slight shrug. "I can bear misfortune far better than you can."

Candamir lifted his cup and snorted.

Osmund turned serious again. "Well, I've come to see that it was a mistake. Today I thank Odin that Siglind rejected me and that he opened my eyes in time."

"Opened your eyes? What are you talking about?"

"She has chosen the carpenter god."

Candamir looked at him, disbelieving. "And that's all? Good grief, Osmund, you were starting to scare me. I thought you knew some dreadful secret about her..."

"It's dreadful enough," Osmund interrupted him.

Candamir put his elbows on the table. "Now, remind me who it was that kept Brigitta from throwing my Saxon's book in the fire on our journey here because Siglind was so attached to it? After all, didn't you *know* that she had accepted Austin's god?"

"I did, but a man in love is always a fool, Candamir. I was foolish enough to believe she would forget this accursed god once she realized that in truth I was the one she was looking for. But she was already completely under his spell, and I didn't want to believe it."

"Is all that really so awfully important?" Candamir replied dismissively.

"You're asking that? You, of all people, who built such a splendid temple for Odin with untiring energy and creativity?"

"It really isn't all that splendid, you know. It's big and it has a nice roof, that's all. And I built it because Brigitta kept pestering me, and because I was afraid she might be right when she said the earthquake was a warning from the Father of the Gods."

"Certainly she was right. Odin *did* elect us, and naturally he places special demands on us. And remember all the old stories, Candamir—

how easily Odin turns away from those who disappoint him or who no longer serve him. If we wish to keep his favor, we must never stop trying to please him."

*What a small-minded god,* Candamir heard Austin's voice saying in his head, and the thought shocked him. He searched for something conciliatory to say to his friend. "This has nothing to do with Odin. I wish to take a wife, that's all. And I wanted to tell you because… because…oh, you know damned well why."

"And I appreciate your consideration, but your fears were unfounded. I put Siglind out of my mind long ago. And you should do the same. Oh, no doubt she's a beautiful woman, but she has deserted the faith. And she's dangerous. Your Saxon's god would never have gained such power over so many of our people if she had not turned to him."

What really frightened Candamir about these words was that they sounded so honest. Osmund hadn't just talked himself into believing them in order to get over Siglind's rejection. He really believed them. "But Austin's god doesn't have power over anyone here in Catan," he said. "And what harm can it do that Siglind has turned to him? He's harmless, after all."

"He is *not* harmless. He is provoking our gods. Has it ever occurred to you that maybe she is infertile because she has angered the gods?"

Yes, it had occurred to him, but he resented that Osmund put his finger on this wound so directly. "I don't give a damn! I have done my duty to the gods. I've done what I can. But I want to have her, and I don't care if she can't have children. After all, I have a healthy son."

Osmund nodded. "I hope the gods will let you keep him."

Candamir felt an icy shiver running down his spine. "Oh, Osmund, I really had no idea that you thought so badly of Siglind." He sounded troubled.

Osmund didn't answer right away. "No, I don't think badly of her," he finally said. But he was no longer her friend, he had to admit, even though he had told her he was on Thor's Night. "I think she has been misled, and the consequences can be dangerous for all of us, especially for you, if you really take her as your wife."

Candamir sighed, shrugged his shoulders, and looked at his friend helplessly. "I'm going to do it just the same, no matter what you say, no matter what happens. I simply can't do anything else."

"Then you're a fool," Osmund said, smiling despite himself.

*Yes, but a happy fool,* Candamir thought, clinking cups with his friend.

In the second week of Wind Moon, which had earned its name in the new homeland as well, Candamir's house was finished. Like most of his neighbors before him, he too gave a great feast on this occasion. The guests cheered wildly as Jared and Osmund, with the help of two slaves, carried the finished high seat into the hall and the master of the house took his place on it for the first time.

As his brother-in-law and fatherly friend, the smith took it upon himself to wish Candamir much happiness in his new home and the good will of the gods.

Candamir listened gratefully, but his eyes kept wandering surreptitiously through the room, shining with pride. He still had no wall hangings and few dishes on the shelves along the hearth wall, and all but one of the tables for the banquet were borrowed, but none of that was important. The room was large and had two wide windows that could be closed in bad weather, as they were this day, with solid shutters. The hearth was wide enough for Heide to hang two large cauldrons over it. Right behind it was the bedroom that in the morning was flooded with the light of the rising sun and where, the next day, he expected to wake up for the first time with his wife.

He exchanged glances with Siglind, who was sitting next to him on the bench and nodded to him with an encouraging smile.

When everyone followed Harald's invitation and drank to Candamir's health, he raised his cup of mead, thanked the smith for his fine words, and thanked the guests for coming and for the presents they had brought. Finally, he said, "When I look back a year, I can hardly comprehend everything that has happened, how much happiness has been granted to me and to us all. Last year at this time I scarcely dared to hope I could get my household through the winter. We suffered hunger and cold, and the world was dark. But today we complain about how much work it is to harvest all the fruits of the field and the forest and to milk all our cows." The guests chuckled softly. Candamir smiled faintly and lowered his eyes in embarrassment, but he continued without hesitation. "Since you know me, you'll not be surprised to hear that I never was really happy, despite the abundance and beauty that Odin has given us in our new homeland—not until recently, when at last I could convince the woman I wanted to give me a chance." He paused briefly for effect, and even though everyone could guess whom Candamir meant, they all held their breath. He looked up again. "I want you to know that it is my wish to take Siglind as my wife. She brings as a dowry the grain, seed, and livestock that she received from you as payment for your roofs, among them three sheep. Since she has neither father nor guardian, she must speak for herself. And so I ask you, Siglind, will you be my wife?" He stretched his hand out toward her.

She rose and put her hand in his. "Yes, I will," she answered solemnly.

Thunderous applause broke out, and everyone cried out their congratulations to the young couple. Asta got up and ran to her sister-in-law to embrace her before all the others. Many people had risen from the benches and crowded around them, including Osmund. Candamir knew him well enough to see that his friend's smile was a little forced, but he was grateful nevertheless. They embraced briefly, and Candamir felt relieved. He wasn't troubled in the least that Inga and Brigitta remained seated on the benches and had no words of congratulation for him or his fiancée.

It was late by the time the final guests said their farewells. Only Harald, Asta, and Hacon had remained, and they followed Austin, who led the couple to the back room. He closed the door against the curious gazes of the remaining servants, who had the thankless task of cleaning up the hall before going to bed.

"Hacon, I think we can do without your presence," Candamir said coolly.

His shoulders drooping, the boy was about to turn away when Austin said, "Stay here." Then, turning to Candamir, he said, "This time, for a change, you'll have to do what I say, Master, and not the other way around."

Candamir stared at him for a moment, flabbergasted, then nodded in resignation. "Just don't forget that tomorrow everything will be the way it was."

"No." There was a hint of a smile at the corner of Austin's mouth, but he quickly regained his solemnity. "Since the two of you have already announced publicly that you wish to get married, I don't need to ask you. But I must point out that this union is inviolable in the eyes of my god, and your vow unites you for your whole life."

"Get on with it, Saxon," Candamir said. He had other plans for this night.

Austin pretended not to have heard him. "Then I would like to have the rings now."

Candamir looked at him, baffled. "What rings?"

"You must exchange rings, otherwise it's not official."

"And you don't tell me that until now, you worthless, shifty, crafty…"

"Here they are," Hacon spoke up shyly. He held out the palm of his hand to the monk and his brother. In it were two narrow silver rings, one small, the other large, but they both had the same engraved wavy pattern. The silver had a deep, rich sheen and sparkled in the light of the two wax candles standing on the wall chest.

"What…is that?" Candamir asked.

Hacon gathered his courage, looked his brother in the eye, and smiled. "My gift to you."

"And didn't they come out beautifully?" Harald asked in a soft voice, but with undisguised pride of his apprentice. "There's not just iron ore in the mountains in the east, you know. We also found copper and silver, and when Hacon heard that you needed rings, he decided to try his hand as a silversmith. There was almost nothing I could teach him about it. He has a natural talent."

In disbelief, Candamir studied the fine jewelry.

"Yes, they're really beautiful," Austin said, clearly feeling that his patience was being unduly strained. "Can we perhaps proceed now?" He took the rings from Hacon's hand and gave the small one to Candamir and the large one to Siglind.

The couple turned to him again, and he asked them to repeat after him: "With this ring I take you, before God, as my wedded husband… my wife, and promise to hold you and honor you in good times and in bad, till death do us part."

Candamir and Siglind looked deeply into each other's eyes as they exchanged their vows, and when each had placed the ring on the other's finger, Candamir was astonished to see that both of them fit perfectly.

Austin spread his arms out, murmured some odd-sounding magic words in a foreign language, then made that strange cross-shaped sign with his right hand, and, as if that weren't bad enough, Hacon and Siglind imitated the weird gesture. And then it was over.

Candamir waited for a moment, cringing, but there was no roll of thunder, no lightning bolt struck him down. He sighed with relief, and not waiting for an invitation from the priest, embraced his wife and kissed her passionately.

Austin turned away, shaking his head in displeasure.

When Candamir finally let go of Siglind and stepped back, his gaze fell on the sparkling ring on her finger, and he turned to Hacon. For a moment they looked at each other uncertainly. Then Candamir took a deep breath. "Fine, then. So be it." He placed the hand with the ring on Hacon's shoulder and said, "Thank you, Brother."

It wasn't much, but Hacon felt as if a huge weight had been lifted from his shoulders, and he closed his eyes in relief. At the same time, he quickly put his hand on Candamir's before his brother could withdraw it, and squeezed it briefly. They didn't say another word to each other. But as his family was moving toward the door, it was Hacon Candamir was looking at when he said, "Asta, take Gunda along. I don't want to have her in the house anymore, and I know you have good use for her. I am giving her to you as a gift. But I do want the boy as soon as he is old enough to go without his mother's milk. What happens to the child she is carrying doesn't concern me."

Asta nodded, showing neither her relief nor her sympathy for Gunda, who would one day lose her son. "As you wish. Thank you, Candamir, and goodnight."

Candamir waited until the door had closed behind them. Then he walked slowly over to his bride, his eyes shining, and placed his hand on the bronze buckle holding up her jumper.

"Candamir..."

"What?" He loosened the first clasp, and the short chain that bound the clasps together made a soft, clinking sound.

"I...thank you. I know it wasn't easy for you. Thank you that you did this for me." She put her arms around his neck and looked up at him.

He smiled and surrendered willingly to the magic of those blue eyes. "No, it wasn't. But I promised to, and moreover, I was indebted to Austin's god. Now we're even."

"But..."

He placed a finger on her lips and shook his head. "Shush, we'll talk about that tomorrow. Now I want to know what you look like with nothing on but this ring."

The yearly cycle of sowing and harvesting was gradually coming to an end in Catan. The fields had been tilled, and now the time for slaughtering, smoking, and salting the livestock was at hand. The settlers, however, saw no reason to slaughter as many cattle as before. Since there was no snow in Catan and apparently no freezing temperatures, they expected the grass would continue to grow and they could continue to graze the cattle all winter long. They wondered why they bothered to make all that hay.

Around the middle of Hunter's Moon, just before the heavy rains began, the last of the houses was finished, and Ivar, the captain of the *Sea Arrow*, who had drawn the worst lot, moved in with his large household. Now only the mill was missing, but its construction was a large, complicated project, and they had decided to put it off until the following year. Austin had seen watermills in his homeland, but he had little knowledge of how to build one. Olaf was the only one who had been interested in how they were constructed. He had visited a number of mills on his many trips and could have told the settlers about them, but from now on they would have to do without his advice. It didn't matter—they could grind the little rye they had just as well with hand mills, and if they harvested wheat and barley in the following year, there was still the possibility of getting a large millstone and having it turned by an ox. Candamir had once seen that in the land of the Franks.

There were still dozens of important things to be done—storehouses, barns, bathhouses, and stables had to be built, and they had to continue clearing the land whenever the weather allowed. The drowsy winter lull forced upon them by the snow, ice, and darkness in their old homeland simply did not occur here, and Harald noted that if they didn't take care, they would keep working all year without interruption, and that couldn't be healthy.

Finally, at the beginning of Yule Moon, the gray rain clouds withdrew and the sun appeared again. The cool, steady breeze finally became too much for Candamir, and he could no longer control his longing for the sea. He spoke with Osmund and Jared and some of the others, and they all agreed they had tired of trout and longed for a decent fish from the sea. And so they prepared the *Sea Dragon* and left for a few days of ocean fishing.

They caught a rich catch of large fish—some over four feet long—that were similar to the cod and hake in their old homeland, but also smaller fish that were tender and unbelievably tasty. Candamir enjoyed the carefree days on the ocean, the uncomplicated camaraderie that was possible only in a place where there were no women far and wide. And in the evenings, he and Osmund sat on deck wrapped in furs, talking and drinking together the way they used to. Jared and Sigurd, who at home were both courting young Margild, fought every night, offering the other fishermen quite a show. It was magnificent.

But after five days, Candamir's yearning for the sea had been satisfied, and his longing for his wife overcame him. The others also felt it was time to return. They had cleaned the catch of the first few days, hanging them out on lines to dry, but they wanted to bring home as many fresh fish as possible, so the women could smoke them.

The wind had turned to the east, forcing them to row upriver, and before they reached their destination, the sky had become overcast again and a heavy, icy rain began to fall. Dripping wet, frozen to the bone, and bearing a heavy crate on his shoulder, Candamir finally arrived home as night was falling.

"Welcome home, sailor," Siglind cried, abandoning her work at the loom.

He put the box down with a loud clatter and wrapped his arms around his wife, slipping his left hand down the back collar of her dress. "I've brought you some wonderful fish for the Yule festival," he whispered, his face pressed into the plaits of her hair.

She passed her hands over his back. "That's very good of you, but you're all wet and cold. Come over to the fire and warm yourself up."

"I could think of a better way," he murmured.

"Yes, I'll bet you can," she said in an equally hushed voice. It sounded conspiratorial, and they looked one another in the eye and laughed. But then she shook her head slightly and said, "We can eat right away."

He was starved. "It smells wonderful," he replied, taking her hand in his and drawing her to the table. "Saxon, bring me a drink."

"Yes, Master. Shall I heat up the mead?"

"Don't bother."

Candamir settled down on his high seat with Siglind at his side. After only five days away he could see his house through fresh eyes, noticing how much had changed since they moved in. As untiringly as Siglind had roofed houses all summer and autumn, she was now occupied day in and day out at the loom. A beautiful hanging covered the wall between the windows and the high seat, and benches were padded with colorful cloths and carefully tanned furs. On the table stood two oil lamps that Tjorv and Nori had crafted from the soft limestone in the grassland. One had a handle in the shape of a coiled snake, and in the other, with a little imagination, you could make out a raven's head. A cheerful fire crackled in the hearth, a cauldron of rabbit stew with fresh herbs and mushrooms hanging above it infusing the room with a marvelously rich aroma.

Candamir took a deep breath. "I must say, it's wonderful to be home again."

"Well, I certainly hope so," Siglind remarked dryly, then took her cup and drank to him. Her eyes twinkled merrily.

Heide placed wooden bowls and spoons on the table. "You brought back some beautiful fish, Master. I'll start smoking them right away."

"Do that."

"That's at least something that will remind us of Elasund. May Odin forgive me, but a Yule festival without snow is very strange," the old cook said.

"You're homesick, Heide," he teased her.

"I'm only a stupid, ungrateful old woman," she grumbled, dishing out the stew while the servants came to the table.

"Well?" Candamir asked with a full mouth. "What news is there?"

Nori waited politely to see if the mistress of the house had something to say. And when she didn't, he spoke up. "I would like to get married, Master."

"Really?" Candamir looked at him curiously. "Who is the lucky woman?"

"Freydis. One of Eilhard's slaves."

Candamir nodded. He was familiar with old Eilhard's maid. She had been Margild's nurse, but since Margild herself would soon be getting married—though it wasn't clear yet to whom—a nursemaid was hardly needed any longer in the old warrior's house. Freydis was a few years older than Nori, he guessed, and she had a crippled foot, but otherwise she was healthy and could probably still bear children. Candamir had no objections to the marriage.

He looked at Siglind. "What do you think?"

She nodded approvingly. "Go ahead. God knows we could use another pair of hands here. I hope Eilhard is not asking too much."

Nori poked around in his bowl of stew. "He wants a sheep," he said meekly, his head bowed.

Candamir sighed. *Everyone* wanted sheep. The little mountain goats provided them with good wool and milk and didn't really taste that bad either—at least not the kids—but sheep were nevertheless as sought after as gold and silver in the old homeland. And presumably for just the same reason—their very scarcity made them valuable. Before, a sheep would have been a ridiculous price for a healthy slave woman in childbearing years. Now it was actually too much. But sheep, unlike silver coins, couldn't be divided, and he could see that his servant cared very much for his Freydis.

"I'll talk with Eilhard," he promised Nori. "We really can't spare a single one of our sheep, but two of them are pregnant. Perhaps I can talk him into taking the third one."

Nori beamed. "Thank you, Master. And may I build a pit house for us out in the yard?"

"I have no objection if you don't neglect your work."

Nori gave a deep sigh. Clearly, he could hardly contain his happiness. With reawakened appetite, he continued eating and remarked between mouthfuls, "She's already pregnant, you know. This is a good deal for you."

"If the child doesn't die," Candamir said dryly. It amused him that his slave was trying to sweet-talk him into the deal.

"Oh, it won't," Heide said confidently. "We've been here for nine months, and only two children have died. In Elasund, as many as that died in a month, and in winter, often more."

She was right, Candamir realized with astonishment. But it wasn't really so surprising, for in the old homeland a child usually died due to cold or lack of food—if the women had not had enough to eat during their pregnancies, they had often suffered miscarriages or gave birth to frail children with no chance of surviving. Of the seven children his mother had brought into the world, only he, Asta, and Hacon remained, and their family was considered fortunate. Osmund's mother had lost seven or eight children, and he was the only one to reach adulthood.

Austin was following his train of thought. "Not only do the herds grow faster here than in Elasund," he remarked, "the number of people is also quickly increasing."

Candamir grinned and nodded. "Because, fortunately, not everyone here leads as chaste a life as you."

With that, he rose, took his wife by the hand, and led her to their room. The remaining servants smiled indulgently, but it never ceased to shock Austin how unashamed these people were.

Candamir and Siglind certainly saw no shame in making up for everything they had missed for the last five days. They tore each other's clothes off, hastily and clumsily, and made love first passionately, then tenderly, and it made no difference to them who heard.

From the very outset, Siglind had been an uninhibited and inventive bedmate, but today she seemed intoxicated, and he was only too happy to let her sweep him away. He lay on his back and held her, eyes closed, still a bit out of breath. Siglind had nestled her head against his shoulder, listening to the strong, regular beating of his heart and passing her index finger over the scar on his belly: Haflad's little reminder of Yule festival the previous year, for which she had developed a peculiar fondness. After a while she let her hand slide farther down.

Candamir bit on his lip and laughed softly. "O mighty Tyr...you are insatiable, woman."

"Just tell me when you're getting tired," she cooed with feigned sympathy.

He seized her impertinent hand, and the other one as well, and bound them together behind her back with his own hand, rolling them both over so that he was now lying half on top of her. "Just so that your high spirits don't get the better of you," he warned her gently.

"You don't frighten me," she replied, trying unsuccessfully to free her hands.

Candamir looked at her, delighted, and laughed at her vain struggles. "Are you going to tell me what makes you so fearless?"

"My happiness," she answered, her struggles ceasing. He let her go, and quick as a flash she took her arms out from under her back and embraced him. "We're going to have a child, Candamir."

He let out a cry of joy, took her face in both hands, and kissed her. He was not really surprised; he knew this fertile land had brought about this miracle. He thought that this was perhaps the best day of his life, and he felt strong and invincible as he thrust inside her.

It was late, the nearly full moon had risen and shone through the window, but they were still talking. They talked about the future, argued about whether Austin's god had made this pregnancy possible, or whether—as Candamir preferred to believe—the magic of Catan had caused it, that and the exceptional power of his semen, of course, which earned him a jab in the ribs. They discussed what Heide and Austin had noted during supper, of how much better the chances were here of a child surviving into adulthood, and without noticing it, Candamir laid his hand protectively on Siglind's still-flat belly before finally drifting off to sleep.

Candamir was sure he had slept for only a moment when he was awakened by the feeling that something was terribly wrong. He sat up, and the first thing he saw was the wide, terror-stricken eyes of his wife.

She stood motionless alongside the bed, and a huge, shadowy form was right behind her, clutching her right breast in one hand and holding a blade to her throat with the other.

"Get up, Candamir. Slowly," Olaf said in a soft voice.

For a moment, Candamir could not move, paralyzed by the realization that the Norns had apparently decided to make the best day of his life also the last.

"Don't keep me waiting too long, or I'll cut her throat, I swear."

Candamir swung his legs off the opposite side of the bed from where Olaf and Siglind stood, rising slowly and groping with his foot for the knife he always put there at night. But then he remembered that Siglind had removed his belt as soon as they came into the room and had dropped it carelessly to the ground. His knife was out of reach.

Candamir turned to Olaf. "What do you want?" He knew this was a stupid question, but he could think of nothing else to say.

Olaf pushed Siglind to the foot of the bed and smiled, almost indulgently. "I've come to settle accounts, Candamir. And because you owe me the most, I'm beginning with you." He pulled a leather strap from his belt, which he had apparently prepared in advance. "Stay where you are," he ordered. Then he took his knife between his teeth, quickly bound Siglind's hands behind her back, and tied the loose end of the strap to the bedpost, without letting Candamir out of his sight. Then he took the knife in hand again and held the needle-sharp point to Siglind's throat.

"Now come here."

"Don't do it, Candamir," Siglind said calmly. "It would be better for him to kill us both right away."

Olaf slapped her across the face with the back of his hand. "Don't even dream of that happening yet. Just hold your tongue."

"Leave her alone." Candamir barely recognized his own voice. Quickly, but not so fast as to threaten Olaf, he stepped into the moonlight. Never in his life had he wished so much for a pair of trousers. He tried to emulate Siglind, who carried her nakedness like a festive gown and met Olaf's glare with defiance.

"Just come a step closer, lad," Olaf ordered with a ghastly smile, and when Candamir was standing directly in front of him, Olaf jammed his knee into his groin with full force.

Candamir had suspected this was his intent, but that didn't make it any better. With a muffled cry, he dropped to his knees, both hands in front of his groin, his eyes squeezed shut.

"You damned, cowardly dog!" Siglind cried out, and it sounded so strange, so completely out of character that even Olaf saw through it. "You can shout all you want," he told her as he tied Candamir's hands behind his back. "Your slaves are no longer in the house, and we are all alone, pretty girl."

Through the narrow slits in his eyes, Candamir could see Siglind tugging at her fetters, but it was hopeless. Olaf understood how to tie a knot, and the bedpost would certainly not give way. Candamir had built this bed himself and knew how sturdy it was, but he was shamed by Siglind's determination and furious at his own weakness. He tried to stand up and push Olaf away before the straps were firmly knotted around his wrists. But he was too slow and breathless, and too worn down by the pain in his groin. Olaf pulled the knot tight so that the leather cut into his skin, and Candamir remained on his knees on the cold ground, realizing he had been beaten. "What did you do with my servants?" he demanded.

"I'm taking them along. I need more men."

"Oh, you do? And how will you keep them from running away?"

"First I'll scare the two imbeciles that you inherited from your father, and then I'll give them a woman. That should do it. I'll cut your Saxon's heel tendons so he'll never run anywhere again. His skill in the art of healing among other things is useful, but I can do without his feet."

Candamir twisted his hands, sensing the straps loosening just a bit. "So you'll try to establish another settlement with slaves?" he asked, astonishment overcoming his fear for a brief moment. "You're a fool, Olaf. What can you offer them that they don't have here?"

"Oh, freedom—or at least something they think is freedom—women, a life of leisure, and your rye, your sheep, and the rest of your provisions," he replied. And with deceptive gentleness, Olaf took Candamir by the forearm and pulled him up to his feet, while stroking one of his buttocks unambiguously.

Candamir felt his innards and his testicles shrivel and could not completely suppress a moan of horror.

Olaf laughed contentedly while patting the other one. "Unfortunately, I don't have time to do it with both of you, but I think I'll just take your beautiful queen along with me. Then I can devote myself to her at my leisure, and she'll be useful to me in many ways. But I have been pining away for you for such a long time, Candamir, and I can't wait a moment longer."

Candamir was in a daze as Olaf led him toward the chest on the wall, but in the middle of the large room he suddenly pulled himself loose and kicked Olaf in the shins. His intention had been to break the bone, but the cracking sound he had hoped for failed to materialize. Nevertheless, Olaf let out a hoarse cry of pain and cursed, but he reacted very fast. Skillfully jumping aside, he avoided the next kick, and at the same time hit Candamir in the stomach with one fist and in the larynx with the other. Candamir staggered, trying to push Olaf away with his shoulder and fling him against the wall, but Olaf grabbed him from behind and squeezed his throat.

He did everything he could to shake him loose, but he was getting less and less air, and he finally started to lose consciousness. With alarming suddenness, Candamir lost all the strength in his legs and collapsed onto the floor. But before he passed out, Olaf let go of his throat and pushed his fettered hands up between his shoulder blades, forcing his upper body forward. Candamir went crashing down with his forehead onto the cover of the chest. He struggled to breathe in long rattling gasps, while his defeat and humiliation brought hot tears to his eyes.

Olaf kneeled behind him, using his left hand to press Candamir's hands upward while fumbling around in his clothing with his right. Candamir turned his head to one side, and through the veil of his own hair he saw Siglind standing barely five steps away. Her face was frozen, her gaze tortured, and as he clenched his teeth to prepare for the pain, she fulfilled his unexpressed final wish and closed her eyes.

When Candamir felt Olaf's skin on his own, he was finally overcome with panic. With a desperate cry of protest he threw himself back, although he was sure the move would break at least one of his overstrained shoulders.

Olaf seized one of the stone candlesticks that had fallen down from the chest and beat Candamir over the head with it. "Now that's enough," he grumbled as Candamir's body became limp. Olaf laughed softly. "Yes, that's just the way I want you…"

"But you won't get him."

Before Olaf could look up, a fist struck him on the temple, and he fell to one side. With a furious snarl that hardly sounded human, he wheeled around and could scarcely believe what he saw.

"That was pretty respectable for a craven like you, little monk." Olaf took his time getting to his feet and made sure that the Saxon got a good look at his private parts before casually tying up his pants.

Austin looked him steadily in the eye. In his left hand he held a knife, and his right was still clenched in a fist, and somehow he didn't look at all like a man unfamiliar with battle.

It occurred to Olaf that he could just as well be dead now, and with rising concern he recognized Lars's weapon in the Saxon's hand. "Where is my son?" he asked, pulling out his own knife.

Austin moved back a step. "I don't know, but he was alive when I left him. Go, Olaf."

"No," Siglind said hoarsely. "Kill him. Don't let him get away."

Austin didn't look at her, but he shook his head. "Only if there is no other way. Don't be a fool, Olaf. Leave!" He pointed toward Candamir, who was still lying half on the ground and half on the chest and beginning to stir. "He's coming to, and..."

"Father?" Lars's muffled voice could be heard through the window. "Father, come quickly. We must leave. One of these damned slaves woke the whole village! Quick, we must get away!"

With a curse, Olaf stepped to the window and jumped out.

For a long time, Austin stared out into the silvery moonlight with a frown. He heard furtive steps in the grass, quickly receding. Somewhat farther away he could just barely hear voices shouting, but it was quiet behind the house.

Trembling, the Saxon let out a sigh, stepped to the window, and quickly closed the shutters. Then he took a woolen cover from the bed and, averting his eyes, wrapped it around Siglind's body before cutting her hands free. Then he walked over to Candamir, cut off his bonds, and was about to take him by the arm when Candamir wheeled around and rammed his head into Austin's groin. The Saxon had anticipated something like this, and quickly stepped back to escape its full force. "It's all right, Master," he said calmly. "He's gone. Everything is fine."

Candamir raised his head like a dog recognizing the sound of a familiar voice. And when he perceived who the speaker was through his strangely clouded eyes, the tension subsided and his body slumped against the chest. He pulled his knees up to his chin and buried his head in his arms.

Austin fetched a blanket for him as well and patiently held it out to him, knowing better than to touch him again. Finally, Candamir saw the blanket and wrapped it around himself, giving a small nod to Austin in thanks.

"I'll leave you alone for a moment," the Saxon said, smiling weakly at Siglind as he headed for the door.

Candamir raised his head. "No, wait. How…what…"

"Soon, Master. Just be patient for a moment. I'll get you a cup of mead, and then I'll answer all your questions. But be of good cheer, everything is all right."

*I'm a wreck,* Candamir thought in disgust. He sat there on one corner of the bed, shaking, the blanket wrapped tightly around his hips. When he felt Siglind's presence, he took her hand but was unable to look her in the eye. "I'm so sorry," he kept murmuring. "I'm so sorry."

"There is no need," she replied firmly. "Nothing happened to me, nor to you either. Pull yourself together, Candamir."

"I'm trying."

"Then try harder."

Her tone of voice—half indulgent and half severe—helped him overcome his horror. Gradually he got over the stiffness in his limbs, and the trembling subsided. When he finally raised his head, he saw that she was completely clothed. Finding his strength again, he stood, shook off the blanket, and pulled on his trousers.

A good while passed before Austin knocked on the door. Candamir had regained his composure sufficiently to sit calmly on the bed. His wife leaned against his chest, between his bended knees, and his left hand rested protectively on her belly.

"What happened?" Candamir asked, worrying about his servants, his belongings, and his neighbors. "What have we lost?"

The Saxon shook his head and stepped closer, carrying two full cups. "No one is dead, as far as I know. Olaf came on foot with Lars and six of his men. Just to attack you. At least that's how it looks."

Candamir nodded. "That's what he said. I was to be first."

"And he wanted his ship. I imagine he succeeded. In any case, they broke into the house, and all four of us awoke to find someone's hand over our mouths. Everything happened very fast and quietly. They must have practiced. They took us on board the *Sea Dragon*, along with your sheep, your horses, and your grain. There they tied us up and told us how good everything would be for us in the wasteland." With a faint grin he held the cups out to them. "Master, Mistress, it's high time you had something to drink. That would make me feel better."

Siglind accepted gratefully, and Candamir also took a cup in his left hand. At the same time, however, he reached out for Austin's wrist, which bore an ugly burn. "How did you get that?"

Politely but firmly, the Saxon removed his hand. "I burned off my bonds with a torch. It was the only way. No one was guarding us. They were all busy preparing to cast off and stowing away all your things. I sent Tjorv and Heide to awaken the village. Nori wanted to at least try to save your sheep—for not completely selfless reasons, one could assume—and I came here because I feared for your life."

"You saved more than just that," Candamir said mockingly, as he was gradually regaining his composure. But his eyes revealed that he had not meant it as a joke.

The Saxon gestured as if to say "anytime," and Candamir noticed that his other wrist had suffered a burn that was just as bad. "Someone has to tend to your hands, and I must go down to the river and see what's happening."

"Stay here," Austin replied. "You look fairly battered and ought to lie down and rest. Osmund and Harald will take care of everything. And no matter what Olaf has taken, the wind is in the east and we can't overtake the *Dragon*."

"No, you're right." Nevertheless, Candamir stood up. "But if I don't show up, there will be rumors and everyone will believe…that something happened which in fact almost *did* happen. I couldn't bear that."

Austin shrugged. "I understand."

But Candamir didn't make it to the shore; he had scarcely reached the door of his house when Osmund, Harald, Hacon, and many others burst in.

"Candamir!" Osmund took him by the shoulder. "Thanks be to Odin. I was sure you were dead."

Candamir gave a smile that was bolder than he actually felt. "Once again, I've been luckier than I deserve."

"Your wife?" Asta asked anxiously.

Candamir shook his head. "Don't worry, nothing happened to us. But how is everything else? Where are my slaves?"

Heide and Tjorv stepped forward, their heads bowed shyly, unaccustomed to people standing aside for them. "Nori is with his sweetheart, Master," Tjorv said nervously. "He was able to get your sheep and horses off the ship before Olaf came back and the *Dragon* set sail."

Candamir briefly touched his arm. "At least all of you are unharmed."

"But your grain is gone, I fear," the smith said. "Siward and Berse set out with the *Wolf* to pursue Olaf, but they won't catch him."

"No," Candamir agreed gloomily. "That is hopeless." He rubbed his forehead, so exhausted that he could scarcely stand on his feet.

His neighbors misunderstood the gesture. "Don't despair, Candamir," Osmund said quietly. "We'll help you. We all have enough, and..."

Candamir looked up and smiled. "Oh, that's very good of you, but fortunately it's not necessary. Olaf did not get all my grain, not even a third." When he saw their surprised faces, he raised his hands. "Well, we had to figure that something like that was bound to happen, didn't we? Most of my grain is in a shed that I've built in the forest on the Temple Island. I only stored here what didn't fit there. Things will probably be a bit tight, but there will be enough. Don't tell me I'm the only one to have taken such precautions?"

There was a short silence before the smith replied. "No, my grain is stored in a hidden room underneath the smithy."

"Don't get the idea that you're smarter than everyone else, Candamir," Haldir teased him, "but I won't tell you where I've hidden mine. I'm not crazy, after all."

One man after the other admitted that he had stored his seed, his flour, and anything else of value to him in a safe place.

"Well, this time we got off easy," Brigitta said as they were getting ready to leave. "But who can say we will be as lucky the next time?"

The very thought of a "next time" gave Candamir goose bumps. "You're right," he said. "It isn't enough to hide our provisions like the squirrels. We must think of something else." *But we don't need to do it tonight,* he thought with relief.

Osmund was the last one to leave after he had looked his friend over again carefully and convinced himself that Candamir wasn't holding something back.

"Everything is all right," Candamir assured him once again.

Osmund nodded and turned to go. "Very well then, goodnight, Candamir. I guess I should look in on Jared. He probably is badly shaken."

"Yes, I'm sure." Candamir sighed. "Goodnight, Osmund." He closed the door, spoke a few words with Heide and Tjorv, and also with Nori, who was just coming home with the sheep and horses they had retaken, and then went back to join Siglind and Austin.

Meanwhile, his wife had applied one of the Saxon's own notorious ointments to the burns on his wrists. Austin sat on the chest, and Siglind was bent over him applying bandages.

Candamir leaned against the door, staring through narrowed eyes at the piece of furniture he had built so lovingly, and decided to chop it into firewood the next morning.

"Well, Austin," he said, folding his arms and looking the Saxon straight in the eye. "You did more for me and my wife than any man can expect from his slave. I owe you a great debt."

Austin stood up and moved a step closer to him. He shook his head and replied, "I didn't do it as your slave, but as your friend. Therefore you owe me nothing."

"I would say then that the debt is even greater," Candamir said. "If there is any wish of yours I can fulfill, I want you to tell me."

Austin didn't stir, but kept his eyes fixed on Candamir just as he had on Olaf. "I...I could be tempted to take you at your word," he said finally.

"Make an exception to your iron rule and yield to your temptation," Candamir suggested.

Austin pulled up his shoulders and rubbed his nose as if he were struggling for the necessary determination to speak his wish. "Then... set me free."

Candamir nodded. He wasn't surprised.

Siglind was horrified, though. "But Austin, as Candamir's slave you enjoy his protection. If you are free..."

"If I'm free, I can do the work of the Lord," he interrupted her.

"And lose your life in doing so?"

"If it is His will, yes. If not, no. We shall see. That is neither in my hands nor in Candamir's."

"There's a difference between trust in God and stupidity," she said impatiently.

"Is there? If you find it, let me know," he replied tersely and glanced at Candamir. "What do you say?"

Slowly, Candamir walked toward him. One step in front of him, he stopped and looked down with a solemn face at the frail little man. "I release you from my services, but not from my friendship."

He stretched out his hands, and they grasped one another briefly by their forearms.

"And so I will leave your services but not your friendship," Austin replied, just as solemnly. Then he lowered his hands and walked toward the door. "*Dominus vobiscum*," he said softly. "Good night, Candamir. Good night, Siglind."

# Part IV: Hagalaz

# Honey Moon, Year Seven

"It's starting to get light over there," Candamir said, pointing toward the north. He had to shout almost at the top of his voice to be heard over the sound of rain and rolling thunder. His worthy colt, Buri, an ordinarily brave and spirited three-year-old, recoiled each time there was a flash of lightning. His sand-colored coat had turned dark in the pouring rain, and his black tail whipped nervously from side to side. Candamir patted him reassuringly on the neck. "Easy, boy, it's all right. It will stop soon, you'll see."

"May Odin grant that you are right," Osmund grumbled. He was steering the wagon, which was being drawn by two strong oxen. Roric and Nils were sitting in the empty wagon bed. For days they had begged their fathers to take them along, and finally they agreed. But now the boys wished they had stayed home. They took great pains not to show their discomfort, but Roric had inconspicuously grabbed hold of the Thor's hammer hanging on a leather strap around his neck and begged his patron god to stop the lightning and thunder soon.

All four were wet to the bone, and they were still at least two hours from their destination. The towering mountains already seemed so close, Nils thought in amazement.

Osmund looked briefly over his shoulder. "Is everything all right back there, men?"

The two boys nodded.

"If you're cold, you can take the saddle cloth from Hacon's horse," he suggested. "I'm certain it won't tell on you."

The boys didn't hesitate. Roric stood up, swayed back and forth a little on the rolling wagon, then jumped down nimbly and took the saddle cloth from the docile gelding tied behind. He climbed back onto the loading area, spread out the wool blanket, and wrapped it around his shoulders and those of his friend. They pulled the blanket up to their chins, snuggled up well, and exchanged grins.

"Won't Uncle Hacon's fire go out in weather like this?" Nils worried aloud.

Candamir shook his head. "No, because his fire is burning..." A mighty clap of thunder interrupted him in mid-sentence, and he gestured dismissively. "When we arrive you'll understand why not." This time, it was he who cast a suspicious glance at the black storm clouds towering over their heads.

Yet his faith in the gods was not misplaced. In a final burst, Thor reminded them again what he could do, so that even the oxen turned white around their noses, as Candamir asserted later. But soon the sky turned blue again, and the onshore wind drove the storm clouds southward. The sun came out, and only a few more isolated drops of rain fell from the sky.

Osmund pointed straight ahead. "There, just look," he said to the boys. A beautiful rainbow appeared over the mountains.

"Bifrost!" Roric cried out in delight.

His father nodded and smiled a little. "So it is."

"But tell me, Father, if that is the bridge leading to the home of the gods, why don't we just cross it and ask Odin whether we can live in Valhalla?"

"Because that is reserved for the bravest of warriors, as you know very well. No man alive may live there. And don't you think that we're well enough off where we are?"

Roric suppressed an impatient grimace. He had no memory of the old homeland, the legendary voyage to Catan, or the first difficult years. He knew nothing but Catan as it was today: a land of abundance and mild climate. "But of course, Father," he answered, a little annoyed—but thankful at least for being spared another lecture about how grateful they should be. "I don't really mean that I'd like to live there, I'd just like to have a look at it, out of curiosity."

"Yes, I can understand that. The problem is no one has ever found where the bridge starts."

"But what is so hard about that? It's right in front of us, in the valley between the Asi and the next mountain in the south. That's pretty easy to see."

"If you went there, you'd see you are mistaken," his father predicted, having difficulty keeping a straight face.

Nils opened his mouth, but closed it again quickly when he caught the warning glance from his father. *But Austin says that the rainbow isn't a bridge at all, but just a picture that God paints in the sky,* he wanted to say. *A sign of peace between him and his creatures.* He knew that from the story he was especially fond of, about Noah and his great ship. How could anyone find the beginning of a rainbow, not to mention climb up one, when it really wasn't there at all? Nils would have liked very much to know that, but he had remembered just in time that his father had promised him a whipping the next time he began a sentence with "*But Austin said...*" And so he held his tongue and turned around to look back. The route behind them consisted of two narrow, but clearly recognizable ruts with a strip of grass in the middle. It extended westward, straight as an arrow, and disappeared over the crest of a grassy hill. Ox carts did not often travel between the village and the mountains, but over the years the heavy, iron wheels had cut through the topsoil, and the bare, white rock showed through. And it wasn't only the carts that used the road. On horseback or on foot, men sometimes went to the mountains to get silver or copper, or to look for gold. Now and then, one of them found some, and Nils's Uncle Hacon fashioned wonderful rings and bracelets from it, and even a bowl to collect blood in the temple.

After a while, the slopes became steeper and the road climbed steadily. It wasn't difficult for the oxen to pull the empty carts up the slope, but they were as lazy as they were strong, and they became slower and slower until Osmund cracked the reins across their wide backsides to urge them on.

As they came up out of a little hollow and rolled over the next ridge, they finally saw the blockhouse and the oddly shaped smelting furnace in front of it. Hacon waved, having spotted them while they were still some distance away.

Four years ago, Harald and Hacon had decided it was foolish to cart the ore from the mountains back to the village before separating the iron from the slag first. And so they had built this little outpost at the highest spot they could still get to with an ox cart. Ten days ago, Hacon had set out for the mountains on foot with two of Harald's slaves. They had climbed high up onto the craggy slopes of the Asi, had dug farther along the tunnel there, and while the servants carried the ore back down, Hacon loaded the smelting furnace. He loved being out here at the foot of the mighty mountains, and he loved the hours of toiling in the glowing heat as much as the hours spent waiting during the slow smelting process.

Yet after ten days with the ill-humored slaves, he was happy for the arrival of his brother. Once the cart and rider had arrived at the blockhouse, Hacon warmly greeted his brother, his friend, and the two little boys, ordering one of the slaves to fetch a pitcher of beer for the new arrivals.

Without saying a word, the man disappeared into the hut.

Candamir gazed after him and shook his head. "Aren't you ever afraid that they could bash your head in and flee into the wasteland?"

"I am," Hacon confessed with a grin. "I never can sleep the first night I'm out here. But Harald swears they are loyal. They are Latvians, and he says they are all sullen and gloomy, and that it doesn't mean anything. And since I am standing here alive before you, we can assume he is right."

Candamir, Osmund, and the boys got their beer, and after Nils had had some, his curiosity—which according to his stepmother was even more unquenchable than his father's thirst—was aroused.

"Is that the oven the iron is baked in, Uncle Hacon?"

Hacon nodded. "You could put it that way. Come along and I'll show you how it works. But be careful, it's very hot."

The boys and their fathers followed Hacon to his smelting furnace that looked like a giant, upside down basket. The young smith pointed down at the bottom. "First you have to dig out a pit. Then you build the walls of the furnace with brick, do you see?" He pointed at the long, thick blocks of clay. Up above, they were inclined inward, almost forming a roof, but in the middle there was a circular opening where the smoke came out. "You stack in the iron ore and glowing coals alternately, up to the top."

"What's this hole for?" Roric wanted to know, pointing to a small opening in the lower third of the brick wall.

"For the bellows," Hacon explained. "You supply air to the fire, which makes it burn very, very hot."

"And so the iron is smelted out," Roric concluded with a fascinated shake of his head.

"Actually, it's the slag that's melted out and is deposited down below. A layer of iron forms over it. Then the iron has to be heated again to a much higher temperature in the smithy before it can be worked on."

"And how long does it take from the time you light the fire till you can take out the iron?" Nils wanted to know.

"With a furnace this size, about one day. We charged it before sunrise, and so we can open it soon. But I want the two of you to go to the wagon then and stay there, do you hear?" It got so hot deep in the furnace that it would take another day before the iron had hardened and cooled enough to safely touch. "A smelting oven is no place for little boys like you," he added with a look of reproach at his brother.

Candamir raised his hands and sighed. "Unfortunately, my son is not as docile as yours."

Ole, the second boy Gunda had given birth to scarcely a year after Nils was born, was just as dark-haired and gray-eyed as Nils, Candamir, and Hacon, but he was such a quiet, obedient child that Candamir had concluded with relief that he could not possibly be the father. This had not diminished his anger toward his former slave girl—quite the contrary. Even after Hacon and Gunda had married, Candamir had not forgiven her. However, he had long ago made peace with his brother. Hacon had become a skillful smith and, over the years, had grown so tall and strong that even Candamir had been unable to outwrestle him at last year's midsummer festival. After nearly an hour, as their thirst became greater than their determination to win, they agreed on a draw.

"Let's start loading the wagon," said Osmund, never able to remain idle for long. He pointed at the iron that had been extracted in the days before, which lay next to the hut like a pile of gray sponges.

"You still have all of tomorrow," Hacon replied.

But Osmund shook his head. "Roric and I are going to climb the Asi tomorrow, isn't that right, lad?"

Roric nodded, his eyes beaming, but it was Nils who told his uncle, "And if they find gold, Osmund wants to have his big drinking horn coated with it. Can you do that?"

Hacon passed his hand over his nephew's shock of hair. "I could try, but I won't hold my breath until Osmund and Roric have actually found their gold."

Nils gave him a conspiratorial grin. "That's no doubt wise, Uncle," he whispered.

Candamir gave him a quick rap on the head that Hacon remembered so well. They looked quite harmless, but you could feel them for hours afterwards.

"You're talking too much again, Nils. Go and get some cheese, bread, and meat from the wagon. For almost a week Hacon has had nothing to eat but dried meat and hard bread."

"All right," the boy replied, rubbing his sore head absentmindedly. Osmund signaled to Roric to help his friend.

Hacon often felt pity for his six-year-old nephew, who was raised in the same haphazard way as Hacon himself. In contrast with Candamir, Osmund was a very patient father who devoted much time to his sons, especially his eldest. Nevertheless, Roric was a quiet, shy boy who often appeared troubled, while remarkably Nils seemed to be the happiest child Hacon had ever known. The fact perplexed him, for he couldn't remember being particularly happy in his childhood.

"How is your wife?" he inquired, uncovering the furnace with his brother.

The bricks felt glowing hot to Candamir, and he cursed under his breath and put them down as fast as he could, while Hacon took them and stacked them up neatly as if they were quite cool.

"Well," Candamir said, blowing on his fingers. "Very round and heavy, but that doesn't bother her, you know. Perhaps the baby will already have come when we return."

"Well, may God grant that this time it's a boy," Hacon couldn't keep from saying.

Candamir shrugged and smiled with atypical indulgence. He was used to being teased about his wife, who had given birth to four beautiful, healthy daughters, but no son so far. It didn't matter to him. He adored his daughters. And moreover, he had Nils. "As far as I'm concerned, we can round it out at a half dozen girls before we start on the sons," he said.

"And what other news is there?" Hacon asked, ignoring his brother's boast.

Candamir knew what Hacon was particularly curious about, something everyone wanted to know who had been away from home. Had Olaf and his gang of thieves come back? And if they had, did they attack my house?

"Everything is fine," Candamir replied reassuringly. "Who knows, maybe Olaf has some doubts, since they had to leave the last two times with nothing but bruises. It's possible they have decided it's healthier to make an honest living and have gone south."

Hacon smiled wistfully. "That's simply too good to be true, which is why I have trouble believing it."

"Well, so do I," Candamir said with a sigh, and they laughed.

The people of Catan knew how to defend themselves, and when they had realized that they had brought along a dangerous enemy from the old homeland, they didn't remain idle. They fashioned a protective wall around their village, not a palisade or stone wall as Eilhard and Siward had first suggested—for no one really knew how to build a large stone wall, and the execution of such a complex project would have tied them up for months. Instead, they took Siglind's suggestion and planted a hedge of thorns instead. "Let's use the advantages of this country for our protection," she had said. "In this fertile ground and in this mild climate, plants do not stop growing even in the winter. If we plant a hedge around the village of this hawthorn-type shrub that we see growing everywhere in the forest, we'll soon have an enclosure that no enemy can penetrate."

And she had been right. Now, after six years, the hedge was higher than a man and five feet thick, and they tended it with care and devotion. It circled the village in a wide arc and extended down to the bank of the river on the east side as well as on the west. On the east side toward the grassland, and on the north side toward the fields, they erected enormous spiked iron gates. Harald and Hacon had worked on them for weeks. As soon as the sun sank below the treetops in the west, the gates were closed.

Olaf and his men still managed to steal their cattle from the fields that lay outside the enclosure, but the greatest danger came from the river. Between the Yule Moon and the Planting Moon in the spring, so much rain fell on Catan that the river became a raging torrent, and Olaf could neither sail the *Sea Dragon* upriver, nor cross it on rafts. But from Honey Moon into late autumn, the men in the village had to patrol the shore at night, and at Austin's suggestion and with his help, Harald had cast a bell which hung in the village meadow on one of the lower branches of the ash tree, which had grown quite tall. Thus all the villagers could be warned and called to arms if Olaf and his men crossed the river. Since they had had the bell, two attacks had been successfully fended off. But after the second failed attack, Olaf had landed outside the enclosure along the north bank of the river and had set fire to the wheat fields.

"Brigitta still hasn't recovered from her sickness. If you ask me, before this spring is over, she will deliver us from her presence," Candamir said, changing the subject.

"Candamir," Hacon murmured reproachfully, guiltily looking around.

But Candamir had made sure that neither Osmund nor the boys were nearby when he said it. "Who are you trying to fool?" he replied. "You and Austin in particular will give thanks and sacrifices to your god when she has finally left this world."

"We don't make thanks offerings to our god," Hacon began to explain, but Candamir interrupted him.

"Maybe that's the reason he tormented you by keeping her around for so long. Who knows? But no one lives forever, not even Brigitta, and you won't mourn her any more than I will."

"That's right," Hacon said, then turned his broad back to Candamir and piled up the last of his bricks carefully alongside the kiln. Four years ago, Haldir had discovered a clay pit south of the wasteland, a half day's march from the coast, and they used this clay to make bricks and dishes. The clay had to be brought back by ship and on pack animals, and for this reason, people used it sparingly. Haldir and Thorbjörn were so delighted with the discovery that they had built themselves new houses of baked bricks. Their neighbors laughed at them, but Haldir warned they would stop laughing when Olaf burned the village down and only their two houses remained standing.

"I'll not grieve for Brigitta," Hacon continued, "but not do I wish her dead."

"Sure, sure," Candamir said dismissively. "Because your god forbids such evil thoughts."

"Not just for that reason. But she was always with us, as far back as I can remember. The idea of a world without her worries me."

Candamir folded his arms, regarding his brother with an indulgent smile. "Sometimes I am reminded that you're only twenty-one years old, Hacon. Only sometimes. Usually you are smarter and more prudent than I. But it's childish to complain about the way things change."

Hacon nodded. "How right you are, Brother." Just like the rest of the world, their community had of course also changed since they arrived in Catan. Not only had old Eilhard died, but Siward too, as well as a number of other men and women. And Hacon, Wiland, and Godwin, along with the rest of their whole generation, had grown up, married, and fathered a large number of children. The population of free men as well as slaves had practically doubled, Austin had recently reported. "No, I have no reason to complain about change, for so many good things have happened to us here. But I have to wonder what will happen when Brigitta dies."

"What would change? Osmund's wife will lead the ceremonies in the temple and favor us regularly with an oracle reminding us to serve Odin with greater zeal, just as Brigitta always did. She will take over Brigitta's role and do everything Brigitta always did, for she is her loyal disciple. Everything will be as it was," Candamir concluded. "Only she'll be prettier to look at," he added after a moment.

Hacon smiled, wondering briefly why Candamir so rarely mentioned Inga by name. "Austin thinks we'll miss Brigitta and want to have her back when she's gone."

Candamir nodded. "Austin has a very strange inclination to suffer. For years, Brigitta has been opposed to him, his god, and everyone who prays to his god—that is, to you and my wife as well. Really, only Austin can hope that things stay the way they are."

"You're wrong, Candamir. Austin is deeply angered that our faith is so poorly regarded. But he's afraid things will get worse when Inga takes Brigitta's place."

"Nonsense," Candamir replied impatiently. "She's Osmund's wife."

Precisely, Hacon could have answered, but he preferred to drop the matter. For years, Candamir had closed his eyes to how Osmund had changed, and he became positively disagreeable if anyone tried to get him to see things more clearly. Siglind tried, from time to time, but to no avail. Hacon, unlike his fearless sister-in-law, had never taken any great pleasure in quarreling with Candamir.

"Come, let's go to the hut," he suggested instead, placing his hand on Candamir's arm for a moment. "If we leave the Latvians alone with the cheese too long, there'll be nothing left for us."

"It seems to me that they have too little respect for you, probably because you're much too lenient," Candamir grumbled.

Hacon took the comment in stride, used to his brother's jabs. "They do what I tell them, and I don't expect anything more. Also, they are Harald's slaves, not mine, so it's not up to me to teach them respect. I don't have any slaves, Candamir."

Candamir raised both hands pleadingly. "Let's have no sermon about the equality of all men and their immortal souls, Hacon. Show me some pity and spare me this nonsense until we have eaten at least."

When they arrived home five days later, Siglind greeted her husband at the door of their house. Her enormous belly had disappeared, and Candamir saw that she wasn't carrying one, but two little bundles, and he understood why she had become so particularly large in the weeks before his trip to the mountains.

He cautiously took his wife and two new children in his arms. His hands passed down over Siglind's hips and waist, perhaps not quite as slim as they once had been, but nevertheless, as wonderful to him now as on the day of their wedding. With his thumbs, he pushed aside the little blond braids from her temples before placing his lips on her forehead. Then he let her go and pointed somewhat indelicately toward the abdomen of the infant in her left arm.

Siglind shook her head earnestly. "Heidrun."

Without much hope, he pointed to the second child. "Heidlind, I assume."

"That's it."

He turned away, placed his forehead in his hand, and began to laugh. "Now we have the full half dozen."

Siglind smiled and shrugged helplessly. "I'm sorry, Candamir."

"Oh, don't be silly." One after the other, he took his two youngest daughters in his hands, carefully studied their tiny little faces, and kissed them on the forehead. Heidrun woke up and began to cry. He handed her back to Siglind and carried Heidlind, who wasn't much bigger than his outstretched palm, into the house himself. He put his free arm around his wife's shoulder and asked, "Was it hard?"

She shook her head. "No, not at all."

Siglind gave birth to her children with an ease that was the envy of many other women. Not only did it arouse jealousy but suspicion as well. Her labors hardly lasted longer than two hours, and rarely was a cry of pain heard, and perhaps worst of all, she managed to keep her figure despite her growing brood. The only thing that spared Siglind from the outright hostility of her neighbors was her inability to bear sons. She had lost her fourth child after only three months, and Brigitta had hinted that surely this was the son that Siglind was denied because she had slandered the gods.

"Heidrun came before Heide could get Asta," she told Candamir.

"Apparently Heidrun is just as full of impatience and uncontrollable curiosity as her mother," Candamir said.

"Look who's talking," she protested. Then she turned to the open door and called out, "Nils? Where is my sweet little rascal? Come here, you scamp, and say hello to your new sisters!"

Nils's slightly grubby face appeared at the door. "A girl again?" he asked breathlessly.

"Two," Siglind replied.

With beaming eyes, Nils stepped into the house, and when Siglind bent down to him and put the little bundle in his arms, he held it with care and skill. If there was anything in the world that Nils knew all about, it was little sisters.

"Twins?" he asked, incredulous. "And will they look exactly the same, just like the twin calves last spring?"

"Yes, I believe so," Candamir answered, holding Heidlind alongside her sister. "Can you tell them apart?"

"New sisters always look the same," Nils explained to his father. "All newborns do."

"What nonsense," Siglind said.

Secretly, Candamir agreed with his son. But before he could express his opinion, Irmgardis came running out of the nursery that had been partitioned from the hall, demanding her father's undivided attention.

Candamir placed the baby back in Siglind's arms and greeted his eldest daughter—the only one who had his jet-black hair. He swung her up and whirled her through the air, and she responded with an exuberant cry of delight. Then she put her arms around his neck. "Girls again," she confided to him with a sigh. "And this time two at once."

He picked her up in one arm. "That doesn't matter, little elf. If they bring me as much joy as you do, I'll have no reason to complain."

Irmgardis smiled at him confidently. She knew he meant it. In contrast to many other girls, she knew she was not a disappointment to her father, but had a definite, even important place in his life.

Siglind beckoned to Freydis, who was a great help to her in caring for the children. Nori's wife came hobbling over and took the two babies back with her into the small nursery. Candamir settled down on his high seat while his wife and the two older children took their places on the benches to the right and left.

Old Heide greeted the homecomers with her usual cantankerous hospitality, brought a pitcher of beer for her master and mistress and milk for the children, and then put a plate of bread and cold beef on the table. Father and son helped themselves hungrily.

"And what did you see?" Siglind asked little Nils.

Her stepson gave a lively description of the trip, the storm, the enormous smelting furnace, and Osmund and Roric's vain search for gold on the slopes of Mount Asi. Siglind listened patiently, expressing her astonishment and admiration at his little heroic deeds.

From the very first day she had been quite fond of Nils and showed him the same affection as her own daughters. Thus the boy had not the slightest suspicion that his father's wife might not be his real mother. Both Siglind and Candamir dreaded the day when Nils would learn the truth from some indiscreet gossiper. They knew they should be the ones to enlighten their son of this fact, but the right moment had simply not presented itself. For the time being, Nils accepted without suspicion Aunt Gunda's adoration, and if she sometimes became too affectionate, a dark look from Candamir generally restrained her.

The golden afternoon sun shone brightly through the window in the southwest wall that looked out over the village meadow. Candamir had to squint, but it never would have occurred to him to close the shutter. Even after six years, he considered these windows, and the light they provided the hall, a precious gift. He closed his eyes, enjoying the play of sunlight and shadow cast by the ash tree branches on his eyelids, and felt his daughter's little hand resting on his knee. For a moment, he was completely in harmony with the world.

The spell was broken by the sound of Godwin's heavy footsteps. "Godwin, come in. Drink a cup with us," Candamir invited his faithful apprentice.

The smith's son did not have to be asked twice. "Welcome home, Candamir, Nils," he said, taking a foaming cup from Heide and nodding his thanks before sitting down on the guest side of the table. Godwin was stocky and more thickset than Harald. Some considered him ill-humored, or even sinister, because he viewed the world skeptically and told everyone exactly what was on his mind, traits he had no doubt inherited from his mother. Candamir, however, found him uncomplicated, his sincerity refreshing, and his trade skills beyond question.

"Well?" he asked his young apprentice. "Who has incurred your well-deserved wrath today?"

Godwin smiled grimly. "Siwold was over in the workshop a while ago and complained that the chest was larger than what he had ordered."

Candamir nodded, unconcerned. Siwold was Siward's eldest son and, just like his father, found fault with almost everything. "He wants to bring the price down, I assume."

Godwin sniffled disgustedly. "Ten spans wide, he said. I made it ten spans wide, and I don't know what he's complaining about."

"Maybe your hands are larger than his," Siglind replied.

Godwin nodded into his cup. "If he weren't so afraid of work, his hands wouldn't be so small."

Candamir grinned slyly. "I'll have a talk with him and make it clear that he can't pay less because he got more than he asked for."

Candamir had never gotten around to becoming a farmer like most of his neighbors. Unlike them, he had also stopped clearing new land at some point. The fields he had, he used as grazing land, and Siglind took care of the large fruit and vegetable garden surrounding their house. But they didn't grow any grain. They simply didn't have the time.

After all the houses had been finished, Candamir had quickly learned that carpenters were still needed. Berse, the shipwright, had returned to his real trade—building boats, rafts, docks, and now and then even a regular ship. But everyone wanted furniture—beds for themselves and their growing families, cabinets for their household goods, chests for their clothing, looms, butter churns, and wooden buckets. And everyone wanted barns, stables, cattle pens, and privies. And just when Candamir thought there was nothing left to do, people started coming and asking for renovations and additions to their houses. Young people grew up, married, and wanted their own houses. The village grew until it threatened to explode inside the hedge.

So the two carpenters were kept quite busy, yet Candamir found time to indulge in his old passion of breeding horses. Every man, boy, and even some of the women wanted one. So now and then he rode out into the grassland, captured a yearling or a pregnant mare, broke it in, and trained it until it was a reliable mount for even the most inexperienced rider. And people paid for their houses and furniture, as well as for their mounts, with grain and sheep—the only currency of value in Catan. Sometimes, Candamir truly didn't know what to do with all the sacks of grain. In Elasund he would have been a very well-to-do man.

"You had better let Austin speak with him," Godwin said.

"Austin?" Candamir asked in amazement. "Ye gods, what does he have to do with Siwold?"

Godwin spat contemptuously. "Recently, Siwold has become a follower of that wretched, crucified god. Just like his brother."

Siglind said sharply, "If you spit on the floor in my house again, you can go and eat in your pit house in the future." She thought highly of good manners, and moreover, she didn't like it when someone denied her god the respect he deserved.

Godwin lowered his head remorsefully. "Sorry," he grumbled.

She nodded politely.

"Well, I can't see what the gods have to do with Siwold's chest," Candamir said. "Either he'll pay me the agreed-on price, or I'll bring the matter up before the *Thing*. Then we'll see who is in the right."

"And that, in turn, has a lot to do with the gods," Siglind remarked. "Or haven't you noticed that it's practically impossible to get justice in the *Thing* if you are a follower of the new faith?"

Candamir waved her off dismissively. He had heard enough of these lectures—the alleged discrimination against the Christians in the village was one of the topics Siglind often got worked up about. He folded his arms and grinned at her. "Well, if that's the case, I can at least be certain I'll be paid the agreed price."

"Inga?" Osmund called, entering his hall after handing over his team of oxen to a slave in the courtyard. "We're back!"

"Your wife is not at home, Master," said a shy voice that seemed to come from the hearth. "She has gone to Brigitta's house."

Osmund had to squint to see the girl who was speaking. Inga preferred to close the shutters during the day in the warm months to keep the heat out.

But his eyes quickly adjusted to the dim light in the room. With a smile, he greeted the young slave at the fire. "Birte. Are you all well?"

"Yes, Master. Sit down and rest after your long journey. I'll bring you something good to eat right away," she promised.

"And open the shutters," he said, settling wearily on his high seat. "It's as dark here as in a longhouse in Elasund in the winter."

She went to the window opposite the high seat and pushed the shutter open. Then she turned to him. "It's strange. I can hardly remember the winters in the old homeland."

Osmund nodded. Birte had been only eight years old when they left Elasund. She was the daughter of Inga's nursemaid, and Osmund had bought her from old Siward two or three years earlier for a splendid ewe. Just like the young Frankish girl who had belonged to Thorbjörn and now cared for Osmund's two sons and his daughter. And he had given two sheep for each of the strong young slaves he had bought during the previous year. It didn't matter, he could afford it. And while wealth and possessions were not as important in Catan as in Elasund, since everyone in Catan had enough to live on, the fact remained that if Candamir was well-to-do by the standards of the old homeland, Osmund was filthy rich.

He owed these fortunate circumstances to his skill in raising sheep, a talent he had been known for in the old days as well. What had begun with the three animals given to him so reluctantly by his uncle shortly after their arrival had become not only the largest, but by far the best herd of sheep in Catan. And there was still enough of a shortage of sheep for them to be sought after by everyone. Thus it was that Osmund, at one time nothing but a pauper, could now afford to have the pick of the slaves. He and his family wore the most expensive clothing made in Catan—nothing garish or showy, but still of superior quality. The same was true of his fine wall hangings and his silver mead cups, oil lamps, and meat platters.

Birte handed him a silver cup and was about to turn away, but he took hold of her wrist and gestured for her to take a seat on the bench.

"Don't you want something to eat?" she asked with a furrowed brow.

He shook his head. "Later. How is Brigitta?"

"Not well, Master," the girl said with a troubled look, lowering her head. "She's not eating anymore, your wife said, and she's getting weaker by the hour. I'm afraid...the end is near."

He nodded, his face betraying no emotion. No one could have guessed the happiness this news brought him. Finally the old witch was making room for Inga. Finally the oracle could be fulfilled...

He raised the cup to his lips and swallowed deeply. The mead was sweet and robust, the way he liked it. A feeling of well-being came over him. He put the cup down on the table and put his hand on his slave's shoulder.

She raised her head and was a little surprised at the way he looked at her, an almost roguish smile on his lips.

"Go to the bathhouse and fill the tub," he said abruptly. "I am dusty and I want to bathe."

"Yes, Master."

"But not alone."

"Then I'll come along and scrub your back," she promised with a smile.

Osmund grunted contentedly. "That sounds wonderful."

Birte stood up. "Where is Roric?" she asked, shoveling a few glowing coals from the fireplace into a stone bowl in order to bring the water in the bathhouse to a pleasant, lukewarm temperature.

"Down at the river with his brothers and sister and the nurse. We met them as we came back. They're going fishing, I think."

The maid nodded with relief. She had a special weakness for the quiet, dreamy Roric, and she didn't want him to come home only to find himself in an empty house while she passed the time with his father in the bathhouse. She knew the boy was anxious by nature.

With the stone bowl on her hip, she went to the door and turned around once more. "Take your time with your cup of mead, and then come. Not too soon, or else the water won't be warm yet."

"I'll try to be patient," Osmund promised.

Austin's house was the strangest one Hacon had ever seen. Half hidden behind hazelnut bushes and small, gnarled apple trees, it stood in the midst of an herb garden between Candamir's house and Harald's smithy. As a free man, Austin naturally had the right to clear farmland, till the fields, and keep large herds of cattle like everyone else, but he hadn't done anything like that. He had a cow that went by the name of Godiva, a sow, and a few chickens. His modest need for grain and vegetables was more than met by the donations he received for healing sickness and caring for wounds, or for his salves and tinctures. There were always bundles of herbs hung from the rafters of his little house to dry, and a long wall with shelves full of pots and jars. But the most outstanding characteristic of the bright, one-room cottage was all the books it held, along with the tools for making them.

Austin made parchment from animal skins, cut them into sheets of uniform size, drew lines on them, and then painted them all over with his little runes. Then he sewed them together and tied them into a wooden, leather-bound cover. In addition to the Latin Bible, there were already five complete works standing on one of the shelves along the wall—a treatise on the healing herbs of Catan, the Rule of St. Benedict, a collection of myths and songs that the people of Catan had brought with them from the old homeland, a Latin grammar book, and naturally the chronicle of Catan that had long become a book in its own right, and that Austin continued to add to.

Hacon still felt strange in the presence of books. They no longer scared him, but filled him instead with curiosity and a strange excitement, somewhat like the prospect of great adventure.

"What are you working on?" he asked in greeting, ducking past the aromatic bunches of lavender and chamomile hanging down.

Austin sat at the table bent over his innumerable sheets of parchment. Without looking up, he replied, "The saints' calendar. I've decided to put aside my translation of the Bible for the time being. It's more important to write down those things I only retain in my memory, such as the liturgy, or the Rule of St. Benedict, which is already finished. This also includes the lives and the feast days of the saints, as they must not be lost." When the ink started to run out, he set down the quill and looked up with a smile. "Welcome home, Hacon."

"Thanks." Unasked, he sat down alongside the monk on the bench and looked over Austin's shoulder. The lines on the page were close together in two columns. Here and there a new paragraph began, each time with a date.

"*The eighteenth of August,*" Hacon murmured as he read. "*On this day we celebrate the feast of St. Helen, the mother of the Roman emperor Constantine, who was the first emperor to convert to the true faith. After the pious emperor had heard the word of God from the bishops, he asked his mother, Helen, to set out toward the east into the land of the Jews, with an escort of soldiers, to search for...*" At this point, the text broke off. "Search for what?" he asked.

Austin smiled mysteriously. "Wait and see. You may read it when I'm finished."

"No, I don't want to wait," the young man protested. "Tell me. Come on, Austin."

"Read five verses from the Bible out loud for me, and translate them—for once, without any mistakes—then I will satisfy your curiosity," his teacher offered.

Eagerly, Hacon stood up and carefully washed his hands in the bucket of water alongside the door before reverently taking the thick, well-worn book from the shelf and opening it somewhere in the middle, in Psalms. He read a short passage and then translated it seamlessly.

Austin listened with his arms crossed and a very contented smile on his face. Hacon was an outstanding pupil. Siglind, too, had learned reading and Latin, and she frequently came to Bible study at his house, principally, Austin suspected, to keep her promise to God and to him. She was serious in her effort to learn the word of the Lord and live accordingly, yet since she married Candamir, he and her children were the center of her life, not God. The same was true for Wiland and Asta, and almost all of the forty or so followers he had won over in recent years. But it no longer worried him. He knew not everyone was called to a life for God, and he had after all not gone forth in order to convert an entire people into monks and nuns, but to try and save their souls from perdition. Why should he object if they carried on their own worldly life too. But Hacon was special. The more he learned, the more his thirst for knowledge and spiritual longing continued to grow. And while Hacon was a skilled smith and had married the unchaste Gunda—and might father a dozen children by her—he was becoming Austin's brother in Christ. Their relationship often reminded Austin of his own youth in the monastery and the abbot who had quenched his thirst for knowledge, teaching him everything he knew and making him the man he was. Whatever course Hacon's life took, the monk was deeply grateful to God for sending him someone he could pass this knowledge on to.

And so he told Hacon about Helen's search for the cross on which our Lord Jesus Christ had died for mankind, a search finally crowned with success. But he did not fail to note the cruel acts the emperor's mother had committed to reach her goal, and soon they were involved in an animated and scholarly debate over whether the end justified the means.

Before they had reached a conclusion, Candamir appeared in the little hut. "I'm very sorry to disturb this little chat…"

Hacon frowned and turned around, while Austin remarked with a sigh, "I'm sure that's a lie, Candamir, and so you have brought another sin down upon yourself. My hearty congratulations on the birth of your daughters. May God's blessing always be with them."

"Thanks," Candamir said. "But it's not he who will be their patron god, but Loki and Baldur. Just so that's clear."

Austin shuddered involuntarily. He had nothing against Baldur—on the contrary. The noble god of light was the most beloved of all the gods for his gentleness and whose treacherous murder, according to the belief of these people, would someday bring about the great battle that would end the world. Of all these barbaric deities, Baldur was the only one the monk could relate to. For he was a sacrificial lamb, pure and innocent, almost like Christ. But Loki? "You are placing your daughter under the protection of a liar and traitor, of the devil himself?" he asked, bewildered.

"I'm never quite sure what you mean by that word," Candamir replied. "Loki is the slyest of all gods, and therefore his protection is powerful—if it serves his purposes to grant it. It's true that he's unreliable and malicious, but he's part of the world of the gods, just as maliciousness is part of the world. Your religion suffers from its denial of everything that isn't good, as if it simply weren't there."

"And your religion suffers from the fact that it just accepts everything that isn't good instead of fighting against it," Austin replied heatedly.

"You're a fool, and you always will be, Saxon," Candamir said, shaking his head. "You want to change the nature of things, yet you assert that your god made the world the way it is. How can you be so bold as to question his work? What will you do next, rebel against the fact that the leaves fall from the trees in autumn or that every life must end?"

Hacon looked expectantly from one to the other. When Austin's and Candamir's words and worlds collided, as they so often did, their disputes brought him astonishing insights.

"I'm not rebelling," the monk said, "but we need not simply accept evil in the world as we do a leaf falling from a tree. God has provided us with reason and a heart so that we can fight against the evil, above all in ourselves."

"O mighty Tyr, he manages to contradict himself in the same breath," Candamir grumbled in mock despair.

Austin shook his head. "Someday, you too will understand it."

"Yes, and on that day there will be snow on the slopes of Mount Asi."

*That day may come,* the monk thought. *Greater miracles are performed every day by God and his saints.* He shrugged his shoulders stolidly. "We shall see. I have baptized your daughters, and so it doesn't matter which idols you have commended them to, for God will protect them even from malicious Loki."

Candamir sighed. He had long ago resigned himself to the fact that Austin would always have the last word in these disputes, for his zeal was far greater than his own. Uninvited, but by no means unwelcome, Candamir took a seat on the bench. "I didn't come to listen again to you offending my gods, Saxon."

"No? Why did you?"

"I need a sheet of parchment, a rather large piece. I want to put it in front of the window of the nursery. Newborns are delicate and prone to illness, and if I cover the window with parchment, I think the light will still come through, but the heat, the rain, and the cool night wind will not."

Hacon looked at him, astonished. "That's a splendid idea," he said. "Maybe our Ole would not catch cold so often if we did that too."

"I can't spare enough parchment to cover every window in Catan," Austin warned.

"Yes, I know. When it comes to your beloved parchment, you're pretty stingy," Candamir replied, grinning. "In return, though, I'll build you a little cabinet for your books. With a door, so they'll be protected from dust and dampness."

Austin smiled broadly. "You'll have your parchment."

"Good. Siglind sends word that she wants you to come to dinner. We'll drink a cup of mead to the health of Heidrun and Heidlind. That is, a cup of mead for each daughter, of course."

"I'll be glad to come if you promise not to make me keep up with your drinking this time."

"You have my word," he promised, smiling, and turned to his brother. "You come along too, Hacon. Bring your family, and let's celebrate a bit, how about it?"

"Agreed."

"Good." Candamir stood up. "I'm going over to Harald and Asta's house."

"Is Osmund coming along to the celebration?" Hacon inquired as casually as possible. He knew that Austin never felt quite at ease when he was sitting at a table with Osmund.

"I haven't gone over there yet," Candamir replied. "After all, we were gone for more than a week and have only been back two hours. It's best to give Osmund a little time to catch up on things after returning from such a long absence," he concluded with a wink.

Austin blushed as Candamir strolled out into the herb garden that filled the mild spring air with the most splendid fragrances.

"Go, child," Brigitta said. Her voice had become nothing but a whisper, but it was still astonishingly clear. "You've done everything you can for me. Now go."

"Don't send me away," Inga begged. "I can't leave you all alone."

"I'm not alone," the old woman replied, pointing with a feeble gesture to her three ravens. Of her three original companions, only Skuld remained. The other two had preceded Brigitta to the other world, and their successors were snow-white Catan ravens. And so now, two white birds and a black one perched at the foot of the deathbed, as quiet and devoted as ever. A faint gleam, like the memory of a loving smile, came into the opaque yellow eyes of the old woman as she viewed her loyal companions. "No, don't worry, my child. I am not alone."

Inga felt goose bumps on her arms and back. She knew that this was a final farewell. "Oh, Brigitta!" She no longer tried to hold back her tears. "What shall I do without you? I just can't…"

"Oh, but you can. You know everything you need to know. And you have everything you need—the runes, the incantations, and soon you'll have the ravens as well. In addition, you have your husband and his son to fulfill the prophecy. So just stop whining and complaining."

Inga couldn't help but laugh. She took Brigitta's ancient, mottled hands in her own and kissed them lovingly. "You're right. Forgive me. Of course I can. I willingly take the burden from you that you have borne so long yourself."

"Yes, it ought to rest on younger shoulders than mine. The gods know that," Brigitta grumbled. "And now, away with you. Let's not drag this out so long. Send me my wretch of a son. He has given me little cause for joy, but I'd like to see him once more, just the same."

Inga bent over, kissed Brigitta on the forehead, and then released her hands. "I'll go and get him for you. Have a safe journey, Brigitta."

Her wrinkled eyelids closed. "Farewell, Inga."

She didn't need to go to Haflad's house at the north end of the village, for he was sitting on the ground in front of his mother's hut, crying like a little boy.

Inga laid her hand on his shoulder sympathetically. "She is asking for you."

He nodded, rose clumsily to his feet, and walked over to the door. Just seeing the ungainly, gray-bearded Haflad crying so bitterly made it easier for Inga to dry her own tears. She was calm and filled with a consoling, melancholy peace as she crossed the village meadow and turned westward.

But her calm only lasted until she got home. As she walked into her yard, she first passed the bathhouse, and the sounds that came through the board walls were unmistakable. Alma, the Frankish nurse, had once accused Birte of making such a racket when she was with the master in order to let all of Catan know that he had selected her. Inga had overheard the maids squabbling quite by accident, and she had thought to herself that Alma certainly was talking big, considering she gave her master a bastard child every year as regularly as mares delivered foals. Nevertheless, the Frankish slut had a point, Inga had to concede. Birte's cries of joy could probably be heard as far as the wasteland.

Disgusted, Inga turned away and briskly walked across the yard and into the house. Inside it was hot and stuffy. With an angry frown she noted that someone had again left one of the shutters open, and she slammed it shut. She would have liked to make more of a ruckus, like breaking dishes or screaming—it didn't matter what it was, as long as it would drive the sound of Birte's voice out of her head. Dispirited, she collapsed on the bench alongside the high seat, put her head on the table, and covered her ears with her forearms.

She didn't know how long she had sat there motionless, given up to her grief. When she heard the voices of children at the door, she jumped up, ashamed of her self-pity. Siward, her five-year-old son, came storming into the hall just ahead of his sister Rutild and the nurse with her own children, while Roric brought up the rear.

"Mother, Mother, we caught a trout!" Siward announced excitedly, proudly handing her a dead, battered fish.

She passed her hand over her son's blond hair. "That's great, my boy. Tell me how you did it."

Siward recounted in great detail the story of his successful catch. Every sentence began with "And then I..." His little sister kept interrupting him, though he poked her with his elbow to make her be silent. Inga listened to them with a loving smile, pulled them up onto the bench on either side of her, and put one arm around each of their shoulders.

Alma took her own children back outside as inconspicuously as possible and led them to the cowshed to see if the slaves had begun milking yet, hoping they could spare a drink of milk for the little ones.

Roric remained alone at the door to the hall. His little hand wrapped around the doorpost, clenching it tighter and tighter the longer he had to listen to his brother's tall stories.

"It's not true," he said softly, his head bowed.

"And then I carefully tugged on the line, just as Father taught me to do," Siward said.

"That's not so," Roric murmured.

"And then I pulled the fish in," Siward concluded triumphantly.

Roric was speechless. Slowly, almost hesitantly, he entered the hall and stood alongside his father's high seat.

Out of the corner of her eye, Inga saw something moving and turned her head. "Well, Roric, you're back."

He smiled at her shyly, nodding.

"And have you found your gold, lad?"

"No," he confessed, embarrassed. "But I'm the one who caught the trout. Siward's lying, Mother. I caught the fish."

For a moment, there was silence. Then Siward began to cry, dramatically. Inga took her hand from his shoulder to show him she was not taken in, but it was Roric she was looking at.

"I am not your mother."

It sounded gentle, one might even have thought sympathetic, but the way she looked at him was not just indifferent, but hostile—a strange mixture of shame and malice. Roric had often seen this look, but he had never been able to understand it. He was too small to comprehend that he, who looked more like his father than any of his siblings, was called on to atone for his father's transgressions.

"Roric, take your brother and sister outside with you," Osmund said, standing in the doorway. "I'd like to speak with your mother alone for a moment."

When Candamir arrived at Osmund's house, he could hear the couple quarreling from ten feet away.

"She's dying!" Inga's voice was not really loud, just raised a bit, but the door was open. "And while she is on her deathbed you have nothing better to do but..."

"The sooner she draws her last breath the happier I will be," Osmund replied sharply. "And this is not about her, or my doings, but about Roric. You have broken your promise. Again."

"Osmund..." She sounded fearful.

At that Candamir beat a hasty retreat. This was none of his business, and he didn't want to hear it. He strolled down to the shore to wait until the argument had subsided, when a voice behind him remarked dryly,

"Yes, that's wise, Master. You are well advised not to get involved in these matters."

He turned his head. "Birte." He couldn't help but smile. She was truly a beautiful girl. Her dark hair fell down her back in wet curls, and her damp dress was clinging to her voluptuous breasts, leaving little to the imagination.

She sat down boldly next to him in the grass. "When they argue, we all quickly find something to do in the yard that can't be put off." She pointed to the right where a few raspberry bushes were standing. "Above all, he does."

Roric was kneeling in the grass by the raspberry bushes and holding a stick in his right hand. A puppy with a gray, curly coat was jumping around him trying to snatch the stick away from Roric. Osmund raised watchdogs with just as much success as sheep.

"His father gave the puppy to him," the maid explained. "It was the strongest in the whole litter and will surely be a splendid dog. But a dog's devotion cannot replace a mother's love."

"You have a very loose tongue," Candamir said, with more surprise than reproach.

Birte shrugged. "Yes, I know."

"Perhaps things would be simpler if you showed your mistress a little more respect."

She shook her head. "Oh, you're mistaken. I have the greatest respect for her. She's a wonderful woman, an outstanding midwife and healer, and very bright. She knows everything about the gods, just like Brigitta. She will be a worthy successor. But…all her cleverness fails her when it comes to her husband, Master."

Candamir nodded. He knew the girl was speaking the truth, but he didn't care to discuss these things with her. Instead, he said, "Be a little more discreet."

"But why?" she asked. "He does what every healthy, normal man does. That is, everyone but you," she added teasingly.

He shrugged and smiled. "That's probably because I don't have such beautiful young maids."

He had never broken his promise to Siglind, but it still embarrassed him, and he tried without success to keep his loyalty to his wife a secret. Birte, after all, was right. What Osmund did was completely normal. Fathering many children with many slave girls was a sign of prosperity, something every man was proud of. And having a large number of children had never been more important than now.

"I just can't understand what she's getting so upset about," Birte continued, sighing. "She is one of the most highly regarded women in the village, and everyone respects her, but she acts as if we were going to take something away from her. That's ridiculous, isn't it? I don't care if she gives me a hard time because of it, but he is the one who has to take the heat." She pointed surreptitiously at Roric, who was romping about with his puppy in the grass, unsmiling. "And that's really very unwise of her, you know. She has no love for the poor little fellow, yet that's the only thing the master wants from her."

And that was just the problem, Candamir knew. He smiled and pinched Birte on the cheek. "I'll say it again—you talk too much. Do be careful. If you can get me a cup of beer without being noticed, then be so good as to do it. I'll try to cheer up Roric."

"That's very kind of you, Master," the maid said with a warm smile. "No one can do that as well as you can."

"Lifelong practice," Candamir explained as he rose. "He is just like his father."

Candamir awoke with a throbbing head and a burning belly, as if he'd swallowed hot coals.

"Mead—never again," he grumbled, turning on his side and pulling a pillow over his head.

"I've heard that vow all too often," Siglind replied, unimpressed, mercilessly yanking the pillow away. "Get up, Candamir, you lazybones. The sun is shining in Catan."

He knew he couldn't expect the slightest bit of sympathy from his wife. "The sun shines in Catan almost every day."

She put a cool hand on his forehead. "Get up just the same. The men are gathering by the ash tree. Something has happened."

They could imagine what that was. Without further objection, Candamir sat up and rubbed his eyes. "Where are the twins?" he asked in surprise, for usually the youngest child shared their bed as long as it was being nursed.

"I took them to Freydis. They were crying so loud, and I didn't want them to wake you up. I don't have enough milk for two, Candamir."

"Then let's buy a wet nurse." He had no objection if a slave nursed his children, because he wanted his wife's breasts to stay just the way they were, especially since he was only allowed to admire other women's breasts from a distance.

Siglind nodded. "Freydis can no longer handle the children alone as it is, and our Heide is getting old. I'll ask Sigurd's wife. She has a young slave girl, her cook's daughter, who had a baby herself last week."

"Do that." Candamir suppressed a yawn. "Tell Sigurd he'll get the horse that he's been hankering after for weeks whenever he comes by my meadow."

Candamir rose from their bed and stepped to the big clothes chest under the window, where a bowl of wash water awaited. He washed his face and hands, and the cool, clear river water made him feel better. He brushed his teeth thoroughly with salt, and to get the repulsive taste out of his mouth, he chewed the rosemary twig that lay next to the saltbox before spitting it out the window.

Siglind had clasped her fingers behind her back and was leaning on the bedpost observing her husband. She loved to watch him when he was so completely lost in thought, and admired the play of the muscles under his light-colored skin. As Candamir reached for his horn comb, she walked over to him. "Let me do that," she offered.

He handed her the comb and sat down on the stool. Siglind undid the narrow braids and combed his hair very carefully in order not to make his headache worse. As she stood behind him, her gaze fell on the dreadful scars covering his back even after all those years. Thoughtfully, she passed her finger over them.

Candamir cast a questioning glance at her over his shoulder.

"So much time has passed," she said. "And so much has happened. We've seen so many fateful days."

"And today is another one," he answered, taking her hand and pressing it briefly to his lips.

Siglind nodded and began to re-plait his hair.

"Actually, I can do that very well myself," he said, embarrassed.

"I know. But this way I'll have you to myself a moment longer. You just got home, and when you leave, I won't see you again for days."

Patiently, he held still until she had finished. Then he turned around to her. "I wish, too, that the old witch had waited a few more days," he said with a sigh. "But when did she ever do things according to our wishes?"

"True," she murmured, a trace of bitterness in her voice. Brigitta had often made her life difficult. Siglind had not only become a Christian, but made no secret of it as others did. The fiercer Brigitta's attacks on Austin and his god had become, the more defiantly Siglind displayed her faith. And ever since Siglind had entered the temple at last Yule ceremony with a silver cross around her neck, Brigitta had stopped speaking with her, even cursed Hacon in front of the assembled villagers for making the cross in the first place. After that, neither Siglind nor Hacon had ever gone to a temple ceremony again.

Candamir pulled Siglind onto his lap, and when he placed his arm around her he felt, despite his wretched condition, an unmistakable stirring in his loins. But it was just five days since she had given birth, and he knew he had to be patient. "Even for old Brigitta we cannot hold a vigil of more than two nights, for the days are already getting warm. All in all, the ceremonies will hardly take longer than a week, and then we'll have time to…"

"Don't say it," she interrupted him, laughing. "Let's make a pact not to utter the words 'son' and 'beget' anymore in a single breath. Perhaps it will work out if we don't talk about it."

"Agreed." It was worth a try, in any case.

Candamir got dressed with great care, choosing a pair of dark brown trousers made of light wool, and shirt of soft calf leather that Siglind had embroidered in green yarn along its hems and neck. Then he put on his solid, ankle-high boots with dark green decorative laces so long that he could tie them crosswise almost up to his knee. After he had put on his belt holding his knife and pouch and had donned his sword, Siglind looked at him with an appreciative nod.

"Don't tell me," he said before she could speak.

"What?"

"Oh, something about a drunken good-for-nothing in fine clothes, or whatever happens to be going through your mind at the moment."

She stood on the tips of her toes and kissed him on the cheek. "You're mistaken." It was true that she was displeased when he drank too much, which happened frequently, as there was an overabundance of barley, hops, and honey. But she was certainly not the only wife with this problem, and unlike many other men, Candamir was no danger to his family at these times. "I was actually thinking how dignified you look, appropriate to the occasion."

"Very well." He took her hand and led her into the hall.

Nils and Irmgardis were already sitting at the table with their sisters and the slaves. Freydis was feeding the small children. "The twins have fallen asleep," she said.

Without being asked, Heide brought Candamir a hearty breakfast of fish soup and sour cabbage. "Here, eat, Master. Who knows when you'll have time to do so again."

He had been certain he would be unable to eat anything, but now he pounced on the tasty food with a ravenous hunger.

"What's going on, Father?" Nils asked, pointing out of the open window. "Why are the men gathering?"

Candamir broke off a piece of bread. "I'm not sure, but I assume old Brigitta has died."

"Oh," Nils said apprehensively. He knew that "dead" meant "no longer here." In Brigitta's case, it was no great loss to him, in contrast to when Tjorv died of gangrene last winter after injuring his hand with a chisel. For Nils, Brigitta was only a mysterious and ancient woman who had something or other to do with gods. But he could tell it was an important event that would probably ruin his great plans for the day.

"So aren't we going to visit Berse today?" he asked with unmistakable disappointment.

"I think not, no," Candamir replied tersely.

Berse was working on a ship for Candamir. The hull was finished, and Candamir had intended to spend one or two days with Berse and his sons after his return from the mountains helping out with the railing and deck work. He had promised Nils he would take him along, and the boy had been looking forward to it greatly. Now his shoulders fell and he lowered his head over his bowl of milk.

"Stop whining, lad," his father scolded. "Didn't you just get back from a trip? Here at home there are chores to attend to, aren't there? Why not think about them for a change? And if you don't learn to control yourself, I'll never take you anywhere again."

Nils scrunched down even lower and sobbed silently to himself.

Siglind cast Candamir a withering look. In her opinion, he was much too gruff and impatient with his son, just as he used to be with his brother, and he always seemed to forget that Nils was only six.

She gathered Nils on her lap. "No doubt you'll be going to Berse's in a few days," she said consolingly. "We aren't in a particular hurry for our ship, are we?"

Nils wiped his eyes with his sleeve. "No, Mother," he murmured sheepishly.

"*No, Mother*," Candamir teased him, perfectly mimicking the whining voice. And he continued in the same tone: "I know you don't think much of buying this ship, Mother. We are on an island somewhere far out at sea, so where in the world should we sail to?"

Irmgardis laughed at her father's antics, and Siglind couldn't help but join in. But she said, "A perfectly good question, to which I still don't have a satisfactory answer."

"Fortunately, there's no law requiring a man to answer all his wife's questions," Candamir murmured into his bowl.

The truth was there was no satisfactory answer to give. He wanted to sail around Catan. He wanted to head out to sea again in the fall to go fishing with a few friends. But for all these ventures, he could have borrowed the *Wavewolf.* He just wanted a ship. He had never really gotten over the loss of the *Falcon.* All his ancestors had been seafarers, and the longing for the sea was in his blood. "I don't need a ship any more than you need the accursed silver cross around your neck," he had replied when first they had this debate. "I just want my ship the way you wanted your cross."

And while a silver cross was far less expensive than a ship, that argument would not hold. For Hacon, who would be co-owner of the new *Falcon*, was contributing the most to this acquisition and promised the shipwright new axes, planes, and other tools.

"If you like, I'll go over to see Berse with Nils," Godwin offered. He lived with his young wife in a pit house in the yard that was so small that they took their meals with Candamir and his family.

But the master of the house shook his head with determination. "You must keep working on Haldir's cart. He's getting impatient."

Godwin shrugged and nodded.

"Sven," said Candamir, turning to the young slave he had bought to replace Tjorv. "Go and give Godwin a hand. Nori, you take the horses to pasture, and bring them back before the gates are closed."

The servants nodded.

Osmund appeared at the door to the hall. He greeted Siglind with a cursory nod.

"I'm coming," Candamir said, standing up.

"She sent Haflad shortly after midnight," Harald said.

He stood in the shadow of the ash tree, surrounded by the free men of the village. The women and slaves had also come in great number and were sitting a bit farther away in the grass listening to the smith's report. "She told me that much of what she had to say would not please some of you, therefore she wanted to relate her final wishes to me so that you would give them the necessary attention." He lowered his gaze a moment, a little embarrassed. Harald was probably near his forty-fifth year, Candamir estimated. His beard was gray, and he was considered the wisest man in the village by all. Yet he always seemed a bit uncomfortable in the leading role.

To save his brother-in-law some discomfort, Candamir broke in. "She did the right thing. It's clear to everyone here that you will truthfully relate her wishes and not weigh them against any personal interests."

There was a general murmur of assent.

"Continue, Harald," Candamir asked politely.

The blacksmith nodded."We are to lay her out in the temple, where she is close to the gods, and hold a deathwatch for her as we see fit. Since she was a wise, venerable woman, I suggest that twelve men watch over her from now until the day after tomorrow at dawn. She doesn't want us to burn her corpse, but we are to bury her on the south shore in sight of the Temple Island."

This last request was met with an astonished silence.

"And she also said that all who come after her should also be buried. For this ground, she said, is sacred, and everyone whom Odin has led to Catan must lie in Catan's earth and be given generous gifts to ease their way to the other world, so that those waiting for them there might see how Odin has favored us."

You could see in their faces that they were starting to understand. Austin could hardly believe his ears. It was the first—and last—time the old witch gave a command in keeping with his own beliefs. Tjorv had been the first of their community of believers to die, and it had grieved Austin deeply to see the corpse of the faithful servant burned, for it was told that one day all saved souls would experience the resurrection of the flesh, but poor Tjorv would forever be a sad little pile of ashes.

"Whatever she leaves behind in the way of possessions, we are to divide up as we see fit," the smith continued. "They are mostly ingredients for her potions and powders and the like, but also a few pearls, a little gold, and amber. I suggest that Inga take what she needs of Brigitta's things and the rest be divided between Haflad and Roric, for they are Brigitta's only descendents."

The men expressed their agreement, but Sigurd asked, "Inga? Why Inga?" His wife also knew a lot about herbs and old songs and in his view could also lay claim as Brigitta's successor.

Harald nodded, as if he had anticipated the objection. "Brigitta saw many things in the hours before her death, she said. It is surely no secret that Inga was her preferred choice as a successor, but she said it was also the will of the gods, and the gods would give us a sign that not even the blindest of blockheads among us could overlook. Ahem…her words, not mine."

A chuckle went through the crowd, relieving some of the growing tension. Nobody had truly loved Brigitta—except for Inga and presumably Haflad—for most had their own stinging memories of Brigitta's sharp tongue and malice. But she had been an important person, and consequently it was important to follow all the rules of propriety when she was buried.

"What sort of sign?" Jared wanted to know.

"I imagine we will know that when we see it," the smith replied, casting a questioning look at Osmund.

"I don't know any more about it than you do," Osmund said. "When Haflad brought the news that his mother was dead, Inga went out into the forest. She said she would come back at the right time, whatever that means."

"Then there is only one message left for me to pass on to you," said Harald, looking around. "Listen carefully, and I'll tell you exactly what she said, word for word: 'And the gods showed me that the renegade traitor will bring great misfortune to Odin's people. Only the worthiest among you can defeat him. You must elect the worthiest man as your leader, if you wish to escape disaster.'"

Silence fell over the meadow as each person pondered this message.

Candamir exchanged glances with Siglind, her face mirroring his own discomfort. Brigitta's last message seemed treacherous. Neither of them believed that a leader would be good for their community. Siglind had spent much of her life under Cnut's tyranny, and her account made it clear to Candamir how dangerous it was to give a single man so much power. What was the difference between a leader and a king?

"What does 'elect' mean?" Gunda asked Austin in a whisper.

"Choose," he replied just as softly.

Although Candamir, Hacon, and Harald had asked Austin several times to join them at the *Thing*, he preferred to stay in the background and only speak when directly asked a question. For free or not, he still remained an outsider, regarded by many with suspicion.

"Now, the 'renegade traitor' doesn't confront any of us in a duel, unfortunately, but attacks us in our sleep," Haldir said. "So what use is a worthy leader if there is no open battle into which he can lead us?"

Jared turned pale. As always, a painful feeling of shame came over him when his father and his brothers were the objects of discussion. As he turned around, looking for support, he met the kind gaze of his wife. Jared and Margild were one of those couples for whom a marriage of convenience had turned into a love match. They were very devoted to each other, and Candamir liked to tease them about acting like lovebirds.

Osmund always tried to help his cousin through difficult moments, this time defusing the mounting anxiety some by suggesting, "We mustn't dismiss Brigitta's prophecy only because we can't understand its meaning immediately. This prophecy comes from a wise woman who was close to the gods. Let us go to the temple and lay out Brigitta's body, as was her wish. Those of us holding watch will have the time and peace to contemplate her message, and perhaps then the gods will show us the way."

The temple had changed over the years. Statues of the gods, almost as tall as men, surrounded the sacrificial stone in the center. Most of them had been made by Berse, who was very proficient at carving, because all his life he had made animal heads for the bows and sterns of ships. The carvings on the beams and timbers had been finished long ago, as all the men had worked on them at every sacrificial feast, and the walls of the temple were covered in red inside and out with the blood of the sacrificial animals that was painted on them at every festival.

The sight and, above all, the odor of so much animal blood, coupled with the heathen rituals, made Austin ill and was the reason he rarely came near the temple. But Candamir assured him that only on the day of the burial would there be such a sacrificial feast, and he asked Austin to bring a large quantity of his lamp oil to the temple. The Saxon perfumed his oil with herbs, and two days and two nights was after all quite a long time to leave a body unburied in the early summer heat.

The bier stood between the sacrificial stone and the spring, and twelve men had taken position around it. Their heads bowed reverentially, as motionless as the statues of their idols, they surrounded the dead woman, whose orifices had been sealed in accordance with custom, and whose face was covered by a linen cloth.

Next to each of the watchers stood a burning oil lamp, so that the center of the temple was brightly lit, and restless, misshapen shadows darted across the walls. Austin made the sign of the cross before stepping out of the darkness and setting the clay jug of lamp oil in front of Candamir.

"Now leave," Osmund whispered. His voice was soft, but unmistakably harsh. "Off with you. You are desecrating this place and disturbing the peace of the dead."

Austin did not take offense. He knew it was enormously difficult for these men to stand still, to fast, and to be silent for hours. After all, it was not in their nature to perform such exercises of asceticism and reflection. Thus it was hardly surprising that they became grim and irritable when they had to do so.

The monk glanced at the shrouded corpse, a shiver running down his spine at the sight of the two white ravens and a black raven crouched motionless at its feet. All of a sudden, he feared that Brigitta might move, or even sit up. *Rest in peace, old witch,* he thought. *But rest.* And with relief, he took leave of the heathen temple.

On the morning of the third day, they laid Brigitta to rest. A few slaves had dug a large pit on the uninhabited shore of the river across from the island, and the women had prepared the burial gifts—bread, meat, fish, and mead for sustenance, and a pair of solid, new shoes for the long, dangerous journey, Brigitta's little handloom, a small wooden box with pearls, and, the most important gift of all, her little sack of runes. The women and girls arranged all these offerings around a bed of straw padded with soft furs and the finest wool blankets. The men carefully rested the bier on this bed.

As the bearers were climbing out of the grave, there was a familiar cawing sound, and Brigitta's ravens came winging over from the Temple Island, landed in the grave, and settled down again at the feet of their dead mistress.

The men of Catan, all of whom were standing together around the grave, exchanged looks of amazement.

Haflad groaned, climbed back down into the grave, and tried without success to chase the birds away, who only pecked irritably at his hands.

"What now?" Harald asked helplessly.

"Shall we kill them before we erect the grave mound?" Jared asked uncertainly.

"*Sacred* birds?" Osmund replied incredulously. "What's more, *Brigitta's* sacred birds? I'd think that through again if I were you."

"Close the grave," a voice behind him said firmly.

Everyone wheeled around.

"Close the grave," Inga repeated. "In olden times it was customary for a loyal dog, a horse, or even a devoted slave girl to be burned or buried with a dead person of high rank. This is the proper thing to do. Don't touch them, but bury them with her."

No one spoke. Everyone stared at the young woman, a few of them open-mouthed. Inga was wearing a simple, white robe without any embroidery, decorated only with a golden Thor's hammer hanging around her neck on a leather cord. She looked majestic, but what astonished the crowd were the birds. Inga was carrying three white ravens. One was sitting on each of her shoulders and another on her left forearm, exactly the way Brigitta had carried her own ravens. Inga had apparently tamed these three new ravens in the two days she had spent in the forest. Yet everyone knew it was impossible to tame the white Catan ravens as they were shy and avoided people. No one but a priestess would be able to do that…

Harald cleared his throat before saying, respectfully, "Behold the sign! I think this is the answer to the question about Brigitta's successor, isn't it?"

He looked at Sigurd. The young shipwright lowered his eyes and nodded.

Osmund walked toward his wife and took her right hand. The people lined up to make a passage for them as he led her to the open grave. Silently, Osmund and Inga looked down on the corpse and its magnificent burial gifts.

Inga nodded with satisfaction. "Well done," she said, stepping back so that the men could close the grave and build the mound over it.

She turned to Jared, who was holding his shovel. "Open your hand," she told him.

He silently obeyed her command, stretching out his hand to her.

She let a few little seed corns trickle into his hand. "Scatter them on the grave mound when you're finished."

Jared nodded. "Fine. What is it?" he asked curiously, looking at the little gray-green kernels in her hand.

"Water hemlock," she explained. "It protects the peace of the dead from pixies and evil river spirits."

"I'm sure it does," Austin whispered to Siglind. "But it's very poisonous to people and animals."

Inga heard him. She turned her head and stared at him for a long moment.

The young witch, with her three snow white ravens, seemed just as weird to him as the old one. But he returned her gaze with equanimity, and even a small forced smile. The passion burning in Inga's eyes was equal to his own, and he knew he had made a mistake; it would have been wiser to have shown a little humility just this one time. But because she was a woman, he could not.

The slaves had brought the sacrificial animals to the Temple Island, and the Catanians returned with their boats and rafts. Candamir had selected his finest young bull for this solemn occasion, but he could not completely suppress a sigh. The bull was gazing at him, trusting and unsuspecting, and Candamir returned his gaze and patted him on his sturdy shoulder. "No hard feelings, young fellow."

Nils stood at his side, nervously fingering the wreath of flowers that the slave girls had made for the bull, and said in a choked whisper, “Please, Father, don’t do it.”

Candamir looked down at him, shaking his head. “We’ve already discussed this a dozen times. We *must*, and I think it’s time you stopped this silly fuss. You can’t get like this every time we slaughter an animal, Nils, for we have to *eat*.”

“I know.”

“Very well then.” He crouched down in the grass in front of his son and pulled out the amulet that hung around the boy’s neck. “Here, just look at this.”

Obediently, Nils took the amulet in his hands and looked at it with an almost reverential smile. “Odin.”

Candamir nodded and put his hands on his son’s shoulders. “We are his chosen people, you in particular, for you were the first one born in this land, you know.”

He nodded.

“For this reason he is your patron god, and he watches over you every day, every hour. You can count your blessings that you have the wisest and greatest of the gods as your protector. Don’t you think it’s the least you can do to part with this dumb beast without tears, in his honor?”

“Of course. But…”

“No, Nils, there is no but. Do it, or go back home with your mother and Austin.”

“I want to stay!” It was the first time he was allowed to take part in a temple ceremony. Roric, who was nearly two years older than he was and whose father had taken him to the temple since he was a small child, had already told him so much about it. Nils was excited and full of anticipation.

“All right then,” Candamir said. “Then you know how you have to behave. I don’t want to hear any whining or crying when the animals are slaughtered. Don’t embarrass me, or you’ll cry a lot more when we get home. Is that clear?”

Nils nodded.

Candamir smiled and nudged him gently on the shoulder with his fist. "Then run and get your friends."

The little boy discreetly patted the bull on its knee and raced off.

The men started to drink as soon as they arrived on the island. While they chopped wood, lit the large fires on both sides of the sacrificial stone, and made all the other preparations, beer and mead flowed freely. Almost all the Catanians of both sexes had come to the temple festival. Only one or two slave girls in each household had stayed behind with the smaller children. Naturally, there wasn't nearly enough room for all these people in the temple, large though it was, and so they had reserved places inside for the freemen. Only Austin and those two dozen of his followers who dared to openly confess their new faith stayed away from the ceremonies.

Candamir knew that Siglind detested these festivals as much as Austin did, but nevertheless he asked her, "Won't you just come this one time? For Inga? It is her first ceremony, and surely she is nervous. And isn't she your friend?"

Siglind frowned, and then she shook her head with a little laugh. "Oh, she hasn't been that for a long time. I never cease to be amazed at how blind you pretend to be."

While Inga and Siglind had once been close, like so many other things, that too had changed. Siglind had no great need for female confidants, as she had Candamir to share her life and thoughts, and for every thought he refused to understand, she had Austin. The only women she called friends were her sister-in-law Asta and her slave woman Freydis, both of whom had converted to the new faith.

"No, believe me; it's much better for me to go home."

He shrugged in resignation. "As you wish."

"Do you think it would do any good if I reminded you to drink moderately?"

He grinned. "No."

He wrapped her in his arms, put his big hands on her backside without any embarrassment, and then, regretfully, let her go.

The light was dim in the windowless temple. The two fires had already burned low, and the circle of oil lamps around the spring gave off as much smoke as light.

The men sat close together on the ground and talked. The quiet that had been observed during the vigil had been broken, but as Osmund and Thorbjörn brought in the first sacrificial animal, the murmuring subsided.

Candamir's young bull obviously had a sense of foreboding, for it kept turning its head nervously and rolling its eyes as it looked around, but Inga had calmed the animals with a potion, as Brigitta had taught her. The two men led the bull up the slight incline to the sacrificial stone. Then taking their places to the right and left, they held the rope tight around the animal's neck.

A hush fell over the crowd as Inga entered the temple. She wore a robe unlike anything they had seen before—a wide, blood red cloak with a hood that completely shaded her face. Both were embroidered with magic symbols, runes, and pentagrams. Her feet were bare, and the cloak came down to her ankles. It was closed in front, but the neck was so large that Candamir was not the only one to wonder whether she was wearing anything underneath.

She stood before the bull, her head bowed, and the animal seemed to sense something of her calmness, and suddenly stood completely still. The fear was gone from its eyes. With a sudden, fast motion, Inga pulled a dagger from her sleeve and slit the bull's throat in a skillful, fluid motion. The sturdy beast went down on its knees almost at once, and it took all of Osmund's and Thorbjörn's strength to prevent it from falling over too soon.

Inga bent over and raised the large golden bowl that Hacon had made. Its edge was set with pearls, turquoise, and other valuable stones that could be found in Catan. Softly, the priestess began to sing to Odin as she collected the red, gushing blood. The monotonous melody was the same one Brigitta had always hummed, but Inga's voice was more powerful and gave more weight to the words. When the vessel was nearly filled to the rim, Inga turned around to the crowd.

Osmund and Thorbjörn released the rope. Four slaves stepped silently toward the sacrificial stone in order to finish bleeding, skinning, and preparing the flesh of the dead animal. Among the slaves, it was considered a great honor to be chosen for this task, but it was not without peril. Anyone who made too much noise or interfered in any other way with the ceremony could expect no mercy from his master.

But all eyes rested on Inga, who held the heavy bowl up in her outstretched arms and continued singing. Finally, Inga set the bowl down on a three-legged stool, raised her hands, and threw back the hood. Here and there, people could be heard gasping. Inga wore her splendid, blond hair loose, held back only by an ornately engraved copper headband.

"Goodness, Hacon," Candamir muttered. "You have outdone yourself again."

But it wasn't the hairpiece that took their breath away, it was her face. Her forehead and cheeks were adorned with small, red runes. These symbols made her face so completely unrecognizable that it seemed as if they were seeing her for the first time, a majestic and frightening vision.

She dipped a little switch into the bowl of blood, touching the forehead of Odin's statue in front of the sacrificial stone. "Hail to thee, Father of the Gods, inventor and creator of all things, who has given to us the crown of your creation!"

"Hail to thee, Odin," the assembly murmured.

Blood ran from the god's forehead into his eye, over a cheek, and finally dripped off his chin.

Inga turned toward the figure flanking Odin on the right. "Hail to thee, bold and mighty one, who protects the gods and their homeland from all their foes!"

"Hail to thee, Thor."

"Hail to thee, giver of life, who bestows the blessing of fertility on the earth, man, and beast."

"Hail to thee, Freyr..."

One after the other, she praised the gods, sprinkling them with blood, just as Brigitta had done before. For since arriving on Catan, the old woman had slowly and carefully guided the people back to the half-forgotten rites of their ancestors, teaching them that men could strengthen the power of the gods with sacrificial blood. Many, at first, had been shocked by this ceremony, but over time they grew accustomed to it, so no one recoiled now when Inga dipped her switch in the bowl again and sprinkled the believers with blood. Their heads lowered reverently, they made room for her to move farther back into the crowd, sprinkling as many as possible with the fortifying blood. When the bowl was half empty, she handed it to the man sitting in front of her.

"Sanctify the temple with the blood of the sacrifice, Candamir."

Candamir rose and took the bowl from her. For a moment he stared into her painted face, feeling an almost uncontrollable urge to tear the strange robe from the priestess, throw her to the ground, and rape her. He was troubled not just by the force of this desire, but the nature of it. All the images that suddenly shot through his head were revolting. With a shake of his head, he freed himself from this spell and looked Inga in the eye. Her pupils looked unnaturally dilated, her gaze distant, as though she weren't looking at him or the temple, but at something else altogether.

"What are you waiting for?" she asked sharply.

He blinked, turned away, and carried the sacrificial bowl over to the wall of the temple where he placed it on the ground before immersing both hands into it. He wiped his palms all over the wall, covering it with a new, bright layer of blood, thankful he was already quite drunk, for he still didn't care very much for this honor. And when he suddenly discovered his son in front of him, smiling at him conspiratorially before dipping his own little hands in the blood and zealously adorning the lower part of the wall, Candamir had the overwhelming sensation that what they were doing here might be dangerous, even a portent of doom.

With each animal slaughtered, with each cup the men drank, the mood intensified. Without pause, the slaves roasted and cooked the meat, distributing it to the people in the temple, who fell upon the food with great gusto and with high spirits as at every other festival, but with every sacrifice the tension in the temple seemed to increase. Not even the odor of the roasted meat could dispel the smell of blood, and several of the men worked themselves into a strange frenzy, drinking the blood before they spread it on the walls.

By the time they finished eating the fifth of the nine sacrificial animals, night had fallen. The doors in the gable walls of the great hall were pushed open to let the smoke out and allow the cool evening air in. Many of the Catanians seized the opportunity to get a little fresh air, relieve themselves, or attend to other urgent needs.

Candamir saw his foster brother disappear into the forest with the priestess and was not surprised to see Osmund in such a hurry. For a moment he envied him so much that he became angry, but then he slumped down in the grass, held his forehead in his hands, and mumbled, "Mighty Tyr, just what is wrong with me?"

"It's bloodlust," he heard a familiar voice say from out of the darkness. "Don't worry, it will pass."

Candamir jerked his head up. "Austin…what are you doing here?"

The monk left the shadow of the oak tree where he had been hiding and sat down next to Candamir. The waning moon was only half full, but it gave enough light so that the two men could see one another.

Austin held a sleeping child in his arms. It was Nils. "I thought I would take him home."

"That's very good of you. But what is it that brought you here in the first place? You've always avoided the temple feasts and won't even come to the island when they are celebrated."

Austin nodded. "I wanted to see what Inga would do. How she might proceed differently from Brigitta. Every new generation has its own character. I just wanted to have a look at her."

Candamir supposed it was always important to know one's opponent, and that was true not just on the battlefield. "And?" Candamir asked. "What is your opinion?"

"I suspect it's the same as yours. I took the liberty of watching you inside there, and you didn't look very happy."

Candamir brushed off this assertion with an impatient gesture. "I'm in a bad mood because I have had to stay away from my wife for four weeks and couldn't take another woman, thanks to the foolish concessions to your god that you and she extorted from me. It's no wonder a man would have weird and gloomy thoughts."

Austin nodded, even though he didn't believe that this was the real reason for Candamir's restless state of mind. "Come along home," he suggested.

Candamir grumbled. "What would I do there? I'm far from drunk enough to go home yet, but you should clear out of here before someone recognizes you. That would only cause trouble."

"Yes, absolutely," Austin said, but he didn't stir. "Why do you wish to stay here when your heart tells you that what they do here isn't right?"

"But it is right," Candamir said heatedly, though under his breath. "It is old and venerable."

"In your eyes that never was justification for anything."

"Your ancestors did it as well!"

"But we freed ourselves from it, and you want to do that too."

"Oh, don't start in with that again. I'm staying here, even if only to prove to myself that I can stand it." Shocked at this rash, humiliating confession, he clapped his hand in front of his mouth. When he finally lowered his hand again, he grumbled in disgust, "What nonsense I am speaking. Go, Austin. You always draw things from me that I don't want to say. You had best go before you fall victim to my gloomy mood."

"Very well then." The Saxon rose, sighing, but he still couldn't bring himself to leave Candamir there in that dreadful place. As he hesitated, Nils stirred in his arms, swallowing with a choking sound. "Father," he murmured sleepily.

"Here I am, my boy," Candamir replied, jumping up and taking the child from Austin.

"I had a horrible dream."

"No wonder, Lord knows," Austin murmured to himself.

"Hush," Candamir said, pressing the small, warm body carefully to him. "Now you're awake, and the dream is gone."

"No, it's still here, I know it. If I close my eyes, it will come back."

"Unfortunately, it's often that way with bad dreams," his father had to admit.

"But I didn't cry when they slaughtered our bull," Nils said, his voice clearer now. He was struggling to stay awake.

"No, you were magnificent. Very brave."

"Are we going home now, Father?" He was trying to sound very matter-of-fact and grown up, but the anxiousness in his voice was unmistakable.

Candamir quickly exchanged glances with Austin. Then he nodded. "Fine then, let's go home."

# Hay Moon, Year Seven

"Was it something like this you had in mind?"

Candamir straightened up from his work and lowered the heavy plane. His brother stood in the doorway of the workshop and held both hands out to him.

Curiously, Candamir stepped closer, and when his eyes had adjusted to the light, he recognized what Hacon had brought him—an iron blade longer than his arm, the upper edge smooth and the underside armed with small, dangerous teeth.

Candamir took it in both hands, almost reverently. "Oh, Hacon, that's *perfect*!" His eyes were sparkling.

His brother smiled contentedly. "Shall we try it?"

"Absolutely!"

As eagerly as two young boys, the brothers went over to Candamir's workbench. They often had the opportunity to work together since so many articles of daily use were made of wood *and* iron: tools, plows, arrows and spears for hunting, barrels and carts, and many other things. Candamir had told Hacon about the saw two weeks before. He had once seen a carpenter using one in a village on the Elbe River, and this strange tool had fascinated him. Berse didn't think much of saws, though. "For as far back as anyone can remember, we have built our houses, furniture, and ships out of wood, and we have always been able to get by just fine without any newfangled tool," he had grumbled at the suggestion.

Moreover, something like what Candamir was describing was probably unsuitable for working with fresh wood, anyway.

But this wasn't the first time that Candamir had ignored Berse's objections when it came to their craft, and some of his experiments had been successful. For instance, he used fewer and fewer of the young, green conifers than was customary when making furniture, but let the oak and beech wood cure for a few years before making chests, tables, and carts from it. And he noticed that these pieces of furniture never warped, as the others often did. Candamir's tables didn't wobble; his chests and doors could be opened and closed without sticking, even in damp weather. But this hard, cured wood required completely different tools, and so Candamir dreamed of having a saw.

Without saying a word, Hacon forged a saw blade according to Candamir's description, and since Candamir had some time ago crafted the wood frame for it, all they needed to do now was insert the blade. They forced the blade into the split ends of the frame, which formed a rectangle, open at the bottom. Then they fastened the top and bottom of the blade with the little iron pins that Hacon had brought along, sticking them into the previously bored holes. Eager to try it out, they headed to the small yard behind the shop and attempted to cut four cartwheels from a thick tree stump like slices of sausage with a knife.

Siglind was sitting on a side bench with Asta and Gunda, facing the garden. The children were romping about between the fruit trees and berry bushes that were already heavy with fruit. Nils was on his best behavior today, generously allowing Ole to take his toy ship for a sail over an ocean invisible to grown-ups. The three women and at least the older children should have been out in the meadow making hay, but since it was so dreadfully hot that day, they decided to spend their time making cherry preserves and sitting in the shade instead, leaving the mowing of the fields in this scorching heat to the slaves.

Siglind and Gunda each had a large bowl of cherries in their laps and a small knife in their hands with which they skillfully removed the pits from the fruit before tossing it into the cauldron at their feet. Asta was the only one who did nothing but sit, her hands folded on her big belly.

"Oh, how marvelous it is to loaf," she remarked cheerfully. "Austin must be wrong. Something as wonderful as this *cannot* be a sin."

The two others laughed.

Solvig, the new nurse, came out of the house. "Heide says you must bring the cherries soon, Mistress, or she won't be finished with them before she has to cook supper."

"Very well. Then take the cauldron inside—it is almost full, anyway. We'll do the rest tomorrow."

Happily, Siglind and Gunda stopped working and started nibbling on the cherries while the slave carried the big pot back into the house.

"What's wrong with her?" Asta asked after the young girl had left. "She looks as though she has been crying."

Siglind raised her hands, baffled. "I just don't know. She's a mystery to me in every way. No one knows who the father of her son is. She's deathly afraid of Candamir, so I assume someone has violated her."

"But surely not Sigurd," Asta said. "After all, he only has eyes for his Britta."

The shipwright's son had married Siward's widow just two weeks after the old grouch had died, and because of their indecent haste it was generally assumed that Sigurd and Britta had been lovers long before she was widowed.

Siglind shrugged. "That doesn't necessarily mean anything. But I don't think it was Sigurd. And what does it matter? The child is born, and Solvig should have gotten over her fright. She must have noticed by now that she has nothing to fear from Candamir. Nevertheless, she's unhappy. But she doesn't take it out on the children, and she is a good nurse."

Gunda, who had lived among these people as a slave for many years, still saw things from a different perspective than her sisters-in-law. "It may be something completely different," she offered. "Maybe she loves one of Sigurd's or Berse's slaves and can't stand being separated from him."

"Then she ought to open her mouth and say so," Siglind replied impatiently. "Surely a solution could be found for something like that."

"Opening your mouth and saying something is not always as simple as you think," Gunda replied, but before Siglind could ask her to explain, a very unusual sound interrupted their exchange.

"Oh God, what is that?" Gunda cried out fearfully.

"A saw," Austin replied, as he came walking up from the river holding a large wooden tub, "and I've told you a hundred times you should not take the Lord's name in vain."

"Forgive me, Austin," Gunda murmured. She knew very well that the monk didn't like her, and she was still a bit afraid of him.

"A what?" Siglind asked.

"A saw. You cut up wood with it, and occasionally your fingers and hands and feet, or whatever gets in its way. The next thing you hear will be a cry of pain."

The women laughed, unconcerned.

With a disgusted grimace, Asta pointed to the contents of his tub. "What do you have there?"

"Boiled lambskins," Austin explained in delight, looking at the milky concoction and the spongy skin floating in it. "You can make the very best parchment from it, you know. Unfortunately, it's rare for anyone to slaughter a lamb here."

Naturally, most people preferred to let their lambs grow up and produce offspring, but just two weeks before, at the midsummer festival, some of the more successful breeders had donated a lamb, nevertheless, and Austin had declared he would make a bid for the skins that they couldn't refuse.

"And what will you do with this especially fine parchment?" Siglind wanted to know.

Before the Saxon could reply, the anticipated shout came from behind the carpentry shop, and the sounds of the blade stopped. Startled, Siglind and Gunda jumped up, and only Asta remained seated. In her condition you just didn't jump up anymore, no matter what had happened.

After a few moments, Candamir appeared from behind his workshop. "Siglind, could you…oh, Austin. It's good you're here."

"Did Hacon hurt himself?" Gunda asked anxiously, walking over to him.

As usual, Candamir acted as if he hadn't heard her, took the tub from Austin's hands, set it down quickly on the ground, and tugged on the monk's sleeve to follow. For once, Gunda overcame her shyness of Candamir and followed too.

Hacon was sitting on a pile of wooden beams, tightly holding his right forearm with his left hand and making a loose fist with his right. A steady flow of blood was trickling from his fist onto the ground strewn with wood shavings, his brow covered with sweat.

Austin sat down alongside him. "Let me have a look."

Hesitantly, the young smith held out his right hand, but turned his face away.

"I'm afraid he's really been hurt," Candamir said nervously.

Carefully, Austin opened the fist and inspected the injury. There was a gaping wound straight across the palm of his large, calloused hand.

"Oh, Hacon!" Gunda cried out, putting her hands to her cheeks.

Candamir glanced at her disdainfully.

"Please get me some warm water and clean linen, Gunda," Austin asked. "And don't worry. It will be all right."

Hacon swallowed. Underneath his short beard, you could see his Adam's apple twitching up and down. He waited until his wife was out of earshot before asking, "Do you really believe that?"

Austin wasn't sure yet. If Hacon had severed a tendon, then this hand would never again swing a hammer. "Move your fingers," he said.

Hacon obeyed, then let out a groan and instinctively closed his injured hand into a fist again. But Austin had seen that all four fingers and thumb had moved.

He patted him on the shoulder. "Yes, I think you were lucky. It will heal."

"If it doesn't become gangrenous," Hacon added gloomily.

"Right."

"And how long will it take?"

"A long time," Austin predicted. "And you will be patient and look after your hand until I tell you that you can use it again, is that clear?"

Hacon nodded meekly.

The monk placed his hands on his thighs and stood up. "I'll get you a cup of mead."

Hacon knew what that meant and turned his face away with a shudder. "Are you going to sew up the wound?"

"I must."

"It's not as bad as you think," Candamir consoled him, speaking from experience.

His brother glanced at him suspiciously. "But actually a little worse, huh?"

Candamir chuckled and patted him on the shoulder. "You heard him, it will heal. That's the only thing that counts."

Still, he didn't want to watch. So before Austin began his gruesome work, Candamir stole away on his trusty Buri with Ole and Nils seated in front. The three of them rode bareback through the north gate of the enclosure and out onto the meadow to see how the haying was progressing. Everywhere on the meadows, men, women, and children were busy working. They mowed the tall grass with long-handled scythes, and those coming behind spread it out to dry. To protect themselves from the sun, they had wrapped scarves around their heads, partially covering their mouths and noses from the prodigious dust.

Candamir stopped by one of his meadows and reined in his horse. "How are things going, Sven? Are you making good progress?"

The young slave straightened up and pushed his scarf down below his chin before answering. "Yes, Master. We are making good progress. I have never held such a good scythe in my hands."

Candamir smiled proudly. "My brother made it."

The servant nodded appreciatively. "I know. The women can stay home tomorrow again, if you ask me. The most we need are a few boys to turn the hay."

Candamir nodded and tapped his son on the shoulder. "Tomorrow morning you'll go out with Sven and Nori, Son."

Nils grimaced furtively, but said, "Yes, of course, Father."

"Don't forget to bring the horses in from the pasture tonight," Candamir said as he left.

Nori and Sven barely suppressed a grin. Hardly a day passed that their master did not remind them to do that.

When Candamir returned with the two boys, the shadows in the garden were already lengthening, and in the northwest dark clouds towered up. He left Ole and Nils with their little boat and entered the house.

"Your brother went home on his own two feet," Siglind said, putting a bowl of buttermilk down in front of Candamir after he had taken his place on the high seat.

"The mead really went to his head," she continued. "The whole time Austin was sewing, Hacon kept telling him dirty jokes. I think that no wound has ever been sewed up as fast."

Candamir grinned, but then he added uneasily, "This saw is a wonderful thing, Siglind. It doesn't matter what Berse thinks—it will make many things possible that we couldn't do up until now. But I wish I had never said a word about it to Hacon. If he runs a fever…"

Siglind sat down and took his hand. "Come now. Don't be disheartened. He's healthy and strong. Everything will turn out fine, you'll see."

He nodded, but didn't say what they both knew—even healthy, strong, young men could get gangrene and die. He ran his hand restlessly over his throat and neck and tried to shake off his gloomy thoughts. "I think a storm is coming."

Siglind clicked her tongue. "Now, of all times, in the midst of the haying. But you're probably right. It has been dreadfully oppressive all day. The morning milk was even sour by noon."

"Don't worry about the hay. It will dry out again. Anyway, I'm sending Nils out tomorrow with the slaves."

"Don't you think he is still too young for such hard work?"

"No, I don't think so. It really isn't hard work, and it's time he learned that bread doesn't grow on trees. He's spending far too much time with Austin."

But before Candamir could draw Siglind into a quarrel, the slaves returned from the fields and Heide called the children in for the meal. Little Ole sat with them at the table. It didn't bother him to have wound up at their house—there was so much coming and going between Candamir's and Hacon's family that the boy felt at home there. Yet as the storm broke, he became anxious and started to cry for his mother.

Candamir stood up with a sigh, picked his nephew up from the bench, and took him under his arm like a bundle of clothing. "Come here, lad. Stop whimpering. I'll take you home," he said, looking at his wife and rolling his eyes. "I'll be right back."

She smiled at him. "You have a soft heart."

"Don't believe it," he grumbled, stepping out into the pouring rain with the squirming little bundle under his arm.

It was a typical Catan storm: the booming thunder and flashing lightning were enough to make your knees shake. Ole began to cry, and Candamir hurried on.

It was only a short distance—past Austin's cottage and Harald's large smithy and house, and then through his garden, and finally into Hacon's yard. Candamir swung open the door to the house. Gunda was sitting alone by the table with her little daughter in her lap, eating halfheartedly. Startled, she looked up when she heard the door. The fire was already banked, and it was getting dark in the house. Candamir put Ole down on his feet and, breaking with habit, spoke directly to Gunda. "Where is Hacon?"

"I don't know." Her voice was thin and dispirited. "He woke up about an hour ago and left the house. Oh, Candamir."

He turned his eyes away from her and somewhat roughly pushed the little boy into the room. "There, go to your mother, Ole." And in Gunda's general direction he added, "I'll go and look for him."

"Thank you, Candamir."

"I'm not doing it for you," he replied tersely, the door slamming behind him.

He had no trouble guessing where his brother had gone. If he had such a dangerous injury to his hand, he would have gone to his workshop too, to take pleasure in the tools he might never use again and to implore the gods for help. A dim light coming from the window of the small smithy told him he had been right about Hacon's location.

Candamir was searching for the right, lighthearted greeting as he pushed open the door to the tidy little workshop. But the vision before him took the words right out of his mouth.

Hacon knelt on the floor, and towering over him was a large, dark figure that Candamir immediately recognized from behind. *This can't be,* he thought. *He can't have come through the hedge unnoticed.*

With one of his heavy boots, Olaf was standing on Hacon's right hand, which Austin had bandaged so carefully, and was now shifting his weight and bearing down even harder on it. Hacon covered his eyes with his free left arm.

"Tell me, Hacon," the tall figure was saying in a voice that was as rough and deep as ever, but ingratiating, almost polite. "When and where can I find your brother alone? I'm sure you know. Come on, lad, tell me…"

Candamir stood on the doorstep paralyzed, and the nameless fear that had hung over him ever since the last time they met seized him once more. Hacon finally lowered his left arm and looked up at Olaf. His face and even his lips were almost white, and he was sweating. Blood from the wound that had opened up again ran out from under Olaf's boot. "I have no idea, Olaf," Hacon replied deliberately. "I have converted to the Saxon's religion and therefore had a falling-out with Candamir. We have become completely estranged, and I don't know anything about his daily routine."

Olaf frowned. "Perhaps it will jog your memory a little if I put your injured hand in the forge? I see you still have a nice fire…"

There was an audible scraping sound as Candamir pulled his sword from its sheath. It was double-edged and light, about one pace long, with a short, one-handed hilt, perfectly balanced and lethally sharp. No sooner was it out than Olaf let Hacon go, drew his own weapon, and whirled around.

"You were looking for me, Olaf? Here I am." Candamir stood in the doorway, his feet slightly apart, holding his precious weapon in his right hand.

Olaf's sword was of equal quality. During one of his raids, he had taken it from Siward, who had lamented its loss until his death. With a contented smile, Olaf scrutinized his opponent. "Candamir…one of the gods must truly be with me today."

"I don't think so." Candamir stepped back toward the door and with his left hand beckoned Olaf to follow him.

Although the sun had not yet set, it was dark. The rain fell heavily, like a sheet of glass, and from time to time the darkness was illuminated by bolts of dazzling lightning. Candamir stopped ten paces from the smithy, raised the sword over his shoulder, and charged at his enemy with a bloodcurdling battle cry.

At the last moment Olaf stepped back a pace and parried, the blades crossing with a loud clashing sound. Olaf dodged to the side and thrust at him from below, but Candamir fended off the blow with a downward slash of his sword.

Hacon stood in the door of his smithy, holding his left hand protectively around his right and following each of their moves fearfully. The tempo of attack and counterattack was dizzying. For the observer of this life-and-death struggle, the pace seemed much too fast for either of the opponents to master and control.

Olaf was the more experienced fighter, and more prudent than Candamir, it seemed, yet Hacon also could see that his brother was faster, and even stronger. In the bursts of lightning, the opponents seemed to vanish among his fruit trees, moving in the direction of the hedge. Blow followed blow in even faster tempo, bright clangs ringing out when the blades clashed, and dull sounds when one of them struck a tree.

After a few moments Candamir was wet to the bone, and the crashes of thunder were so deafening that he instinctively ducked. He was retreating, and Olaf was setting the pace now with rhythmic blows, forcing him further and further back toward the hedge. A tickling at the back of his neck warned Candamir that he had little room to maneuver, and he took a huge risk by ducking under Olaf's next blow, whirling around, and reaching out to attack his opponent from the side.

He almost managed to land a blow, and it was only by chance that Olaf had shifted his weight to his left foot and could pull back in time. He leapt backward and pulled out his knife.

"Watch out, Candamir!" Hacon shouted, and at the next moment he noticed a shadow to his left. Before he could turn around he felt a cold blade at his throat, and a voice whispered in his ear. "Don't worry about your brother. You have other things to worry about."

"Lars…" Hacon hadn't seen Olaf's son for more than six years. He didn't see him now, either, for it was too dark, but he recognized his voice.

"Put your hands on your back, Hacon," Lars ordered him in a muted voice.

"Why bother? I am unarmed, as you can see, and if you want to kill me, I won't be able to stop you." He thought of Gunda, of Ole, and of his little daughter, and it grieved him to leave them. He knew Gunda would be inconsolable—she was so dependent on him and his protection—but he was careful not to let his despair show in his voice. "Don't keep me waiting, Lars. For old time's sake…"

Lars laughed softly in his ear. "I don't want to kill you. You have a very good chance of coming out of this alive if you put your hands behind you."

There was a new flash of lightning, and Hacon could see that Candamir was being hard pressed by his opponent. He stood with his back to the hedge, and Olaf strode toward him with both weapons drawn.

"I won't do that," Hacon replied.

"Then I'll just have to help you out," said another voice that Hacon did not recognize at first. He turned his head and could barely make out a form on his other side.

"Gunnar?"

Olaf's third son nodded silently, grabbing Hacon's right hand and yanking it back. Hacon bit his tongue, and his knees gave way.

With a desperate tug, Candamir freed himself from the hedge's thorny embrace, and Olaf's sword severed the branches where Candamir's chest had just been.

"You had better give up," said Olaf. He was out of breath.

"Why?" Candamir panted. "What good would that do me?"

"I don't want to kill you."

*No,* Candamir thought, *I know that.* He was not certain which was the more dangerous opponent—Olaf, or his own fear that seemed to dull his senses and slow his reactions. His right hand was sweating so much that he was in constant danger of losing his grip on the weapon. *Pull yourself together,* he scolded himself furiously, struggling to remain as calm and cool as he had been in his youth when confronted with an enemy trying to kill him. He wouldn't allow Olaf to take him alive, so how was this different from before? Was it possible that seven years without fighting had made him so soft that he could no longer get through something like this?

That thought sharpened his resolve, making him more prudent. He rolled his shoulders and relaxed his grip on the sword, grabbing it hard at just the right moment to parry Olaf's next thrust and striking back at his adversary with all his strength. The situation suddenly changed—now Olaf was retreating. Candamir had drawn his knife as well, no longer paying any heed to the thunder and rain. Narrowing his eyes, he saw well enough, even after the dazzling lightning flashes, to recognize his opponent's blade. Blow by blow he pressed Olaf back in the direction of the smithy and kept intensifying his pace. But then he got caught in a bramble, almost lost his balance, and his sword fell out of his hand.

With a triumphant smile, Olaf stepped up to him and raised his sword just as a bolt of lightning hit the young walnut tree on his left, splitting the trunk in two. At the same instant came the crash of the thunder, paralyzing the combatants as well as the onlookers. At once the split trunk burst into flame. Candamir and Olaf broke eye contact and stepped back, but they were not quick enough. The split, burning crown of the tree tipped in their direction and fell right on top of the two combatants.

Hacon, Lars, and Gunnar all shouted with fright, rushing toward them. Now the pouring rain worked to their advantage, as it doused the flames and left the tree smoldering. It nevertheless took a long while before they succeeded in pulling off the branches. What finally met them was a horrible sight that haunted Hacon's dreams forever after: Candamir and Olaf frozen in a firm embrace, like a pair of dead lovers. Olaf had come to rest on top, and his clothes were burning. He couldn't feel it, though, because Candamir's knife was protruding from his back.

"O mighty Thor," Lars murmured hoarsely.

Candamir's tunic had been scorched on the arm and shoulder, and a bloody cut ran across his forehead. Hacon bent over him to see if his brother was dead or alive, but at that moment a hard object struck him on the back of the head, and he never saw the next flash of lightning.

Hacon was awakened by a wonderfully gentle, rocking motion. He opened his eyes and saw above him a starry sky of stunning beauty. *The storm has passed,* he thought. *Soon we'll arrive at our new homeland.*

Then a pain in his right hand brought him back to the present, and he sat bolt upright. "Candamir?"

"He's unconscious," Lars's voice said from out of the darkness.

Hacon turned his head. Lars was standing at the helm and gave Hacon only a brief, blank look before turning his eyes forward again. The *Sea Dragon*, Hacon realized. As he got up on his knees and looked over the railing, he saw something unexpected—the ocean. In the dark night, it sparkled with the cold reflected light of the stars, and here and there little crests shimmered on the waves. For a moment, Hacon felt jubilant. Unlike his brother, he had only once in his life set out on an ocean voyage—one that had been very difficult indeed—but the love of the sea was in his blood, just as it was in Candamir's.

Yet Hacon's joy didn't last long. He looked around the deck and discovered his brother's motionless form nearby on the port side of the ship. Kneeling beside his brother, he could tell that Candamir was breathing, but deeply unconscious. Someone had taken off his upper garment, crumpled it together to make an untidy pillow, and placed it under his head. It was too dark to see where and how severely he was wounded.

"What's wrong with him?" Hacon asked.

"No idea," Lars replied. "I think he was hit on the head when the tree fell on them or something like that. We'll just have to wait and see."

"And your father?"

"My father is dead." It was impossible to guess how Lars felt when he said that. It sounded matter-of-fact.

"Nevertheless, you're not going to kill us?"

"Not right away. The purpose of our trip was to come and get you."

Hacon was flabbergasted. "What in the world do you want from us?"

"We only want *you*. We need a smith, Hacon. We wanted your brother only to guarantee your loyal service."

Hacon nodded. His mouth was dry, but his voice sounded very calm as he answered, "Well, I'll do whatever you want, but it will take a while before I can begin."

"Yes, I saw your hand. That doesn't matter, we have time. Those who live in the desert learn patience. You will see."

At sunrise Hacon counted a crew of ten: Olaf's sons Lars, Gunnar, and Leif, and seven former slaves who now wore their hair long and carried weapons on their belts. Hacon knew them from before, but they would not look at him now, and those who did regarded him with hostility and malice. Before he could speak to any of them, Gunnar blindfolded him.

"Don't take the blindfold off," he warned him. "It will be better for you if you don't know exactly where we're taking you, do you understand?"

Hacon nodded.

It was hard for him to estimate how much time passed, since he couldn't see anything. But he guessed it was two or three hours after daybreak when they landed. A man led him off the ship and a short distance over rocky ground before forcing him to his knees. He waited, motionless, listening, and after a while he heard the heavy groaning of wood upon wood. Apparently the ship was being rolled ashore with the use of tree trunks and then probably hidden behind some rocks. So that was why those who had sailed down the west coast had never seen a trace of Olaf's ship.

Hacon heard a groan and groped about with his hands. "Candamir?"

"Where am I?" his brother asked wearily.

Hacon touched something that felt like an arm, and whispered urgently, "Lie still and keep your eyes closed, Brother."

"Hacon…what happened to Olaf? Where is he? What did he…"

"Hush, do as I say. Olaf is dead, but Lars and his brothers have taken us as captives."

He received no answer, but Hacon heard how Candamir's breathing was becoming faster and more labored.

"What's the matter with you, Candamir?"

"I…have no idea. Olaf is dead?"

"He is."

"Did I kill him?"

"In a way. You have every reason to be proud."

"I…I feel dizzy."

"Just be very still. It will pass, you'll see." Hacon got no answer and assumed his brother had lost consciousness again. Before long the ship's crew returned, and Hacon could hear how they were gasping with exhaustion.

Suddenly someone ripped the blindfold from his eyes, taking a tuft of hair along with it, or at least that was how it felt. Hacon looked around. As he had expected, they were in a narrow, rocky bay.

"Get up on your feet," Lars ordered. Then he kicked Candamir as hard as he could in the ribs. "That goes for you too. Let's go—we have a long walk ahead of us."

"Where are we going?" Candamir asked, confused and struggling to sit up.

"You'll see that soon enough. Let's go now."

Lars hoisted Candamir to his feet, and Gunnar tied his hands together in front of him.

"I want your hand to heal as fast as possible, so I won't tie you up," Lars told Hacon. "But if you try to run away, or attack one of my men, or cause us any other kind of trouble, I'll kill Candamir."

Lars and his brothers led them up a steep, rocky hill. When they got to the top, they looked down into a seemingly endless, black and brown wasteland of hills and crevices, and in the middle of it stood the fiery mountain. On this day it was dormant, but its summit was shrouded in a thin veil of smoke or steam. Hacon and Candamir stared toward the east, not saying a word. The dreary wilderness extended out to the horizon.

"There you are," Lars said softly behind them. "Welcome to the wasteland."

They walked down the hill through a kind of gully that looked like a dry streambed running between two low-lying, cone-shaped hills. After twenty paces they were cut off from the sea breeze, and the cool morning air suddenly turned oppressive. The peculiar streambed led around a little hill on the right, where they unexpectedly came upon a dozen horses. They were smaller and sturdier than the horses in the grassland that Candamir had tamed and bred. Their coats were shaggy and lighter in color, and their manes were short. Iron rings had been driven into the rocky soil, and the horses were tethered to them by reins in groups of two or three.

Lars and his men untied them and gave them some water from leather skins they had brought along from the boat. The animals drank thirstily, but each one received only a few swallows before the men closed the water skins and mounted the horses.

Lars nodded at Hacon. "Since my father didn't come back, we have an extra horse, and you can ride it."

Candamir stared in fascination at the animals' hooves, which were covered in thick layers of leather. "Shoes," he murmured. "It's just as Osmund suspected."

"Let my brother ride," Hacon asked. "There's nothing wrong with me, but he can scarcely stand up."

Lars slowly stepped up to him. He looked very much like his father, as did Jared. He was as tall, and his eyes were as bright—and his gaze could be just as penetrating. "Now listen here, Hacon. We have somewhat different customs here. If I tell you to do something, it's not a suggestion and it's not a request, but an order. You will ride and Candamir will walk. Is that clear?"

Hacon did not reply at once, loath to give in so easily. But a glance from his brother and a furtive gesture of his fettered hands let him know that he should obey. Only then did Hacon nod at Lars and swing himself onto the back of the little horse.

The column set out slowly in a southeasterly direction. Lars rode at the head of the column, holding Candamir on a rope. Hacon came next, flanked by Gunnar and Leif. The other men followed two by two. After about a hundred paces they had to leave the flat gully, and Candamir's feet encountered for the first time the true nature of this soil—uneven, sharp-edged, and treacherous, pockmarked with ankle-deep craters. After a good half hour, he fell for the first time, skinning both knees and shins hard enough to feel blood flowing down his legs. After another hour, one of the characteristic sharp rocks that covered the ground penetrated his left sole, and after that he limped.

"How far is it?" Hacon asked.

"We'll be there by sunset," Gunnar replied.

*O mighty Tyr,* Candamir thought.

Before the morning was half over, it was hot as a furnace in the wasteland. The air was shimmering above the ground, which seemed to soak up the rays of the sun like a sponge and then reflect the heat back. To Candamir the world looked strange and unreal. His head was hammering dully, he was dizzy, and everything swam before his eyes. He was also terribly thirsty, but what worried him most were his feet. They hurt, and with each step he felt moisture in his shoes that could only be his own blood. He narrowed his eyes and tried to look down at his feet, but he couldn't see them clearly, nor could he see the ground, and thus he stumbled at every step.

Around noon, Lars ordered a short halt. They had come around a hill and were now at the foot of its north slope, but because the sun stood high in the sky there was no shade. In this desert there was no shade anywhere, Gunnar later told Hacon, and therefore even the gods were afraid of this place.

"Every man and every horse will get half a cup of water," Lars told them, "that is, everyone except Candamir."

Hacon looked at his brother. Candamir had sunk to his knees as soon as the column came to a stop, and he was now lying on his side, his arm in front of his face to protect himself from the sun. When Gunnar gave Hacon a half a cup of water, the young smith dismounted and shook his head. "I'll drink when my brother drinks, and not before."

Gunnar turned around questioningly to Lars, who shrugged indifferently. "He'll learn not to refuse his ration a second time. Save his share for Leif, so that he doesn't give out on us again before we arrive home." The men laughed, and sixteen-year-old Leif hung his head in shame.

No one got anything to eat. *Aren't they all hungry?* Hacon wondered, as his stomach had started to grumble some time ago. Lars and his men all looked slim and athletic, but not emaciated. *And why should they be,* he thought bitterly. *They've lived well all these years from the work of our hands.*

When Lars pulled him back to his feet, Candamir had trouble standing. His condition had gotten noticeably worse during the break. He was tormented by thirst, his head was pounding, and everything was wavering before his eyes.

"How far?" he asked.

Lars folded his arms and looked at him, his lips curling in a scornful little smile. "At this snail's pace, five or six hours."

Candamir nodded. He wished he hadn't asked, for he knew he would never make it.

Lars, Hacon, and the other men mounted, and they moved on. Gradually the land changed, and the jagged chain of hills became a broad plain. But the type of ground they were walking on remained the same, and even though they were drawing away from the fiery mountain, it still towered up on their left. Nothing was stirring in this desolate land; nothing even grew to offer the eye and the spirit some relief from the endless, dark brown expanse.

When Candamir fell for the second time that afternoon, he knew it was the end. He wouldn't be able to get up again. The sole of his left shoe had a tear from the toe to the heel, and his foot was so badly cut that he left a bloody print behind at every step. But even worse than his foot was his thirst. Bewildered, Candamir wondered if he had died without noticing it and was journeying to the horrors of the underworld.

Lars pulled on the rope. "Get up on your feet!"

Candamir didn't budge.

"Now come on, let's go."

There was no answer.

"You think you can't go on?" Lars asked. "I'll prove you wrong, you'll see." He opened the big leather pouch he had put down in front of him on the horse's bare back along with the water skin, pulled out a rolled-up whip, and slid to the ground. Candamir recognized at once the soft clinking of the lead weights at the end of the straps.

"Lars...," Gunnar began hesitantly.

But his brother raised a finger and cut him off. "You will be quiet!"

Hacon climbed down from the horse, but before he could utter a word of protest, Lars wheeled and hit him in the chest with the straps. Hacon did not cry out as uncontrollably as he had when Olaf had used the whip on him, but the shock of the sudden pain was still the same, and he could not entirely suppress a cry of outrage. Candamir raised his head like a dog detecting a familiar scent. "Stop," he murmured. "Stop it, Olaf..."

This time the straps landed on his back. "I am not Olaf," Lars said calmly. "Olaf is dead. *You* killed him."

"I would say that Thor killed him," Hacon said, though he did not believe it. "*He* sent the lightning that split the tree that buried your father. And if you want me ever to lift a finger for you, you'll leave my brother alone now."

Lars turned to him, more in control of his temper than his father, but just as terrifying. His eyes were strangely cold and completely devoid of feeling. Hacon found it impossible to imagine that Lars could love a woman, cradle a child, or show any human impulses. Lars was like this bleak land.

"Whether it was by Thor's hand or Candamir's is of no importance," he said matter-of-factly. "Your brother was always the bane of my father's existence. He is responsible for his downfall, his banishment, and his death. And now he will pay for it." He turned his head and pondered for a moment the man lying at his feet. Then he kicked him in the ribs. "You know that, don't you?"

Candamir had closed his eyes tightly, but he nodded.

Lars again looked at the younger of the brothers. "And you will obey me, both of you. If one of you defies me, the other one will pay for it." His father had introduced this principle, as many of his followers were siblings or had come together as couples over the years. In an environment like this, everyone felt the need to be close to another human being, and Olaf quickly learned to use this vulnerability to his advantage. "So, what do you say, Candamir? Will you come along now, or must I first flay the skin off Hacon's back?"

Candamir never would have believed he could find the strength to stand up again. But he did, and lowering his head and looking no one in the eye, he hobbled a few steps over to Lars's horse, as if he were waiting impatiently to get started again.

Barely an hour later, Candamir fell down again, and this time he could not be moved either by kicks and blows or by insults and threats. When Hacon bent over his brother, he thought he was dead. He couldn't see him breathing, but when placed his hand on his chest, he felt a slow heartbeat.

Hacon straightened, shaking his head. "You're not going to get him on his feet so easily this time, Lars."

"I guess we'll just have to see…"

"Ye gods, Lars, be reasonable," Gunnar said. "It's getting late. If we want to arrive before nightfall, we've got to hurry. And you won't get anything out of Candamir if he dies on us now. You ask me, it looks like he's about to do that."

Lars gave in reluctantly. "Go ahead then, load him on Leif's horse. He can walk a quarter of a mile and then one of the others can spell him."

Hacon watched in astonishment at how nimbly Leif and the other men scrambled over this impossible terrain. Apparently this was something you could learn if you had six years to practice. After they had loaded Candamir onto the sturdy, patient horse like a sack of flour, they made much better progress, and when the sun was sinking over the western edge of the wasteland, they finally arrived at their destination.

A steep slope led them down into a deep hollow, more like a hole in the ground than a hollow, actually, Hacon thought. It was some ten fathoms deep and the shape of an irregular circle, perhaps twenty paces in diameter, and in the rock face there was an opening, also nearly round in shape.

Lars made a scornful gesture of welcome. "Don't be shy now, Hacon, ride on through. This is Olaf's castle, probably the only really impenetrable fortress in the world."

He was not exaggerating. The opening in the side of the rock led to a spacious cave that was used as a stable for cattle and horses. The animals, which were for the most part stolen, stood along the rock walls in a thick layer of straw. The straw, too, had clearly been stolen, and it was apparently cleaned and replaced on a regular basis, for the odor here was no worse than in any ordinary cattle barn. The men dismounted and gave the horses to two of Haflad's former slaves who had been keeping watch.

"Where is the *jarl*?" one of them asked.

The word sounded strange to Hacon. He knew it meant a great master or the head of a mighty household, but not even in Elasund had Olaf taken that title for himself. Things were clearly different here.

Lars replied, "He's standing in front of you. My father is dead. We buried him at sea last night with his weapons and finery."

The news brought looks of shock, but no sign of grief.

"Take care of the horses and then come into the hall," Lars commanded. "We have a lot to talk about."

Two of the men seized Candamir, who was still unconscious, and pulled him roughly from the back of the horse, but Hacon came forward and offered to carry him.

"But your hand is injured," the older one objected.

Hacon smiled weakly. "I can manage just the same."

Taking Candamir's hand with his own uninjured one, he pulled his brother onto his shoulder as if he were no heavier than a bundle of hay. The men exchanged surreptitious glances and nodded appreciatively. Lars, too, noticed this effortless show of strength, as he took a torch from a holder in the rock wall and walked farther to the rear. In the flickering light, Hacon could see that the cave was much longer than he had assumed, but after just thirty paces the ground fell steeply—how far, only God knew. Hacon peered over the edge and saw nothing but a bottomless black hole, spanned by a bridge of wooden planks a full pace wide. He crossed it with his brother on his shoulders, and when he looked back, he realized the bridge could be pulled up. Lars was right, this place was indeed impregnable.

Beyond the chasm there was a wide, downward sloping corridor from which, here and there, passageways opened up to other caves. Some lay in the dark, so Hacon wasn't able to make out anything, but in others torches were burning, and he saw strangely round rooms—like huge air bubbles in the rock. In one of these, three women were working at a fireplace. The smoke rose straight up and disappeared. There had to be a vent to the outside, he realized in astonishment, and during the day, there might even be a bit of natural light here.

The passageway in the rock wound its way over uneven ground and finally opened into the largest underground chamber Hacon had ever seen. It was higher and wider than any hall built by the hand of man could be. The part illuminated by the torches was probably thirty paces wide and fifty long. Behind it everything was dark, but the cave still seemed to go on.

"Here," Gunnar said, pointing to the wall on his right where a few blankets were lying on the ground. "Put him down there, Hacon."

Hacon was grateful to put down his burden and carefully laid his unconscious brother on the ground. He tried again to feel for Candamir's heartbeat. It was unchanged. When Hacon stood up again, he saw the wall shimmering with a greenish or reddish color here and there, signs of copper and iron, he knew, and he wondered briefly whether Lars would let him mine the ore here, right in his home.

"You must be thirsty, Hacon. Here, drink this."

Olaf's beautiful Irish slave girl, whom he remembered well, stood before him and held a gold-adorned drinking horn out to him. Hacon took it gratefully and drank. It was water. He had never heard of drinking mere water from a horn, but perhaps these were the simplest drinking vessels to get here, or maybe the water was so precious that these grand cups were appropriate.

"Do you think I could have just a little more? I have to try to give my brother some, and to take care of his wounds."

"I'll bring you as much as you want," she promised with a shy smile. "We have plenty of water."

Gunnar was standing nearby and saw the look of surprise on Hacon's face. Pointing to the dark end of the hall, he said, "Back there is a lake, a natural cistern, you could say. In the wasteland it rains just as much as it does everywhere in Catan, you know. On the surface, the water burns off very fast in the sun, but it finds its way through the porous rock into this cave and flows into a natural basin. It's enormous, and even in the summer it's never dry."

"The water tastes very good," Hacon said.

Gunnar nodded. "We have learned to appreciate it. The first few weeks, before we found this place, were horrible."

"I'm not surprised."

As boys, Gunnar and Hacon had played and fished together in Elasund, getting into all kinds of mischief. They had experienced the voyage to the new homeland, the storms, the landing, and the beginnings of a new life as friends, and now they were enemies.

The Irish girl came back with a bowl of water, and Hacon was relieved that she gave him a pretext to end the faltering conversation. "I must go and look after my brother, Gunnar."

The younger man nodded. "It looks as if he won't last much longer."

"Yes. Do you have any medicinal herbs here?"

Gunnar snorted in amusement. "Not much grows here, you know. All we have is dust and stones, nothing else."

Hacon could not do much for his brother. It was impossible to get him to drink, because he could not swallow. And so Hacon cleaned out the wounds with the clear water. Candamir's feet were a terrible mass of blood and dirt, and Hacon spent most of the time working on them. Despite all his efforts, he could see they were beginning to swell. He unwrapped the bandage around his own hand, inspected the wound and stitches critically, and bathed them in water as well. In spite of Olaf's efforts, the stitches seemed to have held, and there had been no swelling around the wound. The palm of his hand was not hot to the touch, and Hacon could find no sign of infection. That gave him reason to hope. He washed the bandage with the remaining water and wrapped it around his hand again as best he could. And with everything he did, he prayed to Jesus Christ, as Austin had taught him. He did not allow himself to think of home, of Gunda and his children, of Asta, Harald, and Siglind, and the concern they all must feel for the two brothers. Nor did he abandon himself to his worry for his sick brother. Instead, he confidently placed their fate in God's hands, and as always he found consolation and strength in this.

He brushed Candamir's sweaty hair from his brow more lovingly than he ever would have dared had his brother been awake. "I wish I could sing for you, as you did for me," he murmured. "But I'm afraid if I sang, it would just make you want to leave this world once and for all."

Candamir's mouth suddenly quivered, and it looked for a moment as if he were smiling.

"Candamir?" Hacon asked hopefully, shaking him gently by the shoulder. But he got no answer.

More than two dozen men and women came to the hall for supper. According to the estimates they had made at home, ten men and eight women were among the outlaws now, in addition to Olaf, his four sons, and two daughters. But Hacon saw that things had changed here as well—Olaf's sons and daughters had grown up, just as he had, and a healthy crowd of children romped around the hall. And he discovered one of Ivar's slave girls whom everybody thought had drowned while swimming in the river, and a Jute who had belonged to Haldir and had never returned from a hunting trip on the south shore. Even here in this infertile wasteland, the community had thrived and grown.

"He fell in battle," Lars told his silent listeners. "He had captured the smith, but then his brother came upon the scene..." Faithfully he described what had happened and how they had entrusted his father to the ocean that night. "I think that was the proper thing to do," he concluded. "No one knew and loved the sea as he did."

Everyone nodded in agreement.

After an appropriately long silence, the Irish girl asked, "Do you want me to bring the smith something to eat, jarl?"

"Absolutely," Lars replied. "We want him to keep up his strength, after all."

The young woman stood up and filled a bowl from the cauldron around which they were sitting on blankets of fur and wool. There was no furniture of any kind in this magnificent hall. It seemed to Hacon that they needed a carpenter just as much as they needed a smith. With a grateful nod, he took the bowl the girl brought him. It contained a rich soup with beef, which he ate greedily.

"Ketil," Lars continued, "you'll go back to the coast tomorrow with two men and the pack animals to get the cargo from the ship."

The man nodded his agreement, but asked, "What are we picking up? Just so I know how many animals we'll need."

"Take them all. It's heavy stuff. Iron, an anvil, and all kinds of tools."

Hacon felt a pang. "Is that so? So you simply cleared out my workshop, did you?"

Lars frowned and looked at Hacon over his shoulder. "You won't do us much good without your tools."

Hacon realized then that they would never let him go—he already knew too much about them. He did not believe he would ever find the way back to this cave again, for every part of the wasteland looked the same to his eyes. Nevertheless, for Lars it was a risk.

Hacon slept deeply and dreamlessly alongside his brother. When he awoke, he saw that Candamir still had not regained consciousness, and his heartbeat seemed slower and weaker than on the evening before. Hacon's attempts to get Candamir to drink a little water were still unsuccessful, and his hopes began to fade.

Lars suddenly appeared at his side and asked bluntly, "Is he dying?"

Hacon shrugged sadly. "I don't know. But…he seems to be fading."

"I hope he's suffering," Lars replied. "That's the least he owes me for my father's life."

Suddenly, Hacon was seized by such a powerful anger that he was unable to contain it. "Your father only got what he deserved," he spit. "No, that isn't true. He got off much too easy. For years he intimidated us and did everything he could to sow discord between my brother and me. He made our lives miserable, just for his own amusement. He was a monster!"

Lars nodded hesitantly, as if he were not sure whether he should agree with this assessment. "He also had another side," he said unexpectedly. "He could be completely different."

"Yes, when it served his purposes. I'm happy that he's just fish food now!" Hacon said with uncharacteristic malice. "And if you had any brains at all, you would be too."

Lars did not retaliate, as his father would have done. He just shook his head and said, "Don't make the mistake of believing I am different from my father. I am the son he always wanted, the one Jared could not be."

"Then I have nothing but pity for you, Lars," Hacon replied.

Candamir's mysterious unconsciousness lasted five days and nights. Hacon feared for his brother's life and hardly left his side. Nevertheless, during this time he witnessed the comings and goings of Olaf's castle, as domestic life took place primarily in the large hall. Situated deep in the bowels of the wasteland, down here it was always night. Yet, the inhabitants had learned to sense when the sun rose in the outside world, and they got up when the day began. There was no shortage of stolen lamp oil and tallow, so there was no need to skimp on torches, and during the day little lamps stood on the ground everywhere, covering the walls of the cave with a warm glow and making the minerals and ore sparkle. Hacon could not help but admire the surprising beauty of this place.

The inhabitants of the cave took their breakfast together before heading out to perform their various tasks. The women prepared the meals, kept things in order in the hall, spun, wove, sewed, and cared for the children. The men milked and herded the cows and took on almost all work that had to be done outside the fortress. The morning after their arrival, Ketil and a few others had set out for the coast with all the pack animals to bring back the spoils they had left on the ship, as Lars had commanded. Since the men who had carried out the attack and brought Hacon and Candamir to the fortress had not been able to also take the heavy cargo back with their horses, a tiring march to the coast was necessary—in the blazing sun, one day out and one day back. Hacon could see how difficult life was here, how much these people lacked, things that he and his family and neighbors took for granted.

Lars, too, frequently had to travel beyond his fortress, leaving Gunnar in charge in his absence, as he did on the fifth day. Gunnar took the opportunity to visit Hacon briefly.

"Your brother looks better," he said in amazement. "And you can see that he's breathing."

Hacon nodded. "Yes, I think he's recovering. He's sleeping now."

"Hm, don't be offended, but I'm afraid it would have been better for him to have died. Lars really has it in for him."

"So I have noticed. But if he wants me to make new weapons and tools for you, he should think carefully about what he's doing."

Gunnar nodded, but he didn't look very convinced.

"And what about you?" Hacon asked. "It doesn't seem to me that you hate Candamir for having killed your father, at least indirectly."

"No, I don't." Gunnar grinned guiltily and shrugged. "I feared my father, just like everyone else here did. He took good care of us all, but he was a very harsh jarl. Lars will no doubt be like that in his own way, but he is only my brother. That's different. I think…I'm relieved that my father is dead."

Hacon was silent for a moment before asking in a soft voice, "But you must realize that as a result everything has changed? Your father was a criminal convicted by the *Thing*, but you weren't, nor were your siblings or anyone else here. I'm convinced the *Thing* could decide to let bygones be bygones. You…you could return."

Gunnar raised his eyebrows, looked at Hacon, and shook his head. "The former slaves among us certainly would not find your suggestion attractive."

"Everything can be negotiated," Hacon said vaguely.

Gunnar scoffed at that. "Just cut it out. I can imagine why you're trying to tempt me, but you can save your breath. It may seem to you that life here is unbearable, but we have gotten used to it. We prefer it to toiling in the fields. We can make our own rules and don't have to take orders from any *Thing* or any wicked witch. We are *free*."

"You are outcasts," Hacon replied, barely suppressing his disdain.

"Don't you see, that's the reason we despise you," Gunnar said, and it didn't even sound unfriendly. "Some people here hate you too, especially the slaves. I merely despise you, for you think your way of living is the only one that's good. You think you are better than we are. But what is your life like? You toil from morning to night, you have a few children, and then you lie down and die."

"And what do you do?" Hacon asked curiously.

"Whatever we like. We rule over this land and even over you. We let you work for us. In truth, you are the slaves."

"Your freedom is unbridled lawlessness," Hacon said. "The land you have supposedly conquered is only dust and stone, as you said yourself. What is so desirable about that?"

"Perhaps you'll understand when you have been with us a little longer. And you're wrong—it's not just this desert that belongs to us. Yesterday my brother headed south with a few people to get new horses and some extra cattle. The south is as rich and fertile as the area you have settled. And it all belongs to us."

"Then why do you live here and not there?"

Gunnar grinned at him. "To be near you. We don't want you to forget us, and we don't want any unnecessarily long trips when we bring back your grain, hay, and cattle."

Hacon frowned in disgust. "You must have noticed by now that we are no longer easy prey."

"And you must have noticed that we find a way around every protective measure you think up. It's rather an entertaining pastime."

"Then tell us how you did it," Candamir said suddenly. "How did you get into the village this time?"

"Candamir!" Hacon was startled and jumped to his feet. "You woke up!"

Candamir nodded, but kept his eyes on Gunnar, who eyed him condescendingly. "You'd really like to know that, wouldn't you?"

"Yes, I'd really like to know that," Candamir admitted.

Gunnar hesitated for a moment, but the urge to show off was greater than his caution. "All right then, why shouldn't I tell you—it doesn't matter. We watched your people bringing in the hay. Then we wrapped scarves around our heads and faces, just as they did, and slipped through the gate into your village unnoticed. I even carried a bale of hay right up to the door for my dear brother Jared." For a brief moment, his sneering face turned dark. Then, shrugging his shoulders, he concluded, "Before we brought you on board the *Dragon*, I sneaked back and set fire to his blasted barn."

"Oh, Jared," Hacon said, burying his face in his hands. Jared, his wife, and his two slaves had, with very few hands, worked so hard to get ahead. The fire in the barn would probably set them back years. As it was, Jared did not have an easy life, for each time his father had attacked the village he had to put up with hostile glances and abuse, and some people would not speak to him for weeks.

Candamir cast a warning glance at his brother. Hacon knew what he was trying to convey to him. *Don't let him notice how they hurt us with their attacks.* And naturally, Candamir was right, Hacon knew, but he was not as good at covering his emotions as his brother. Yet, he simply lowered his hands and folded his arms in front of his chest. "Oh well, he'll make out all right. Jared has many friends in the village, fortunately. Anyone who has brothers like his really doesn't need enemies."

Gunnar rose abruptly and walked out.

"Well done, Hacon," Candamir said. "You have angered the only ally we have here."

Hacon gestured dismissively. "We can do without the friendship of such a scoundrel."

"Speak for yourself," Candamir scolded him wearily. "I don't particularly care to have his affection, either, but now that it looks as if I am to live a bit longer, I'd like to do that as a free man again as soon as possible."

Hacon smiled with relief. "It's good to hear that you can be grouchy again and make plans. How do you feel?"

"Awful. And thirsty."

Hacon fetched him a drinking horn full of water.

Candamir sat up carefully, took the horn in both hands, and emptied it thirstily. When he had finished and set it down, he was out of breath. "What…what happened? Where is Olaf?"

"You don't remember?"

"Only partially. I can remember that Olaf attacked you and we fought in your garden. It was pouring. A thunderstorm? Yes. Yes, it was a thunderstorm. Then I can't remember anything else until I came to on the rocky shore. What happened?"

Candamir listened attentively, a slight frown on his face, as Hacon filled in the details. When his brother had finished, he nodded. "Too bad, I would much rather have killed him myself."

"Well, it was your knife that pierced his heart. I think you can be quite satisfied. And in view of the fact that we're captives here, it's no doubt better for everyone to think that Thor had his mighty hand in it."

Candamir smiled glumly. "I doubt that will save me from Lars's vindictiveness."

Candamir was right. For when Lars came home that night and saw that his prisoner had awakened and appeared more or less healthy, he regarded him with such a look of malevolence that it caused a painful stab of dread in his gut. Lars walked over to them and looked down on the two brothers. Candamir rose from the ground, even though his feet were still in such wretched shape that he could hardly stand.

"My father used to say that he didn't need to enslave men to make them follow him, and therefore everyone was free in the wasteland," the young jarl said.

Candamir nodded. "Anyone who treats his sons like slaves risks nothing by treating his slaves like sons," he replied.

Lars ignored him. "Since my father is dead, I'm free to set up new rules." He nodded to two of his men standing nearby. "Place him in chains and cut off his hair."

Before they could seize him, Candamir clenched his fist and struck Lars in the face. He was not yet back to his full strength, but it was enough to break Lars's nose. With a cry of alarm, the men fell on him and beat him, kicking him as he lay on the ground until Lars called them off. Candamir felt the rusty chains on his wrists and ankles, realizing they had everything here, of course, that had been aboard the *Dragon*.

In disbelief, Candamir stared down at his hands while Lars's men pulled him to his feet. His father's frequent prophesies that he would come to a bad end had led him to expect almost anything, but never this. A brave man of high standing never allowed himself to be enslaved, because he was never captured alive, yet the fetters on his hands and feet indicated otherwise. And with the perfect lucidity that sometimes accompanies a shock, he realized it had even been his own choice. For five days and nights he had been at death's door and then decided to turn around and come back—to accept this, because he wanted to see his wife, his son, and his daughters again. He was not yet ready to give up all hope and leave Catan. The awareness that his hunger for life was greater than his fear of dishonor shamed him, but it also strengthened his determination.

In the middle of the hall they forced him to his knees. Someone seized him roughly, sawing away at his hair with an apparently very dull knife. *Oh, Hacon, they* really *need you here,* he thought with clenched teeth. A thick, black handful landed on the floor in front of him, followed by a narrow plait, and then a second, until his hair grew into a small mound. He squeezed his eyes shut to keep from bursting into tears.

# Harvest Moon, Year Seven

Dusty and exhausted, Osmund returned home as dusk was falling. His household was sitting at the supper table, and they could all see that he was in a gloomy mood.

At a silent signal from Inga, the maids led the children outside. Then one of the slaves fetched a mug of beer and put it down on the table in front of the high seat. Only the two dogs that had been lying unnoticed near the hearth jumped up and greeted him joyfully. Osmund patted them on their heads and tugged on their ears absentmindedly. Ignoring the beer, he then slumped onto his seat, looked at his wife, and shook his head in despair.

"Nothing at all?" she asked hesitantly.

"No, not the slightest trace. It's *impossible* for anyone to live there."

Ten days before he had led a search party out into the wasteland to look for Candamir and Hacon. They had arrived there after a two-day march, filling their water skins before entering the wasteland. Yet, after only three days, they had to turn back in order to reach the first spring alive. Haldir, Thorbjörn, Godwin, and Sigurd had been part of the search party as well as a few others whom Osmund considered to be among the best and most fearless in Catan, but they all had been overcome by thirst and finally urged Osmund to abandon these senseless expeditions, for sooner or later one of them would die.

This had been their third search. Each time they had gone to a different place in the wasteland, and once they had taken a ship to explore its western coastline. But except for a few dark and possibly bloody footprints, they had been unable to find the slightest trace. Even Osmund knew that it was pointless.

"I'm so terribly sorry, love," Inga said helplessly, putting her right hand on his large one and pressing it tenderly. Osmund did not pull his hand away at once, and for that she was thankful, but after a few moments he carefully freed himself and stood up restlessly. "Just look at me, I haven't even wiped the dust from my hands," he said, and noticing that all his servants had fled at his sight, he prepared to fill a bowl of wash water himself.

But Inga motioned to him to stop. "Stay seated, I'll bring you some water. Rest a bit and refresh yourself."

He nodded gratefully and sat down again, drinking deeply from his beer mug. When she returned holding a bowlful of water, he washed his hands and face, pressing the fresh linen cloth to his face a moment longer than necessary. Then he put down the cloth and looked up at her with a forced smile. "And how have things gone for you here at home, my beautiful priestess?"

She gave a slight shrug. "Fine. The children, sheep, and slaves are well. The harvest is proceeding smoothly and will soon be over. Odin was well disposed toward us again."

"To us, indeed, but why not to Candamir? Can you explain to me how the gods could permit him to fall into Olaf's hands? They always loved him. How could they so suddenly abandon him?"

Inga sat down alongside him on the bench. "You know the answer, Osmund. Don't think that I don't grieve for what happened to Candamir and Hacon," she added hastily, before he got angry. It was a lie. She grieved for neither one of them, for Candamir had always had more of Osmund's love than he was entitled to, and Hacon prayed to the accursed carpenter god and fully deserved whatever happened to him at the hands of the renegades. But she kept these feelings well hidden. "I can't sleep any more than you can at the thought of what Olaf is doing to them. But the gods have not abandoned them; it is the other way around. You know that quite well, having warned Candamir often enough."

"Nevertheless." He shook his head helplessly. "He didn't deserve what happened."

"No," she agreed, though she wasn't even sure of that. She let a few moments pass before suggesting, "Let me get you something to eat. You must be hungry after the long march, and it's of no use to anyone if you make yourself sick with your worries."

"I'm not hungry."

"But Osmund, you..."

He stood up abruptly. Her concern annoyed him just as her sympathy did, which he distrusted anyway—perhaps unjustly. He knew that he was about to take out his despair on her—just as he took so many things out on her—and a guilty conscience was the last thing he needed now. He smiled and kissed Inga on the forehead. "I have to go and speak with Siglind. She must be anxiously awaiting news." *News that I don't have,* he thought to himself, despondently.

"Yes, of course you have to do that, my love."

Osmund walked slowly along the river to the other side of the village, for he dreaded bringing this bad news to Siglind. The sun had disappeared behind the treetops, but overhead the clouds were still aglow, transforming the river into a band of mist and fire reminding him of the fiery mountain. During their last night in the wasteland, they had seen it glowing again, and shortly before daybreak, a tremor accompanied by a distant rumble had caused the earth to shake. The mountain was sleeping fitfully, and Osmund was sure it was a bad omen. As slowly as he walked, he eventually arrived at Siglind's garden, peaceful in the fading twilight. The fruit trees and berry bushes stood in a pleasing jumble that offered a nice contrast to the neat plots of herbs and vegetables. He could see why all the children loved this garden, for it had something magical about it. It was a wonderful place to hide, and nibbling on apples and berries was expressly encouraged. He regretted he hadn't brought Roric along. Hesitating for a moment at the door, Osmund composed himself and pushed it open.

Siglind was sitting at the table with her household, just as Inga had been at his home, and Gunda and her children were visiting. Osmund's gaze swept over the empty high seat that he and Jared had built. He raised his eyes and saw that everyone sitting around the table was staring at him, and no one had any difficulty interpreting the look on his face.

Gunda buried her face in her hands and broke out in tears. Osmund glanced at her with a fleeting look of contempt—he despised her just as much as Candamir did. Then he looked into Siglind's eyes. Before he had figured out what he was going to say, little Irmgardis asked, "Did you find my father and my uncle, Osmund?"

He walked over to her and lifted her up from her seat. "No, Irmgardis. I'm very sorry. I did what I could, just as I promised you, but unfortunately without success."

She too began to cry, but in contrast to Gunda's hysterical wailing, this little girl's heartrending sobs were hard to bear. Osmund did not put her down though; he endured her sadness, believing he deserved this punishment for his dismal failure.

Siglind rose from her place by the high seat and put her hand on Nils's bowed head. Her movements were peculiarly slow, as if she was exhausted or ill, but her face was simply solemn. "Solvig, take care of Irmgardis," she asked the young nurse, before turning to her guest. "Let's go outside for a moment, Osmund. It's such a beautiful summer evening."

He had great admiration for her composure. A queen indeed, even though she always asserted she had left all that behind long ago. They sat down next to each other on the bench at the side of the house. Darkness was falling fast, and only a glimmer of light could be seen through the window, but the fragrance of the garden was more intense and intoxicating in the evening air than in the sunlight.

"This time we searched the eastern side of the wasteland, keeping the mountain on our right," he said. "But it was the same as last time—we found no sign of man or beast, nor any signs of habitation. I could swear that by now we have searched every inch of this desert, without the slightest success."

She could hear the hopelessness in his voice and started to stretch out her hand toward him, before withdrawing it quickly. "Thank you,

Osmund. I probably can't really imagine all you have done, but be assured I am very grateful to you. I…" But she could not continue. It wasn't that she had expected a different outcome with this new search. She knew how poor the chances were. Nevertheless, she had been hoping, against her better judgment. And now she didn't know how she could go on without this hope.

The crickets were chirping in the grass around the fruit trees. It was a peaceful, constant song, and they listened to it for a moment with rapt attention. Finally, Siglind said softly, "We…had six years together, quite a bit of time. But they seem to me like a single moment, and I wonder if this is really to be all I was entitled to."

"Yes, I remember that I asked myself the same thing after Gisla had died." He broke off, so horrified at his lack of consideration that he quickly put his hand over his mouth, as if wanting to take back the thoughtless words.

"So you believe he is dead?" she asked calmly.

He didn't reply at once.

"Tell me, Osmund, please."

He turned and looked at her directly, so that she could see the whites of his eyes, his face only a shadowy outline. "Yes, that's what I believe deep down. More than six weeks have passed. They would probably keep Hacon alive that long because they need him. But Candamir…"

When the two brothers had been discovered missing, Osmund, Harald, Austin, and a few others had examined the scene. They had found signs of a fight, gashes caused by swords on tree trunks and bushes, a tree split by lightning that had obviously been moved by someone, and the empty smithy with a prominent bloodstain on the hard-packed dirt floor. Outside they hadn't discovered any blood, but it had been raining hard. It hadn't been difficult to figure out what had happened: Olaf and his men had come to abduct a much-needed smith, and the older brother had arrived on the scene and tried to stop them, obviously without success. Clearly, they had taken him along as well, possibly as a way to put pressure on Hacon. And Osmund doubted that Candamir would endure this type of imprisonment and all its horrors for long—it was simply unthinkable.

"But I may be mistaken, and as long as this possibility exists, I won't give up. I will broaden the search. The more I get to know the wasteland, the less likely it seems to me that they really are living somewhere there. Next time I'll look farther south."

But she could tell from his voice that he himself no longer believed he would find anything. "You ought not to do that, Osmund. Your life is here, with your family and your wife."

He sat there motionless, his hands wrapped around one knee, his eyes fixed on her. "I don't think I'm ready to give up yet."

"Although deep down, as you say, you're convinced you're chasing an illusion?"

He realized then she was crying, her hoarse voice giving her away. Instinctively, he took his hands from his knee, put them gently on Siglind's arms, and moved a bit closer to her. At first she stiffened, but she simply could not resist the temptation of his broad shoulder and buried her face in it, weeping over her loss, first bitterly, then furiously, and finally sadly. Osmund held her patiently, passing his hand gently over her back. Her grief was painful for him, but at the same time he wished this moment would never end.

Passing his lips over her hair so gently that she didn't even realize it, he promised, "I'll keep looking. You have my word. With or without hope, for I need certainty just as you do."

And he wanted to bring Candamir back to her. At that moment he wanted him more for her than for himself, although he was only too aware of how dependent he was on Candamir, how much he needed him to be able to carry on from day to day. But as clearly as he recognized that, he also knew something else. If his worst fears were confirmed, he would leave Inga for this woman. He would defy the anger of the gods and renounce the power promised by the oracle, without looking back.

# Autumn Moon, Year Seven

Hacon took the melted iron from the fire in the long-handled stone ladle and poured it into the stone mold. The mass, glowing white and viscous, took the shape of a sword—the cast-iron core that would later be covered with a steel blade. Hacon smiled inadvertently as he always did when one of his projects began to take shape, but a moment later he grumbled, "I can't believe I'm standing here forging weapons for these scoundrels so that they can use them against our people someday."

Candamir stepped back from the bellows. "Make them faulty," he suggested. "Make them so they'll break the first time they're used to strike a serious blow." As he sat down on the rocky soil, his chains jingled softly. He scarcely heard the sound anymore.

"Sure, Candamir, that's a magnificent idea," Hacon scoffed. "And what do you think Lars will do when he finds out that his new sword is defective?"

"We just have to be gone by the time he notices it."

Hacon did not reply. He looked around his extraordinary smithy. It was in one of the taller, strangely spherical caves that had a vent to the surface. A little daylight even came through the hole in the vaulted ceiling. Nevertheless, the light was always dim there, the air was full of smoke, and it was as hot as the hell Austin had described to him in such vivid images. Just as in the great rock hall and in the other inhabited chambers, the ground had been smoothed by a thick layer of dark gray, powdery sand that could be found in near inexhaustible quantities in the desert. It looked like coarse-grained ash, quite suitable for the life they led here.

Hacon had come to hate this place. Nevertheless, he believed he would spend the rest of his days in this smithy, for it lay deep in the bowels of Olaf's castle, and the bridge over the chasm, the only route to freedom, was guarded day and night.

Hacon sat down alongside his brother to wait until the slug had cooled. "But not even you know how we might accomplish that."

Candamir cast a longing glance at the melted iron in the mold that would soon be made into a superb weapon. With a sword like that, he would gladly have taken on the two watchmen at the bridge. If only he had not been tied hand and foot. If only Lars hadn't searched the smithy and his two prisoners every evening for weapons, and hadn't checked meticulously on the whereabouts of every single ball of iron ore.

"No," he had to admit. "But it's about time we came up with something."

Hacon looked at him anxiously and nodded. His brother's voice sounded calm, but he knew that Candamir wouldn't be able to hold out much longer. Lars and his men humiliated him every chance they got—beating him, kicking him, and spitting upon him, even though he hardly ever gave them a reason to, obeying each of their often absurd commands in silence. They made him pay for the fact that they were outcasts. And they let him go hungry. Candamir had lost as much weight as after the last winter famine in Elasund. And he endured everything they did to him with an unflagging self-control that Hacon never believed his brother possessed.

After Hacon's injured hand had healed and he had started to work again, things improved a bit, for he needed Candamir's help working the bellows, fetching water, holding a slug in the tongs while he hammered it into shape—in short, he always found something for his brother to do so that he could protect him some from Lars's cruelty. But in the evenings, when the inhabitants of Olaf's castle gathered in the hall after their day's work to eat and drink, there wasn't any way he could protect Candamir. His brother had ordered him not to protest and never to beg on his behalf. "You must swear to me, Hacon," he had said. "Not a word, no matter what happens."

"But..."

"No buts! We must deny them at least that satisfaction, understand? Act as if it didn't matter to you."

"Aren't you afraid it will just egg them on, just to get some reaction from you?" Hacon asked uneasily.

Candamir had turned his face away. "What I'm really afraid of is that I could get used to this, that sooner or later I might start to believe I am what they are trying to make me. And I must prevent that at any cost, so swear to me."

And naturally Hacon had given him his word. But every night for the past three months he entered the hall with a knot in the pit of his stomach.

"Just assume we did get across the bridge," Hacon said in a low voice. "Then what? Should we steal two of their horses and try to make our way north?"

Candamir chewed nervously on his thumbnail. "No," he answered hesitantly. "No, I don't think so. We couldn't water the horses, for we must be prepared to go without water."

"*What?*"

"There would probably be a few unpleasant questions if both you and I suddenly filled a water skin at the well and walked toward the bridge with it, wouldn't there? We must get out quickly and without warning, or we won't have a chance."

"Without water we won't have a chance in the wasteland either," Hacon said.

"But we will, if we go at night."

"Oh, it's getting crazier and crazier!"

"Shush..."

"Candamir, how are we supposed to make it through this country at night without breaking all our bones?"

"With caution and a little luck. And perhaps some moonlight. We'll head northeast, and I figure if we leave shortly after sundown we'll reach the edge of the forest by the next evening."

A march of a night and a day, in searing heat, and without water. *You'll never make it,* Hacon thought dejectedly. *Not in your condition.* But he kept his doubts to himself. He had already offered more than enough objections. Moreover, he had learned in recent weeks that his brother had undreamed of reserves. So who was he to judge what Candamir could or could not do?

"It sounds like it's worth a try," he lied.

Candamir made a mock grimace, followed by a weak shadow of that endearing happy-go-lucky smile of his. "But there's still the little problem with the bridge. We can't…"

He stopped short, interrupted by a dull rumble that seemed to rise out of the earth before gradually subsiding. This had happened more or less frequently in recent weeks, but this time it lasted longer. As little stones started to rain down on them, Hacon rested his forehead on his drawn-up knees and wrapped his arms around his head for protection, praying silently.

The quake stopped as abruptly as it began.

Hacon didn't move at first, but whispered to Candamir, "If they can feel that at home, I'd rather not know what Inga has to say about it."

A sharp elbow struck him between the shoulders. "Stop mumbling like an old woman. Just look at that."

Hacon raised his head. "What?"

Candamir pointed to the ceiling. Hacon didn't understand what his brother meant at first, but suddenly the smoke from the forge dissipated and a bit of blue sky became visible. The small hole in the ceiling through which just a ray of daylight had fallen a few moments ago had become at least twice as large.

The two brothers looked at each other, a wild hope welling up within Hacon. "Perhaps…perhaps we don't need to cross the bridge at all."

Candamir put his finger to his lips to quiet his brother. He could hear hasty steps along the subterranean corridor. Several men rushed past the smithy to the entrance of the castle, presumably to see if there had been any damage and to survey the fiery mountain. Hacon and Candamir continued working quietly until Lars poked his head through the entrance to the smithy. "Is everything all right here?"

"Of course," Hacon replied. "How do things look out there?"

"The same as always." The young jarl entered and checked the slug in the mold. The edges, which had been white hot, were gradually turning red. "My sword?" he inquired.

Hacon nodded.

"When will it be finished?"

"In three or four days."

"Very well. Next, you'll make one for Gunnar."

"As you wish, Lars," Hacon replied coolly.

Lars started to look around a bit more carefully, and the brothers feared he would notice the room had gotten brighter and the hole in the ceiling larger. Panicked, Candamir considered tipping a bucket of water on the glowing mold, for that would have provided enough steam and confusion to distract Lars from the changed lighting conditions, but it would have ruined the mold and the repercussions would no doubt be brutal. Before he could decide what to do, Leif appeared at the smithy entrance. "Oh, by Odin's balls, is it hot here! Lars, can you come along? One of the horses has bolted and run away during the quake…"

Lars cursed, quickly following his brother in the direction of the bridge. Hacon and Candamir exchanged relieved looks. They waited patiently until things had calmed down in the castle, and then Candamir climbed onto Hacon's shoulders to inspect the low ceiling. The air hole was now large enough that he could put his fist through it.

"Just watch out!" Hacon gasped, looking up. "What if someone up there saw your hand?"

Candamir reached up a little higher with his arm and suddenly felt warm sunshine on the back of his hand. "Oh, Hacon," he whispered. "The ceiling is no more than a hand's breadth thick."

"It's a miracle that no one has fallen through yet and landed in the forge," Hacon murmured, putting a hammer into his brother's outstretched hand. Very carefully, Candamir tapped on the roof, afraid the sound of the hammer would arouse suspicion. With every tap, he was able to break off small pieces of the porous stone, which fell to the floor around Hacon's feet.

"If I wanted to, I could make an exit for us right away," Candamir said, hoarse with excitement.

"No, come down. I've got to rest, and we ought to think carefully about what we're going to do," Hacon replied.

He let Candamir down, fetched a red-hot knife blade from the forge, carried it to the anvil, and began hammering on it. Between each blow, they exchanged a few whispered words.

"We mustn't act too hastily," Hacon said. "You need shoes." Candamir had nothing left to wear but his frayed and holey trousers—everything else had been taken away from him. "And you can't cross the wasteland in chains."

Candamir nodded reluctantly. His cautious brother was right. "Can you open the cuffs on the chains?" Candamir inquired.

"Certainly. But not without making a lot of noise. Since we want to leave at nightfall, we must think of something else." He examined the fetters carefully. The chain on Candamir's feet allowed him only short steps, and Lars never tired of making fun of the way Candamir walked. But it was long enough to be able to melt the middle link in the forge without burning his feet. The chain on his hands was a bit longer and would be no problem at all. "I'll open one link on each, but just a bit. Not enough to attract anyone's attention, but before we leave you can unhook it and then move your hands and feet freely. We'll do the rest when we get home."

"Agreed."

Candamir enlarged the hole in the ceiling until he could push through one of the numerous pieces of leather Hacon used to protect his hands from hot objects. He covered the hole with the leather, and then covered that with the loose ash he could feel above. Since he couldn't see what he was doing, the camouflage was not expert, but the piece of leather was dark brown like this land, and so they simply hoped for the best. They were going to widen the hole over the next few days to form an exit, camouflaging it like this as they worked. Candamir hoped that it would take no longer than two days. The thin, porous stone was easy to chip away, but Hacon had to continue his work on Lars's sword to keep from arousing suspicion, and naturally they could only work on the ceiling when no one was around. Regardless of their progress, Hacon wanted to open Candamir's chains in two days. They planned to steal some shoes just before they left. It shouldn't be hard, as all who slept in the hall at night placed their shoes alongside their beds. In addition, they planned to use Lars's horses as an example and tie a double layer of leather around their shoes to protect their feet while crossing the wasteland.

Two evenings later, the mood in the hall was particularly boisterous. The men drank more than usual, laughed too loudly, and scarcely took the trouble to lead their female companions beyond the light of the oil lamps before they pulled them to the ground and pushed up their skirts.

As usual, Hacon sat next to his brother close to their bed along the wall, even more afraid than usual. *Please, God,* he begged fervently, *make them leave him alone. Give us at least a chance, that's all I ask.*

But it was inevitable that sooner or later Lars would turn to look at Candamir, who was lying on his blanket with his eyes closed, trying to ignore the odor of roasted meat that hovered in the air more intensely than usual. The women had served a sumptuous feast. There was beef, a few chickens, even a sheep they had slaughtered and roasted on a spit. Candamir had long ago become accustomed to an empty stomach, and he could deal with that. But to suffer hunger with these tempting odors in the air seemed just as impossible to him as it had been for Hacon in the storage shed all those years ago.

"Hacon!" Lars bellowed from the middle of the hall. "Come, do us the honor and eat with us! And bring my slave along to wait on us..."

"O mighty Tyr," Candamir said softly, but immediately sat up.

Hacon nodded to Lars in agreement, washed his hands in a bowl standing next to his bed, and whispered to his brother, "Be careful with the chains. If they open up now, it's all over." He had not opened the links in question any farther than necessary, but chains could be treacherous and often opened at the most inappropriate moment when they had a weak link—intentionally or not. "Just remember, when we get home you can eat until you burst, but if you make a mistake now..."

Candamir nodded and got to his feet quickly, partly to escape Hacon's admonitions. The brothers stepped out into the light. Hacon took a seat between Gunnar and one of Olaf's former slaves, while Candamir stopped in front of Lars, staring down at his bare feet.

"Bring me more mead," Lars commanded, although his cup was still half full. "It isn't bad at all. Did your beautiful queen make it, huh? What do you think?"

"That's very possible," Candamir replied. He had learned that Lars was never happy until he had gotten an answer to such questions.

Lars emptied the cup in a mighty gulp and then held it out to him. Candamir carried it to the place along the wall where pitchers and platters were standing. "Bring a piece of the roast to your brother!" Lars called after him. "We want him to stay strong. What would you like, Hacon? A piece of mutton? A chicken, perhaps?"

"Whatever you say, Lars," Hacon replied wearily.

Candamir filled the cup with mead, picked up a clean wooden plate from a small stack on the ground, and placed a juicy piece of roast ox on it—saliva filled his mouth, and his gnawing hunger made it hard for him to stand up straight. His hand started to tremble as he placed the meat on the plate. Candamir cursed himself silently, commanding his hand to be still. The trembling lessened, and he even managed to wipe his fingers on his trousers instead of licking them.

He brought the cup to Lars and the plate to Hacon, without looking either of them in the eye. Hacon had averted his eyes just as he had, but Lars followed each one of Candamir's steps with a broad smile. "Do you know why we're celebrating tonight?" he asked jovially.

It wasn't hard for Candamir to guess, but he knew very well that if he expressed his suspicion, he would not be able to rein in his temper, and so he merely shook his head.

"We're setting out tomorrow for the coast, and the day after tomorrow, we'll head out to sea. We should reach the mouth of the river by evening, and then we'll row upstream to see what your dear neighbors have in their barns."

Hacon, who had not touched his beef, set the plate on the ground.

Lars took another drink, and a little mead ran from the corners of his mouth, trickling down to his beard. He was drunk. *Good,* thought Candamir. *Drink a few cups more, and there will be even less of a chance that you'll hear us tonight when we slip away. And the longer it will take for you to wake up tomorrow morning and notice we are gone.*

"Don't you have anything to say about that?" Lars asked impatiently. "You're not even batting an eye."

For the first time, Candamir looked directly at him. "May the spoils of your trip be as great as you deserve."

The men sitting around whispered angrily, and Lars frowned. With silent looks, Hacon tried desperately to warn his brother to be sensible.

"I'm thirsty!" Gunnar suddenly cried out and held up his cup. He was as drunk as his brother. "Don't just stand around, Candamir, bring the pitcher! And you'd better fill another one right away," he ordered. Candamir turned, and the dangerous moment passed.

As so often in recent weeks, Hacon looked surreptitiously at Gunnar and tried to guess what he was really thinking. He hated them, he had said, and in fact he seemed to be completely indifferent to their fate, usually just looking on passively as Lars played his cruel tricks on Candamir. Still, he seemed to take no pleasure in them and never took part himself. And sometimes he did or said something that made things a bit easier for Candamir, as he just had—though never in such a way as to attract attention. It was too bad about this man, Hacon had thought many times. Gunnar was probably just as decent a fellow as Jared, and if he had been older and had had a choice, he would probably have decided quite differently back then…

"Hacon? Are you asleep?" Lars asked sharply.

He jumped. "Excuse me, what did you say?"

"I asked whether my sword will be ready by tomorrow morning so that I can take it along."

"No, I'm afraid it will take another few days," Hacon replied stiffly. "A good sword takes a week—that's just the way it is."

"Hm," he grunted. "Perhaps we should put off our trip for a few days. I really meant to take this sword along."

Candamir stepped into the brightly lit circle, holding a heavy pitcher in each hand, and filled all the cups that were presented to him. He moved more slowly and awkwardly than usual, for he was terrified that the chains would give him away. The trembling in his hands had gotten worse, and he felt dizzy with hunger, so that each time he filled a cup he spilled a little mead. At first they just laughed at him, but then they kicked him.

Hacon looked on impassively, just as he had promised Candamir, but he clenched his hands into tight fists without noticing it.

Candamir staggered around the little circle like a blind beggar, kicked from all sides on his ankles, his shins, and finally the hollow of his knees. Instinctively, Candamir stretched his arms out to maintain his balance. The chain tightened with a rattle, but didn't come apart. However, one of the heavy pitchers slipped from his hand and landed on Lars's head with a deep, hollow thud; its contents spilled over Lars's face and chest and into his lap.

At any normal feast such a mishap would have caused riotous laughter, but here the laughter was halfhearted and strangely muted, subsiding quickly. Blinking his eyes, the jarl looked down and tried unsuccessfully to wipe the sticky brew out of his eyes. As inconspicuously as possible, the young Irish woman came running, picked up the pitcher from the ground, took the second one out of Candamir's hand, and went around the circle herself filling the cups. But if she had hoped this would put an end to the unpleasant silence, she was wrong.

"It seems that my slave is feeling rebellious," Lars stammered.

"It was an accident," Hacon said.

Candamir shot him a glance, his face dark and harried.

Lars looked up at Candamir and frowned. "If it was an accident, then apologize."

Hacon started to pray again.

Candamir swallowed, but he knew what was at stake. "I apologize," he said in a voice devoid of expression.

Amazingly fast for such a drunken man, Lars kicked his feet out from under him. "That isn't good enough!"

Candamir landed hard on his knees.

"Try again," Lars ordered him. "And it had better sound convincing, or I might decide to pay your beautiful queen a little private visit and…"

That was as far as he got. With a truly tormented cry, Candamir rushed him, grabbed Lars's knife from its sheath, and put it to his throat before Gunnar and one of the other men could pounce on him and pull him back.

Lars was uninjured except for a thin trickle of blood running down his neck. He fingered the little wound and seemed to marvel how things had gotten to that point so fast. The two men held Candamir down on his knees, and Gunnar grabbed him by his hair, forcing his head back while he placed the knife he had seized from him to his throat. "Shall I?" he asked his brother.

"No." Lars was still squinting like an owl in the sunlight. "Get me the whip, Leif," he ordered. Then he rose ponderously to his feet. "I'm going to beat you to death, Candamir, damn you. I swear I'm going to beat you to death…" He staggered a step to the side.

"Do it tomorrow, Brother," Gunnar suggested. His voice sounded like a mixture of good-natured ridicule at the jarl's drunkenness and cold fury at the attempt on his brother's life. "Do it tomorrow morning when you're sober and you've got all your strength. Let him sweat for a few hours, huh? He's not going anywhere."

Lars hesitated for a brief moment and then nodded. He was very pale. Although nothing had really happened to him, he had been shaken by the sudden attack that had almost cost him his life.

Gunnar grabbed Candamir by the hair and yanked him to his feet and out of the circle just before Lars abruptly vomited on the floor.

Gunnar did not look back, but merely grimaced in disgust as he hustled Candamir back to his bed and pushed him to the ground. "Sweet dreams," he growled.

The hall resounded so loudly from the revelers' snoring that you might think the next earthquake had come. The boots Candamir had stolen reached to his calves, and his hands trembled worse than ever as he put them on, carefully stuffing the foot chains inside so that they wouldn't rattle as he walked. Then he rose and silently followed Hacon to the smithy.

They did not speak. Hacon groped about for his tools and wedged them into his belt. Both brothers were sweating, and their hearts were in their mouths. Hacon bent down and took his brother on his shoulders again. Candamir pushed aside the piece of leather covering the hole, stuck his arms through, and boosted himself up out of the hole. Then he dangled the long end of his chain down into the smithy, so Hacon could grab hold.

Not only was Hacon a tall, muscular man, but he was also carrying heavy tools. And Candamir was weak and half starved, but he knew he only had to pull Hacon up about three feet before his brother would be able to boost himself the rest of the way. But as Hacon grabbed the edge of the hole, one side crumbled and Hacon fell back. The chain clattered, and it seemed to Candamir like a deafening noise.

He could hear soft cursing coming up from the dark hole in the ground. "Grab hold again, and don't move," Candamir whispered. "I'll pull you out."

With great difficulty, he was able to pull Hacon up, and finally they both lay panting for a moment on the rocky earth still warm from the sun. Candamir thought he wouldn't be able to go one step farther. Then he felt Hacon's hand groping for his own. Hacon opened his fingers and put something in his brother's hand. "Eat, Candamir. But take a little time for it, otherwise it won't agree with you. In the meanwhile, I'll tie the leather around our shoes."

It was the large piece of beef that Candamir had brought to him that evening. As the confrontation between Lars and Candamir escalated, Hacon had quickly slipped the piece of meat under his clothing.

"Shouldn't we share?" Candamir asked with a full mouth.

Hacon was working at his feet, first wrapping two layers of thick leather around them and then pulling the laces tight. He smiled and shook his head. "No, I don't want anything."

Candamir ate with relish. The meat tasted as good as he had imagined it would. "I had hoped you were going to say that."

Luck seemed to be on their side at last. A bright third-quarter moon shone in the cloudless night sky over the wasteland, and when Candamir had gotten his "overshoes" and had eaten his long-overdue meal, they set out on their way. Even without the moonlight, they would have been able to make out the fiery mountain. It was enveloped in a reddish glow that night and showed them the way. They figured they would have to go somewhat to the left of it to take the shortest route home.

They walked silently and quickly, stumbling along in fear of being pursued, but when they knew they were out of sight of Olaf's castle, their pace grew slower and steadier. The night was pleasant and mild, and a gentle wind cooled their damp foreheads. Silence lay over the desert; the only sound was a soft rustling from time to time, caused by a stone coming loose, or possibly some small nocturnal creature darting away from them.

It was Candamir who finally broke the silence. "I'm sorry, Hacon. I almost ruined our chances. I hope you can forgive me."

Hacon was astonished. As far as he could remember, this was the first time his brother had ever apologized to him. "Sure, Candamir, I can easily do that. You showed more self-restraint than I ever could have. But tonight he simply pushed you too far."

Candamir kept his eyes on the treacherous terrain. "I just hope he doesn't carry out his threat."

"To do that they'd first have to get into the village. Since the hedge is so high and we have the bell…"

"You know very well that it can happen just the same. After all, they found their way into the village to get you and me."

"Yes," Hacon admitted grimly. Then after a moment he added, "Well, there is no way we can get there before they do if they really set out tomorrow. All we can do is pray."

"Then do that, pray to your god. You're so loyal to him that perhaps he will listen to you."

"Or perhaps your gods will listen to you. We should both try our luck."

Candamir did not reply. He had long ago stopped speaking to his gods, but not because he thought they had abandoned him. What had happened to him was not their fault, but Olaf's, Lars's, and his own—he had no reproach for his gods. And if he should actually make it back to his family alive—something he didn't consider especially probable, but nevertheless possible—then he would have every reason to be thankful to them. But he had drifted far away from his gods. He couldn't have said why that was, or exactly when it had happened, but they had become pale shadows of their former selves.

All night long they continued in a northeasterly direction without stopping, and at daybreak they were almost up to the fiery mountain. It towered in the east, perhaps twenty miles to the right. The lighter it became, the paler the reddish glow grew over its summit, until it was covered in nothing but light smoke.

"It's sleeping fitfully," Hacon said as they stopped to rest for a moment on the hard ground.

"It was that way the year we arrived," Candamir replied, a bit out of breath. Small black dots danced before his eyes. The night's walk over difficult ground had put a strain on him. "It will quiet down again, you'll see."

Hacon nodded and looked his brother over carefully. "Are you all right?"

"Of course."

Hacon took his hammer and a gleaming new chisel from his belt. "Let me take off these chains. They are just dead weight."

Candamir made no objection to that, eagerly stretching out his left arm. But as Hacon placed the chisel on the connecting bolt between the ends of the cuffs, he admonished, "Watch out. I still need my hands."

Hacon raised his head in an unusually bold grin. "Do you remember what you told me when we tried out the saw?"

"No, what did I say?"

"Trust me." The hammer came crashing down.

Candamir was soon rid of his insufferable fetters, though he felt as if he had aged a few years. But his newfound freedom of movement gave him renewed courage, just as Hacon had hoped, and when they started out again, Candamir's gait seemed as easy and agile as before.

Not until around noon—later than Hacon had expected—did the extent of Candamir's exhaustion become apparent. He became silent and grim and walked with his head down. His skin hadn't been exposed to the sun in nearly three months, and it began to redden. Hacon pulled off his tunic and pleaded with his brother until he put it on. "We'll take turns," Hacon told him. "We'll each wear it for an hour, and then it's the other's turn."

Candamir nodded and looked toward the north. They could make out a faint shadow on the horizon that might be a band of clouds, but they fervently hoped that it marked the edge of the forest. It seemed terribly far away. They were still in the middle of the wasteland, and dark brown stone baked hard by the burning sun was everywhere. They became so thirsty that Candamir completely forgot his hunger.

By early afternoon, Hacon had to take charge, making all the decisions for both of them. Candamir was still able to put one foot in front of the other, but his head nodded at every step, and his pace became slower and more halting. Hesitantly, Hacon put an arm around his waist to lead him, and the fact that his brother allowed him to do so really worried him.

The shimmering, hot desert air played cruel tricks on their eyes. If the fiery mountain had seemed close enough to touch the night before, now the forest seemed to cling to the horizon and never come any closer. Hacon was tormented by thirst as well. His throat was dry, and his tongue seemed to be swollen and sticking to the roof of his mouth. He thought back on the voyage to the new homeland and the endless days in the storm when they had suffered a similar thirst. He searched for something small and smooth enough for his purposes, but he could find nothing except dead earth, nothing that would even have a faint resemblance to a pebble. Then a thought came to mind, and he stopped.

"Take off your ring, Candamir."

For the first time in hours, his brother lifted his head. "What?"

"Your wedding ring." Hacon took his own from his finger and put it in his mouth. "You must suck on it—that helps against thirst, believe me."

Slowly, Candamir raised his right hand. "Do I still have my ring?" he asked incredulously.

"Yes. Lars wanted to take it from you, but I gave him a line about the ring being a present from the gods and Brigitta giving it to you during the temple dedication, and that it was of too little value to risk Odin's anger. Do you remember?"

Candamir shook his head.

That was no more than three weeks ago, Hacon estimated with worry. He took his brother's hand and pulled the ring off. It came easily—the silver band fitting more loosely than before. Hacon wiped it on his trousers, as the ring was encrusted with a black layer of dust. Then he placed it between Candamir's lips. "Here, but don't swallow it."

The hottest time of day in the wasteland was in the late afternoon, when the dark ground began to radiate its stored heat. It was during this part of the day that the hazy shadow first appeared on the northern horizon. Even if Hacon hadn't known there was a forest there, he would have recognized it then.

The two hikers hadn't felt a breath of wind all day. They only noticed it had been there when it died down, and in a few heartbeats the air became thick as paste, much too hot to breathe. Candamir walked another hundred paces before stopping. For a moment he stared intently to the north and then fell like a slaughtered ox.

Hacon crouched down beside him and shook his shoulder. "Candamir, get up again, let's go. It's not so far now, perhaps another hour." Or two.

He didn't answer.

Hacon shook his shoulder again. "Candamir, can you hear me?"

"Yes."

"Then get to your feet. Come on! You can't give up on me now, so close to our goal, do you understand?"

"I can't go on."

"Then try harder!"

Candamir was too exhausted to be indignant, but nevertheless he raised his head and growled, "How dare you…"

"That's what you always used to tell me."

Candamir gave a fleeting smile before burying his head in the dirt again. "But I know what I'm talking about."

Hacon feared he might be right. It was just like Candamir to push ahead without complaining and then fall down when his strength was utterly depleted. Hacon probably would have started whimpering hours ago. Well, at least that way you didn't catch your traveling companions by surprise, he mused briefly.

"Candamir, please!" he pleaded. "You can't just lie down here and die."

"Oh yes I can." He didn't want to quit, but he knew he had nothing left in him. Since noon he had suffered from cramps that had gradually worked their way up his legs. Now his feet as well as his legs were completely numb.

"Come now, let's try just once again. Just once," his brother begged him.

Candamir allowed Hacon to pull him back onto his feet, but then he staggered and fell down almost immediately. "You see," he muttered, closing his eyes. He was not unconscious, but had simply gone to sleep. It was not thirst that threatened to kill him, but fatigue.

Hacon crouched down beside him and wondered whether they could risk staying here a few hours until the sun had set and it had gotten cooler. But his instincts told him that his brother's condition would not get any better by waiting. On the contrary, Candamir needed water soon, and until he got that he would not be able to get back onto his feet again.

Hacon carefully placed a hand on Candamir's chin, opened his mouth, and took the ring out before he choked on it. But even that did not wake him, nor did he stir when Hacon put the ring back on his finger. Candamir's sleep seemed unnaturally deep, though restless. Hacon saw his brother moving his cracked lips, and when he bent over him, he could just barely hear the word, "Siglind."

"You're not yet ready to leave this world, Brother," Hacon scolded him. If Candamir had heard him, he could have told his brother that he had known this for some time.

Hacon took his brother by the hand and sat silently beside him for a while. He knew he could do one of three things—he could go on alone and come back and give him a decent burial later; he could lie down and die with him; or he could pray for a miracle and try to do the impossible.

As a boy, he had ardently wished he could be as bold as his brother. As a man, he had come to have greater appreciation for other virtues. But in this moment, he wished he had the courage born of despair so highly praised in many songs, the courage to begin a task that could never be completed. With all his senses he felt the vanquishing power of the desert, the sticky heat on his skin and in his eyes, the smell and taste of the lifeless dust, and the sound of nothing, the all-encompassing silence. It was monstrous, powerful enough to rob men bolder than himself of their last bit of courage.

"Then you simply have to do without courage," Hacon finally murmured to himself. When he stood up, his limbs were heavy as lead, and he felt old. Nevertheless, he leaned over his brother, sat him up a bit, and hoisted his motionless body onto his shoulder. The sun hung over the wasteland like a molten coin and cast a golden glow over the darkening desert, giving it a completely unexpected charm, but Hacon paid it no heed. Instead he looked steadfastly ahead toward the edge of the forest.

Later he had trouble remembering his long march through the desert. All he could recall were isolated feelings and moments. On that long journey his spirit had shrunk to a small, blue flame. He couldn't hold thoughts for more than a few heartbeats; he didn't pray, nor did he worry about the attack on the village, or the safety of his family and neighbors. He summoned all his strength for the sole purpose of placing one foot in front of the other and never interrupting the rhythm of his constant, long strides. He didn't see the sun set, didn't feel the heat dissipate, he only stared down fixedly at the ground and at his feet so as not to stumble. For he knew he must not fall.

And so, a good hour after nightfall, he reached the shadow of the trees, which began suddenly, without transition, where the wasteland ended. He did not know this forest, but it was so much like the one bordering their fields that Hacon immediately felt at home and secure. He cocked his head to one side and heard the murmuring of water somewhere in front of him.

Almost joyfully, he laughed to himself. His back, neck, shoulders, and arms ached as if he had been carrying an iron yoke for days. With each step, his brother seemed to grow heavier. In the future, Hacon vowed, he would have more patience and sympathy for the poor oxen that plowed their fields and pulled their carts. Yet when he heard the water, he was overcome by such a feeling of euphoria that all his aches and misery seemed to melt away. He steered his way toward the babbling sound, through ferns and grass which reached over his knees, and soon he came to the gentle bank of a brook. More roughly than he intended, he let his brother down into it.

Candamir did not move at once, but the cool, prickling water finally roused the little life he had left in him. He opened his eyes and began groping about in the mud at the bottom of the brook.

Hacon had dropped down in the water beside him and drank three or four mouthfuls before reason made him stop. Then he lay down on his back, groaning, and splashed the water over his sunburned face.

"Hacon," Candamir mumbled, sounding both confused and incredulous.

The younger brother sat up and rolled his unburdened shoulders. "We did it, Candamir. Drink. But just a bit. You're weak, and I fear you may be running a fever. So be careful."

Candamir sat up, plunged his hands into the water between his knees, and drank and drank, until Hacon intervened, grasping his brother's hands. "Why don't you ever listen to me?"

Candamir did not pull his hands away, but just looked at his brother. "How...how can this be? What a strange miracle. I...you..." His eyes wandered about restlessly.

Hacon smiled. "Don't rack you brains over it. We're here, and that's the only thing that counts. Your memory will come back."

"But..."

"How do you feel?"

Shaking his head in confusion, Candamir replied, "Thirsty, hungry, and tired."

"Then drink and sleep. Tomorrow morning I'll catch a few trout, and then..."

"Hacon, why am I here and not dead in the wasteland?" Candamir said, cutting him off. "What's the meaning of this? What happened?"

Hacon lowered his eyes in embarrassment. "I carried you here."

"You *carried* me? But we had at least five miles still to go!"

"About that, yes."

"That...that's impossible."

"Nonsense. After all, you hardly weigh more than a straw."

Candamir turned away, scooped up some more water with his hands, and drank again. Then he stood up unsteadily, waded out of the little brook to the grassy shore, and threw himself on the ground. When Hacon followed a few moments later, Candamir had already fallen asleep.

Two days later they reached the south shore of the great river. The sun was already skimming the treetops on the island in the middle, and just across from them lay the village meadow.

"The houses are still standing," Candamir murmured.

"Yes, everything looks as it always did," Hacon said with relief, carefully examining the river. Now, after the dry summer, the current was slow and safe for a good swimmer. "What do you think? Can you do it?"

"I'm not an old man, Hacon," came the curt reply, and without waiting Candamir waded into the water. Hacon sighed and followed him.

The last two days, Candamir had been reserved and moody. They had gotten up at sunrise on the first day and wisely taken the time to catch and fry a few trout, setting out right after, eating while they walked. Water and food had helped them to quickly overcome the toil and deprivation of their desert crossing. Candamir's fever was gone, and the muscle cramps did not come back either. Despite their greatly improved circumstances, Candamir remained silent for most of the hours they spent walking through the forest. *A simple "thank you" would have been sufficient,* Hacon thought to himself, but he waited in vain. When he could no longer stand his brother's silence, he asked, "Would you rather I had left you behind to die?"

Candamir glowered at him before replying, "If you can restrain yourself from boasting of your accomplishment, I'd appreciate your keeping to yourself what happened."

Offended, Hacon remained silent for the remainder of their journey. Only hours later did he realize that Candamir had not answered his question.

Side by side they arrived at the far shore. Candamir's knees were weak and he was short of breath, but he wasn't going to let his brother see how exhausted he was.

The village meadow lay deserted in the evening sunlight. They were grateful to be spared the curious glances and questions for the time being. Candamir said goodbye to his brother with a curt nod and entered his yard. No one was there. He hoped fervently that this only meant they were all at supper, but suddenly a high-pitched voice came from behind. "What are you doing here?"

Nils, Candamir realized. Slowly he turned around so as not to frighten the boy.

Nils was standing there, perhaps five paces away, between him and the orchard. "Who are you?" It sounded half scared, half defiant.

For a moment Candamir was so shaken by the fact that his son did not recognize him that he could neither move nor answer. With growing dismay, he realized that the boy was holding a knife in his small fist.

Slowly Candamir sank to his knees in the grass. "It's me, Nils, your father." He held his hands out to him. "Just come and look at me close up and you'll see that I'm telling the truth."

The child's little red mouth formed a circle of pure astonishment. But his sea-gray eyes shone. Nils recognized his father's voice, and with a shout of joy cast the weapon aside and wrapped his arms around him.

Candamir embraced him, laughing, and lifted him up. "Well, well."

"But your hair is so short that I thought you were a foreign slave and…"

"Hair grows back, you know. Where is your mother?"

"She's with Austin. He's wounded."

She was alive, she wasn't captured, and that was all Candamir could take in at first. It was only after a moment that he grasped the second half of what Nils had said. "Wounded? Badly?"

"I don't know."

"Did Lars's men do that?"

"No, Osmund did. Father, why do you look so different? It's not just your hair, it's something else, but what is it?"

"Osmund wounded Austin?"

"Yes. Now I see! You're so thin!" Nils placed a hand over his mouth and giggled. Since he knew little about sickness and even less about hunger, it seemed funny to him to see a skinny man.

Candamir knew he had to go to Siglind at once. He grinned conspiratorially at Nils and patted him on his heavy black head of hair. "Are your sisters well?"

The boy nodded.

Candamir put him down. "Then run into the house and tell them I'm back and I'm well. And so is your uncle. I'm going to see Austin."

He was about to turn away, but Nils pulled him back by the hand. "Austin is here at our house. His house burned down."

Candamir stooped down, picked up the dangerous weapon from the grass, and recognized it as his own. "Where did you get my knife?" he asked as he walked toward the house with Nils.

"We found it next to the fallen walnut tree after you had… disappeared. Mother put it in the chest, but last night when the robbers came, she gave it to me."

*Poor child,* Candamir thought, *you're too young to be the man of the house.* He put the sharp blade carefully into his cloth belt before entering.

Only the slaves and the children were in the hall. He placed a finger on his lips to forestall their boisterous welcome, then scooped Irmgardis up in his arms. She clung to him like a kraken, so he carried her with him to the back room.

Siglind looked up when she heard the door opening. Slowly she rose from the stool alongside the bed and took a step toward him. "Oh, the Lord be praised," she whispered. "It's true, he wasn't lying…"

Candamir went to his wife, pulled her to him with his free arm, and pressed his lips to her mouth. Siglind stood up on her tiptoes as always and wrapped her arms around his neck, along with Irmgardis. They stood like that for a few moments, and Candamir supposed that he and Siglind would have stayed that way for hours, but their daughter had other plans. "I have a loose tooth, Father!" she announced. "Here, just look!" She opened her mouth wide and put a finger on one of the tiny lower incisors.

Candamir let go of his wife and duly admired the loose tooth. Then he set Irmgardis down. "Tomorrow we'll think about what we'll do with it after it falls out," he promised.

"Are you going to make me a little box for it?"

He nodded. "If you're a good child now and go to Solvig and finish your bowl at supper today for a change."

She gave him a sorrowful look, lamenting the injustice of a world in which parents could put conditions on every promise. But apparently she wanted the little box very badly, for she left without further objection.

Candamir sat down on the stool and pulled Siglind onto his lap. Carefully, she placed her hands on his face. He closed his eyes, but when he felt her lips on his forehead, he opened them again and then they simply looked at each other. Nothing of what he saw surprised him. She had worried, suffered, and grieved. He smiled more lightheartedly than he actually felt, and with his little finger wiped away the tear that ran down her cheek.

Then he looked down at Austin, who lay motionless in their bed, his eyes closed. He was terribly pale, and the unaccustomed shadow of a beard covered his chin. "What's wrong with him?"

Siglind turned back the cover a bit, revealing a bloody bandage covering the Saxon's slender chest and right shoulder. "He has a sword wound and has lost much blood, but this morning the bleeding stopped. If he doesn't run a fever, he'll make it. In any case, I hope so. I really don't know very much about these things, and Inga refused to treat him. Fortunately, Heide knew which herbs to use to stop the bleeding and where to find them."

"Osmund attacked Austin with a sword?" he asked incredulously.

She shrugged with a helpless look and nodded hesitantly. "In a way."

"Tell me how it happened."

"Yes, but not here. Let's go out. He's sleeping peacefully now and doesn't need us."

In celebration of Candamir's return, Heide killed a few chickens, apologizing that supper would be a little late because of that. Siglind placed two cups on a board along with a pitcher of mead, a generous helping of bread, and some delicious goat cheese, then carried it out into the garden. Under the apple tree they sat down in the grass close together and kept their silence as Candamir ate.

"Take your time, otherwise it won't agree with you," she warned.

"Yes, Hacon said that too," he answered with a full mouth. "But it's not true. Anything agrees with me except hunger."

"How is your brother? Did they almost let him die of starvation too?"

He shook his head. "They fattened him up because he had to work for them, but also, I now believe, to turn us against each other. Lars is a wily scoundrel, just like his father. Anyway, it was just as well they fed Hacon so generously, for the day before yesterday, he carried me more than five miles through the wasteland. It took two, three, maybe even four hours—I have no idea. And that…embarrassed me so much that I've treated him like dirt ever since," he concluded, with a disarming, remorseful smile.

Siglind took him by one hand. "Don't worry. You'll make up for it," she said confidently.

Candamir nodded, even though he wasn't so sure his brother would ever forgive him. He tore off another large piece of bread from the fresh, soft loaf. "I must go over to Osmund's house. He must be worried about us as well."

"It almost drove him crazy," she replied in a strangely matter-of-fact way.

"Then I had best go over right away. But first I must know what took place here last night."

"They came after midnight. The watchmen at the river discovered the *Dragon* and sounded the alarm, but this time they had brought their women along, who plundered Thorbjörn's barn as well as a few others while our men were fighting with theirs at the shore. When the women had taken their plunder to the ship and given a sign, Lars and his men withdrew—all except Gunnar."

"Gunnar?"

She cast a brief, sad look at him and nodded. "He surrendered to Osmund. He wanted to leave the wasteland and come back to us. He said he was sorry for what he had done and how his brother had treated you. Hacon, he said, had got him to thinking about how he might be able to start over again with us, now that his father was dead. He said he was ready to work as our slave for seven years as atonement for the harm he had done us."

"An acceptable offer," Candamir said.

She nodded. "Harald and Jared thought so too. Jared was beside himself with joy to have one of his brothers back. Even when Gunnar confessed that he had been the one who had set fire to his barn, Jared was ready to forgive him everything on the spot. But Osmund…" She broke off, as if she had suddenly lost heart.

"Well?"

"He didn't believe a word Gunnar said. He ordered two of his men to tie him up, and then he asked him where you were. Gunnar replied that you had fled the night before with Hacon. But Osmund didn't believe that either, and he held Gunnar's feet to the fire to force the truth out of him."

Slowly Candamir put down the piece of bread. "Oh, Osmund," he said softly. "Truest of all friends. You picked out exactly the wrong one…"

"That's what Harald and a few others said, too. They were inclined to trust Gunnar, but the majority sided with Osmund, and he…showed no mercy. Gunnar's screams woke up our children, and other children as well everywhere on the meadow. The women scolded Osmund and insisted he stop, but he paid them no heed. Finally, Austin intervened. He simply got a bucket of water and put out the fire, then stood in front of Gunnar to protect him. Osmund drew his sword and put it to Austin's throat.

"'Go ahead, kill me, and we'll both know it doesn't have the slightest thing to do with this poor boy,' Austin said. He was completely…fearless, or at least he gave that impression. Osmund was so furious; I have never seen him like that before. He took another step forward and pressed harder with his blade. 'Get out of my way,' he threatened him. 'If you don't, I'll do this community a long overdue favor and release us all from you and your accursed god.'

"Austin didn't budge an inch, and at the very moment Osmund was going to strike, the smith pulled Austin aside so that the blade wounded him only superficially." She had to stop for a moment because tears were coming to her eyes. She had been sure her gentle friend would die, and the horror of it all was still very much on her mind.

"And while the ruthless villain was still standing there dazed, wondering where his innocent, defenseless victim had suddenly gone, noble Jared carried his wailing brother into the house, and the gruesome scene came to an end," a soft voice said behind them.

Candamir jumped to his feet. "Osmund!" He laughed and put his arms around his foster brother. "A happy end, it seems to me."

Osmund squinted, reciprocated the embrace briefly, and then drew away. "It remains to be seen if this is the end of the story. Welcome home, Candamir. I had almost given up hope of ever seeing you again."

"Yes," replied Candamir solemnly. "I thought the same myself."

"I hope my words didn't offend you, Osmund. It was not my intent to speak ill of you," Siglind said stiffly, rising from the ground.

He nodded almost imperceptibly.

"Oh, come on," Candamir said impatiently. "You know how fond she is of the Saxon, Osmund. And last night none of you could know that Gunnar was telling the truth. His feet will heal, and so will Austin's wound, and we can forget the whole story."

*Just as you always try to forget everything that's disagreeable to you,* Siglind thought. But this was hardly the right moment to point that out.

Osmund nodded hesitantly, then looked Candamir over carefully from head to foot. His gaze lingered on his friend's shorn head. Candamir began chewing nervously on his thumbnail, as had become his habit. He knew that he looked like a worn-out slave, and that alone was embarrassing. He considered not leaving the house until his hair was long again and he was back to normal weight.

"I wish I'd killed Gunnar," Osmund said.

Candamir took the thumb out of his mouth and shook his head. "But he was the only one who helped us." He thought back on the horrible scene in Lars's hall. *Oh, ye gods, was that really just three nights ago?* "Without him we would never have been able to escape. Without him I'd probably be dead now."

Osmund simply stood there, his arms dangling, and for a moment he appeared not to know what to think or to say. Candamir put a hand on his shoulder. "Come along inside and join us for supper, and then I'll tell you what it was like."

"I'd really like to," his friend replied, "but I can't. Today is the equinox, and Inga is waiting for me at the temple."

Candamir released his hand on Osmund's shoulder. "Then come tomorrow."

Osmund hesitated. "Come to my place," he finally said. "I don't want to enter your house as long as the Saxon is there. Good night, Candamir, Siglind." Then he turned around and disappeared into the dusk.

Candamir stared after him in disbelief.

Siglind took his hand. "You were away a long time," she said gently. "Many things have changed here."

During supper, the mood in Candamir's hall was unusually tense and quiet. They were all happy that he was back home, but it was embarrassing to the slaves that their master looked like one of them—only skinnier. Nils besieged his father with questions about his battle with Olaf and life in the wasteland, and Candamir replied. But Siglind could tell that he was too exhausted for that and had not yet overcome the horrors of his captivity. She decided to put an end to the conversation before Candamir's mood changed and he snapped at the boy.

"Godwin, would you be so good as go to your father and Asta and to the other neighbors to tell them that Candamir and Hacon have returned and they are well? They'll all be so relieved to hear it, and we shouldn't keep them waiting."

The young carpenter rose and set out on his way with the happy news.

"And you go to the bathhouse," Siglind whispered to Candamir.

"But it's dark," he protested in surprise.

"Do it just the same," she advised him with such a promising smile that he raised no further objections.

In the bathhouse, two little oil lamps were burning, and in their warm glow he found not just a wonderful, warm bath prepared for him, but alongside the tub, a bed made of furs, blankets, and soft feather cushions. It was then he remembered that his own bed was occupied. No sooner had he stretched out in the water than his wife entered. Without saying a word, she took off her clothes, climbed into the bath with him, and they made love gently, fervently, in a tight embrace. Then she washed him from head to foot, as if he were a little boy, and he submitted to this, feeling with closed eyes how she washed away the fear, anger, and despair of the last three months along with the desert dust.

Finally, he climbed out of the tub, dried himself casually, and reclined on the little makeshift bed. A mug of beer had been placed nearby. He drank deeply and gave a sigh of pleasure. "You must really have missed me," he said. "This is the first time you have tempted me to drink."

She sat down beside him, wrapped her arms around her raised knees, and looked at him with a smile. "I thought you must have had very little mead or beer recently."

He shook his head. "Only water. On good days. It was like during our winter famine, only warmer."

She wasn't deceived by his mocking tone. She lowered her eyes and took his hand. "Only yesterday we learned from Gunnar that you had killed Olaf. And I was so relieved, because I knew you had been spared what you feared most of all. But then the thought came to me that Lars surely would try to get vengeance. He admired his father so much."

"And is indeed a worthy successor."

She didn't reply to that, but waited till he had emptied the beer mug and stretched out. Then she blew out the lights and lay down with him. She had hoped he would talk when it got dark, but he fell asleep at once.

Shortly before dawn, he woke with a start from a confusing nightmare that had more to do with Gunnar's feet than with events in the wasteland. He shook off the ugly images and awakened his wife, who willingly took him in her arms even before she had opened her eyes. Only then did he tell her what she wanted to know, as the first gray light of dawn gradually seeped through the cracks in the board walls. It was distasteful to him, but he knew it was the best way to put behind him all that had happened. And he kept almost nothing from her, telling her things that he could never have confided to anyone else.

"And now it's your turn," he finally said. "What happened here? Ye gods, what happened to Osmund?"

Siglind was suddenly restless. "Let me trim your beard while I tell you, may I?"

"Please do. But there's nothing you can do to make me handsome before my hair has grown back."

"There's nothing that will ever make you handsome," she replied with a grin. They both laughed, mostly because it sounded so marvelously normal, as if everything was just as it used to be.

Siglind borrowed his knife, raised his chin with her finger, and set to work. "On Midsummer's Day there was an earthquake."

Candamir held still. "Yes, I know." They had felt it also in the wasteland. "I imagine that Inga didn't let the occasion pass without demanding more rituals and sacrifices."

Siglind nodded. "She ordered Austin, me, and the other Christians to take part in the midsummer festival. We didn't. Then Harald told us that during the ceremony in the temple, she called upon everyone there to fight the 'false god and his servants' who were a constant offense to Odin. And that's what they have been doing ever since. They cast insults at every chance, they throw stones at Austin, and in the *Thing* they do whatever Osmund tells them. Inga has forbidden Roric and little Siward from playing with Nils, and all three of them are unhappy about that."

Candamir listened incredulously and with increasing anxiety. He seized her by the wrist, took the knife away from her, and pulled her down next to him on the blanket.

"At the last *Thing* they decided to prohibit the wearing of crosses," Siglind continued, her hands folded in her lap. "Whoever does so must pay a fine of one sheep and one horse to the temple."

"*What?*"

"Since then I've worn my cross under my dress, for I was alone and feared for my children. Moreover, I didn't want them to get their hands on your wonderful horses. But Austin...well, you know him. If he had had an even larger cross, he probably would have hung that around his neck just to defy Inga and Osmund. Since he owns neither sheep nor horses, he couldn't pay the fine, but they took his cow and his pig, and a week ago someone set fire to his house."

"O mighty Tyr..."

"Fortunately, he wasn't at home. We had met in the smithy to celebrate mass. We have to do it again in secret, as we used to."

"And did they burn all his books?"

Siglind shook her head. "He suspected that something like that might happen and gave his books to the smith for safekeeping, as well as his supply of parchment and ink."

It was quiet for a moment. Finally Candamir murmured, "I think I must have a word with my foster brother."

Siglind put her hand on his arm as a warning. "Be gentle with him, Candamir. He went to look for you, you know. Four times he went out into the wasteland with a group of men to look for you—always without success. And each time he came back, he seemed more desperate. I think that's what made him so unforgiving."

"That? Or his wife?" Candamir asked sharply. "She is worse than Brigitta, an absolute snake in the grass."

*So you know that?* Siglind thought, surprised, realizing that she had underestimated her husband. She nodded uneasily. "Whatever it is that's bothering her, apparently it's no longer enough to just make poor Roric pay for it. Now she's out to get everyone not of her faith."

Candamir pulled Siglind close to him and put his chin on top of her head. "Don't be afraid any longer. I'm back now, and I have no intention of disappearing again. I'll bring Osmund to his senses—you'll see."

Siglind pressed her lips to his shoulder. She did feel safer having him here. But she doubted he could persuade Osmund to give up the course he was now pursuing, as he seemed quite beguiled with the power he suddenly had. And he was acting from deep conviction. The events of the last few months had made him more unbending than was his nature, but he hated Austin and his god with a passion, and sometimes she couldn't shake the feeling that he hated her, too.

Suddenly restless, she extricated herself from Candamir's arms. "There," she said, pointing at the stool near the chest of firewood. "I picked out your best clothes. Get dressed and then let's go and see how Austin is doing."

When they entered the hall, the members of the household were already awake and getting ready for breakfast. Heide was cooking buttermilk soup, and Freydis was spreading honey on rye bread. Candamir snatched a piece, grinned impudently at his maid's indignant protest, and, still chewing on his bread, followed Siglind to the bedroom.

Austin was sitting upright in bed leaning on a pillow. He was still pale, but when he caught sight of Candamir he broke out in a wide smile. Stretching out his left hand he said, "I dreamt I heard your voice. So it is true."

Candamir took Austin's hand and squeezed it so tightly it nearly broke the monk's bones. "It's true. Here I am—not entirely unscathed, perhaps, but alive. And how are you, my foolish Saxon friend?"

"The same. At least better than I could have dared to hope the night before last."

They exchanged knowing smiles, but had no opportunity to go over what had happened. "Above all," Siglind interrupted, "Austin needs rest. Go and have a good breakfast, Candamir, and tell Heide to bring Austin a bowl of soup."

Candamir made no objections, but before leaving the room turned and asked, "Is there anything I can do for you?"

The Saxon nodded eagerly. "Get me my Bible. It's at Harald's house."

"I know. I wanted to stop by there soon, in any case."

He went back into the hall, ate an enormous breakfast, and began receiving an unending stream of visitors, all of whom wanted to see Candamir with their own eyes. He was grateful to them for their concern but troubled by all the uneasy, furtive glances. Silently he praised his wife for her foresight; at least the fine clothing she had picked out gave him a bit more self-confidence.

"Ah, I think I've got it now," Hacon said optimistically. He was sitting at a table in Harald's house studying one of Austin's books and running his finger along the lines of tiny runes.

The smith, Asta, Godwin, and Jared stood around, gaping at him as if he were juggling colorful little balls or speaking in verse.

"Here—*Yarrow, also called woundwort, is a pretty plant which grows to a height of between one span and an ell. It can be recognized by its feather-shaped leaves and the tight, white to pink paniculate umbels. The plant flowers from early May through October.* That is, from Honey Moon through Wind Moon, therefore still at this time. *Since it is sun-loving, it grows mostly alongside fields and in meadows in Catan, but rarely in the forest, just like chamomile, eyebright used for curing eye ailments, and Hypericum, also called St. John's wort, which likewise...* Heavens, Austin, why must you always be so wordy," Hacon murmured impatiently, skipping over the next few lines and then finding what they wanted to know: *"Burns can be treated with a yarrow compress that relieves pain, promotes healing, and prevents gangrene. For each compress, take two large handfuls of blossoms and boil them in a small pot of water for as long as it takes to pray ten paternosters before straining them. Soak clean linen bandages in the liquid and place them on the wound. Repeat the treatment at noon and at vespers."* Hacon looked up. "That's it."

Jared went to the door. "Thanks, Hacon. I won't forget this favor."

"I'll come with you," Asta offered. "I know where yarrow grows."

In the doorway, they almost bumped into Candamir.

Asta embraced her brother. "Oh, Candamir..."

Embarrassed, he patted her shoulder briefly before pulling away and looking at her flat stomach. "Well? How many came out?"

"Only one," she replied. "A boy. We named him Candamir. It was meant as...a sign of hope."

Candamir smiled and nodded at the smith curtly, but they knew him well and could see that Candamir was moved.

He turned to Jared. "How is Gunnar?"

Jared looked away, embarrassed. "Probably about the way you would like."

"I believe you're mistaken. Is he feverish?"

Jared shook his head. "My Margild is tending to him, and Hacon read to us from the Saxon's book telling us what we have to do," he replied before making his exit with Asta.

"Noble Hacon," Candamir murmured after the door had closed. "A man of many talents—smith, scholar, life-saver."

Hacon turned his head and glared at him. "Did you come over here just to make fun of me?"

Candamir stepped up to him and placed a hand on his shoulder. "No, I came to thank you. I...well." He raised his hands again and smiled bashfully. "I felt embarrassed, Hacon. You must understand that."

"No, I don't," the young smith growled.

"Don't be so hard on him," Harald gently scolded his former apprentice. "It was a shock for your roles to be so suddenly reversed, and now he has made up for his mistake."

Hacon grumbled.

Harald gestured to Candamir to take a seat at the table. "Here, lad, try Asta's sheep cheese..."

Candamir readily accepted, but remarked with a shake of his head, "Suddenly they all want to fatten me up. I'll gain weight again, you'll see. It just won't happen in a day."

Harald nodded, but nevertheless looked at him with concern.

"Austin is better," Candamir reported. "He's awake now and wants his Bible."

"Praise be to Jesus Christ," Hacon murmured, crossing himself. "I would have stopped by to see him sooner, but I didn't dare go to your house." His tone still sounded cool.

Candamir placed his elbows on the table and leaned forward a bit. "I know you're furious, and it's just what I deserve. So beat my brains in if you like. But at the moment we can't afford the luxury of quarreling with one another, do you understand?"

Hacon looked at him for a moment. "I'm not sure, Candamir. You usually enjoy quarreling with me so much."

"Candamir thinks we have serious problems," said the smith, who never tired of being the intermediary between his two brothers-in-law.

Hacon nodded. Gunda had told him about the events of the last few months, just as Siglind had told Candamir, and Hacon could hardly believe how great Gunda's fear was of Osmund and Inga and how much had changed here—as if he had been gone for three years, not three months. Hacon absentmindedly passed his hands over Austin's book of herbs, and sighing audibly, he said, "Fine, you are right. Let's think about what we should do."

Candamir spent most of the day in his workshop, as there was a great deal to be done there. Godwin had not been able to handle all the work himself, and orders of tables, chests, beds, carts, and even new buildings had piled up.

Almost every hour, Heide or one of the other maids came and brought cold chicken from the day before, cheese, bread with honey, and pies, and although Candamir scolded them and told them they shouldn't go to such a fuss, he ate it all anyway—for the most part without washing his hands, so that everything he ate was garnished with wood chips.

Many neighbors and friends also stopped to visit him in the carpentry shop. They came to express their thanks and admiration for slaying Olaf, or to make sure he knew that they were waiting more urgently for their new furniture than anyone else, or just to express their concern at the events of recent weeks.

Candamir listened to them attentively, but his hands were never idle. He hadn't been aware of how much he had missed his work, the feeling of his tools in his hands, and the fragrance of wood, resin, and glue.

A number of them also came to advise him to turn the Saxon out of his house and forbid his wife from associating with him and his god.

"My wife chooses her friends and her god the way she pleases, and any of my neighbors who have had their house set on fire by a wicked scoundrel will find shelter in my hall," Candamir replied heatedly.

"You had better watch out," Godwin warned him after Haflad had gone storming out. He was not the first to have done so.

"Why?" Candamir inquired, puzzled. "Why shouldn't I say what I think in my own home? Haflad and I rarely agree, but that never kept me awake nights."

Godwin nodded grimly. "But those who think the way he does are now in the majority."

Candamir shrugged it off. "The way you put it, it sounds like we are separated into hostile camps."

Godwin did not reply.

After they had finished their day's work, Candamir washed up with a bucketful of fresh water that Nori had brought him from the river, before they headed out to care for the horses. The stable was at the east end of the yard, as close as possible to the gate in the hedge, for at this dry, mild time of the year the horses went out to graze for a few hours every day.

Buri pricked up his ears when he heard Candamir's voice and turned his head toward his master expectantly. Candamir patted him on the neck. "Have you missed me, old pal?" He took a few apples from a box of windfalls near the stable door and fed them to his beloved horses. The three foals had grown a lot since he had seen them last, and Nori told him all about their adventures and growing pains.

"The sorrel was limping on his near fore for almost three weeks, and I simply couldn't figure out what was wrong. Then he caught a fever and I was really worried. But he wouldn't let me look at the hoof in order to really know. Honestly, Master, he was kicking like a billy goat. Finally, Austin made the little fellow so drunk on beer that he couldn't stand up and became as meek as a lamb. Then the Saxon made a small cut in the hoof and discovered an ingrown splinter of wood."

Candamir listened, stroking the foal's shaggy mane. "You were lucky, weren't you, little fellow?"

Nori nodded. "If they drive Austin away, many will miss him, men and beasts alike," he prophesied gloomily.

"What makes you think such nonsense?" Candamir asked, annoyed.

The servant shrugged. "Everyone says it's going to happen—all the slaves, I mean."

Candamir waved him off impatiently, took a bridle from a hook on the wall, and put the bit between Buri's teeth. Without another word, he led the fine, light-colored stallion out into the evening sunshine and swung himself up on his back.

The distance to Osmund's house was not far enough to require a horse, but Candamir longed for the company of his beloved Buri. The stallion possessed every virtue that men value in a horse—he was tireless, loyal, brave, and fast as an arrow. But the two things Candamir loved most about him that evening were his innocence and silence—two characteristics he wished many of his neighbors possessed.

He took a lengthy detour along the hedge, pondering Nori's words. He knew that slaves often had a sixth sense for what their masters were thinking and for every quarrel that was brewing, as their lives, or at least their well-being, often depended on recognizing these warning signs in time.

The stillness of the evening was soothing after such a busy day. In the stables, most of which faced the hedge, slaves were busy milking and mucking out the stalls. Children were playing with balls or wooden swords in the gardens. In an orchard he saw a pair of lovers standing in a tight embrace, while in the next garden a young lad was consoling his little sister who was bitterly crying over a broken wood doll. Before his exile to the wasteland, Candamir was not sure he would have been able to appreciate the simple beauty of this evening. He realized that he loved this place he had helped to build, and that, in seven short years, he had put down roots here deeper than those he had had in Elasund.

Osmund's stables also lay close to the hedge. They were among the largest, because of the vast number of sheep he kept. Candamir wrinkled his nose as he rode by. He still thought that sheep smelled worse than any other farm animal, with the possible exception of goats, and he had never regretted his decision to keep only as many as he needed to clothe his household. Behind the pens, close to the river, was a windowless shed where Osmund kept his wool, and Candamir heard a soft whimpering as he approached.

He dismounted, opened the padlock with the key left in the lock, and pushed through the heavy wooden door. In the wedge of evening light entering the little room, he saw Roric kneeling on the ground, trying in vain to hold back his tears, his arms wrapped around the neck of a dog that looked almost as unhappy as he was.

"What's the matter, Roric?" asked Candamir, crossing the threshold and crouching down in front of him.

Startled, the boy looked up, but then he immediately lowered his eyes again. "You're back. Thanks be to Odin."

"You mean nobody told you?"

Roric shook his head. "I…we have been in here since yesterday."

"Ye gods, what have you two been up to?"

Roric passed his hands through the shaggy coat of his loyal companion. "He didn't do anything. I was with Nils. And she caught me."

"Your mother?"

He looked at Candamir again with his deep blue eyes, and despite his tears, his anger was evident. "My father's wife."

Candamir was relieved to hear that Roric had apparently given up searching for affection where none would be found. But this cold fury—so unnatural for an eight-year-old lad—was disconcerting.

The brave front quickly crumbled, however. "She…she said if the robbers, the pixies, or the evil river spirits came to get me, I had no one to blame but myself. And I was so terribly afraid last night," Roric concluded, with embarrassment. His mouth was quivering. "I just saw that the light coming through the cracks is slowly turning red, and I realized she means to leave me here another night. I don't know if I can stand it, and I am so terribly hungry."

*Bitch,* Candamir thought with disgust. He stood up and took the boy's free hand in his own. "Come along, Roric. You've been in here long enough."

Roric pulled his hand away and withdrew further back into the darkness of the shed. "No, please. That will only make it worse. She'll smile and act as if she has forgiven me until you go home. Then she'll start scolding again and won't give my father any peace until he beats me. It won't take much to get him to do it, for he hates it when I'm disobedient."

"Well, it's the same with all fathers, you know. And they are right. A good son obeys his father, that's the rule. And so a disobedient son is not a good son, and that naturally grieves a father."

Roric nodded, barely concealing his impatience. He had heard this lecture before.

Candamir held the door open for him. "A good son also obeys his father's foster brother. Come now, lad, you must eat. And your friend here is surely just as hungry as you are. If you want, you can ride back to the house on Buri."

He didn't know which of his tacts proved more persuasive, but in any case, Roric stepped out of the stuffy shed, and when Candamir set him down on the horse's back, the boy beamed. Candamir took the reins so that Buri wouldn't get too high-spirited when he noticed he had an inexperienced little rider, and the puppy followed them, wagging its tail.

When they arrived at the door, Candamir helped the boy down and placed a hand on his shoulder, pushing him in front of him. "Forgive me, Inga, for overruling your judgment. Roric objected to coming along, but hungry men have to stick together."

She was standing at the hearth tasting what the maids had cooked. With the large wooden spoon in her hand, she turned around and smiled. "Welcome home, Candamir."

Even without Roric's revelation, he could easily see that her smile was as deceptive as a calm sea under stormy skies. "Where is Osmund?" he asked.

"Out by the beehives. He insists on helping to bring in the honey."

"Ye gods." Candamir shook his head and grinned. "I hope he doesn't faint again, or supper will surely be late tonight."

Osmund appeared in the doorway and said with a laugh, "Don't worry, the bees were kind to me." As he walked by, he placed a hand on Candamir's arm. "Come and sit down. Birte, bring my guest a drink." He walked over to the bucket of water next to the hearth and washed his hands and face, smiling to his wife in passing. Then he sat down on his high seat and winked at his eldest son. "Free already?"

Roric shuffled his feet in the rushes on the floor, embarrassed. "So you know…," he mumbled.

Osmund nodded and exchanged a quick glance with Candamir, who had trouble concealing his astonishment. So Osmund had knowingly let the boy spend a night in terror, just one day after Lars and his men had attacked.

"Candamir brought me out," Roric said.

Osmund nodded. "A smart boy knows who his friends are, doesn't he?"

"I only wonder what may have led Candamir to look around in our wool shed," Inga murmured, putting a jug of mead down on the table. "Was he perhaps feeling cold and looking around for a fleece to warm him up?"

Candamir poured himself a drink, caught Roric's pleading look, and replied to Inga, "The dog barked. I thought perhaps he had been locked in there by mistake, so I went to have a look. I hope you don't mind. Just go and count your fleeces if you're afraid I have stolen one." He took no pains to conceal what he thought of her qualities as a stepmother in general and of this whole matter in particular.

"Oh, of course I have nothing against it, quite to the contrary," she replied sweetly. "I only wish you were as concerned about your own domestic affairs as you are about ours."

Candamir grimaced in disgust, raised his cup to Osmund, and drank.

Osmund reciprocated the gesture, but before putting the cup to his lips he said to his wife, "We're not in the temple here, but in *my* house, where my friends will be treated with civility and respect."

They were sharp, clear words, and they were spoken in the presence of Roric and the slave Birte. Inga stared at her husband for a moment as if he had slapped her, then she blushed, and fighting to control her tears mumbled, "Of course, Osmund."

He nodded without looking at her again, and she turned away like a maid who had been rebuked. Candamir knew it wasn't particularly kind of him, but he was quite pleased to see her humiliated.

Shortly afterwards the remaining household and the younger children arrived, and they all greeted Candamir joyfully. Osmund had slaughtered a lamb in celebration of Candamir's return home, and the servants brought it to the table on a spit. His foster brother was moved by the gesture and ate with shameless relish.

After the meal, the two friends left the hall with the pitcher and their cups of mead, just as they had done innumerable times in the past, strolled down to the river, and sat down in the grass to talk. It was rather dark, but an unearthly glow over the mountains in the east signaled the moon would soon be rising.

"Siglind told me how you kept looking and never gave up on us, and I want to thank you for that, Osmund. I know the wasteland, and so I know that hardly anyone would have set out to search a second time. You did it four times, and that's something I can barely imagine."

Osmund shrugged. "I just couldn't believe that you had been swallowed up by the earth. And I thought that if I looked hard enough, I would simply have to find you and the den of thieves. Where are they hiding out?"

"They call the place Olaf's castle. It's a series of caves, one of them very large. Lars claims it's impregnable, and I'm afraid he may be right." He described to Osmund what the caves looked like.

"They could be starved out," Osmund remarked, with unmistakable excitement.

Candamir nodded hesitantly. "Perhaps. But it would take a long time, for down below they store all the provisions they have stolen, and they have a limitless supply of water. If they took the livestock across the bridge before they drew it in, you could count on your siege lasting three months before they'd get hungry. If you sent a force to besiege the castle, how would you feed them there for that long? Where would you get enough water? Lars would have all the advantages on his side while we'd be left to die of hunger and thirst in the desert. Anyway, you'd first have to find the entrance to the cave again. I don't think I could. Everything there looks so much the same..."

For a while they weighed the implications of such a long and tedious campaign. But finally Candamir broached the subject that had caused him the greatest worry since returning home. "Osmund, why do you forbid your sons from visiting Nils? I know he's often wild and impetuous, but…so was I."

"You still are."

"Perhaps. But have you ever watched them when they're together? Haven't you seen how much calmer Nils is when he's with Roric, and how much more light-hearted Roric becomes when he's with Nils? Isn't it just the way it used to be with you and me? They're good for each other, and they like each other's company, so what's the problem?"

Osmund did not reply at once, as if he were carefully weighing his words.

Candamir grew impatient at his silence and asked, "Do you think my son is cowardly, or dishonest, or do you find some other fault in him that might be dangerous to your sons?"

"There is nothing cowardly or dishonest about Nils, Candamir," he replied, trying to placate his friend. "But he's dangerous nonetheless. It's not he," Osmund said, anticipating Candamir's outraged protests, "but the influences he's exposed to. Do you realize how much time he spends in the company of the Saxon? That he's learning to read his runes, that he neglects his duties in order to go and listen to his stories? That has all happened more frequently since you were gone, because Siglind does nothing to stop it. On the contrary, she encourages it. Your son mocks the gods, Candamir."

"*What?*" Candamir was astonished.

Osmund nodded. "He told Roric that our gods are powerless idols and that only the crucified carpenter god could bring you back home again."

Candamir shook his head in disbelief. "It doesn't sound at all like Austin to tell the children such nonsense, but you can be sure I'll have a talk with him, and with Nils also."

"I'm afraid that's not enough."

"What do you mean?"

"You yourself have fallen under the influence of this Saxon without noticing it. Even while he was still your slave you listened to him and allowed him to mislead your wife and your brother to worship his god. I have never been able to understand that, and many other men feel the same way. I have come to realize that he has cast some sort of spell on you. All those who were in favor of killing him back then were right, and I was wrong. Rarely have I regretted anything as much as this error. But I will make up for it."

"Osmund…"

"The Saxon is the renegade traitor, Candamir."

"He is *what*?"

"He's the one that Brigitta's last oracle warned us of. Don't tell me you forgot."

But he had. With everything that had happened in recent months, he had actually forgotten about Brigitta and her malicious, ambiguous oracle. "Oh, Osmund, I just can't believe that you would pay any attention to the foolish talk of a dying witch."

"It wasn't foolish talk." Osmund's voice sounded sharp. "All her oracles have come true. The very fact that we are here should give you a little more respect for her perceptiveness. But as I said, you too are under the spell of the traitor."

Candamir could no longer sit still. He stood up, folded his arms, and looked down at Osmund, shaking his head. "So you think I'm so weak that I've simply fallen under a magic spell, do you?"

"No, not weak, just gullible and good-natured. His magic is strong. The very fact that so many of our people have been taken in by him—not the least of whom is your wife, who has just as strong a will as you do—proves that."

"He's *not* a traitor! Fine, he's perhaps a little strange and easily gets carried away with things that concern his god, but there is nothing about him that is evil or malicious. He does nothing with his powders and salves except help his fellow men."

"Indeed!" Osmund jumped to his feet as well. "And those who take his powders and salves one day are praying to his god the next. Don't you find that strange?"

"That's not true. He doesn't bewitch them, he cures them. Most of the time, at least. Shall I tell you what I think, Osmund? You're embarrassed that you were wrong when you wanted to roast Gunnar, and the Saxon was right. You want to forget that as quickly as possible, and you want everyone else to forget it as well. That's why you want to get rid of Austin."

By now the moon had risen over the mountains, and Candamir could see Osmund shaking his finger at him. "And I'm telling you, Candamir, it's a provocation to Odin and all the other gods that we tolerate him here in our midst. It's a constant offense. He's the renegade traitor, so he must go, and I don't care how. But I will defeat him, just as the oracle predicted."

"I see." Candamir spoke in a soft but unmistakably contemptuous tone of voice. "So you consider yourself to be the worthiest among us whom we must choose as our leader, do you?"

Osmund did not dispute that, and replied in a much calmer voice, "Remember Brigitta's words shortly after our arrival in Catan: Odin chose me as the first to set foot on his land. That must have some significance, mustn't it? And if it does, then you are chosen as well, for you were the first to have a son in this land. It's up to us, you and me. That's why I had hoped to share this burden with you."

Candamir shook his head. "We are all chosen, Osmund, everyone who has set foot on this wonderful island. And it's therefore up to each of us to guide his own fate in this better homeland. A good people should have a good king, you once said, but I say a good people do not need a king."

"But they do," Osmund countered. "A threatened people need someone to protect them."

"From Austin?" Candamir asked with grim amusement.

"From all dangers, particularly from those the people don't want to recognize."

Candamir snorted. "I see you consider yourself wiser than the rest of us. So, worthy Osmund—only one head can wear a crown. Take it, I don't want it. Carry your burden alone." He turned away, furious.

"No, Candamir, don't leave like that," Osmund said.

Candamir wheeled around. "Why not? What point is there in talking if you believe you've been called by the gods to higher things, and that I am a foolish weakling who has fallen under a spell without even noticing it? In this case, what could we possibly have to say to each other?"

"I didn't mean to offend you. And I never said you were foolish or a weakling, for you aren't. But...you're so hopelessly stubborn. You always were, and it sometimes drives me to despair. You just refuse to recognize the signs; you won't see the long hand of Odin, who has planned all of this. Didn't it ever occur to you that perhaps my mother died only so that you and I would have the chance to grow up as brothers and rule over Odin's land in brotherly unity?"

The presumptuousness of this idea made Candamir shudder. He realized that he was fighting a losing battle. "Your mother died because the time the Norns had intended for her had run out. That was all."

"But Candamir..."

He raised both hands to silence him. "Let me go home. I know you want only the best for all of us, but no matter what you say, you won't convince me you're right. So let's stop before we say things to one another that we will later regret."

Osmund nodded hesitantly. "Fine, as you wish. Maybe we shouldn't have spoken about it today. You've just returned and have gone through an ordeal..."

"Osmund, I would have told you the same thing three months ago or three years ago. In this question we simply have different points of view. That's no reason for despair—it's happened before. But I'll say one thing to you: keep your hands off my Saxon. If you feel yourself called to be that leader, find yourself another victim to walk over so you can rise to your new glory. For if you touch him..." He broke off.

"Yes? What then?"

"Then...there will be discord between us. Don't do it, I entreat you. He is harmless, just like his god. What could they possibly do to threaten our gods?"

Osmund stared at him, shaking his head. "Either you have really fallen under his spell, or you care more for him than you do for me," he said in bewilderment.

Candamir turned away. "Choose whichever is easier for you to live with."

He mounted his horse and rode home without saying goodbye to Inga. When he got to his house, he was tempted to rouse Nils or Austin, or both of them, from their beds and make them suffer for the fact that they had mocked the gods and thereby caused all this misery. But Nils lay between two of his sisters, and they were all sleeping so peacefully that Candamir couldn't bring himself to let out his anger on them. And the monk had disappeared.

"Where is he?" he grumbled as he entered the bedroom and found only his wife there.

"I thought you would be pleased that we have our bed to ourselves again," Siglind replied sleepily. "He got up, even though I didn't think it wise, and went to Hacon and Gunda's house."

"Splendid," Candamir said sarcastically. "Together they can worship his accursed god until the heavens come crashing down upon us."

She propped herself up on her elbows. "What's the matter with you? What happened?"

"Nothing!" he snapped at her, struggling clumsily to take off his clothes.

Siglind looked at him in silence as he threw back the covers and lay down beside her. She didn't move. It was always hard to figure out how drunk he was when he returned from an evening with his foster brother, and normally it didn't particularly worry her. Tonight was the first time he frightened her.

He saw that in the way she looked at him, and he was ashamed. Turning his back to her, he pulled the covers over his shoulder. "We quarreled," was all he said.

"Not for the first time," she said.

"But never like this! Austin is responsible for everything. He made Nils tell Roric that our gods were powerless idols."

Siglind could guess how the argument had gone, and the fact that Candamir was already here, that he had come home so upset, told her whose side he had taken. But she realized she was walking on thin ice. "Austin often appears haughty when he's talking about the power of God. He says himself that pride is his worst failing, but believe me, he didn't instigate Nils to say anything like that. Austin himself said it to Jared, who had come to him in despair to ask for his advice after you disappeared. Nils happened to be nearby and heard it. When Austin noticed the boy was present, he made him promise never to repeat to others what he had heard. But you know how children are."

"It's getting better and better. Nils not only offended the gods, but broke his word. Just you wait, son…"

"Candamir." She placed her hand on his shoulder to calm him, but he shook it off. "Nils was so terribly unhappy when you suddenly disappeared. And Roric was not exactly blameless in the matter. He told Nils that your capture was a punishment from the gods for your faithlessness. And he, in turn, probably had heard that from one of his parents—Inga, I presume. They quarreled, just as you and Osmund do. They are just like their fathers. Even grown-ups sometimes say thoughtless things when they're upset. Now you're home again. Why can't you just let the matter rest? Haven't we all suffered enough? Can't we simply each thank our own gods that you're back and pick up our lives again?"

He thought about it for a moment. "I don't know," he said. "I don't even know if I want to, or if Osmund will let me."

"But why is it that Osmund gets to decide about this? Who is he that he should have such power?"

"The king of Catan," murmured Candamir before he could catch himself.

Siglind sat up. "What was that?"

Candamir turned around to face her. "That's what he wants to be. He thinks he has been chosen."

She snorted. "What modesty! Just what makes him think that?"

Candamir reminded her of Brigitta's last oracle and explained how Osmund had interpreted it.

As she listened, her eyes got larger and larger. "Oh, Jesus Christ, stand by us," she finally whispered. "He wants to banish Austin."

Candamir nodded. "And I told him I wouldn't allow that. I think it will have to be taken up at the next *Thing*."

They both knew that for years Osmund had held a majority there, and that, ever since his wife had become the temple priestess, few dared to vote against him even if they disagreed with him. But neither Siglind nor Candamir wanted to discuss that subject in the middle of the night, when worries and fears were far more powerful than in the light of day. He reached out to her instead, and she laid her head on his shoulder, but neither was able to sleep very much.

# Wind Moon, Year Seven

A semblance of normalcy had returned to their lives. Candamir toiled from early morning to late at night in his workshop and at the various construction sites in the village. Hacon shared Harald's smithy just as he used to, for making a new anvil was a long, complicated task, and he simply did not have the time for it. But the mood in the village was strangely tense. There were people who refused to use Candamir's services under one pretext or another, turning to Berse instead. He heard the same thing about Hacon: Thorbjörn had come into the smithy to order a new hammer, but insisted that Harald make it. When Hacon indignantly asked for the reason, Thorbjörn had simply walked away. Candamir didn't make out any better with Haflad and a few others.

Nevertheless, he went to sea to fish with a few friends, as he did every year before the autumn rains began. He was aware that it was a bad time to leave the village, but his need for the freedom he had recently regained overcame all reservations. He wanted to stand on the deck of his ship, his hand at the helm, and look out across the open sea to his heart's content.

It was the first long trip with the new *Falcon*, and both Hacon and Candamir were very pleased with its performance. Wiland had come along, as well as Jared and Gunnar, but for the first time Osmund was missing. He had claimed that he simply had no time this autumn, but Candamir was not the only one to know that this was a pretext.

Since their quarrel, Osmund had avoided him, just as he had avoided Osmund. The fact that most of the young men on board the ship were Christians had no doubt influenced his decision as well. In Osmund's place Candamir had taken Austin along—who hadn't wanted to go at all—for he feared for his safety.

It was not uncommon for a rock to come flying from behind a tree when the Saxon walked through the village, and someone had poisoned his few scrawny chickens, which aside from his books were the last of Austin's worldly possessions. He suffered it all with the silent satisfaction of the born martyr, but Candamir was furious and troubled by these vile acts that were unusual for his neighbors, and he had given the Saxon no peace until he had agreed to go along.

As always, the fishermen drank too much, brawled occasionally, and behaved dreadfully in every respect, but for Austin, too, it was a profitable fishing trip: the evening before they returned, Jared was baptized.

Silently, Candamir observed the solemn, quiet ritual, and when it was over they heard him murmur, "Woe to us if Osmund hears about this."

Jared's devoutly bowed head snapped up, and he asked Austin, "Must I tell him?"

The monk shook his head. "Your belief is your concern alone."

Jared nodded, a little ashamed at how relieved he felt. Helplessly, he looked at Candamir. "Osmund has always been so kind to me. I don't want to disappoint him."

"Oh, we certainly can't allow that. We must be considerate of noble Osmund at all costs," Gunnar said.

Candamir looked at him and frowned, but didn't rebuke him. It was not surprising that Gunnar despised Osmund. He was still suffering from constant pain in his feet and could limp only a few steps before he had to take a rest.

"He is and always will be your cousin, Gunnar," Candamir finally reminded him. "And he's not the way he seems to you."

"Really?" the young man asked. "Or am I perhaps the only one to see him for what he is while you only see what he used to be?"

"And what, do you think, makes your sight so much sharper than ours?" his brother asked angrily.

Gunnar looked at him and shrugged. "Six years in the desert."

Candamir usually stood at the helm when they were sailing, observing his companions. Some gathered at the bow with Austin at sunrise to begin the day with a prayer, while the others praised Freyr for the abundance of fish in the sea, calling upon their patron gods for help when the nets were so heavy that they could scarcely lift them out of the water. But none were offended by the ways of the others. And Candamir kept wondering why everything was so much more complicated at home.

As they sailed up the river with their good haul, Candamir was determined to try again to come to an agreement with Osmund and his adherents. But when he got home he learned that Siglind had fled to Harald's and Asta's house with the children because she feared for their lives.

"What happened?" Candamir asked when he found his family in the smith's hall.

Siglind was sitting at the table with an untouched cup in front of her. She looked small and pale and discouraged—not herself. He stood behind her and put his hands on her shoulders.

"Someone painted the Hagalaz rune on our front door," she said. "In blood. I told Solvig to wash it off, but the next morning it was there again, along with a second one on the door to the bedchamber. Someone broke into our house to threaten us, Candamir."

He exchanged glances with Harald, who shrugged helplessly. "I told her to come here. She couldn't stay there alone."

"Hagalaz…," Candamir said.

It was an ominous rune that stood for hail and the destruction it wreaked, but also for any threatening force of nature or the anger of the gods. And the really tricky thing about Hagalaz was that because it was shaped like an H, you never knew if you were looking at it or at its mirror image, because they both looked alike. The reversed image stood for loss, pain—and discord.

"Someone waited until I left my house for a week and then threatened my wife and children with a Hagalaz rune." Candamir seemed stunned. "Who…who would do such a thing? Not Osmund. Never. You can say what you want, but I'll never believe that."

Harald shook his head. "But the very fact that his name occurs to you proves how serious things are."

Candamir lowered his eyes. "You're right, I should be ashamed of myself." He sat down next to Siglind and took her hand in both of his.

"No, you have no need to be ashamed," the blacksmith said. "It would be more useful if you asked yourself why such a terrible suspicion even comes into your head."

Candamir knew the answer. He had been thinking these things over the last few days. "Because Osmund is poisoned by his hatred of the Saxon and the carpenter god. He thinks they're standing between him and what he wants—a community living in peace, unity, and prosperity here under his rule. That's what he's dreaming of, what he believes in, and to reach this goal, no price seems too high. To attain it, he is even prepared to go out into the wasteland and lay siege to Lars and his people in their impregnable fortress. And whoever is not with him…" He couldn't go on.

"Is against him," Harald concluded. "That applies even to you. I see I am spared the task of opening your eyes for you."

"What shall we do, Harald? I mean, I can't allow him to drive the Saxon away. By what right? For what reason? Must I bow to the tyranny of my foster brother in order to live in peace?"

"No, there is another way."

"And what would that be?"

Harald folded his massive arms on the table and leaned forward. "Brigitta's oracle. I know you think it's all a trick and she said these things because she could foresee the situation we are in now and wanted to strengthen Osmund's position. Nonetheless, we can make use of this oracle."

"How?"

Siglind immediately knew what Harald meant. "You killed Olaf, Candamir—the man who in truth was the 'renegade traitor,' as everyone here knows. *You* must take the position that Osmund is yearning for. Only if you become the leader of this community will all of us still have a future here."

Candamir shook his head, took his hand out of hers, and stood up, avoiding their expectant gazes. "You can forget that! I…I don't want to be this leader."

The smith nodded sympathetically, but replied, "Still, if Brigitta did see those things she told me, then it will happen, whether you like it or not, lad."

In the two weeks before the autumn *Thing*, the weather remained dry, but it was unusually oppressive for that time of year. There was no wind, and the sultriness weighed as heavily on their bodies as the tense mood did on their spirits.

The rift in the community became larger and harder to ignore. On the one side were the supporters of the new faith and all those sympathetic to them, fearful of the claims to power that the young priestess and her husband asserted. On the other side were Osmund and Inga's supporters, who met more often than usual in the temple on the island and insisted that their gods alone should rule, because this was, after all, Odin's land. In some cases this rift even ran through a family. Thorbjörn and Haldir hardly spoke to one another anymore. The case of Siward's children was even worse: Siwold and Wiland had converted openly to Austin's god, while their sister was the highly esteemed priestess of the old faith, and the siblings treated one another with undisguised hostility. These rifts frightened everyone, as they had set out from Elasund as one community and had lived as such on the island for almost seven years. Naturally, Osmund's group said that the Saxon was responsible, for he was, after all, the only outsider among them, the foreigner. *He is not the one throwing stones at you and your family or poisoning your cattle,* the others replied, *but it's you who are doing those things and want to tell other people how to live and what to believe.*

Everyone anxiously awaited the *Thing*, for they hoped that some clarification would come out of the meeting. Even the most obstinate ones on both sides realized that things could not go on like this. But on the evening before the meeting, the earth began to rumble.

It was that terrible, threatening thunder that seemed to come from the bowels of the earth and was usually followed by the weak tremors that were so common here. This time, too, the ground trembled, but the rumbling persisted and slowly grew louder, gradually subsiding again until it was very soft, but never completely dying out.

Siglind came running out of the house, looked around, and found her husband on the bank of the river.

"Oh, Candamir, what can that be?"

He put his arm around her shoulders and shook his head. "I don't know, but it comes from the southwest."

The sun went down quickly behind the trees, as it always did, but it didn't get really dark. A strange red glow flickered in the sky above the other side of the river.

"Oh, Jesus Christ, save us," Siglind whispered. "The fiery mountain has awakened in anger..."

"No, I don't think so," Austin said softly. They both turned around. "The fiery mountain is thirty-five or forty miles away," the monk continued in a hushed voice, pointing toward the red glow in the southwest. "This is closer."

"But what is it?" Candamir asked, perplexed.

"I'm not certain," Austin admitted. "I think...we are seeing the birth of another fiery eruption."

The earth continued rumbling, casting columns of fire and glowing red balls into the air that looked like comets. From time to time it trembled in its birth pangs, and then the people along the shore felt a quivering underfoot. There was no sound at all except for this soft rumbling, and the silence of the eruption made it all the more powerful.

"How far away do you think it is, Austin?" Candamir finally asked, spellbound.

"That's hard to estimate in the dark. But far enough that we needn't fear it," the monk said. "It can't be any closer than twenty miles, or we would certainly hear it."

So it was somewhere in the middle of the forest that he and Hacon had crossed, Candamir concluded. It was incredible. Great showers of sparks rained down, and he wondered how much of the forest was burning. Would the streams of fire they saw shooting up into the sky crush every tree and shrub? And where would they stop? And what would be left when the fire had gone out—another wasteland?

"I hope you're right," he murmured.

"Yes, I hope so too," Austin admitted. He was as fearful as everyone else about what was happening in the southwest. What difference did it make whether it was ten, twenty, or thirty miles away? Once again, God had released the power of his elements, and it was terrible to behold. "I think I'll go to the smithy and pray."

"I'll come along," Siglind said hastily.

Candamir did not like to see her leave, but he knew she would feel better thinking she was doing something useful instead of simply standing around here idly watching the sky burn. He nodded and took his hand off her shoulder. Before she and Austin were even five steps away, Candamir had turned back and was staring up at the sky again.

"Father, are Odin and Jesus Christ angry at us?" Nils's voice roused him from his contemplation.

He picked the boy up so that he wouldn't tumble into the river. "It looks that way, yes, at least one of them is."

"Which one?"

"I don't know, Nils."

An especially large ball of fire shot into the air, and it seemed to be heading right toward them, before descending and disappearing like all the rest. Cries of horror rose up along the river, and the women and even some of the men threw themselves on the ground and covered their heads with their arms.

Little hands clutched at Candamir's tunic, and Nils buried his face in his father's shoulder, crying softly. Hesitantly, Candamir turned away and carried him back to the house.

The servants were standing together by the door and also staring toward the south. Candamir put his son in Solvig's arms and said, "Here, take care of him and his sisters. Take them to bed and sing to them, and no wailing and weeping in front of them, do you understand? It's miles away, and nothing will happen to us here."

She swallowed visibly. "Yes, Master." But it was obvious she didn't believe a word he said.

Candamir turned to his older slaves. "Heide, Freydis, keep an eye on her and see to it that she doesn't frighten the children."

Nori's wife nodded and hobbled into the house.

"Do you really believe we're safe here, Master?" the old cook wanted to know.

"Of course," he said brusquely. "Don't be silly, Heide. It's way beyond the river."

"That may be, but how do we know that what's going on there today won't happen here tomorrow?"

He looked at her and shook his head. "Of course we can't know that. But cheer up. Tomorrow there will be enough blood and tears here in any case; the gods can spare themselves the trouble of casting fiery balls at our feet."

She lowered her eyes and nodded anxiously.

Candamir placed his hand on her wrinkled forearm for a moment and then went back down to the riverbank. For a while he stood there watching the eerie spectacle in the night sky, and then he set out along the river, heading west. Everywhere on the village meadow, people were standing around in small groups and looking toward the south. Some responded to Candamir's greeting with a murmur, while others remained silent.

Austin was giving his followers a final blessing, and they all made the sign of the cross. Only a pitifully small group had sneaked into the smithy this evening—many didn't dare to be seen with the Saxon at present.

"Do not be afraid," Austin told them before they stole away into the night. "It's not Odin's anger that caused this fire to break out, but the hand of God which created this volcano in the first place, as well as everything else on earth. If it is a warning, it is not a warning to us."

They nodded earnestly, and some even seemed a bit consoled. One by one they said goodbye and left the dark building by the river. Siglind, Hacon, and Gunda waited until the monk had stored his implements away in the ancient, cracked sealskin pouch. "Be our guest tonight, Austin," Hacon invited him. "You can tell me a little more of what you know about mountains that spew fire, and we can pray together for Candamir's success tomorrow at the *Thing*."

The Saxon smiled and shook his head. "Since I'm not at all certain that Candamir really wants to succeed, I would rather avoid this matter. Thank you for your hospitality, Hacon, and I'll be glad to come. But go now and leave me here alone for a while. I need to have a serious talk with God."

Hacon and Gunda walked toward the door, but Siglind objected. "I don't know, Austin. I don't feel comfortable with you being alone anywhere, even for only a short while, and certainly not on a strange night like this."

He smiled and led her to the door. "I stand here on hallowed ground. Nothing can happen to me here—God and all his saints are watching over me. Besides, ever since this matter with the Hagalaz rune, it has seemed to me that you're not much safer than I am. Hacon, would you accompany Siglind home?"

"Of course." He held the door open for his sister-in-law, and after hesitating a moment, she stepped outside.

When they had gone, Austin sank to his knees on the hard ground of the smithy and became engrossed in prayer. Unfortunately, he was not one of those few blessed spirits who had ecstatic visions as they prayed. But through years of practice, he had learned to become very quiet and empty and simply listen to what the Lord had to say to him. Even that was a great art, for often the word of the Lord was so terrible that it was much easier to turn a deaf ear to it. But Austin had left all his fears and doubts behind him. He felt that his work was almost finished.

"Just tell me the meaning of these signs, Lord," he whispered. "I am listening. Show me the way, and I will follow. If you wish to be merciful to me one more time, then hold your protecting hand over your people here and enlighten the hearts of those still walking in darkness. In return, I am willing drain the cup to the last drop, as bitter as it may be."

"That's just as well," a hushed voice whispered behind him.

Austin did not jump, for he had already felt the draft from the door. He also did not turn around and did not even move when two powerful hands gripped his throat from behind and started to choke him.

Osmund, too, was standing on the bank of the river with his back to his house, watching Odin's fireworks in fascination. When he heard the rustling steps in the grass he asked softly, "What have we done?"

Candamir stopped beside him. "It's not too late yet. Let's try to find another way, Osmund."

Osmund turned his head and looked at Candamir. His eyes were peculiarly small, his face rigid—hostile, it seemed. But Candamir knew this face better than his own. He saw that Osmund felt just as desolate as he did.

"Where, Candamir? Where can we find this other way? I can't go back. But how can I make you understand that it's Odin's will I'm carrying out? That this warning is directed at you?" He pointed up at the fiery sky. "If the situation were the other way around, I probably wouldn't believe you either."

Candamir gestured dismissively with his left hand. "It's surely nothing new to you when I tell you that the gods and their intentions don't especially interest me, is it?"

"No. You're completely indifferent to them, yet they love you just the same. As far back as I can remember, I have been trying to understand that."

"Osmund, if you and I challenge each other tomorrow at the *Thing*, there's only one way for it to end. You probably have more followers, I won't deny that, but only by a very few votes. The two sides are almost equal. What we are risking here is a war where father will fight against son, and brother against brother."

Osmund nodded.

"I can't allow this to happen," Candamir continued, "for that would have unforeseeable consequences, and I have sworn, after all, to do what I can to prevent blood feuds."

"That was a foolish oath," Osmund said critically.

"That may be, but it still stands."

"So?" Osmund lifted his hands helplessly. "What do you expect me to say? I have no idea what to do. I don't understand how we ever came to this deadlock, but the gods just have a peculiar sense of humor. And tomorrow you will..."

"Osmund," Candamir interrupted. "Listen to me. I'm ready to accept your claim to power."

"*What?*"

"Why not? We both know that you are the smarter and more prudent one, and perhaps it's supposed to be that way. All my life I have blindly trusted you, so why not now? I have only one condition."

"The Saxon."

Candamir nodded. "Don't banish him. I forced him to come here with me, and therefore I feel obligated to him. If you insist, let the *Thing* decide to make him a slave again. I'll take him into my house and see that he causes you no more trouble."

Osmund folded his arms and looked at him steadfastly. "It's not my intention to send the Saxon away."

The relief in Candamir's face was so great that for a moment Osmund was tempted to leave it at that and say nothing more. That would probably have been even the wiser decision, as Odin would have it. But he realized he was incapable of deceiving his friend that way.

"Austin must die, Candamir. He is the renegade traitor, don't you remember? He wants to bring misfortune to Odin's people. He has already brought us enough misfortune, and to fulfill the prophecy, I must destroy him."

Candamir cleared his throat, which had suddenly become as dry as dust. "Osmund, I beg you as I have never begged you before..."

"Spare yourself the trouble. While you and I are standing here talking, his blood is already running into the pretty bowl that your brother made for the temple."

Austin lay on the sacrificial stone and wondered whether Inga had ordered the men to hold his arms out to the side in order to mock him and his god. And just like Christ on the cross, he too was naked and felt ashamed of it. *Were you ashamed of your nakedness, Lord, when they nailed you to the cross and mocked you and cast lots for your clothes? Are you with me?*

No more than fifty people stood before the altar in a semicircle. Inga had invited only the most steadfast among her believers to this secret ceremony, for what they had to do here tonight hadn't been done in living memory, and she wanted to avoid having the holy ritual disturbed by the timorous and fearful.

She ended her song and slowly turned around to her victim. As always, her face was completely shaded by her hood, so that the priestess became a ghostly presence, the tool of her gods. Her robe shone blood red in the glow of the fires that flanked her.

Slowly and deliberately, she proceeded to the stone and pulled the knife from her wide sleeve. The blade flashed in the glow of the fire. A soft murmur passed through those assembled like a sigh, but at once silence returned.

"Behold, Father of the Gods, the sacrifice we bring to you," the faceless figure cried, raising her arms up high.

Austin looked where he thought Inga's eyes might be. *"In God have I put my trust: I will not be afraid of what man can do unto me."*

He spoke his psalm in Latin, and the hand with the sharp, murderous dagger trembled. "Be still!" the voice hissed.

*"They continue to revile me and their minds are set on destroying me. They band together and lie in wait for me, they follow my footsteps, they yearn for my life."*

Thorbjörn suddenly deviated from the prescribed course of the ceremony, bent over the fettered victim, and punched him in the face. "Enough of your magic spells and curses," he growled.

Austin tasted blood and swallowed something that probably was a tooth. At the same moment he felt a sharp, stabbing pain on his lower forearm. Thorbjörn raised up the arm, and Inga held the golden sacrificial bowl beneath it. A steady, but very thin flow of blood dripped down into the bowl.

*Why not my throat?* Austin wondered with confusion, and he continued murmuring, *"In God have I put my trust: I will not fear what man can do unto me...I owe you what I have promised..."* He jerked his head to the side to avoid a second blow. *"I owe you what I have promised, oh God, and shall give my offering of thanks to you."*

Thorbjörn's next blow did strike him, however, and for a moment he was dazed. Blinking, he watched as Inga also made a cut in his right arm and collected his blood. Finally, she placed the bowl on the three-legged stool and threw back her hood. The red runes on her forehead and cheeks never failed to have their effect. Many of the believers held their breath and reverently lowered their heads.

The priestess dipped her switch into the bowl and sprinkled the assembly with the sacrificial blood.

"Hail to thee, Father of the Gods, inventor and creator of all things, who has given to us the crown of thy creation!"

"Hail to thee, Odin..."

*Hail to thee, mighty one*, came next, the monk knew, but apparently Inga was not yet finished appealing to Odin, for she continued: "Take this offering that we consign to the sacred flames to appease thy anger, so that thou will no longer rain down thy fire on thy people. Behold, he who reviled and scorned thee shall burn..."

It took Austin a moment to realize what she was saying, but then he was seized with horror. He closed his eyes. Now he realized why the sacrificial stone beneath him was covered with a layer of straw. The witch meant to burn him without first cutting his throat.

Ever since they had seized him in the smithy he had struggled with the sadness of having to depart this world so soon. He knew that such emotion was unworthy of a man of his position—he should be rejoicing and marching resolutely toward the world to come. Nonetheless, he grieved over his farewell to this wonderful land that he had become so attached to, and above all the people whom he loved. Yet he knew that the separation would be only temporary and had consoled himself in the belief that his end would be easy. He had apparently been mistaken.

Thorbjörn and his companion Oswin tied the ropes they had wound around Austin's wrists to the iron rings at the foot of the sacrificial stone. In ordinary ceremonies these served to restrain strong bulls and horses—an Anglo-Saxon man of God could not hope to rip them from their anchorage. As the priestess raised a pitcher and poured the warm, thick liquid it contained over the sacrifice and the straw on the altar, Austin recognized the fragrance of his own lamp oil. He wanted to beg God to forgive her, but he was unable. For she knew what she was doing…

A piercing cry rent the silence of the temple. "Fire!" It was all the more shocking as it was a man's voice. "Oh, Odin, save us…"

All those gathered in the temple spun around. Ivar, the otherwise imperturbable captain of the *Sea Arrow*, stood in the rear and with a trembling finger pointed up at the east end of the roof. Flames were indeed licking at the wooden shingles there, and they were quickly spreading. They had already eaten a hole in the roof right over the sacred spring, and even as the assembled group stared up, spellbound, a fiery ball broke through and seemed to float down languidly, landing in the stone basin of the spring, where it continued burning.

The sight was so horrifying, a portent of such ominous power, that they all were thrown into a state of panic.

"Odin is hurling his fire down upon us!"

"The carpenter god wants to burn us all!"

"Everyone out! Flee!"

"A ball of fire! A ball of fire!"

They all screamed and cried out at the same time as they rushed toward the western portal. Thorbjörn and Oswin also left their posts and fled. Only Inga remained in the temple. She scarcely seemed to notice what was going on around her. Singing softly, she thrust the prepared torch into the fire on her left, without even paying the slightest attention to the fire behind her. And so she didn't see the three shadowy forms that slipped through the east door of the temple, around the fire in the spring basin, and crept silently toward the sacrificial stone.

Inga raised her arm, holding the torch above the altar, but Candamir seized her wrist and pulled it back. At almost the same moment, he slipped the dagger out of the sheath in her sleeve and put it to her throat. "I'm going to twist your arm behind you now," he said. "You can drop the torch first, or you can hold on to it and your butcher's coat will go up in flames. Have it your way."

Inga was a smart woman and had no trouble interpreting the tone of voice. Without hesitation, she let go of the torch. Candamir twisted her arm so violently that she cried out.

In the meanwhile, Siglind and Hacon had arrived at the altar. Hastily they untied Austin, and because Hacon knew his Saxon friend, he loosened his own belt, pulled his knee-length tunic over his head, and held it out silently to Austin. He pulled it on without taking the time to wipe the oil off his body.

It had been dry all summer, and the autumn rains had not yet arrived. The temple roof burned like tinder. Candamir gazed upward and watched sadly as his work was consumed by flames. "Let's get out of here," he whispered, shoving his fist between Inga's shoulders. "Let's go. You and I are leading the way."

"You'll pay for this, Candamir," she promised. "This is a sacrilege that not even Osmund will forgive."

*I know,* Candamir thought, but he pushed her out the door without another word.

The believers had come together on the meadow and looked fearfully toward the southwest where the sky was still glowing red, and then into the interior of the temple, where burning shingles rained from the roof.

When they saw Candamir and realized he had seized their priestess and was threatening her with the sacrificial dagger, they fell silent.

Siglind and Hacon followed, with Austin in their midst. The crowd became restless again and was murmuring indignantly. "If one of you moves," Candamir warned them, "I'll cut her throat, and you'd better believe me. There's not much that I would stop at tonight."

As they weighed the seriousness of this terrible threat, Hacon led Austin from the clearing and headed southward. When they had disappeared among the trees, he let him go. "Can you run, Austin?"

"Yes."

"Then go. Who knows how long Candamir can hold them back. Swim across to the south bank and go to the bay where we stopped when we were fishing and found all the mussels. Do you remember?"

"Surely. But Hacon..."

Hacon shook his head, turned Austin around, and pushed him ahead. "Run! Wait there three days, and one of us will come to get you if we can. If not...you'll have to manage on your own."

Austin nodded, but turned around briefly once more and embraced him. "God bless and protect you all." Then he disappeared between the trees. Naturally, no one knew how things looked on the south shore, if the bay with the mussels was still there, or if it had become a sea of fire. But God had just shown him once again what miracles He was capable of, and the monk placed himself in His hands without hesitation.

As they had agreed, Hacon waited until he estimated that Austin had reached the shore of the little island in the river. Only then did he turn back to the temple clearing. As soon as she saw that the rescue was successful, Siglind disappeared in the other direction and returned to her children. The men had needed her because she was the only one light enough to climb onto the temple roof without being heard. Moreover, she knew as well as Candamir which spot in the roof lay directly above the spring. But as soon as her task was complete, they had agreed she would return home, for no one could know what might still happen that night, and their children ought not be left home alone longer than necessary.

When Hacon returned, the entire roof of the temple was ablaze, illuminating the clearing. He nodded at his brother, and for a brief moment, Candamir closed his eyes. He wasn't sure whether it was relief or fear that made him feel so weak in the knees.

He pulled himself together, removed the sharp blade from Inga's neck, and let go of her right arm. Then he stepped back a pace and almost respectfully handed the dagger back to her, handle first.

She stared at him, but did not take the knife. Without stirring, she said, "Seize the traitors."

Her loyal followers did not have to be asked twice. They eagerly rushed at the two brothers who had thwarted the sacrificial offering to the gods, with Haflad and Thorbjörn in the lead, binding their hands on their backs and kicking them viciously.

"Let us lock them in the temple, Inga," Ivar suggested. "Odin demands a blood sacrifice, you said. They have taken it from us, and so they must assume that role."

Inga looked into Candamir's eyes, her own eyes shining. The thought had an almost overpowering appeal. She knew it was unwise, but the temptation was irresistible…

"Wouldn't that be just, Candamir?" she asked calmly. "That you should perish along with your temple that you have destroyed?"

He looked over at the burning temple. Flames were licking at the blood-red walls now. The fire was consuming the beautiful building with such a loud roar that the rumbling of the earth could no longer be heard. Or had the earth become silent? Candamir wondered.

Hacon spoke up. "I would think that over very carefully, if I were you, for no matter what becomes of us, you will have to continue living with your husband."

Inga's transfigured expression vanished, and she nodded reluctantly. She knew that Hacon was right. "Go home," she ordered her believers. "Tell Osmund and the other men that Candamir thwarted the sacrifice and burned down the temple, and for this reason the *Thing* must take place tomorrow at the ash tree. Thorbjörn, Oswin, you stay here and guard the traitors. Bring them to the *Thing* in the village tomorrow." She turned and headed southward.

"Where are you going?" Thorbjörn asked in surprise. "You can't catch the accursed Saxon anymore, and it's certainly dangerous over there."

Inga jingled the little pouch on her belt. "I must consult the runes, and I must do so at Brigitta's grave."

Like Candamir, Hacon held his head down and tried not to look into the many faces of those who had already gathered for the *Thing*. It was quiet on the village meadow. The earth had fallen silent again, but the fiery spectacle of the night before seemed to have robbed everyone of their voices, even the birds.

When the temple had burned completely and the quiet of the night had descended again on the island in the river, the rumbling had gradually lessened and finally died away. The glow on the southern horizon, however, remained until the sun came back and outshone it.

Osmund stood near the trunk of the ash tree, his arms folded. Thorbjörn left the two brothers with Oswin a few steps away from the sacred tree, then walked over to Osmund and tried to whisper something to him, but Osmund waved him off. Osmund's gaze wandered over the assembly, and then he spoke up in a clear voice. "Many but not all of you know that last night we were going to fulfill Brigitta's last oracle. For a long time, I had harbored the suspicion that the Saxon, who prays to the false god, was the 'renegade traitor,' and when Odin in his wrath rained fire down upon the forest in the south, the priestess and I decided it was time to act and destroy the traitor." Coolly, without disclosing his hatred of Austin, he told them what they had planned to do with the Saxon. Then he raised an accusing finger at his foster brother. "But Candamir and Hacon thwarted the sacrifice and helped the traitor to flee."

Candamir, unable to tolerate Thorbjörn's grasp any longer, freed himself with a sudden tug. Then he moved two paces toward Osmund and also turned around to address the assembly. "That is true. And yet the earth stopped thundering, proving that it wasn't Austin who roused the ire of the gods. It is ridiculous to think that he was the renegade traitor, and you all know that."

*We know nothing of the sort,* most of the faces seemed to be saying. *We know nothing anymore with certainty. The sky burned, and we are afraid. So tell us what it all means.*

They could both sense that this bewilderment worked to Osmund's advantage. For a moment their eyes met, and they guessed at one glance what the other was thinking.

"How did you do it, Candamir?" Osmund asked softly. "I know it's of no importance, for we really have other things to worry about. Nevertheless, this is what I have been wondering all night—how did you do it? Did you persuade the Saxon's god to throw a ball of fire at our temple?"

Candamir smiled grimly. "No, I had no time for that. I had to act fast, you understand, as your wife was about to burn Austin alive." Here and there sharp gasps could be heard. This detail had been omitted from Osmund's previous account. "Siglind climbed onto the roof of the temple and removed a few shingles right over the spring. I had wrapped an armful of hay in a piece of parchment—that was our fireball. Siglind took quite a risk: first she set fire to the roof, then to the fiery ball, and then she threw the ball down into the spring."

"How did you know that the parchment would keep burning in the water?" Osmund asked in astonishment.

Candamir shrugged. "I didn't. I simply took a chance."

"Your luck has never let you down, has it?"

"Yes it has, Osmund. Recently, in fact, it hasn't been a very faithful ally. But I had to take the risk, because what you were about to do was a terrible crime. This man has never harmed any of us. You have been wrong about him. But you didn't want to listen to me, and therefore we simply had to do something to prevent your crime, that's all. We did nothing more than that."

"No? Didn't you destroy the statues of the gods? Didn't you defile the temple and burn it down?"

"It was only a house. I can build you a new one."

"And didn't you threaten the life of the priestess, my wife?"

Candamir lowered his gaze and nodded. "I regret that. But if you wish to know the truth, I regret the loss of the temple even more, for it was the most beautiful thing I have ever built. Yet both of these, it seems to me, are a small price to pay for the life of an innocent man."

The men at the *Thing* exchanged surreptitious glances and hesitantly looked at the two adversaries. In the past, Osmund and Candamir had always been regarded by their neighbors as one entity; hardly ever had one been mentioned without the other. Yet what a contrast they presented now. Osmund stood tall by the holy tree, handsome, almost noble in appearance. And next to him, Candamir: tied, gaunt, his clothes and face covered with soot, and moreover, his hair short and shaggy like that of a slave. And yet it seemed to many of them that he had the greater strength—and more importantly, that right was on his side.

Osmund sensed the indecisiveness in the *Thing*, but before he could take the next step, Harald rose from the grass, walked over to them, and cut Candamir's fetters, and then Hacon's as well. Here and there, the men grumbled, and the smith turned around to them and said with atypical passion, "Neither of them has violated a law! On the contrary. They saved the life of a free man who had not been judged by the *Thing*. They preserved the law. *You* wanted to break it."

"But Harald," Thorbjörn protested, "the Saxon is an evildoer! He casts a dangerous spell on people with his salves."

"That's nonsense," the smith said. "He is a good man, just a bit different from us. Strange perhaps. Is that really so terrible? Are these differences so unbearable to you that you must destroy them? What would you call a man who is so afraid of what he doesn't understand, Thorbjörn?"

"Think carefully whether you want to call me a coward, because there would be consequences," Thorbjörn said, placing his hand on the hilt of his sword.

Harald smiled at him. "I can't remember having said the word 'coward.'"

"This accursed Saxon doesn't scare me, but I know he's dangerous. Osmund and Inga are right. He was the one Brigitta referred to in her last oracle, and thus it was right to sacrifice him to the gods. Your own son agrees, or he certainly wouldn't have been in the temple last night!"

Harald hadn't known that, and it was a blow. He turned around to Godwin, who looked back at him defiantly. Neither father nor son said a word.

"You're not the only one to be ashamed of his family, Harald," Haldir said.

"That's true," Wiland agreed, turning to his sister and his brother-in-law. "You placed yourself above the *Thing* and wanted to shed the blood of an innocent man, Osmund. Harald is completely right—your crime is worse than Candamir's and Hacon's, and therefore I disown you and dissolve all bonds between us. And I call my god, Jesus Christ, as witness."

"And now you are breaking the law, for the *Thing* has forbidden the worship of this god," Inga responded sharply.

Siwold, their oldest brother, stepped up to Wiland. "And on the day after, every man who voted for it had one more sheep than the day before, didn't he? Just how did that happen? Did Odin bring them here personally and put them in the pens?"

"That's a lie," Osmund protested. "That's not true, Siwold, and you will take that back."

Siwold drew his weapon. "Really? And what will happen if I don't? I know it's true, because I've seen it with my own eyes and I can count!"

Osmund drew his sword as well.

"No, wait," Candamir said. He stepped between the two men, placed one hand on each of their chests, and pushed them apart. "Wait. It's a sacrilege to spill blood at the *Thing*, and you know that. No matter what you say, you are brothers-in-law. Your son's are cousins. Do you want to burden them with the duty of killing one another?"

"I'm not eager to," Osmund admitted, "but I'll not permit anyone to accuse me of corruption at the *Thing*."

"Osmund." Candamir briefly rubbed his forehead. "If you fight each other, we'll just be exactly where we are now, but blood will flow, and your family will perish in a blood feud, and all for no reason. For the discord is really between you and me, isn't it?"

Osmund lowered his sword, seemed to forget Siwold for a moment, and turned to his foster brother. "Discord, Candamir?"

Candamir nodded. "Didn't you bring it into my house?"

Osmund's eyes widened for a brief moment, but he quickly regained control of himself. "Would you tell me what you're talking about?"

"The Hagalaz rune that you painted on my door."

"And what makes you think that I did it?"

"Do you deny it?"

Osmund shook his head but kept looking straight at him. "No, you're right. I did it because I couldn't think of anything else to do. It was a last attempt to bring you to your senses, to show you what you are risking."

"But it did no good."

"No," said Osmund, with a note of honest regret in his voice.

"You're the one who let it come to this," Inga chided Candamir. "I accuse you, Candamir Olesson, of offending the will of the gods by preventing the fulfillment of the oracle. You protected the renegade traitor who wants to bring misfortune to Odin's people. And so you yourself have become a renegade and must pay for it."

*Damn you,* Jared thought furiously. A moment ago he had hoped that Candamir and Osmund could somehow reconcile, even if he couldn't see how—and then she came and poured oil on the fire. He looked at her in astonishment, no longer able to see anything in her of the girl he had once been so much in love with.

"I've heard enough of this now," he said in a soft voice, though everyone heard him in the tense silence and all heads turned. "It doesn't matter how often you say Austin is a traitor. Just because you decide to interpret the oracle this way doesn't make it true. You all know very well who the renegade was, who betrayed us, and who wanted to bring misfortune upon us. That was my father, and Candamir defeated him. So if any of us is to be chosen as our God-given leader, he should be the one."

Osmund looked at him in disbelief. "Jared..."

"I'm sorry, Cousin. I know I owe you loyalty and gratitude, but what you require of me is my soul, as Austin would put it. And that you will not get. In this matter I can't side with you, for you are wrong." He looked all around him. "And you all know that, if you're honest with yourselves."

A murmur went through the group that soon grew to an uproar. It was just as Candamir had expected: the opposing sides were of equal strength, and the emotions were much too strong. If they let it come to a vote, they would set off something that no one would be able to control anymore.

Candamir stood at the bank of the river, stared down at the ground, and made the most difficult decision of his life. He knew very well what he had to do, but he was not sure he could.

When the uproar died down, Thorbjörn said, "We keep going around in circles, but there is a simple way to learn the will of the gods, isn't there? A *holmgang* is the only solution."

Candamir and Osmund looked at one another.

A holmgang was a duel that took place according to strict rules and precluded subsequent blood vengeance. The rules were many and complicated. Everything was prescribed: the size of the staked-out battlefield as well as the type and number of weapons and shields. Some rules were good, others were bad, some made sense and others did not. And the most important rule was that only one of the combatants would leave the battlefield alive.

Osmund was deeply troubled but willing to fight. Candamir could see that clearly, and he was not surprised. That was the way Osmund was. He thought he was fulfilling the will of the gods and serving the well-being of his people, and that right was on his side. For this reason he was convinced he had to follow this course, once taken, to the end, irrespective of what it cost him and where it finally led. This conviction was so deeply ingrained in Osmund that he could never give it up, for that would have meant denying who he was. And so he was ready to enter into battle with his foster brother—even though he would be the loser in the end, no matter the outcome.

Candamir understood all of that, but he felt for a moment like the world had come to an end when he realized that Osmund was ready to kill him. For nothing. Nothing but a dubious goal that he hadn't even set himself. Candamir could no longer bear his gaze. He shuddered, turned away, and shook his head.

"Count me out," he told the *Thing*. "I will not spill the blood of my foster brother, nor burden him with staining his hands with mine, only because you don't agree on the oracle of a dead, old witch."

"It's more than that, Candamir," Inga reminded him. "You are still on trial."

He nodded. "You can spare yourself the trouble of reaching a verdict. I..." He found it incredibly difficult to say it. Again he looked at Osmund, not sure whether he was seeking advice or vengeance. Osmund shook his head silently but pleadingly.

Candamir smiled sadly and pronounced his own sentence: "I'm leaving. I...I'm going into exile."

Again there was an uproar. Men, women, even slaves cried out all at once and gestured excitedly. Only Siglind was silent, like a rock in a stormy sea. She stood barefoot in the grass, in a simple blue jumper that Candamir loved so much because it was the color of her eyes. Her blond hair shone in the bright morning sun. And he was consoled when he saw her like that, for she nodded to him, even smiled a little, though tears were running down her cheeks.

Slowly she stepped forward from the back row, where she had been standing among the other women, until she was at his side. "Wherever you go, you will not go alone."

He lowered his head and placed his arm around her shoulders.

"Grant us two days' time," he said, looking in Osmund's direction. It sounded more like a demand than a request. "We have a few preparations to make. If I remember correctly, every man sent into exile is allowed a grace period of one or two days, even murderers and traitors, aren't they?" He wasn't able to conceal his bitterness.

Hacon and Gunda glanced at each other briefly, nodded, and then the younger brother joined them. "We will come with you."

Candamir raised his hand to object. "Hacon...you need not do that. I don't think anyone insists on that."

"On the contrary," his brother answered with determination. "I do. I cannot stay here."

Wiland took his place beside him. "That holds for me as well. Any place where a man can't believe what he wants to is no place for me, either. I hope you still have a little room for me and my people on your ship."

"Wiland!" Candamir protested. He practically begged him, saying, "Do you have any idea what you're doing? Do you know what that means?"

"Oh yes." *We'll simply start all over again,* he thought. *And we will do it the way* we *want to.*

At almost the same time and without saying a word, Siwold and Harald joined the small group of exiles.

"Harald…" Osmund spoke for the first time since Candamir had announced his decision to leave. His face was grim, but his eyes were full of fear. "Harald, you can't do that. We need a smith." *So you need a smith,* Candamir thought. *You can do without a foster brother, but not a smith.*

Harald nodded curtly. "I'll leave my Latvians here, as they'll not want to move away. They've been working in my smithy for twenty years and can do almost everything I can."

"But…"

"That's the most I can offer you, Osmund, for if you let Candamir go, I can't stay here."

Haldir joined him. "I could offer you some more places on my ship…"

Gradually they came forward, the Christians and all those who felt that no man had the right to tell another what to believe. Many struggled with their decision, many wept openly and without shame. But they came and stood at Candamir's side, and the group increased until it included practically half the settlers.

Jared and Gunnar were the last. With their heads bowed, they quietly joined the group of exiles.

"Oh, Jared," Osmund muttered, his distress showing in his voice.

Candamir refused to look at Osmund. *He wanted to kill me,* he reminded himself. *He was ready to kill me. For his accursed gods, for his power, and because I got the woman he wanted.* Now that he saw where all the lies and his self-deception had led him, he was finally able to admit that to himself. But it didn't help. He felt sympathy for Osmund just the same, and grieved at the loss of their friendship.

"I am sorry, Cousin," Jared confessed sincerely. "For your sake, I would have preferred to remain, and yet you are the one driving me away."

It was a bitter parting. Everyone going into exile had loved the beautiful village on the river, for they had dreamed it, planned it, and built it themselves. And they were all leaving dear friends behind here.

Before the meeting broke up, Candamir and Osmund exchanged one final grim glance, and that was all. It was the same for most of the rest of them. They left behind brothers, sisters, children, or parents, and no one doubted that it was a final farewell. They were going away because they knew no reconciliation was possible, and because it seemed to be the only way to avoid a fratricidal war.

The children and the slaves also felt dejected as they packed the dishes and wall hangings in the trunks, dismantled the high seat, took their crops on board, and prepared the livestock for loading. Candamir cleaned out his workshop himself, wrapping his finest tools in cloths soaked in oil and stashing them safely in a solid box. He left his second set there for Godwin.

They all moved along sluggishly, as if their hands and feet were unwilling to do what their will commanded. No one could really believe they were leaving this place.

"Where are we going, Candamir?" Hacon asked when the exiles gathered in the smithy the evening before their departure.

His brother slowly raised his shoulders. "You know as much as I do. To the south."

"To the south?" Haldir repeated skeptically. "To the place where fire rained down just a few nights ago?"

Candamir shook his head. "To the south coast of Catan, I meant. As far away as possible from here and the wasteland."

Harald agreed. "Let's journey south until we catch sight of the mountains that Berse spoke of, and look for a place on the other side, on the southeast coast, perhaps. Then the mountains will lie between us and everything we leave behind. If we wish to start all over again, we must really cut all our bonds, otherwise it may turn out that everything was in vain, and war may still break out."

"Then you be our leader, Harald," Candamir said. "I'm...too confused." Perhaps he had also lost heart. The idea of starting over again, clearing forests, building houses, anxiously awaiting the first harvest, practically paralyzed him. "I see only darkness when I look into the future."

His sister came up from behind and placed her hands on his shoulders. "It's the grief over your foster brother that weakens your body and spirit, but that will pass, Candamir, you'll see. Believe me, I know what I am speaking of."

"She's right," the smith murmured. He too was unhappy over the final break with his son and blamed himself, but he seemed resolute now.

Candamir shrugged, but remained silent.

The others talked a while longer, but they spoke more about the distribution of people and animals on the ships than about their destination, for this was Catan, and they were confident that the land was rich and the soil would be fertile, no matter where they settled.

Just as in Elasund, Candamir spent the last night before their departure on board his ship. As long as there was a bit of daylight, people came from all over, bringing a keg of mead or a sack of grain, but darkness had finally descended.

Now alone, he buried his head in his arms and wept. He cried for a long time, for there were so many things to mourn. It felt strange—the tears seeped into his beard and tickled his cheeks and chin, but nevertheless he found it difficult to stop. He was devastated by the loss of his friend and the chaos that lay before him. It was small consolation to him to know he would do it all over again exactly the same way and that he didn't know what he might have done better.

When he finally heard Siglind's soft steps on the deck, he wiped his eyes and nose determinedly with his sleeve, but made no attempt to hide from her the depths of his misery.

She sat down cross-legged alongside him. Without saying a word, he took hold of her hand and linked their fingers together. The waxing moon shed a faint light, causing the silver in their wedding bands to shimmer softly.

"It will be a better life, Candamir," she said in a low voice.

"That's also what we believed when we left Elasund. And just look what it all has come to."

"That was not your fault."

"It was my fault as well as Osmund's, but that's not really of any importance. Only now do I see what a fool I was to believe that everything would be better because the land was better. I was lulled into a false sense of security and forgot how fleeting everything is that man creates. Osmund's father once said that no happiness could last, because it was only lent to us by the gods. But I have come to believe it can't endure because we ourselves keep running toward the abyss. And I don't know...if I really want to start all over again."

"Oh, but you do," she replied. It sounded forceful, but he also heard the smile in her voice. "You are one of those people who always start over again when they fail, until they're satisfied with what they've done. That's the way you are about building a house or a chest, and you're that way too with everything else. And I tell you, this time you will succeed."

"Why are you so certain?" he asked, puzzled.

"Because this time you're taking far fewer old burdens on board your ship, and you're finally getting the chance now you always wanted: a completely fresh start. And everyone going with us wants the same thing."

He shook his head skeptically. "Even two people never really want the same thing. How do you expect two hundred to agree?"

"Well, at least they agree on what they *don't* want."

He pulled her closer and put both arms around her. "Yes, I guess that's a start."

The sun had barely risen over the mountains the next morning when they set out in their five ships. It was cool; apparently autumn was finally at hand. There was a gentle breeze from the west, so they used the oars and with the help of the current floated quickly downriver.

Although there was not much need to steer, Candamir stood at the helm. Then disobeying his father's commandment, he looked back. No one was there to watch as they left. The village meadow lay deserted in the thin morning fog.

Osmund had not come.

Candamir knew that it had been a foolish hope, yet he felt the disappointment like a new ache in his heart. He clenched his teeth and determinedly looked straight ahead.

"I just hope the accursed Saxon is still alive and where he ought to be," he murmured to himself.

Hacon, who this time had volunteered to sit at the first rowing bench, smiled to himself. "Oh, I can't imagine that even a burning sky and rain of fire would be enough to destroy him."

And he wasn't disappointed. In the early afternoon, two hours after they had reached the open sea, they arrived at the bay they had sent Austin to. From far off, they could see the small, wiry form with the flaxen hair, waving with both arms. Candamir and Hacon exchanged a grin.

They didn't need to cast anchor, for Austin had run down to the sea and was swimming toward them eagerly. When he reached the *Falcon*, Harald let down a rope ladder and Austin climbed nimbly aboard.

They received him with cheers. Even those who were not followers of his carpenter god were happy, nonetheless, to see him alive and unharmed.

Hacon embraced him, overjoyed, and after a short, awkward hesitation, Candamir followed his brother's example.

"Welcome on board, Saxon."

Austin smiled at him, but his eyes were full of sorrow. "I hoped and prayed to God to see you again in this world. But at the same time I was afraid that our meeting would mean the breakup of your community, and that is something I deeply regret, Candamir."

Candamir dismissed the little speech with a wave of his hand. "Would you be relieved or disappointed if I said it had nothing to do with you?"

Austin briefly cast his eyes heavenward. "I'd be dismayed, for then you'd be telling a lie again."

They laughed, and Candamir was surprised at how lighthearted he suddenly felt.

"Did you bring my books along?" the Saxon inquired.

"Of course." Candamir pointed with his thumb in Hacon's direction. "He even insisted on bringing along all the unused parchment."

Austin gave a smile of relief. "God bless you, Hacon."

"Tell us about the firestorm," Hacon asked.

"I didn't see much more of it than you," Austin admitted, "since I walked along the south bank of the river in order not to get lost and to find the bay again. But once it seemed to me as if there were a large forest fire some miles away to my left. I fear it's as I thought, that there's a new well of fire near the edge of the wasteland, perhaps enlarging it."

"May Odin protect Osmund and all the others," Candamir murmured. "I hope the tremors will subside now that our dispute has been settled."

*"Settled" is perhaps not quite the right word,* Austin thought, but he knew what Candamir had given up in order to avoid bloodshed and admired him for this decision—this wisdom that stood in such fundamental contradiction to the traditions he had grown up with.

The monk took a deep breath of the salty sea air and then looked around on the ship curiously. "I must say…it really looks like Noah's Ark, even more than on our first voyage. This time, even the cattle and horses are peering over the railing just like in the picture I once saw of Noah's ship."

By now even Candamir knew the story of the flood, because his son and oldest daughter wanted to hear it again and again, and he replied,

"Well, I hope we will be spared the rain. We tried again to limit ourselves to the necessities, but with even less success than when we set out from the old homeland, I'm afraid. The larger animals simply found no room down below, for the storeroom is full of sheep, sacks of grain, and iron."

"Let us pray that the *Falcon* doesn't sink this time."

"Yes, speak to your god and put in a good word for us. We will anchor the ship in one of the many coves overnight, but if there is a storm we must hope to find one very quickly."

Austin nodded confidently. On Catan they had seldom experienced severe storms, and this trip couldn't be compared with the last one, for this time they would always stay within sight of the coast. "And where are we going?" he asked curiously.

"South."

Under sunny skies and fair seas, they sailed down the coast. Most of the settlers were seeing this part of Catan for the first time. They viewed the wasteland in anxious silence, but after they had passed it they couldn't stop praising the beauty of the forests and hills of Catan. Yet it was the sea that excited them even more than the coast. Looking out across the broad, shining ocean, many realized now for the first time how much they had missed this sight. Nils, Ole, and their younger brothers, sisters, and friends were seeing the ocean for the first time in their lives. After they had overcome the initial awe of this vast and strange expanse, they too were enchanted by it, and when the ships entered a bay in the evening and the settlers went ashore, the children frolicked exuberantly in the shallow water, admiring the breaking waves.

On the fifth day they caught sight of the southern foothills of the mountains, and after they had passed them they began their search. They could all see that the coast on this side was different. "Gentler," Berse had said, and they had to agree with him. They left the cliffs behind them, and the bays became shallower, with long sandy beaches, and the colors and contours were softer. But that wasn't all. The wind and surf on the east side of Catan were noticeably gentler than in the west, and for this time of year it was unusually warm.

Finally, on the morning of the seventh day, Candamir led the little fleet out into the sea a good mile from the coast, and there he cast overboard the bundle of posts comprising his high seat.

His companions looked at him timidly, wondering if this was a delayed outburst of anger at his foster brother, who had given him this gift. But Candamir laughed and shook his head, pointing at the posts bobbing along in the waves. "Look, they're drifting toward the coast. Come, let's see where they lead us."

They had to row again, for the wind was only a gentle breeze that morning. But the current was weak as well, so they had no difficulty keeping an eye on the drifting high seat. First it drifted southward a ways, and then the current unexpectedly changed direction and pushed it toward the northwest.

"I hope your high seat won't take us back to the place we started," Hacon said nervously.

Candamir stood at the bow with his arms folded and shook his head. "We could hardly be farther from that place than we are here," he said. Then he shouted over his shoulder, "More to the starboard—are you blind?"

The high seat washed ashore in a crescent-shaped bay over a half mile wide. The shallow shoreline was covered with coarse sand, but after about fifty paces it sloped up gently to a grass-covered chain of hills that extended above the entire crescent.

After they had cast anchor and gone ashore, they climbed these hills and discovered a large forest on the other side that seemed to consist mostly of pines with wide tops and thick, gray bark. The higher the morning sun climbed, the more intense became the resinous fragrance of these strange trees. They were rooted in rich, dark earth.

Candamir took in deep breaths of the fragrant trees before turning his back on them and looking down at the sea. Harald and Asta stood on the beach talking. He saw the smith making the form of a ship with his huge hands and pointing out to sea and southward. Maybe he was discussing with his wife whether it was possible and practical to bring the ore from the mountains by sea. Hacon, Gunda, and Austin stood with their feet in the water admiring a seashell that the sharp-eyed Saxon had found in the sand and was apparently using as an opportunity for another learned discourse. Everywhere on the beach, as well as on the crest of the hill, people stood together in groups of two or more talking with each other, and by their gestures one could see they were making great plans.

Candamir was so absorbed contemplating his companions that he hardly paid attention to the beauty of this land. Then Siglind walked up from the beach, stepped to his side, and placed her arm around his waist. "So what do you think?" she asked. "A good place, isn't it?"

He nodded pensively. "Yes, a good place. When we left Elasund, I always thought about what kind of house I would have in the new homeland someday. I still clearly remember thinking about it that night on the Cold Islands, shortly before I found you."

"Oh, you did? And what sort of house was it going to be?"

"A hall looking out over the sea, at the top of a gentle, grassy hill, with the sea breeze blowing through the door. Back then I never thought of anything like windows." He shrugged with a smile and kissed her on the temple.

"A hall looking out over the sea," she repeated.

"Yes."

Siglind pointed toward the forest down below them. "There's all the wood you need."

"I see it."

"Well? What are you waiting for?"

*END*

# Endnotes and Acknowledgments

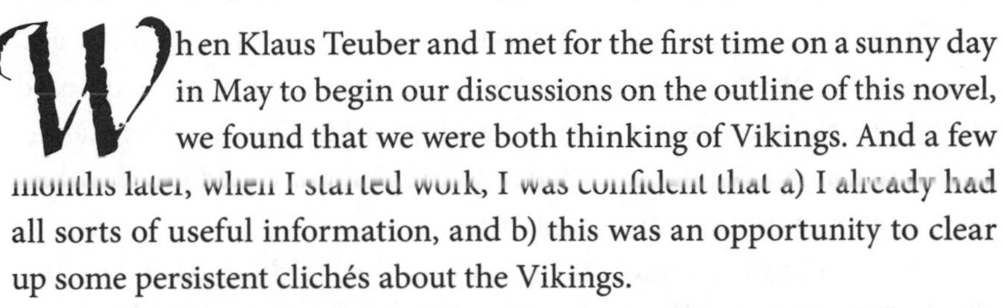

When Klaus Teuber and I met for the first time on a sunny day in May to begin our discussions on the outline of this novel, we found that we were both thinking of Vikings. And a few months later, when I started work, I was confident that a) I already had all sorts of useful information, and b) this was an opportunity to clear up some persistent clichés about the Vikings.

As so often happens in life, things turned out quite differently. During my research I found out how much my view of the Vikings was still colored by English and European historiography molded by the perspective of the victims, and how thoroughly I had to revise some aspects of it. On the other hand, some of the above clichés were well founded. The tendency toward immoderate use of alcoholic beverages, for example, was not malicious gossip, but a fact. In the sagas there are detailed descriptions of lusty drinking orgies and their consequences that really exceeded all bounds of good taste.

Every historical novel is fiction and can never be an exact account of past events. That's true of this novel in particular, since all the characters and places are fictional. For this reason I have avoided any references to our present calendar. But despite all the freedom that fiction affords, I have nevertheless endeavored to reconstruct as precisely as possible the historical and sociocultural background. This holds for types of ships, houses, clothing, weapons, and all the articles of daily life as well as for religious beliefs and social structures, even though the sources are often incomplete or problematic and there are conflicting opinions about many matters. The latter is likewise true for the place of women, which in my view has often been overestimated. It's true that a woman could leave her husband while retaining her personal property, and that moral restrictions were not as severe in the pre-Christian period as they were later. But the society of the people we call Vikings—who incidentally never called themselves by that name—was a male-dominated macho world, and women's rights did not apply to those who were without means or in bondage.

Many of the rites and customs described here are historical fact, including the use of ravens to search for land, collective urination after the *Thing*, painting the walls of the temple with sacrificial blood, and determining the site of a settlement by tying up and throwing overboard the posts of a high seat to see where it drifted. Death by snakebite, unfortunately, is also documented, and there is more evidence for than against that human sacrifices took place.

Truly fascinating to me was the world of the Nordic gods and myths. These stories are peculiar and profound, comical and tragic, beautiful and repulsive, strange and yet familiar. I took the liberty of inventing such a story, even if, naturally, it could not measure up to the originals, and those who think that my tale of Odin and Tanuri and the far-off island bears markedly Tolkienesque traits are entirely right. I hope that will be understood as an homage to the great master I revere so highly and whose work in turn was inspired by the *Edda*.

As in the past, many people assisted me this time as well in my research and the evolution of this novel; above all, my husband Michael, to whom once again I offer my most sincere thanks. As always I would also like to thank my sister, Dr. Sabine Rose, for her medical advice, honest opinions, and creative suggestions; Alfred Umhey for the invitation to peruse his fascinating archives, and the wonderful books he lent me (and which he allowed me to keep for so long!); Michael Jäger for the stimulating conversations during long automobile trips, and for many other things; Olaf Höger and especially Hermann Stolle for answering my questions on cereal agriculture; Tina Steinhauser for her good suggestion on some secondary material; and H. C. Steinhauser for very useful material on keelsons, mast anchors, and other strange things.

My special thanks, this time, goes to Klaus Teuber, who has honored me with his confidence, invited me to Catan, and thus made this whole wonderful adventure possible.

And I would like to thank Lee Chadeayne, who translated this novel from German into English, for his willingness to take on a manuscript of such monstrous length, for his creativity, and his literary skill, as well as his collaborator Ingrid G. Lansford, and finally my brilliant American editor Ingrid Emerick for giving me a new awareness of "showing" and "telling" and for her magic touch that made all the difference.

# About the Author

Photo Copyright: Olivier Favre

Rebecca Gable taught Anglo-Saxon language and literature and worked as translator of English and American novels by such authors as Elizabeth George, Neil Gaiman, and Kevin Baker before writing full-time. Her eight historical novels have been international bestsellers, translated into several languages, and in 2006 she was awarded the Sir Walter Scott Prize, Germany's most important award for historical fiction. *The Settlers of Catan*, her novelization of the popular board game, is her English-language debut. Rebecca lives with her husband in Mönchengladbach in Western Germany.

# About the Translator

Translator Lee Chadeayne is a former classical musician, college professor, and owner of a language translation company in Massachusetts. He was one of the charter members of the American Literary Translators Association and has been an active member of the American Translators Association since 1970. Most recently he translated the best sellers *The Hangman's Daughter* by Oliver Pötzsch and *The Copper Sign* by Katia Fox.